TOR BOOKS BY LINDA GRIMES

In a Fix

Quick Fix (forthcoming)

IN A FIX

Linda Grimes

A TOM DOHERTY ASSOCIATES BOOK • NEW YORK

IN A FIX

A Tor Book
Published by Tom Doherty Associates, LLC
175 Fifth Avenue
New York, NY 10010

www.tor-forge.com

Tor® is a registered trademark of Tom Doherty Associates, LLC.

ISBN 978-0-7653-6855-3

Tor books may be purchased for educational, business, or promotional use. For information on bulk purchases, please contact Macmillan Corporate and Premium Sales Deportment at 1-800-221-7945 extension 5442 or write specialmarkets@macmillan.com.

First Edition: September 2012
First Mass Market Edition: June 2013

Printed in the United States of America

0 9 8 7 6 5 4 3 2 1

For Bob, ever the because to my why

IN A FIX

The ideal vantage point for observing a half-naked man was definitely across the rim of a crystal champagne flute. Especially when the champagne was expensive, the backdrop was a postcard-perfect Bahamian beach, and the man was *that* one.

He had muscles in all the right places under summer-bronzed skin. Hair on the long side, wavy, and breeze-blown, streaked naturally by the sun. No phony salon highlights for him. When he flashed a smile it was sparkly clean, bright, but without that annoying Chiclets perfection. The icing on the beef-cake: he didn't even glance at the bikini-clad beach babes strolling by, some of them close enough to reach out and touch. His ocean-blue eyes were mine alone.

God, I love my job.

He slid into the chair across from me at the

boardwalk bistro and lifted a bottle of Dom from the ice bucket. "Another glass?" His question was moot—he was already pouring.

I shrugged. What the hell. There's always room for more champagne.

He filled a glass for himself and raised it. "To us."

"To us," I echoed, gazing into eyes that had the late-afternoon sun glinting in them like miniature whitecaps on a stormy sea. (Normally I gag when overwrought poetic comparisons pop into my head, but this time I was too busy heaving a happy sigh.)

"Mina, I thank heaven every day for the piece of luck that brought you to me."

"No, I'm the lucky one," I gushed. The sentiment was surprisingly true. Sure, his words were corny. But he was sincere, and that made it romantic.

It was enough to make me wish I really were Mina.

My client's soon-to-be fiancé—Henry Howard Harrison III, nicknamed "Trey" for the "III"—took some bills from the wallet he'd just retrieved from our bungalow and anchored them under the ice bucket. He pulled me out of my chair into sun-warmed arms.

"Let's go back to the house," he whispered, one hand chasing goose bumps down my back. When he got to the top of my sarong he slipped his fingers beneath it. My breath caught in my throat, hampered by the sudden pounding in my chest, and I leaned in for a kiss that would have knocked my socks off, if I'd been wearing any.

Damn. I could almost feel guilty about taking money for this.

Before I was overwhelmed by . . . um, let's call it remorse . . . he yanked the brightly colored cloth off my waist and ran away with it, tossing me a wicked grin over his shoulder. I was left standing, stunned, in a thong bikini I would never consider wearing as myself.

The corners of my mouth lifted. But I wasn't me right now, was I? I was Mina. Wilhelmina Augustine Worthington, to be precise. Rich, pretty, pampered . . . and having fun. I gave chase.

I reached the front porch of the bungalow minutes after my quarry, puffing from the run. Really, Mina should exercise more. The trouble with borrowing somebody else's aura is that you get their level of fitness along with it. Not that I'm one to talk. My favorite aerobic activity is reading steamy romantic thrillers. I figure an increased heart rate is an increased heart rate. Why quibble about methodology?

I dabbed my dewy brow with the sarong before tying it back around my waist. I'd found it snagged on a wood-encased garbage bin on the boardwalk—a distraction, no doubt, to slow me down. Obviously our boy liked games. Okay by me. I was ready to play.

"Tr-hhhey?" I wheezed as I went in, blowing silky strands of black hair out of my face. Make that almost ready. But I was sure I'd be fine in a second. Slow breaths, in . . . out. There.

He wasn't in the living room or dining area. It was one big open space, tastefully furnished in expensive beach modern, and there was no seminude male figure in it. It wasn't something I'd overlook. The kitchen was a bust, too.

The door to the bedroom was ajar. Ah. *Perfect.* I took a second to adjust my bathing suit top, knowing Mina wasn't the type to approach even a spontaneous romp in bed with boobs awry. They were great boobs, too. I'd miss them when the job was done.

No signs of life in the master suite. The bed was still made, which wasn't odd since we hadn't actually been to bed yet. Trey had flown in after I'd arrived, and he'd met me on the beach. I always like to have my first encounter with a significant other in a public and fairly lively place. The distractions help smooth over any small inconsistencies I might show before I get a bead on what I'm dealing with. Trey hadn't presented any great difficulties—he was pretty much exactly how Mina had described him when she hired me. Adonis incarnate.

Just thinking about him made the king-size bed look a lot emptier.

"Trey? Honey? Where are you?"

No response.

I'm cool. I can get with a good game of hide-and-seek. But he wasn't in the closet, or under the bed either.

The bathroom. He was probably in there, just

waiting to fill up the tub and play dock the submarine.

Okay, that was a crude and totally un-Mina-like thought.

Not that I could help it. When you grow up with a bunch of guys and a propensity for eavesdropping, crudity is the default mode when sex is on your mind. It's a situational hazard. Still, I tried hard to stomp it down, along with other vestiges of my real identity—Ciel Halligan, Facilitator. Intrepid Fixer of Other People's Problems. (Yeah, I know. Goofy. What can I say? I read a lot of comic books as a child.)

My job is made possible by a genetic quirk that allows me to adapt my aura into an exact copy of another person's. No, it's not shape-shifting, which is a crock, by the way. Give me a break. Shape-shifting on a biomolecular level? Directed cell morphology—the actual physical changing of tissue—takes time, and lots of it. It wouldn't be practical. Aura adaptors deal in *energy*. Much faster, and quite a handy trait for someone in my line of work.

Guess you could say I'm a kind of life coach. At least, that's my cover with all but the select few nonadaptors who know about us. Only instead of teaching people how to solve their own problems, I just do it for them. My clientele tends to be more comfortable with delegating than learning.

The only tricky part of the job is getting the internals right. The personality. But this time I was determined to stay totally in character on the job.

Looking, smelling, and sounding exactly like another person wasn't enough. To give a believable performance I had to immerse myself in the client's psyche as well. Otherwise, the whole illusion could collapse around me like a bad soufflé, and I couldn't afford that. I had bills to pay. Big ones. If I screwed this job up, I could say bye-bye to my business.

Alas, the bathroom was empty, the large array of foaming agents and botanical oils on the counter untouched. Huh. This was getting a little weird. Oh, well. I'm flexible. He had to be around here someplace. While I waited for him to emerge, I ran a handy brush through Mina's hair. Primping in front of a mirror was certainly in character.

Wait a second . . . that's odd. There was a smudge on my forehead. I peered more closely at my reflection. It looked like—

I grabbed a tissue, moistened it, and dabbed the spot. Sniffed it.

It *was* blood. When had I . . . ? I scrubbed my face clean. No cut. It wasn't me.

The sarong. It must have been on the sarong. I pulled it off and examined it. Sure enough, there was a still-damp (ick!) splotch, camouflaged by the gaudy, crimson-flower print. I did a quick personal check, even though I knew good and well it wasn't that time of the month for Mina. All clear.

So what happened? Had Trey tripped and skinned his knee? Maybe he'd gone to the resort's clinic to get it bandaged. But why would he do that when he had someone right here, ready and willing to play doctor? No, he must be hiding. I just needed to be patient.

I twitched. I don't really do patience.

My eyes settled on Trey's luggage. I hesitated, but only long enough to come up with a plausible excuse to use if he caught me: But, honey, you were gone. I found *blood*. I thought something was wrong—I *had* to search for clues.

I shrugged. Worked for me.

The bags contained the usual well-off bachelor vacation assortment. Casual clothing, a few dressier duds, a shaving kit with some wonderful-smelling toiletries, a velvet ring box, a spare bathing suit—

Whoa. Back the expectation train up. A ring box? Had Mina turned the reins over to me prematurely? I flipped open the hinged top and was nearly blinded by the flash from the solitaire. I whistled, long and slow. That sucker had to be at least three carats. High clarity, emerald cut, platinum setting. The man was serious.

Well, bite me. Now I couldn't in good conscience employ any gratuitous persuasive techniques to obtain the marriage proposal Mina so desperately wanted. That part of the job was officially over as soon as I found the ring—professional ethics wouldn't allow otherwise. (Professional ethics *suck*.)

My disappointment was interrupted by the sound of Mina's cell phone.

On the other hand, it occurred to me with expedient clarity, I would be derelict in my duty if I didn't give the job my full effort until that ring was on my finger. So I dove for the phone and answered with Mina's sexiest hello.

"Mina, get out of the house."

"What? Who is this?"

"Get out. *Now.*" It was Trey, his words tight with fear.

"Trey? What's the matter? Where are—"

I was cut off by another voice, darker, with some sort of accent I didn't recognize. "Miss Worthington, I suggest you do as Mr. Harrison says. Take your phone. You will be contacted shortly." *Click.*

What the . . . ? *Crap.* I clutched the cell and ran out the front door. Twenty yards later I was knocked off my feet by a teeth-rattling blast. When I looked over my shoulder, there was a pile of debris where the bungalow had been.

Chapter 2

Dust descended, choking and blinding me. *Holy freaking cow. She was right.*

Coughing, I pushed myself up and stumbled toward the boardwalk, where a group of evening strollers stood transfixed. An elderly woman was the first to come to my aid, taking my elbow and leading me farther away from the destruction.

"Are you all right?" she asked, concern pouring from her kind eyes.

My still-ringing ears made out a muffled British accent. She looked awfully familiar, but I couldn't place her. Probably just one of the tourists I'd seen around the resort over the course of the day.

"I-I'm fine. I think." My voice shook more than I thought it should, and my body started to follow suit. I sat down abruptly, right there on the edge of the boardwalk. Guess my legs weren't taking the situation too well. Still, buzzing in the back of my brain like a two-hundred-pound mosquito was *damned if she wasn't fricking right.*

"She" was my mother, whose favorite saying when I was growing up was "God punishes right away." Mom popped that little gem out every time one of us kids got hurt while doing something naughty. And here I'd only been *contemplating* having sex with somebody else's boyfriend, and *kaboom*! If that wasn't right away, I didn't know what was. Sure, the sex was contractually sanctioned by my client, as per our working arrangement, but God probably didn't care about loopholes.

Though, as loopholes go, you have to admit it's a great one. Not much can top your client telling you, after serious consideration of the clause in question, "Well, I guess if you're being me, then he's not really cheating, right?" (Yeah, I know. My clients can be kind of out there, bless their gotta-have-what-I-want-when-I-want-it hearts. If people weren't so impatient for results, I wouldn't have a business.)

I glanced skyward warily, on the lookout for any residual fallout from on high. No lightning bolts, so maybe I was being let off with a warning. A fierce flash of joy at still being alive swept through me, making the urge to jump up, shake my fist and yell, *Ha! Missed me!* almost impossible to resist, but I managed. I hoped God gave extra credit for restraint.

The old lady turned to one of the gawkers and spoke firmly. "Young man, do find some water, if you would be so good." The boy kept gaping.

"*Now*, please. Go." He went, snapped out of his fixation by her command. She might look like a dowdy old tourist, but authority fairly dripped from her. After turning back to me she said, "Now then. Was there anyone else inside with you? I noticed you had a companion earlier today."

"No. My friend wasn't there. I was alone."

"Fortunate," she said, looking quite pleased. "I doubt anyone could have survived that." She gestured toward the remains of the bungalow, shaking her head.

A middle-aged man in a Hawaiian shirt, linen pants, and leather sandals came running from the direction of the resort's office, stopping when the dust got too thick for him. He put his hands to his head, grasping for hair that hadn't been there in quite a while.

"Holy shit. What happened?" He turned toward us, homing in on me. He knew it was my bungalow—he'd been the one to handle the rental. I waved weakly and shrugged.

"Miss Worthington—thank God you're okay." He rushed over and went down on one knee next to me. For a crazy second I thought he might propose.

"Hi, George. How's tricks?" I quirked a smile at him, not much caring how Mina would've reacted under the circumstances. I figured shock was a big umbrella for any possibly inappropriate behavior.

"I don't know what to say . . . I don't know how this could've happened . . . you are okay, aren't you?" He scanned my arms and legs (dirty and scraped but not bleeding much), then rose and looked frantically around. "Oh, my God—where's Mr. Harrison? He's . . . he's not . . . ?" The last was a horrified whisper.

"Relax, George. Trey was out."

George looked like he wanted to ask more questions, but was interrupted by the sound of approaching sirens. The water boy returned, bearing designer water in small plastic bottles. When I reached for one I realized I had Mina's phone in a stranglehold. I was trying to pry open my fingers when it rang. I dropped it like it had stung me.

Good Samaritan lady picked it up and handed it to me. I checked the number—it wasn't one I recognized from Mina's file—and spoke cautiously. "Hello?"

"I see you made it out in time. Smart girl." Same voice as before, the one who had Trey.

"I try." What else could I say in front of all these people?

"Another word of caution, since you've proven yourself adept at staying alive. The police will be questioning you soon. Tell them you were about to cook something. When you turned on the stove, it made a funny noise and flamed up. You couldn't see a fire extinguisher, so you left the cottage to get help. You don't know anything else."

"But—"

"The evidence they find will support your story. If you say anything else, next time you won't get a warning. Understood?"

"Yes, but—" *Click*. ". . . what about Trey, you

asshole?" I finished in a whisper, impotently, and jabbed the end-call button with my thumb.

The Good Samaritan cleared her throat. I glanced up and saw her mouth twitching a smile into submission. Guess she heard me. "The authorities will want to speak with you soon. Perhaps you'd care to come to my cottage afterward and clean up a bit? It's right over there, and I may have something you could wear until you have an opportunity to shop. I doubt your own clothes are salvageable."

I looked down at myself. Blushed. Adjusted my top. There wasn't much I could do about the bottoms. "Thanks."

"You sit there while I see if I can expedite the matter." She strode off, posture perfect, straw hat riding atop her head like a crown.

That was it. I knew who she reminded me of—she was a dead ringer for Queen Elizabeth. Which could only mean one thing. My cousin Billy was spying on me.

I waited until we were in the Queen's cottage before I turned on her. Two policemen and three insurance adjusters had just grilled me, and I wasn't in the mood to put up with any nonsense. "What the hell are you doing here?"

"I beg your pardon?"

"I know it's you, so you can cut the innocent act."

She backed half a step away, like she thought

perhaps I had a screw loose. Crap. Maybe it *wasn't* Billy. Maybe the blast had addled my brain. "I, uh, I'm sorry. I thought for a minute you might be . . . I mean, you look like somebody I know."

"I'm quite certain we've never met, my dear. By the way, my name is Edith Hathaway. How do you do?" She extended her hand hesitantly. I took it, still not entirely certain of her, but deciding it was better to take her at face value until I was thinking more clearly.

"I'm Mina Worthington. Please, call me Mina."

Her hand was warm and dry, softly wrinkled. "So nice to meet you, Mina. Shall I show you to the lavatory? You can have a good wash while I find you something to wear." She led off briskly.

Her bathroom was a lot like ours had been before it was blown to smithereens. A stack of plush, sea-green towels waited on a stand between the glass-enclosed shower and the soaking tub, along with an assortment of flowery-scented soaps.

"You go ahead and start, dear. Take your time. I'll find some clothes for you and leave them on the vanity."

After she left I reached into the shower stall and turned on the water. While it warmed up I slipped off the bathing suit. Regardless of the skimpy garment's sex appeal, I can't say I was sorry to get rid of the wedgie. My envy of Mina's lifestyle was rapidly ebbing.

I grabbed a rosebud-shaped soap and stepped under the hot spray. *Aaah . . . bliss.* I lathered quickly, top to toe. Rinsed. Looked for some shampoo. There was none at hand, so I assumed it must be in the little guest basket on the vanity, and stepped out to reach for it.

Queen Elizabeth was leaning casually against the sink, ankles crossed, shampoo bottle in hand, enjoying the show. "Looking for this, dear?" There was no mistaking the leer.

I snatched the bottle and leapt back into the shower. "You are *such* an ass."

"Why, whatever do you mean? And wouldn't you like a little help washing your back? I'm wonderful with a loofah, you know."

"Billy Doyle, get out now or I swear I'll knock that phony aura right off your sorry carcass. Wait for me in the living room."

"Aw, come on, cuz. Let me have another peek. This is some of your best work yet—a true masterpiece."

I squeezed a blob of shampoo onto my head and started scrubbing. "Go away, you pervert."

"*Sorority* sisters, Ciel," he reminded me for the umpteenth time. True enough. We weren't actually cousins. Our mothers were both Tri-Delts. Couple that with being BFFs ever since their respective adaptor parents put them in the same preschool, and it was natural they'd be honorary aunts to each other's offspring. "Technically, that's not pervy. And don't forget I'm a bastard. There's that, too," he added, just to bolster his argument. Also true. Billy was Uncle Liam's son from a prior relationship. He seemed to think that gave him license to behave as family or *not*-family, according to whim.

"Trust me, I could never forget that! Now leave, before I squirt shampoo in your eyes."

He left, chortling a queenly chortle. I was going to kill him.

"Why are you here?"

I was dressed in elastic-waist, aqua polyester capris and a shapeless, floral-print blouse. All I needed was a huge handbag and some orthopedic sandals, and I could make my reservations for Leisure World.

My interfering cousin eyed me with approval. "Oh, you look lovely, my dear. Simply lovely."

I narrowed my eyes. "Answer the question."

"Okay, okay. Don't get your knickers in a twist. Mark just asked me to check on you." Mark was my oldest brother's closest friend, practically a part of the family. (People with aura-adapting capabilities are a relatively small population, and tend to stick together.) He was also the object of my unrequited childhood passion.

"Why would Mark ask you to do that?"

Billy cocked his head and shrugged, his mannerisms sitting oddly on the Queen's frame. "Why does the spook do anything? Overdeveloped sense of protectiveness, maybe? Either that or the sadistic pleasure of making me watch you fawn all over a dumb piece of meat."

"Trey isn't dumb!"

He wagged a regal finger at me. "Ah-ah-ah, my dear. Remember your professional detachment."

I looked at the ceiling. No guidance there. "You're

such an idiot. I don't believe Mark sent you at all. And didn't he warn you to stop calling him a spook?"

"As I recall, we *both* got that warning. Besides, semantics. He's the spookiest spook they have, the very wet dream of spookdom, and you know it. They would kill to have more like him."

"Apparently they have you," I said, still cross.

"No, they don't. Every now and then I do a favor for Mark, that's all."

"Favor, is it?"

"A compensated favor, yes," he said with a cheeky grin. "One does have to pay the rent."

"Yeah, right. Like *you* ever have any trouble coming up with cash. Why are you really here?"

"Like I said, to keep my eagle eye on you. Seems Mark's afraid you might slip up with your little homegrown business, and give yourself away. I'm here to help make sure that doesn't happen. Think of me as a business tool."

I snorted. "Don't know about 'business,' but 'tool' fits." Then it hit me. "He pays you to spy on me?" I couldn't keep the shock out of my voice. Making money by helping Mark on his assignments was one thing, but turning me into a business transaction? That was going a little far, even for Billy.

"What'd you think? That I can't tear myself away from you?"

"No," I said sincerely, though of course it was exactly what I'd been thinking. I'd noticed him in the background on previous jobs—which I never could've done if he hadn't intended it—and had assumed he was just indulging his inborn urge to bug me.

He shrugged. "I'd do it for free if I could, but I gotta make a living. Mark knows watching you keeps me from pursuing more lucrative endeavors, so he tosses something extra my way to make up for it, that's all."

"Lucrative? Huh. You sure 'illegal' isn't the word you're searching for?"

"Eh. Potato, potahto."

No point in getting into a morality discussion with Billy. He lived by his own code. "Look, I'm careful, all right? Anyway, I think you just enjoy tormenting me with your presence. Can't I have one job without you showing your face?"

"Well, technically, I don't show *my* face."

True. On my last job, he'd appeared as Brad Pitt, only with buck teeth. The one before, he was George Clooney with a pot gut. He got a kick out of adding a twist. I was surprised he hadn't given poor Liz leprosy, but maybe he thought being old and a Windsor was bad enough.

"You know what I mean. You're worse now than when we were kids. At least then you only pulled my hair and pinched me when our mothers weren't looking. Now you're trying to ruin my career."

He drew himself up with a look of injured innocence. Exasperated, I turned my back—never a smart move where Billy is concerned, but it's hard not to trust the Queen. The yank and pinch were simultaneous. I whirled on him, but the bugger was too fast. He'd already made it across the room.

"Feel better now?" he taunted.

"You . . . you . . ." I took off after him. "You never grow up, do you?" I grabbed a bright yellow pillow off a club chair and threw it at his head.

He caught it effortlessly as he danced around the couch. "Look who's talking." If the Queen could have seen her doppelgänger, she would not have been amused. But I was.

Oh, hell. I never could keep a good mad going with Billy. Giving in to laughter, I plopped down on the sofa. He sat next to me and took my hand. "I keep telling you, just come work with me. My jobs are way more fun than this boring stuff you do. Plus, I hardly ever get blown up." (I huffed. He winked.) "The pay is better, too. What do you say? Shall we ditch this place for greener—and I do mean *greener*—pastures?"

"Tempting, but Mom made me swear never to work with you. She even got out the Bible."

"What? I can't believe she doesn't love me anymore! My own aunt."

"Oh, she loves you to pieces. She just doesn't trust you as far as she can spit. And, yes, that's a direct quote."

Billy laughed and squeezed my hand. "Smart woman, your mother." The ghost of masculinity beneath the small, elderly persona he was projecting comforted me in spite of myself.

"God, Billy, what's going on here? Trey disappeared between the bistro and the bungalow. I waited—"

"All alone," he interrupted. "Worried. Distressed.

So very horny." This said in a proper, upper-class British accent.

I broke up again. "Stop. I'm trying to explain things to you." I told him about Trey calling, and the guy with the weird accent.

"I gather you don't want to tell the cops about the phone calls. Do you think that's wise?"

"I don't know! All I could think about was Trey getting killed if I said the wrong thing. *Maybe* the police could rescue him, but . . ." I dropped my head to my lap and hid behind a sheet of black hair.

He patted my back. "Yeah. But." I felt him leave, and when he returned he had two beers. He popped both cans open and handed one to me. "The odd-accent guy didn't give you any idea what he wanted?"

"Not a clue. I'm waiting for the next call. I assume there will be instructions." I sipped gratefully. My throat was still sore from all the dust. "Gee, Your Majesty, shouldn't we at least pour these into glasses?"

The Queen chugged her beer and followed it with an openmouthed belch. Most unregal. "Nah. Liz is a common girl at heart. Word in the palace corridors has it she sneaks down to the local and knocks back tequila shots on her birthday. Oh, wait— maybe that's just when I'm there."

I looked at him sideways, doubting the real Queen had ever grinned so impishly. "Does Mark know you snatched a reigning monarch's energy? I don't imagine he'd approve."

"Pish. He doesn't care, as long as I don't cause

an international incident. No one here recognizes Liz, anyway, not when she's out of context."

"No one?" I raised my eyebrows and took another, much longer, drink. Mina's burp was barely a whisper compared to the Queen's.

"I suppose it's possible the management is under the impression they have a member of the royal family here incognito."

"And might one assume you are getting the royal treatment while you are here?"

"Call it a perk," he said with a twinkle.

"Well, as long as you *are* here, make yourself useful and help me figure out what to do. Should I call Mina and tell her what happened?"

"Is she the sort to take bombing and kidnapping in her stride?"

"She's more the sort who wants everything taken care of and presented to her in a neat package. Like the engagement she contracted with me to deliver—" I vaulted to my feet. "Oh, shit! Shit, shit, shit!"

The Queen rose, too. "What? What's the matter now?"

"The *ring*! Mina's engagement ring—I left it in the bungalow, and now it's . . . it's . . ."

"Relax. Diamonds are hard. They'll probably find it when they sift through the debris."

I tried to calm down. "Yeah . . . yeah, I guess you're right. Sorry. It's just that this whole job centers around getting that ring. I'd hate to disappoint Mina." Not to mention see my business go down the tubes. But there was no need for Billy to know how imminent failure was.

"Heaven forbid. So, you squeezed the proposal out of him?" He gave me a congratulatory clap on the shoulder. "Good for you, cuz. But when did you manage it?"

"Well, he hasn't exactly popped the question yet. While I was waiting for him earlier, I just sort of . . . um, came across the ring."

"Snooping, were you?" he said, happy as a frat boy at a kegger to catch me admitting to something naughty.

"I was just looking for some clue as to where he might have gone," I said, chin up. "I don't make a practice of it."

"Right. I know that." His eyes said otherwise.

"Look, it was part of the job. It's not like I snoop in regular life."

"Oh, no. You're an absolute angel. Angels don't snoop."

"You are *not* helping." Glaring, I grabbed his beer can and squashed it one-handed. Did the same to mine. His, at least, had been empty. I stomped into the kitchen to look for the recycling bin, my hand dripping.

"You know what your problem is?" he called after me. "You're tense. If all this had happened after you'd boinked Trey, you'd be a lot more relaxed right now. And that, my love, is something I can help you with."

Uh-oh.

Chapter 3

I dropped the cans on the counter and ran back to the living room, wiping my hand on the seat of my pants as I went. Too late. There was Trey, every spectacular inch of him. He ditched his old-lady shirt—and bra—and was about to drop his pants as I caught his arm.

"Billy, you can't just assume Trey's—"

"I can and did." Trey's voice, the very pitch and tone. He maneuvered me into his arms and kissed my neck.

Geez, he smelled good. All beachy and manly. How had he gotten rid of the Queen's perfume so fast? My knees started to buckle—only a little, I swear—so I pulled away fast, to give him a piece of my mind. Only then I saw his lips, and he smiled the non-Chiclets smile, and I forgot what I was going to say. I think my mouth fell open.

He stopped and let me go. Two seconds later he was Billy, the real Billy, and he didn't look pleased. Handsome as hell, yes, but not happy.

Truth is, Billy in his natural state is nothing to sneeze at. It was hard for me to be objective, having known him all through his snotty grade school and awkward teenage years, but adulthood had been good to him. He had dark brown hair, which he kept fairly short because of its tendency to curl, and inky blue eyes, fringed with lashes so black and thick they would make any woman—not just me— green with envy. When we were six, I told him he had girly lashes, and he promptly took his mother's manicure scissors and cut them off. Which was a really dumb thing for him to do, and I still don't know why I got the spanking for it.

Add tall to the equation. Six-foot-one, tennis- player trim. Oh, and dimples when he smiled. Shirt- less was a good look for him, too—a smattering of dark chest hair, and muscles that showed but didn't bulge like a gym rat. I halfway suspected he liked to spend time behind odd auras just to get a break from the hordes of willing women who tended to accumulate in his wake like sharks after chum. Frankly, his good looks annoyed me.

Once my post-exposure-to-Trey wits returned, something occurred to me. "Hey, when did you get close enough to Trey to pinch his aura? And why?"

He shrugged. "Clumsy old Liz almost slipped on the steps to the boardwalk right as Trey was on his way down to the beach this afternoon. He did the gentlemanly thing and steadied me. Some energy must've accidentally rubbed off."

Yeah, right. Like anything was ever accidental with Billy. He still looked a little grumpy, though, so I let it slide with "Oh."

"You shouldn't get personally involved in your jobs. It only leads to trouble," he said, a little too autocratically for my taste.

"Excuse me? *You* are telling me not to get involved? Mr. Nail-It-If-It-Wears-A-Skirt?"

"It's different with men. We're built for meaningless sex. You're not equipped to deal with it."

"What?" I narrowed my eyes at him. I only hoped it worked as well with Mina's face as I knew it did with mine. "Of all the sexist, chauvinistic, paternalistic, patronizing—" I sputtered, increasing the volume with each word, "egotistical, idiotic, asinine . . ."

The amusement was building in his eyes with every new adjective I threw at him, and it wasn't long before it dripped down into his dimples. By the time I was close enough to wag my finger in his face, he was back to his sunny self. He grabbed my shoulders and kissed me on both cheeks. "Easy to rile as ever, cuz."

I shrugged him off. "I will never understand why you weren't drowned at birth."

"I'm hurt." He tried—unsuccessfully—not to smile.

"Yeah, right."

"Truly. I'm crushed. This hurts worse than when you kicked me in the nuts."

"Oh, geez. How many times do I have to apologize for that? We were in fifth grade, for Pete's sake. Get over it." He'd told me he was wearing a cup for soccer practice. I was merely seeing if it worked. I can't help it if I have an inquiring mind.

Before we could continue down memory lane—which tended to be a rocky path for us—my pocket sprang to life. Mina's cell. It buzzed again as I fished it out of the polyester cavern.

Billy stopped me before I could answer it. "Wait. Who is it?"

I checked. "Looks like the same number as before. I better take it."

"Let me." When I hesitated, he held out his hand impatiently. "So I can hear the accent."

"But if it's not me, he might—"

"So it'll be you." He took my hand, borrowed some of Mina's energy, and all at once we were twins. I'd say it was disorienting, but I was used to that sort of thing. It was only a little weirder than usual this time because he was still topless.

I handed him the phone. He kept holding on to me, because a secondhand aura takes a little longer to absorb. As long as he was poaching off me it didn't matter. "Talk to me," he said in a perfect imitation of Mina's perky voice.

"Show-off," I mouthed to him. He turned away from me, pinching my fingers more tightly than necessary.

"Yes, I understand . . . Where? I'm afraid I don't . . . yes, of course. No, I haven't said anything about you, I swear . . . Her? Just some old tourist who offered me use of her shower . . . no, of course I wouldn't . . . Wait! What about Trey? Is he—" He closed the phone and let go of me.

"Well?"

He looked at me like I was a slow child. "Since when is a Swedish accent difficult to recognize?"

"Is that what it was? Huh." I totally suck at recognizing accents, other than your standard BBC America British. I can imitate any dialect connected to an aura I'm borrowing, no problem. I just can't identify them. My mother tells me I'm like someone who can play an instrument by ear, but can't read music. Whatever. I wasn't going to admit a weakness to Billy.

He shrugged. "Might be Norwegian, but my money is on the Swedes."

"So what did he say? What am I supposed to do?"

"Mina will be following instructions to the letter, for the meantime."

"Okay, I'm prepared for that. But you have to be a little more specific."

"No, I don't." Still projecting Mina's aura, he reached for his shirt and slipped it back on, not bothering with the bra. "Right now I'm going shopping. If you want to come along, I suggest you slip into something a little more regal."

"Oh, no you don't!" I grabbed his arm and spun him around. Not difficult, since in his current incarnation we were evenly matched, to say the least. "You are not hijacking Mina. I can take care of this myself."

"Listen, Ciel, you're great at your job, but this is different. This is dangerous. I can't let you do it alone, and since Mina can't show up with anyone, I'm afraid I'll have to fill in for you."

"That is so not going to happen," I said in my best stand-up-to-Billy voice.

"Here's the deal, Ciel. I am walking out the front door as Mina. If you want to follow me as Mina I can't stop you, but you'll blow your whole job here. Is that what you want?"

"Billy, be reasonable. You don't know Mina. You might slip up. If I had her file here for you to read—"

"Don't worry. I've read it."

"What? How did you . . . you broke into my office!"

He shrugged. "Of course I did. How else could I track you?"

A nasty realization hit me. "You've done it before, haven't you? Gone through my private files?"

"Well, how did you think I found you all those other times?" he said in a perfectly reasonable, albeit Mina-ish, voice.

"I thought my mother told your mother."

"You tell your mother where your jobs are but not me?" He looked incredulous.

"She worries."

"I worry, too." He certainly had Mina's pout down pat.

"Yeah, but I don't care if I worry you," I said, feeling mean.

He gave my hair a tiny yank. "Yes, you do."

"Do not."

"Never mind. I have some shopping to do before my big meeting. If you want to come along to the mall, you best get changed. If you get my drift."

"Shopping? Are you crazy?"

"We have some time to kill. Coming or not?"

I sighed, heavily and melodramatically, the way I'd learned from my mother. (He ignored it, the way he'd learned from every male in my extended family.) "All right, already. Hand over a bit of the royalty," I said, not seeing an alternative, since I wasn't about to let him out of my sight until I found Trey.

He took my hand and shifted to the Queen long enough for me to tap into the energy, and just as easily donned Mina's aura again. Call me shallow, but going from a firm, young body to one that's . . . well, not . . . isn't entirely pleasant. I shook out my arms—ack! the jiggle!—and flexed my muscles. Aside from the bingo wings, I was fine. When you project an aura, you're limited by the age, size, and reflexes of your subject. Lucky for me, Liz was spry.

Billy held up the sturdy-looking brassiere he'd taken off earlier, not even bothering to tone down his grin. "Here. You might want this."

I looked down at my new, gravitationally challenged bosom and sighed. "Give it over. I'll be back in a second—and don't you dare leave without me."

* * *

"Mina would never wear leopard spots," I hissed at Billy after the tarted-up salesgirl left us to hunt down more "perfect for you" clothes.

I was still having a hard time believing a shopping expedition was necessary, but Billy had assured me he was acting on orders to go about Mina's normal day before going to the designated rendezvous point later. He figured the Swede didn't want Mina traipsing off to meet him too soon, in case any stray police officers were still hanging around, and might be inclined to follow her. Since shopping was as normal as breathing for Mina— and nothing would've kept her from replacing her blown-up wardrobe—here we were, being normal.

"Says you. I happen to like it." He twisted and turned in front of the three-way mirror, getting the full effect of Mina's to-die-for body in the clingy halter mini dress.

I shuddered. "You would. But Mina happens to have taste. I thought you said you read her file. Did you even look at the pictures of her closet?"

"She's on vacation. Believe me, nobody who owns a thong bikini like the one you were wearing earlier would hesitate to be seen in this."

"That was beachwear, and she only wore it to get Trey's undivided attention. Normally she's more reserved."

"All right," he said, still unable to take his eyes off his reflection. "You go find me something then."

"I will. Stay right there."

Halfway out of the bimbo department, I started to suspect I'd fallen for it again. Why do the work yourself if you can get somebody else to do it for you? Both our mothers were still under the impression Billy couldn't load the dishwasher properly. All he'd had to do was let one piece of heirloom china fall through his fingers while in transit from the sink to the bottom rack, and he'd never been asked to help again. When I'd dropped a crystal goblet—mostly by accident—all I'd gotten was a stern warning to slow down and be careful.

In the grown-up women's department I selected several appropriate outfits, stepping though the aisles as rapidly as I could while maintaining a nonchalant, just-an-old-lady-shopping attitude. I could've moved faster, but I didn't want to attract undue attention to my royal presence.

"Excuse me . . ." I was interrupted by a sturdy, middle-aged woman with hair too blazing blond to be natural. Her outfit screamed American tourist. ". . . but you're . . . aren't you . . ." She checked the surroundings. No one nearby. ". . . *her*?"

Guess I hadn't been nonchalant enough.

She looked so puppy-dog hopeful, I hated to disappoint her. Meeting the undercover Queen was probably the most exciting thing to happen to her in . . . well, ever, from the looks of her awed expression.

"Not actually, no." I smiled and patted her hand.

"But you sound just like her."

"Yes, we Brits all sound alike, don't we?"

"Oh, I get it," she said, and scrunched one eye up in the biggest, most obvious wink I had ever seen. "Don't worry. I won't tell anyone."

"No, really. I'm not the Queen."

"Uh-huh. Gotcha." Another wink. Popeye had nothing on her. I didn't have time for this.

So I winked back. "I was hoping I could shop anonymously. It's so difficult to do back home."

Positively thrilled, she started to curtsey, but caught herself. "Oh, yes, Your Maj—er, ma'am. I understand. But, first, could I ask a question?"

"Of course." *Just hurry, damn it.*

"Did you do it? Not you personally, I don't mean—but did you order it?"

"I beg your pardon?"

"You know . . . Diana." She was practically salivating. "Don't worry, I won't tell anyone," she added under her breath.

Oh, geez. People. "Well, just between you and me . . ." I whispered conspiratorially.

She leaned in closer, tickling my nose with piña colada fumes. "Yes, yes?"

"NO! Monarchs aren't allowed to do that sort of thing anymore, you twit."

"Oh." Her disappointment was palpable, but she made one last stab at a royal scandal. "But if you *could* have?"

I gave her my frostiest royal glare and marched back to the dressing room. Shoved four complete outfits at Billy and said, "Don't say a word. Just try these on, and let's get the hell out of here."

Chapter 4

Billy dumped the shopping bags on a chair in the living room. "Be a love and put those things away for me, will you? I have to rush."

He had elected to wear one of Mina's new outfits out of the store, and it was a vast improvement over the Queen's resort wear. Now clad in white linen walking shorts, a blue silk shirt worn open over a white cami, and fashionable marina moccasins, he captured the real Mina. And I felt dowdier than ever in my geriatric attire.

I ignored his request and followed him to the master bedroom, where he slipped into the closet and opened a small wall safe hidden behind scads of floral print blouses. He withdrew a wad of bills, tucked them into Mina's new straw handbag, and tossed it onto the bed next to the one I'd been carrying.

I appealed to him once more. "Look, it's my job. My responsibility. Whatever has happened, I should be the one to take care of it."

"No." Simple, direct. He reached back into the safe and took out a gun.

My knees gave, and I sat down—hard—on the bed, feeling dizzy.

"Ciel? You okay?"

"No! I'm not. What the hell do you have that for?"

"What, this?" He held up the gun and shrugged. "Thought it might come in handy if I got into a tight spot, that's all."

"Guns are dangerous. You could get hurt."

He tucked the small firearm into the back of his waistband, under the shirt, and sat next to me, taking my liver-spotted hand in his beautifully manicured one. "The idea is more to prevent that from happening."

"What did that man say to you on the phone? Where are you going?" My voice quavered. I'd like to claim I did it on purpose, to manipulate the information I wanted out of Billy, but the fact is, I was upset. Post-explosion Confronted with a Gun syndrome, or something.

"I know how to use it, you know. Expert marksman ranking. You don't have to worry."

"That's not what I asked. And I'm not worried." I tried to hold back the petulance, but some may have slipped out.

"Of course not." His tone was too kind, his hand

too gentle. I felt my eyes fill. If Liz weren't past the age, I'd swear she had PMS.

"*Where?*" I pressed, spoiling the demand with a sniffle. Stupid crybaby aura. British stiff upper lip my ass.

"Not far. I'll be back soon, I promise." He gave me a hug, letting a little of his own comforting self leak through. For a second, I thought he might relent and tell me where he was going, but instead he tugged one of my short, gray curls. "And I don't fall for waterworks, so dry up, toots."

I pushed him away. "Go ahead. Leave. Take your stupid gun with you, and when you get yourself killed, don't come whining to me."

He grabbed the purse and let Mina's silvery laughter carry him out of the room. "Stay here, Ciel. Behave yourself, and I might even bring you a present."

"Unless it's six-foot-two and wearing Trey's bathing suit, I'm not interested," I called after him.

"Check the bookshelves, Edith. You might find something there to keep you entertained while I'm gone." I heard the door close behind him.

The sound I emitted in his wake was terse and rude. I'm sure the Queen did not regularly make use of the raspberry, but it expressed my feelings perfectly. I *hate* waiting. And I wasn't interested in anything Billy might keep on the Queen's bookshelves. Knowing his propensity for adding twists to his celebrity auras, it was probably a fine selection of royal erotica.

What I needed to do was think of a good way to explain this mess to Mina if Billy didn't get Trey back. It was one thing not getting her proposal—or that gorgeous ring—but coming back without even her boyfriend? I groaned. This situation was *not* going to enhance the word of mouth I was depending on to grow my business. Not that I'd have a business left if this job went south. I palm-rubbed my eyes and flopped backward on the bed. Hit my head on something scratchy. My eyes flew open.

Uh-oh.

I reached back and discovered Mina's new handbag. Billy had grabbed the Queen's—or rather, Edith's—by mistake. Easy enough to confuse the two, especially for a guy. Same size, both straw with leather handles. The only big difference was, one was stuffed with a crap-ton of large bills.

I jumped up and ran for the door. No telling what the kidnapper might do if Billy didn't have the money to exchange for Trey.

Too late. Billy had snagged a bicycle from the resort's guest supply, and was already well down the road. Mina didn't have a rental car—she always used a resort driver. And of course Billy wouldn't want a driver along. He was supposed to come alone, so the bike made sense. I debated calling out to him, but knew it would be futile. He was too far ahead. I'd have to follow, and hope I could catch him before he got to where he was going.

You were supposed to check in with the resort's activities office before you took a bike, but they relied on the honor system. I figured kidnapping qualified as an exigent circumstance, so I didn't hesitate to grab the one single-seater left without asking, only to find it had a flat rear tire. *Crap*. Of course, there were scads of tandem bikes available. This place was geared toward couples. Could one person even ride a bicycle built for two? I sucked in a deep breath and hauled a bulky beast away from the rack. Guess I'd find out.

Okay, technically, yes, but it wasn't easy. First thing I realized was a tandem bike is heavy on the ass-end, and awkward as hell to steer around curves, especially with an over-eighty body at the pedals. Second, it's a lot hotter in the Bahamas when you're on a bike than it is when you're on the beach. Who knew royalty could perspire so much?

I made it to the road without falling off, which was a minor miracle in itself, and then narrowly avoided head-on collisions with an airport van and a truck full of watermelons as I wiped the sweat out of my eyes. The driver of the truck helpfully pointed out, "The left, you idiot! We drive on the left here!"

Huh. Like I wasn't trying.

I pedaled for what seemed like hours, but was probably a few miles, tops, barely managing to keep Billy in sight. Thought I'd lost him for sure when he abruptly turned off the road, but as I caught up to that point I saw it was a dirt path, almost hidden amid the dense vegetation. Wheezing, I ducked my head beneath the overhanging branches, and kept going. My aged butt took a beating, but at least the bike stayed upright until I came to a clearing.

The building Billy pulled up to was long and

low, and had seen better days. He left his bike leaning against it, and disappeared through the door—
without the money, dammit!—before I could gather
enough breath to call his name.

Shit. There was only one thing to do now.

I dumped the stupid bike where I stood, happy
to be done with it, and started speed-walking toward the building. Not a particularly graceful look
for anybody, much less the Queen, but my legs were
too shaky to run, and at least it got me there without dropping me on my ass. As soon as I pushed
the door open a few inches I was smacked in the
face with a heady aroma. Rum. Old barrels lined
the perimeter of the large space, most of them topless, some knocked on their sides. The place was
run-down and dusty, probably abandoned years
ago.

Tied to a pole in the center was Trey, in all
his half-naked splendor, arms stretched taut behind him. Billy, staying true to his Mina form, had
run to him, and was fussing over him big-time while
the Swede looked on, gun in hand. I wanted nothing more than to join the Trey love-fest, but common sense prevailed. Edith wouldn't do it, so I
couldn't either.

Not knowing precisely the best way to handle the
transfer of funds, I cleared my throat. All eyes swiveled my way. Hard to say who looked more surprised to see me—Trey or the kidnapper. Billy just
compressed his Mina-mouth into a what-the-hell-
are-you-doing-here line of displeasure. I answered

him with an it's-not-my-fault shrug, and held up the straw bag.

They all kept staring. Geez, had I grown a third boob? "Mina got our purses mixed up," I explained, plastering a cheery smile on my face. When it appeared they still weren't grasping the significance, I added, "I thought she might require hers? You know, the one with the money in it?"

The kidnapper cocked his head. "How thoughtful of you. Put it there, on the floor." I complied, leaving it a few yards from his feet. Without taking his eyes off me, he said, "Mina, bind our elderly friend—"

"What? *Me*? Why tie *me* up?"

"—and secure her to that crate. See that you do a good job. I will be checking."

The crate was old and splintered, crawling with indigenous insect life. *Oh, crap!* Were those spiders? I sucked in a breath, almost choking on my own spit. "Really, this isn't at all necessary," I said, trying to sound reasonable as I digested the possibility that multilegged microdemons from hell would be creeping up my legs within seconds.

"I'm afraid it is. You won't be continuing with us. But don't worry. You won't be stuck here for long. A guard swings by every day or two."

Okay, screw reasonable. "Now, you wait just a doggone minute, buster!" I said in my sternest voice, only slightly strangled by panic. Remember what I said about patience? Well, I don't do spiders either.

The Swede gestured toward a pile of rope, then pointed the gun right at Billy, who reluctantly obeyed orders. While he tied my hands behind my back, he whispered near my ear, shielding his mouth with a fall of his Mina-hair. "Relax, cuz. They're not venomous. Now, do me a favor—make some noise."

A day or two tied up in a smelly old warehouse? With spiders? Who cared if they weren't venomous? They were *spiders*. Hell *yeah*, I'd make some noise. "Nooo! You can't leave me here!" I hollered, struggling against my bonds. "*Pleeease!* I, uh, I have asthma. If I can't reach my inhaler I'll have an attack. I could *die*! I don't want to DIIIIE—"

The Swede approached, looming over me, his gun inches from my temple. "Silence! You are lucky I don't kill you now and be done with it."

Ack. I slammed my mouth shut. Right. Silence. I could do that. Gun trumps spiders.

Billy took over as noisemaker, backing away and screaming wildly, faking the fear that would be normal for Mina under the circumstances. At least, I hoped he was faking. It would be nice if one of us remained cool-headed.

The Swede turned his attention—and his gun—from me to Mina. "Shut up! Or I will shoot you both."

While Billy and I had been throwing our respective fits, Trey had been busy freeing himself. Apparently Billy had slipped him something while ooh-ing and aah-ing over him—a sharp something, judging by the blood dripping from Trey's fingers.

Billy *was* awfully fond of blades. As I stared in openmouthed admiration of his escape skills, Trey snuck up on the kidnapper from behind, doubled up his bloody fists and brought them down, mallet-like, on the side of the man's neck.

Nighty night, asshole.

I had a much easier go of it on the way back to the resort, sitting on the rear seat of the tandem and letting Trey do the steering, as well as ninety percent of the pedaling. Trust me, his legs were up to the task. *Glutes, too, from the look of them*, I thought, glancing down and enjoying the view between my handlebars.

Trey had thought it best to leave the Swede tied up at the warehouse, and phone in an anonymous tip to the police later. He didn't want having to deal with the local cops to interfere with the rest of his and Mina's vacation. Also, if the newshounds got wind of a rich American being kidnapped there'd be a feeding frenzy, so I could see his point. Given the sensitive nature of my own involvement, I wasn't sorry to keep prying eyes away from us. Heck, I was just happy to have him back, so I could wrangle the proposal out of him. Once I handed the ring over to Mina, collected my fee, and paid off a few dozen creditors, I'd be breathing a whole lot easier.

After we were safely back at the Queen's bungalow, and Trey's hands had been seen to—they weren't badly cut after all—I offered drinks, sure that Trey and Billy were as thirsty as I was.

"Sounds marvelous—here, let me help," Billy said, squirming. Trey had kept "Mina" snuggled up against his naked torso since we'd dropped the bikes off, even as I'd put bandages on his fingers, and Billy apparently wasn't thrilled with the situation.

Trey, proving to be as nice as Mina claimed, said, "No, babe. You sit. I'll help Edith."

Billy parked himself on the sofa, fine with waiting as long as it didn't involve Trey's flesh pressed against his. Trey followed me to the kitchen, where I set him to the task of getting the glasses while I checked the refrigerator to see what Edith had handy. A lot of beer, a few soft drinks, and a pitcher of lemonade. Thinking it to be in character, I chose the lemonade, and almost dropped it when I felt Trey's manly body pressing up close behind me. I jumped. Trey didn't have a thing for old ladies, did he?

"Easy there. It's me," he said, voice low.

Huh? "Er, yes?"

"Billy, cut it out," Trey said. "We don't have much time before I have to get back out there to Ciel."

I stiffened. Trey knew Mina wasn't Mina? And that Edith was supposed to be Billy? How did Trey know Billy? I turned slowly and looked up—far up—into his eyes. "Um, yes. Ciel," I said, frankly at a loss.

"What's the matter with you? I asked you to keep an eye on Ciel and next thing I know, her bungalow blows up."

Mark! Trey was Mark.

"The bungalow was hardly my fault," I said, mind racing. "Hey, where is Trey, anyway? Is he all right?"

"Same place he's been all week—on assignment. I would've filled you in earlier, but Trey thought he'd be back in time for this trip. Unfortunately for all of us, he got held up. Didn't want to explain his moonlighting to Mina, so I'm filling in."

"But that's not Mina," I pointed out.

"I couldn't exactly tell Trey it wouldn't be Mina with him on vacation, could I?"

"Right. I, uh, know that," I said, still trying to wrap my mind around Trey working for the CIA. "I just wondered if Trey was still, you know, healthy."

"Yeah, as far as I know. He's pulling out for good after this job, going legit. Wants to start a family with Mina, the whole nine yards."

"And he couldn't just wait and propose for himself?" I couldn't resist asking. Geez. Men.

"Mina was expecting it this week. He didn't want to disappoint her."

Ha. Shows how much he knew. Mina wouldn't have hired me if she'd been expecting it. "Well, shouldn't we tell Ciel what's going on now?"

"Are you crazy? She'd blow up if she knew we've been keeping tabs on her, even if it is for her own good. And she'd never believe I'm just doing a favor for Trey."

You got that right, I thought. *And I can damn well take care of myself.* The main reason I started my own business was to get out from under the overprotective thumb of my family. And now I find out Mark is in on it?

"Yes, but do you really think it's wise to keep something like this from her?" I elbowed him out of my way and set the pitcher on the counter. Trey's six-pack deflected my jab with barely a flinch. Stupid muscles. "Sorry. I slipped."

"If she finds out it'll be that much harder to keep an eye on her in the future. Don't worry—it'll be fine. Ciel never needs to know."

Oh yeah? Well, I've got news for you, buster . . .

Mina's voice interrupted us from the living room. "Hey you two, do you need any help? You putting the moves on my man, Edith?"

I tittered as loudly as I could manage. "Oh my, no," I called back. "Just borrowing a little of his strength to carry the drinks for me. You keep your seat—we're on our way."

Mark leaned down close to my ear. "Listen, you have to fill in as Trey for me later. I don't think Ciel will let him get away from her again, and I need you to keep her occupied while I finish dealing with the Swede. Take her for ice cream or something."

"Ice cream?" I pushed a smile across my teeth. So, now he was trying to treat me like some kid and keep me out of the grown-ups' business?

"Yeah, or something like that. You know what to do. Be affectionate. Be cuddly, like Trey would. She'll expect that. Anything short of sleeping with her—if Ciel ever found out that wasn't the real Trey, she'd kill us both. So improvise."

Oh, I'd show him improvise. I gestured for him to carry the tray of drinks. Once his back was turned I gave him another gesture. Yeah, I know. Childish. Ironic, huh?

I knew I should let them both in on the little farce we unwittingly had going. But the more I thought about it, the more pissed off I got. They could just stew in it for a while, as far as I was concerned. The kidnapper wasn't going anywhere for a while; I had some time. Mark thought Mina was me, and Billy had no way of knowing Trey wasn't the real Trey. They didn't dare reveal themselves to each other.

"Trey" put the drinks on the coffee table and sat down next to "Mina." He laid his arm over Mina's shoulders, making Billy squirm. Interesting. Just how far would Mark take this charade if he didn't get the opportunity to switch places? Would he follow through with it all the way to the bedroom? The panicked look in Mina's eyes told me Billy certainly thought so. *Interesting.* Bet I could make Mark squirm, too, if he thought he had to, say, pretend Trey was impotent just to avoid sleeping with me. He wouldn't relish explaining to his friend why he'd had to give him a sudden case of performance anxiety, would he? Because, thinking I'd be giving a full report to the real Mina, Mark would have to explain not rising to Mina's expectations. So to speak.

Mina stood as Trey was about to pull her closer.

"Excuse me. I have to use the restroom. Edith, could you show me where the spare soap is?"

"It's on the vanity."

"I already used that up."

"There's more under the sink." I relaxed back into my club chair and put my feet up on the ottoman.

"Silly me. I looked there earlier and didn't see it. Could you show me? Please?"

I sighed and got up. Billy made a beeline for the guest bathroom and was tapping his foot impatiently when I got there. He pulled me in and shut the door behind us.

"We have to switch back. Now."

"We can't—we don't have time to trade clothes. Trey will get suspicious if I don't go right back out. Besides, you're just as good at Mina as I am. You can keep her."

"No!"

"Why not?"

"Because Trey misses Mina." He looked at me meaningfully. "A lot."

I played dumb. "Yeah. So?"

"Cuz, I will do a lot in order to look out for you without risking your cover, but I will not sleep with Trey."

"But you expect me to?"

"Hell's bells, Ciel, you *want* to!"

"That was before I found the ring. Now it goes against my professional ethics. You, on the other hand, have no ethics, so it shouldn't bother you."

"I draw the line at sleeping with other men."

"I have to get back out there to Trey. He'll wonder what's taking so long."

"Ciel, by God, if you don't make an opportunity to switch places with me before bedtime, I'll . . . I'll . . ."

"What? Pull my hair?" I smiled sweetly and left.

Chapter 5

My plan was simple: payback. Watching the two of them dance around each other, both trying to get me off by myself to make a switch, would be balm to my wounded pride. I might even let them spend the whole night together. It would serve them right. Who cared if the kidnapper had to spend more time tied up in the dusty old warehouse? He'd been planning to leave me there, so it served him right. I hoped the spiders were crawling all over his sorry kidnapper ass.

Billy's behavior I could almost understand. Our sparring went back to childhood, and neither of us would miss an opportunity to jab the other. He was a merciless tease, but I knew he cared for me underneath it all. Just on general principle, though, I couldn't pass up a chance to cause him a little discomfort.

But Mark. I couldn't believe how easy it was for him to deceive me. Oh, not how easy in the capability sense. Any competent adaptor could pull it off. Easy in the not-a-twinge-of-conscience sense. *That* ticked me off.

After the lemonade was served, Mina immediately became concerned with Trey's wardrobe, or lack thereof. "We have to find you something to wear, pumpkin. Edith was kind enough to take me shopping—maybe she and I should go out and get you a few things, too." Behind Mina's eyes, I could see Billy grasping for a way to separate himself from Trey's bare skin.

Mark jumped at the idea, at least partially. "That would be great, babe, but don't you think Edith has done enough for us already? Maybe you could run out and get me something while I keep her company here." He looked at me pointedly. Getting a little anxious to make the switch, was he? Fat chance.

"The stores are all closed by now," I said pleasantly. "But not to worry. You lovebirds are welcome to my spare room tonight. Tomorrow you can go shopping together." Twin glares met my perfectly reasonable suggestion. You just can't please some people, I thought with inner glee.

Ignoring the visual arrows, I moved the conversation forward, as any good hostess will. "I must say, Trey, we were all so relieved when Mina told us you were out at the time of the explosion. But, Mina, you must have been *horrified* when you found out he was kidnapped."

Billy caught on. "Well, yes, of course I was—you know I was. I was terrified someone would hurt my pumpkin." He looked at Trey, letting tears fill Mina's eyes. However annoying Billy could be, at least you could trust him to remain in character on the job.

Mark narrowed Trey's ocean-blue eyes at me, telegraphing mayhem at the Billy he thought I was, and pulled Mina closer to his naked chest. "I'm sorry about that, babe, but I'll make it up to you." He leaned over and whispered into Mina's ear. I didn't catch what he said, but judging from the way Billy jumped up when he was done, it hadn't been well received.

"Are you quite all right, Mina? You've gone pale." And I was loving every chalky bit of it. If I could make Mark equally uncomfortable, I'd be a happy old woman. How dare he try to foist the job of not sleeping with me onto Billy? If he didn't want to sleep with me, he could darn well not sleep with me himself.

"I'm fine. Except . . . this is a little embarrassing to say, but I think I just started my, um, monthly. Since all my stuff blew up, I don't have any, uh, you-know-whats. You wouldn't happen to have any on hand, would you, Edith?"

Slick. Billy always could think on his feet. I pretended to be flustered at the forthrightness of the question. "Oh, my. I don't know. I mean, I don't . . . for myself it's no longer . . . well. Perhaps there's something in the cabinet under the sink?"

"Let's go look, shall we?" Billy took me by the

arm, none too gently, and led me back to the guest bathroom.

"We have to stop meeting like this." I batted my eighty-odd-year-old eyelashes at him.

"You. Clothes off. Now."

"I beg your pardon?"

"We are switching right this minute, or I swear I'll spill the beans to Trey. Screw your business."

"What on earth did he whisper to you?"

"He told me he bought some special supplies at the resort shop when he went back for his wallet earlier."

"So?"

"The 'special supplies' are condoms. Fruit-flavored. Mina's favorite." A shudder went through him.

"F-F-Fruit? Oh, my gawd!" True, they were Mina's favorite, but how did Mark know? Unless Trey told him. Guys do talk. And Mark was probably trying to pay Billy back for giving him trouble, not knowing it was really me. What better way than to have Mina entice Billy's Trey persona with the condoms later, when Billy was under orders not to follow through? Hee! This was working out even better than I'd hoped. I doubled over and stuffed half my hand in my mouth to keep my howls of laughter contained.

"Ha-fucking-ha. Come on. Get those rayon rags off right now. Don't worry—you haven't got anything under there I'm not already intimately acquainted with." He didn't wait for me, but unbuttoned my blouse and yanked on my sleeve.

I sat down hard on the plush bath mat. I couldn't help it—my legs stopped working. My hand dropped away from my mouth as I tried to steady myself, and I'm afraid some unqueenly guffaws may have escaped the confines of the room.

Within seconds the door swung open. Trey's eyes widened when he saw us there, me splayed on the floor, one arm pulled upward by Billy's attempt to disrobe me, and Billy bent over me, reaching down my back to unhook my bra. We froze.

"What's going on in here?" Mark looked positively flummoxed. Mr. Unflappable himself. Not much, but it was something. I supposed it was time to come clean.

But first I had to enjoy it a little more. "Care to join us, big guy? The more the merrier."

Billy was the first to recover. "Trey! Help me. I think Edith has had a stroke or something. She started talking nonsense and ripping at her clothes. I thought I'd better get her to lie down." The boy was quick.

Mark was over me in a flash, pushing up my eyelids to look at my pupils, moving one finger back and forth in front of my face to see if I could track it. "Can you smile for me, Edith?"

No problemo. In fact, I was having trouble not smiling.

"Good. Now can you lift both your arms for me at the same time?"

I did.

"Great. Now can you tell me how you're feeling?"

"I'm feeling like you're a big jerk, *Mark*."

His eyes narrowed, and Billy jumped in with, "Mark? Is that you? What are you doing here?"

Mark looked over his shoulder at Mina. "I'll explain later, Ciel. Or maybe I'll let Billy here do that." He stood up and booted my royal posterior. Not hard, but still.

"Ouch! I'm not Billy. *I'm* Ciel. Mina is Billy."

Mark looked from me to Billy and back again. "At the risk of repeating myself, what the hell is going on here?"

I pulled myself up and shrugged, rebuttoning my shirt. "Nothing. Billy stole Mina from me and wouldn't give her back, so I had to take the Queen—" Something occurred to me. "Hey, did you know Trey might be Mark all along?" I asked Billy. If he had, I was gonna kill him. Twice.

"I did *not*. If I had, I never would've gone after him."

"Thanks a lot. See if I ever hire you again," Mark said.

"Only because I'd have trusted you to get out of the mess yourself," Billy explained, with a pretty Mina-smile, and then turned on me. "In any case, *you* shouldn't have followed me. For God's sake, you saw me take the gun. I had it covered."

"Yeah, well, it didn't look 'covered' to me. Quite the opposite, in fact."

"Jesus, Ciel, I'd just gotten there. I was still assessing the situation."

I got right up in his pretty face, and jabbed his shoulder with my age-spotted hand. "Right.

Because it's so easy to 'assess' when you have a gun pointed at you. If you'd tried to go for yours, you could've been killed, and Trey—I mean, Mark—too!"

"I had it under control," he said, voice escalating to match mine. "Mark would've been free in another minute even if you hadn't arrived when you did, and believe me, the two of us wouldn't have had any difficulty taking down the Swede."

"And how in the hell was I supposed to know—"

A piercing whistle made us both wince. Trey's ocean-blue eyes were stormy, and the non-Chiclets were nowhere in sight. "Both of you—quiet." We obeyed. Very few people didn't obey Mark when he used that tone. For the space of two hard looks—one for Billy and one for me—there was silence. "Now, then," he said at last, softening it with a hint of amusement around his eyes. "I'm hungry. What do you have to eat around here?"

Half an hour later Mark, Billy, and I were seated around the glass-topped dining table, drinking beer, ready to chow down on newly delivered pizza. We had closed all the blinds and dropped our assumed auras as soon as the delivery boy left, a huge smile on his face at the size of his tip. All things considered, it was just less confusing to be ourselves for a while.

Since there was a severe shortage of men's clothing around the place, Billy was wearing Edith's pink flannel robe, and Mark was still in Trey's bathing suit. I'd snagged one of Mina's new outfits for myself, a floaty, multicolored drawstring skirt and matching spun-rayon tank top. The top was big and the skirt way too long, but it was miles ahead of anything in Edith's wardrobe style-wise.

Yes, I'm short. My own hair is strawberry blond, my eyes are pale green, and "voluptuous" is not a word you'll ever hear associated with my true form. Try to ignore the freckles. I know I do.

Mark, looking too damned delicious in Trey's trunks, glanced at the clock on the wall. His build was similar to Trey's, but his hair was a darker blond, and his eyes a shade of gray that oscillated between dove-soft and cold as steel. His features were sharp and rugged. If Trey brought to mind country clubs and polo, then Mark made you think back alleys and street fighting. Seeing him in his own form never failed to make my hormones do the happy dance. Billy's dark curls and dimples were probably, from a strictly objective point of view, every bit as swoon-worthy, but the pink robe tended to detract from that.

Billy's voice interrupted my mini-reverie on Mark's physical virtues. "Nice job at the warehouse, cuz. Your screams sounded so *authentic*." One of his hands crawled across the table toward me, squashing any hope that my reaction to the spiders would go uncommented upon.

"That hand gets any closer, and I swear to God I'll smash it," I said, my mostly full beer can held poised for attack. Mr. Crawly retraced his steps.

Mark gave my shoulder a squeeze, looking at

me with what could have been pity, but I chose to believe was sympathy and understanding. He let go too quickly to suit me, and turned his attention to systematically devouring slice after slice of a Meat Lover's Special. Between bites he grilled me about everything Trey- and Mina-related.

". . . so, was there anything—anything at all—in Mina's dossier that might point to a non–Agency-related reason for Trey's abduction?" He timed the final question to coincide with his last swallow of beer.

"No," Billy and I answered simultaneously.

I glared at Billy, who flashed me his best dimples-and-lashes look of pure innocence. *Note to self: beef up security at my office.*

"Okay," Mark said. "But we better look at it again. I'll have a copy sent over in the morning. In the meantime, I have to go check on our new friend." He dropped a kiss on the top of my head (a waste of good lips), ruffled my hair, and was Trey again before he got to the door.

"Wait a minute," I called after him, my mind backspacing to what he'd said about Mina's dossier. "You mean to tell me you have a copy of Mina's file, too?" Damn it, was there anyone who didn't have access to my office?

"Later." He lifted one hand in a casual wave, without turning around, and let himself out.

I turned to Billy, who was studiously selecting his next slice and avoiding my eyes. "Billy," I started in conversational tone, "how did Mark get the file from my office?"

"About that . . ." He cleared his throat and took another swallow of beer before continuing. "Well, you see . . ." He looked at me and must've seen the murder in my eyes. I'm no good at hiding my feelings when I'm in my natural state. "I suspect he has people for that sort of thing, don't you? Clerical help." He took a humongous bite of his new slice.

"Did you give a copy of Mina's file to Mark? Or did you make him steal his own?"

He chewed thoughtfully, taking his time before swallowing. "There's no good answer to that, is there? I'm screwed either way. You probably won't even be mad at Saint Mark, you're still so besotted with him."

"That is not true!" I felt my cheeks flame.

"Is so. Why else do you think you were so attracted to Trey? You've worked plenty of jobs with good-looking men, and never turned into a quivering mass of hormone-rattled goo before. You were obviously picking up on his underlying Mark vibe."

Oh, my God—was it true? Did I subconsciously know it was Mark all along? Was I really that miserably stuck on him? I spat a piece of thumbnail into my napkin. *Shit*. I hadn't even been aware I was chewing it. I pushed my chair away from the table, not hungry any longer.

"Don't worry, cuz. Your secret is safe with me." He leaned back, a smug look on his face. Probably because he had successfully diverted my ire from his wavy-haired head.

"You're being ridiculous. *If* I was attracted to

anyone, it was Trey. Mark is too good an adaptor to let any of himself slip through. If I responded at all, and I'm not saying I did—"

"Right."

"*If* I responded, it was a purely physical reaction to a nice male specimen. That's *all*."

"God, you're cute when you're mad. By the way, I like your hair short like that, sticking out all over, kind of post-modern punk."

My hands flew to my head and smoothed my flyaway tresses. I'd gone short since the last time Billy saw me—but not, I stress, "punk"—in hopes it would make me appear older. Wearing my hair long had made me look about fourteen, and I was sick of getting carded in bars. I was also sick of my cousin's barbs.

He winked. "Unclench your fists, cuz. I'm not wearing a cup today and I'm feeling rather defenseless." His eyes softened, losing their teasing glint. "I meant what I said. You're adorable, you know that, right?"

I dropped my head back and stared at the ceiling. "Uh-huh. I'm irresistible. Just ask Mark."

"He cares an awful lot about you."

"Yeah, I know. I'm the little sister he never had." I grabbed the pizza box and trudged toward the kitchen. "You have no idea how frustrating it is to really, really like someone who only sees you as an annoying relation."

Billy gathered the empty beer cans and followed me. He crushed them one at a time and tossed them in the bin while I shoved the leftover pizza into the fridge. "So, you 'really, really like' Mark, huh? You mean, like, *like* like?"

I had to admit it sounded pretty juvenile. "God. I'm pathetic, aren't I?"

"Absolutely," he said, draping an arm over my shoulder. "But on you it works." He kissed my forehead and walked me back to the living room.

"If I'd had half a brain when I was growing up, I'd have gradually adapted myself to be tall and curvaceous as soon as I was through puberty. Now everybody in the family knows what I really look like, so I can't do anything about it." I shrugged out from under his arm and sprawled backward on the couch.

"Not even you can hold an aura forever, Supergirl. Somebody would have caught you eventually," he said reasonably, sitting next to me and pulling my feet onto his lap. *Gaaaah*. There is nothing better than a foot massage, except for chocolate, and maybe sex. I felt my whole body relax as he worked the arch of my left foot with strong, gentle fingers. Make that a big maybe on the sex. Nothing I'd experienced in that department thus far came close to being as good as a foot massage. He switched to my right foot. "Now, which speech do you want—'Appearances Are Shallow' or 'It's What's on the Inside That Counts'?"

I felt a tug at the corner of my lips. "Neither. I'd rather bitch and moan some more."

He went on massaging. "If you must. But could you give me a heads up when you're done, so I'll know when to start listening again?"

I peered at him from beneath half-closed lids. "It's easy for you, you know. You'd be singing a different tune if you still looked like your sixth-grade school picture," I said, just to be evil.

He laughed in good-natured agreement, and started in on my toes. "Not a good year for me. If I'd been capable then, I'd have gone to school every day looking like the teenage heartthrob of the week."

I suppose it's just as well our talent doesn't emerge fully until adulthood, even if it does make middle school hell. "What about now? Are you really as gorgeous as you look? You aren't fudging it even a tiny bit?"

"You think I'm gorgeous? I'm flattered." He batted his eyelashes so fast I could almost feel a breeze.

"Oh, come on. You know you are—why else would all those women chase you? Stop avoiding my question. Do you cheat or not?"

He hesitated. "Well, there is one part of me I alter on occasion."

"I knew it!" *His eyelashes. It had to be his eyelashes.* "What is it?" I sat up eagerly, but kept my feet where they were. They didn't want to leave yet.

"Promise you won't tell anyone?"

"Yes. Now spill."

"If you must know, Miss Nosy, it's my"—he turned away from me, pained—"my manhood."

I poked him in the belly with my big toe. "Oh, come on. Get serious."

He looked wounded. (He did wounded well.) "Fine. Be that way. See if I ever open up to you again," he said, with just the right amount of hurt in his voice, so I knew he was full of shit.

"Golly gee, Tiny, I'm sorry. It was insensitive of me not to take you seriously. Hey, I got some e-mail the other day that might help with your problem. Want me to forward it to you?"

"It's obvious you don't understand the true nature of my dilemma. The fact is, if I don't scale it down to normal proportions, I demoralize my pals at the gym and frighten the women I date." He laughed when I rolled my eyes, and shoved my feet off his lap. "My turn. Time to pay the piper."

"It's really not a fair exchange, you know," I pointed out after he plopped his feet onto my thighs. "There's a lot more acreage here than you have to cover with me."

"Whine, whine, whine. Shut up and knead."

At least they were nice feet, clean and well kept. I applied myself as assiduously as he had, tit for tat. The temptation to tickle was strong, but I knew from experience I'd never come out ahead in that game. "When do you suppose Mark will be back?"

"Why? Planning on waiting up for him?"

I shrugged. "I'm thinking about it." He laughed and wiggled his toes, drawing my hands to where he wanted them. "Well, it does involve Mina," I said, tackling each little piggy in turn. "I should know what's going on. Aren't you going to wait up?"

"Nope. Not my client. I'll be sleeping the sleep of the blessedly conscience-free. You can have Mark all to yourself."

* * *

"Howdy?"

I jumped at the sound of Mark's voice, quiet though it was. "Howdy" was his childhood nickname for me, short for Howdy Doody, who had more freckles than I did when I was ten, but not by much. Leafing through magazines—and, okay, maybe dozing a tiny bit—I hadn't heard him enter the bungalow. Super Spy was just that stealthy.

"Sorry," he said, sitting next to me sideways, one knee up, ruffling my hair before he draped his arm over the back of the sofa. "Didn't know I'd be so late. You should've gone to bed."

He was fully dressed now, having gotten hold of some faded jeans and an equally faded Hawaiian shirt. On him, faded looked good. (Admittedly, I'd never seen anything on him that *didn't* look good.) I tossed the magazine onto the coffee table and stretched, stifling a yawn. "I wanted to talk to you. What'd you find out?"

"Not much. Yet. I'm taking the Swede back with me on a company plane—I just stopped by to leave Billy some travel clothes, and both of you new passports. 'Trey' and 'Mina' are booked on a flight tomorrow—we'll talk more about it when you're back."

Well, that was quick. Guess it pays to have connections in high places. "Did you get in touch with Trey? Does he know Mina is okay? If he heard about the explosion, he's probably worried to death."

"Not yet, but we will. In the meantime, I have something for you." He dug into his pocket and pulled out a battered ring case. Opened it and held it out to me. My heart thudded against my ribs, jolted by past fantasies of precisely this moment— Mark giving me an engagement ring. Like an idiot, I stared at it, sparkling in the soft light of the table lamp. Mocking me.

"You gonna take it, or do I have to get down on one knee to make your job officially complete?" he joked.

I took it and snapped the case shut. "Thanks," I said, jumping up and heading to the guest room before he could read my face. Not that he could have failed to realize my pathetic crush on him over the years, but I was kind of hoping he thought I'd outgrown it. No need for him to know my girlhood passion blazed on. It was embarrassing enough that Billy was aware of it. "I'll just put it with Mina's stuff."

He followed, taking my arm and turning me back toward him. "Hold on a second. I have to go . . . hey, are you okay? What's the matter?"

I swallowed hard. "Nothing. I'm fine. I just . . . it's been a day. You know?"

His arms circled me gently, pressing me to his chest, and mine automatically went around his waist.

"It's going to be fine. Billy will take care of

everything tomorrow, and you can put this whole thing behind you. And, Howdy . . . I know it pisses you off, but I'm not going to stop watching out for you." His lips pressed against the top of my head briefly. "You get some sleep."

Yeah, right. Like that was gonna happen now.

Chapter 6

Billy and I got to the airport early, after driving through a raging storm, so I had plenty of time to work myself into a state of near-frozen panic before we boarded. I'm not the best air passenger, even under ideal circumstances. Toss in some bad weather and I stiffen up like a nun in a whorehouse. Not precisely in character for jet-set Mina, but frankly I didn't give a flying fig.

As soon as we were airborne, Billy signaled the flight attendant. She came at once, bearing booze. The hundred-dollar bill I'd seen pass from Billy's hand to hers as we boarded might've had something to do with her alacrity.

"No, thanks," I said, gripping the armrests and shuddering as the plane bounced. Even the sight of Mina's new ring on my finger didn't comfort me. It wasn't like I could give it to her and call the job done, not before the real Trey was notified.

Billy took the glass from her and held it to my lips. "It's medicinal. Drink." We bounced again. I drank. Fast, not even tasting it.

"What was it?" I asked, staring straight ahead and ignoring the clouds floating past the window in my peripheral vision.

"Only the finest Tanqueray martini. Wasted on your taste buds, apparently. Breathe."

I gulped some air. "I don't think it's doing anything for me."

He downed his drink in two quick sips and called for refills. I shook my head at the flight attendant, but I was invisible to her. Ensnared as she was by Trey's killer smile, she wouldn't have noticed me if I'd stood on my seat and danced naked.

"Bottoms up, sweetheart," Billy said, pouring the second one past my lips, not giving me a chance to refuse. He popped my olive into his mouth and chewed. "Don't worry. You'll feel better in a minute or two."

"I dunnoh . . ." But he was right. My grip on the armrests gradually eased.

He smiled. "There now. You're not scared anymore, are you?"

I thought about it, somewhat amazed. "No. Not at all." In fact, I felt pretty good. I snuggled up to Trey's manly bicep as a wave of euphoria settled over me. "You're wonderful. Martinis are magic, aren't they?"

"I've always thought so," he said, eyes alight.

"Now, have I told you about a little organization called the Mile High Club?"

I swatted him. "I'm not *that* drunk."

He laughed. "Too bad."

The landing at Reagan National Airport was bumpy, or maybe that was just me. But after staying lubricated with magic martinis for most of the flight, at least I was no longer stiff. In fact, I was so un-stiff Billy had to help me down the aisle.

"Can't hold her liquor," he stage-whispered to the amused flight attendant as we passed. I would have denied it vehemently had I been capable of forming coherent words, but she probably wouldn't have believed me anyway after I stepped on her foot.

The first thing we noticed after we deplaned (and by "we" I mean Billy—I wasn't noticing much of anything myself) was a TSA agent who seemed excessively interested in the pair of us. It wasn't until Billy gripped my upper arm and hurried me into the midst of the crowd stampeding toward baggage claim that I picked up on something being out of whack.

"Wha's—what's up?" I said. Billy let my mush-mouth moment pass without comment. It was the least he could do after pouring the martinis down me.

"TSA does not customarily greet arrivals—they are more concerned with departures. They also do not use the kind of badge that guy was wearing, nor do their officers speak into their badges. Plus, the blue of his shirt is at least two shades off."

I craned my head to get a better look. He gave my arm a small shake. "Eyes front, cuz."

"He's not following us, if that's what you're worried about," I said, a small burst of adrenaline having cleared my mind somewhat.

"Yet. He's giving us space because he thinks he knows where we're going."

"But we're not?"

"Oh, we are." He maneuvered us over to the restrooms. "But not as Trey and Mina. Meet me in two minutes right here. Get comfortable," he said, adaptor code for be yourself.

Luckily, there was a free stall, so I could change right away. I switched shirts with one from my carry-on. Figured that would have to suffice clothing-wise. Billy was waiting when I returned. He'd done the same.

We continued to Arrivals at a more leisurely pace, which was good because Mina's shoes were at least an inch and a half too long for my feet. We'd gone through customs in Nassau, so we could leave the airport without that delay. As we passed the baggage claim area we saw a uniformed driver holding up a sign with Trey's name on it.

"Aw, how thoughtful," I said. "Mark ordered us a limo."

"Think again, cuz," Billy said, guiding me away from the man, toward the taxi stand, with one hand on my waist.

Oh. Well, crap. Guess Trey and Mina were still on somebody's radar.

* * *

I live in D.C., not too far from George Washington University, in a condo I rent from my oldest brother, Thomas. He held on to it after he moved to a bigger place because its location made it such a good investment. When I decided to start my own business, I grabbed at his offer of cheap rent, figuring there were worse places to live and work than D.C. For one thing, it's far enough away from the family homestead in New York that I'm not dropped in on by an endless parade of well-meaning relatives.

And, okay, D.C. is the closest thing to a home base Mark has. That might have had a *little* something to do with my decision. He used to room with Thomas, and still stops by the condo occasionally. Sometimes even stays overnight in his old room, which is now my guest room. I keep hoping he'll wander across the hall some fine night, but I'm not holding my breath.

By the time the cab dropped Billy and me at my building I was slightly more functional. Not precisely sober, but Billy only had to steady me with one hand on my elbow as we walked to the condo.

I punched in the code to unlock the front door. It stayed locked. Tried again.

"Damn it. Somebody must've changed it while I was gone."

"Here, let me." Billy, of course, got it on the first try. I hate people who can hold their liquor.

My stomach contracted the instant he turned on the lights in the living room. "Shit. What the fuck happened here?" he said, echoing my thoughts. "I don't suppose you left it this way?"

I stared blankly, trying to take it in. My mind kept fighting me. Finally I said, "No. I may not be Martha Stewart around the house, but I usually manage to keep the cushions on the sofa and the TV off the floor."

"You stay here. I'll check the rest of the place."

No argument from me. If whoever had done this was still here, I was in no hurry to meet him. A minute later he was back. "It's the same upstairs. The stuff I keep in your guest room is all there. You'll have to check your room and see if anything is missing. Come on."

I followed him reluctantly. When I got to my bedroom door I froze, sucker-punched again, even though I was expecting what I saw. My comforter and sheets had been ripped from the bed and strewn on the floor, my clothing yanked from hangers in the closet, my underwear pulled out of my dresser drawers. Bile crept into my throat at the thought of some stranger handling my intimate apparel.

Billy laid a hand gently on my neck. "Hey, you okay?"

I wasn't, but I nodded anyway. "Why would somebody do this?" On top of everything that happened in the Bahamas, it seemed a little much to just be bad luck.

"Obviously whoever did it thought you had something he wanted."

"But I don't have anything. My furniture is all secondhand. My TV and stereo are crap. I don't even have any good jewelry."

"How about a computer?"

"My laptop!" I rushed to the desk and rustled beneath the scattered papers. "It's gone."

"Anything vital on it?"

Say, like backup copies of confidential client files? Oops. "Uh, no, of course not. Well, maybe a few . . . never mind, it doesn't matter. It's password protected."

Billy snorted. "Oh, now we can rest easy. Please don't tell me you used the security software that came with it."

"Of course not—I'm not stupid. Mark set something up for me when I got it."

"Should be okay then." Approval, if somewhat grudging.

I looked around at the mess, trying to survey it dispassionately. "What do we do now? Call the police?"

"No. We'll call Mark and let the spooks handle it. I suspect whatever this is, it's more up their alley. Besides, I'd prefer Mark to run interference between us and anyone official. But first let's look around and figure out what else is missing."

After a thorough search, I said, "My diary."

"The green suede one, or the cute little pink one with unicorns?"

I closed my eyes and counted to ten under my breath. "Green," I ground out. I hadn't used the pink one since middle school, which I was sure he knew darn well.

"Well, you shouldn't keep a diary if you don't want people to find it," he said, without an ounce of shame. "Anyway, I wouldn't worry too much about it. If I couldn't decipher your mumbo-jumbo, I doubt our thief can." That was some consolation, at least. I'd developed my own secret code at an early age. Growing up with three brothers and a very annoying pseudo-cousin will drive you to extremes to ensure some privacy.

"It's not like I wrote anything important in it, anyway." Unless you think schoolgirl fantasies about a certain spook are important.

Billy wanted to make the call, but I told him it was my condo so I should be the one to do it. Mark answered after the first ring, sounding alert in spite of the late hour. "What's up?"

"Nothing much. Somebody broke into my condo, trashed the place, and took my laptop."

"Shit. Is Billy still with you?"

"Yeah."

"Put him on."

"No. You can talk to me."

"Ciel, I need to ask—"

"Ask *me*," I insisted.

"Never mind. I want the both of you out of there now. Tell Billy I said to use full caution. You know where I am." *Click.* Didn't anybody say good-bye anymore?

"Well?"

"We're supposed to go to Mark's place using 'full caution,' whatever the hell that means."

Billy seemed to understand. He smiled and said, "How good are you at projecting drunken college boys?"

Oddly, I didn't have a single drunken college boy in my repertoire, but that was okay because Billy had plenty to choose from in his. It was easy enough to borrow one—Billy called up an alcohol-riddled specimen of undergrad manhood and took my hand. After a few minutes I had a good enough take on the image. And the smell. Ew. I felt myself getting woozy again on the beer fumes alone. Once I was set, Billy dropped the fragrant aura and brought out another one for himself, a much finer example of campus masculinity.

"Hey, why'd you give me the overweight one with pimples?" I protested, my new voice cracking. Good thing the waistband on Mina's skirt was expandable.

"It was the first one handy," he said in a pleasantly deep voice, looking at me through only slightly inebriated bedroom eyes. Handy, my ass. "Now come on. Get changed and let's go."

Billy visits D.C. a lot, and keeps as many clothes at my place as he does at his own in New York. I suspect he has stashes everywhere he frequents, because he never seems to be at a loss for something to wear, no matter which aura he's using. His jeans were all too tight for my new persona, but he had a pair of cargo pants that had been stylish once upon a time. They were intended to be worn baggy but, sadly, on me were not. Mina's ring—back in its case—fit neatly into one of the side pockets, though, so that was good. I couldn't risk leaving it at my condo now. The old black T-shirt was a slightly better fit than the pants, but the picture of Bart Simpson mooning the world wasn't exactly my cup of tea.

We made it to the street unobserved. Once there, we blended in with a group of similarly jovial college kids as we made our way to the closest major road to get a taxi. One of the girls was a tall, big-bosomed brunette who cozied up to Billy like a kitten to cream. Her T-shirt was emblazoned with a "Slippery When Wet" road sign. Huh. I'll just bet.

"You're in my chem class, aren't you?" she purred.

I missed Billy's answer because another girl in the group—short, plump, and still in full orthodontic regalia—swayed into me. I steadied her the best I could, and was mortified to feel my projected penis start to twitch when my arm accidentally brushed her breast. See, this was exactly why I generally prefer not to assume a male aura—I never quite know how to deal with an appendage that has a mind of its own. (Granted, this one seemed to be twitchier than most I'd experienced.) It is also proof positive a man's penis acts without consulting his brain, because there was no way my brain was the slightest bit turned on by the unfortunate girl beside me. Not that I would have been even if she'd been a super model, but damn.

As we rounded a corner, I saw a cab and quickly hailed it. Billy laid a happy frat-boy kiss on Miss Boobs before I shoved him into the backseat and climbed in after him. He leaned over me and rolled down the window. "See you in chem class," he called out, and blew her a kiss.

I elbowed him in the gut, garnering a satisfying "Oof!" He pushed himself off my lap. The cabby was familiar with the address I gave, so I settled back, trying unobtrusively to adjust myself.

"Got a little problem there, cuz?" Billy said under his breath.

"Why did you choose this aura for me?" I whispered back furiously.

"You mean old 'Boner' Benjamin? No special reason. Just thought he'd make good cover."

I narrowed my eyes to murderous slits. "You do know I'm going to kill you in your sleep someday, don't you?"

Chapter 7

Mark lives on a thirty-foot sailboat he keeps anchored in southwest D.C. Lucky for me, it requires maintenance from time to time—that's usually when he shows up at my place to borrow his old room. I guess he figures I'm less likely than Thomas to have overnight visitors he might disturb (sad but true). Well, other than Billy, but Mark doesn't really care if he disturbs Billy. If they both show up at the same time, they flip a coin for the couch.

He was waiting on deck for us when the taxi let us off at the marina. Billy and I stumbled our way over and boarded, with me narrowly avoiding an unintentional dip in the Potomac when Mark grabbed me by the waistband and hauled me back to safety. Which says a lot about his strength because, believe me, Benjamin was no lightweight. I was relieved to avoid the dunking, even though the cold water might have helped with my continuing, um, problem.

"Steady there, Ciel," he said quietly.

"What makes you think I'm Ciel?" I whispered back, embarrassed by my clumsiness.

"Because there's no way Billy would take that aura for himself."

"How do you know Bo—uh, Benjamin?"

"Who do you think gave him to me in the first place?" Billy answered for him.

"And you felt compelled to pass him along to me why, precisely?"

"You've heard of 'pay it forward'?"

I clutched my twitching crotch, drawing gleeful laughter from Billy and a look of restrained amusement from Mark. I stomped off toward the cabin. "I will see the two of you inside," I said as imperiously as my cracking voice would allow.

The windows were mostly covered by the mesh hammocks Mark had rigged in front of them to make extra storage space, so I assumed it was safe to resume my own identity, which I did with an explosive sigh of relief, holding my pants up with one hand so they wouldn't fall off. I parked myself at one end of the table. Billy chose the opposite end, but I was still close enough to kick him, so I did, right on the shin, with a shoe that was now about ten sizes too big for me.

"Ouch! What was that for?" He switched back to himself as he rubbed his injured limb.

"You know very well what that was for, and you're lucky I didn't aim farther north." I slipped out of the clown sneakers and tucked my feet up under me.

"Hey, I got you here safely and without being followed. Those were Mark's instructions."

"Oh, so 'full caution' means 'use the horny drunk slob' aura? Must be some secret spy code I'm not privy to."

"Children, children," Mark said as he closed the cabin door behind him.

I wasn't quite through bitching yet. "How do you guys put up with *that*? It's like having a gerbil wake up in your pants when you're least expecting it."

They both cracked up, though Mark recovered faster. "Not every guy's gerbil is as jumpy as Benjamin's," he patiently explained.

Billy was more than willing to elaborate. "Some of us have our gerbils well trained. Take mine, for instance—"

"No! You can just keep comments about your gerbil to yourself." I scooted around the banquette, making room for Mark to sit. "I want to hear what Mark knows. What did you find out from the Swede? And is it connected to my condo getting trashed?"

He hesitated, obviously considering how much—or how little—he could get away with telling us.

"Everything," I said, knowing full well he'd say only what he pleased. Sometimes I like to pretend he listens to me. Just another one of my spook fantasies.

Before he answered, he retrieved a bottle of Scotch and two glasses from the galley. He put one in front of Billy, the other at his own place, then turned to me. "I think I have some of those wine coolers you like somewhere in the back. Just a sec, I'll see."

"You still drink those glorified juice boxes, cuz? We really need to work on your palate."

I lifted my chin. "Thanks anyway, Mark, but I'll just have what you're having."

Mark paused to give Billy a Look, but fetched another glass. He poured a generous amount for each of us, neat, careful not to skimp on mine. Crap. Now I had to drink it. I don't even like Scotch, but if I ever wanted Mark to start seeing me as older, maybe I should quit the teeny bopper drinks. Billy had been getting adult treatment from the time he turned twenty-one, and we were the same age, damn it. (All right, so he had a couple of months on me. Well, five. Okay, almost six. Big whoop. Everyone knows girls mature faster than boys anyway.) I lifted my glass and took a hearty swig, figuring the sooner I downed it, the sooner it would be gone. I only choked a little. Billy didn't say anything—his shin was still within reach—and neither did Mark.

After taking a much smaller sip, Mark began carefully. "Trey has been with us peripherally for years. His import-export business is a legitimate family operation—one of the reasons he was recruited by the Agency to do occasional jobs for us. At the time, he wanted to be more than just a trust-fund boy, but now that he's ready to marry and settle down he wants out. He agreed to one last job, since it had been in the pipeline for months."

I was puzzled. "Why didn't you just do the job for him and let him off the hook? Then he could have proposed to Mina himself."

"I offered, but it would have taken too long to bring me up to speed on the details. Besides, he thought he could zip over to Sweden, do what needed to be done, and be in the Bahamas in time to pop the question himself. I was only there to cover his ass in case he got delayed."

"So what happened?" Billy asked.

"Don't know yet. We lost contact."

Two creases materialized between Billy's dark brows. "Shit. That's not good."

Worry wasn't a look I was used to seeing on Billy, and it concerned me more than the simple facts Mark had stated. Something was very wrong.

"No, it's not good. But don't invite trouble—it might just be a mechanical failure. Dead battery in his satellite phone, maybe," Mark said, smiling reassurance at me.

"That's a crock. Stop treating me like a kid," I said, not in the mood to be reassured.

He gave me a quick once-over, noting, I was sure, the baggy clothes I was drowning in, probably looking like a twelve-year-old boy. I stared him down.

"Okay," he said. "Somebody tried to grab Trey in Sweden last week. He got away, checked in with us once, and that's the last we heard. I think I was taken in the Bahamas—when I was Trey—because somebody picked up on me—him—being there. So far the

Swede hasn't coughed up much information, other than he was getting paid a whole helluva lot of money to return Trey to whoever had him before."

"Did he tell you who that was?" Billy leaned forward, intent.

"Not yet, but he will."

"How can you be sure?"

Mark looked at me with eyes so remote they left me chilled. "I'm sure," he said quietly, and sipped his drink.

"Oh." I leaned back, shrinking into my clothes even more, trying not to let my imagination loose.

Mark swore softly under his breath. "Are you going to throw up? Do I need to get you a bowl?"

I glared at him. Once upon a time I'd had starry-eyed visions of joining the Agency myself. Mark had tried to discourage me, explaining calmly and reasonably why he thought it wouldn't suit me. When I persisted, he took me aside and painted graphic word pictures of some of his wetter assignments. (And by wet, I don't mean water. Think redder.) He held my head tenderly over the toilet while I puked my guts out, and then asked me a simple question: if I couldn't hear about stuff like that without losing my lunch, how would I handle being in the middle of it?

He had a point. That's when I decided to start my own business instead.

Of course, he wasn't overly thrilled with my career as a facilitator either. Thought there was too much exposure inherent in building my clientele. As far as Mark was concerned, the less known about our kind, the better. His bosses knew there were more like him, naturally (hard to keep something like that from the top echelon of the CIA), but Mark had worked out some sort of deal that entailed them leaving the rest of us alone in exchange for his exclusive services.

He was right about there being safety in anonymity—all adaptors know that, and try to preserve it. But heck, you can't live in a total vacuum. And it wasn't like I was renting billboards or taking out banner ads on popular websites. Referrals from friends and family worked for me. Discreet word of mouth, too. Kind of like with a traveling poker game. People might start to suspect something funny was going on, but as long as they couldn't pin it down, it didn't matter.

"No, you don't need to get me a bowl. I'm fine," I said.

"You sure, cuz? You do look a little greener than usual, even for you."

I glared at him, too. "Shut up, Billy." I downed the rest of my Scotch and pushed my glass toward the bottle. "You, Mark—keep talking. If they only wanted Trey, why call Mina and tell her to come to the warehouse?"

Mark poured, a much smaller amount this time, and let Billy field the question.

"Leverage over Trey—threaten Mina, and Trey was more likely to give them what they wanted."

"Why not grab her at the same time, then?"

Back to Mark. "Only one guy—even with a gun, it's hard to control two grown people. Much easier to nail one down, and then add the other using the first one as bait. If Mina had been first on the scene, she would've been taken."

"Okay. But why blow up the bungalow?"

Mark shrugged. "That was a simple 'we mean business' statement."

It made a warped kind of sense. "The men at the airport?"

"Probably activated when the Swede didn't come through with Trey in the Bahamas."

"So where's the Swede now?" I had to ask. I just hoped the answer wouldn't make me hurl.

"I dropped him off with some people who have a few more questions for him. They'll let me know when he comes out with something useful."

I took a deep breath and drank the Scotch. It didn't taste quite as bad this time. "All right, then. Unless there's been a tremendous coincidence, somebody has connected me to Mina. Why else would my condo be ransacked?"

"Somebody must've been watching Trey for quite a while. He never uses his own name when he travels for us, but obviously he can't change his appearance all that much. If someone tagged him on a job, it wouldn't be impossible to keep him under surveillance, leading right back to his private life. They'd know about Mina, probably followed her to your office. I only hope they don't know what you really do for your clients."

"My office! Do you think they've been there, too? Maybe we better go——"

"Hold on there, Wonder Woman. I have somebody

watching the building. He'll call if anything looks suspicious outside. We'll check inside ourselves first thing in the morning."

"But—"

"But nothing. You and Billy need to sleep. So do I. We are all going to take a nice nap."

"I call the double berth," Billy said quickly, patting the cushion beneath him.

"Sorry, bud. That's mine. And the quarter berths are loaded with some extra gear I've been storing. One of you can have the V-berth, and one of you will have to make do with that." He pointed to the short banquette sofa across from the dinette.

Billy took one look at the narrow cushions and said, "Well, that's a no-brainer. Shorty, the couch is all yours."

"Thanks a lot," I grumbled automatically, though I was just as happy not to get stuck up front. The V-berth didn't have any windows, and I tend to be claustrophobic.

Billy heaved himself up, chucked me under the chin, nodded to Mark, and left with a cheery, "Night, all." He crawled into his pointy but ample accommodations and pulled the privacy curtain shut behind him.

I looked at the Scotch, considering one last nightcap—the rich, smoky flavor was starting to grow on me—but Mark removed temptation from the table before I could reach for it.

"You too. Off to bed with you."

Just as well. I yawned my acquiescence and unfolded my legs for the two-foot journey across the floor. Stood. Stepped. Fell on my ass. Damn baggy cargos.

Mark hooked me by my armpits and lifted me easily—almost right out of my pants. I dove for the waistband, and bashed my face into his chest. He steadied me before I fell again.

"Ow," I said, cradling my nose. "Geez, are you wearing armor?"

"You okay?" He moved my hand, and gently probed the length of my nose. "Not broken, anyway."

I scrunched up my face, testing. "Yeah, I'm fine. Nothing bruised but my dignity."

He smiled, eyes shifting to the dove-gray that always made me go all soft and gooey inside. "A few more scars there will hardly be noticed." He ruffled my hair and kissed the top of my head. "Good night, Ciel."

Damn, I was getting sick of the hair-ruffling, head-kissing routine.

Maybe it was the Scotch doing my reasoning for me, but I decided this was a fine time to do something about that. So I reached up, dragged his face down to lip level, and planted a big one right on his mouth. I called upon some of my recently acquired job-related expertise and kissed him for all I was worth, slowly and thoroughly, working my body closer to his.

I pulled back before he did, which was somewhat gratifying. He looked totally stunned, which I chose to take as even more gratifying.

"Hey, Mark," I whispered, savoring a power I'd

never before felt around him. "I think your gerbil jumped."

His eyes widened, and I could swear he was blushing under his tan.

"Good night," I said before he could respond, and laid myself down on my bunk, my back to him. He didn't say anything else, but a minute later a pillow and a blanket landed on me. I smiled. For once I'd gotten the upper hand with Super Spy.

The frigid shock of a piece of ice jerked me upright. I shook my T-shirt away from my back and glared lightning bolts at Billy.

"There. That ought to do it," he said, removing himself to a safe distance.

Mark shook his head in wonder. "You are a brave, brave man."

"Just a hungry one. If we don't leave soon, I know we won't have time to stop for breakfast," Billy said, with emphasis on the final word.

"Breakfast?" I said hopefully, and yawned, tugging the oversized shirt down over my knees. I had ditched the pants during the night.

"See? She's easily distracted from her murderous impulses by thoughts of food, especially if her brain hasn't started functioning for the day."

"Good to know," Mark said. "Come on, Ciel. If you don't hurry up, it'll be daylight and you'll have to put on Benjamin again."

I dragged myself to the head. Anything to avoid that aura. After making quick use of the facilities, I did a cat-wash at the sink. Mark kept extra tooth-brushes in the cabinet, thank goodness. Post-Scotch morning mouth was not a sensation I wished to live with for long.

Once I was clean, and as clearheaded as I was going to get before ingesting massive quantities of caffeine, I realized I didn't have anything to wear. Shit. I did not want to assume Benjamin again just so something would fit—it would feel like putting dirty clothes back on after a bath. Yuck.

"Mark!" I hollered as I opened the door, holding a towel in front of me for decency's sake. "I need—"

He was standing there with a small stack of clothes balanced on one hand like a waiter's tray. I recognized them as some I had left on the boat after a day trip with Mark, my parents, and Thomas the previous summer. It was the spare set my mom had insisted I bring, she being sure I would fall off the boat at some point during our outing. She's such a worrywart. (Okay, so I did fall off, but only once, and I dried off in the sun after Mark pulled me out of the bay, so I didn't really need the change of clothes.)

"Bless your mind-reading little heart," I said, and closed the door in his smiling face.

Mark's face . . . smiling . . . lips . . . *Oh, shit!* Had I really?

I had. Goddamn Scotch. I knew I hated it for a reason. It was a treacherous drink, an *evil* drink, and it made people do stupid things. How was I going to look him in the eye again?

Chin up, that's how. Face it head-on. I slipped

into my jeans, T-shirt, and green hoodie. *You look him right in the eye and . . .* I swallowed . . . *and you pretend it never happened. Act like you don't remember.*

Yep. Selective amnesia: the better part of valor.

I went back out to the main cabin, looking everywhere but at Mark. "Didn't I leave some shoes here, too? I can't wear Billy's. They'd fall off my feet."

"There—in the net," Mark said. Nothing unusual or awkward in his voice. Good. This might work.

I found my old docksiders and slipped them on, sock-less. "Okay, I'm ready. Let's go."

Mark led the way. Billy got to the exit next, but stopped short of leaving. To play the gentleman, I thought, and let me go ahead of him. I should've known better. As I got closer, he puckered up and held out his arms.

"What are you doing?" I asked, not bothering to hide my exasperation.

"Waiting for my good-morning kiss. You gave Mark a good-night kiss. Fair is fair."

"You saw?" Mortification now complete.

He shrugged. "Heard a thunk. Had to investigate."

"Ass." I slugged him as I passed. "That's for the ice cube."

"Ouch," he said, rubbing his arm. "Sheesh. You are so grumpy before your coffee."

Chapter 8

My company headquarters is located on the third floor of an old office building in the heart of D.C. I rent office space from my brother. As with my condo, no way would I be able to afford the primo location without the family discount. I think it's Thomas's way of keeping tabs on his little sister, and I should resent it, but he's so damned nice about the whole thing I mostly don't. Still, as soon as I was financially able, I'd be saying toodle-loo.

The only drawback to the current arrangement is that I'm surrounded by lawyers—no offense to anyone in the legal profession. If lawyers can be offended, that is. Thomas claims not; I'll defer to his expertise.

When we got to the building, Mark pulled around back and parked in Thomas's reserved spot, which took some major cojones. Nobody but my brother ever parked there, on pain of . . . well, I don't know what, because to my knowledge no one has ever dared try it.

Billy unlocked the back door and quickly disarmed the security system. There was no sign of forced entry. Ditto the door to my suite, with its simple brass plate reading "Ciel Halligan, Facilitator." (I still felt a burst of pride every time I saw that. My business might be small, and currently holding on by a financial thread, but it was *mine*.) When Mark punched in the code to open the door, I didn't bother to ask how he'd come by it. Obviously, my life contained no secrets.

We passed through the tiny reception area, straight back to my office, which is minimally but tastefully furnished with leftovers from the lawyers who've moved to greener pastures. The dark, heavy wood of the antique desk, along with the burgundy leather chairs, gave an air of ancient reliability to the place, or so I told myself. It sounded better than "stuffy."

First thing that caught my eye was the rock. In the middle of my desk, atop a piece of cream-colored parchment, was a smooth, black stone. It was about the size of my palm, with some sort of symbol carved into it. Mark zeroed in on it immediately. He gave me a questioning look.

"Well, it sure wasn't there when I left for the Bahamas," I said.

Mark stopped me when I would have reached for it, snapped a few pictures of it with his cell phone, and sent them whizzing off into cyberspace.

Using a tissue from the box in my desk drawer, he lifted the rock by its edges and examined it more closely. "Looks Norse to me," he said. "Probably wiped clean, but we'll let the lab guys check it anyway."

"What does the note say?" I asked, my stomach rerunning the sick feeling I'd had at my condo.

Billy read it aloud, leaving it where it was. "'Dear Miss Halligan, please give this to Miss Worthington, as a token of our regard.' That's all, and then it's signed with the same symbol as the stone. Now, what could that mean, do you suppose?"

Mark's phone buzzed; he listened for a minute before disconnecting, placing the rock back on top of the parchment at the same time. "It's a rune. Mannaz—the equivalent of the letter 'm.' It means 'man.'"

"But why leave it here with me?" It didn't make sense.

"Somebody wants Trey to know they've been following Mina. It's a threat." Mark's mouth was grim, his eyes cold. He was pissed. "Howdy, check your files. See if anything's missing."

The room where I keep my backup computers and paper files was tiny, more like a large walk-in closet, and something in it was different. Not ransacked, like my condo, but disturbed. "Someone's been in here," I said.

Billy gave the room a once-over. "Yeah? Looks all right to me. How can you tell?"

"I'm not sure. But something is making the hair

on my arms stand up." I scanned everything, floor to ceiling. My eyes stopped on the bottom drawer of the last filing cabinet on the wall opposite the door. I pointed to it.

"There. It's not quite closed. I always close the drawers all the way." I shrugged. "It's one of my things. So, unless one of you left it partially open after you were through pilfering my files . . . ?"

"Nope, I'm not that sloppy," Billy said, unapologetic.

Mark didn't grace the suggestion with a response. Of course *he* wasn't careless. He took a pen from a half-full box on one of the shelves and used it to open the drawer. The files looked the same as always—tidy. I may be a little messy at home, but I keep my office organized.

"I don't see anything missing, but you better check for yourself." He handed me the pen.

"Why bother? I'm sure you know them as well as I do." I smiled sweetly. I think. Maybe I just bared my teeth.

"As a favor to me," he replied, taking me by both shoulders and pushing me down to drawer level.

"All right, all right." I shrugged his hands off, trying to ignore the tingle they left behind, and was as careful with the pen as he'd been. Damned if it would be my fault if the perp's prints got smudged.

"Everything seems to be in order," I said minutes later, after a careful perusal.

"Doesn't really mean anything," Billy said. "They

probably made copies and put the files back afterward. Or faxed themselves copies from the handy little machine right there, like I did."

I stood, planted my hands on my hips, and looked from one to the other. "We are going to have to have a talk. You can't just treat my office like—"

"Later." Mark took me by one of my jutting elbows and hustled me back into the main office. "Somebody's coming."

"Geez, what do you have, super hearing?"

He pushed me toward my desk. "Sit down and look busy," he said quietly, and slid back into the file room. He left the door open a crack.

I finally heard it—footsteps in the corridor. Who would be coming in at this hour of the morning? Cleaning staff maybe, or some newbie lawyer trying to rack up billable hours. *Or whoever left the rune, still here in the building,* I thought, grateful I wasn't alone.

The door to my reception area opened. "Ciel? You here?"

Ah. Thomas.

"Yeah. Come on back." I met him as he came into my office. He pulled me into a bear hug instead of giving me the usual peck on the cheek. Medium tall, medium build, medium-brown hair. Gorgeous face. Why did all the men in my life have to be better-looking than me?

"What are you doing here so early?" I said when he relaxed his hold enough for me to breathe.

"I heard about the bungalow." He held me away from him, examining me from top to toe. "Are you all right?"

"She's fine. I told you I was going to drop her at your place after we checked her office. You could've waited," Mark said when he and Billy joined us.

Thomas gave them both a hard look. "And I told you to keep Ciel out of your business."

"Our paths crossed unexpectedly," Mark said. "I had Billy keeping an eye on Ciel after I found out about her involvement with Mina Worthington. I was there, too, so she was never in any real danger."

"Oh, yeah? Nearly being blown up isn't real danger?" Thomas tended to puff up into full grizzly mode when he perceived a threat to his baby sister. I know it's because he loves me, but it's annoying as hell.

"A little close for comfort, you have to admit," Billy said matter-of-factly to Mark, and ignored the flinty glance that followed. I guessed we weren't going to bring up my close encounter with the kidnapper.

"Don't worry. She's officially uninvolved now," Mark assured Brother Bear. "You take her for a few days while Billy and I get a handle on things."

"Excuse me?" I turned on Mark and jabbed him in the chest with my finger. It might have made more of an impression had my fingernail been long enough to be felt through his shirt. "I am not an object to be passed back and forth between you *men*." I swung back to Thomas and poked him, too. "Just because I rent space from you doesn't mean you can tell me what to do. You're not my father."

"Shall I get him on the phone? Or maybe Mom? Would you listen to them?" God, I hate that reasonable tone lawyers invariably fall back on.

"No, no, and no! I can make my own plans and take care of my own problems." I stopped short of stamping my foot.

"This isn't your kind of problem, Ciel. Let Mark handle it."

"Mina is *my* client, so she is, de facto, my problem." I didn't stick out my tongue either, but I wanted to. It is incredibly difficult not to revert back to childish behavior when you're surrounded by the Boys Club.

"And you can deal with her any way you like, with Mark's permission."

"Uh-oh. Probably could've phrased that better, Tommy boy." Billy was leaning casually against the wall, arms crossed, a smile playing at one corner of his mouth.

I rounded on him, finger out and at the ready. "And *you*. You're no better than the nanny twins. Sneaking around, spying on me like I'm some incompetent boob who can't keep herself out of trouble."

He stood up straight, raising both hands in the air. "I surrender. You're absolutely right, I couldn't agree with you more. Men are pigs. Girl power!"

Grrr. I stomped around to the back of my desk,

drawing power from its massive proportions. "Get. Out. Of. My. Office."

All three of them looked at me for about a second, and then went on as if I weren't there.

"By the way, whose piece of shit is in my parking place?" Thomas said, his tone deceptively casual.

"That would be Mark's," Billy said. Mark changes cars the way most people change socks. Makes it harder to keep tabs on him, I guess.

Thomas glanced at his Rolex. "The tow truck will be here in about three minutes. Just so you know."

Mark laughed. "You lawyers are retaliatory bastards, aren't you? Hey Billy, do me a favor, will you?" He tossed his keys across the office. Billy caught them and left, looking happy to make his exit.

Mark strolled over to my desk and perched one leg on the edge, his knee pushing aside my second-hand mahogany pen caddy. "Okay, Ciel. There is a way you can help." He ignored the warning look on Thomas's face.

"How?" I eyed him suspiciously.

"Tell me where you sent Mina. It'll save me time if I don't have to check out all your hidey-holes."

Thomas relaxed. I think. Sometimes it's hard to tell with him. Mark looked at me blandly.

"You mean there's actually something you don't already know? How refreshing." I sat and, careful not to disturb the rock and parchment, readjusted my pen caddy. (Territorial? *Moi?* Just a tad.)

He shrugged. "I could find out easily enough, but why waste time? Look, I just want to make sure she's still all right."

"Why wouldn't she be? No one but me knows where she is—I don't keep that information in the files here." On my laptop, maybe, but he'd made that safe, right? It would be rude to question his competence by bringing it up now.

"You don't think anyone—anyone at all—might have been watching when she left?"

"We were careful. I'm *always* careful," I said, my eyes unconsciously seeking the reassurance of the polished leather album full of thank-you cards and letters from my satisfied clients. At least *they* all thought I was good at my job, great even.

"I'm sure you are." The patience in his voice went down a notch. "And that probably suffices for most of your jobs, but this one is different. Whoever took Trey will be looking for Mina, too."

"And they'll find me. Give me a bodyguard if you're so worried, but Mina is fine where she is."

"Can you be absolutely certain?" Thomas piped in, maddeningly reasonable again.

"Yes." *The laptop, Ciel.* "No! I don't know, let me think." I swiveled my chair toward the window behind me so I wouldn't have to look at the two of them staring holes into me. The view wasn't much—another old building across the street—but at least the dawn was beginning to cast a rosy glow on it. The thing was, they were right. Even if the laptop was secure, how could I be positive Mina wasn't at risk?

I have three undisclosed locations where I send my clients while I'm filling in for them: a remote island beach, a secluded cabin by a lake in upstate New York, and a middle-of-nowhere dude ranch. They're all run by trusted associates, and cost a mint to maintain. On the surface they are ultra-exclusive getaway spots for wealthy people who need some time alone, which has the advantage of being basically the truth. If ever investigated closely, however, they would appear to be mental health facilities for members of the moneyed set who may have had a small nervous breakdown.

Thomas thought of the camouflage—he said no one would be likely to let it slip that they'd spent time in a mental institution, no matter how exclusive. If someone *were* crazy enough to blab . . . well, if they tried to explain me, and what I do for them, they'd only confirm the necessity of their stay in such a place. Machiavelli was a piker compared to my big brother.

I heard Billy reenter the office. "What's up with Ciel?" he asked in an exaggerated whisper.

"She's thinking," Thomas whispered back, equally audible.

"Good grief—stop her before she hurts herself." Back to normal volume from Billy.

I slowly spun my chair around to face the three of them. Choosing to ignore Billy's rudeness, I said, "I'll call and check on Mina. If you'll wait in the reception area?" I indicated the door with my hand.

"Not good enough" was Mark's terse response.

"Why not?" I asked.

"Well, for one thing," Billy said, with a significant look at Mark, "somebody in a rent-a-dent out front appeared to be awfully interested in this building. Or rather, he was until I started to approach him. He took off before I could discuss it with him. Disappeared before I could get back to your car, so there was no way I could follow."

"Crap. Do you think it was whoever left the rock and went through my files?" I said.

"I supervised the security on this building myself—trust me, nobody got in without my knowledge," Thomas said.

I pointed at the rune. "Yeah? How do you explain that, then?"

He shrugged. "I put it there. A messenger delivered it the other day—said it was a gift for one of your clients. Seemed harmless enough, so I brought it up."

Mark pounced on the information. "What did he look like?"

"Scrawny little guy in bicycle shorts. He makes deliveries here all the time."

"Not much help there. Did he say who it was from?" Billy said.

"Just a friend of Ciel's client. Said Ciel would know who it was," Thomas said.

"Well, obviously I don't. But what about my files? If the messenger wasn't in here, who messed with them?"

That made my brother shift uncomfortably. "I may have checked them myself after I heard about the explosion on the news—stop giving me the evil eye, Ciel. I had to see where you were, didn't I? Believe me, I was not reassured when I found out, either."

"Fine," Mark said. "At least we know no one has been in Ciel's office—"

"Other than every fricking one of you," I said, putting my glare on wide-beam.

"Other than us," he conceded. "Tom, I'd like the number to the messenger service." Thomas left, with a nod. "Ciel, I need to know which location—a call won't be enough. I want to get some people on site."

"There's a security guard at each—"

Mark snorted.

"They're good at what they do," I insisted.

"If they were good enough, they wouldn't have to take pissant guard jobs at secluded resorts."

Pissant? Ouch. "Yeah? Well, *you* ran their background checks. If they're no good, you can blame yourself."

"They're good enough for general security, which is what you need. This situation has gone beyond that."

Billy interrupted with an appealing show of dimples. "Come on, cuz, tell Mark what he wants to know so he can get on with his job. You know he's not going to let up on you until you do, and that's just annoying to all of us."

Much as I wanted to keep on arguing, I knew Billy was right. "Fine. She's at the lake house. Now, do you want me to call or what?"

"No need. I'm on it." Mark pulled out his cell phone, dialing as he left the room, pausing only to take a slip of paper from Thomas, who rejoined us.

"And just what am I supposed to do now?" I hollered after Mark, not expecting a response.

Thomas filled the void. "Mom called. She said to remind you about the party. You, too, Billy."

We groaned in unison. My mother, the inimitable Aurora "Ro" Halligan, along with Billy's mom, Maureen "Mo" Doyle, threw a party every autumn. Everyone in New York's adaptor community came. There are more of us than you might think—at least sixty or seventy in NYC alone. Most major cities have at least a few. There's probably a common ancestor, way back down the line somewhere, who started the ball rolling with a mutated gene. That little gene has really branched out during the intervening generations.

The party was the one social event of the season where adaptors could let their hair down and just be themselves. Attendance by the hostesses' family members, while not technically compulsory, was strongly encouraged, to the point where if you didn't show up you'd best be dead. Or at least hospitalized.

"Come now. It's not so bad." My brother dismissed our misery with a wave of his hand.

"How can you say that after last year?" I said.

"The fire was put out quickly, and the catering staff didn't press charges," Thomas said, his voice projecting calm evaluation of the facts.

"Only because you bought them off," I said.

Thomas shrugged. "Come on. Nero apologized, and Mo did get a new kitchen out of it."

"Mommo gets a new kitchen every other year, regardless of smoke damage," Billy pointed out. His mash-up of "Mom" and "Mo" had begun shortly after Auntie Mo had married his dad, and had stuck. "And as I recall, you weren't even there last year, so you have no solid basis for underplaying the calamity."

My ears perked. "What do you mean he wasn't there? I saw him myself, chatting up Felicity Belgrave. Mom was thrilled—she has high hopes that Thomas will settle down and give her some grandchildren so she can lord it over Auntie Mo." I smiled sweetly at my big brother, savoring the one topic that could rattle him. He was far from ready to give up his bachelor lifestyle.

He coughed, and didn't meet my eyes.

"What?! Who'd you pay off to be you for the evening? Nobody's good enough to fool Mom for long."

Billy cleared his throat and nonchalantly buffed his nails on his shirt.

"It couldn't have been you—you were chasing me around all evening as Attila the Hun."

"Only most of the evening. Every now and then I would let Auntie Ro discern just a shade of Thomas beneath my barbaric exterior. A masterfully subtle performance, if I do say so myself."

"But I saw Thomas after the unmasking was complete, and I saw you, too."

"Yes, but did you ever see us at the same time?"

Thomas gave Billy a sour look. "I had assumed confidentiality was a part of our agreement. See if I ever hire you again."

"And I had assumed 'hired' meant I would be paid for my work. Seems we were both mistaken."

Thomas laughed. "Are you sure you won't consider law school? You'd be a natural."

"Sorry. You legal beagles lead too exacting a life for me. I prefer the freedom to follow my fancy." He sauntered around the desk and pulled me up. "Lead on, Fancy."

Chapter 9

Mark stood at the end of the otherwise empty corridor, speaking softly into his phone. When he saw the three of us he held up one finger, said a few more words, then ended his conversation. He slipped the phone into his front jeans pocket, where the ultra-slim gadget barely made a bulge, and gestured for the three of us to join him.

"What's up?" Billy asked.

"Okay. The Swede works for some wacko neo-Viking splinter group bent on restoring masculinity to Scandinavia." Derision seeped through his carefully neutral voice.

"Vikings? You have got to be kidding me," I said, picturing a bunch of tall, blond barbarians running around in horned helmets.

Mark looked faintly embarrassed. "Yeah, I

know. But I guess it's no weirder than some of the other shit going on in the world."

Billy grinned and held up fingers on either side of his head, simulating horns. Great minds think alike. "No, this is definitely weirder."

I giggled.

Mark gave us both a quelling look. "It is what it is. This group wants to reclaim their heritage of strength and honor."

Billy nodded. "The world can always use more strength and honor. And helmets. You can never have too many helmets."

Thomas silenced Billy with a backhanded slap to his shoulder.

"Trey connected with the Vikings six months ago," Mark continued, "and has been trying to figure out whether they're a legitimate threat or just out to grab some headlines."

"Why Trey?" Thomas asked. "Isn't he a little green for anything other than courier work?"

"Normally, yes. But he had a legitimate business reason to be in Sweden, and, frankly, it didn't seem like this neo-Viking thing would amount to much. I mean, this is a group that started out as a bunch of men who were tired of being told by society to 'pee sitting down,' as they so colorfully put it. Hard to take that seriously."

"I'm going out on a limb here, and assuming they meant that metaphorically," Billy said.

"One hopes," Mark said, lips quirking. "Anyway, the group has grown recently. It's showing signs of expanding to America, for fundraising mostly, at least so far. Sweden doesn't want them taking a page from the IRA playbook, and has requested we take a closer look. There've been some rallies, a lot of blustering. No public violence, but picking up steam to the point where we couldn't ignore them as a possible future threat, no matter how ridiculous they seem."

"Ridiculous or not, they're after Trey," Thomas said. "Did your organization drop the ball somewhere, Mark?" The accusation was clear.

"Come on, Tom, be fair," Billy said, all seriousness now. "Do you have any idea how many radical splinter groups there are to keep track of in the world?"

"Only one I care about right now—the one affecting my sister." Thomas was usually a reasonable guy, only not so much where his family was concerned.

"You're right," Mark said. "No excuses. I should've looked into the Vikings more closely as soon as I knew about Ciel's connection to Mina. You have my apology, Tom."

Thomas nodded, somewhat mollified, and Mark picked up where he left off. "Trey was in the process of delivering some intel to his liaison with the Swedish security police when he was grabbed. We don't know how he got away, and we don't know where he is now. The Vikings are still looking hard for someone. We assume it's Trey. He knows enough not to risk communication with us under the circumstances."

"What do you need me to do?" Billy said.

"Gotland," Mark said at once. "Island off the coast of Sweden. You know it?"

"Ah, yes. I visited once, with a friendly SAS flight attendant who hailed from Visby. Charming place." The faraway look in Billy's eyes gave me a good idea of just how friendly the flight attendant had been.

"Great. Visby is the last place Trey was known to be, and there's a good chance he's still on the island. Get there as quickly as you can. Travel commercial, don't draw attention to yourself. Once you're there, make a show of wandering around. Act touristy. Trey trusts you—our best hope is that he'll make contact."

"*You* know Trey?" I asked Billy, once more feeling out of the loop.

Billy shrugged at me, and spoke to Mark. "What do you want me to do if I find him?"

"Get him off the island and to our safe house outside Stockholm without being picked up by the Vikings. If that's not feasible, learn whatever you can, leave him hidden, and get yourself out. In the meantime, I'll be checking with some of my contacts here."

"What about me?" I asked, wondering how I was supposed to fit into all this cloak-and-dagger stuff.

"You stay put until you hear from me," Mark said. "Once we have Trey back, you can wrap up your job."

"You expect me to wait around, twiddling my

thumbs, while you're out tracking down my client's fiancé?"

He cast a wary glance at Thomas. "Since I have no desire to be eviscerated by your brother, wait is exactly what I expect you to do. Thumb twiddling is optional."

I was about to tell him what he could do with *his* thumbs when Mina's cell phone rang. I'd kept it with me ever since I'd taken it out of the bungalow right before the explosion. If I wanted to salvage this job, I had to maintain the facade.

"Crap. It's Dragon Mama," I said, referring to Trey's mother. She and Mina were not on the best of terms. Reluctantly, I morphed into my client, wincing as my clothes suddenly pinched. "I have to take this."

"Mina?" she said before I'd even gotten half my hello out. "Is that you? Where's Henry? Why isn't he answering his phone?" Trey's mother was the only one who called him Henry. He hated it. "Tell me he wasn't in that explosion I saw on the news. My *baby*! Where is he? Which hospital did they take him to?"

"Calm down, Mrs. Harrison. Trey is fine."

"His *name* is Henry. That awful nickname makes him sound like something a waiter carries. I did not go through twenty-eight excruciating hours of labor to give birth to a serving piece!"

I winced. I *knew* that. "Um, yes. Henry. Henry is fine. That wasn't us. It was, uh, the bungalow next door. Tr—Henry has just been busy, um," I crossed my fingers, "helping people." What else could I say?

If she thought Trey was hurt, nothing would keep her from rushing to his side.

"You're lying to me—I can tell. Oh, my God! He's dead. You're afraid to tell me he's—"

"NO. He's great, I swear. Oh, look—here he is now. He just got back." I covered the mouthpiece and pushed the phone to Mark, whispering wildly, "You have his aura—do something!"

With an I-really-have-better-things-to-do look, Mark slid into Trey's aura. I held on to him the whole time, leaning in close, trying to hear both sides of the conversation. From what I could make out, Dragon Mama was lobbying for a visit. "How are you, Mother?" Mark said, his cadence perfect. "Yes, I'm fine . . . no, don't do that . . . Mother. Stop. Breathe . . . I'll let you know. It may be a while . . . here, Mina wants to say something."

I tried to back away, shaking my head madly. He caught me by the wrist, and grinned as he slapped the phone into my hand, dropping Trey's aura and abandoning me to the verbal mauling of Mina's future mother-in-law. By the time I hung up I was dazed, confused, and practically anoxic from how tightly my jeans squeezed Mina's luscious curves. Which no doubt accounted for me promising the Dragon I would personally see to it that Trey would make it home in time for her birthday, whenever the hell that was. I'd have to check Mina's file.

When I was myself again, and my head cleared, I saw Billy had left. Thomas and Mark had gone back into my office to talk. Their conversation ceased abruptly when I joined them.

Mark spoke first. "I'd better be on my way. Tom, good to see you again. Ciel, I'll let you know as soon as we recover Trey. Sorry for any inconvenience the Agency may have inadvertently caused you."

Trying to keep it official now, was he? I don't *think* so. I planted myself squarely in the doorway. "Thomas, isn't there something you have to do in your office? Actually, here," I dug into the front pocket of my hoodie and took out Mina's ring, "could you keep this in your safe for me? I need to speak to Mark for a minute before he goes."

With a sympathetic glance at Mark, Thomas said, "Sure. Come on up when you're done, sis— I'll take you to lunch later." I stepped out of the way, briefly, to let him pass, and then blocked the door again so Mark couldn't escape.

"Look, Ciel," he began as soon as we were alone, giving me the dove-soft eyes. "I know you don't like this, but it can't be helped."

I resisted the pull. "Mina is my client. Anything that involves her involves me. *You* seem to be under the impression I'm still some sort of kid you can push to the side."

He stepped closer, invading my space, but I held my ground, putting a hand on his chest to stop him. I wasn't going to let him crowd me out of his way that easily. He stared intently at my face for several seconds before his eyes took on a look I'd never seen before, at least not directed at me. *Hot.* Leaning in close enough for me to feel the warmth of his body and his breath on my neck, he said, "Is that what you were trying to prove last night, Howdy? That you're not a kid anymore?"

I sagged against the doorframe, my mind spinning like an anemic hamster in a rusty wheel at the reminder of my drunken kiss . . . and at his closeness.

Don't pass out, don't pass out, don't . . .

He continued speaking, softly, his words tickling my ear. "Maybe Scotch isn't your drink."

I cleared my throat, dragging myself back from the brink of idiothood. "So next time I'll have bourbon," I said, keeping my voice jaunty in spite of my nerves. His laugh came in a short burst, like I'd surprised it out of him. I thought for a second he'd move his lips closer to mine—he was staring at my mouth—and felt my eyes get big in spite of my bravado. Flirting with him wasn't nearly as easy sober. But he just took a deep breath, pulled me away from the door, and left me standing there, wobbly.

"Later, Howdy."

Later? As in "see ya later, kid"? Or was he promising something more? When my head stopped whirling at the prospect, I realized I was still firmly in possession of the piece of my mind I'd been planning to give him. And he was doing exactly what he intended all along: leaving me with my brother.

Goddamn stupid hormones.

If I had to wait out the Trey-saving mission, I figured I might as well do it where I could be more useful. With Mina. Keeping an eye on her, just in case . . . Okay, so I was still feeling kind of edgy about that laptop. But first I wanted to make sure I'd done everything I could to help locate that fiancé I guaranteed her. Finding the guy was kind of crucial to my career cred, after all. You have to look at the big picture if you're going to succeed in the business world.

Alone in my office, I dug back into my files to see if we'd overlooked anything—anything at all— that might be helpful in the hunt. Some tiny clue to where he might be hiding from the Vikings. The first thing that struck my eye, about as pleasantly as an errant squirt from a grapefruit, was Trey's mother's birthday: tomorrow.

Crap. I could've sworn I had at least a few weeks—enough time to be certain it wouldn't be my problem. And here I'd practically taken a blood oath on the head of Mina's firstborn child that Trey would be there to watch his mother blow out her candles. (Ha. Dragon Mama could probably *light* the candles with her breath.)

No avoiding it. Before I went to hang with Mina, I'd have to fix things with Trey's mother. I locked up my office, and ditched Thomas with a promise to connect with him later. It wasn't a complete lie, since I'd already established through my earlier interaction with Mark that "later" was an inherently ambiguous word. I didn't like deceiving my brother, but I had no choice. He wouldn't like what I was about to do. It would worry him, and worrying him wouldn't be nice, would it?

Honestly, sometimes I'm such a considerate sister I surprise even myself.

My condo was still a mess. I ignored it and went straight to the closet in the guest room, where I dug through Billy's stash of clothing until I found some things I thought would suit, and put them on.

Time for a test run.

After saying a brief prayer the aura wouldn't prove to be as twitchy as Benjamin's, I closed my eyes and searched my mind for the residual energy I'd absorbed while holding on to Mark during his brief talk with Trey's mother. Sure, it was a second-hand aura—I had yet to meet the real Trey—but between the little I'd intentionally taken then and any I'd absorbed from my exposure to the aura through both Mark and Billy in the Bahamas, I thought I could pull it off.

When I opened my eyes and looked in the mirror I was rewarded with the sight of the gorgeous, non-Chiclets smile. Maybe not perfect, but close enough for horseshoes or hand grenades. And hopefully dragons.

Chapter 10

LaGuardia was bustling when I landed, but at least I didn't have to retrieve any suitcases from baggage claim, Trey's luggage having been blown into nonexistence. All I had was a small carry-on bag I'd borrowed from Billy's extensive stash of aura accessories to hold the few essentials Trey would have replaced before this short trip home.

On the way to the taxi stand I was intercepted by an age-defying platinum blonde who might as well have been wearing an "Ice Queen" name tag. She had a hint of a smile, but that was probably because her latest facelift was still pulling a little tight. Trey's mother.

She rushed to my side. "Henry! Let me look at you. Are you all right? You scared me to death."

"Happy Birthday, Mother. You look younger every year." I kissed her taut cheek and gave her a brief hug, just as Trey would have. I'd reread my files on the plane, trying to pack in every bit of info about him Mina had provided. "But you didn't have to come to the airport."

"Don't be silly," she said, preening under my flattery. "I have the limo. Why wouldn't I come?"

"Fine then," I said, hitting her with the non-Chiclets. "And thank you."

"Where's Mina? I thought surely she'd be with you—the pair of you are joined at the hip these days. Unless you've had a falling out?" Hope gleamed in her eyes.

"Mina flew straight home to reassure her parents."

"I see. She didn't think it was important to stop here on the way and wish me a happy birthday herself . . . well, never you mind. I'm sure your thoughtfulness will rub off on her eventually. If you're together long enough."

Trey wasn't an eye-roller, so I suppressed *that* urge. But I was seriously starting to question Mina's judgment about marrying into this family. Sure, Trey was wonderful enough, but geez, think of the holidays. There wasn't enough Valium in the world to make sharing a turkey with this woman bearable.

On the up side, I sensed repeat business in my future.

The limo looked just like the one in Mina's dossier. Once we were settled in the backseat, I tried my best to be the kind of son I knew Trey was. "So, Mother, how have you been? Busy as ever with the girls?" The "girls" were the doyennes of one of the most exclusive country clubs in Connecticut, where the Harrisons kept their country home. Trey's parents divided their time between there and a penthouse near Central Park.

"Not so busy that I don't have time to miss my only son horribly," she said, with what I'm sure she thought was a pretty pout.

Before I had to fish out the appropriate response, a small crackle indicated the intercom had connected. "Will we be making any stops before going home, ma'am?" the driver inquired, sounding suitably obsequious.

"No, Lars. Straight home."

I tensed. "Lars? What happened to Joe?"

"The stupid man had an accident last night—a car accident. Can you imagine? He's supposed to be a professional driver."

"Is he all right?" I asked.

"Oh, he'll be fine. He won't be driving for a while, though, so the limo people sent Lars to fill in. I only hope he can find his way around town—I certainly don't want to waste my time giving directions to every place I go."

I stared at the back of the chauffeur's head through the glass barrier. The man wasn't especially fair-haired. He hadn't spoken or done anything to draw attention to himself when he'd put my bag in the trunk, but the name was enough to make me wonder. The more I wondered, the more I worried about Mina.

At the next stoplight, I caught the chauffeur staring at me via the rearview mirror. I didn't like the look in his eye. It was . . . smug, somehow, like he knew something I didn't.

That was it. I was heading to the lake house ASAP. But I couldn't leave Trey, and by proxy Mina, holding a relationship time bomb with Dragon Mama either. Somehow I had to leave this woman smiling when I left. But how? Hmm . . .

"Mother, since we're already out, how about I take my best girl out for a birthday lunch? Bouley okay?" I said, naming her favorite (exceedingly expensive) French restaurant.

"*Darling!* That would be marvelous! Wait until I tell the girls—oh, I know! I should ask them to join us. They *love* you. This is going to be so much fun! You are the best son *ever*."

Geez. Dragon Mama *and* the girls? Guess it was true what they said. No freaking good deed goes unpunished.

The impromptu birthday party went amazingly well, if I do say so myself. We'd stopped off at the Harrison home, so I could make a quick change into the casual-elegant clothing Dragon Mama required of her escort, while she marshaled her ranks. Nothing tickled her more than a chance to show off how much her only son adored her. She even managed to keep her Mina attacks to a minimum. Plus, all the commotion helped disguise the fact that I was rather shaky on the more minute details of Trey's behavior, never having spent time around the actual guy.

Four hours of being giggled and cooed over by the Ladies Who Lunch was enough to make me look back fondly on my time in the rum warehouse with the spiders. But at least Trey made such a superb showing (smiling and nodding helps a lot in these situations) that Dragon Mama wasn't even too bent out of shape when he got a "business text," and had to beg off dinner later. The things I do for my clients.

I'd gallantly refused Dragon Mama's offer of the limo, claiming she'd need it herself, which earned me an enraptured "*Darling!*" and an air kiss. My search for ready transportation took me several blocks east, into territory I didn't visit often, but apparently Trey did. Before I could hail a passing taxi, a warmly welcoming voice boomed out behind me. "Mr. Harrison?"

I turned slowly and saw a short, round, mustachioed shopkeeper poking his head out of a tobacco store. He obviously knew Trey. Crap. Can't anything ever be easy?

"Hi . . ." I glanced at the name of the shop, and risked it. "Enzo. How are you?"

His mitts engulfed my hand. "Come in, come in," he said with a broad smile, and waited while I preceded him into the shop. Whew. Guess he *was* Enzo. "I've been expecting you."

I racked my brain for any pertinent info from my files. Came up blank. "Uh, great. So, do you have my . . . ?" I paused, realizing I didn't know a damn thing about Trey's tobacco habits.

"Your 'special order'?" He looked from side to side, saw nobody near, but still whispered. "The finest Cubans my shop has ever seen." He held one finger to his lips. "Shhh."

"My lips are sealed," I said.

The bell on the shop door jangled after Enzo slipped into the back room. The charming proprietor poked his head back out to assure the new customer he'd be with him shortly, and then disappeared again, leaving me alone with the addition to the shop: a tall, bulky blond. No horned helmet, but my inner alarms shrieked anyway. With good reason. After sweeping the room with his eyes to make sure we were alone, the man walked right up to me, not even pretending he didn't know who I was.

"We know where Mina is. If you wish her to remain safe, you'll come with me now. Quietly."

Great. Just freaking great. How long had I been followed? Did Lars tip somebody off? And which Mina did he mean? Me-Mina, newly home from the Bahamas, or the real Mina? Did they know about the lake house or not, for cripe's sake?

I smiled. Strangely, the non-Chiclets appeared to have no effect on him. Go figure. "I believe I'll take a pass on tha—*agh!*" His fist was in my stomach, doubling me over, before I could finish my sentence.

Sonofabitch, that hurt. Nobody had ever punched

me before. I decided I didn't like it a bit. Sucking in air as I tried to straighten up, I was struck by the look of pleasure on his face. Fucking sadist.

"As I said, you will come with me. Quietly," he repeated.

Nodding my compliance, I pretended to need assistance to move. When he leaned in to take my elbow, I stomped on his instep, grabbed his crotch, and twisted. Hard. Then, while *he* tried to breathe, I carefully placed my other hand behind his neck, and slammed his face into the antique wooden counter. He crumpled.

Damn. Now *that* felt much better. I could get used to having muscles.

Looking down at him, I said—quietly, since that seemed so important to him—"And *I* said I'd take a pass, asshole."

After explaining to Enzo how his customer had tripped over his own shoelaces (which I'd taken the liberty of untying before the genial proprietor returned with the Cubans), I caught a cab and gave the driver Billy's address. He wouldn't be there, of course, but I needed a place to reconnoiter, not to mention recover from my debut punch in the gut.

Billy's official residence is a wallet-gutting East Village loft. He bought it right after he graduated from college, had it renovated, and furnished it with a heavy emphasis on black leather and steel. Nobody in the family questioned him too closely about how he could afford it. Some things you didn't want to know.

The kitchen took up one corner of the large open space. It had black cabinets, gray granite countertops, and stainless-steel appliances. I found a plastic bag, loaded it with crushed ice from the refrigerator door, and stretched out on the couch. Thor Thunderfist had missed my ribs, but I was still going to have a hell of a bruise to adapt away.

I hadn't seen anyone else around Enzo's, so I didn't think I'd been followed. But, to be on the safe side, I dropped Trey's aura and kicked off his pants, leaving me in a baggy, dress-length (on me) men's silk T-shirt.

I had to think. What was I going to do about Mina? If the Viking in the shop was telling the truth, they knew about my lake house, and she wasn't safe. I could call and have her moved right away, but what excuse would I give? Besides, maybe they were trying to flush her out. Moving her might expose her to even more danger.

What I should do was stick with my plan to go check on her myself, and stay with her until I heard from Mark that they'd found Trey. That way I wouldn't have to upset her needlessly. Question was, how to get there? Also, as whom? Not me—if Mina saw me as myself, she'd expect me to hand over a ring, and explanations would be awkward. Better go with being a new employee.

I dialed Hilda, my faithful, overworked doer-of-everything for the lake house. Told her I'd be sending some help her way ASAP, and that the new-hire would know the password to give to Pete, the security guard. Didn't go into details, because heaven only knew who might be listening. Figured I could explain more when I got there.

Now I just had to come up with a good way to get there. If Billy were around, I would ask him for a suggestion, but . . . *Billy. Now there's an idea.* But did I dare? I thought of all the times my cousin had pulled a fast one on me. Oh, hell yeah. I dared.

Chapter 11

Sunlight from the open air side of the garage bounced off the chrome like bullets off Superman's chest. The cherry red hood gleamed as wetly as a freshly lacquered fingernail, and the white top glistened like a movie star's caps. It was one damn fine car. And now I was finally going to get my chance to drive it. He would *kill* me if he ever found out, I thought, shivering with delight.

There are few things on earth Billy values as highly as his 1957 Chevy Bel Air. The boat on wheels was a college graduation gift from his father, just as it had been a gift from his grandfather to his father before him. Family legend has it that Billy was born in the backseat, and left there by his real mother when she walked out of Uncle Liam's life forever, but nobody will talk about it much, least of all Billy.

Suffice it to say, Billy feels a strong attachment to his car. Which is why he never lets anyone else drive it, keeps it in a garage that costs him almost as much every month as his loft, and tips the attendants extravagantly to see that no harm comes to it.

I squelched a twinge of guilt when I opened the driver's side door. Surely he would understand the urgency of my situation. I didn't have a car; he did. I needed it right now; he didn't. It was simple, really. And since he was in Sweden—safely on the other side of the ocean—I was just going to have to *assume* permission. It was the logical thing to do. Besides, who knew when I'd get another opportunity as good as this one?

It started like a charm, the hum of the engine penetrating me from my seat up, making me aware of the singularly male part I was sporting, and I felt another, even stronger, burst of guilt. I'd never projected Billy before. It was considered the height of bad form to use another adaptor's aura without express permission. Adaptors had better reason than most to be touchy about privacy issues. But, honestly, how else could I get the car? Billy had made sure the attendants wouldn't let anybody but him near his baby. When you really thought about it, I'd *had* to do it.

Satisfied my reasoning was sound (well, sound enough), I put the car in reverse and eased it out of the parking place, glad none of the parking attendants were around to see how gingerly I was maneuvering—that wouldn't be in character for Billy at all. Fortunately, I had three levels of driving in circles to perfect my technique before any-one was likely to see me. Easy-peasy.

I was leaning back and driving one-handed by the time I got to the exit, and waved casually as I passed the pudgy young man in the booth. Since I knew Billy paid by the month, I didn't bother to stop, even though it might have been a good idea, seeing as how the gate wasn't all the way up.

The sound of metal on metal reverberated in my head like the screech of a banshee.

Shit! I slammed on the brakes and gripped the steering wheel with both hands. After a brief pause I heard the awed voice of the kid in the booth. "Damn, Mr. Doyle. Look at your car!"

I forced my eyes open and surveyed the damage. The decorative twin ridges on the hood now had distinctive, paint-free gouges from the front of the car to just shy of the windshield. I swallowed, wondering if I had time to stop for touch-up paint on the way to the lake.

"I have some red fingernail polish my girlfriend left here . . ." the kid ventured helpfully. Maybe he was psychic.

I sighed. "Thanks anyway, but I don't think a manicure is going to cover it," I said, while in the back of my head my mother's voice echoed: *God punishes right away.* No shit.

I got out of the city with no further vehicular mis-haps. After the kid had lifted the gate—there was no damage to *it*, thank goodness—I told him I'd appreciate it if he never reminded "me" of the incident, and slipped him one of the hundred-dollar bills I'd borrowed from Billy's closet safe. (What? I was going to pay him back. Someday. Probably after I collected my final payment from Mina. *If* I finished the freaking job, which I needed the borrowed Benjamins to do. So I *had* to take the money. If I didn't, I'd never be able to pay it back.)

As soon as I was safely out of the city I stopped at the nearest rest area, found a stall in a deserted ladies' room, and changed both clothes and auras. Maria Rossi, one of my former clients, would be playing the part of the new hired help, giving me the excuse I needed to stick close to Mina until I knew the real Trey was safe.

Maria was an overripe peach of a woman, still beautiful despite the extra twenty pounds she carried, the silver in her hair, and the crow's feet that framed her eyes. My job for her had been to reconnect with her estranged father before the old man died. Maria had been afraid the cantankerous old goat would leave his millions to his ancient cat in a fit of pique, instead of to her own blameless offspring. In spite of the blissful reconciliation I contrived, I still hadn't been paid. I'd taken the job on spec, knowing Maria would only be able to afford my fee if the inheritance came through. (Yeah, business decisions like that might have a little something to do with my current financial situation.) As far as I knew, the old guy was still alive and kicking. I'm guessing the cat didn't last long, though, once the real Maria got back into that house, so I did expect to collect my fee eventually.

In the meantime, I didn't feel too bad about borrowing her aura as a down payment.

The family cabin in the Adirondacks (gifted to my fledgling business in a show of support from my parents) had been the ideal location to take us kids when we were first getting used to our aura-adapting abilities. Far away from the prying eyes of the public, we could practice changing auras, polishing our skills in private until we were sure of ourselves. The ability doesn't spring into existence overnight—it appears gradually after puberty, and takes concerted effort to perfect.

I was about to turn onto the private road that led to the lake house compound when a small, black pickup truck cut me off. I jammed on the brakes and let loose with a string of Italian curse words as I skidded to a halt. In my line of work, you have to have a passing familiarity with a lot of languages, and colorful phrases come easily to me in times of stress. One mishap with Billy's car was more than enough for me.

The man got out of his truck and strode toward me. He looked like a middle-aged gardener, weathered, but appealing enough in that worked-outside-your-whole-life kind of way. Probably a landscaper hired to do some seasonal work for one of the bigger estates around here. Maybe he was lost. Still, that was no reason to cut me off. I got out of the Chevy and slammed my door. "That's a private road, mister, and you're blocking my way," I said. No point in mincing words.

He stopped a pace away. "Ciel, what are you doing here? You're supposed to be with Thomas."

Shit. "Mark? I thought you were looking for Trey."

"I was. I *am*. But I wanted to check on Mina for myself."

"Well, now that you know I'm on it, you can just toodle along. You know, save Trey, save my job. Both would be good."

"Better idea—you head back home, and let me handle it from here."

"No can do. Hilda's expecting a new hire, and I'm it. Can't disappoint her, now can I?"

I must have looked determined, because he didn't push it. "Fine. We'll give Hilda a two-fer." Suddenly he was as Italian as Maria. Still middle-aged, but now drop-dead Mediterranean gorgeous.

"Mark, this isn't necess—"

"It's Gianpaolo. Now, what's our last name, *cara mia*?"

Pete buzzed us through the electronically controlled gate after Mark gave him our phony names and told him that "the asparagus is good in Holland this time of year." (What? You can't tell me *anybody* would guess that pass phrase. Even Mark didn't know it until I told him, and that's saying something.)

Mark was at the wheel, having hidden his truck

in the underbrush on the other side of the main road after transferring a small duffel bag to Billy's trunk. (He'd insisted on driving the last leg down the private road because "Gianpaolo's just that kind of macho guy.") We'd reached a stalemate. After I told him about the Swede in the cigar shop, he was more determined than ever to check things out, and I wasn't about to leave without seeing Mina for myself.

He parked the Chevy under a tree. God help the bird that dared poop on it, because I wasn't in a forgiving mood where Billy's car was concerned, and I knew how to make a slingshot.

We left our luggage in the trunk and went to the main cabin, where the extremely cheerful Hilda Perkins greeted us. Sixty-ish, with a cushiony figure of the sort that invited hugs, she was thrilled to learn she was getting not only indoor help, but outdoor as well. From the look on her face you'd think it was Christmas morning. Geez. I was going to feel like such a bitch when I had to tell her she couldn't keep us.

Hilda, of course, knew about aura adaptors. She was a nonadaptor member of another adaptor family—the gene doesn't always carry through to the next generation—and so could be trusted. Her husband had died several years before, and her children were grown, leaving her without anyone to take care of. My clients filled the gap. Mark and I had decided not to mention who we really were unless we had to—no chance of Hilda slipping and calling one of us by our real name that way.

"Mr. and Mrs. Rossi? So happy to meet you. I hope you had an easy drive," she bubbled.

"Fine, fine. It was smooth sailing the whole way," Mark lied. "You are Mrs. Perkins? But I wasn't expecting someone so young."

I tried not to roll my eyes. Great. Now Hilda probably thought I was an ass for telling the new hired help she was old.

"Oh, I'm no spring chicken." She wiped her hand on her apron before extending it to Mark, who held it just a shade too long, flicking his eyes up and down her body, pausing for a beat at chest level. If he kissed her hand, I was going to slug him.

I cleared my throat. Hilda broke away from Mark and held her hand out to me. Her grip was firm and no-nonsense, just as I remembered it. It had been one of the reasons I had hired her in the first place—I hate a wimpy handshake.

"I'm happy to meet you, too, Mrs. Perkins," I said.

"Please, call me Hilda."

"And you must call me Maria. My husband is Gianpaolo."

"You may call me Johnny, if you like." He gave Hilda a dazzling smile, one that bordered on being a little too friendly.

I don't know why that should irk me so much, but it did. "You must forgive my husband, Hilda. He is an incurable flirt. If he gives you any trouble, just tell me, and I will—how do you Americans say it?—neuter him."

Her smile froze, and I could tell she was torn

between welcoming us with open arms and sending us on our way before she even let us in the door. Her need for help must have won out, because she lapsed into a weak laugh and said, "Oh, you are so funny! I can tell you're going to be good company around here." She didn't look quite as thrilled as when she first saw us, though, so maybe she wouldn't be too sorry to see us leave after all.

Hilda guided us into the kitchen, and explained our duties over iced tea and sandwiches while continuing to dodge Mark's attempts to flirt with her. I decided to give her a raise. When I could afford it.

After our business was concluded, Mark went to fetch our bags while Hilda showed me to our room. Call me stupid, but it just then occurred to me that we'd be sharing a bed. It wasn't even queen-size—only a double. My stomach did a backflip, and the sandwich I'd just eaten almost made a return trip.

Get a grip, Ciel. Isn't this what you've been dreaming about forever?

But that was before, back when I knew I didn't have a snowball's chance in hell of it happening. Ever since I kissed him, I was wavering. Did I really want to sleep in the same bed with him? What if he tried something?

Or what if he didn't? my shriveled up little ego said.

I wasn't sure which would be worse.

But I have a pretty good idea which would be more fun, my inner slut (who has never had much opportunity to become an outer slut) said.

I was going back and forth with myself, and had

about come to the conclusion I should tell Hilda that Gianpaolo snored like a buzz saw and ask if we could have separate rooms, when Mark returned. Hilda left as soon as he entered the room. He closed the door behind her.

Gulp. When in doubt, attack.

"What the hell were you thinking, coming on to Hilda like that? Geez, she's old enough to be your mother!" I said, quietly but forcefully, fists on ample hips.

"Jealous, *cara mia*?"

"Don't you *cara mia* me, you old goat. And I'll thank you not to harass my hired help."

He came over to me, close enough to whisper. "Maria. Darling. I'm simply trying to set up a logical escape route for us. If we need to stay for a while, I'll behave myself around dear old Hilda. If we need to leave quickly, I'll do something slap-worthy and get us fired."

Oh. Well, that sort of made sense, I guess. "What if she doesn't fire us, huh? What if she decides a fling with the new yardman might not be such a bad idea?"

"If that's the case, we'll make sure you're close enough to discover your husband's indiscretion. You can throw a god-awful fit and quit for the two of us. Either way, it works."

I nodded grudgingly. "All right. But just so you know—if you do anything that makes Hilda quit, I'll kill you."

He pulled me into a bear hug and lifted me off my feet. "That's what I like about you Mediterranean women. You're so fiery." He kissed me full on the mouth, fast and hard, and dropped me on the bed, stunning me into silence. Which was probably his intention.

He dug through his duffel until he found what he was looking for.

"Where are you going?" I asked, my lips still tingling.

"To check the perimeter. Pete will stick close to the cabin until I get back. I ran into him when I was getting the bags, and told him I was additional security you'd hired in the guise of a grounds-keeper. Even repeated your asparagus code phrase for him." Was that a wink? From Mark? "He said he'd stay within shouting distance of Mina."

I acknowledged the wisdom of his actions with a nod. "How long do you think you'll be?"

"Couple of hours at least. If I'm not back before bedtime, don't wait up. Just toss a blanket and pillow on the floor for me; I'll be fine."

Damn. So much for *that* worry. It was quickly replaced by a new one when I got a closer look at what he'd taken from his bag: a gun.

"Do you think you'll need that?" It was still hard for me to imagine any real danger here—it had always been a safe haven.

"Nope." He patted his lower back, a spot covered by his shirt. "I already have one. This is for you, in case anything comes up while I'm out."

"But . . ."

"But what? You know how to use it."

I couldn't deny that, since he was the one who'd

taught me. I could shoot. I even enjoyed target practice. It's the idea of firing at anything alive that gives me the heebie-jeebies.

"What if Hilda notices it? It would be tough to explain why the new maid packs heat."

"Your shirt's loose enough. Lift it up a little. I'll help you put on the holster."

"That's a holster? It looks like an elastic band."

"It's a belly holster. You can hide your gun under your rather impressive rack."

I felt myself starting to blush. "You noticed that, huh?" I said nonchalantly.

"Hard to miss. Now, stand up and lift your shirt so I can get this on you before I leave."

The wide elastic was snug. More than snug. It felt like a damn girdle. "Hey, I do like to breathe, you know."

"Sorry. It has to be pretty tight so it won't slip." He finished up, then added the gun.

"You sure that's real? It looks too cute."

"Hey, don't knock the mouse gun," he said with an easy laugh that had me wishing we could work together like this all the time. It was fun. Relaxed. Well, as relaxed as you can get while arming yourself against a possible Viking attack.

"Mouse gun, huh? Yeah, it looks like it might come in handy for hunting rodents."

"Don't let its appearance fool you—it'll get the job done with people. Especially at close range, which is the only place you'd need a gun. If you're far enough away, either run or hide."

I have no moral objection to either of those things. "Gotcha," I said. "Run. Hide."

He lifted my chin and looked into my eyes with Gianpaolo's soulful brown ones. "But if you have to use the gun, shoot to kill. Understand?"

I swallowed. "Uh-huh."

"I mean it, Ciel. No fucking around—you aim like I taught you, and you fire."

I saluted. "Yes, sir!"

He shut his eyes briefly, his equivalent of an eye roll. "Just stay close to the cabin. Check on Mina. I'll be back as soon as I can."

Chapter 12

The gazebo had a gorgeous view of the lake, but Mina, parked at the table in its center, appeared oblivious to the beauty surrounding her. A thermos of something was at hand—milky, unsweetened coffee, if she was staying true to her dossier—and a bunch of magazines were laid open in front of her. As I got closer I could see they were all wedding-related—*Bride*, *Modern Bride*, *The Knot*, you name it. She had a notebook and pen, and was furiously taking notes. Gave me a twinge to see how much faith she had in my abilities.

I approached slowly, giving her ample warning of my presence. "Hello. I'm Maria Rossi, Hilda's new assistant. You must be Miss Worthington."

She nodded, wedding-dream glow spilling from every invisible pore. "Yes, I'm Mina. Hilda told me you were coming. I'm sure you'll love working here. It's a fantastic place," she said.

"I can see that. Peaceful as well as beautiful, isn't it?"

"Absolutely. I'm thinking I may need to see about finding a place here myself after . . ." She glanced at the array of magazines and blushed.

"You're planning your wedding—but how wonderful!"

Still looking embarrassed, she said, "Well, it's not exactly official yet, so don't let the cat out of the bag. Let's just say I'm daydreaming a little."

A little? Looked more like a full-scale battle plan. But as long as she was keeping herself happy—and busy—it was all good for me.

"Then I'll leave you to your dreams. It was nice to meet you."

"Please stay. Would you like some coffee? Hilda always packs an extra cup, in case she can make time to join me, but it doesn't look like she's coming today."

"Thank you. I'd like that." I sat on the bench across the table from her. "So, have you chosen a dress yet?"

She poured. "I have it narrowed down to three." After handing me the cup she turned two of the magazines around so I could see better.

"This one." She pointed at a simple satin sheath, one that would drape seductively over every curve. "Or this one . . ." A lacy mermaid type, again sure to show off her gorgeous figure. The third was pure Cinderella, huge and floaty. I tried hard to keep the appalled look off Maria's face.

Mina glanced away, her cheeks turning pink. Guess I hadn't been entirely successful. "I'm only considering that one for nostalgia's sake. It looks just like the wedding dresses I used to imagine when I was a little girl."

Something must be wrong with me, because I never even thought about wedding dresses when I was a girl. Or weddings, for that matter. I've always had it in the back of my mind that I'd be married some day—in the foggy distant future—but I've never given much consideration to the details. Maybe I lack the wedding gene.

"They're all beautiful. You could carry off any of them," I said warmly, feigning matronly interest in all things nuptial.

"Thanks. You're sweet. I guess I'll just have to figure out which one will go best with whatever kind of wedding I—well, we—decide on. If he asks, of course." She knocked on the wooden table.

"Of course he will," I said with an air of old-world mysticism. "Trust me. I know these things."

She leaned in eagerly. "Really? Are you psychic or something?"

"I wouldn't say psychic. But I get impressions, and they are rarely wrong. You are giving me a strong impression of wedded bliss." Then, unable to resist playing the clairvoyant, I added, "I see a ring on your finger very soon."

She looked at her empty hand, wistful. "I don't suppose you can see what it looks like?"

I closed my eyes, picturing the ring that was now sitting in Thomas's safe at work. "Emerald cut diamond, three to four carats, simple platinum setting."

Her mouth dropped open a tiny bit. "Wow. That's a pretty detailed vision. I'll let you know if it comes true."

The sound of a motorboat drew my attention to the water, but I tried not to let it worry me unduly. Probably just a lost boater. It happened occasionally—a lot of these properties look alike from out on the lake. They'd pull away once they got close enough to see the great big "No Trespassing" sign posted at the end of the dock. And if they didn't notice that, it looked like Pete was on his way to meet and greet them.

The boat pulled up right next to the sign. A man hauled himself out, followed by another, who tied the boat off in short order. The men were big. They were blond. They looked like—

Shit. *Vikings!*

Pete approached them, easygoing. From his gestures I could see he was amiably explaining the no-trespassing policy.

No, Pete! They are not friendly lost people. Get out your gun!

As if he'd intercepted my thoughts, one of the blonds shrugged, then casually reached into his jacket, pulled out a gun, and shot Pete in the chest. The guard—one of the friendliest guys I had ever met; it was why I hired him, stupid me—fell first to his knees, then forward onto his face. The Vikings stepped over him and looked our way.

My mind rejected what I saw. I *couldn't* have been followed. Nobody knew I was a middle-aged Italian woman—it was impossible.

Regardless of the impossibility factor, my body jumped into action. They must be after Mina. Somehow, someone had figured out my nifty client hideaway.

I grabbed Mina by the arm. Pulled her upright and out of the gazebo. "Come on!"

"What's going on?" She looked over her shoulder and saw the boat. "Who're those—"

"Now!" I yanked for all I was worth—Maria's heft was worth quite a bit—and got us both speeding toward the cabin. Counting the length of the dock, we had a good two-hundred-yard head start, but that would disappear quickly when those long-legged neo-barbarians got it in gear. I had to get Mina hidden, and fast.

We plowed through the back door into the kitchen. I shoved Mina toward Hilda. "Get her to the attic. And call an ambulance for Pete. Quick!" Though, honestly, I didn't see how he could still be alive, not shot at that range. But I couldn't think about that now.

Hilda was a gem. She didn't question me further, just grabbed the confused Mina and pulled her down the hall toward the smallest bedroom. The attic stairs were accessible through the closet there.

As soon as they were out of sight, I dropped Maria's aura and called up Mina's. Except for the clothes, I was identical to her current appearance, and I was banking on the Vikings not having gotten a good look at which of us was wearing what when we took off from the gazebo. Once they saw Mina heading away from the cabin they'd be unlikely to stick around to make a thorough search for anyone else.

I went back out the same door I'd just entered. They were closing in fast. After making sure they got a good look at my new face, I took off toward the trees, reaching for the gun now flopping around in the much looser belly holster, praying I could switch off the safety while on the move. If luck was on my side, I'd make it to the woods before I had to shoot them. Maybe Mark could have the bodies taken care of quickly, so we wouldn't have to traumatize Mina and Hilda any more than necessary. I just hoped I could bring myself to pull the trigger when the time came.

An image of Pete—good-hearted, reliable, friendly Pete—hitting the dock after the Viking shot him reran itself in my head. I decided pulling the trigger wouldn't be a problem.

Didn't matter. Luck was not on my side. I was sacked like a rookie quarterback before I got the gun disentangled from the holster. I grunted and tried to kick my legs, but they were plastered to the ground by two hundred–odd pounds of Scandinavian he-flesh, his head planted on my posterior.

When you can't fight, holler long and loud. That, I decided, was my brand-new philosophy. "Who the HELL are you? What's going ON here? Do you have any idea how much TROUBLE you're going to be in when the police get here?"

I was flipped over onto my back. The second Viking—the one who wasn't still wrapped around my legs—clapped a hand over my mouth.

"I suggest you remain quiet." Yep. Accent.

"Mmmphh," I continued, to no effect. So I squeezed my tongue out between my teeth and tickled his palm with it (bleah—engine oil), which startled him into easing the pressure just enough for me to bite him. Hard.

"Ouch!" He jerked his hand away. "You bitch. Don't you know the human mouth has more germs than a toilet seat? You could give me an infection."

I pushed up to a sitting position, spitting to rid myself of the rusty taste of his blood. "So sorry. What was I thinking?" Then I gulped in a huge breath and roared, " HE-E-E-LP!"

The hand came back, harder. This time he knelt behind me, and clamped my nostrils shut with his other hand. Oh, shit—I couldn't breathe. The son of a bitch was going to suffocate me.

Chapter 13

I woke up in a small, dark, musty-smelling place. I was tied up and gagged, and had one hell of a headache. The gun was gone. No surprise there. Near as I could tell, I was still Mina. An aura tends to hold through sleep, unconsciousness, or whatever, until an adaptor makes a conscious decision to drop it. I wiggled my shoulders back and forth as much as possible, gauging the boobage. Yep, plenty there. Definitely still Mina.

On the plus side, I wasn't dead. Unless God had a really warped sense of humor.

I was lying on something soft—some sort of fur, judging by the ticklish feeling on the back of my neck. That might account for the aroma, too. Were the Vikings smuggling bearskins? Or maybe it was beaver skins. I wrinkled my nose. Whatever they were, they didn't seem to be overly processed.

There was a humming noise in the background. Sounded like an engine of some sort. Had the Vikings taken me back to their boat? But it didn't really feel like we were on the water.

A sudden dip in the floor beneath me, followed fast by a rise, jostled me over onto my side. Turbulence. Shit. I was on a plane. Tied up, gagged, stuffed in a small compartment, and on a fucking airplane. I tried really hard not to think about my claustrophobia. Fat lot of good that did me.

I sucked in air through my nose at an increasing pace, the musky fur adding to my sudden queasiness. Crap. It would not be a good idea to vomit with a gag in my mouth, so I pushed myself over onto my back, trying to get my nose as far away from the skins as possible. To stave off panic, I closed my eyes and searched my brain for images of wide-open places. Cloud-filled skies, fields of spring flowers, rolling plains—*No!* Cut that last one. It made me think of rolling *planes*, and only made the turbulence harder to take.

Better just to try and figure out the situation. Okay, I'd been unconscious. How long had I been out? Where on the plane was I? And most important, how much longer would I be stuck here?

I didn't have much time to ponder it. The door opened and a big silhouette took its place. I squinted and squeaked, trying to push myself back against the wall. I couldn't tell if it was one of the Vikings who had grabbed me or not—all I could see was golden halo atop a linebacker body.

"You are awake."

Bright guy.

"If you promise not to make any noise, I will let you out. Do you promise?" His voice was deep, a little singsongy. Sounded Viking to me, but I knew better than to trust my opinion on accents.

I nodded. "Mmm-hmm." What the hell did he expect me to do? Shake my head and go back to sleep?

He removed my gag first, probably testing to see if I'd keep my word. I remained silent, except for gulping in air, so he untied my hands and legs. I stretched as much as space allowed and rubbed my arms, trying to restore circulation. He helped me to a sitting position. My head swam and the world got all black around the edges. I must've been drugged up pretty good.

"Take it easy. You will be better soon."

"I'm all right. Just give me a second." My voice was raspy, my mouth dry and nasty-tasting.

He waited patiently. Once I was seeing clearly again, I could tell he was the tackler. Not in nearly as much of a hurry now as he was the last time I saw him.

"What's this about?" I asked. "If you're holding me for ransom—"

"I told you to be quiet."

"But—"

He reached for the gag. I shut up.

"Come with me," he said.

My legs were wobbly, so I didn't mind him holding on to my shoulders as we walked down the aisle as much as I might have otherwise. He stayed close behind me, bending his head to avoid bumping it on the ceiling. It was a small cabin—well, compared to a commercial jet, anyway—maybe a Gulfstream, maybe a Lear. I'd flown on corporate jets before, during other jobs, but not so often that I could tell them apart. I was never crazy about spending time in the air, but those rides had been a hell of lot more fun than this one.

We approached the Viking I'd bitten. I felt a tiny burst of pleasure at the sight of his bandaged hand, and hoped his worst fears of infection came true. He was sitting on the sofa that stretched along one side of the cabin, talking with a man who didn't look remotely like a Viking. More like an Indian, the Native American kind.

In fact, he looked a whole lot like Jay Silverheels, the guy who played Tonto on *The Lone Ranger*, my favorite TV western. I had such a crush on him when I was a kid—he was way cooler than the masked man. My dad had recorded the whole series, and I used to make Billy watch the shows with me over and over, even though he teased me relentlessly about my crush on Mr. Silverheels. Just thinking about Tonto made me smile at the black-haired Viking. "Hey, you kind of remind me . . ."

The words died in my mouth when I saw the look in his eyes. Uh-oh. Guess he wasn't a fan of westerns. O-kaaay. *Not* Tonto. The un-Tonto it is. *Nonto.*

I sat where the big guy behind me told me to, across from the others. "As long as you are quiet, you may stay out here in the cabin. If you make trouble, you will be given another injection and put back into the luggage compartment."

I gave him the double thumbs-up, not risking a single word.

"Would you like something to eat or drink?"

Okay, so maybe he wasn't entirely bad. "Some water would be good," I said, voice still scratchy. "Pellegrino, if you have it," I added. "I don't really like Perrier." What the hell. As long as I was Mina, I might as well stay in character.

Nonto was studying me, his face motionless. I had a strong urge to stick my tongue out at him, but I resisted.

"Watch out for her," the other Viking said. "She bites."

"Only when I'm being kidnapped," I said, plastering a big, phony smile on Mina's face. "By the way, where are we going?"

He flexed his bandaged hand into a fist. "Perhaps we should take you to a veterinarian and make sure you don't have rabies," he said. All right, he was going to be Nasty Viking. From the looks of him, he'd enjoy the role. Nonto still hadn't said anything.

Slightly Nicer Viking returned with the Pellegrino, the bottle still unopened, and a commercially wrapped sandwich. Maybe it was his way of showing me the food and water weren't drugged. *Geez, Ciel. Get a grip. Why would they need to drug your food and water when they have shots they can give you, you idiot?* Okay, so I wanted to believe somebody here was halfway decent. What

was so wrong with that? *Damn. This is probably
how Stockholm syndrome starts*, I thought as I
sipped the water.

"We are taking you to your boyfriend," Nice
Viking said after he sat in front of me. His seat
faced mine.

"Nils!" Nasty Viking cut him off.

"You have Trey, too?" I piped up. "Where is he?
Is he all right?" Now I really was concerned. If
they had the real Trey, why were they still after the
fake Trey?

"He is healthy. You will see him soon."

"Nils." There was a warning in Nasty Viking's
voice.

"You worry too much, Per. There can be no
harm in telling her. If she knows she is going to see
him, perhaps she will be a better passenger."

I wondered briefly why Nasty Viking was named
for a fruit, but decided it didn't really matter in the
grand scheme of things. Probably meant something else in Swedish, anyway.

"Where is he?" I repeated, pressing my advantage with Nils. (That name I recognized, thanks to
Bruce Springsteen's E Street Band.) "Why did you
take him? And me? Does this have something to
do with his import business?" I scooted forward in
my seat, trying to react how Mina would under the
circumstances. "Oh, my God—is he smuggling?
He can't be. He would never do anything like that.
He's—"

"*Håll käften!*" Per said.

I looked at him blankly. Hole shefton? What the hell did that mean?

"He wants you to be quiet. It means 'hold your jaw,'" Nils explained.

Well, how rude. I looked down Mina's perfect nose at Per. "Didn't your mommy teach you any manners?" I said.

He reached across the aisle and grabbed my arm, half-pulling me out of my seat, scaring the bejeezus out of me. Talk about overreacting. His grip would leave a bruise for sure, if I let it show. Which I wouldn't. I didn't let myself wince either—no way would I give this creep the satisfaction. "Oooh, tough guy," I said. "You're not half the man my Trey is!" (I know! But it just slipped out. When I'm scared, I bluster. It might be stupid, but it's better than pissing yourself.)

He squeezed my arm harder, twisting it until I was afraid it might break. "You overstep yourself, Miss Worthington. A lady should know better. But perhaps you're not so much of a lady. Perhaps you would like proof I am more of a man than your Trey could ever be. Is that why you taunt me?"

Uh-oh. The gleam in his eye pegged him as a certified resident of Crazy Town. I tried to pull away. Saw that Nonto behind him appeared to be enjoying the show. Yikes. Guess I should have gone with pissing myself.

"Per. That's enough." Nils had risen. He took Per by the wrist, his knuckles whitening with the pressure he applied. "Remember the plan."

Per glared at Nils and let loose a string of Swedish I couldn't begin to decipher. Nils listened patiently, but didn't loosen his hold until Per let go of me. "I will sit with her."

"Fine. We will move up front," Per said. He headed for a seat as far away from me as he could get, and Nonto followed him without adding anything to the conversation. What was he, mute?

Shaky, I leaned back in my seat. Almost made a comment about Mr. Loony Tunes, but decided not to press my luck. Instead I said, "If you could just tell me *why*—"

"I am afraid I cannot tell you any more than I already have."

"But—"

He shook his head, a single time. A definitive no. I sighed. "Can you at least tell me if Trey and I are going to come out of this alive?" I said, a little wistfully. I really was curious about that. When I die, I think I'd rather do it as myself.

"If you do as you're told."

"Well, color me obedient," I said, and tried to twist my mouth into something resembling a cooperative smile. "But I think it's only fair to warn you, there are some pretty powerful people who won't be happy to find out I'm not where I should be. They'll be coming after you."

"Let's not dwell on unpleasant business for now. Surely there are nicer things we can discuss."

Okay, so much for threats on my part. "The weather, maybe?" I suggested. "I do hope I'm appropriately dressed for . . . ?" I raised my brows.

"Don't worry about your clothing. We will supply you with something suitable before we arrive at our destination."

Per called out from the front, interrupting us.

Nils stood. "You will excuse me?" he said.

"Of course," I said, nodding graciously, like I had a choice. Since we were being so polite and all.

Mostly just to keep myself occupied, I opened the sandwich and bit into it (turkey, a little dry, but tasty enough on an empty stomach), all the while straining to hear what they were discussing. Unfortunately, the exchange between Nils and Per was in Swedish. They switched to English when they addressed Nonto, but they also lowered their voices even more. All the words blurred together until one jumped out at me with frightening clarity: ". . . bomb . . ."

Cripes. Bomb? Did I really hear that?

I tried to swallow, found I couldn't, so I spit congealed turkey and bread into a napkin and shoved it between the seats. Geez, these clowns were supposed to be the great restorers of masculinity to Scandinavia? *Hey, guys, real men don't use bombs!*

Damn it all to fucking hell. I tried really hard not to think about how much trouble I was in. And what if I wasn't the only one? What about Billy? Had he made it to Gotland safely? Was he on Trey's trail, or had the Vikings caught him, too? And Mark? Had they gotten him, back at the lake house? Did they shoot him like Pete? Jesus, I could *not* think about this now—I'd go crazy.

I closed my eyes and attempted to focus on

something more pleasant, like how when I was out of this mess I was going to treat myself to a pedicure. I don't even like pedicures. It's boring as hell to sit there and stare at the top of somebody's head while they mess with your toenails, but it was better than what I was doing now. Boredom had suddenly become a lot more appealing.

I must have dozed off—a residual effect from the drugs, I suppose—because next thing I knew Nils was shaking my shoulder. "It is time to ready ourselves for landing. If you will come this way?" He indicated the back of the plane.

"Can't I just buckle my seat belt here?"

"First you must change your clothing."

"Oh." I looked from one end of the plane to the other. There didn't seem to be anyplace that offered a great deal of privacy, other than the lavatory, and that would be a tight fit.

"I will hold up a blanket for you, if you like," Nils said, his eyes crinkling at the edges.

"Um, thanks." I got up and headed to the back. On the last seat was a pile of cloth that looked more like bed linens than clothes. I looked back over my shoulder at Nils and raised my brows. He nodded. I shrugged and reached for the garment, unfurling it as I lifted.

There were two pieces—an ankle-length, ivory-colored dress with a rounded neckline and long sleeves, and a dark brown overtunic made of some roughly spun fabric. Okay, this was weird.

"Are you serious?" I asked.

"Quite," Nils answered, and offered no further

explanation. He squeezed by me and retrieved a green, fuzzy blanket from the closet where I'd been stowed. Shook it out and held it between me and the male eyes on board.

"Hurry, please," he said. Now would be a good time to do something, if I could think of a damn thing to do. But even if I could incapacitate Nils, I'd still have the other two to contend with, not to mention the pilot.

I sighed and began shedding my Maria clothing. I left on her granny panties (elasticized, so they wouldn't fall off) and bra, since they were better than nothing. I did take an extra moment to unhook the bra and tie the back into a secure knot to make it fit a little better. Not perfect, but it was wearable. The ivory dress went on easily enough. The hem grazed the floor and the bodice was a bit snug, but all in all it was a good fit.

I checked to see if Nils was looking; he wasn't. More "nice" points for him. How many nice points did you have to earn to counterbalance kidnapping someone? Not wanting to push his limits, I hurriedly pulled the brown, sleeveless tunic over my head. It hugged Mina's curves pretty snugly, but I could breathe.

"Are you finished?" Nils inquired, still polite.

"Yeah, I think so. Unless you have some ancient shoes to complete the ensemble. So, what's up with this outfit, anyway? Are we going to a costume party?"

He lowered the blanket. "Your own shoes will suffice for now," he said, ignoring my questions.

Fortunately, Maria's sensible walking shoes were not a bad fit for Mina, and I'd already proven I could run well enough in them. Not fast enough, obviously, but well enough. It remained to be seen if I could work up any speed in the medieval garb. I'd sure as hell test it out as soon as I got the opportunity.

Per interrupted us, a small, black leather bag in his hand and a smile on his face. That couldn't be good.

"So, back to my seat?" I said brightly to Nils, deliberately not looking at Per.

Nils shook his head. "I'm afraid not."

Per stopped right behind Nils and opened the bag. He removed a syringe.

My heart walloped the inside of my rib cage. I *hate* needles. I've never even had my ears pierced—if I want to wear earrings, I adapt myself lobe holes. "Look, there's no need—"

Nils took my hand, gently at first, but clamped down when I tried to yank it away. I pulled harder, putting my whole body into it. I lashed out with my free hand. It was captured and held fast. I kicked anything I could reach, but the damned dress rendered the attempts useless.

"Stop screaming. No one can help you here," Per said.

Funny, I hadn't even considered that. Nor did I particularly care. I got my mouth as close to Per's ear as I could. Screeched loud and long. Mainly just noise, but I think I squeezed out an "asshole" and a "dickhead." Possibly a "motherfucking, boybuggering, shit-eating douche-nozzle," too. My mouth was pretty much on autopilot, so it's hard to say for sure.

My chain of description was unceremoniously interrupted by the back of Per's hand slamming across my mouth. He didn't leave it there long enough for me to take a hunk out of it this time, so the only blood I tasted was mine. It made me fight that much harder.

Didn't do me a lick of good. Using both his arms and one of his legs, Nils immobilized me while Per pushed my sleeve up and jabbed the needle into my arm.

Chapter 14

When I came to again I was on a bed in a tiny, dimly lit room. My head hurt and I had to pee. But at least I wasn't gagged, and I wasn't on an airplane. I felt good about that.

There was a wooden dresser against the opposite wall, and a whitewashed nightstand with a quaint oil lamp on it to my left. A simple country bedroom, it appeared. I bounced once to test the mattress. It was comfy enough. If one of my wrists hadn't been handcuffed to the iron headboard, it might have been a nice place to wake up from a nap.

I didn't have an old rag stuffed in my mouth, so I supposed the Vikings expected a shout out from me when I woke up. "Hello?" I croaked. Guess I was a little hoarse from all that screaming right before Per jabbed me. I mustered some saliva, swallowed, and tried again. It was a bit louder this time, but still nothing to brag about.

"Is anyone there?"

Cue the crickets.

Suppressing an unreasonable flash of panic at being abandoned by my captors, I assessed my situation. I was still in medieval attire, with no idea why. Judging by the light filtering through the red-checkered curtains of the room's lone window, it was either dawn or dusk. I'd know in a few minutes, when it got either lighter or darker.

Since I appeared to be alone, I figured no harm could come of taking a look around. I flipped through my mental files for an aura with the smallest hands possible. It would have to be Molly, Billy's youngest sister. Ten years old and tiny, still anxiously waiting for the famous Doyle growth spurt to hit. She had long, dark hair, eyes exactly like Billy's (all the Doyle kids do, courtesy of their father), and more energy than a hummingbird on crack. When I used to babysit her, the only way I could keep her entertained was by playing "twins" with her. Have to admit, that was fun for me, too. I loved having an excuse to bat the legendary Doyle eyelashes.

Molly's hand slipped easily from the handcuffs. Once free, I almost changed right back into Mina so my clothes would fit, but decided I would be faster and lighter on my feet as Molly. I hauled up my dress, slipped out of my shoes, and tiptoed to the window. Peeked out, careful to keep my face from showing, in case anyone was outside. No tall blond men, no dour Native American, only a bunch of trees to one side, and a barn to the other. Beyond the barn was an old farmhouse. All right, then. A country farm. I must be in some sort of guest cottage.

Still treading softly, I scurried to the bedroom door, Molly's teensy feet soundless on the wooden floor. There was no lock. They probably hadn't thought they'd need one, what with the handcuffs and all. Little did they know what I was capable of . . . and my problem was going to be making sure they didn't find out about those capabilities while I made my escape.

No squeak when I opened the door—good. The bedroom was directly off the living area, where the furnishings were pure Ikea. Inexpensive, modern, serviceable. The kitchen, if you can call a stove, a sink, a minifridge, and two small cupboards a kitchen, occupied one end of the room. A pine table with four chairs around it served as a room divider. If there was a bathroom, I didn't see it.

The back window looked out over a small yard, with closely cropped grass blanketing the ground right up to the edge of the woods. Just beyond where the trees started I noticed a small building, barely wider than its door.

Ah-ha. An outhouse. Lovely. Well, any port in a storm. I didn't want to risk getting caught, but not nearly as much as I didn't want to wet myself, so I crept out the front door and scanned the area. All clear. I ran to the privy and slipped inside.

Ugh. It wasn't a bad outhouse, as outhouses go, but the atmosphere left little doubt as to its function. The seat—basically, a hole in the wooden planks—looked well-sanded, so maybe I wouldn't wind up with splinters in my ass. Lucky me.

Pressing matters seen to, I stepped out and scanned the area, turning my mind to what I should do next. Run for it? Tempting, considering the bad vibe I'd been getting from Per. That man would take any excuse to slap me silly, just because of a little bite. What a baby.

Nils hadn't hit me, but he'd sure as hell held me down while Per had jabbed me with the needle. Couldn't count on him for help, no matter how polite he was. I needed to get gone, and fast, before they got back. Running was hardly practical, though, considering I had no idea where I was. How close was I to a town? Might be too far to walk, even if I had a clue which way to go.

Maybe there was a phone? I hadn't seen one in the cottage, but the big farmhouse might have one. But what if that was where the Vikings were? Crap. Couldn't risk it.

What I needed was a vehicle of some sort. A car, or even a motorcycle. A map that had a big "You Are Here" X-ed onto it wouldn't hurt either, I thought wryly. Hmm . . . The barn? It was big enough to hold a car, or maybe there was one behind it. That was more likely—I'd check there first.

The only thing behind the big, old building was an equally old fertilizer truck. Full of shit, from the smell of it. Still, it had wheels, and I couldn't exactly afford to be choosy. I morphed back into Mina (Molly was too little to see over the steering wheel) and reached for the door.

As I was climbing up onto the seat, I heard the sound of an engine in the distance. *Shit*. Someone was coming. I left the truck—regretfully—and peeked around the corner of the barn. Saw Per and Nonto get out of a Mini Cooper. No way would I be able to make a quiet getaway in the monster truck with them so close—I'd be caught for sure. *Damn it*. I'd have to get back to my bed and wait for a better opportunity.

Nonto retrieved a few sacks from the backseat— groceries, it looked like—while Per headed straight to the front door. Not a helpful sort, apparently. If he checked on me right away, I was sunk.

I waited until Nonto was almost to the porch, then made a dash for the cottage, moving as swiftly as my long dress allowed. The sky was definitely darker than it had been earlier, so we were on the downhill side of the day. Once around to the back of the house, I saw what I hoped was the window to the bedroom. If it was locked from the inside, I was screwed.

It wasn't. It gave, with only minimal resistance and not a lot of noise. I heard voices from the front of the house, and the sound of cupboard doors closing. I might just have time.

Bracing my hands on the sill, I hopped up and swung my hip over. Ducked my head into the room, pulled my legs in behind me. The voices were getting louder, heading toward me. I couldn't take time to close the window.

I changed into Molly as I dove for the bed, slipped my hand through the cuff, and was back to being Mina before I could complete a breath. Just in time, too. Per strode through the door, a pompous smirk plastered to his face.

"Well, well. *Den lilla hunden* has awakened from her nap," he said.

"So it would appear," I said, ignoring what he'd just called me. I figured whatever it meant, it wasn't likely complimentary.

He looked from me to the window, where the cheap cotton curtains were moving with the breeze. His brow furrowed and he swung his head back to me. I kept Mina's expression blank.

"Nils thought you needed some fresh air?" he asked, his tone making it clear he didn't approve of his partner's considerate treatment of me.

"How should I know? I just woke up." I rattled my handcuffs. "Hey, can you undo me here? I could use a ladies' room."

"You will have to wait." He walked to the window, closed and locked it. "When your hero returns, perhaps you can prevail upon him to see to your needs. Though I must warn you, we have nothing so fancy as a 'ladies' room' here." He smiled unpleasantly and left.

The son of bitch. If I hadn't already taken care of matters, I'd pee all over his bed just to spite him. I found myself actually missing Nils. At least he was courteous. And he *had* kept Per from breaking my arm. That was nice of him. Where was he, anyway? The only voice I could hear belonged to Per, saying something about shampoo and body wash in English to Nonto.

What the heck? They were in the middle of a kidnapping and discussing toiletries? I listened harder, but wasn't able to make out every word.

". . . new product . . . unlikely women will . . . only men who need . . . be no problem," Per said.

"Have you considered . . ." Nonto's voice at last. Well, whaddya know. He wasn't mute after all. ". . . could harm . . ."

"It's a chance we must take," Per said, his voice closer.

The front door opened and shut. "I sometimes think you are willing to take too many chances." Nils's voice. I was relieved to hear it.

"And I sometimes think you need to use some shampoo," Per answered him.

Huh? What kind of comeback was that? Maybe it was a Swedish thing.

My door opened and Nils filled it. His hair looked clean enough to me. "Ah, you are awake."

I bit back a smart-ass comment and nodded. "Where's Trey? You said you'd take me to him."

"And so we shall. Later." He set his jaw, and I knew was the end of that topic for the moment. In a more solicitous vein, he added, "Have you been up yet?"

"If that's your way of asking if I need to pee, the

answer is yes. Your buddy didn't seem inclined to let me off my leash." I jingled my special bracelet.

He took a key from his pocket and freed me. "I'll show you to the toilet. I'm afraid we don't have indoor plumbing here in the cottage."

"Yeah, well, I'm dressed for the olden days, so lead me to it. I'm sure I'll manage. By the way, what does '*den lilla hunden*' mean?"

"The little dog. Why?" He looked at me curiously.

Pretty much what I'd expected. "No reason," I said.

I put my shoes back on, hoping Nils would assume I'd kicked them off when I woke up. Guess he did, since he didn't comment on it. I wasn't exactly thrilled at the idea of spending more time in the outhouse—especially now that it was even darker outside, and God only knew what kind of creepy-crawlies liked to hang out there in the murk.

Once outside I gestured toward the farmhouse. "How about there? Any chance they have a working toilet?" If I could get a look inside, maybe figure out where a phone was, I could sneak back later and call for help.

"Sorry. We only have access to the cottage. The farmhouse is locked."

"And, heavens, we couldn't break in, could we? Why, that would be illegal," I said, widening my eyes. He acknowledged the irony with a tight smile, and led me to the crude facilities, where I went through the charade while he waited nearby. One would almost think he didn't trust me. Nothing crawled up my legs, as far as I could feel, and I removed myself from the fumes as quickly as seemed reasonable.

I looked around after I got out, pretending it was all new to me, and noted there was still only the one car. Wherever Nils had been, he hadn't returned with a vehicle.

"Hey, is that a Mini?" I asked, trying to sound excited in a rich girl way. "They are so cute. I wanted to get one, but my parents got me a stuffy old Mercedes instead. No fun at all."

"Poor you," Nils said, clearly amused.

"Seriously, may I look at it?"

"Why would you want to? Surely you've seen one before." He eyed me with something hinting at suspicion. Time for a wistful sigh.

"Well, it's something to do to stay outside a little longer, isn't it? I'm not really looking forward to being chained up again." That much was true.

He cocked his head. Shrugged. "All right. But only for a moment." He took my hand and led me toward the car.

"Afraid I'm going to make a break for it?" I said.

"No. You are smart enough not to do that. But the ground is uneven here, and I wouldn't want you to trip and fall."

Yeah, right. Well, he needn't worry. I wouldn't be trying to run right under his nose. I just wanted to get a look inside the Mini to see if maybe, just maybe, Per had left the keys in the ignition. I knew how to hot-wire a car—Billy showed me when we were in high school—but that didn't work well with the newer models, and I didn't want to waste time searching the cottage for the keys later if I didn't have to.

I figured there was a good chance all three musketeers would sleep tonight without one of them standing guard, since they would think I was stuck in the cuffs. If I could get away with the only available car, they wouldn't be able to catch me. It wasn't like the fertilizer truck could keep up with a fine piece of German engineering like the Mini. And so what if I got lost? I'd reach someplace civilized eventually, and figure out how to contact help then.

Nils extended a hand toward the dark green import as we neared it. "Look—here is your dream car. Do you really think it would satisfy a woman of your refined tastes?" It looked ridiculously small next to him when he stopped beside it, almost like a toy.

"Oh, my tastes tend to be quite simple," I said, running my free hand over the white car top, and bending over to look inside. There was still enough light to see the keys hanging in the ignition. *Yes!* I thought. Only maybe I kind of thought it out loud. Oops.

Nils brought his head down to my level to see what had me so excited.

"Um, *yes*, look at that—leather seats!" I gushed. "See? Good things come in small packages."

"I can see that," he said, only he was looking at me and not the car. *Yikes!* He wasn't getting ideas, was he?

Duh. What man wouldn't be getting ideas about Mina? *Improvise, Ciel. Maybe you can use this.*

I straightened up and moved away from the car, taking Nils with me, since he still had hold of my hand. Darned if I didn't slip on a loose stone and stumble up against the big Swede, and heck if I didn't accidentally brush my breasts up along the side of his rib cage as I righted myself. His swift intake of breath told me if he *had* noticed the key, it shouldn't be in his mind long enough to make a lasting impression. Mission accomplished.

"I'm sorry—I guess you were right about the ground. I'm not usually so clumsy."

His hand tightened on mine. I looked away, hiding my victory smile. "I, um, guess we should go back in now," I said.

"In a moment." Nils's voice was soft. Inviting.

I tried my best to avoid meeting his eyes, but he caught my glance when I peeked up at him, and pulled me closer. Geez. He was going to kiss me.

Should I let him? Would that make him more kindly disposed to help me? I didn't want to—oh, hell, who was I kidding? A tiny part of me (the unthinking, stupid part) kind of did want to. I was curious. Hello? Viking hunk. What normal, heterosexual woman *wouldn't* be curious? But, I decided, Mina wouldn't want him to—she would be too worried about Trey to even think of it—and I had to be Mina. So I pulled away.

Right after the first minute or so.

I *know*. It was wrong. I mean, here I was making

loose with somebody else's morals. Honestly, I was just going to take a little sample, and then fly into a mortally offended routine, but you know how it is when you have one itty-bitty bite of Ben and Jerry's Cherry Garcia, with the best intentions not to have any more than that, and before you know it the whole pint is gone? Yeah, it was kind of like that. The thing of it was, Nils was a pretty good kisser, which sort of took me by surprise. Could kidnappers be good kissers?

And then I felt queasy—the ice cream analogy holding up only too well—because here I was betraying Pete's memory. I mean, even if Nils hadn't been the shooter, he was still an accomplice. But I could hardly claim to be offended now. Not when I'd let it go on for so long. So I kept it simple. "I shouldn't have let you do that."

He smiled, not looking like a killer at all. "I'm glad you did."

I shook myself. *Mina. Damn it, remember who you are!* "Just don't do it again. I'm practically engaged!"

"So?"

"What do you mean, *so*? Trey is the man I love, and for all I know you've killed him. I saw one of you kill Pete, and you're probably going to kill me, too, for God's sake!" I balled up a fist and slammed it against his chest.

He pulled me back to him, but only to wipe away a few stray tears sliding down my cheeks. *Gawd.* Was I actually crying? Damn aura leeching—Mina must be a crier. How embarrassing. But at least it seemed to be gaining me some sympathy. That couldn't hurt, could it?

"First of all, who is this Pete? The man on the dock?"

I nodded, more tears springing forth. I'd really liked Pete.

"It is unfortunate he was in the way," he said, voice tight. Was that regret I heard in his tone? I wanted to think so, but I couldn't be sure. "But Trey is not dead. And I am not going to kill you."

"Ha. You won't have to—Per would rather do that himself," I countered.

"Per will not kill you. I promise." Then he added, almost as an afterthought, "If you cooperate with us." I shivered, afraid once more. Every time I felt myself start to trust this guy, he said something to snap me out of it. Maybe he was just an extremely courteous sociopath.

"What about the other guy? He might. He looks pretty shifty."

"Not him either."

"Who is he, anyway, and why is he working with a bunch of Swedes?"

"That I cannot tell you. Now, perhaps we really should go back in. Per is watching from the window."

I pushed away from Nils and swung my head toward the house. "Oh, shit! Did he see? Was he watching?"

"What does it matter? It isn't his business."

"He'll think . . ." I stopped and swallowed, feeling shame I knew was unreasonable. While I was perfectly willing to use Mina's charms to manipulate Nils, I certainly didn't want that asshole watching. Especially if it might lead him to think I was up for grabs.

"He will think you were trying to enlist my aid," Nils said matter-of-factly. "It is not an uncommon tactic."

I felt my eyes get big. Was I that transparent?

Laughter rumbled through him. He turned back to the Mini and retrieved the keys. "It wouldn't have worked, anyway," he said when he looked at me again.

"I'm sure I don't know what you mean," I said, masking my disappointment with as much innocence as I could gather.

"Distracting me with sex so I wouldn't handcuff you tonight, and then taking off in the car after we are asleep. You don't know where you are—you would get lost. Besides, I still would've handcuffed you. Sex with handcuffs can be exciting, *ja*?"

Chapter 15

Nils handcuffed me back to the bed, but didn't attempt any funny business. I couldn't help feeling some part of him was decent, hard as it was to reconcile that with him being buddies with someone like Per. Guess he just really didn't like to pee sitting down.

At least he left me a pile of the latest American gossip rags, including my favorite, *World Wag Weekly*. There must be a large English readership in Sweden if he could find it here. I hoped it might help distract me, and it did. Page six especially, where an article headlined "Undercover Liz" caught my eye. Sure enough, the reporter had an exclusive with an American tourist in the Bahamas. The lady claimed she'd helped Queen Elizabeth with her shopping, and that the monarch had let it slip she would've had Diana killed if it had still been within the Royal Prerogative. Geez. The woman must've been on the phone to a reporter within minutes after Billy and I left the store. Good thing nobody really believed these stories.

An hour or two later—it's hard to keep track in a clock-less room—I heard snores and decided to risk some recon. Morphing into Molly once again, I freed my wrist and then returned to the Mina shape that had become normal for me. I rolled as quietly as possible off the bed and crossed quickly to the dresser. Faint light filtered through the curtains—could it be dawn already? Then I remembered where I probably was. Summertime sunrise comes early in Sweden.

I opened each drawer gingerly, searching for anything blunt and heavy. Nothing but some ratty old long johns and thick woolen socks. Damn. I'd have to check the kitchen.

As before, the door cooperated. No telltale squeak gave me away. I could see three forms sprawled and sleeping, one on the sofa and two on the floor. The loudest snorer was one of the Vikings. Must be Per. Surely Nils wouldn't make sounds like that. I eased myself out of the bedroom and tiptoed over to the kitchen.

Ah-ha! On the stove was a cast-iron skillet. Perfect. Precisely how hard did you have to hit someone on the head to knock him out without killing him? I wasn't sure. Guess I'd just have to bash away and hope for the best. And hit all three of them in rapid succession; otherwise, I'd risk one or two of them waking up before I was done. Couldn't imagine any of them, not even Nils, taking kindly to this part of my escape plan.

I'd hit Per last—his snoring might cover up any sound the other two made. The Indian would be first. He was on the sofa, and farthest away from Per. Then Nils, and finally the asshole. I felt bad about hitting the first two (well, not so much Nonto—I was ambivalent about him), but I was kind of looking forward to introducing Per's head to a cooking utensil. It would be like dessert after an unappetizing meal.

I crept closer, raising the skillet with both hands as I went. Geez, it was heavy. With this sucker, you could weight-train while you cooked.

The three of them continued to sleep soundly. Nils was on his back, head pillowed on a chair cushion, hair mussed, eyes moving rapidly beneath his eyelids, and the merest hint of a smile playing on his lips. He must be dreaming. About Mina?

I paused. He'd been polite to me. Nice, really, if you compared him to Per, and ignored the fact that he'd maybe been the one to shoot Pete.

Damn it! I couldn't do it. I was going to wuss out. I couldn't bring myself to risk killing him. Shit. What kind of woman couldn't hit a man with a frying pan? I couldn't even carry out a fucking cliché. Disgusted with myself, I lowered my arms. Now I'd have to sneak back into my room and spend the rest of the night berating my cowardice. I *hate* berating my cowardice.

Unless . . .

I hadn't planned to look for the keys until the

gang was safely dispatched, but since they were so soundly asleep, I might as well try anyway. I scanned the room, searching the tops of the end tables, the dining table, and the bookshelves on my way back to the kitchen nook. I thought about putting the skillet back on the stove, but decided against it. Heavy and awkward as it was to manage, it was still the only weapon I had at hand. Holding it tightly with one hand, I used the other to push the empty grocery bags out of the way, and immediately stifled a whoop.

Pay dirt!

The keys were there, next to a bunch of receipts. Guess even criminal organizations have to keep track of expenses. I pressed the simple key ring tightly into my palm—didn't want to be given away by any stray jingles—and snuck back to my room. I figured my best shot at getting out of the house undetected was through the same window I'd come in earlier.

On my way across the room, my left foot found the one floorboard in the house that creaked. I cringed at the sound and stood frozen until I could be sure the snoring from the next room continued. Various snorks and rumbles reassured me.

The window slid open easily, once I remembered to unlatch it. Between the long dress and the unwieldy frying pan, it was difficult to haul myself through, but I managed, going out feet-first and dropping soundlessly to the ground. (Mostly. Unless you count the muffled "Shit!" when I banged the skillet against my knee as I hit the grass.)

I turned around to shut the window behind me—anything to help dampen the sound of the car engine—and jumped back when Per's head popped out of it, a snarl on his lips. Reaching for me, he gave a big shout-out to his buddies.

Crap! I raised my arms and brought them down swiftly, bashing his forehead a good one. *Pan, meet Per. Per, pan. There, intro complete.* His eyes widened for just a second before they fell shut, and he slumped over the sill.

I dropped the skillet and ran for all I was worth, *fuckity-fucking* under my breath all the way to the car. Keys still in a death-grip, I yanked the car door open, dove in, and pulled most of my dress in behind me. With trembling hands, I found the ignition. Cranked it. The car lurched forward, then jerked to a stop, rattling my teeth.

Right. Manual transmission. Okay, I *knew* how to do this. Didn't do it often, but I *could*. Clutch. Stick in first. Turn the key. The engine roared in my ears as a wild-eyed face appeared in the driver's side window.

Fuck!

This Nils looked like he could kill me without blinking an eye. I should've bashed him while I had the chance. See what you get for being nice?

I locked the door with one hand at the same time I released the clutch and stomped on the gas. Repeated the clutching process, gaining momentum with each shift. Surely he couldn't keep up with a speeding car—he'd have to let go, or else risk getting dragged.

Or he might just give a mighty heave with his legs and wind up on top of the car. *Shit!*

I stomped on the gas, veered to the right, and found myself in the wooded area behind the farm, slaloming between the larger trees and mowing down the smaller ones. Nils pounded on the car top, sliding from side to side above me. I caught glimpses of his feet through the windows. Why didn't the idiot just get off? Did he want to die?

I pulled to the left, and narrowly avoided turning the Mini into a Christmas tree ornament. Found myself bearing down on a primitive-looking horse.

Oh, for the love of . . . ! What was *with* this place?

The horse stood still, calmly gazing at me while chewing on a mouthful of something green. The trees to either side of me were too big and too close together to risk veering again, so I braked. Hard.

What else could I do? I couldn't hit the horse. I *love* horses.

Nils flew off the top of the car and landed with a thud in front of the placid beast. I shoved the gearshift into reverse, reacquainted the accelerator with the floorboard, and was back to the farm road by the time the crazy-eyed Viking was on his feet.

Chapter 16

I drove as fast as I dared, letting instinct lead me. When you have a sense of direction like mine, that's risky, but what choice did I have?

Eventually I got to a real road. Paused briefly, trying to figure out if one direction had any notable advantage over the other. None that I could see, so I eeny-meeny-miney-moed, turned right, and floored it, for the first time in my life hoping a cop would pull me over. No such luck. The tree-lined road, dappled with pinkish-gray, early-morning light, was deserted. I wasn't charmed by the fairy-tale beauty of the setting. There were ogres in these woods. Fricking big Viking ogres with needles, and I had to get away.

After a mile or so I came upon a long driveway, at the end of which there was a farmhouse. I slowed to a stop, but stayed on the main road. Did I dare take the time to see if anyone was home? What if they didn't speak English? Or didn't have a phone? Or worst of all, what if they knew Per or Nils?

I stepped on the gas. Better not risk contact with anyone until I was in a more populated area. A couple of more miles down the road I saw a blue destination sign, slowed just enough to read "Visby," and sped onward. Fantastic. I sort of knew where I was, then. Visby was the town Billy had been heading for on Gotland. Not that he'd be easy to find, but I felt better just knowing he was in the vicinity. If I could find a phone, maybe I could even track him down.

I knew I was getting close when I saw the old stone wall in the distance, and the Baltic beyond it. Three black spires rose from a sea of red-tiled rooftops, maybe some sort of church. I remembered Billy telling me about the wall—it dated from medieval times and surrounded the town—but he'd extolled the virtues of the beautiful Swedish girls a lot more than the buildings, so I wasn't as up on the architectural details. I just hoped the town wasn't so medievally picturesque that I couldn't find a public phone.

I ditched the car in a stand of trees. It was no good to me anymore, and might be a liability if Nils had called ahead and warned anyone to be on the lookout for it. It was going to be hard enough to blend in, dressed as I was, and there was no point in dropping Mina's aura until I could find less identifiable clothes. Besides, I'd draw even more attention to myself tripping over my hem.

The noise hit me first, before I even got close to the gate—happy babbling, raucous laughter, and lots of singing of the decidedly unsober sort. My puzzlement grew as I passed though the gate. Groups of people strolled the bricked and cobbled roads, making merry in languages I didn't understand. Mostly Swedish, near as I could tell, but also some German (possibly), a soupçon of French (maybe), and even a little Japanese (okay, that one was a stab in the dark). Most of them were dressed as oddly as I was. What was going on?

I kept to the smaller roads and avoided eye contact with anyone until I came upon a group of jolly, English-speaking inebriates, and smiled at a girl dressed in garb similar to my own. She smiled back and said, "Isn't this the coolest place? Too bad the festival is only once a year."

Festival? Okay, that would explain the clothes. I'd been to Renaissance Faires in the States—guess this was similar. "Yeah, too bad, " I said, feigning a touch of tipsiness. "Um, I seem to have lost my friends. You haven't seen any big, blond Viking types, have you?"

Laughter rolled through the group. Yeah, okay, it *was* kind of a stupid question.

One dark-haired, skinny guy, dressed as some sort of robed medieval scholar, said, "You're kidding, right? This place is lousy with Vikings. Kind of trite, if you ask me."

I shrugged. Thought about explaining that my Vikings wouldn't necessarily be in period costumes, but decided not to waste the time. "It's our first visit here. They figured they'd go with tried and true."

One of the other girls, a dreamy-eyed, golden-haired princess type, said, "Oh, I love the Vikings. They're so . . . well, *so*." The last word was carried on a sigh; the scholar rolled his eyes.

"Um, yeah. So so," I said.

One of the guys—a large, generic peasant with longish, super-curly brown hair and black-framed, squishy glasses—pulled a cell phone from his pocket and began texting someone. I almost salivated. There was my link to Billy.

The scholar tried to grab the phone. "You doofus—you're not supposed to have that. We all agreed to play it real," he said with a scowl.

The peasant twisted away, blocking him with his back. "My phone is a part of me. It doesn't count."

"You dipshit."

The peasant merely sniffled, wiped his nose on his sleeve (he could have a cell phone but tissues were too modern?) and continued texting. I edged myself between the boys. "Excuse me. Could I possibly borrow your phone when you're through? I accidentally left mine at the hotel, and it would sure save me a long trudge back if I could call my friends and see where they are." I put forth my best damsel-in-distress vibe and smiled, stopping just short of batting my eyelashes.

"Sorry. Can't spare the minutes. Roaming charges are already killing me," he said, his thumbs never pausing.

"But . . ." I was about to offer to pay him for his damned minutes, but of course I had no money.

"Put it away, turd. You're ruining the experience." The scholar was getting seriously bent out of shape.

"Screw you." The thumbs never missed a beat.

Dreamy girl tried to intervene. "Come on, Phillip. Lay off him—he's only checking on Emmie."

The peasant turned beet red. "I am not."

"Jesus. She doesn't want to hear from you, asshole!" Phillip might have been a scholar, but he was not the soul of tact.

Assho—er, I mean peasant boy—turned and walked away, his eyes locked onto the two-inch display. Phillip, totally irritated, followed him and, after pretending to go in from the left, grabbed the phone from the right. He threw it into the nearest rosebush.

"Hey! That is not cool, jerk!" Peasant boy shoved Phillip aside and dove in after his prized possession, ignoring thorns and curious passersby alike. "If you broke it—"

"Get a life, jackhole."

"That wasn't very nice, Phillip," the first girl I'd approached said.

"It's tough love. We took him on this trip to get his mind *off* the bitch, didn't we? How's he gonna do that if he keeps contacting her?" Phillip explained patiently.

As much as I wanted to get my hands on that phone, I had to admit Phillip had a point. Unrequited love was painful, but clinging pathetically never got anyone to requite. Trust me, I know. Much better to moon longingly from afar. Well, maybe not better, necessarily, but less embarrassing in the long run.

The dreamy princess reached down and tugged on Peasant Boy's pants leg. "Come out of there, Kevin. You're getting all scratched up."

"I don't care," he said, his voice thick. I suspected he wasn't so much hunting for his phone now as he was giving himself a moment to recover.

"Leave him," Phillip told the girls. "Kev, we're going. See you back at the hotel later."

"Fine," Kevin said, and stayed in the bushes.

The rest of the crew waved and set off down the narrow, cobbled road, debating the relative merits of forcing fun on someone recovering from a broken romance. I stayed where I was, still hoping to convince Kevin he really wanted to let me use his phone. As the sound of his friends receded into the distance, it was replaced by suspicious snuffling noises coming from the bushes.

Oh, God. He was crying. What was I supposed to do with a crying, barely post-adolescent peasant boy? I had problems of my own.

I nibbled a nail and tiptoed away. Got about five steps before I stopped and turned back. I couldn't leave him like that. Poor kid. He was really hurting.

I cleared my throat. The quiet sobbing stopped.

"Kevin? Are you okay?"

"Go away."

"I will, but first I want to make sure you can get

out of there all right. You, um, your clothes might get caught on the thorns. Just come on out and then I'll leave."

He took a deep breath and started backing out. Sure enough, the branches grabbed him mercilessly, clinging to him even harder than he was clinging to his lost love. I plucked them away as best I could, holding branches aside while he finished extricating himself. He stayed on the ground, knees up, elbows hooked around them, staring into the middle distance.

I checked him over as casually as I could, figuring the last thing he needed right now was mommying. His face and arms were crisscrossed with tiny red lines, but I didn't think he'd need a transfusion. Nodding my approval, I deadpanned, "So, that was a pretty impressive dive there. I give it a solid nine point five for form and a nine point seven for originality."

That got me a ghost of a smile.

"Yeah, well, ten years on the swim team will do wonders for your technique," he said. "Normally I make it a habit to land in water, though."

I chuckled. "Did you at least find your phone?"

"Yeah." He held it up by the flip top, leaving the bottom dangling by one hinge. "For all the good it does me."

Well, damn. Stupid Phillip.

"I don't suppose you carry a spare?" I asked, not too hopefully, seating myself gingerly beside him, trying to avoid grass stains. Not that I should care. They weren't my clothes.

"If I'd known what an asshole Phillip would turn out to be, I would have."

"Hard to know stuff like that in advance," I said. "Well, I guess I better, um, head back to my hotel."

Finally looking in my direction, he squinted his eyes, pushed his glasses up, and said, "Hey, I've seen you before. This afternoon at the hotel. You were coming out of one of the second-floor rooms when I was getting off the elevator."

Huh? "Really? This afternoon?"

"Yeah, only you were in other clothes. Modern ones. Guess it was before you changed."

My first thought was, *You're delusional, kid*. My second thought was, *I just found Billy*. He was trying to connect with Trey. What better way than to be visible as Mina?

"Oh yeah. Right," I said. "Say, are you heading back to the hotel now? Maybe we could walk together. I hate to admit it, but I'm a little lost. No sense of direction." I tacked on a self-deprecating shrug for good measure.

Kevin sat himself up a little taller, cleared his throat and said, "Sure. I'm not really in the mood for more partying, anyway." We walked along in silence for a while, Kevin taking the lead. He was still immersed in his cocoon of gloom, but I did catch him flitting glances at my chest, so I suspected he'd pull himself out of the mire eventually.

A short stroll brought us to a four-story structure that fit right into the medieval town. The white facade had a pinkish cast in the early-morning

light, and the steeply pitched roof was lined with
dormers. Looked like a nice hotel. Not that I'd expect anything less from a place Billy would deign
to stay.

"Would you like me to walk you to your room?"
Kevin asked once we were inside, motivated perhaps by courtesy, or more likely by loneliness. I
looked around the gorgeous reception area, with its
intricately carved wooden check-in desk and plastered archways, pretending it wasn't new to me.

"Well, about that . . . see, my friend has the key,
so I have to wait for hi—uh, her to get back. I'll sit
here in the lobby. I'm sure she won't be much longer." I just hoped the other Mina came along soon.
I had to warn Billy about the Vikings before he
found himself snatched off the street with no idea
about my previous contact with them.

"I'll wait with you," Kevin offered magnani-
mously.

"No! I mean, that's not at all necessary. You go
on to bed." Despite the sunrise, it was still the middle of the night by the clock. "Really, I'll be fine
here. Look—there's a nice, comfy chair for me."

I needed him to get gone, so I could slip out of
Mina's aura before I ran into my twin. I'd been
afraid to drop her before, because there was no way
I could've explained being a different person if the
Vikings had caught up to me during my thrilling
getaway. Now they might find it odd to see another
woman in clothes exactly like the ones they had
provided for me, but they couldn't be certain there
was a connection.

Kevin plopped down in an elegantly upholstered seat beneath a mural of a medieval outdoor scene. "No, the least I can do is keep you company, since you waited for me to get out of the bushes, even after I didn't let you use my phone. That was pretty cool." I suspected it was more that he didn't have anything better to do, being without his cell phone, but I couldn't say that. Resigned, I parked myself next to him.

"So," I said, turning my chair slightly so I could see out of a nearby window, "where are you and your friends from?"

He said either Indiana or Iowa, or maybe Idaho. Something with an "I" anyway. I wasn't exactly paying attention, because outside the window intermittent groups of tall, blond men kept walking by and I was fighting the urge to jump up and run the other way. Still, it would be rude to let him know his conversation was less than riveting, so I said, "Um, that's nice. I've heard it's really fun, er, there."

"Oh, yeah. Sure. Fun," he said. Then he added something about dentist offices and walking over hot coals, but a couple of the Viking types from outside chose that moment to enter, so my heart attack got in the way of hearing him clearly. They weren't Nils and Per, but they might've been.

"Coals, dentist . . . yeah, I hear you. No fun at all." I scanned the room for less open places to wait. The pair of men went to the desk. Within a few minutes, an attendant came. They spoke to her in what sounded like Swedish—I'd have to be an idiot not to recognize it by now—and she answered them in kind, handing them a piece of paper. One of them looked casually over his shoulder at me and Kevin, but his eyes didn't linger. He pulled a cell phone out of his pocket and spoke softly into it as they left the lobby for the lounge.

I directed my attention back to Kevin. His mouth was still moving and he didn't appear confused, so I guessed our conversation was going all right. I broke in. "Uh, excuse me, Kev—you don't mind if I call you Kev, do you? No? Thanks. Listen, do you think if I asked at the desk, they'd let me back in my room, even without ID? I mean, if the girl there recognizes me? I really need to get some sleep."

He looked a trifle disappointed, but said, "They might. It's worth a shot."

Apparently someone else thought so, too. Literally. The bullet whizzed above my head and embedded itself in the wall behind me, leaving me with a fine coating of plaster dust, and the running stag in the mural without a head.

I counted myself lucky it wasn't the other way around.

Chapter 17

"Whoa! What was that?" Kevin jumped up, blocking me. Chivalrous I'm sure, but stupid. I grabbed his arm as I dove for the floor, bringing him with me.

"Stay down!" I said, lifting my head only enough to get a gander at the door. It was closed. No one had come through it unless they were invisible. I scanned the lobby; nobody there either. The person behind the desk had ducked. I looked more closely at the window next to the door and saw the small hole with a spiderweb of lines radiating from it. _Okay._ Somebody outside was trying to shoot me. Or Kevin, I supposed, though that didn't seem as likely.

"Kev, where's your room?"

"Second floor, right down the hall from yours. Why? You wanna go there?"

A second bullet hit the wall, lower than the first.

Now the stag was missing a leg. "Might be a good idea," I said.

"Right." He started rolling sideways toward the stairwell. Kevin might not have been the sharpest crayon in the box when it came to girls, but he knew how to make an exit. I followed his example. My legs were so tangled in my dress by the time I got to the door, I couldn't crawl through it when he held it open for me. He grabbed my elbow and yanked me past him, giving my rear a final shove over the threshold before he followed me.

As soon as the door swung shut behind us, he helped me to my feet. I grappled with my dress, loosening its grip on my knees and hauling the hem up to my thighs. *There. That should make the stairs easier.* I flew up half a flight, realized Kevin was lagging, and looked back. He was standing on the bottom step, mouth agape, staring at Mina's lovely limbs.

Geez. "Come *on!* We have to get to your room before they follow us."

He gave himself a small shake, like a poodle after a rain shower, and started climbing. "Yeah, right. I'm coming."

That would explain the expression on your face, I thought wryly.

Kevin's room was the third one down the corridor on the right. I tried not to watch while he fumbled in his pocket for the key, giving him a chance to adjust himself without too much embarrassment. After my recent experience with Benjamin, I empathized.

The room was larger than I expected, with a pair of twin beds, and a wing chair by the window. One of the beds was as rumpled as the young man in front of me; the other was made with military precision. Either he occupied the room alone, or . . .

"That's Phillip's," Kevin said. "He's kind of anal about neatness. Among other things."

I shrugged. "Hey, don't knock a clean-freak roommate. I had one in college, and never once had to clean the bathroom myself."

"Yeah, that's a plus. Phillip's my roommate back at State. If I toss my dirty clothes onto his side of the room, sometimes he'll even do my laundry."

I laughed. "I like the way you think, Kev."

He grabbed a pile from the chair and tossed it onto Phillip's bed. "Sit. Please. Can I get you something to drink?"

I stayed by the door, listening for telltale footsteps. "Sure. Water, if you have it handy."

He pulled a plastic bottle out from under his bed. "It's not exactly cold."

"As long as it's wet." I gulped half the bottle. Escaping kidnappers was thirsty work.

Kevin stared at me. I could see the wheels turning behind his eyes.

I sighed. "Go ahead. Ask."

"Okay," he said. "What's going on?"

"It's kind of a long story."

He sat on the edge of his bed, elbows on knees, chin in palm. "I got nothing better to do."

Still no noise from the hallway, so I crossed to

the window and checked the street below. Nobody hanging around with a gun. I turned to Kevin and sat in the chair he had so thoughtfully cleared.

"We-e-ll," I started, brain whirling madly to come up with something plausible. Best to keep it from Mina's perspective, I decided. "Look, I shouldn't tell you this. It might not be safe for you to know."

"Worse than getting shot at?" He had a point.

"They were shooting at me, not you. For now. If you hang around me, though, I can't guarantee they won't add you to their hit list." I pushed myself up from the chair. "In fact, I should probably get out of here right—"

Kevin stood and blocked the path to the door. "Come on. You have to tell me more than that. Maybe we should call the police."

"Not feasible, Kev. The local cops would only complicate the situation."

"What situation?" he persisted.

How could I explain something I wasn't sure of myself? "Okay. Some Swedes kidnapped my fiancé." Kevin's face fell a little at the mention of a fiancé, but he recovered nicely. "I'm not sure why. Maybe just for money—he's got plenty—but nobody has asked for a ransom. I came here because it's the last place he was seen before he disappeared. Now I'm a target, too."

"I still think we better call the police."

"If we do that, they might kill Trey. I can't risk it. Listen, I'm going to leave now. Pretend you never saw me, okay?"

The room door opened with a bang. Kevin and I

dove for the floor between the twin beds at the same time. Luckily for me, he landed first, or I would've been squashed like a bug.

Phillip strolled in, followed by the girls. They looked down at us, eyebrows rising in unison. The princess's mouth dropped open. "K-Kevin? What . . . ? I mean, I thought . . . what about Em?" she wailed.

"Glad to see you're recovering there, bro," Phillip said. Sardonic, straight up, with a twist of envy.

"This isn't what you think," I said, pushing myself off a dazed Kevin.

The princess's hands perched on her hips and her voice hardened. "Here I thought you needed some psychic space to get over that bitch Emmie, and you take up with the first slut you meet in Sweden!"

Ah. So that was the way the wind was blowing. I glanced at Kevin, who looked about as bewildered as a boy could.

"Listen, you two. I think you may have the wrong idea here—" I started.

"Ha!"

"Cool it, Jennifer. Let her talk," Phillip said, grabbing all the clothes from his bed and tossing them onto Kevin's. He smoothed his duvet, picked a piece of lint off it, and stepped back. The kid really was too anal.

I stood up, leaving Kevin on the floor staring openmouthed up at Jennifer. Boys can be so oblivious.

After clearing my throat, I began again. "See, after

we realized we were staying at the same hotel, Kevin kindly offered to walk me back, and to wait with me until my roommate could bring me my key. While we were talking downstairs, some gunshots were fired into the lobby, so we got out of there as fast as we could. Since I didn't have my key, we came here. When you came in so suddenly we were still feeling a little skittish about the shooting, so we dove for cover. It's simple, really." I looked at Kevin, trying to signal that I didn't want to go into the rest of it with his friends. Apparently, subtlety was wasted on him.

"Don't forget to tell them about your kidnapped fiancé."

Thanks, Kev. "Yeah, I was getting to that."

Hope flared in Jennifer's eyes—I guess the idea of the boy you like getting shot at is better than the idea of him hitting on some strange woman—but Phillip's face maintained a healthy skepticism.

"Well, you see—" I choked to a stop when I saw Mina's face peek in through the doorway. "Billy!" I yelped. Panicking, I pointed at my face and shook my head, willing him to understand.

He got the hint, and pulled out before the others saw him. When he poked his head back in a second later he was a completely different woman. Same basic build, but redheaded, a little older and longer in the face, and absolutely gorgeous.

"Knock, knock. I'm looking for a friend of mine," Billy said in a smoky voice.

I crossed to him at once. "Billy, there you are. I've

been looking for you for hours. Guys, this is my roommate, um, Wilma. Only she hates to be called that—who wouldn't?—so everyone calls her Billy. Right, Billy?"

"Right you are, darling. I'd sue my parents for saddling me with that name if I could, but it turns out the courts won't allow that."

"Is she here supporting you through your ordeal? That is just so sweet!" Jennifer gushed. At least she no longer wanted to assassinate me. That was something.

"Um, yes. That's exactly what she's doing—helping me find my fiancé. She's had experience with kidnappings before."

Billy looked sideways at me. "Yes, indeed. A friend in need, and all that. In fact, I have a few leads to discuss with you, so maybe we should get back to our room. Ta, all." He took my elbow and began backing toward the door.

"Wait," Kevin said, finally getting to his feet. "What if it's not safe? Don't we need to find out who shot at you?"

Again Billy stepped up, speaking rapidly as he continued pulling me out of the room. "I'm on it. I've just been speaking with the police—undercover, very hush-hush—and they are taking it from here. I saw them a few blocks away, chasing someone—the shooter, no doubt. Thanks for looking after my friend. I'm sure everything will be fine now. Go on about your vacation. See you around." He closed the door behind us and dragged me down the hall.

"My God, Ciel. What the hell are you doing here?" he said as soon as we were alone in his room.

"It's kind of a long story."

"I'm listening."

I took a deep breath and filled him in on everything that had happened since we parted company back at my office, minus a few insignificant details, like me maiming his car and Nils kissing me, but I included pretty much everything else.

Billy looked impressed when I got to the part with the frying pan. "Beaned him, did you? Think you killed him?"

"Oh, God—I hadn't even thought of that! What if I did? I could be a murderer!" I felt a little sick.

"Nah. Self-defense. Justifiable homicide at worst."

"Gee, thanks. I'll sleep ever so much better now," I said, with a twist of my mouth.

"Don't worry, cuz. It's harder to kill somebody than you might think. He might only have permanent brain damage."

I cut him a look. "Give me your phone. I'm calling Mark."

"Can't use a cell. Someone might be listening. Hey, how did you find my hotel? I didn't even know where I was staying until I got here."

"Dumb luck. I bumped into Kevin and he recognized me as you. Told me I was staying here. I figured you must have been playing Mina to find Trey."

He shrugged. "It seemed the easiest way to get his attention. I've been all over this damn burg, trying to be as visible as I can. Guess that's pointless now, if you're sure the Vikings have him."

"Who knows? *They* seemed sure. And you're lucky the Vikings didn't snatch you off the street— Mina is not exactly the safest face to wear in public anymore."

"So drop her already," he said, with a tug on my hair.

"Then my clothes won't fit," I grumped.

He kicked off his heels and reverted to himself, going from chic to preposterous in a blink of his lovely lashes. "You think you have problems." He grinned and began disrobing.

"Billy, I'm standing right here."

"What? You don't expect me to hang around in this dress, do you? For one thing, I'm about to split it." He turned his back to me. "Be a pal and unzip me."

I complied, tugging hard on the zipper, which was strained almost to the breaking point. "What if our new buddies down the hall pay an unexpected call?"

"I'll switch back and they'll see a beautiful redhead in a generic hotel robe." He shrugged and went to the closet. "Here's one for you, too. Change in the bathroom if your modesty insists."

I caught the robe he tossed at me and did as he suggested. It was akin to slipping out of too-tight shoes—the relief was profound and immediate. I didn't even half-mind seeing my skimpy figure in the mirror. It felt right.

What I did mind was putting the clean robe onto my less than fresh body. The gleaming white porcelain of the tub was irresistible. I twisted the hot-water faucet, and poked my head out the door while the water warmed. "I'm going to take a quick bath. Anything you have to tell me that can't wait ten minutes?"

"Nope. Indulge yourself—go for fifteen. You hungry? I'll order room service."

My stomach growled. "Ravenous. Order a lot."

The hot water felt too good for a purely hygienic dip (besides, there were bubbles) so the fifteen minutes stretched to twenty. Maybe half an hour. Long enough to get pruney, anyway. I heard the door to the room open and close a few times, and picked up on some muffled voices, which I tuned out. Billy could handle the waitstaff without my input.

When I came out, I found a spread fit for a queen. The small table was laden. Excess side dishes, left on trays, overflowed onto the bed. A stand held an ice bucket with a bottle of champagne and two glasses, each containing a single raspberry. Next to the glasses was a note in Billy's careless scrawl.

Taking care of a few details. Back soon to pop a cork and celebrate your escape.

"Geez," I said to the empty room. "I said order a lot, not the whole menu."

Oh, well. Billy was nothing if not extravagant in his gestures. The assortment of breads, fruits, cheeses, pickled herring, smoked salmon, thin-sliced roast beef, ham, hard-boiled eggs, caviar, and—praise God—pastries was not out of character for him.

I sampled small pinches of everything, trying to be polite and wait until he was back to share the meal with him. He'd better hurry, though, because I didn't know how long I could hold out.

A few minutes and one dry piece of hard bread later, I was pacing when my eyes fell on the champagne glasses. They were the short, saucer kind, not flutes. Maybe it was just my whirling mind looking for a distraction, but the raspberries made the stemware look like nothing so much as inverted boobs. I popped one of the berries into my mouth and considered the glass thoughtfully. I'd read somewhere that the champagne saucer was supposedly modeled on the perfect breast of one of Napoleon's mistresses. *I wonder . . .*

What the heck, why not? I was alone. I was curious.

I was bored.

So I opened my robe and tried one on for size. *Hallelujah!* It fit. I even overflowed a tiny bit. Not bad, I thought. Not bad at all. Inordinately pleased, I ate the berry from the second glass, and poured my other boob into it. Holding the glasses in place, I looked down at myself, thinking it was maybe not so horrible to be less endowed than Mina Worthington. At least I shouldn't sag much by the time I was sixty or seventy.

A throat cleared, loudly. And it wasn't mine. *Shit!*

My eyes flew up to meet Billy's. He was standing across the room, staring in shocked fascination, dimples bracketing a wide grin. Damn. I hadn't even heard the door squeak.

"You win. Your raspberries are better," he said, eyes aglow.

I whipped myself around, removed the glasses, and resecured my robe. Not looking at him, I stumbled through an explanation of Napoleon and his mistress, which sounded totally stupid when I heard it out loud, so I quickly changed the subject to the humongous amount of food he'd ordered.

The teasing glint lingered in his eyes, but he followed my conversational detour willingly enough. "I wasn't sure what you were in the mood for. But don't worry. It's on Mark."

"Do you always abuse your per diem when you do a job for him?"

"Pretty much. He's used to it." He plucked a raspberry from the dish of fruit and held it between his lips for a second before he sucked it into his mouth. I blushed and gave him a dirty look. He laughed, picked up another and threw it at me.

I dodged it. "You're never going to let me forget this, are you?"

"Not if we live to be a hundred." He held out a chair for me, like the gentleman he wasn't.

I lifted my chin and sat, refusing to look at him. Standing behind me, he leaned down and said, "Come on, cuz. Lighten up. You have nothing to be embarrassed about."

I ignored him and reached for the gooiest,

sweetest-smelling confection on the table. "I'm not listening to you."

"So I've seen your raspberries. Who cares? What's a little fruit between friends?"

I pressed my lips together, trying to look mad, but gave up when he started juggling berries from the bowl. He was pretty good. "Okay," I said. "I can see where it might be a little bit funny from your point of view. But can we please drop it now?"

He caught three berries with his mouth, in rapid succession, and slid into the chair across from me. "Sure. But I reserve the right to bring it up randomly in the future."

"Hmph. I expect no better of you. Only"—I chewed the corner of my lip—"not in front of anyone, okay?"

He leaned back and cocked his head. "Of course not. It's more fun torturing you privately." But his eyes softened.

I relaxed and bit into my pastry. "My sweet Lord," I mumbled around a glob of creamy heaven. "What is this? It makes getting kidnapped totally worth it."

"That, I believe, is called a 'semla.' It's made with marzipan." He poured each of us a glass of champagne while I stuffed my mouth.

"To staying alive," he said after I swallowed. We clinked glasses and sipped.

I made short work of the rest of the semla, and went for something with a hard chocolate shell on top next. "Oooh, this is even better!"

"Yeah, yeah. The Swedes know their sweets.

Now, here, try this. You need to eat something healthy." He handed me a piece of hard bread topped with sliced hard-boiled egg and caviar.

I looked at it skeptically. "I dunnoh . . ."

"Come on, cuz. If you don't want eggs, try some roast beef or cheese. You can't live on carbs alone."

"Bet I could," I said. But I took the sandwich anyway, and even enjoyed it. The salty burst from the caviar was just the thing to top off all the sugar. "How can you eat so fast without spilling a crumb?" My own lap was littered with bits of bread crust, stray crumbles of cheese, and smears of fruity pastry filling.

"Efficiency," he said, wiping his mouth with a napkin that was still as clean as when he started, except for a bit of whipped cream he'd wiped off my chin.

I leaned back in my chair and groaned. "I ate too much."

He eyed the shambles in front of me. "You think?"

"Yeah, and I'd do it again." I tossed my well-adorned napkin at him, stretched my arms high over my head, and sighed. "You know what would make the evening complete?"

He grinned devilishly. "Raspberries for dessert?"

"Ha-ha. Aren't you funny. Guess again."

"A foot massage followed by eight solid hours of sleep?"

"Mmm . . . you read my mind."

"Sorry. All you're going to get is a few hours of shut-eye, sans massage. I'm going out for a bit. I'll

try to contact Mark from a public phone somewhere—they can't have all of them tapped."

I pushed myself away from the table. "I'll come
with you. Mark might have questions for me."

"Nothing that can't wait a while. You need to
rest."

"No. Trey's still in danger. Somebody tried to
shoot me—no telling what they'll try to do to him.
And speaking of the shooting, the police will probably want to talk to me."

"Mina has already given all the information required to the nice officer in the lobby."

"So that's where you went. God, you're handy."
I smiled gratefully. I hadn't really wanted to face
an interview with the local constabulary.

"You're welcome. But while I may seem omnip-
otent, I'm not actually God."

I tried to give him an ego-withering look, but
wound up laughing instead. "Go away."

"I will. After you're all tucked in."

I glanced at the bed, still covered with trays of
partially eaten food. All of a sudden I was too tired
to move myself, much less all the debris, and
maybe a tad queasy. "No, I'll just rest here for a
second, and then we can go together."

He shook his head and snorted, then cleared the
bed for me.

"I *said* I was coming with you."

"Just lay down for an hour first—we can wait
that long." He would've carried me to the bed if
I'd let him. As it was, he held on to my upper arm

until I was ensconced up to my chin in the soft linens.

"Don't you leave without me," I mumbled as my eyes shut. If he answered, I didn't hear it.

Chapter 18

It was a tug-of-war, and I was pulling for all I was worth. My fingers ached with the effort of holding on, but it was no good. I was losing.

"Come on, Ciel. It's time to wake up. Don't make me get the ice."

Damn. I let go of the covers—unwillingly—and pried one eye open. Squinted up at Billy. Oh, yeah. I was no longer Mina. I was me. And Billy was himself, too. Black jeans, black T-shirt, black eyelashes surrounding his inky blue eyes. Why did he always have to flaunt his eyelashes at me?

"Go away. You said I had an hour." I reached behind me for the pillow and pulled it over my head.

"That was six hours ago. Sorry, but that's all you get. We really have to move now."

I pushed the pillow down to my waist. "I was out that long? Ugh. It feels like minutes."

"Yeah, well, exhaustion will do that to you. Not to mention the residual effects of whatever little drug cocktail the Vikings gave you." He snagged my arm and pulled me to a sitting position. "Up you go. Time to get dressed." He reached for the belt of the robe I was still mostly wearing and started to undo it.

I slapped his hand away. "Hey, naked under there! Please."

"Okay, here's the deal. Your clothes are on the bed beside you. I'll turn my back while you change. If you don't accomplish that in two minutes, I'm doing it for you, modesty be damned. Starting . . . now."

Yawning, I contemplated my situation. I was normally a fast dresser. Two minutes meant I could technically sneak in another forty-five seconds of sleep.

"One minute, thirty seconds left."

Crap. Somebody was speeding up time. It wasn't fair. Still sitting, I dropped the robe from my shoulders and reached for the bra and panties Billy had provided, wondering briefly where they had come from but not awake enough to be overly curious. I was too used to him just happening to have whatever was needed at any given time. He'd always had a knack for procurement.

The bra went on first—a lacy little pink number with good support. Not that my boobs needed a lot of support, except for maybe the moral variety. Still, this scrap of skimpiness actually made me look like a girl. I should let Billy do all my lingerie shopping. "Hey, how'd you know my bra size?"

"I took a champagne glass with me. One minute."

Oh yeah. Right. No comment.

Next, I slipped into the panties, which matched the bra in both laciness and skimpiness, with both legs at once, rolling backward to bring them over my hips. Same routine with the jeans, which were too long—I was used to that with jeans—but fit well enough otherwise. I automatically double-folded the leg bottoms into neat cuffs, and then went for the zipper.

"Forty-five seconds."

"Button fly? You got me *button fly*? Hey, I should get extra time for that!"

"Thirty."

I fumbled with the fastenings, my fingers tripping over themselves. "No freaking fair," I mumbled.

"Ten."

I skipped the top two brass irritants and grabbed the shirt. Thank goodness it was a pullover—

"Five."

—a forest-green, scoop-neck tee. I hauled it over my head and yanked it down over my boobs.

"Four-three-two-one," Billy finished rapidly. "Ready or not . . ."

He turned back to me with a devilish glint while I tried to shove my arms through the sleeves. "Not bad," he said. "I didn't see a thing. But you're backward."

"Aargh." I pulled the sleeves back off, reached under the shirt from below, and twisted it around, all the while retaining coverage. "Three questions. A, what's the sudden rush? B, where are we going? And C, why didn't you wake me sooner?"

"Taking those in reverse order, C, I tried to wake you an hour ago. You assured me—with wide-open eyes and utter sincerity—that you were conscious and capable, so I left to arrange transportation. B, you'll see when we get there. And A, the police were called away to referee a jousting dispute, leaving the hotel unguarded. I'd like to be gone before the Vikings send reinforcements."

I finally finished buttoning my jeans. "Oh. Well, C, sorry. You know I can't be trusted where sleep is concerned." I paused to glare at him. "B, I don't like surprises. And A, give me some shoes so we can get the hell out of here already."

He had already checked out as whoever he'd checked in as, which was anybody's guess, so as soon as my shoes were tied I grabbed the smaller of two backpacks that Billy had dropped on the bed. We left through an inconspicuous back exit, and mingled with the hordes of festival revelers cluttering the cobbled road. Jostled by the foot traffic, we passed stall after stall of crafts, clothing, and food.

The smell of roasting meat wafting through the air made my mouth water. After the spread I'd plowed through back at the hotel I thought I'd never want to eat again, but apparently my stomach disagreed. It cried out for a turkey leg and a tankard of ale, but Billy refused to be sidetracked by my need for sustenance. At the first corner he took the lead and steered us upstream against an onrush of medievally clad incomers to the city.

"I'm feeling a little underdressed," I remarked, loudly enough for Billy to hear over the clamor.

"Don't worry, we won't be here long. There's the way out. Step lively, cuz." We approached one of the gates in the wall.

As luck would have it—my luck, anyway—coming through the gate, dressed authentically as Viking warriors, were Nils, Per, and the Indian. Shit. Granted, Nonto didn't look as much like a real Viking as the other two, but he was no more out of place than the Japanese shutterbugs crowned with horned helmets who had come in ahead of him. Per had one hell of a bump on his forehead, and two black eyes blossoming beneath it. Mina probably wasn't his favorite person in the world at the moment. I dug in my heels and pulled Billy back to me.

"What?" he said, clearly annoyed to be stopped.

"There," I whispered urgently, jerking my head toward the trio. "That's them."

Billy turned boldly toward them and stared. "That's who?"

Nils and Per were scanning the street, looking for something or (gulp) someone. Per's eyes passed over me without wavering, but something about me gave Nils pause.

I stepped behind Billy, instinctively trying to hide. "*Them*," I said. "The ones who kidnapped me. No, don't look."

He dragged me out to his side, slung an arm over my shoulders, and bent down to kiss my cheek. While he was eye level, he whispered, "Relax. You're not Mina anymore. They can't possibly recognize you."

"Oh, yeah." I shrugged. "Reflex. Guess I'm a little jumpy."

He straightened and went back to openly watching my kidnappers. Each of them carried an animal skin bundle. They were too careful with them, not allowing them to bump anyone, which seemed a little odd. I wondered what was so special about—

Crap.

I remembered the snatches of conversation I'd overheard on the plane. "They're going to bomb the town."

"What are you talking about? Why would they do that?"

"I don't know, but I heard them talking about it on the plane, and they definitely said something about a bomb. I'm sure of it."

"And you're just *now* telling me this? Jesus, Ciel!"

"Well, I didn't think of it before, what with escaping and running for my life and all. Sue me."

"You could've said something back at the hotel. I would've hauled your ass away from this island as soon as I found you."

"That's your fault—you got me distracted with all that food, and then I was too sleepy to think straight, and—"

"All right, all right. Calm down. And come on."

I pulled him to a stop. "Wait! They're headed into the town center—we have to follow them, see what they're up to—"

"I'll get back after them once you're safely out of here."

"That might be too late. I told you, they might have a frickin' *bomb*. We have to stop them."

"And how do you propose we do that? There are three of them and only two"—he looked down at me—"one and a half of us."

"I don't know! But we have to at least see where they're going. Come on." I took off, pulling Billy behind me.

The Vikings turned a corner a block ahead of us, disappearing down a narrow roadway lined with houses covered in climbing roses. When I rounded the bend, I stopped short, and Billy plowed into the back of me. The Vikings had come to a halt and were having a little conference.

I whirled to face Billy. "Quick, go back!"

"Too late. They've seen us."

"Okay, then . . ." *Think.* "Uh . . ." I grabbed him by both arms and leaned back against one of the houses standing directly next to the street, pulling him against me. All at once I was flanked by fragrant red blossoms, with only my pack to protect my tender back from the thorns.

"What are you—"

"Play along," I whispered urgently, hiding my face behind his shoulder, trying to pretend we were just another madly in lust young couple roaming the streets.

"Ooooh," he said, barely audible, delight spreading across his face. "Well, aren't you the quick thinker." He gathered me close and leaned down, only too willing.

My eyes narrowed and I glared at him. *Pay attention*, I telegraphed with a jerk of my head toward the trio. He gave a barely perceptible shrug and said, softly, "Your idea."

His lips hovered near mine. Even annoyed, I couldn't help noticing how sweet his breath was. And I *had* dragged him into it. Oh, hell, I thought philosophically. Duty calls. My eyelids drifted shut. Surely there was nothing wrong with kissing your cousin if it was for a good cause.

"No, don't close your eyes." He pulled his head back a fraction. "Look over my shoulder."

"Your head's in the way."

He shifted obligingly, bringing his mouth down to the side of my neck. I stood on tiptoe and tried to focus on the Vikings, but it was a little hard to concentrate, what with the tickle of warm breath sending goose bumps down my arms.

"Can you see them?" Billy asked.

"Huh? Wha—um, yeah. They're still talking. I can't make out what they're saying—oh, cripes!— they're looking this way. What should we do?"

"Relax," Billy said under his breath, intently focused on what he couldn't see behind him. "Tell me which way they go when they move out. In the meantime just pretend you can stand me, okay?" His lips connected with my neck, and I melted into him with a small moan and an involuntary wiggle.

"That's the spirit," he whispered.

I forced my eyes back open and saw the smirk on Per's face. Nils had already turned away, obviously more polite than the jerk. Nonto's face was as impassive as ever. No surprise there. Nils started pointing toward the other end of the street, and Nonto tapped Per's arm to get his attention back where it should be.

"I think they're getting ready to move," I said, moving my lips as little as possible.

Billy twisted me a quarter-turn, to better his view. "Hold on. Two of them are headed back this way."

He brought his mouth to mine, this time connecting quite thoroughly. I heard footsteps approaching behind me, and the closer they got, the more thorough Billy got. When his tongue touched mine I felt it in places his mouth was nowhere near. *Ack!* How could that happen? This was my bratty cousin, the bane of my existence, and I was tingling at his kiss?

Oh, my God—I'm a perv, too!

The footsteps passed by and faded, and Billy disconnected. I just stood there, eyes shut and mouth open, wondering what the hell had hit me.

"Ciel? Are you all right?"

I opened my eyes to find Billy staring at me quizzically. *Honorary cousin,* I told myself. *And step. Don't forget step. Not pervy.* "Uh, yeah. Fine, fine. Let's go."

"Wait a second. If we follow too closely they'll catch on. Besides, I have to figure out who to go after."

I disentangled myself from his arms and looked both ways. Nils continued down the street we were on, and the other two had gone back to the one we'd been on before we turned.

"Why don't we split up?" I suggested.

"Nope," Billy said, grabbing my arm and holding tight.

"But how else can we keep track of them all? You follow those two—the blond is Per, and he's a mean son of a bitch, so watch out for him. I'm not sure about the Indian. I'll follow Nils."

"Uh-uh. Not gonna happen."

"Look," I said in a reasonable tone. "Don't worry about me. Nils isn't all bad, for a kidnapper. He was nice to Mina." Kind of. Right up until he tried to stop the Mini with his bare hands. "I don't think he'd hurt a woman—" No matter how crazy-mad he looked the last time I saw him. "—even if he caught on to me following him—"

Billy gripped me harder.

I continued, speeding through the words ahead of his objections. "—which he won't, because I'm going to be very, very careful. Besides, what can he do to me in this crowd, anyway?"

He looked torn, but the seconds were ticking away, and he couldn't come up with a better plan.

"Okay," he said finally. "There's a cell phone in your pack. Any number in the contacts will connect you with me, no matter who it says it is. Speed dial is your friend. Call when you find out where he's going and do not, under any circumstances, approach him. Understand?"

I nodded, and he loped off after Per and Nonto. I turned to catch up with my quarry, walking as nonchalantly as my quivering knees would allow while still keeping him in sight. I might've overstated my case to Billy a tad. But even if I couldn't be certain about Nils, I knew one thing for sure. He was better than Per.

Chapter 19

I didn't know where Nils was headed, but he was in a hurry to get there. He wasn't running, but with legs as long as his, he was hard to keep up with—if the crowd hadn't hampered his movement, I would've lost him.

He had passed his fur bundle to Per before they separated, so whatever was going on with that would be Billy's problem. The explosive possibilities worried me to an almost paralyzing extent, but I'd known Billy my whole life. There had never been a scrape he couldn't get himself out of, and there'd been some doozies. I'd just have to pray his luck continued.

Nils's flaxen hair glinted in the sunlight as I followed his bobbing and weaving head through the crowd, until he stopped abruptly and looked down. There were too many people between us for me to see what drew his attention, and I couldn't get closer without shoving aside a couple of buxom peasant girls who were obviously enjoying a ringside view of his masculine charms. When he squatted, I forgot my inbred courtesy and squeezed myself as far as I could between the Valkyries.

It was a small boy, three or four years old, hanging on to a wooden sword half again as long as he was. A circle had formed around him, creating a mini-arena for the Hägar the Horrible wannabe. Nils showed him where and how to grip the handle, then whispered something into his ear. The boy nodded and giggled, his whole face lighting up. Nils stood, patted the boy's head, and took off at a good clip.

Keeping low and employing my elbows, I made it past the Viking gals. The boy, however, was another matter. He stepped in front of me, raised his sword and growled menacingly. Well, as menacingly as a preschooler could. Normally, I would've found him adorable, but I didn't have time for adorable.

I moved to the right, intending to step around him. He moved to his left, blocking me. More growling. I searched for some sign of parental supervision. A couple dressed in simple linen garb looked on indulgently. No help there.

I feinted to the left, and jumped back to the right when the kid tried to block me again. I was feeling pretty good about outwitting him when I felt a hard *thwack* across the seat of my pants.

"Ow!" I hollered and whirled back to face him,

glaring, which seemed to delight the little heathen, so I shifted my visual daggers to the responsible couple. They laughed and shrugged. *What's a parent to do?*

I had a pretty good idea what a parent could do, and it involved the kid's backside instead of mine. Not having time to get into a philosophical discussion on child rearing, however, I turned my attention back to Nils.

Who was no longer in sight. *Shit.*

A quick three-sixty revealed plenty of blond heads, not one of them Nils. I took off in the direction he'd been going, receiving a final sword-poke on the behind as a parting gift. I chalked it up to birth control inspiration, and ran through a break in the throng, trying to catch sight of Nils again before he turned down one of the side streets. I really, really didn't want to have to call Billy and tell him I lost somebody as big as Nils. He'd never let me live it down. Especially if he found out I was outfoxed by a three-year-old.

I was passing a narrow side street when a brawny arm reached out and grabbed me, pulling me out of the busy river of humanity and down the quiet cobbled lane, moving fast. Nils was taller from my own perspective than from Mina's, but otherwise unmistakable. I scrambled to keep up with his long stride, taking at least two steps for each of his, and would've fallen several times had he not been half-lifting me as we went.

I might have screamed, if I'd had the breath, and

if I had a reasonable way to explain my situation to the cops. As it was, it would be easier to go with the flow and see what Nils wanted. As long as we stayed out in public, I figured not much harm could come to me. Besides, it was the only way I could find out what he was up to—it's not like I could follow him anymore, now that he was on to having a tail. Even if I could discreetly change auras, he'd still be wary.

He pushed me into the narrow space between two buildings and blocked the view from the street with his body. Guarded speculation swept over his face when he took a closer look at me.

"Why are you following me?" he asked, his voice calm, not at all threatening.

"Uh . . ." I said, displaying my typical quickness.

He waited patiently, saying nothing, still holding my arm.

"Well," I began again, shrugging. "I, um, like your costume."

His eyes narrowed and he quirked his mouth in disbelief.

"No, really. It looks so much more authentic than the other Vikings I've seen around here. Is that hand-woven cloth? I was going to ask you where you found it, so I could get one for a friend. He'd look really cool in something like that."

"I don't think so. Try again, Miss Halligan."

He knew who I was? Shit. *Not* good.

"Wh-who?" I stammered. "I think you must've mistaken me for somebody else."

"You are Ciel Halligan, the 'facilitator'—whatever that is—Mina Worthington visited in Washington, D.C., three weeks ago."

I didn't bother with denials. "You seem to know a lot about me."

"A bit. You look quite nice in jogging shorts when you walk in the park near your home, for instance. Though you really should try actually jogging. You might like it."

Crap. He'd been watching me? For how long?

"I also know you're working for Miss Worthington. In what capacity are you employed, may I ask?"

I lifted my chin. "You may ask anything you like. Doesn't mean I'll answer."

His grip tightened. "You would be wise to tell me what you know of Miss Worthington's whereabouts, at the very least. Then perhaps you may continue your holiday unencumbered."

"Unencumbered by what?" I said, sounding cockier than I felt.

"By me."

Gulp. Okaaaay. Thinking fast, I smiled in what I hoped was a flirtatious manner. "I don't find you cumbersome at all," I purred. Or meant to purr. Maybe I squeaked. The whole femme fatale thing was a lot easier when I was covered by Mina's aura.

He laughed at me. I didn't know if I should be relieved or offended.

"If you say so. But your boyfriend might not feel the same. Shall we find out?"

I cleared my throat. "Oh, you mean that guy I

was with? He's not my boyfriend. He's just someone I met at the hotel. You know how it is—pay a
little attention to someone and they think they
own you. Thank goodness I finally shook him.
Whew!" I wiped imaginary sweat from my brow.

"It did not look as if you were anxious to rid
yourself of him a few minutes ago."

"What can I say? I was trying to let him down
gently. A kiss for the road. Pucker up and sayo-
nara." I shrugged, but suspected my blush was
leaking despite my effort to adapt it away.

"I see," he said, his amusement plain. "Well then,
since you do not find my company cumbersome,
you may come along with me."

"Gosh, that's kind of you, but I have some
friends I have to meet. Maybe another time."

I tried to disengage my arm from his grip. He
wasn't cooperating.

"I think they will have to wait for you. Unless,
of course, you wish to take me to Miss Worthington now?"

"Not possible, I'm afraid."

"Then you will have to endure my company for
a little longer." He lifted one corner of his mouth in
a fetching half-smile.

"What if I scream?" I inquired matter-of-factly,
willing to reconsider the option now that I had the
breath to back it up.

He tilted his head to one side, considering. "A
small scream would likely go unnoticed. Go ahead,
if it will make you feel better. But if you become

too loud I shall have to take measures to mitigate the noise."

"My, don't you have just the best command of the English language," I said drily.

"Thank you. Now, shall I block my ears or not?" His eyes crinkled at the corners, and try as I would, I couldn't dislike him entirely. Of course, I hear a lot of women just loved Ted Bundy, too.

I released a long-suffering sigh. "Oh, don't bother. I'll come along with you quietly. Heck, who knows when I'll get another chance to see Visby on the arm of such a realistic barbarian."

He loosened his grip, sliding his hand down far enough to grasp mine. "Good, then. Come along."

Like I had a choice.

We stopped at the far end of a particularly narrow road. The house on the corner was small, sided with dark, wooden planks, and separated from the bricked lane by a narrow stone stoop. The door—a lighter wood—was surrounded by the ubiquitous roses, these a buttery yellow. They set off the heather green doorjamb beautifully. Very picturesque, if you had time to appreciate that sort of thing, which I really didn't, but wished desperately I did.

Nils knocked on the door with a heavy hand. After a moment it was opened a few inches, and half a face appeared. The milky-blue, rabbit-lashed eye squinted suspiciously at me, and a muffled voice asked something in Swedish. Nils responded, and the door swung open far enough to allow us to enter.

The room was clogged with large men. They weren't all blond—there was plenty of brown hair, lots of red, and even some black. Relatives of Nonto, maybe? What they all had in common was their period clothing—to a man, they wore Viking regalia, and wore it well.

Being eye to sternum with so many hulking examples of masculinity left me a little breathless, and I don't mean in the good way. More like the impending panic attack way. Feeling suddenly too tiny, I eased myself backward until my pack bumped up against Nils's chest. He pushed me toward the center of the room. The men stepped aside and formed a circle around us. There was a short silence, followed by a burst of Swedish, each Viking making an attempt to shoehorn in his own question or comment.

Nils gave them a minute to get it out of their systems, said something loud and terse, and they all shut up. He continued speaking, explaining how and why he happened to have me, I supposed. They must have bought it because they dispersed, heading off to various parts of the house. Those who stayed kept wary eyes on me while they went back to what they'd been doing before we got there: stuffing lightweight plastic bags with colorful pieces of paper, and sealing them.

I stared for a minute, waiting for the lightbulb over my head to switch on. A feeble flicker was the best it would do. "Flyers? You're advertising?"

"It is one aspect to our campaign, yes," he said.

I picked up one of the leaflets and studied it. A

half-naked, excessively well-built blond barbarian was flanked by shapely, adoring young women, each holding a rugged-looking bottle up against his chest. I don't read Swedish, but it didn't require a lot of translation.

"You're selling men's shampoo?" I didn't even try to mask the incredulity in my voice.

Nils flushed. "That's not shampoo. It's body wash."

"Oh. Well, that makes all the difference. Selling shampoo might not necessitate kidnapping, but *body wash*, now that's something else entirely."

I guess sarcasm sounds the same in any language, because Nils snatched the paper away from me and threw it back onto the pile I'd plucked it from, to the snickering delight of his comrades in arms. He quieted them with a grim look, took me by the elbow and hustled me toward the stairs, which were narrow enough that he had to walk behind me on the way up. The top floor was even more cramped than the bottom. There were only two doorways off the dimly lit hall; Nils directed me toward the one on the right. The room was cozy, its scant space filled with rustic antiques. The centerpiece was an old iron bed. Great. *Déjà vu.*

"Huh. Got your handcuffs handy?"

He looked at me sharply. "So, you have spoken with Mina. Quite recently."

Oops. "Um . . ." I searched my brain for plausible deniability. When I couldn't find any, I shrugged.

"You are a puzzle, Miss Halligan. I had thought

to leave you here while I took care of some business, but I now believe I must take you with me after all. Perhaps you will do the smart thing and guide me to Miss Worthington."

"I already told you—not possible."

"That is a shame." He sounded genuinely regretful, which made my stomach twist.

"Look, there really has been some sort of misunderstanding. Sure, I know Mina, but—"

"Let me have your pack."

"Huh?"

"Your knapsack." He didn't wait for it, but slipped it off my shoulders.

I let go of it reluctantly. Heck, I didn't even know what was in it, other than the cell phone that was my only connection to Billy, but giving it up gave me a pang, like losing a security blanket.

Nils unzipped it and dumped the contents onto the bed. Along with the phone, there were toiletries, a few changes of underwear, an extra pair of jeans, a sweater, and Mina's medieval maiden outfit.

Crap. Guess Billy thought I'd like a souvenir.

Okay. Stay calm. I could brazen this out. It wasn't like there weren't dozens of costumes just like it all over Visby. Nils couldn't know for sure it wasn't mine, so I kept my face bland.

"What?" I said. "Can't I have a costume?"

He didn't say anything. He merely picked up the linen dress, shook it out, and held it up against me. It was a good four or five inches too long. "Maybe," he said. "But not this one. Now, where is Mina?"

"Look, Nils, I'm not taking you to Mina. Face it."

"We shall see." He tossed the dress back on the bed, took my phone, and scrolled through the contacts list. He seemed satisfied with what he saw there, and punched the call button.

He paused, waiting for the connection to go through, staring at me the whole time. When he finally spoke, my stomach fell.

"Miss Worthington? How nice to hear your voice again—our recent time together was cut far too short. However, I have had the good fortune to meet a friend of yours. Ciel Halligan. Here, I'll put her on."

Chapter 20

"Mina, this is Ciel. I'm okay. You got that? I'm—"

Nils pulled the phone away from my ear. "You see, Mina, what I tell you is true. I'm sure you'd like to see your friend again, but maybe I'm wrong. You don't seem to want to see your boyfriend again very badly, after all."

He paused, listening to whatever Billy was making up on the spur of the moment. Trust Billy to be prepared for any contingency—Mina was obviously one of the contacts Billy had listed, so it was "Mina" who answered.

"So you say . . . yes, I understand about panic . . . no, Ciel is fine—for the moment—but I believe she would rather continue her vacation without me. Once you're safely back with me, I will let her go."

I grabbed for the phone. Nils was faster than

me, and held it out of my reach. So I yelled. "No, don't do it—I'm fine! He won't hurt me. Really, I'm—"

Nils swept my legs out from under me with his foot, pushed me face-first onto the bed, and held me there with one knee. "—*oof*, fine, I swear, don't listen to—" A resounding smack on my backside interrupted my desperate reassurances. "OUCH!"

Before I could yell anything else, Nils stuffed part of the quilt into my mouth and held it there while he went on talking. I *mmphphed* helplessly against his protected fingers.

"Really, Mina, I think it would be best for all concerned—certainly for Trey and Ciel—if we arranged a meeting. Yes? Very good. The Maiden's Tower in thirty minutes. Outside the wall. Any vendor will be able to direct you there. Oh, and if I notice a police presence, or anything out of the ordinary—and I must warn you, I have a good eye for such things—your friend Ciel will be staying with me, and it will be a long time before you see her or Trey again."

He hung up and released me. I spit out the quilt, balled up my fist, and slugged his jaw.

I'd never seen anyone look quite so shocked. "Ow! What did you do that for?"

"You hit me first, you fucking prick!"

He sighed, scrubbing at his face, as if he could rub the pain away. "It was necessary to convince Mina to come."

"It *hurt*!" I didn't know why I should be so surprised, but I was. Viking or not, deep down I hadn't believed he'd hurt *me*.

"It wasn't so bad. I didn't hit you hard, only enough to make some noise. You didn't leave me a choice."

I sat up, arranging myself into a more dignified position. "She won't come, you know. She's smarter than that," I said huffily.

"She will come," he responded, way too confident, and dialed a number. He spoke rapidly in Swedish. I heard Per's name; the rest was gibberish. Crap. If there was anybody I didn't want to see again, it was that asshole.

"Listen, Nils, can't we talk this over? Whatever you're involved with, it isn't worth the kind of trouble you'll be in once the police find out about this. It's not too late—"

"You are wrong. It is much too late." He reached for Mina's costume and held it out to me. "Here. Put this on."

I refused to take it. "Oh, no way, buster. Uh-uh. I am not putting that on—" I stopped myself before I said "again."

"Yes, you are."

"Forget it."

His face was an implacable mask. I hate to resort to whining, but I'm not above it when the situation warrants. "Come on, it's way too long for me. I'd trip all over myself in it."

He reached beneath his tunic and retrieved a large knife. It had a carved wooden handle and a lethal-looking blade. My mouth went dry, and I was beginning to regret hitting him. Just how pissed off was he? "Whoa, now, big guy. Let's not be hasty—" I backed away.

He looked from me to the knife, and back to me. "You really think I would use a knife on a woman?" There was genuine shock in his voice.

"Well, you did hit me," I said, thinking it wasn't such an unreasonable assumption.

He emitted a short, disgusted sound, and neatly sliced the bottom six inches off both the dress and tunic. Returning his knife to its sheath, he said, "I don't have to use a knife to make you put on the dress." He stabbed the words into me with eyes sharper than his blade. I think he was kind of miffed that I'd even entertained the notion.

I snatched up the dress and tunic, pissed as hell myself, mainly because he was right. In my current form I was no match for him, and it wasn't like I could switch auras in front of a nonadaptor. Jutting out my chin and flashing him the evil eye, I said, with as much authority as I could gather, "No, but you do have to leave the room. I won't change in front of you."

He opened his mouth to protest, but after studying my face he said, "Fine. Just so you know, that window is stuck shut and I have men posted in the back garden."

After he closed the door behind him I checked the window and backyard anyway. He hadn't lied. So much for that big idea. Resigned, I changed as fast as I could, wanting to get myself decently covered before he thought better of taking his eyes off me. The dress and tunic fell gracefully over what few curves I had rather than molding to them, as they had Mina's, but with Nils's alterations the fit wasn't too bad. I was stuffing my clothes into my backpack when he rejoined me.

"You won't be needing that."

"But—"

"Leave it," he said, taking my hand and heading for the stairs.

Nobody from the herd of Vikings in the living room questioned him as we left the house, and my attempts at conversation as we hurried through the streets fell flat. I might as well have been talking to the town wall.

The longer he was quiet, the more nervous I got. All I could think about was Billy rushing headlong into a trap, hindered by Mina's aura. Because he would come for me, I had no doubt about that. And Nils wouldn't release me without seeing Mina, so Billy would have to be Mina. He would be just as helpless as I was.

I tugged on Nils's arm, which had about as much effect as a toddler yanking on a rottweiler's leash. So I dug in my heels and leaned backward with all my weight. That at least slowed him down, but only long enough to swing me over his shoulder. My breath left me in a *whoosh*. I couldn't believe he'd do that right in front of all the people wandering the streets with us. Was he nuts?

"Put me down, you Viking pig!" I yelled. Well, in my mind I yelled, but a shoulder in the solar plexus tends to hamper the necessary breath support, so it came out as more of a wheezing whisper. I doubted I could be heard more than a yard away.

Frustrated, I pounded on his back with both fists. Seemed my earlier comparison of him to the town wall wasn't too far off the mark. Stone would have been softer. Kicking my legs didn't work either, since he held them tightly to his chest, no doubt protecting his precious manhood.

Didn't matter, I told myself. People would notice. Some Good Samaritan would help me, or call the police, or at least question Nils long enough for me to get away.

That's when I heard the applause start. A few random claps at first, then, after Nils addressed the crowd in a stentorian growl of indecipherable Swedish—with a decidedly macho overtone—a thunderous ovation erupted. The crowd parted to make way for us. If I'd been upright, my jaw would've dropped. The idiots thought we were street performers. Freaking bunch of drunks.

Nils leaned forward. For a second, I thought he was putting me down, but when I realized he was bowing, I gave up. It was too fucking surreal to do otherwise. I hung my head and stared at the firm, perfectly formed ass moving beneath his tunic, and entertained myself by imagining a steel-toed boot planted there.

After a few minutes, the crowd grew bored with watching me being hauled around like a sack of potatoes, and dissipated, but it wasn't until we were outside the wall that Nils spoke to me.

"We are almost there. Will you behave if I set you back on the ground?"

My first impulse was to tell him to fuck off, but I bit my tongue. Comments like that, while exceedingly satisfying for a moment, didn't tend to enhance one's situation in the long run. I settled for crossing my fingers and saying, "I'll try my best."

I guess it was good enough for Nils, because I found myself back on my feet, facing him. The blood that had been pooling in my head left it in a rush, and I had to grab his forearms to keep from falling. He obligingly held me upright by my elbows until I was steady.

Once my head cleared I gave him the dirtiest look in my repertoire. He had the grace to try to look ashamed, but he couldn't keep his eyes from crinkling at the corners.

"If you laugh, I swear to God I will kick your big, hairy Viking balls."

His eyes widened a bit, but he said, "They really aren't so hairy."

"Hairy or not, it'll feel the same to you."

He shrugged. "I doubt you could kick so high in that dress."

"Try me," I grated out, reaching down to lift the dress up far enough to let me maneuver.

"No, no, that's okay. I won't laugh." He glanced appreciatively at my calves before he settled his face into blankness.

I dropped the hem—it's not like he would've stood still and let me kick him anyway—and looked around. There weren't as many revelers on this side of the wall. "So, what now?"

"Now we wait for Mina."

"I already told you, she won't come."

"We shall see." Still maddeningly sure of himself.

"Look, I'm not going to let you trade me for Mina. You have to know that."

"No, I don't expect you will." Way too agreeable.

It finally dawned on me. "You have no intention of letting me go, do you? You're just using me to get Mina back. I'm bait."

He shrugged, the barest trace of an apology in his eyes. "It would hardly be wise to set you free to go to the police, now would it?"

If he hadn't grabbed both my hands, I would've slugged him again, but he was ready for me this time. Despite Herculean effort, I couldn't get free. So I did the clichéd feminine thing, and stamped my foot—right down on top of his. (Hey, a cliché had served me well with the frying pan.) It may not have worked as well as when I'd had Trey's weight and muscles at my disposal in the cigar store, but it didn't go unnoticed. Nils swore under his breath in Swedish. At least, I'm pretty sure it was a swear word.

When he didn't budge, I did it again, more out of frustration than spite, though spite *may* have factored in a teensy bit. Same word from him (yeah, definitely a swear word—no mistaking the tone this time), and a shake, followed by, "Stop it! Don't make me think this would be easier with you unconscious."

I thought briefly about morphing into a carbon copy of him, just to shock him into letting me go, but it was too risky—somebody might come upon us at any second. Besides, my dress would split.

"Damn it," I said, after letting out an angry breath. "I don't understand you. You were nice enough to me—" I caught myself, coughed lightly, and continued. "Mina. Mina said you were the good one. Why are you being such a jerk now?"

He cocked his head and studied me. After a moment, he sighed and said, "I am trying to help you. I *like* you, Ciel. You are brave and funny. You have a sharp mind, an even sharper tongue"—I squirmed at that—"and a great right hook," he added with a rueful smile.

"Really?" I said, kind of flattered at that last bit.

"Truly. My jaw is still sore." He was teasing now. Actually, that made me relax a little. If he was teasing me, it probably meant he wasn't planning to kill me.

"You can let me go now, you know. I won't hit you again."

He shook his head. "You would run. For now you must trust that I know best."

"Why should I?" I said peevishly. "You're a part of some wacko group that gets off on dressing funny and killing people. And kidnapping," I added. "Let's not forget *that*."

"There's more to it than you know. I can't tell you everything, but one small thing I can say . . . if you promise to tell no one."

A secret? That could be useful. I dropped the

peevishness. "I promise." Which was a big lie, and I couldn't even cross my fingers, gripped as they were in his big hand. I wondered if God made allowances for extenuating circumstances, or if I could look forward to another explosion in the near future.

"I am trying to get Mina back before Per finds her. He is very angry with her, and she wouldn't be safe if he finds her first. I am sorry to have to use you for this, but I can think of no other way."

"Oh, so now you're the hero. Right." I didn't worry as much about sarcasm as I did lying. If God held sarcasm against you, I'd have been blown to kingdom come before I was out of grade school.

"Not a hero, no. But Per has gone too far. Men should not hurt women."

Ha. Says the man who'd whacked me on the bottom not half an hour earlier. Guess he didn't count that. And *I* didn't happen to think men should hurt other men either, but at least he was halfway on the right track.

"Is he the one who shot at her at the hotel?" I asked.

"Not personally, no. But he ordered it."

"Mina said she may have, um, conked him on the head a tiny bit?"

"Oh, yes. She gave him quite a headache—one he won't forget or forgive easily. It is best he doesn't find her."

A chill settled in my stomach. "Let me go when Mina gets here. Let us both go—"

"That I cannot do. It wouldn't be safe for either

of you. Per has too many men looking for Mina. So, now. Can I trust you to say nothing about this to anyone? It would not go well for me—or for Mina's fiancé—if Per found out."

"Do you really have Trey somewhere?"

He held his breath for a few seconds, coming to a decision. "Yes. We have Trey. He has information we need, but is not being cooperative. Per believes Mina may be useful in convincing him to be more forthcoming. I must keep that from happening. Per is planning to kill them both after he finds out what Trey knows."

I pulled away as far as I could, considering he was still holding my hands securely. "Why do you even need Trey?"

"He was the one who approached us, and Per was perhaps too anxious to include a wealthy American in our ranks. Access to money is always handy. Now that he has been exposed as an infiltrator, Per is determined to stop him. But first he must find out what Trey has already told his superiors."

"You know what? Per is an asshole."

He lifted one side of his mouth in a rueful half-smile. "Per is a fanatic. Fanatics tend to be extreme."

"Okay. An extreme asshole."

Laughing, he finally let go of my hands. "You are the most astonishing girl. I wish I could—" He stopped and stared over my shoulder. I looked behind me to see what had distracted him.

Another neo-Viking strode toward us. The good news was the newcomer wasn't Per. The bad news was that it was Per's buddy, Nonto, carrying an animal-skin bag that looked to be loaded with something heavy. If he was here, how far behind could Per be? My stomach sank.

"Ahiga?" Nils said. Huh. So that was his name. "What are you doing here? We are not supposed to meet until later."

Ahiga didn't answer. He kept walking until he was right next to us, pushed me as far away from Nils as he could, and walloped him upside the head with his bag.

Chapter 21

Nils crumpled, leaving me standing there staring at the black-haired Berserker.

"What the hell did you do that for, you big oaf?" I slammed his chest with the heels of my hands, surprising him enough that he actually fell back a step.

I knelt beside Nils and ran my fingers over his face. I didn't think his jaw was broken, but he was going to have a hell of a bruise.

"Uh, Ciel?" the big guy—Ahiga, Nils had called him—said.

"What?" I said, testy and not much caring that he was twice my size and could break me in half with one hand. I felt the back of Nils's head where it had hit the hard dirt. No bleeding, no indentation. Good.

"Ciel, what are you doing?"

"I'm checking to see—oh, my God!" I whirled

my head around to get a better look. "Billy? Is that you?"

"Of course it's me, you twit. Didn't you know I'd come for you?"

"Well, yeah, but I was expecting Mina. That's how you answered the phone."

"Go up against Hulk Hogan there in Mina's aura? Do I look like a complete idiot to you?"

I scanned him from head to toe and raised one brow. "If the moccasin fits . . ."

"Never mind. I answered as Mina because I heard the Mina ringtone. The phone I gave you had some of my auras listed in the contacts, with all the numbers forwarded to my phone—I figured you'd catch on when you saw them, and call whichever me you needed most."

"I didn't exactly have the opportunity to phone you myself," I said wryly, looking at Nils for signs of consciousness.

"Relax. He's not dead. Now, come on. We have to get out of here. There are a few too many of my European brethren roaming the area for comfort. Mark is waiting for us on the boat."

My heart skipped a beat. "Mark is here?"

"Yeah. He's the surprise I was telling you about back at the hotel. He flew over on a company plane and rented a sailboat. It's at the marina—he thought it would be easier to get you and Trey off the island if we bypass public transportation. Less hassle, less explaining, no waiting for new documents."

My mind raced ahead. "But that's great—we can take Nils, too."

"You're not getting the picture here, cuz. Nils is one of them. The bad guys. He's going to be rounded up with the rest of them once we're sure Trey is safe. Then Trey will testify against the bunch of them," he said, his voice low and level.

"Nils might not be alive to freaking testify against if we don't take him with us," I whispered back, exasperated. Why could Billy never see my side of things?

"And how do you propose we do that? Ahiga is strong, but I can't carry your buddy there all the way to the marina. Besides which, we don't need the attention that would bring us," he said, his voice not quite as soft.

"Then we'll just have to wait until he wakes up, won't we?" I said, taking my own voice up a notch.

With noticeable effort, Billy brought his voice down. "Time, Ciel. We. Don't. Have it."

"Don't blame me—you're the one who hit him," I said, trying but failing to follow suit.

"Damn it, I was saving you!" he shouted.

"That's beside the point!" I matched him decibel for decibel.

"AHIGA!" a horribly familiar voice boomed out from the direction of the gate.

We both stopped short and turned to look.

Crap. It was Per.

My head snapped back to Billy. "Just play along," he said, suddenly calm. He positioned himself between me and the oncoming mini-horde, lifting one arm in greeting to Per and the men who were with him. All were costumed similarly—the perfect Viking swarm.

Per spoke heartily as they approached. "What is the yelling about, my friend? Have you found a nice Swedish girl to amuse yourself with until—" He stopped when he saw Nils.

The men—fifteen or sixteen of them, it looked like—formed a loose circle around us. Per stepped toward the center and looked down. "What happened here?" he said to Billy.

"I don't know," Billy said. "I just got here myself. This lady says she found him like this, and was checking to see if he was hurt or just passed out drunk. She got a little overexcited when I told her to leave and let me handle it." He turned to me and said, "You can go now, miss. We'll take care of him."

I pushed myself up off the ground, careful not to look directly at Per. "Uh, sure. Hope your friend is okay. See ya." I hurried toward a space between two of the barbarians.

"Wait," Per said, taking hold of my arm and turning me to face him. "You're not Swedish."

I cringed at his touch.

"I know you," he said slowly, staring hard, processing my face.

The Vikings behind me closed ranks. I saw Billy's fists clench, and willed him not to do anything stupid. He relaxed his stance—somewhat—when Per dropped my arm.

I smiled, hoping I didn't look as nervous as I felt. "I don't think so. I'm sure I would remember if we had met. You're, um, striking." Especially with that huge purple bruise spreading down your forehead, and the double shiners. But I decided not to mention that. Didn't seem like something he'd take kindly to being reminded of.

"No, I do know who you are. You're the Halligan woman, the one working for Mina Worthington."

"Who?" I said.

"Don't play dumb. I don't have time for it. Tell me what you did to Nils—did you drug him? Or sneak up on him and hit his head with a rock, perhaps?" He paused, a sneer on his face, a threat in his too-quiet voice. I got the idea he didn't like women much. Probably had mommy issues.

I was about to address the subject with him when I caught a warning look from Billy, who was now situated to the left of and slightly behind Per. I kept my mouth shut.

"Cat got your tongue?" Per said. "No matter. Nils has always been weak-headed when it comes to women." He looked down and kicked his colleague's leg lightly. A small groan came from the prone Viking, which seemed to satisfy Per. "It could be you have taught him a valuable lesson." He turned back to me. "So, Miss Halligan, it seems we have happened upon you at an opportune time. Tell me, where is Mina?"

"I have no idea," I said, seeing no point in denying who I was. Then, just because his fearless leader charade got on my nerves, I added, "And I wouldn't tell you if I knew." (Yeah. Bluster. Like I said, it's a reflex.)

Billy winced, but of course couldn't say anything. Fortunately, Per was too busy staring at me like I was dog shit on his shoe to notice anything odd about his faithful Indian companion.

"Oh, I think you will tell me anything I want to know, Miss Halligan. I really do."

I swallowed hard. Note to self: learn to keep your mouth shut.

He turned to two of the men and said, "Karl, Lennart—see to Nils. Take him back to the house. Get a doctor if you must, but use someone we know."

They each got a shoulder under Nils's arms and hauled him to his feet. His head flopped to one side, but his eyelids were starting to flutter and he was making an effort to get his legs to support him.

"I'll take the woman," Billy volunteered. He wouldn't want to be around when Nils woke up. "She'll talk for me."

"No, Ahiga. I'll take care of our little friend. I need you to go to our booth in the town center and see that the samples are ready to be distributed after our package is sent. Tell the men to prepare for delivery."

"But—" Billy started, then heard Nils groan and thought better of it. "Right. Don't worry. I'll take care of it," he said to Per while looking straight at me. My mouth dried at the thought of him leaving, but I managed a minuscule nod. He'd be back for me somehow.

Watching him march off without me left me so scared I wanted to vomit. I drew in slow, deep breaths until I could control it, then chanced a glance at Per. He was watching me intently, sucking down my fear like it was blood and he was a tick. The fucking misogynistic asshole. I narrowed my eyes and stuck out my chin, refusing to feed him what he wanted.

Instead, I watched Nils. He was almost back to the land of the living. One of his human crutches spoke encouragingly to him in Swedish, and he mumbled something back. At least he was alive. I took some comfort from that. As much as I hated to see him go, I hoped Karl and Lennart got him away from here before he started questioning why Ahiga had clobbered him. Billy needed time to ditch that aura.

"Walk with me, Miss Halligan," Per said, sounding as pleasant as I'd ever heard him, which made the fine hairs on the back of my neck stand at attention.

Not seeing a ready alternative, I fell into step beside him. The others trailed a few feet behind us. Rocks in various hues of pink, gray, and black dotted the expanse between us and the sea, where the Baltic lapped against a strip of white sand. If I hadn't been strolling with a monster, I might've enjoyed the view.

"Ciel, isn't it? Such an unusual name. It means 'sky' in French, doesn't it?" He got a faraway look in his eye, as if something had just occurred to him. "May I call you Ciel?" he continued conversationally as we walked along the strand.

I shrugged, not trusting that any words coming

out of my mouth wouldn't get me into even deeper trouble.

"Ciel, then. Are you quite sure you can't be more helpful about Mina? She is a client, not a friend, *ja*?"

"I don't betray clients," I said, aiming my tone for neutral but hitting cold instead.

"But this situation isn't in your job description, is it? Whatever it is you 'facilitate' for Mina doesn't include you getting hurt, does it?"

"What it doesn't include is *her* getting hurt."

"Mina will come to no harm in the long run, if she cooperates. She has access to something we need. That is all."

Yeah, I thought wryly. Trey. And I already knew the harm Per was willing to do Mina. It wouldn't help me to let on, though, so I kept my eyes forward and said nothing.

My silence sparked speculation. "If it is a matter of money, whatever she is paying you, we can offer more."

"I don't need your dirty money." I would have spit, but that's a bit melodramatic even for me.

"I see. You are an idealist, one who must always take the moral high ground. In my own way, I, too, am an idealist. What I have learned, though, Ciel, is that sometimes the high ground is a dead end. Sometimes one must step around a lesser ideal in order to obtain a greater one. Do you understand?"

Step around? Try stomp all over. He sounded as benign as a philosophy professor giving a lecture to a slow student, but I knew better. "It seems to me, if you easily cast aside the so-called lesser ideals, then your loyalty to any greater one would always be in question," I said, matching his lofty tone.

His mouth tightened. "There we must disagree."

I shrugged again, and we walked in silence until we came to a huge wooden structure, weathered gray from the elements. A long, thick-timbered arm was positioned on an axle between two A-frame supports, with a massive counterweight at the bottom holding it in an upright position.

Sheesh. Talk about your phallic symbols.

At least fifty Vikings mingled near it. They weren't exactly standing guard, but they had the effect of keeping the tourists a fair distance from it. My curiosity got the better of my reluctance to speak to Per. "What's that?"

"That," he said, pride evident in his voice and stance, "is the Visby trebuchet. It is a replica of a medieval war engine designed to launch artillery from a great distance. This one has a range of almost two hundred meters with a limestone projectile. Less for something heavier, but still impressive."

"Oh. Well, not that I don't appreciate the sightseeing tour, but why are we stopping here?" His almost human behavior was starting to make me antsy.

"Shortly we will send a package into town via this attention-getting delivery system."

I stared at the machine, which suddenly took on a more sinister aspect. "*That's* how you're going to bomb the city?" I said, appalled.

"You know about that?"

Oops. Probably shouldn't have let that slip. "I'm just guessing."

He didn't seem to mind my knowing. That wasn't good—it meant he didn't think I'd be talking to anyone about it in the near future.

"It seemed appropriate, given the medieval theme of the festival," he said.

How could he be so cavalier about it? "But why? Why do you want to kill all those innocent people? What have they ever done to you?"

He looked puzzled. "Kill them? Who said anything about killing them?"

"You did. You just said you were going to bomb them, for God's sake!"

"Yes. With advertisements. Why would we kill our potential customers?"

"Customers?" Then the connection came to me. The shampoo. The body wash. "Is this how you finance your group? You're trying to ram some sort of new masculine agenda down Sweden's collective throat by selling men's toiletries?"

His smile gave me the creeps. "You are well-informed, aren't you? Yes, restoring the true masculine ideal to Sweden is our goal. Getting our products into the hands of the men is one way we're going about it."

I was unable to suppress a derisive snort. "Shampoo and body wash will make men more manly? Hello? I think you must have some wires crossed somewhere. Ever hear the term 'metrosexual'? Your target demographic probably isn't the most macho group out there."

"Not at first, no. But they will be after they use our soap and lotions for long enough," he said. I must have looked blank, because he continued. "Steroids, Miss Halligan. Surely you've heard of them."

"Steroids," I echoed, shocked. "You're lacing your toiletries with steroids?"

He didn't deny it; he only stood staring at the huge catapult with smug satisfaction, the arrogant bastard.

"Don't you know how dangerous that is?" I asked, biting back the "you idiot" I desperately wanted to add. See? I can learn. "Even in a controlled situation the side effects can be horrendous. With no monitoring, no dosage warnings . . ." What he was proposing was tantamount to poisoning a large segment of the population.

"There may be a few bad reactions, yes, but on the whole it will make men's lives better. They will be stronger. More willing to listen to what we have to say. In the long run, more likely to vote for someone who supports our platform."

"Good God. You sound like a freaking politician." It was so ridiculous I almost laughed, but the glint of fanaticism in his eyes killed the mirth in my throat.

"Politics is the only true path to power. To do the country any lasting good, one must eventually pursue that course, yes."

"Don't you think that maybe, just maybe, it

should be a man's own decision whether or not to shrink his testicles down to the size of raisins?" Contempt colored my voice as I shot a quick glance at his crotch.

His laugh was an ugly sound. "If these so-called men had any balls to begin with, they wouldn't be in need of our help. And, no, Miss Halligan, I don't find it necessary to use our products. Would you care to see for yourself?"

"I'll pass on that," I said with as much scorn as I could summon. "I prefer men who aren't clinically insane."

He stepped closer, looming over me, and whispered, "And do you know what I prefer, you little bitch? I prefer that you tell me immediately where I can find Mina. You have one more chance."

"Or what? You're going to slap me around in front of all these people? You get off on that, don't you? Hurting women?" I taunted. Stupid, I know, but I was too pissed off to care.

His face darkened. He opened his mouth to speak, but a middle-aged, long-bearded buffalo of a man interrupted our little tête-à-tête.

"It's time to turn the engine to face the wall. The men are ready," the man said in surprisingly good English.

Per's face relaxed. His whole demeanor changed to that of someone who'd just received an unexpected gift.

"A moment, Sam." Per looked at me, speculation glittering in his eyes. "Can you swim, Miss Halligan?"

Huh?

He didn't wait for an answer.

"Sam, tell the men to winch up the arm, and bring me some leather straps." And then, more softly so the people beyond the Viking human shield wouldn't hear, "We have a volunteer for a test flight."

Holy shit. He couldn't mean that, could he? "Sam, wait!" I called after the retreating man.

The buffalo started to turn back to me, but continued on his way when Per gave him an abrupt hand signal.

"You'll get no help from Sam just because he is a fellow countryman of yours. He is my brother-in-law, and quite loyal to our cause."

"Listen, Per—"

"Tell me where Mina is."

"I don't know!"

"I don't believe you," he said.

"Look, she could be anywhere. She might be on her way home to the States by now. How about we just slow down here until you check the airports?"

"I'm afraid you will have to do better than that. Ah, here is Sam back." He took the straps from him.

"No, really. I don't know, I swear." I hated the pleading that had crept into my voice. Not so, Per. He liked it fine.

"Take her arms, Sam. Hold her still."

Knowing it was useless, I took off, getting not even two steps before I was jerked to a halt by the back of my stupid dress. A hand came down over my mouth and stayed there until a gag—a filthy-tasting linen rag—replaced it.

A fence of Vikings blocked the actions from any curious passersby. Hell, they probably would have thought it was just another show, anyway, the oblivious sheep.

With the help of a handy Viking knot ace, Per fashioned a harness snugly around me. My hands were tied in front of me, and my ankles bound. It took two of them to carry me over to the trebuchet. I managed to kick one of them in the gut, but eventually I was laid beneath the archaic device and held in place, my shoulders and feet pinned to the ground by large hands.

Per straddled me, placing his feet on either side of my hips, and looked down at me from his great height. He held a hook connected to a long rope in one hand, and appeared to be enjoying himself.

"One last time. Where is Mina?" he said.

I would have gladly kicked him in the nuts if I could get my legs free. "Uck oo!" I said instead, as loudly as the gag permitted. He got the gist.

"Very well, Miss Halligan. As you wish."

Now, I thought, would be a good time for Billy to show up. I looked around at all the Viking faces, keeping a chokehold on my panic, searching for some clue as to which one he might be. There was no indication.

Per attached the rope to my harness. Hooked the other end of it to the long arm of the trebuchet. When he spoke to his men, excitement glazed his voice.

"Take off the safety lines and hand me the trigger rope."

Chapter 22

Okay, changed my mind. If this was a cruel ruse meant to make me talk, it was now officially working. *Boy*, would I talk. I'd talk until my tongue cramped, make shit up, say whatever I had to. Just as soon as he took this damn gag out of my mouth and let me.

Twisting and squirming, I tried to convey my newfound sense of cooperation to my captors. Either Per wasn't buying my change of heart or, more likely, he didn't care. He pulled the trigger rope, and the men holding me let go and scrambled sideways.

My mind refused to accept what my eyes had seen. No way had he really done that. It had to be a fake rope, one rigged to look like the trigger. Still, I couldn't rip my eyes away from his face during the oddly elongated pause. He stared back in near orgasmic delight.

Then I was gone, yanked backward with a force that left my stomach behind. Up and over, like a kid living the dream of completing a loop around the swing set, only taken to nightmare proportions. Somewhere past the top of the arc, the hook disengaged from the engine's arm and I was launched, trailing the rope like a kite tail.

Instinctively, I tucked my knees up and my head down, squeezing my eyes shut against that last nasty image of Per's face. Unable to scream, or to flail my bound arms and legs, I tumbled end over end, dizzy and disoriented.

The space between my heartbeats fluctuated wildly. Faces flashed in my head. Billy with his teasing grin. Mark with dove-gray eyes. My parents. My brothers, aunts, uncles, every aura I'd ever assumed—all strobed in and out, vying for possession of my final thoughts.

In the end, they all lost out to the great big overriding *OH, CRAAAAP!*

I slammed into the water butt-first, with a whack that made Nils's earlier smack on my bottom seem like a caress. A small, dispassionate part of me wondered, for a split second, if I had just set the world record for cannonball dives. Then the pain hit, paralyzing me, and the icy shock of the water squeezed the remaining breath out of me like a fist, shriveling the frivolous thought.

I sank, at first unable to move my limbs at all, utterly undone by the hurting, until something— sheer panic, I suppose—kicked in and set my arms and legs in motion. Ignoring the pain, I grappled with the ropes around my wrists for a frenzied moment before it occurred to me to employ the same technique I'd used to slip out of the handcuffs. Concentrating, I called up Molly's aura once again.

The sleeves and hem of my dress accordioned with my shrinking limbs, held in place by my bonds. My shoes fell off. I worked my arms back and forth frantically, until the rope released its grip.

Hands free, I mermaid-kicked to the surface. Ripped the gag out of my mouth. Sucked in air, frankly surprised to be alive. Pushing aside my gratitude—no time, and besides, it could be premature—I shoved my sleeves up and set to work on my legs. The rope clung to the coarsely woven cloth of the tunic like squid to its dinner. I slipped under, over and over again, spraying the salty Baltic out of my mouth and nose every time I resurfaced.

I finally freed myself, only to have the sea immediately grasp my oversized clothing, stretching it well below my legs, dragging me down. Crap. I'd have to shed that, too.

Except I couldn't, because the leather harness was still on me. The knots, pulled tight from the stress of the launch, and now soaked through, were impossible to work loose with my frigid fingers. I tried slipping the whole contraption over my shoulders, but Molly wasn't quite narrow enough for that.

Shit! Damned if I was going to die like that asshole expected me to. I switched back to myself so the dress and tunic would be more manageable, and to conserve the little energy that projecting an aura takes. The clothing was still a weight on me, but at least I'd be able to keep my head above water longer than I would as Molly.

I spun slowly in place, orienting myself. There was a sailboat that might be close enough to hail, but for all I knew it was loaded with more Vikings. I hoped I hadn't already been spotted.

When I turned further, and spotted the shore, my heart sank. It was farther away than I'd hoped, judging by the apparent size of the men standing at the water's edge. Per's merry macho maniacs were all lined up, looking outward. Probably checking to see if my body would sink or float. Swimming directly toward land might get me out of the proverbial fire, but I'd be right back in the frying pan.

I scanned the coast for an empty spot. My arms and legs were rapidly tiring—no time to waste on decision making. To the right was the city, where God knew how many more Vikings waited. Striking out to the left seemed the more prudent choice.

I kept my arms low, barely lifting them above the water, not wanting to draw attention to myself with broad movements. Maintained a course parallel to the shore, hoping the waves would block a clear view of me.

If I could get far enough down the coast before I headed for land . . . if I could make it out of the water . . . if I could run to the cover of the trees without being noticed . . . then I might actually survive.

Of course, my brilliant plan would only work if I could keep my arms and legs moving—an "if" that was looking more doubtful by the second. I couldn't even gauge my progress reliably. The island was too far away, and too large, to use as a marker. For all I knew, I was swimming in place.

Shut up, Ciel. Thinking like that won't help.

I put one arm in front of the other, digging through the water, focusing on getting back to dry land alive. Finding shelter. Finding Billy and Mark. And, above all, finding a fucking way to come down on Per like a sledgehammer.

Unfortunately, no amount of focus could make my legs any less heavy. Within minutes I couldn't tell if they were moving at all. My feet were completely numb. Fingers too. I knew my arms were working only because I saw them continue to rise and fall.

Breathing had become a problem, too. I was inhaling more of the sea with each stroke, and wasting valuable energy ridding myself of it. It would be so much easier if I didn't need air. If I could just slip under the water and glide along like a fish, emerging only when I was beyond sight of the horde. If I didn't have to *fight* so damn hard to stay at the surface.

In fact, that seemed like a pretty good idea, when I really considered it. Logical. Swimming mostly underwater would conserve energy, which meant I wouldn't need to take as many breaths. It made perfect sense. Not only could I move along much faster, but it would be a cakewalk compared to what I was doing now.

My arms concurred and I drifted under. It felt

glorious to stop, just for a minute, to take a short break. It was helping already, too, because I didn't even feel so cold anymore. Sure, it was a little dark, but that was okay, dark wasn't so bad . . .

Then I was going up again, and it was easy, even simpler than I had hoped it would be. I should have thought of this sooner. It was so effortless, in fact, that I kept right on rising even after I broke the surface.

Huh. Something about that wasn't exactly right. In a second I'd open my eyes and see if I could figure it out.

"Ciel!"

How odd. It sounded like Mark. Muffled, but Mark. Then again, maybe I was dreaming. It kind of felt like a dream.

"*Ciel!*"

No, it was definitely Mark. I willed my eyes to open, and found myself face to face with the hull of a sailboat. I pondered that, but my waterlogged brain couldn't seem to make sense of it.

"Ciel, can you hear me? Let me get the boat hook off you, then I'll get you up here. Ciel! Stay awake!"

Okeydoke, I thought. I would've said it out loud, but it seemed like too much trouble to take the necessary breath. When the tension on my harness slackened I slid down, not really caring much. It hadn't been so bad beneath the water. Kind of nice, really.

A hand grasped my upper arm, hard, and pulled me up far enough for an arm to secure itself around my waist. I fell forward over it as I was hauled aboard, and promptly vomited seawater all over my legs.

Mark laid me on the deck and pushed me over onto my side.

"That's right—get rid of it," he said, gently rubbing my back.

I did as he told me, emptying my stomach, feeling the water, and possibly my lungs, pour out of my mouth and nose. I gasped as I finished, swallowing convulsively. It burned.

"All done?"

I nodded.

"Okay. Let's get you inside."

He carried me into the cabin and set me on a vinyl-covered seat in the dining area. I leaned on the table, resting my cheek on the warm Formica, and began to shiver violently.

Mark fished in his pocket and came out with a Swiss Army knife, which he used to saw through the sodden leather straps of the harness. It was a huge relief to get it off me. Only then did I feel free of Per's grip.

"Wait here," he said, and left me. Like I was going anywhere, except maybe to sleep.

But he was back before I could get my eyes shut. He tossed a towel over my shoulders, unzipped a sleeping bag and spread it out on the banquette sofa across from the table. An instant later he was back to me, rubbing my hair briskly with the soft terry cloth.

"We have to get you out of those wet things. Can you stand for just a minute?"

I tried. Really I did. But my arms wouldn't push me up, and my legs . . . well, I still couldn't quite feel them.

"Never mind." He opened his knife again.

"Whuh . . . whuh . . ." I said, rasping it out, having trouble making my mouth function. Seems it was in league with my arms and legs.

"Shhh . . . it's okay."

He leaned me back and, starting at the neck, sliced downward through the dress and tunic in a series of short, smooth motions. Then he put the knife aside, slipped an arm between me and my clothes, pulled me up to his chest, and peeled the sodden garments off me. While my back was exposed, he unhooked my bra. After he laid me on the sleeping bag, he removed both the bra and my panties.

Great. At long last naked in front of Mark, and I looked like a plucked chicken. A cadaverous blue plucked chicken. *And* I was shivering like a Chihuahua at the North Pole. A half-dead, blue, plucked-chicken Chihuahua, with teeth chattering like castanets. Could it get any worse?

I sneezed, spraying snotty saltwater all over myself and Mark. Wonderful. Never, ever, question if it can get worse. It can *always* get worse.

"Gesundheit," Mark said. He wiped his face with his sleeve, gave me a vigorously impersonal swipe with the towel, and closed the sleeping bag over me, zipping it partially shut. Then he stripped off his clothing, quickly and efficiently, and crawled in beside me.

"Wh-wh-what are you d-d-doing?" I croaked when I finally found my voice. This wasn't exactly the encounter of my dreams.

"It's all right," he said, zipping us in. "Shared body heat. It's the best way to bring your core temperature back up."

"B-but . . . b-b-but . . ."

"It's either this or a warm-water enema."

Eeep. No, thanks. "Th-this w-will do."

He turned me away from him and hugged me, spoon fashion, putting his top leg over mine and his arms around my torso. His body was heavenly hot, and I instinctively sank back against it, my incipient sigh of rapture disappearing into another spasm of uncontrollable shaking.

"It's okay. You'll be warm again soon," he whispered, holding me closer.

"P-p-promise?"

"Yes. I promise. Now rest."

"Sh-shouldn't you be st-steering the boat?" I said, hoping he could hear me over the rattling of my teeth.

"Got someone on it."

"Oh." I kept quiet for a minute, trying to clear my head. There was something I should—"Oh! I have to tell you—"

"Later."

"It can't wait." I tried to turn toward him, but he held me fast.

"Yes, it can. Don't worry. Billy is on top of everything, and we have other agents in place, too. Relax."

"But we have to st-stop them before they start selling the t-t-toiletries," I said.

There was a short pause. "Care to run that by me again? You're not making a lot of sense."

"The shampoo . . . body wash . . . lotions. Laced with steroids. I f-found out, so they had to get rid of me."

"Are you sure about that?"

"Per told me himself. He's proud of the idea."

Mark believed me. I could tell by how he tensed up. "Son of a bitch. We knew they were plotting something, but we've been expecting a big, attention-grabbing Viking raid. We never thought they would strike commercially. The bastards."

I tried to sit up. "Let's go."

He pushed me back down. "You stay right where you are. You aren't going anywhere until you warm up."

"But—"

"There's time."

Since my mind was still almost as sluggish as my body, I gave in and changed the subject.

"How did you find me?"

"Billy called as soon as he saw Per taking you away from town. I was on the boat, waiting to ferry you away from the island. I thought taking it would be the fastest way to follow you up the beach. The plan was to meet Billy just beyond where the Viking ranks were gathered, and from there we were going to figure out a way to go in after you."

My heart thudded at the thought of how fortuitous my rescue had been.

After a moment I asked, "Did you see it?"

"Your flight? Did I ever. I was trying to get to where you hit the water, but I couldn't see you in the waves. I really thought I'd lost you. Again. After Hilda told me you'd been taken . . . damn, Howdy. You've shaved at least ten years off my life in the past few days."

The shared body heat technique must have been working, because suddenly I was feeling much warmer inside. "Did I make a big splash?" I said drowsily. "It'd be a shame if a cannonball like that was wasted."

He chuckled softly. "Huge, Howdy. It was huge."

"You didn't happen to capture it on video, did you?"

"Sorry, no."

"Too bad. It would've rocked on YouTube."

Chapter 23

The mirror in the head was small, so I only had to see tiny chunks of sea-mangled me at a time. That was bad enough. Salt-encrusted hair sticking out at crazy angles, dark freckles polka-dotting a kabuki-white face, red-rimmed eyes. And my lips . . . ugh. Parched out of any semblance of their typical rosiness, so even my one good feature was letting me down.

I had awakened a few minutes earlier, still in the sleeping bag, with a couple of blankets piled on top for good measure, feeling good enough to be disappointed that a naked Mark was no longer sharing his warmth with me. I sighed. Skin to skin with him for that long and nothing had happened. Life is cruelly ironic sometimes. It just goes to show, when you're bargaining with the universe, you'd better be specific or the loopholes will pop up and bite you on the ass.

Clutching the blanket I'd wrapped around myself, I opened a small cupboard under the sink and searched methodically for lip balm. I found a bar of soap, a sample-size bottle of shampoo, a stick of deodorant, shaving cream, and some disposable razors, all of which I was sure would be useful, but not what I wanted first. Was one freaking tube of ChapStick too much to ask?

Maybe Mark had some in his luggage. This wasn't his boat, so surely he had to have packed before he came to Sweden, right? Where there was a man's luggage, there was a toiletry bag. Where there was a toiletry bag, there might be ChapStick. I could go find him and ask.

Or I could just look for it myself. I mean, why bother him?

There were two pieces of luggage stowed near the quarter-berths. One of them was a compact leather duffel I recognized as Mark's, the other a more structured overnight bag. I hesitated. Some might consider an uninvited search an invasion of privacy. Then I remembered my office, and just how much the men in my life, Mark included, respected *my* privacy. Screw it. I went for the duffel.

I sifted through jeans, some khakis, several shirts, and plenty of socks. When I got to the dark cotton boxer briefs, I paused and swallowed, remembering what I'd seen when Mark removed a similar pair before climbing into the sleeping bag with me. Ignoring them, I dug further, until I came upon a small leather case.

Sure enough, there was the lip balm. Also, an electric razor, some ibuprofen, a small bottle of peroxide, a few bandages, and a box of condoms. I felt the blood rush to my cheeks, and told myself to grow up. Mark was an adult. He was a man. Of course he had a sex life. Obviously. One that didn't include me, also obviously.

Unless . . . I supposed he *could* have purchased them after my drunken kiss on his sailboat had opened his eyes to certain possibilities, and he wanted to be prepared if anything, well, popped up between us. (Naïve? Maybe, but I preferred "optimistic.")

I took the ChapStick and arranged everything else back the way it was. The other suitcase was tempting me, but since I'd already found what I was after, I decided to take the high road and leave it. I can be big.

Back in the head, I snapped up the shower curtain, and rinsed myself with the handheld nozzle. Getting the residual salt off me improved my outlook a thousand percent. My short, wavy hair was easily finger-fluffed into an acceptable 'do, and the balm restored my lips reasonably well. What it couldn't do I took care of with a smidge of aura adapting, at the same time as I toned down my freckles and got rid of the baggage under my eyes. I told myself it wasn't really cheating, since I didn't look any different from my usual, pre-dunk-in-the-ocean self. And, dammit, what good was having a talent like mine if you couldn't take advantage of it now and then?

The first thing I noticed when I went up on deck was the spectacular sunset. The bright white orb hovered just between the wispy clouds and the rippling water, turning the sky pink and giving the ocean a golden cast. There was a breeze, but it wasn't cold, and the hot shower had banished any lingering effects from my frigid dip. My only problem was that I didn't have any clothes at hand. I'd wrapped the blanket back around me, two corners crisscrossed in front and tied behind my neck to form a kind of makeshift toga. I was hoping to find something a little more tailored.

We were docked at the marina, surrounded by other sailboats, all of which seemed to have people on deck enjoying the view. At the front of our boat, also appreciating Mother Nature, was a curvaceous young woman with auburn hair that hung past her shoulders. She looked right at home, coiling ropes like a pro.

"Billy?" I said.

She turned, and I saw at once that it wasn't Billy's recent incarnation.

"No . . ." She smiled and approached me.

Okay. I squinted at her suspiciously. "Mark?" I said, a little less confidently. I really couldn't think why he'd need to appear as a woman, but maybe it was his cover for being here in Visby.

She laughed softly. "No again. I'm Laura. And

you must be Ciel." Her words were unrushed, her voice low-pitched and kissed by the south. Even her handshake was genteel.

"Um, yeah." I looked around. "Where's Mark?"

"He had to meet with someone." She studied my face. "Are you feeling all right, hon? You didn't hit your head, did you?"

"No, I'm fine. Fit as a fiddle. Right as rain. Couldn't be better. Who the hell are you?"

Her easy smile was bland, meant to soothe. My stomach was starting to feel a little uneasy as I flashed back to the box of condoms. She and Mark couldn't be . . . could they? But why not? She was beautiful. He certainly hadn't stuck around in the sleeping bag with me any longer than necessary, had he? Why would he be interested in a scrawny, salt-caked Popsicle when he had lovely Laura—who had not one freckle in spite of the red hair—handy? And she knew her way around a sailboat, too, damn it. Mark probably thought that was sexy.

"I work with Mark," she said. Well, I could believe that. She had the same reluctance to part with any excess information.

"At the Agency?" I asked. Might as well get it spelled out.

"Yes." Same bland smile.

"Okay. So, how much do you know about Mark?" *Do you know about his adapting ability or not?*

"I know he's good at his job," she said.

Oh, big help.

I tried another tack. "What did he tell you about me?"

"That you'd been kidnapped by the neo-Viking organization, and we were to extract you."

"Anything else?"

She shrugged. "You're his best friend's baby sister."

True enough, but it still stung. Is that how he'd described me? Not even *his* friend, but his friend's baby sister?

"That's all?" I pressed.

"What else is necessary? Mark needed backup, and here I am."

This was getting us nowhere. Either she didn't know a thing about adaptors, or else she knew Mark was one but didn't think I knew. Neither one of us was going to be the first to give anything away, so I'd just have to wait and ask Mark.

"When will he be back?"

"He said sometime before morning," she said vaguely. "If he gets held up, he'll send Billy back again—"

"Wait—Billy was here? When?"

"Not long after we pulled back into the marina. He went below to check on you and talk to Mark. Didn't you see him?"

I frowned. "No. I guess I was asleep." I felt kind of uncomfortable, knowing Billy had seen me snuggled up naked in a sleeping bag with Mark, though I wasn't sure why I should.

"That's understandable. Almost drowning will take it right out of you. You looked nearly dead when you first boarded."

"Gee, thanks."

"You look much better now. Really," she said quickly.

"Lucky I recover fast," I said, smiling as sweetly as I could. Maybe.

She cleared her throat. "So, can I get you anything? A hot drink or something to eat?"

"No, that's okay. I'm not hungry. I could use some clothes, though, if you happen to have anything handy that might fit me."

She hesitated.

"Actually, I don't even care if it fits—I'm not proud. I promise to take good care of it and return it as soon as I get something of my own." I smiled winningly. Nobody could resist my winning smile.

Except lovely Laura, apparently. She shook her head with regret that verged on being sincere. "It's just that . . ." she began. Didn't continue.

A nasty little suspicion gripped me, tightening my voice. "Mark told you not to give me any clothes, didn't he?" Her eyes got big. I guess my face might have given away my feelings on the matter just a tad.

"Uh . . . not in so many words. He just suggested you might be more comfortable resting in the blankets until he gets back."

"Did he, now? Refresh my memory—when is he supposed to be back?"

"By morning. And if he isn't here by six, then I'm to sail you to the mainland."

"*What?*" I wanted to shout, but managed to keep it to a horrified whisper.

"Don't worry—I can handle the boat. Mark's a great teacher," she said.

Did I detect a hint of double meaning in that? I narrowed my eyes and looked her over.

"Mark's great at a lot of things," I said, carefully neutral, though I felt like shoving her overboard. Which wasn't really fair of me. Mark was the one who could use a good dunk in the ocean.

"If you're concerned about sailing with me at the helm, you needn't be." Her chin went up a notch. Yeah, she had the spook ego.

"Not at all," I said, declining to add that it was moot, since I wouldn't be sailing away from Gotland with anybody, least of all her. No point in getting her antennae up any farther than they already were. "I just hope Mark will be back before then. There are a few details he needs to know about the Vikings." Among other things. Like, that I do not need a fucking babysitter.

"Maybe you should tell me. I've been working closely with Trey, monitoring the group."

"No offense, Laura, but I think I'd rather wait for Mark. After all, I haven't really met you in any official capacity yet, have I?"

She didn't question my reluctance. Guess she understood all about discretion.

"That's fine. Are you sure you aren't hungry? I can heat up some soup if you don't want anything heavy."

Might be good to get her attention focused elsewhere. "You know, maybe I *should* have a little something. Build my energy back up. Do you mind if I wait up here and enjoy the view until it's ready?" I sank down onto the built-in storage bin *cum* bench seat closest to me.

"Not at all. I'll holler up when it's done. Would you like me to bring you another blanket first? Mark will get mad if I let you get chilled again."

Yeah? Just wait until you see him after you lose me, I thought nastily.

Then I felt kind of bad for thinking it, because she really was trying to be decent to me, and it wasn't her fault Mark decided to act like a controlling jerk. But there was no way I was going to allow myself to be carted away from the island with a stranger while Mark and Billy went about their merry rescue operation without me. Trey was my client's fiancé, and I intended to make sure, personally, that he got delivered to her in a timely fashion.

"No, I'm fine," I assured Laura. "It's positively balmy out here, isn't it? I'll come down if I start to feel cold," I promised, fingers crossed in the folds of my blanket.

I didn't waste any time after she went below, padding to the front of the boat and hopping to the dock with only a slight misstep when my foot caught the bottom of the blanket. I righted myself before I fell, no harm done. Not having a clue how long it would take Laura to heat up the soup, I walked away as fast as I could without drawing unwelcome attention. I didn't want to risk still being in view of the boat when she realized I wasn't answering the dinner bell.

The good thing about wearing a blanket was that it would adjust to cover changing auras without much trouble, and keep me decently covered until I could score some clothes. My own face was the last one I wanted to show in town, so I'd have to switch to another one ASAP. But I had to find a dark niche someplace to change—too many people still wandering around to risk it in the open.

The marina was right on the edge of the Old Town, so I didn't have far to cover before I blended in to the confusion of the festival. Finding a spot private enough to make a change was the challenge. I was jostled between groups of various sizes, most of them intent on a single destination. Nobody paid any attention to my odd attire. Maybe they all thought it was just a really miserable attempt at a medieval costume, and were being polite.

After a few minutes, I heard English being spoken—a magnet to my ear. When I saw who it was, I had to stop myself from waving.

"Come on—we have to see the fire show. We can't come all this way and miss it." It was Dreamy Princess girl from the hotel—Jennifer—and she was dragging along a completely smitten Kevin. Ah, youth. They recover quickly.

I continued uphill, against the predominant flow of the crowd, turning at small side streets as I came to them. Eventually I found a house with a real yard. A yard burgeoning with plant life, in fact—the perfect cover. But before I could change, I heard voices.

Disturbingly *familiar* voices.

I froze. Peeking out from the foliage I saw Per's brother-in-law, Sam, the American who had helped launch me. He was walking down the street speaking urgently to several other Vikings, in English, saying something about heading to the southern meeting point because "the little bitch" (guess that was me) had ruined things here. One other guy said not to worry, the "big plan" was still on for tomorrow. And then they were gone, past where I could hear them.

Shit. I had to get back to the boat and tell Laura, at least. As I stepped out of the shrubbery, I was caught from behind in an exuberant hug, my arms pinioned to my sides. Hot breath tickled my ear, and a familiar voice followed it.

"Boner Benjamin might be a good choice . . ."

". . . don't you think? He could help you raise the blanket in front, hands-free, so you won't trip while you're running away."

I sagged. "How'd you find me?"

Billy let me go and I turned to face him.

"I'm just that clever." He grinned, a one-dimpler.

"No, really," I deadpanned.

"Smart-ass. I saw you leaving the boat as I was coming back. You looked so furtive I knew you were up to something."

"Yeah, well, never mind that. We have to get back now—I just heard some Vikings talking. They're heading south for their 'big plan,' whatever the hell that is."

"That's all? Nothing else?" he said. I shook my head. He tilted his skeptically. "Since when do you understand Swedish?"

"They were speaking English. One of them is Per's brother-in-law—he's from America. He helped with my launch."

Billy stiffened, his face setting itself into hard planes. "Which way did they go?"

I pointed. "That way, but don't even think about it—there are way too many of them. Now, let's go." I took off, stubbing my toe on a jagged cobblestone. I muffled a curse, and promptly stubbed a toe on the other foot. I looked heavenward. *Seriously? It wasn't even that bad a word. Besides, extenuating circumstances here!*

Billy debated going after them, I could tell, but stayed with me instead. "Your feet hurt?" he asked.

Duh. "Yeah, and they're cold, too. Got any spare shoes on you?"

"No, but I'll give you a piggyback ride back to the boat if you like."

I hesitated.

He turned his back to me. "Come on, it'll take us forever otherwise. Up you go. I won't drop you."

"Pinky swear?"

He reached over his shoulder, and hooked his little finger with mine. "Pinky swear."

I rucked up my toga and climbed aboard. It was embarrassing, but he had a point about the speed. Once his arms were safely tucked beneath my knees, he said, "Now, why don't you tell me why you were running away from Mark."

"He told Laura to sail me to the mainland if he wasn't back by morning. I am not leaving the island without Trey." I skipped the part about my jealousy of Laura's place in Mark's life. Why cloud the main issue?

"You twit. He just wants you to be safe if he and I get killed, is all."

"Oh, well, that makes it okay," I said, heavy on the sarcasm; nothing Billy wasn't used to.

He moved through the streets at a good pace, backtracking without hesitation, not even breathing heavily. Physically fit people are so annoying. When we got close to the dock I told him to put me down. He refused.

"Your toe is bleeding. You can wait till we're back on the boat."

"Oh, geez. It's not that bad. It doesn't even hurt." I wiggled my legs and shook his shoulders.

"You have absolutely no patience, do you?" he said. "Give it up, cuz. I can out-stubborn you any day of the week."

"I could change into Nils and make you collapse under my weight," I threatened.

"You won't. Too many people around," he retorted equably.

He was right, damn it.

"Wait a minute—before we get there, tell me if Laura knows about adaptors."

"If she does, she's never let on to me. Mark may have told her about himself, but I doubt the walking personification of zipped lips would tell her about the rest of us."

"Great. So I'm stuck as me as long as I'm around her."

He gave my legs an annoyed squeeze. "There's nothing wrong with being you."

"Except that all those Vikings think I'm dead, and I'd really hate to disabuse them of the notion."

"So you'll have to keep your head low. Big deal."

We boarded, and found Mark had returned. He was deep in a quiet but heated conversation with Laura, who looked apologetic and peeved at the same time. I probably wasn't high on her list of favorite people at the moment.

They turned when they heard us. Mark's anger shifted palpably from Laura to me. Billy dropped my legs and pulled me around to stand in front of him, resting his hands on my shoulders. "Look who I found. Slippery little thing, isn't she?" he said cheerfully, trying, I think, to lighten the moment for my sake. It didn't work.

Mark's eyes were definitely at the steel-cold end of the gray spectrum. "Barefoot?" he finally said, his tone a perfect blend of incredulity, anger, and disgust. "And naked under a blanket, after you nearly froze to death? Are you a complete idiot?"

I shrugged off Billy's hands. "I didn't have access to a wardrobe," I said.

"Do you know how stupid it was to leave this boat by yourself? Are you *trying* to get yourself killed? Or one of us, when we have to come after you again?"

I flinched. No way to hide that. I'd heard him speak harshly before, but had never had the full force of it directed at me. Sure, I *may* have deserved that last bit—I hadn't given a second thought to how I might be dragging them into more danger. But, really, did he have to take that tone? "It won't happen again," I said tightly.

"It better not."

"I said it wouldn't. So, do you want to hear what the fucking Vikings are up to, or would you rather keep yelling at me?" I said. It wouldn't hurt to have him think I'd gone off to gather intelligence on purpose.

That got his attention. "What are you talking about?"

"I overheard a bunch of them, the same ones from the trebuchet. They're heading south. Apparently there's a 'big plan,' and it's on for tomorrow."

I could see the thoughts flying, rapid-fire, behind his eyes. "Did they say where, exactly?"

"Not that I could catch."

He nodded. "Okay. Doesn't matter. It still confirms something we've suspected." He skewered me with his eyes again. "So that's why you left the boat—you were playing spy?"

I shrugged. Flushed. Kept silent. What was I going to say? No, I was running away from your girlfriend? I don't think so.

Laura actually looked sorry for me. That was worse than Mark's anger. "I think the soup is still warm, Ciel. I'll bet you could use something in your stomach," she said kindly. Mark cut her an annoyed glance, but visibly relaxed when she tilted her head, slightly, and raised one brow.

"Take Ciel below and see that she eats," he said to Billy, his voice starting to lose some of the harshness. "Have something yourself. Keep her down there until we're under way—sit on her if you have to." The last part might even have been an attempt at humor. I ignored it and asked him where we were going.

"Relax, Howdy. Just a short hop down the coast," he said. Yeah, pleasant enough now, and all because of that cute little signal from Laura. I was about to say something rude, until Billy took my hand and squeezed it.

"Come on, cuz. I don't know about you, but I'm starved. Let's eat."

Mark's attention was already on preparing the boat to leave the marina, with Laura's help. They worked in sync, at ease with each other without talking, which spoke volumes about how often they'd done it before. As I watched, a barrage of flaming arrows dotted the sky just up the coast behind them, part of the fire show I'd heard Kevin and his princess talking about earlier. Mark and Laura paused in unison and looked out at the sight, shoulder to shoulder. They were beautiful together.

Anger doused by a wave of dejection, I followed Billy below.

The soup, a luscious chicken and corn chowder, was beyond compare, and obviously hadn't come out of any can. After administering first aid to my toe, Billy served us both healthy portions. I ate two helpings, torturing myself with visions of Laura as a gourmet cook on top of being a CIA operative and an excellent sailor. She was perfect for Mark. I hated her.

Billy took care of our dishes while I moped at the table. After he finished cleaning the galley, leaving it spotless, he came and stood next to me.

"Bedtime." He tilted his head toward the V-berth at the front of the boat.

I don't like V-berths. Granted, my claustrophobia seemed a petty annoyance compared to some of the things I'd been through in the past few days, but still. "You go ahead. I'm not sleepy yet."

"Well, I'm beat, and I'm not leaving you to your own devices. We've all seen where that leads."

"But—"

"Look, I'm on Mark's dime right now. He's the boss, he said sit on you, so I'm sitting."

I stayed right where I was.

He sighed. Rubbed the back of his neck. "Come on, Ciel. I'm operating on fumes as it is, and if I have to stay up to watch you—and you know I would—it might just push me over the edge. Please?"

He did sound tired. He probably hadn't had any decent sleep since he got to Sweden, poor guy. I guessed I could suck it up and not whine about my discomfort in windowless enclosures. "All right. But I won't sleep."

"Fine. You can lie awake and listen to my rhythmic breathing."

Even with a backpack sharing the space, the mattress-covered compartment at the front of the boat wasn't cramped. I shoved the pack over to one side, and scooted to the other. When Billy followed me in, he left the privacy curtain halfway open so I could glimpse a bit of a window in the main cabin, which helped me a lot. I smiled gratefully at him. He didn't say anything about my phobia, just shrugged and plopped down right in the middle of the mattress. Since there was room, I left a good foot between us when I lay down.

"Oh, no you don't," he said, and pulled me close, settling my head on his shoulder and his arm around me. "I want to be able to feel if you try to sneak out. I warn you, I'm a light sleeper, and I will know if you move away from me."

"Billy, this really isn't necessary. I'm not going anywhere."

"Indulge me."

I sighed and stayed where I was. "Go to sleep."

I tried to lie as still as I could, but I was restless. My mind wouldn't let go of Mark and Laura, up on deck together, sailing along in perfect harmony. I wondered how many assignments they'd shared in the past, and how much time they spent together off the job. I imagined him kissing her right then, in the moonlight, his arms wrapped around her, his fingers tangled in her glorious red hair . . .

"Stop thinking so loud," Billy said, giving me a squeeze.

"I can't help it. God, I'm such a mess. Mark's right. I'm a total idiot." An idiot for mooning over him, was what I meant.

"No, you're not. A little impulsive, maybe, which

may lead to the occasional idiotic behavior, but that doesn't make you a total idiot."

"No, I'm an idiot all right. I wish I could be like you and Mark, good at everything, but I can't. And it's not just because I'm a girl. Look at Laura—"

"Not a difficult assignment," he said, his appreciation plain in his voice.

I gave him a little shove in the mid-section. "See? You think she's gorgeous, too. And she's probably a perfect spy, just like Mark."

"Ah, so that's what this is about. Mark and Laura."

I raised my head and looked at his face. "So there *is* a 'Mark and Laura.' I knew it."

He pushed my head back down. "That's not what I meant. I have no idea if there's a 'Mark and Laura'—he doesn't keep me informed about his love life."

"Come on, there has to be something going on there. Did you see how they work together? How smoothly they started to unmoor the boat, without even talking about it? They communicate without words. I'll bet everything they do together is like that."

He sighed impatiently. "I work smoothly with Mark, too. Doesn't mean I'm sleeping with him."

"You're a guy, and you've known him forever. Of course you work well together." I shifted, adjusting the blanket that was still twisted around me. Billy helped, and then pulled another blanket over the both of us.

"Look, you are great at what you do. How many clients have you helped in just the past year? Ten? Twelve? And every one of them is better off, now that you've fixed their lives. You have a knack for knowing what's needed, and doing it. You should be proud of your track record."

"Maybe," I admitted reluctantly. "Or maybe I've just been lucky so far." Except, of course, with that whole collecting payment thing.

"And maybe you need to get your head out of your ass and stop feeling sorry for yourself."

I huffed an almost-laugh. "Agreed," I said, and followed it with a big sigh. "Don't pay me any mind—I just need to get it through my head Mark is never going to be attracted to me."

"I don't know. You guys looked pretty cozy in the sleeping bag together," he said.

"Ha. There's the proof right there. We were zipped up naked in a single sleeping bag, pressed together like sardines, and he didn't even . . . react."

"Oh, for crying out loud, Ciel. You were an ice cube. His nether parts were probably jumping up into his abdominal cavity in self-defense. Give the guy a break. Besides, do you really think Mark is the kind of man who would take advantage of a situation like that? He can be a ruthless bastard sometimes, but he's not a complete asshole."

"So you don't think it's because I'm totally unat-tractive?" I said. I *know*—fishing. Not cool. But he'd been so nice about my job. Why not go for broke?

"Christ," he said, and twisted his body toward me. "There, feel that? No, I fucking well don't think it's because you're unattractive. Ego all better now?"

Oh, my. The bulge pressing against me was certainly impressive. Not precisely what I'd been going for—I'd been thinking more along the lines of "Of course you're pretty, Ciel"—but, strangely, it did make me feel better. At least somebody was responding to me.

It made me feel something else, too. Tingly. All over, like when he'd kissed me while we were chasing down Per and company. I had tried to repress that, but it came back to me now in a brain-fogging whoosh.

Good Lord. Maybe I'd been concentrating my libidinous energies on the wrong guy. Billy had been teasing me for as long as I could remember, in more ways than I could count—my size, my freckles, my abilities, my career choice, my pathetic love life. I never took his sexual banter any more seriously than the rest of it. He'd been telling me for years that honorary step-cousins weren't perv material—what if he was serious?

I raised my head so I could see his eyes. They were almost black in the dim light, low-lidded, his lashes shadowing his cheeks. He leaned his head toward me. My heart sped up, skipping randomly as I pressed closer to him, my lips parting in anticipation.

He pulled back. "Forget it. I'm not going to be a stand-in for Mark."

Stung, I said, "It's not like that."

"It's exactly like that, and I won't take advantage

of the situation. Regardless of how it may at times appear, I am not an asshole when it comes to women either. Now, for God's sake, let me sleep." He rolled away from me.

I stared at his back for a full minute, stunned by the rebuff. Finally, I turned away from him and buried my head under the pillow, confused. My adolescence had been fraught with dire warnings from my brothers that men were only after one thing, and I'd better be prepared to defend my virtue at all costs.

Ha. Defend my virtue? If I were an egg inside a chicken, *maybe* I could get laid. But I wouldn't put money on it.

Much later, when I was still awake and Billy was sleeping like the dead, I heard Laura bustling in the galley. I knew it was Laura because if it had been Mark, I never would've heard him. The man moves in a bubble of silence.

I'd had time to do a lot of thinking, and figured maybe I owed her an apology for ditching her and a thank-you for the soup. Like I said, I can be big. I rearranged my toga and crawled toward the main cabin. A warm hand around my ankle yanked me back.

"It's okay, Billy. A replacement guard has been sent down. Go back to sleep." The sounds from the galley confirmed my statement.

"Fine. Go. Wake me when breakfast is ready," he said, sleep muddying his voice. He was out again in a split second. I left him, and closed the curtain behind me.

Laura, looking bright and chipper, was pouring the coffee. She smiled at me—a genuine smile, not at all wary. I wanted to still hate her, but I couldn't.

"I'd give you my last penny for a cup of that," I said, smiling in return.

She laughed, a low, musical sound as beautiful as her face, and handed me a mug. "No need for that. It comes free with the pancakes."

"Pancakes? You're making pancakes?" Hope returned to my world, floating on the rich aroma of dark-roasted Arabica beans and the giddy expectancy of maple syrup.

"Mark said you might like that."

"Mark would be right. Where is he?" I asked, casually looking back toward the quarter berths, wondering if they'd slipped in earlier without me hearing, and had slept there together, all snug and cozy in one of the small beds.

"He's been out doing recon since we got here. He should be back soon."

That was a relief. Maybe it was mean of me, but I was glad nobody else had gotten any last night either. Yeah, I can be petty as well as big.

"So, where are we?"

She shrugged. "Some little fishing village south of Visby. Mark can tell you more when he gets back."

I sat at the table, not offering to help. I wasn't about to display my kitchenly incompetence in front of her.

"Listen, Laura . . . I shouldn't have taken off on you like that. I'm sorry."

"Don't worry about it. No harm done." She laid a griddle across two burners on the small stove and started it heating, then gathered the ingredients—she was going to make them from scratch, of course—and got out a mixing bowl.

"No, really. It was a dumb thing to do," I said. "And thanks for the soup. It was delicious."

She paused in her preparations and looked at me like she was debating whether to say something. Mark had probably told her all about my infantile crush on him, and this was where she would sensitively explain their undying passion for each other. My stomach tied itself into a great big knot while I waited for the anvil to drop.

"Ciel, Mark's not always an easy guy."

I snorted. "Tell me something I don't know."

"What I mean is, try not to be upset with him. It's just how he is. He'll steamroll right over you, trying to make you live according to what *he* thinks is best for you." She pointed her wooden mixing spoon at me, giving it a shake for emphasis. "Don't let him."

I sat back, a little shocked. Guess we weren't going to talk romance. I was enormously relieved. "You sound like you're speaking from experience."

"I am. On our first assignment together, I was fresh off the Farm—you know what the Farm is?"

"Yeah, Mark told me about it. It's where baby spooks are born."

"Something like that," she said, stirring the

pancake mixture. "I was a total newbie, and a girl to boot. Mark didn't think I had any business working a dangerous mission—and he considers just about any mission that isn't behind a desk dangerous. He did everything possible to get me kicked off the job and into an office somewhere. He was so overbearing, I almost quit. Luckily, I have a stubborn streak a mile wide . . ."

I felt a bond start to form as I listened to her misadventures with Mark. Damn. This, and she makes pancakes, too. Forget Mark. I was falling for Laura.

I didn't wake Billy up until after my second plate of pancakes. Why take a chance on running short of batter? Besides, I was having too much fun talking with Laura. She'd been totally indignant on my behalf when I related how Mark had made me throw up with his horror stories about tough assignments. Even though she knew he only did it because he worried about me, she said he'd had no right to bully me away from a possible career choice.

It was great to finally have someone see it from my point of view—I was eating it up along with my breakfast. Of course, I couldn't tell her what I really did for a living now, so I gave her the life coach story. She was impressed that I was running my own business, and I basked in the glow of her approval.

When I finally called Billy, he emerged from behind the curtain wide-awake and totally refreshed. He slipped in next to me at the table as he joked with Laura about not letting me near the galley, and complimented her charmingly on her culinary skill.

While she was making more coffee he laid a warm hand on my thigh, caught my eye, and mouthed, *Are we all right?* I nodded. I couldn't stand feeling awkward with him, so I decided I just wouldn't. He seemed to be in accord.

Once Billy was served, and a fresh stack of steaming delectability was left under an overturned bowl to keep warm for Mark, Laura excused herself to go check something on deck. She said she'd send Mark down when he returned. I wasn't precisely anxious to see him again, but it was easier to contemplate after having talked with Laura. It was heartening to know I wasn't the only one he had ever treated like an incompetent child. If she could overcome it, I could, too.

As soon as she was out of earshot, Billy turned to me with the devil in his eye. "So, you sure you're not mad I didn't boink you last night?"

You'd think I'd know not to expect him to remain circumspect while we were alone. He never— well, rarely—embarrassed me in front of other people, but it was his favorite pastime whenever it was just the two of us. I blushed, just the reaction he was going for, I was sure.

"No, I'm not mad. I'm fine," I said, letting my irritation at his reminder seep into the words.

He dug into his stack of pancakes. "Because," he said between mouthfuls, "I'd be happy to oblige. Just as soon as you're over your crush on Mark, and I can be sure it's me in your head as well as your bed. I'm afraid my ego won't have it any other way."

I shot a quick look at the cabin door; luckily, no one was there to hear. "Do we have to discuss this now? I know I was being pathetic last night. You don't have to rub it in."

"Oh, but I do. Payback for my aching blue balls."

"I get it. I'm sorry. It won't happen again." I tried to scoot away from him. He put his fork down and stopped me with a hand on the back of my neck.

"Yes, it will," he said softly. "I'll see to it."

He gave me the kiss I'd wanted a few hours earlier. It was long and slow, and maple-syrup sweet. After the first stupefying seconds, I melted into the experience as fervently as I had attacked Laura's breakfast. Seemed his tongue was every bit as clever, and even more teasing, when he wasn't using it to talk. I was quivering by the time he was done, my heart racing like I'd just run a fifty-yard dash. I might not have balls, but something inside me sure was aching.

He nibbled his way along the side of my jaw until he got to my ear, and whispered, "Try thinking about me for a while."

"Sorry to interrupt y'all . . ." Laura's softly amused southern accent penetrated the haze surrounding my brain. I just about choked, and scooted away from Billy as fast as I could. ". . . but I just saw Mark. He'll be here any second."

Chapter 25

Laura lifted a questioning eyebrow, but didn't say anything else. She just shrugged and left, chuckling. Billy went back to eating his breakfast, cool as you please, while I sat there like a dummy, breathing hard and madly trying to think of something intelligent to say. I had zip.

This was getting too damned confusing for me. I wanted my life to be simple again. I wanted to go back to the Bahamas, be Mina and snag Trey for her. The Trey who owned an import business, not the one who was a CIA operative.

I wanted to have easy, uncomplicated-by-any-emotion-except-pure-lust sex, contractually sanctioned by my job, without being bombed by God. Was that so much to ask? And once my itch was scratched, I wanted to go back to being me and forget about it all until my next job. I was sure I wouldn't be reacting this way to Billy—Billy, for Pete's sake!—or to Mark either if I only had an adequate sex life of my own.

Mark came into the cabin and greeted us with a brief wave, intent upon food. Just what I needed. I could *not* be in the same place as both of them at once, not before I got my feelings sorted out. But I froze.

Mark got a plate from the galley and joined us at the table, sitting on the other side of me. It was too late to move. I was sandwiched between the Rock and the Hard Place.

I felt a little dizzy.

Mark served himself a hefty stack of the golden flapjacks, accidentally grazing my arm with the back of his hand as he reached for them. Goose bumps pebbled my skin; I adapted them away, but not before Billy saw. He reached for the coffeepot, brushing the fine, dark hairs of his forearm against my bare shoulder. More goose bumps, too fast for me to get rid of before Mark noticed them.

"Chilly, Howdy? I suppose we should find you some clothes," he said.

"Might be a good plan," I said, studiously not looking at Billy, who was choking back a laugh behind his napkin.

Mark glanced at Billy, but drilled his eyes into me. "What are you up to?"

"Me?" I squeaked. "I'm not up to anything!"

Billy took pity on me and changed the subject,

asking Mark what he'd found while he was out. Mark cut me one last sideways glance, then turned his attention to Billy.

"They're gathering at the ship-grave site."

"What's that?" I asked, eager to keep the conversation on something that wasn't me.

"The place old sailboats go to die," Billy said, all seriousness except for his eyes. I continued to ignore him, and turned to Mark for the real answer.

"Some Viking burial sites are made up of standing stones in the shape of a boat's hull. Think small-scale Stonehenge for ancient Norse sailors. There are hundreds of them on Gotland, and one group of them in particular, near here, seems to be the focus of neo-Viking attention. They had to leave Visby faster than planned after their little stunt with the trebuchet."

"So they didn't get to launch the flyers?" I was pleased to have inadvertently thrown a monkey wrench in Per's plans.

"Nope. And, by the way, apparently there are fifty Vikings ready to swear you were a dummy."

Billy opened his mouth, but I cut him off with a glare. "Don't say it."

He couldn't suppress his grin, but he didn't make the comment. Instead he said, "I don't suppose Per is a happy camper right now. What do you think he'll try next?"

Mark shrugged. "Not sure, but I'm afraid it has something to do with Trey. Swedish isn't my best language, but from what I could tell they do have him."

"Well, why are we just sitting here? Come on—we have to do something." I tried to stand, but didn't get far, what with the table in front of me and the human bookends blocking me. They each took one of my arms, and simultaneously pulled me back down.

"Calm down, Howdy. We're going to get him."

"I assume you are not including Ciel in that 'we,'" Billy said.

"Of course not. She'll stay on the boat."

"She will not!" I said.

Mark glowered at me. "I thought we had this settled last night. If I recall, your exact words were 'It won't happen again.'"

I glanced at Billy, squirming as I thought of my more recent usage of that phrase, and what it had led to. He gazed back innocently. Clearing my throat, I turned my attention back to Mark.

"That was before I knew the Vikings had Trey."

"Doesn't matter. I'm holding you to your word. You are capable of keeping your word, aren't you?" His eyes hardened even more.

"Damn it, Mark. You're not being fair. I can help—tell him, Billy."

"She can help, Mark."

"There, you see!"

Billy stepped on my words. "She can help by staying on the boat and watching for suspicious activity around here. Leave her a cell phone—she can contact us if she sees anything."

I slugged his shoulder. "That's not what I meant, and you know it."

"That's an excellent idea," Mark said to Billy. "I'm sure Ciel will like it much better than my plan to leave her in the cockpit locker while we're gone. *If* she can be trusted," he added, with a pointed look at me.

Damn him. He knew about my claustrophobia. I didn't like to think he'd really do something like that, but Billy was right about one thing—Mark could be ruthless, especially if he thought he would be keeping me out of more trouble in the long run. He also wasn't known for making idle threats.

I knew a brick wall when I was looking at it. Stubbornness on my part wouldn't break through it, but maybe I could get around it with reason. "Wouldn't it be better for Laura to stay with the boat? What if, um, a storm blows in, and, uh, the hatches need to be battened down or something? I know nothing about battening."

"The weather is fine, Howdy. No storms on the horizon."

"Why does Mark get to keep calling you that? You punched me in the nose the last time I did."

"We were eight. And *you* called me 'Howdy-Doody-In-Your-Pants.' It's not the same thing. Now, shut up. Listen, Mark—does Laura know about adaptors? Because if she doesn't, it could be pretty limiting on you guys to have her along with you. I, on the other hand, could be a big help. I can be whoever you need me to be—you name it, I'll adapt."

"Laura knows about me," Mark said.

Of course she does. Probably every little detail, I thought wryly. "But not Billy or me?"

"No," he admitted. "She suspects there are others like me, but isn't high enough up the food chain to know who they are. As far as I'm concerned, that's need to know only, and she doesn't need to know."

"Well, see? How can she possibly help you in the field more than I can?"

"She speaks Swedish fluently. I need her ears."

Well, shit.

"Okay," I conceded. "That's probably an asset. But I still don't see why I should stay here. The boat will be fine." And then inspiration struck. "Besides, if something does happen around the boat—say some Viking scouts decide to board and check it out—do you really want me in the middle of it? By myself? Using my own judgment? It might be safer all around to keep me closer to you."

Mark looked a trifle perturbed. "Is that a veiled threat, Ciel?"

"No, of course not," I said, trying to copy Billy's innocent look. Hardly veiled at all, really.

"She has a point," Billy said grudgingly. "Besides, if you leave her in the locker she'll throw up. You know, it might be best to wait for the cavalry this time."

"SÄPO will be a while yet."

"Who's Seppo?" I asked.

"More of a what," Mark explained. "It's the Swedish National Security Service. When we realized how damn many neo-Vikings have gathered here, SÄPO decided they needed to bring more men over from the mainland. But I don't think we can afford to wait. After seeing what the Vikings did to Ciel, we know how far they'll go to keep somebody quiet."

Billy nodded his understanding. I looked from one to the other. Their concern for Trey scared me. "I really can help, you know," I said.

Doubtful looks from both of them. Great. Skepticism in stereo.

Okay, so that wasn't going to work. I could lie, of course. Promise to stay on the boat, and then follow them. But I really don't like to lie, and there was that whole God thing to consider.

"I don't want to be left on the boat alone," I finally said, in a small voice. True enough, though it's possible I made it sound more pitiful than accurately reflected my worry. Exaggeration isn't as bad as lying, right? God might trip me or something, but He probably wouldn't blow me up.

Mark's mouth tightened, but I thought I saw concern thaw his eyes ever so slightly. When he finally gave in, I suppressed a cheer. "But there will be no adapting in front of anyone," he said. "We can alter your appearance the nonadaptor way—Laura will help you with that—but there's a risk the Vikings will recognize you. I still think you'd be better off here on the boat, but if you can accept those conditions, you can come along."

I threw my arms around his neck and kissed his cheek, forgetting all about my discomfort with him and Billy. "You won't be sorry."

"Well, *I'm* sorry," Billy said.

Mark gently disengaged himself from my embrace and said, sternly, "One more thing—you follow orders. You don't do a thing that hasn't been okayed by me or Billy. You got that?"

"What about Laura?"

"Or Laura. You are low man on the totem pole. The best thing you can do is stay out of our way, and don't get into any trouble."

"Aye, aye, sir!" I saluted, grinning. I couldn't believe how easy that had been.

He pinched his eyes closed between thumb and forefinger, giving a single what-have-I-agreed-to shake of his head.

Billy gripped the back of my neck, making me shiver with a sneaky caress behind my ear. "Not to worry. I'll watch her."

Mark looked at him sharply. He didn't seem all that reassured.

Laura decided to get Billy's transformation started first, in case Mark needed him sooner rather than later. She gave no indication she'd seen anything amiss earlier. Discreet of her. Mark asked me to come up on deck with him, probably to continue his lecture on the proper behavior of me. Well, he'd said I could go with them and I wasn't going to let him back out, no matter what kind of guilt trip he laid on me.

Ours was the only boat moored at the dock of the fishermen's enclave. Rows of dark-roofed, mostly barn-red cabins were evidence of human habitation, but no one was in sight at the moment. The morning was a smidge on the cool side, but puffy white clouds and a gentle breeze hinted at warmer temps to come. Mark went to the front of the boat, scanning both land and sea for anything out of the ordinary. I followed him forward.

"Go ahead. Lay it on me," I said, steeling myself for more admonitions and orders.

A short, dry laugh escaped him. "I've been hard on you, haven't I, Howdy?"

He was admitting it? "Well . . . yeah. I guess. Kind of."

He checked the rope anchoring us to the dock. Apparently it passed his inspection. "I have to be. Thomas would have my balls for breakfast if I let anything else happen to you."

Now, there was an image. I snorted, but of course in a ladylike way. "Thomas needs to cut the big brother strings. Maybe if he'd get married and have some kids of his own, he'd let up on me. He's worse than any parent."

"He'll settle down eventually. In the meantime, you'll just have to put up with him. And me."

Great. Remote nannying. "What are you, his surrogate?"

He acknowledged his role with a slight smile. "Something like that. Which brings me to what I'm going to ask you."

I set my shoulders and nodded, resigned to hearing yet another request that I behave myself and stay out of trouble, yadda-yadda-yadda. Instead, he looked me right in the eye and said, "What's going on between you and Billy?"

I stiffened. Okay, that threw me. Had Laura said something to him? Was she a great big tattletale? "Huh?" was the most intelligent response I could come up with on the spur of the moment.

"Ciel," he said after gauging my reaction, "you know I think Billy is a great guy. I rely on him—my job would be a hell of a lot harder without him. He's as much like a brother to me as Thomas is. But . . . well, he's not a man I'd want my kid sister involved with, if I had a kid sister of my own."

I felt my face go pink, but was too flustered to camouflage it. "Whatever Laura told you—"

"Laura? What does she have to do with this?"

Oops. Guess she hadn't said anything. "Uh, nothing. Nothing at all. I just thought . . . I mean . . . look, Billy's just a tease, always has been," I finished lamely.

"There's teasing, and then there's *teasing*. Billy is an expert at both. I have a feeling he's shifted direction with you since he saw you kissing me on my boat."

That startled me. "You knew he was watching?"

He shrugged. "You made some noise when you tripped. He would've checked."

Yeah. It hadn't exactly been my most graceful moment.

"I don't think he much liked seeing me in the sleeping bag with you either," Mark added, as if the reminder of my clumsiness hadn't been enough to embarrass me.

"So why aren't you talking to him about it? Why me?" I said, a little grumpily.

"And what do you think Billy would do if I told him to mind his manners around you?"

My lips twitched at the thought. "He'd tell you to shove it."

"Precisely. That's why I'm talking to you."

"What if I tell you to shove it, too?" Because I kind of felt like it.

His smile was broader this time, meant to engage cooperation. "I'm hoping you have more sense."

I reserved comment on that. "So, you're saying you think Billy would hurt me? I can't believe that."

"No, he wouldn't, not deliberately. But he is who he is, and he doesn't have a good track record with women. Or maybe too good a track record, I suppose, depending on your point of view," he said, with an attempt at humor.

I narrowed my eyes and stared him down. "First of all, I am not 'women.' Don't mistake me for one of Billy's bimbos. Second of all, it's not like that." *Much. Yet. Whatever.*

He looked skeptical, but moved on. "It's not only the women. Billy's reckless. You know he's been involved in some pretty dubious operations. I keep him as busy as I can helping me, but he refuses to give up his own business interests entirely. He's going to trip up one day, and I don't want him taking you down with him when it happens."

"He would never . . ." I stopped, since we both knew he might. Billy had always fluctuated between tempting me into trouble and pushing me back to safety. It was like he needed to know I'd follow him, but then didn't want to worry about me. I was used to being the yo-yo companion for his shenanigans. I just didn't like to think he'd play with my feelings the same way.

"Listen, Ciel," Mark said in a patient voice that was starting to grate on me. If he reverted to ruffling my hair, I was going to tenderize Thomas's breakfast for him. "It's easy to get swept up in the moment, especially with a guy like Billy. He's good-looking. Smart and funny. Add the adrenaline of a dangerous situation, and it makes everything feel that much more intense." He looked out to sea before he continued, offering me a bit of privacy from his gaze. "The . . . uh, sensations . . . can go to your head, and you might not be thinking clearly."

I balled up my hands, but kept them at my sides, which showed great restraint on my part. What he was saying might be true, but I sure as hell didn't need to hear it from him. Now, if he were giving me a better reason to stay away from Billy—say, like, "I'm wildly jealous and don't want another guy near you," for instance—it *might* be a whole 'nother ball of wax. But this pseudo big brother crap wasn't doing it for me.

I forced myself to speak evenly. "Don't worry about me. If I can handle your kiss—and I believe I somehow managed not to lose my head there, even after a few drinks—then I'm sure I'll be able to cope with Billy's attention."

He looked at me sideways, apparently amused.

"What's so funny?"

He shook his head, still suppressing a smile. "Nothing."

"Tell me," I insisted.

He shrugged. "That was you kissing me, not me kissing you."

"Oh, so there's a difference?" I didn't say *yeah, right*, but he got the subtext.

"Look, never mind. Forget it."

"No, I really want to know," I said, with an edge to my voice. A smart man might've noted the danger. Not that Mark was one to back away from danger.

"Yes, there's a difference," he said. "And if you'd ever been kissed by me, you'd know it."

I expelled a short, derisive blast of air through my nose. "Much of an ego there, Mark? Gee, I'll try my best not to swoon in your presence."

"Look, Ciel, I may have gone about this the wrong way. I didn't mean to make you mad. I'm just trying to get you to understand—"

"Understand what?" I jabbed his chest. "Reactions?" Jabbed it again. "You're one to talk. If I recall correctly, you—" (Jab.) "—reacted more than I did back on your boat. But *maybe* I'm misremembering." (Jab, jab.)

He took my hand, firmly, the flint back in his eyes. "Stop that." The patience was gone. Good riddance. "Of course I reacted. I'm human. You're human, too. That's all I'm—oh, hell."

He pulled me to him and lowered his head, stopping with his lips mere millimeters from mine.

"Shall we see if your defenses are as good as you think they are?" he said, his voice silk over steel, no doubt intended to make me run away like a frightened schoolgirl.

Ha. Fat chance.

"Give it your best shot, spook," I said, calling up a sneer, sure my anger at him would provide all the insulation I needed.

Um, yeah, about that . . .

Okay, so I was wrong. Turns out one kind of heated emotion isn't that far off another, and sometimes they even morph into each other. Kind of ironic for that to take an adaptor by surprise.

It started out tamely enough, with a brush of soft, warm lips over mine. A quick flick of his tongue gave me a start, but I returned it in kind, showing him he couldn't steamroll me. Easy, peasy. I could do it all day without breaking a sweat. But then his tongue got busier, and I may have made a small noise in the back of my throat.

That was my mistake. He latched on to my itty-bitty response—really, it hardly qualified as a moan at all—and fanned it until I couldn't have backed away, even if I'd been inclined to try. Which, to be totally honest, I wasn't. And this time I couldn't even blame the Scotch.

He was right. It *was* different, different as night and day, and he was definitely night. The summer-in-the-mountains, black velvet, stars-like-fireworks kind of night, so soft and sensual it made my skin go crazy. A little voice in my head—it sounded remarkably like my thirteen-year-old self—started squealing, *This is Mark! Mark is finally kissing you!*

I kept my breathing under control, but I couldn't do anything about my heartbeat. He had to know the effect he was having on me, that he'd accomplished his purpose within the first ten seconds of his lips touching mine, but he didn't stop. He drew it out. I knew why he was doing it, knew I should pull away, but—

Screw it. I kissed him back, letting my hands slide up his chest—geez, he had nice pecs—and behind his neck.

He dropped his arms and pulled me roughly to him, teasing me with his arousal. I pressed against him, and, okay, I wiggled. Only a little—I couldn't help it. A small part of me was angry he was right, that I was so easily sucked into the embrace, but it was subdued by the part saying, *Shut up already! Wiggle some more!* A fine time for my inner slut to make an appearance. She was even worse than my thirteen-year-old ghost of hormones past.

He groaned (breathing heavily himself, I was happy to note) and began inching apart the blanket I was still wearing, dragging the soft pile across my bare skin until it opened in front. A hot hand snaked between the folds, up to my breast, cupping it softly, grazing my nipple with the callused pad of his thumb.

Whoa. Now *there* was sensation, and damned if he wasn't right again. It *was* going straight to my head, where Inner Slut and Thirteen-Year-Old Me were fighting over who would get custody. Inner

Slut won. Thirteen was way too young for a feeling like that.

His mouth left mine—it would have been the perfect time to cry uncle, except I was half-afraid he might listen—and went exploring on my neck, from under my chin to behind my ear and back again. I bit my lip against a whimper. My neck is entirely too sensitive for its own good. As he tickled the pulse under my jaw with his tongue, his hand slid lower, finding my navel and dipping in. I was all set to protest—honest—but then his mouth was right there with mine again, and my lips decided they had better things to do than listen to my brain. I bit his bottom lip hard enough to make him suck in his breath and deepen the kiss. He *had* to be feeling this, too. It couldn't just be me.

"Hey, Mark." Laura's voice jolted me, calling from below. *Crap*. Again? I tore my lips away from Mark's. "SÄPO called. They said they'd—" She stopped when she saw us, both brows jumping this time.

Mark held me against his chest, so she wouldn't see where the blanket had come apart.

"Never mind. Tell you later." She turned and went back below.

Mark held me until my heartbeat slowed. "So, hey," I said finally, avoiding his eyes. "I, um, guess you were right about those sensations, huh? Sneaky little bastards, aren't they?"

I tried to disengage myself, but he held on to me. "Howdy, I'm sorr—"

"Don't you *dare* say it." I pushed away from

him, surprised at the strength of my reaction to his attempt at an apology. Guess I was a little upset at being caught by Laura. Twice. In a short span of time. With different guys. What must she think of me?

Shit. What did *I* think of me?

"But I shouldn't have—" Mark tried to continue.

"No, I'm the one who shouldn't have." I straightened my blanket and got hold of myself. "Look, just forget it, okay? You were right. Lesson learned, Professor Fielding. Class over. Now, hadn't you better go see what Laura wanted to tell you?"

He swore softly. "Yeah, I better. We'll pick this up later, Howdy."

"Hey, Mark," I said as he walked away. "Are *you* the kind of guy you'd want your kid sister to get involved with?"

He stopped and turned back to me, eyes serious. "No. I'm the kind of bastard I would castrate before letting him near my kid sister. Maybe you better think about that."

Chapter 26

Cripes. Think about that? On top of thinking about Billy? Oh, and why not contemplate what a skeeze Laura must think I am, while I'm at it. *Shit*. What in the hell was going on with Mark and Billy, anyway? Did Billy suddenly want me because he thought Mark did? And was Mark interested only because Billy was paying attention to me?

Fuck it all. I made up my mind. I wasn't having any more to do with either one of them after this escapade was over. I was done with the both of them. Finito. I'd redouble security at my office, so they wouldn't be able to track me on my jobs. I'd avoid family gatherings where they might be present—there had to be at least a dozen severe illnesses I could credibly fake as excuses. And if that didn't work, I could always tell Thomas. He'd kill both of them for me.

Back below, I went straight to the head, and rinsed my face with cool water until I felt in control again. I could do this. I could be strong. Helping free Trey from the Vikings would be my focus. Getting him for Mina was my job. Nothing else mattered.

Other than a half-grin and a suspicious twinkle in her eyes, Laura didn't let on that she'd seen anything unusual—thank goodness for inbred spook discretion. I had to wonder, though: if she could be so sanguine about the whole thing, maybe she *wasn't* involved with Mark. Unless the pair of them were a whole lot more open about relationships than I was.

Not that it mattered anymore, of course, since I was no longer interested.

Laura was a whiz with disguises. After being introduced to a bottle of peroxide, Billy bore more than a passing resemblance to Spike, of *Buffy the Vampire Slayer* fame. By the time she was finished with me, my hair was orangey-red, my freckles had disappeared beneath a thick layer of foundation, and my lips looked considerably thinner and paler. She said she hated to mess with my mouth, but that any man who'd ever seen it wasn't likely to forget it, so she had to.

"Your eyes are spectacular, Ciel—I've never seen such a clear, spring green," she said when she was done with my makeup. "Really distinctive. Unfortunately, distinctive is what we're trying to avoid. I have some noncorrective colored contact lenses—could you give them a try?"

I agreed, and chose a plain medium brown. I managed to get them into my eyes after several failed attempts. Not liking the way they felt, I waited until her back was turned, removed them, and adapted my own eyes to the same color. Surely that wasn't cheating. Though judging by the gleeful look on Billy's face, *he* considered it cheating.

She didn't have to do much to herself because she had barely been in view since they'd arrived in Sweden, and of course Mark was free to adapt at will. He didn't have to do a thing except put on a costume, in hopes of blending in at the periphery of the Viking group. Laura, Billy, and I wore typical, touristy day-hiker clothing made of state-of-the-art synthetic materials in various shades of tan. Ho-hum.

The plan was to get as close as we could to the Viking encampment, under the pretext of bird watching. With luck, Laura would overhear enough to tell us if they were holding Trey there, and what their plans were. If our presence was detected and questioned, we would feign total ignorance of anything other than Gotland's bird life.

According to the new passports Laura had modified for us by making good use of a digital camera and compact photo printer, she was now Rose, Billy was Hubert (which made me laugh and him wince), and I was Sarah. Mark gave us a brief inspection after we were fully outfitted. I refused to meet his eyes.

He lifted my chin and said, "Look at me, Ciel."

I did, but kept my lips compressed. I had nothing to say to him. He turned my head from side to side, in full professional mode, his manner giving no hint of the passionate embrace we'd shared. I knew good and well he could tell I wasn't wearing the contacts, but he couldn't call me on it in front of Laura. Finally he said, "You'll do." He barely looked at Billy and Laura as he left, trusting them to handle their disguises without supervision.

Fifteen minutes later, after receiving the designated signal via text message, the rest of us followed. Billy had found a prescription-less pair of black-framed glasses in Laura's bag of tricks, and was wearing them to dorky effect while training his binoculars on every passing feathered creature. He assumed a slightly pigeon-toed walk that totally altered his gait, and would have cracked me up but for the warning look Laura gave me. I knew I couldn't keep up something like that myself for any length of time, so I didn't even try. Laura's transformation of my face and hair would have to do for me.

I hung my binoculars around my neck, got out my book, and tried to look fascinated by nature. It would have been a nice outing under most other circumstances. Heck, if I was honest with myself, I was having fun under *these* conditions, as long as I kept my head in the moment, and didn't think too much about Mark or Billy. No wonder it wasn't difficult for covert agencies to recruit people to do this stuff—it was a rush.

We walked for a mile, maybe a little more, never

far from civilization but sticking to the wooded areas, with Billy checking his compass every now and then in a big, nerdy production. I doubt he needed it—he had the most obnoxiously keen sense of direction of anybody I knew—but it fit in with Hubert's persona. I, on the other hand, would have been lost inside fifty yards, even with the compass. When it comes to directions, I depend upon the kindness of strangers. Honking big landmarks help, too.

As we neared our destination, we came upon our first neo-Viking. The tall, barrel-chested, ginger-bearded fellow seemed amiable enough as he approached, greeting us in Swedish. Laura answered him in kind, and asked him a question, also in Swedish. After hearing his response, she grinned and said, in English, "Pretty good, Mark. I wouldn't take you for a Swede, but you pass—barely—for a somewhat slow Dane trying to speak schoolroom Swedish."

A hearty laugh rumbled through him. "You got me. Now, let's go—I need you to listen for me. I heard Trey's name mentioned again, but couldn't cipher out the details. If we hurry, they may still be discussing him."

"What now?" I asked Billy once they were gone.

"Now we work our way closer to the camp, looking at all of our fine, feathered friends. I need to get myself better situated to help. Presupposing Mark is right about what he heard."

"Okay," I said, falling into step beside him. "Um, how precisely do you propose to get Trey? Their team is a little bigger than ours, in case you haven't noticed."

He shrugged. "I don't think about the bridges."

"Bridges?"

"You know—the ones you cross when you get to them—I don't think about those. Something will come up. There'll be an opening, and we'll take it."

"Oh." It didn't sound like the most reassuring of plans to me, but since I didn't have a better one to offer, what else could I say?

We wandered on, moving quickly without appearing to be rushed, Billy sweeping the area visually with his binoculars, making occasional, clearly audible comments to me about this or that bird. "Oh, my God," he gushed in a loud whisper, sounding like he meant to be quiet but just couldn't contain himself. "Is that a Radde's Warbler? Could it be? It is!"

I lifted my binoculars and pointed them where he indicated. Saw a small, brownish bird with a lighter underbelly, and what looked like long, cream-colored eyebrows.

"Why, yes. I believe you're right. Shall I, um, make note of it?" I said, and then added, ultra-low volume, barely moving my lips, "How the hell do you know what bird that is?"

"I paged through the book while we were waiting for Mark to call. Didn't you?" he said.

Not actually, no. A bit of musical birdsong interrupted before I had to admit it, though. I scanned the area. "Did you hear that? Why, that's a . . . what would you say that is, Hubert?"

"My phone," he said drily.

Well, how clever to think of programming bird-call ringtones, just exactly as bird geeks might do, I thought, irritated for no valid reason. Weren't Billy and Mark just so good at everything. Sailing. Spying. Kissing. Why not ringtones? I kicked a rock.

Okay, so maybe I was ticked about the kisses. Both of them. And maybe, if I were honest with myself, I was more ticked about my reaction to the kisses than the fact that either one of them had kissed me. Ticked and confused.

Crap. Being honest with yourself *sucks*.

Billy slid open the tiny device. "Hubert here." He listened intently for several seconds. "Where? . . . Is he still . . . ? . . . Got it."

My cranky confusion was doused by a sudden splash of adrenaline. "What? Did they find Trey? Is it time?" I whispered urgently. "Are we going to bust him out? Did anybody bring a gun?"

Billy laid his hand over my mouth and spoke softly. "Laura thinks she knows where they have Trey, but they could be moving him at any time. It won't be a simple extraction. We—by which I mean Mark, Laura, and I—are going to try to sneak him out without being noticed by the horde. *You* are going to head back to the boat—"

"But I can—"

"The boat," he repeated firmly. "You will wait there, out of sight, until one of us calls you. Mark decided it was too dangerous for a civilian around their camp after all. The natives are getting restless."

I opened my mouth to argue. Thought ahead to the likely outcome. "Okay," I said instead. Agreeably, seeing as he was in a hurry.

For some reason, that seemed to piss him off.

"Damn it, Ciel. I mean it. If you don't do as I say, next time I'll throw you in the locker myself, screw your claustrophobia. You are *not* going to get into the middle of this and get yourself hurt."

His eyes were thunderclouds behind the dark frames. I got the feeling if he removed the glasses, I'd be struck by lightning.

"I said okay, didn't I?"

He still looked totally suspicious. Huh. Some people.

"So what are you waiting for? Go," he said gruffly.

"All right, I'm going." After two steps, I looked back over my shoulder at him. "Um, which way?"

"The way we just came," he said, not very patiently.

I looked around. "And that would be . . . ?"

"Good God, you mean that, don't you? You have no idea how we got here, do you? Weren't you paying attention at all?"

"Well, I was following you. It got kind of twisty there at the end," I said defensively.

He took a deep breath and walked me over to a large evergreen. "Sit," he said.

I sat, settling myself comfortably on a blanket of rusty-brown pine needles.

"Now, get out your bird book and binoculars, and start finding birds. Do not move from this spot. If a Viking approaches you, play dumb. Shouldn't be tough." The last bit was under his breath as he turned to go, but I heard it.

He fell for that, and he thought *I* was dumb?

Ha. We'd just see about that. I spent a few minutes doing exactly as I was told, sure he would double back and check on me at least once. He did; I pretended to be too intent on following his instructions to see him.

Like hell was I going to walk meekly back to the boat and wait while the big kids played, even if I *could* remember the way back. I had a backlog of missed games in my past, the ones that were deemed by my brothers, and later Mark, to be too rough for me.

Billy would always egg me on to play—at first—but then, just when the game got good, he'd gang up with the rest of the guys and shove me off the field.

I'd swallowed it then, but not anymore. I was an adult, and I'd damn well decide for myself how much danger I was willing to risk, just like the rest of them. If I got into trouble, they didn't have to follow me—it was their choice, and I refused to feel guilty about it.

Once I figured Billy wouldn't come back again I got up and headed out at a ninety-degree angle from the way he'd gone, sure he was too slick to head straight for the encampment. Deplorable sense of direction notwithstanding, I had a pretty good idea of which way to go. For one thing, the Vikings were a raucous group, and they were getting louder, working themselves up over something, so I just followed the noise.

My binoculars helped, too, once I got the hang of aiming them between the trees. The first time I got a clear view of the ship-grave site, I was astounded by the number of costumed men. More even than had been around the trebuchet—a hundred, at least.

The high resolution brought their faces into sharp, close focus, giving me the eerie sensation of being right there among them. When my eyes landed on Per's face he was staring right at me. Startled, I dropped the binoculars. The jerk of the leather strap on my neck snapped some sense back into me—he couldn't possibly see me from this distance.

I lifted the field glasses again, reassuring myself the characteristic sneer warping his grotesquely handsome face wasn't for me. His sight was trained on some other lucky bastard. I shifted slightly to see if I could make out who. Okay, there . . . light brown, sun-streaked hair, slightly too long and somewhat mussed.

My stomach tightened. It was Trey. It looked like his hands were tied behind him, and he was flanked by giants. The side of his face was puffy and a thin line of blood trickled from a corner of his beautiful mouth. Mina was going to be so pissed.

There was no way Mark was going to be able to get him out without more help than Billy and Laura could provide. And it was still a long time before we could expect any backup from Swedish security.

"*Är du borta?*" a pleasantly male Swedish voice rumbled behind me.

I jumped, and dropped my binoculars, the strap jerking my neck downward yet again. Plastering a big, touristy smile on my face, I turned around. Though decked out in the proper gear, he wasn't especially tall for a Viking, nor excessively bulky. Must not have drunk the Kool-Aid yet. Palms up, I gestured my puzzlement. "I'm afraid I don't speak Swedish. Do you speak English?"

He smiled. "Of course. It is necessary in today's world, *ja*? All Swedes must know some English."

I feigned relief. "I'm so glad. Maybe you can help me—I seem to be a little lost."

"I thought this. It is what I asked you when I approached." He seemed pleased with himself.

"I sailed here with some friends," I started. Best to stick to the truth as much as possible. Made things less complicated. Of course, the truth would only carry you so far. "To watch birds. We, um, split up to cover more territory, and get more pictures of, uh, birds." I smiled feebly.

His eyes lit up. "Ah, you are adding to your life list? *Vad bra!* This is good. What have you seen today?"

The smile froze on my face. A bird-watching neo-Viking? Shit. I tried to remember the bird Billy had mentioned. What the hell was it? Oh, yeah. "Riddy's Warbler?" I said, praying it was close enough.

He paused while I held my breath, then said, "*Ja, ja*, this is good. A happy little fellow, this warbler. Have you seen also the *Columba palumbus*?"

What the hell was that? Better claim not. "Not today. So hard to spot sometimes, aren't they?"

He laughed in agreement, but his eyes narrowed on me. "Come," he said, taking my hand enthusiastically. "I shall show you some. I know where there is a huge nest of them."

I tried to stay where I was. "Hey, wait. I can't leave here—my friends might miss me."

"I will bring you back later. They will understand—what birder would miss a rare opportunity to see the *Columba palumbus*?" He pulled me along, leaving me no time to ponder the touch of irony I thought I'd detected in his voice.

He brought me to a huge nest, all right. A huge nest of Vikings. Never letting go of my hand for an instant, he marched me up to a large group of men milling around near the standing stones of the ship-grave. At the center of the men, with a remarkable shiner, was Nils.

"*Hej*, Nils," my bird guide said, followed by more Swedish. I looked at my shoes, willing myself to evaporate. Like most of my wishes, it didn't happen. But, I comforted myself, at least it wasn't Per.

"*Vad har vi här?*" Nils said, which I took to mean something like "what's this?" He walked over to me and raised my head with two fingers under my chin, the familiar half-smile lifting one corner of his mouth . . . until recognition filled his eyes, and his detached control was replaced with shock.

Chapter 27

"She calls herself a birder, and she doesn't recognize the scientific name for a wood pigeon. She must be a spy," my birding buddy gloated. In English, so I'd be sure to realize just how stupid I'd been.

Well, damn. I'd walked right into that one.

"Thank you, Johan. I will take care of this," Nils said, never losing his authority.

My hand was transferred to his, and I felt two small squeezes. I thought I saw relief, and maybe happiness, in his eyes, but my track record with men being what it was recently, I tried not to let myself get too excited about it.

"Come with me, miss. We will have a talk." His words dripped double meaning, and the men around us laughed knowingly.

He led me through the woods beyond the ship

setting, sticking to the side opposite from where I'd seen Per with Trey. Again, I had to move double-time to keep up with his long stride, and again he didn't seem inclined to speak to me until we got to wherever he was taking me. I didn't press it.

Beyond the wooded area was a road, and across the road there was a farm. *The* farm. The one I'd escaped from before. Crap. Right back into the fuckity-fucking frying pan. He made a beeline for it, not stopping until we were in a barn at the far end of a field.

A double row of cows, their heads poking out between the metal bars in front of their stalls, stared placidly at us while they munched on what-ever fine grain product was laid out in front of them. Apparently it was a dairy farm. The aroma was . . . well, it smelled like cow shit. No real grace-ful way to put that.

Once the door was closed behind us, Nils grabbed me up in a huge hug, lifting me from the ground and rocking me side to side. "Ciel? Is it really you? You are alive?"

Laughter bubbled up inside me at his apparent joy. "Yes. I'm alive. But if you don't stop squeezing me so hard, I may not be for long."

"Sorry," he said, putting me down. "But Per said—all of the men said—you were . . ."

"Launched out to sea from that giant slingshot, and left to drown? Yeah, that pretty much hap-pened. I decided not to drown, though."

"My God, I was so angry, so sorry I couldn't do anything—but what have you done to yourself?

You dyed your hair, and your eyes—where are your beautiful green eyes?"

"Oh! Well, uh, I'm in disguise. Colored contacts. Just a second—" I leaned away from him, pretended to take out the lenses, and mimed flicking them into a nearby pile of straw. A quick adjustment, and my eyes were my own color again. "Better?"

"Much. And this . . ." He lifted his arm and wiped my lips with his sleeve, scrubbing thoroughly to rid it of all traces of Laura's makeup. "There. That is what I remember."

"Nils, we have to talk. You have to leave here. SÄPO is coming, they'll be here soon, and you'll be arrested with all the others."

He smiled. "SÄPO is already here. I am SÄPO."

My first thought was, *I knew it! He is a good guy.* I made myself question it, though. "But you're with Per. You kidnapped Mina. You killed Pete, for God's sake! Or let Per do it, which is just as bad."

"I killed no one. That was a tranquilizer pistol. I had to make sure I shot first, because Per's gun had real bullets."

I was so relieved I felt like I could float up to the ceiling. "So Per thought you killed Pete?"

"Yes. With a silencer on the pistol. Fortunately, Pete fell forward, and there was no time for Per to notice a lack of bleeding. After that, Per had no reason to doubt my loyalty to his cause. As for kidnapping . . . well, when one is undercover, one must do many things that are not precisely law-abiding."

"Okay. Right. I understand that. But Per is going

to kill Trey. Soon. We can't let that happen." I grabbed his arm and tried to pull him toward the door. "Come *on*, let's go."

He didn't budge. "No, we must wait."

"What? Are you crazy? We have to go arrest Per—now, before somebody gets hurt."

"I will find a way to free Trey," he said. "But I can't stop things right now. This has been the plan all along—we must catch them in the act of something very bad, or it would only be a light sentence for them. We would like to send them to prison for a longer time."

"How can you be sure Per won't hurt Trey sooner rather than later?" I pressed.

He put his hands on my shoulders, thumbs under my ears so I had to look up into his eyes, and spoke seriously. "Per will not give up the ceremony he has planned for this evening. He believes reenacting a Viking human sacrifice will bind the men to his cause."

"Vikings sacrificed *people*?"

"Yes, it happened. Often slaves from other cultures. In Per's mind, since Trey is American, this makes him suitable. But the timing of the ritual is important to him. He will keep Trey alive until then. I will go back soon and make sure of it. You must trust me on this, Ciel."

"Okay, okay. I believe you. You can stop tickling my neck now."

He stepped back and brought both his hands in front of me, holding them palms up. "I'm not tickling you."

The sensation continued, only now it was creepy. "Then what—*Oh, shit!*"

"What? What is it?" Nils took me by the shoulders and turned me around.

"Get it off! Get it off!" I jumped up and down, waving my arms like a madwoman.

"Wait. Be still . . . I can't . . . it crawled down under your collar."

"Aaaack!" I yanked my shirttail out of my pants and pulled the garment off in a flash, but I still felt tiny legs. My T-shirt came off next. When I saw a small, dark spot scurry across it, I flung it away from me with superhuman force. It landed behind the bars of the farthest stall, right in a fresh, moist pile of cow dung.

Laughter erupted next to me. I narrowed my eyes at Nils, and most decidedly did *not* laugh. He composed himself.

"It was only a tiny spider. It wouldn't hurt you."

I shuddered. "Yeah, well, I hate spiders."

"I never cared for them much either, but I think I like that small fellow." There was a new glint in the big Swede's crystalline eyes as I stood before him in the pretty little bra Laura had rinsed and dried for me after my unexpected swim in the sea. He seemed to appreciate Billy's taste in lingerie.

I picked up my other shirt, shaking it briskly before I slipped it back over my head. "Don't you have a rescue to get to?"

His sigh was full of regret. "I suppose so. But first we must discuss what you will do—"

"Don't worry, I know."

"What do you know?"

"I know I should stay here while you go and do whatever you need to do. I know if Per sees me it could cause all sorts of problems, including more bodily harm to me."

He nodded his approval. "I will come back and get you when everything is over. Now, what will you do while I am gone? It may take a long while."

"Oh, I'll keep myself entertained somehow. I'll talk to the cows. I'll play tag with spiders. Whose farm is this, anyway?"

"My uncle's, but I have a small cottage here also. Not so fine as the big house, but pleasant enough for short visits." Huh. I begged to differ, but of course kept my mouth shut. "I would have taken you there, but it has become our local head-quarters, and Per might find you."

Ugh. "No, no . . . this is fine. Really."

He patted my arm, understanding, and turned to go. At the door, he paused and said, "A neighbor is looking after the cows while my uncle is on vaca-tion. If you hear somebody coming, hide in the third stall on the left. She's a nice cow, and will try not to step on you."

I waited five minutes and followed him, figuring he was more trusting than Billy and wouldn't come back to check on me. I felt a little guilty about de-ceiving such a nice guy, but I really didn't lie to him. My exact words were, "I know I should stay here," not "I will stay here." It wasn't my fault if he wasn't attuned to the nuances of English.

I needed to find Billy and Mark, and let them know about Nils. As close as they might be to the Vikings now, I didn't dare use my cell phone. I'd have to see if I could get their attention quietly. Then maybe they could communicate with Nils somehow before Per's ceremony that evening, whatever the hell that was going to involve. Between all of them, maybe they would be able to save Trey.

Circling the encampment as closely as I dared, which was not close at all, I looked for some sign of Billy or Mark, or even Laura. Maybe especially Laura—she wasn't as likely to jump down my throat for not doing as I was told.

For once in this whole ill-starred adventure, I got my wish. Laura dropped down right in front of me, from the branches of one of the taller pines, landing noiselessly on her feet.

"Ciel? What are you doing here? Billy said he left you guarding a spot closer to the boat."

Guarding? Yeah, right. I laughed out loud at that one. "Thanks for trying, Laura, but I know darn well Billy told you he sat me in the proverbial corner and tied me there with threats. He didn't really think I'd stay, did he?"

She grinned. "He hoped, but I knew better."

"Where are they?"

"Mark's scouting for a likely candidate he can stand in for to get closer to Trey. We weren't able to take him from the Viking's impromptu prison tent—it was too heavily guarded, and besides, Per keeps hauling him out to play his sadistic little games."

I shuddered. "That guy is such an asshole. Where's Billy?"

"He should be up a tree on the other side of the camp, keeping an eye on things from there. If he's not looking for you, that is," she said with a tiny, disingenuous smile.

I flushed a bit, but tried to laugh it off. I didn't have time to explain things to her right now. Not that I understood any of it myself. "Listen, Laura, I found out something important—don't ask me how, I'll explain it later." Or not. "Nils—he's the other guy in charge, along with Per—isn't a neo-Viking. He's with SÄPO. He's undercover, like Trey."

She shrugged. "Yeah, I know. Nils is a pal of mine."

I stared at her. "You know him?"

"Of course. He helped me a lot with my Swedish."

"Does Mark know? Does Billy?" Did every-fucking-body but me know?

"I don't know about Billy, but Mark knows—why wouldn't he? It's why he didn't call in the whole Agency to get you out after you were snatched—he knew Nils wouldn't let anything too horrible happen to you."

I remembered being jabbed with the needle on the plane while Nils held me down. "Huh. Well, that's a matter of opinion."

"Listen, Ciel. I know this whole experience has been hard on you, but if we'd had to go in with guns blazing, our whole operation would've been jeopardized. You understand, don't you?" She sounded sympathetic, and probably was, but I detected the hint of a ruthless streak. Guess it went with the job description.

I sighed. "Yeah, I suppose."

"I knew you would. You would've made a great agent," she said, with either sincere or skillfully faked admiration. I wanted to believe it was real.

"Well, what do we do now?" I asked, determined not to think about anything that would distract me from the task at hand. Time enough to stew later.

"You could be a big help if you head in that direction"—she pointed—"about a hundred yards or so, shimmy up a sturdy-looking tree, and keep your field glasses aimed toward the camp. Call me if you see anything that strikes you as odd."

"Rosie-girl," I said, proud that I remembered her incognito name, "this whole situation strikes me as odd. But I'll do my best."

Chapter 28

The pine I chose wasn't overly tall, but it was densely branched enough to provide good camouflage. I only fell on my ass twice before I managed to monkey my way up high enough to grab a branch. Once seated as securely as possible, I got out my binoculars and looked back to where I'd left Laura. She was hidden too well in the branches of her own tree for me to make her out, but I thought I saw a flash of light from one of her lenses.

I scanned the rest of the area and found I had a decent enough view of the camp. I could make out the shape of the biggest ship-grave, and a boatload (so to speak) of Vikings milling around it. I guessed they'd all start getting more organized when the time for the ceremony approached. Nils had said evening, but that was a pretty broad time frame in Sweden this time of year. Did he mean evening by the clock, which would be here soon enough, I reckoned, or did he mean evening by the setting sun, which would be much later?

I hoped it was the former, because my legs were going to cramp up if I had to sit still for long. Also, I was going to need a ladies' room pretty soon. The urge to pee was only a small nudge in my bladder now, but I knew from experience how fast that could balloon into dire need.

Of course, once I started thinking about it, the need for relief snowballed. Crap. Guys had it so easy. In the first place, most of them had bladders like horses—they could hold it forever, and then pee buckets. Women—me, anyway—weren't so fortunate.

I'd have crossed my legs if I could have without falling. I supposed if I got desperate enough I could climb back down and find a place to squat, but exposing my privates to whatever creepy-crawlies might inhabit the woodland floor was unappealing, and besides, it would take time away from my lookout duties.

There was one other option open to me, however, if I dared.

I lifted my binoculars and did as much of a circular sweep as I could without breaking my neck. No one near enough to worry about, except possibly Laura. Hugging the trunk, I inched around to the side of the tree opposite where she was posted, and adapted to the first small-enough male aura I thought of (Stanley, a code monkey friend of a friend, with no people skills whatsoever, who'd needed help landing a job—I got him through the interview process, and he'd been happily and solitarily writing computer programs ever since), unzipped my fly, and started emptying out. This, I thought with a sigh, was the biggest advantage to being male. You could urinate outside without getting your feet wet.

"Tell me you are *not* peeing on my head," Billy's appalled voice wafted up from below.

Aack! I couldn't believe it. When had he snuck up on me? My stupid luck strikes again.

If I'd been a girl caught peeing, I could've stopped on a dime. Guys do not have the same ability, at least not the one I'd picked. The stream continued for several seconds, in spite of my best effort to bring it to a halt. As soon as I shook off the last dribble, I adapted back to myself and hastily zipped up.

"What are you doing there? You're *supposed* to be on the other side of the camp." When cornered, you may as well attack first.

"What am I doing? Getting wet, that's what. Now, get your ass down here—we need to talk."

"About what?" I stalled.

"About why you're not where you're supposed to be, for one."

Oh, that. "Can't it wait? I'm kinda busy."

"Now." There was a world of threat in that one word. I sighed and started climbing down. If I didn't, he'd just climb up after me. When I got there, he was pouring a bottle of drinking water over his hair and face, scrubbing vigorously.

"Uh, sorry about that. I didn't know you were there. Honest." I stifled my laughter, but not very effectively, so I also kept my distance.

"Jesus, cuz, if I'd known you were into water sports, I'd have worn my raincoat." He sounded grumpy, but there was a hint of laughter beneath his words, so I knew he wasn't really mad.

He stripped off his shirt and threw it on the ground. His pants had somehow escaped the shower, so he left them on, and after a quick rinse of his chest and arms, he shook off most of the water. "Give me your shirt."

"What?" I squeaked.

"Come on, I need a shirt. You have a T-shirt on under it, don't you? I saw Laura give you one. Besides, you have an extra thermal in your pack if you need it later. I didn't get one of those. Silly me, not planning ahead for the odd rain of piss."

I chewed the inside of my cheek. I really didn't want to have to tell him about the spider, or for that matter, the pile of cow dung. It was too embarrassing. He already had enough to tease me about without adding more ammo to his arsenal. "Wouldn't you rather have my thermal?"

"Nah. Too tight for me. The shirt you're wearing looks baggy enough on you that it'll work for me. Come on, give it." He held out a hand, impatient.

"Just a second." I took off the pack and rummaged through it for the thermal. "You know, I think this would fit you. A little snug, maybe, but that's okay—it would show off your manly physique."

"Ciel . . ." he said suspiciously, walking toward me.

"It's your color, too. Tan is just the thing to set off your eyes. It's all about the contrast. I learned that watching *What Not to Wear*." I backed away, holding the shirt up between us. "It deepens them to midnight blue, really attractive."

He followed, until he had me backed up against the tree. Looming over me, he hooked one finger into the front of my shirt, lifted it away from my chest, and peeked down. "Ciel, where's your T-shirt?" he asked conversationally, but his eyes drilled into mine.

"I, um, got a little warm, so I took it off?"

"So it's in your pack."

"No. Because I, uh, lost it."

"Ciel?"

He wasn't stepping back, and neither was the tree. I swallowed again. "That's my name."

"Where did Nils take you when he escorted you from the camp earlier?"

"You saw that?"

"Yeah, cuz. I notice things. Like, your eyes are green again, and the makeup Laura put on your mouth has somehow been rubbed off. Had a little help with that part, did you?"

His voice was still nerve-rackingly even-keeled. It was making me edgy. When I get edgy, I get testy. "Well, if you saw a freaking Viking taking me away, then why in the hell didn't you do something about it?"

"Nils isn't a Viking. He's with SÄPO. I knew he

wouldn't kill you, and my attention was otherwise occupied with trying to find a way to save Trey."

"Wait a minute—you knew all along Nils wasn't a Viking?"

He shrugged. "Not all along. Mark told me after he got here."

"Did you know when you clobbered him on the beach?"

"Maybe."

"Billy, how *could* you?"

His eyes narrowed. "He hit you. I didn't like that."

"But you were going to just leave him there, hurt, on the beach!"

"Look, Ciel, Nils is a professional. He's undercover. I wouldn't have been doing him any favor by taking him out of the game. Now stop avoiding my question. Where did he take you?"

"His uncle has a farm right across the road. Nils had the idea I might be safer there, away from Per."

"Can't fault his reasoning. A farm, huh? That would explain the aroma of"—he sniffed me rudely—"dung."

"There were cows," I said haughtily.

"And was there a handy haystack?" He pulled a piece of straw from the hair at my nape, and flicked it away disdainfully.

"None of your business."

Speculation grew in his eyes. "Better watch yourself, cuz. I think you're getting a little too caught up in . . . things."

"Oh, for God's sake, do you and Mark get

together and compare scripts?" I pushed him away
and stomped off a few paces. My back to him, I
removed my shirt and tossed it over my shoulder at
him, then pulled the thermal quickly over my head.

"Great," he muttered. "Now I get to smell like
piss *and* shit."

"You washed off all the pee, and the shirt will
air out soon. Get over it. Now, if you'll excuse me,
I'm going back up the tree. I have a camp to
watch."

He caught my arm and held me back. There was
something in his eyes I couldn't quite read. "Tell
me you didn't sleep with him."

What? He thought I . . . ? I flushed. With embarrassment at first, but anger quickly overcame that.
What gave him the right to judge me?

"I fail to see how that is any concern of yours,"
I said, my words clipped.

He swore. "For God's sake, you've known him
what? Two days? What are you trying to do, make
up for lost time?"

"What's that supposed to mean?"

"Well, you've only slept with two men in your
whole life—that loser back in college, and the asshole lawyer your brother wound up firing. I'm assuming you must be feeling a little deprived if
you're jumping into the hayloft with the first Viking who kidnaps you."

"What makes you think those are the only two?
Maybe I've slept with every guy I ever went out
with, like you do with your women," I flung at him.

"You haven't," he said, mouth tight.

Okay, now I *wanted* him to think I had slept with Nils. "How can you be sure? Because I'm a girl? Sauce for the goose, Billy."

"Remember when I told you I couldn't decipher your diary? I lied."

"Ha. If that were true, you'd know I never slept with the lawyer, he just spread rumors that I did."

I clamped my mouth shut, upset that I'd given that away. It didn't say much for my appeal that the loser back in college had been the only guy I'd ever had. Or, rather, halfway had. The boy had barely breached the ramparts before his ammunition was spent. It was downright embarrassing for both of us, and he'd never asked me out again. Still, I counted it.

Billy's whole manner softened. He brushed a thumb over my hot cheek. "Don't you see? I just don't want you to get hurt."

My anger left me in a rush. "I didn't sleep with Nils. There was a spider. It fell down my neck. I had to take off both shirts to get it off me, and my T-shirt landed in a pile of . . ." I trailed off when I saw the stark relief in his eyes.

After a minute his dimples appeared. "A spider, huh? Bet you jumped a mile."

"Tell me about it." I shuddered again, just at the memory.

"So, was it a big spider?" His eyes laughed and his hand walked up my arm, fingers wiggling like little legs.

I jumped back and slapped it away. "See? That's just why I didn't want to tell you—I *knew* you'd do that. Now leave."

"Aw, come on. I'm sorry." He pulled me into a hug and stroked my back with a flat hand. No more spider fingers.

I looked up at him. "Billy . . . I have to have a life, too. I can't just watch you guys from the sidelines forever."

He took a deep breath, and let it out slowly while something warred in his eyes. Finally, he gave my hair a tug and said, his voice soft and serious, "Right. I understand. But when you get into the game, just remember I'm on the playing field, too."

Chapter 29

Billy left without another word. I scurried back up my tree, and did *not* think about what I thought I'd read in his eyes.

Instead, I watched the stupid camp until my eyes blurred. Twice I saw Trey dragged from his tent and hauled before Per, who questioned him, slapped him, and sent him back. He must not have liked the answers. Nils was there with them both times; his face tightened when Per hit Trey, and once, when Per was about to use a fist instead of an open hand to strike, he held Per's arm back.

The sun was getting low in the sky when the vibration from my cell phone gave me an unexpected thrill. I dug it out of my pocket and flipped it open. "Yeah. Uh, Sarah here."

"I've heard from our friend." Laura's voice—she must mean Mark. "We're going in. The cavalry has

been held up. Stay where you are and keep a lookout for them, and when they get here, tell them
what we've done."

She hung up before I could argue with her. Did
she think I was just going to sit back and watch the
three of them—well, four, counting Nils—go up
against a hundred Vikings? Those suckers were
big. They had swords, and knives, and God knew
what other kind of medieval weapons . . . and I
would be about as useful under the circumstances
as a parasol in a hurricane. So I stayed put and
prayed SÄPO would hurry their asses up.

Through the binoculars I saw Laura and Billy
approach the camp together, looking like curious
tourists. From their gestures, I could tell they were
asking about the spectacle, maybe inquiring if it
were some sort of reenactment exercise. What
would they do? Make a distraction of some sort, I
guessed, so Mark could get to Trey.

Which one was Mark? No way to know—there
were too many possibilities. Was he even close
enough to Trey to do any good? I just didn't see how
Laura and Billy could create a big enough ruckus to
get the attention of all the Vikings at once. Even if
they pulled out some handy weapons, numbers
alone would overwhelm them.

As if to prove my point, one of the big guys
clapped an arm over Billy's shoulders. Another did
the same from the other side, and *voila!* Billy sandwich. His struggles did no good—he was held im-
mobile.

Only one Viking attempted the same with Laura,

and got a foot in his face for his troubles. Damn. I
didn't know anybody could kick that high, that
fast. The big galoot went over like a felled tree. For
all the good it did Laura. As soon as the Viking
went down, three more were on top of her.

Pain flared at the tip of my left index finger. *Shit*.
I spit out a piece of fingernail and sucked off a
drop of blood. I couldn't just sit here waiting for
SÄPO. I'd be down to my knuckles before long.

I shook my hand. *Shit, shit, shit*. It stung.

Wait a minute—that was it! Shit.

I dropped from the tree, sliding down the trunk
like it was a fireman's pole. I ran—faster than I ever
had before—straight back to the farm. They needed
a distraction, I'd give them a distraction.

The truck was still behind the barn, just where it
had been the last time I saw it. Only this time there
was a man with it. Crap. Apparently Nils's neighbor was getting ready to fertilize the fields.

The driver's seat was empty—the neighbor was
in back of the rig, piping more of the oozy brown
glop into the back of the truck from a holding
tank. The ultimate in recycling—straight from the
cows to the field, to help grow the grass to feed
the cows.

I chewed my bottom lip, debating whether to
enlist the neighbor's aid. He could be a major help,
since he knew how to operate the machinery, but
what if he just thought I was crazy? At best, he
could shoo me off the property; at worst, hold me
until the authorities came. There was no time for
that, or for the lengthy explanations it would take

even if I could somehow convince him I wasn't a lunatic.

So I'd just have to take the truck and do it myself.

How close was he to topping off the tank? I had no idea, and I didn't plan to wait long enough to find out. I snuck to the front of the truck, opened the door just enough to squeeze through, and slid myself into the driver's seat. No keys, but that was okay. It was an old truck; getting it started shouldn't be a problem.

To my right, rising up from the floor below the dash, was a control panel I guessed was connected to the distribution system. I couldn't read the few words printed on it, but I assumed the buttons were "on" and "off," and the lever controlled the flow. I'd find out soon enough.

Scooting to the edge of the seat, I reached under the dash and pulled out a bunch of wires. Selected the right ones, peeled back the insulation, touched them together. The engine turned over at once, purring like a large, loud cat.

Thank you, Billy, for being such a delinquent, and for showing off to me.

I released the emergency brake, jammed the truck into drive, and stomped on the gas. There was a tug when I got to the end of the big hose filling the tank, but it didn't slow me down. Nor did the vision of one very surprised neighbor dancing in my rearview mirror. I pressed the pedal harder and left him to his jig, putting my eyes back where they belonged—on what was in front of me.

Crap! Cars. Coming from both directions on the previously deserted road.

I couldn't afford to slow down, so I sucked in a panicked breath, made an executive decision, and did the next best thing—I closed my eyes and stepped on the gas.

Brakes squealed, and the smell of burning rubber permeated the air. When I dared peek, only two cars had run off the road. Both drivers were waving their arms and making rude gestures, so I knew they weren't hurt. That was good.

Also, I hadn't hit a tree. That was better.

I rattled over the bumpy terrain, dodging pines, butt bouncing on the seat, teeth snapping together in jaw-jarring clashes. It might have been wise to fasten my seat belt. Too late now.

As I neared the encampment, I crossed my fingers and pushed a button. If it didn't work, I'd be shit out of luck. Literally. Then all I'd be able to do was run down as many of the Vikings as I could. The thought made me queasy, but I'd do it to save my friends.

There was a sputtering, followed by a loud, metallic groan. I held my breath. After a small eternity, there appeared the most beautiful sight I ever saw—liquid poo, flying high.

"Woo-hoo!" I yelled to nobody in particular, playing with the lever to adjust the flow. "Get out your parasol, Per, you son of a bitch. The perfect shitstorm is heading your way."

The first of the Vikings to notice me—a few sentries posted on the outskirts—stood and stared, mouths agape, until they finally figured out I wasn't stopping. They jumped out of the way and went running for the gravesite, yelling. I followed, sticking close.

The nearer I got, the thicker the Vikings got, and the more they had to scramble to get out of my way. But none were fast enough to escape the flying shit. They tried, though. Boy, did they try—they parted like the Red Sea, leaving me bearing down on the small central group standing in the middle of the boat grave.

Trey and Laura were held by two Vikings each, gagged, arms stretched out to their sides. Billy was on his knees, hands tied behind his back. One Viking was behind him, with a knife to his throat.

Per, sword in hand, on his way to do something unspeakable to Trey and Laura, was pulled up short by my arrival.

I couldn't plow through the standing stones without doing considerable damage, not only to the ancient site, but also to the vehicle I was in, and quite possibly to the people I was trying to help. So I leaned on the horn and veered left, maneuvering the tank into position for maximum coverage.

The odorous slurry coated them all like fudge sauce glopped on an ice cream sundae. I let loose a hoot of laughter at the look on Per's face—what I could see of it, anyway, covered as it was. Surprise would be an understatement. Total, pole-axed disbelief was more like it.

Even stunned as he was, I didn't expect he'd stand still for long, and he was still too close to Trey and

Laura for somebody in possession of a blade that long. I needed to draw him away. So I got close to the window, plastered on a huge smile, and pointed at my face. And then I finger-waved at him.

Thought his eyes were going to pop out of his head. Geez, you'd think he wasn't happy to see me alive.

While Per stared at me with murderous intent, the Viking holding the knife on Billy moved in a flash, cutting the ropes. He shoved the knife into Billy's hand and retrieved another from the sheath strapped to his own belt.

Billy dove for the nearest Viking—one of the two holding Trey—and, within seconds, sliced both of the guy's Achilles tendons.

Holy crap! And I thought Mark was ruthless. As the man screamed and grabbed his ankles, Billy repeated the process on the oaf holding Trey's other arm, felling him, too.

As soon as Trey was free, he and Billy grabbed one of the Vikings holding Laura. They threw the guy to the ground, where Trey delivered a quick kick to the side of his face, leaving him inert.

The other Viking let go of Laura and ran, slipping and sliding in the ever-increasing pool of slurry. They let him go.

All of that happened in seconds. The screams from the men Billy had sliced and diced broke Per's focus on me. He looked like he might be tempted to bisect the Viking who'd freed Billy—that had to be Mark—and go after Billy and Trey, so I honked the horn to get his attention again. Once his eyes were back on me, I put my thumbs in my ears and waggled my fingers.

See, most people would think that was funny, but Per had no sense of humor. Leaving my friends to the tender mercies of the Vikings who hadn't run off at the first sign of the shit hitting the fan, he hunched over like a maddened bull and ran straight at me.

Oops. Hadn't really thought this part through. I reached to lock the door, only to discover the window was open. I grabbed the handle and twisted for all I was worth. It spun uselessly in my hand, broken.

Maybe I could outrun him. Which, granted, would work better if he weren't already just yards away from the truck and closing fast. Still, I had to try something.

I made myself wait a few crucial seconds, and shoved the door open as hard as I could. Timing is everything. It caught him hard across the chest and face, knocking him flat. Knowing I couldn't count on him being incapacitated for long, I jumped down from the high seat and took off, heading back the way I'd come.

It was less than a minute before I heard a stream of angry Swedish, hot on my heels. Damn. I was hoping for more time before he—

Tackled me from behind. *Déjà vu.* Only this time kidnapping was not in the cards—I was sure he had something more permanent in mind.

I rolled over fast, planning to shove him away

before he dropped his full weight on me. Mistake. It gave him better access to my throat.

Slurry-coated fingers gripped my windpipe, and white-ringed eyes stared down at me. His freshly broken nose canted to one side. The tendons on his neck stood out more with each growling breath he took.

Yep, looked like a classic case of 'roid rage to me. I wouldn't last long at this rate.

So I did it. The forbidden thing. The ultimate taboo.

The Big No-No.

I adapted in front of a nonadaptor. (Hey, I was *desperate*.) Using my last bit of conscious energy, I shifted into a replica of the man pinning me down.

The look that spread over his face was priceless—if I'd thought he was crazy before, it was nothing compared to the total lunacy engulfing him now that he was strangling a living, breathing mirror-image of himself.

His hold weakened, and I gulped in air. Said to him, in his own voice, "This is your conscience, Per. Your higher self. And you've been a VERY . . . BAD . . . BOY."

He squealed like a girl and released me entirely, pushing himself away like I was the devil incarnate, which wasn't too far off the mark at the moment, as far as I was concerned.

I rose up on my elbows, keeping my head as close to his as possible, seeing as how it was having such a beneficial effect on him. He scrambled to his feet, straddling me in much the same way as he had beneath the trebuchet right before he'd launched me out to sea. I did what I hadn't been able to then—I swung up a now painfully tight boot, and kicked him.

Right in his raisins.

He clutched his crotch and fell over sideways, drawing his knees up to his chest. Man, that felt *good*. Who knew causing pain could be so darned satisfying?

As I stood, I heard voices getting closer, and rid myself of Per's aura at once. My feet and waist were supremely grateful. Per was a big guy, and my clothes had been a snug fit. I sincerely hoped I'd never have to don the bastard again.

The first one to reach me was a Viking, caked in brown. *Crap!* It wasn't over yet.

I turned to run, and was once again caught from behind. This time I screamed in frustration, because with all those other voices getting closer I couldn't risk another change. You can claim one person is crazy, but not a whole bunch of people who see the same thing.

"*Tyst*, Ciel. Shhh. It's me."

I shut my mouth and peered closely at him. Under a thick, aromatic coating was Nils.

"SÄPO is here. You are safe."

"Well, it's about bloody time," I said.

He laughed and looked down at Per, still writhing on the ground. "But see—you didn't need SÄPO after all. You truly are an astonishing girl." His smile was ultra-white against the brown on his cheeks.

The new guys who joined us were not dressed as Vikings. As far as I could tell under the slurry, anyway. They gathered up Per and dragged him away, wild-eyed and screaming the whole way.

"Just out of curiosity, what's he saying?" I asked Nils.

He screwed up his brow and shook his head. "Crazy talk—something about witches, and being attacked by his conscience. Perhaps he meant he is having an attack of conscience? Though he doesn't sound remorseful, does he?"

"No, he doesn't. Not a bit." But Looney Tunes enough that no one would believe him if he told them what I did, thank goodness. Breathing easier, I turned back to Nils. "I, uh, borrowed your uncle's truck. I hope you don't mind."

"We at SÄPO call that initiative." I heard the smile in his voice. "Perhaps you would like to stay here and take a job with us? I can get you the proper work permits."

Before I could frame a polite refusal, a very brown Mark appeared, stepping between me and Nils. He must've figured it was safe to drop the Viking aura he'd been wearing, what with being covered in shit from head to toe.

"Ciel? Is that you? What are you doing here? I told Billy to send you back to the boat." His face threatened mayhem, and once I might've cowered under his glare. Not anymore.

I shrugged. "Couldn't remember the way back. By the way, you're welcome."

He opened his mouth, probably to start another

lecture, but stopped when I raised my eyebrows at him.

"Thank you," he squeezed out. "Don't ever do it again." Then he hugged me tight enough to crush the breath out of me, and spoke softly, right next to my ear. "You and I need to talk. When we get back to—"

"Ciel!" Billy skidded to a halt, surfing the sludge, barely stopping himself before he rammed into us. Mark let go of me to steady him. Billy looked even worse than Mark, covered with blood—none of it his own, I hoped—as well as shit.

"Jesus, cuz, that was brilliant! *You* were brilliant! You sure we're not from the same gene pool?"

In his excitement, he grabbed me by the waist, lifted me high, and twirled me twice before setting me back down. Mark was forced to step back.

Hands holding tightly to Billy's shoulders, I laughed with him. "Not according to Auntie Mo. She claims you were part of the package when she married your dad."

"Well, I guess she would know." He leaned closer to me, resting his forehead on mine and lowering his voice so only I could hear. "Welcome to the playing field. Glad we're on the same team—I'd hate to go up against you. You play dirty."

Mark cleared his throat, interrupting our tête-à-tête. "She might've been hurt, you know. In case you didn't think of that."

Billy kept his head where it was, his eyes twinkling just centimeters from mine. "Uh-oh. Coach is mad." Then he straightened up and said, "And without her, the rest of us most likely would have been killed before SÄPO got here. I'm not going to argue with the way things worked out."

"It was luck that SÄPO got here when they did, or we'd all be dead, including Ciel. You really think that's an acceptable risk?" Mark said, giving Billy as hard a look as I'd ever seen.

Billy let it roll off. "Not personally, no. But I think that's up to Ciel to decide."

I could've kissed him right then and there. Except his face was still covered in shit and all, so I didn't.

SÄPO proved efficient at rounding up the stray neo-Vikings. They loaded as many of the medi-evally adorned, brown-caked men as they could find onto buses with armed guards, and sent them to be processed in Visby. The two Billy had put out of commission with his impressive knife work were seen to by agents skilled in first aid. They would eventually be able to walk again, maybe even before they were out of prison.

Per was taken away in a special, heavily armored van, shackled hand and foot. He was still scream-ing at the top of his lungs when I last saw him. I suspected it was just as well I couldn't understand what he was saying.

Nils directed local police officers to an isolated warehouse full of the anabolic steroids used to lace the neo-Viking's line of men's grooming products, as well as incriminating documents related to Per's illegal smuggling activities. The animal skins turned out to be more than just supplies for the neo-Viking recruits to make their leather accessories with— they also hid, in a well-cushioned manner, all kinds of small containers of the illegal muscle-building aids.

Ahiga, a disgruntled employee of the DEA, had been recruited by Per, who was excited by the prospect of expanding his macho empire across borders. He had thought Ahiga, along with Trey, whose legitimate import-export business was a great cover for smuggling activities, would make excellent American contacts. He'd been half-right. Ahiga would be sent back to the States to face charges.

After Trey's CIA connection was discovered because of a fluke in the line of communication (I think that's Company jargon for "somebody fucked up"), Per had been even more determined to maintain his connection to America via Ahiga, especially since the Indian was a major source of the steroids. Happily for testicles throughout Scandinavia, that was one pipeline now cut off.

Once the general hubbub surrounding the arrests was taken care of, I officially met the real Trey for the first time. Even covered in shit, even with a split and puffy lip, his smile still melted me a little. Mina was one lucky lady.

Nils graciously invited all of us over to his uncle's farm to rinse off. Mark declined on behalf of everyone, saying a dip in the ocean followed by a rinse on the boat would suffice until we were back in Visby.

Laura took exception to Mark speaking for her. "Well, y'all can freeze your tushes off if you want to, but I'm taking Nils up on his offer." She took the big guy's hand. They were clearly thrilled to see each other again. "Are you certain you don't want to come along, Ciel? I'm sure there's plenty of hot water."

"Nah. I'll be fine on the boat. You guys must have a lot of catching up to do."

Laura looked from Mark to Billy, firmly planted on either side of me, and cocked her head at me. *Which one?* her teasing eyes asked. I gave a tiny shrug. *Hell if I know.*

Chapter 30

The surreal image in the full-length mirror floated dizzily before me. If I let my eyes go out of focus I looked as poofy as an unsheared sheep fresh from a spin in the tumble dryer.

Crap. Why did she have to choose the Cinderella dress?

I jumped when I heard the door open behind me. My brief moment of solitude in Mina's childhood bedroom was over. Ava Milan, thirty-something Ace of All Wedding Planners, effervesced into the room, brimming with good-natured efficiency.

"You look absotively, posilutely stunning, Mina!" Her worshipful voice did nothing to soften my horror at being decked out in billowing, blinding white from head to toe. I would've felt totally ridiculous had I not also been wearing Mina's aura.

Thank God no one would ever see *me* in a getup like this.

"It's time." Ava flashed me her toothiest smile and made a minuscule adjustment to my veil, which was long enough to double as mosquito netting for a queen-size bed.

I followed her, and with every precarious step down the stairs my feet screamed at me silently. Really, the least Mina could've done was choose comfortable shoes. If I got through the day on four-inch stilettos without breaking an ankle, I'd consider myself blessed. I already had blisters on both heels from all my practice walking, and my toes were cramping like a son of a bitch, and for what? You couldn't even see the damn things underneath the umpteen layers of silk and lace that barricaded me from the rest of the world.

There are times when I hate my job.

Little more than two weeks had passed since my return from Sweden. Mina just couldn't wait any longer than that to live her dream. Really. She *couldn't* wait. She was pregnant.

After everything she'd done to orchestrate this momentous day, you'd think she'd be the last person to leave the actual walk down the aisle to someone else. But it turned out she really was more interested in being married to Trey than in the trappings of the occasion, no matter how much she had entertained herself with the planning.

The truth was, she was more than a little concerned she would never get through the day without decking Dragon Mama, pregnancy hormones being what they are. Personally, I thought that would help set the right tone for future relations with the woman, but I don't get paid to think. Mina wanted beautiful pictures for her wedding album, and blood flowing from her mother-in-law's nose would not provide a happy remembrance to share with her future children.

I sighed. At least I was getting paid well. After I sent her Trey, with a ring, Mina thought I could do no wrong, and was willing to allocate quite a substantial sum to keeping me on retainer for possible future visits with the in-laws. She promised to triple my pay whenever I could find someone to fill in for Trey, too. My business prospects were looking up.

Mina's father met us at the back door, glowing with paternal pride as he held out his arm for me. He was also glowing with two or three martinis, and who could blame him? I'd drink heavily today, too, if I could get away with it.

I smiled at him and whispered, "I love you, Daddy," as we started down the petal-strewn path beneath the tent on the lawn. Fourteen bridesmaids, twin flower girls, and a terminally cute ring bearer had blazed the trail for us.

At the end of the aisle Mina's groom waited. Or at least a reasonable facsimile thereof. Naturally, Mina wasn't going to sit back and allow me to marry the real Trey. No, he was hidden away with his bride at my undisclosed island hideaway, enjoying a private honeymoon after their private— and small—real wedding. The lucky bastards.

Standing in for Trey was Mark. Or maybe Billy.

And therein lay the real source of my discomfort. It was *killing* me not knowing which one of them I was marrying.

Mark had been pulled into a sensitive job as soon as we hit the home shore, and had enlisted Billy's help. When I'd sent out my SOS about the wedding they hadn't been certain who would be available; they'd only sworn one of them would be here. It shouldn't matter who it was—this wasn't really us—but somehow the mass of butterflies swarming in my stomach didn't take that into consideration.

Though we hadn't had a chance to speak privately since the incident on the boat, Mark had hinted, on our way back to the States, that there would be a long talk in our future. But who knew what that meant? I still had a major crush on him— old habits die hard—but it could be *he* was just sorry he'd gotten caught up in the heat of the moment, and wanted to apologize. (Not that the whole thing was entirely his fault. I mean, I *had* wiggled.)

And Billy . . . geez. I didn't know *what* to think about him. It was like there were two of him occupying my head: the one I'd grown up with—my best friend-slash-nemesis—and the one who'd kissed me senseless while eating pancakes, and made me feel ten feet tall when he cheered my victory over Per.

Gaaah.

As the priest spoke words I could barely absorb, I gazed into Trey's ocean-blue eyes and tried to detect some clue as to his real identity. His face gave nothing away. We both spoke the words we were supposed to, and the deed was done. Mina and Trey were married in the eyes of the world.

The kiss. Surely I'll be able to tell after the kiss . . .

No such luck. It was a pleasant kiss, but as unlike Billy's or Mark's as a good adaptor could make it. Not the slightest hint of anything non-Trey detectable, damn whoever the hell it was. Probably Mark. *He* never let any of himself leak through an aura, no matter what.

On the other hand, it would be just like Billy to torment me.

Whoever it was maintained his cover perfectly throughout the posed shots with the control freak of a photographer. My cheek muscles ached from holding Mina's face in a perpetual smile—which wasn't easy with her new mother-in-law poking her nose into every shot—but the groom breezed through the whole session with perfect aplomb. The non-Chiclets smile wasn't nearly as endearing as it once was.

I got through most of the reception with my radiant bride-face on autopilot, pretending to know a multitude of people I'd never met. Mr. Perfect never dropped his facade for an instant.

Finally, just in time to save my sanity, I saw something that infused my smile with sincerity. Two burly members of the catering staff carried out the showpiece of the evening: a breathtaking, six-tiered Matterhorn of a cake.

For the first time all day I didn't care who my

groom was. Mark. Billy. Jay Leno. Hell, he could be Groucho Marx's bastard grandson, as long as I got a piece of that beautiful confection.

Trey and I were about to cut the ceremonial first slice when Dragon Mama insinuated herself into the picture. Again. I gritted my teeth, a trifle peeved on Mina's behalf. And, okay, maybe my blood sugar was a little low. She really shouldn't have tried to come between me and the cake.

"Excuse me, Mother Harrison," I said politely, delighting inwardly at the pained expression on her face when she heard it. For Mina's sake, I didn't snicker. "I think I should probably be the one standing next to *my husband*."

Oh, direct hit! She frosted me with her eyes. "Do call me Helene."

Ha. I'd rather call her "Granny" and watch her face melt. But that would be a major violation of my contract with Mina. She and Trey should have the pleasure of sharing that joyful news with her themselves. Still, there was no harm in poking her just a little, was there?

"But we're family now, Mother Harrison. Or would you prefer 'Mom'?" I kept Mina's smile sweet. Really. It was more fun that way.

"Helene. I insist," she said, ever so drily.

"Okay. Helene," I capitulated. I was sure Mina wouldn't want to call this woman Mom, anyway. "Now, about my husband . . ."

Her eyes narrowed as she warped her mouth into a smile. "Of course. After just a few pictures.

You don't mind, do you? Just in case. You know how it is. So many marriages don't work out, and it would be a shame not to have a picture of Henry in his finery without . . ." She lifted one eyebrow delicately.

My smile stiffened, and I looked to Trey for support. *Count*, he mouthed to me. *Deep breaths. One, two, three* . . .

Right. Good advice, something that could have come from either Mark or Billy. *One . . . two . . . three* . . . I could do this . . . *four . . . five . . . six* . . .

No, I couldn't.

I sidled over to Dragon Mama. "But our marriage will last forever. I promise. For-*ever*. So let's get a nice, cozy shot of the three of us, okay?" I moved closer, took careful aim, and—oops!—accidentally stepped on her foot with my stiletto heel. (Some accidents take more finesse than others.) The screech was music to my ears. I only hoped one of the three roving videographers got a good shot of her tonsils.

Dragon Mama teetered on one foot, leaning over and holding the other with both hands. "Why, you little—"

"Oh, dear," I said, noting how close we were to the cake, and thinking it would be a darn shame if she toppled right into it. Yessirree, a darn shame. So I reached out to . . . um, steady her.

But Trey got to her first, damn it.

He carried her to the nearest chair, shooting me a warning look as he spoke to her. "Mother, you poor thing. Here, sit down." He signaled a waiter to bring ice while he continued to talk over her protests. "You just stay right here and let the staff wait on you hand and, uh, foot."

"But she did it on purp—"

"Don't be silly. It was an accident. Wasn't it, Mina?" he said pointedly. Huh. Must be Mark. Billy probably would have helped me push her into the cake.

I crossed my fingers in the folds of my gown. "Of course it was. I just can't seem to see where my feet are going under this dress. I am so sorry, Mother Harrison—I mean, Helene. Can you ever forgive me?"

Okay, so I played to the crowd a little. Most of them seemed pretty amused by the whole thing. Let's face it—weddings are basically boring. The least I could do was provide a little entertainment.

Noting the avidness of the audience, Mrs. Harrison reined in her temper. I'd have to warn Mina she might want to employ a food taster at any family meals for a while. But at least she would be guaranteed a good number of pictures without her mother-in-law in them, which ought to count for something. Heck, there might even be a bonus in it for me.

Trey and I left Ava the Ace to gloss things over with Dragon Mama while we got on with more important matters. I was perfectly happy once I had cake (dense chocolate fudge under a rich, white butter cream icing, which almost made up for the pinching shoes) and champagne. Nothing like sugar and alcohol to brighten one's mood. Two pieces and three glasses mellowed me out so much, I could even smile benignly at the tug-of-war between the two bridesmaids who conjointly caught the bouquet.

The garter toss was another matter entirely. My sugar- and alcohol-induced serenity fled when bold fingers tickled their way up my leg, overshot the garter by several inches, and settled on the bare skin above my stockings. Hidden as his hands were, Trey—*damn it, which one was he?*—felt no pressing need to maintain decorum.

"Help me out here, hon," he said, eyes aglow with mischief. It had to be Billy. "Tell me when I'm getting warmer." His fingers crawled northward, stopping within centimeters of—

"Hot!" I squeaked. Then again, it might be Mark. His hands had been pretty free and easy on the boat, and he obviously wasn't bashful in public places. Also, after that kiss I was pretty sure he couldn't think of me as a kid sister anymore.

"Sorry, babe. It's hard—"

"I'll bet!" a drunken male voice boomed from among the spectators.

"—working blind." Trey ignored his buddy. "I better take a look, or we could be here all day."

He disappeared under my skirts, flailing his arms in a mad parody of a search. Whoever it was, I was going to kill him. I took aim at the moving lump I judged to be his head, and struck. Connected on my third attempt. "Enough, Romeo!" I said, laughing.

He slipped the garter from my leg and made his exit from beneath my gown—but not before leaving a warm, openmouthed kiss high on the inside of my thigh. Being the professional I am, I didn't gasp. Much.

He shot the elasticized bit of silk and lace, rubber band style, into a group of single men who had been herded together by the bridesmaids, and then led me into a final dance without waiting to see who caught it.

"Can we go yet?" he whispered.

He didn't have to ask me twice. After a flurry of good-byes, the two of us ran the gauntlet through a blizzard of white rose petals, and found ourselves stuffed into the backseat of a limo. I tried my best to tame the dress that kept popping up between us, but it was like playing Whac-A-Mole—every time I mashed one part down, another sprang up. Trey finally subdued it for me.

The privacy barrier was closed between the driver and us. I couldn't stand it for another second. "Okay, who are you?"

Heat flared in his eyes. "It's our honeymoon. I'll be whoever you want me to be."

I swallowed hard, trying to quiet my suddenly pounding heart. Who *did* I want him to be? I opened my mouth to speak, but no words came.

"What's the matter? Can't decide?" He reached over and tugged a wisp of hair that had escaped my satin-flowered headpiece.

Billy. Of course it was Billy. I let out my breath and smiled. "You know what I want, don't you?"

He laughed. "Sadly, I'm afraid I do. You've been limping for the past hour." He reached under my dress and slipped off my shoes one at a time, caressing my silk-encased toes in passing.

Once my feet were on his lap, and my shoulders suitably reclining against a cushy armrest, he started to massage. The cramped muscles relaxed under the pressure of fingers that knew instinctively where to dig deep and where to glide easy. He wiggled my toes back and forth gently, avoiding blisters, loosening joints I'd feared would be permanently bent at stiletto angles. It felt so good I wanted to weep with ecstasy.

I was glad it was Billy. Not that I would've kicked Mark out of the limo, but Billy sure knew how to give a foot massage.

His hands moved up a little. Goody, an ankle massage, too. He took his time, revisiting my feet frequently, until my head lolled back and I closed my eyes.

"Mmmm . . ." I said, which he apparently took as a signal my calves needed attention, too. Since the pressing matter of my cramped feet had been seen to, my aching lower legs agreed with his assessment. I sighed happily. But when he took *that* as an invitation to include my thighs in his tender ministrations, I sprang upright and halted his hands.

"What are you doing?" I said, nerve endings on full alert.

His hands slid back over my calves to my ankles, circling them and pulling me closer as he dropped Trey's aura. I had to clutch his shoulders to keep from toppling over backward.

"The windows are tinted," he said quietly, flattening the highest mountains of material with his elbow. "The driver can't see us behind the screen. The intercom is off. Relax. And lose that aura."

"We'll be in our room soon. We should wait," I said, but since I'd inhaled deeply before speaking, and noticed he smelled even better as himself than he had as Trey, my protest was maybe not stated as firmly as I intended. However, I did *not* give in to the urge to sniff his jawline, which I counted as restraint.

He shook his head. "I can't stay long. Mark is probably already frothing at the mouth. He thought I was jeopardizing the assignment by leaving at all—and, to be fair, he's right about that—so I have to go. But first I want to see *you*."

"But . . ."

He cocked his head and looked at me with those damned Doyle eyes. At this range, that was all it took. I caved. Dropped Mina, leaving myself more buried than ever in clouds of hideously expensive fabric. I felt out of place, but Billy's eyes filled with obvious approval as he reached one hand behind my head to pull me closer.

"Wait!" I said at the last second.

"You said you were tired of sitting on the sidelines. You wanted in the game. So let's play."

"Look, I don't know if I can get used to thinking about you this way. And . . . well, what about Mark? What happened to waiting until he's out of my head?"

He grinned. "After careful consideration, I've

decided on a more proactive approach. You could use a little help pushing the spook out."

"Proactive?" I said, curious but wary. Proactive combined with Billy could be . . . interesting. Then again, we all know where curiosity got the cat.

"That's right. I figure the more of me in there," he said with a tap on my forehead, "the less room for him." He leaned his head toward me.

I drew back again. "But we're—"

"Damn it, Ciel, we are not technically related. I promise you it's not perverted. Besides, you enjoyed it the last time I kissed you. A lot."

"Of course I did—you tasted like maple syrup. You know how much I love maple syrup."

"You love me, too."

"I do n—"

His mouth swallowed the last word. This time he tasted like expensive champagne and wedding cake. How was I supposed to resist a combo like that?

It was futile and I knew it, so I didn't try, not even when his hand slipped back under my skirts. Really, his touch was so light and my heart hammering so heavily, how could I be sure it wasn't just my fevered imagination? And it would be rude to wrongly accuse him. Best to make sure before I—oh, hell, who was I kidding? His hand was there all right, his fingers dancing delicately back and forth, slowly working their way past my garters, until they found what they were looking for, and lingered.

Okay, so protest *was* one option. But honestly?

There's a lot to be said for lingering fingers, especially when they're moving slowly in time with a tongue already doing insanely delicious things to your mouth.

Ditto for a dizzying scent—geez, was that cologne? or just him?—going straight from your nose to points south, adding fuel to the fire. I whimpered. Oh, yes, a *lot* to be said for that. Basically I didn't stop him because . . . well, it felt really, *really* good. It was like there were fizzy little bubbles racing through my bloodstream, tickling every erogenous zone I had, and finally popping against my . . . *OH!*

All thoughts of protest suddenly moot, I pulled my lips from his and buried my face in his neck, trying unsuccessfully to stifle a sound of pure pleasure. I was a little embarrassed about the moaning, but the rational part of me figured it was at least better than screaming, *Yes! I do love you!* No way was I going to jump off *that* bridge first, even if what I was feeling *was* love and not just lust.

He hugged me to him, giving me a moment, then kissed my forehead and raised my chin. "Were you thinking about him just now?" he said softly.

"Huh? Wha—who?"

A smile broke slowly from one corner of his mouth to the other. A happy smile, not a gotcha smile, but I blushed anyway.

"Yeah, okay. I get your point," I said, then raised a brow significantly. Judging from where I was sitting, I hadn't been the only one strongly affected by the kiss. "What about you?"

"No, I wasn't thinking about him at all, actually," he said disingenuously.

"That is *not* what I meant," I said, and then wiggled my hips the tiniest bit. "*That* is what I meant."

He groaned. "Not that I don't appreciate your consideration, but—" He shifted beneath me, finding himself a more comfortable position. "No time. We're almost at the hotel, and we have to change back. Unless you don't mind the driver, not to mention the other hotel patrons, speculating about our activities when we don't emerge from the vehicle in a timely fashion, of course."

At the moment I wished, fiercely, I could say, *Screw it—let 'em speculate*. But I did have an obligation to maintain Mina's dignity while presenting myself as her. I pushed as far away from Billy as I could (doing my best not to press unduly against his lap while I did so—I'm not *that* cruel) and straightened my dress, trying to regain my composure.

"Billy?" I said, doubts seeping back with the distance.

"Yeah?"

"Aren't you worried this will ruin our relationship? I mean, you're my best friend, and I think I'm yours. What if we spoil it?"

He cracked up. "Spoil it? Ciel, the last time we were together you peed all over me and pelted me with cow shit. From *my* standpoint our relationship can only improve."

I narrowed my eyes at the reminder. "Yeah, well, I also stole your car and scratched the hell out of its precious paint." Ha. Bet *that* would help put a damper on his ardor. Sometimes you have to be cruel to be kind.

He only grinned. "I know. But it was brave of you to confess."

"How'd you find out?" I was surprised, because I'd paid a good chunk of Mina's fee to have the Chevy restored and returned to the garage before Billy could find out it was ever gone.

"I got a text message from a certain well-tipped attendant, telling me not to worry, he couldn't even tell I'd ever driven into the gate. Only you and Mark knew I was out of the country. I extrapolated from there."

"Aren't you mad?"

"Nope. It's fixed."

"But I . . ." I swallowed hard, reconsidering this whole confession. Perhaps I'd been hasty. Too late now. He had to know, so I might as well just say it. ". . . borrowed your aura. Without asking."

"Yes, you did. That was bad," he said, stern-faced. Then he was me in a flash, looking ridiculous in his tux. "There. Now we're even." Himself again in a matter of seconds, he continued, "Though if it would ease your conscience to atone in some way, I could always give you a spanking." His eyes teased, but I wasn't entirely sure he didn't mean it.

"Don't even think about it, buster," I said, attempting severity, but failing utterly when I was ambushed by a giggle.

He closed the space between us and draped an

arm over my shoulder. "God, I love that sound. You have the best laugh of any woman I know."

I pushed away, but not far this time. He smelled too good. "That's another thing—you know too many women. And I *do* mean in the biblical sense. You're a man-slut. I'm not sure I should get involved with a man-slut."

"Pish. My reputation has been exaggerated. Besides, I'm seriously reconsidering the benefits of monogamy."

Ack. "Uh, I really wouldn't feel right asking you to do that."

He looked at me for good half-minute, eyes full of speculation. "Tell you what," he said at last. "If you're still crushing on the spook after I have my wicked way with you—and I'm talking a whole night in my bed, not messing around in the backseat of a car—I'll bow out gracefully." And then he winked.

Cocky bastard. "Who says I'll let you have your wicked way with me?"

"I can only live in hope," he said, and kissed me again. It was shorter this time, but what it lacked in duration it made up for in *Zing!* Maybe not quite the same kind of *Zing!* as the first kiss, but as close as you could get without lingering fingers.

"Okay," I admitted afterward. "I like kissing you. I'll *probably* let you do it again. But honestly? I'm not sure about the monogamy thing."

It wasn't just letting go of the idea of Mark either—that fantasy was already loosening its grip on me. But getting involved with Billy would be risky enough without setting myself up for the kind of hurt that could come from expecting something he might not be capable of delivering.

"That's okay. I'll have fun convincing you." He gave my hair another tug, and we changed back into the bride and groom.

It was starting to rain as we got out of the limo; a storm was brewing. Billy carried me all the way to our room and over the threshold, so I wouldn't ruin Mina's stockings. No way was I ever putting those shoes on again.

He changed in record time, ridding himself of Trey's aura and tux with a casual disregard for my presence. I busied myself removing my headpiece and veil, all the while sneaking peeks at his side of the room.

Other than turning his back briefly as he dropped Trey's trousers and boxers (he *would* have to have an ass like a Greek statue, I thought with an inward groan) he didn't seem overly concerned with modesty. Which was a good thing, because the stylishly ripped T-shirt and low-rise jeans he pulled on after donning the oh-so-sexy black boxer briefs didn't do a lot to cover his abs. If I wasn't careful, I'd be drooling all over Mina's gown.

I coughed lightly, calling attention to myself, once again overwhelmed by the Mina-size dress. "Do you think you could give me a hand getting out of this monster before you leave? I know you're in a rush, and I wouldn't ask, only I can't reach far enough behind me, and it might look strange to call the concierge for assistance."

Billy's Adam's apple bobbed twice before he spoke. "Sure. Not a problem."

He stepped behind me, crushing my skirts between us in an effort to get close enough to deal with the tiny satin-covered buttons. There were dozens, and it took a considerable amount of time to get through them, with his fingers brushing against my back and his breath tickling my neck the whole time. When he made it almost as far as my hips I said, "I think I can manage from here."

"Only a few more," he said softly, and continued. When he paused I thought he must be finished, and tried to turn around to say good-bye. He stopped me, slipping warm hands past my waist, up to my breasts, bare now because the bra had been built into the bodice.

I inhaled sharply, but was otherwise motionless as I felt his lips on the side of my jaw. When his fingers began teasing, I lowered my arms and let the dress fall as far as it would.

"Just a taste," he whispered, turning me and lowering his head. The shock of his mouth, hot on my nipple, jolted me back to reality, and I pushed his head away.

"I thought you had to go now," I said.

His eyes twinkled. "More like an hour ago."

"Then why are you—"

"Because," he said, pausing to kiss each pink tip before continuing, "they are right there in front of me."

I laughed at the blunt honesty of his reply. "Maybe you could stay just a little longer," I said, trying to sound nonchalant. "You're already late anyway."

Regret filled his eyes, but when he spoke his voice was resolute. "No. I don't want you to remember the first time we make love as some sort of work-related quickie."

"You're right," I agreed, if reluctantly, and licked my lips. Slowly. (What? They were dry.)

Staring at my mouth with hot eyes, he said, suddenly, "Come with me." Not the words I expected to hear.

"I can't," I said with a tiny shrug, my dress slipping down more with the motion. Oops. "I'm in the middle of a job." I blinked innocently.

He took a deep breath and tugged the bodice back up to cover my chest. "Suit yourself. Either Mark or I will be back in a few days so you and Trey can make a show of leaving the hotel together."

I was surprised to feel a stab of disappointment that he might actually let Mark come back in his place, but didn't let myself comment on it. He slung a small pack over his shoulder and gave me a last kiss, a real toe-curler, half-lifting me with one arm.

Wait just a darn minute . . . Was he trying to out-tempt me? He *was*.

Well, we'd just see about that. After he abandoned my lips I licked them again, because I liked what it did to his eyes the last time, and also, I admit, because I *might* be a teensy bit competitive.

"You're really sure you have to leave?" I said, extra-breathlessly.

He saw through it, and grinned down at me. "Convinced already? Gee, you're easy."

Argh. Points for Billy. I pushed him away, making sure I held the bodice up. "I am not! Go. Leave already. See if I care."

He laughed as he headed for the door.

"What am I supposed to do by myself until you get back?"

"Think about me," he tossed over his shoulder, and was gone.

"I might just think about Mark instead!" I hollered after him, a sorry attempt at a Hail Mary pass.

Silence.

Damn it. I wasn't about to sit around thinking of either one of them. I kicked my way out of the dress, threw on my stand-by "me" clothes and shoes, and quickly dialed the front desk. Told the clerk to hold all calls for the next few days, said the fruit basket and champagne in the suite would suffice, so room service wouldn't be necessary. Grabbed my overnight bag, left a Do Not Disturb sign on the door and ran down the stairs, not trusting the elevator to be fast enough.

I found Billy on the first level of the parking garage, leaning against his Chevy, casually drumming his fingers against the fender, a gleeful sparkle in his eyes.

I pulled up short, stopping a few feet away, breathing hard. "You ass," I wheezed. "You're waiting for me."

He shrugged. "Hoped you might change your mind."

I eyed him suspiciously and gave myself a minute to think. "Okay," I said finally, after I'd recovered enough breath to speak evenly. "Say I do come with you—we have to get some things straight."

"I'm all ears."

"If I'm in, I'm in. No shoving me off the field if things get dangerous."

"Wouldn't dream of it." He said it so earnestly I knew better than to trust him.

I raised a brow.

A smile visited his lips briefly. "Really. I'm past that. I've evolved. Mark's the one you have to worry about."

"He'll be pissed you brought me," I pointed out.

"Yeah. You care?"

I cocked my head and gave it some thought. "Nah. He'll get over it. Oh, and one other thing— give me the keys. I'm driving."

"You must be kidding," he said, his voice appalled. Everyone has his limit.

"If I wreck it, you can spank me," I lied. I mean, what were limits for if not to be pushed?

His eyes darkened and he tossed me the keys without a second's hesitation, swallowing hard. I settled myself into the driver's seat, mentally spiking the ball. *Hee. Touchdown.*

As we exited the garage, a huge *KABOOM!* rocked us, accompanied by a blinding flash. We both jumped as far as our seat belts would allow, and looked around for flying debris. But it wasn't a bomb this time—lightning had struck the tree across the street, and it was coming down fast.

I stomped on the gas, pulling out of the way just as the towering oak crashed behind us. *Yikes!* Had the Big Referee in the Sky called a flag on my play? A girl could get paranoid if this kept up.

Fortunately, Billy started laughing as soon as he realized the tree hadn't smashed his baby, distracting me from impending remorse. After a second I joined in, savoring the adrenaline rush along with him.

Ha! Missed me again! popped into my head as we sped away. But I squelched it before it could take root. Pushing the limits was one thing, but tempting fate was just plain stupid.

First of all, it's not my fault! Not entirely, anyway. I may have written *In a Fix*, but loads of people share the blame for its final incarnation. Just so we're clear on that.

Here are a few of them:

My mother, Elly Clayworth, who might be embarrassed to let her friends read certain parts of the book, but who will act proud anyway. Thanks for providing me with the phrase "God punishes right away." You're right, Mom. (There. Now you have it in print.)

My husband, Bob, who always treated my writing as if it were a serious pursuit, worthy of respect, even when I was just playing.

My children, Annalisa and Sean, and my son-in-law, Mike. If any of them were ever appalled by the "research" questions I brought up at the dinner table, they at least had the good grace not to show it. Much.

My fantastic beta readers and critique partners: Eagle-Eyes Susan Adrian, Elise Skidmore, Kris Reekie, Beth Shope, Pamela Patchet, Julie Kentner, Tiffany Schmidt, Emily Hainsworth, and my Agency Sistah, Tawna Fenske. Seriously, folks. Anything you didn't like, I'm blaming them.

Vicki Pettersson and Joanna Bourne, who blazed trails I was too frightened to set foot on before I saw it could be done.

The CompuServe Books and Writers Community, where I became convinced I might actually be able to make a go of this author thing. Thanks to everyone I met there who encouraged my writing addiction, especially Diana Gabaldon, whose grace and patience with newbie writers is an astounding thing to behold.

And, of course, eternal gratitude to my amazing agent, Michelle Wolfson, who never once gave up on me, and my supremely talented editor, Melissa Frain. The good parts were probably suggested by her.

Finally, my apologies to anyone I've inadvertently left out. Look on the bright side. If the book bombs, you'll be glad your name isn't associated with it.

THE DISTRICTS

THE DISTRICTS

Stories of American Justice
from the Federal Courts

Johnny Dwyer

ALFRED A. KNOPF NEW YORK

2019

THIS IS A BORZOI BOOK
PUBLISHED BY ALFRED A. KNOPF

Library of Congress Cataloging-in-Publication Data
Names: Dwyer, Johnny, author.
Title: The districts : stories of American justice from the federal courts /
Johnny Dwyer.
Description: New York : Knopf, 2019.
Identifiers: LCCN 2019003945 (print) | LCCN 2019005226 (ebook) |
ISBN 9781101946558 (ebook) | ISBN 9781101946541 (hardback)
Subjects: LCSH: District courts—New York (State)—New York. |
Criminal justice, Administration of—New York (State)—New York. |
United States. District Court (New York : Eastern District). |
United States. District Court (New York : Southern District). |
BISAC: POLITICAL SCIENCE / Political Freedom & Security /
Law Enforcement. | LAW / Criminal Law / General. |
POLITICAL SCIENCE / Government / Judicial Branch.
Classification: LCC KF8755.N85 (ebook) | LCC KF8755.N85 D87 2019 (print) |
DC 347.73/22097471—dc23
LC record available at https://lccn.loc.gov/2019003945

Jacket photograph by Ferrantraite / E+ / Getty Images
Jacket design by John Vorhees

Manufactured in the United States of America
First Edition

For Sarah

Justice is merely incidental to law and order.

—J. EDGAR HOOVER

Contents

THE DISTRICTS

Prologue

Two helicopters hung in the gray sky above the federal courthouse. On the street below, a crowd of several dozen cameramen wrapped in weatherproof winter gear trained their lenses on the doorway, awaiting the appearance of the defendant. Upstairs on the twentieth floor of the Daniel Patrick Moynihan United States Courthouse—known as "Pearl Street" for its address along the edges of Manhattan's Chinatown—the security was light. A team of guards acted, instead, as ushers leading reporters, the public, and family members of the man to be sentenced to their respective rows. The crowd waited quietly for the hearing to begin.

The defense attorneys arrived first, passing wordlessly through the gallery, past the bar, before taking their seats at their table facing the judge's bench. The government followed. On this morning, two sets of federal prosecutors represented the Department of Justice. One team had traveled from Washington, where the attorneys had been working for the Special Counsel's Office under the former FBI director Robert Mueller. The other had walked several hundred yards from the U.S. Attorney's Office for the Southern District of New York. When the defendant stepped through the courtroom's door, he held his daughter by the arm as she hobbled toward her seat on a crutch.

Michael Cohen appeared before the court—in many senses—as a typical white-collar defendant in the Southern District. He was a white man, in his early fifties, who had amassed a fortune on the margins of the business world. He wore the mien of legitimacy; he was a licensed attorney who also ran a multimillion-dollar taxi medallion business. When federal investigators pulled apart his conduct in both roles, a pattern of fraud and deceit emerged. This provided sufficient basis to charge him with a range of federal offenses. And when the moment of accountability had arrived, Cohen did what is perhaps most typical of white-collar defendants in this district: he pleaded guilty.

But Cohen was unlike any other defendant to enter that courthouse. He, by his own admission, had committed crimes at the direction of the president of the United States. This day's sentencing covered two sets of criminal charges brought by the Southern District related to these crimes, one a single count brought by the Special Counsel's Office charging him with lying to Congress, the other an eight-count criminal information including charges of tax evasion, illegal campaign contributions, and making false statements to a financial institution. The FBI had kicked off the investigation by executing a search warrant on Cohen's offices, hotel room, and phones nearly eight months earlier. The seizure of an attorney's files was aggressive, but not unheard of in the Southern District. The move by the government immediately prompted litigation—and a cartoonish courtroom showdown drawing the dramatis personae of the Trump affair, including the porn performer Stormy Daniels and her attorney Michael Avenatti. In August, when Cohen allocuted to the president's involvement in the attempt to cover up trysts with Daniels and the *Playboy* playmate Karen McDougal, the admission was sordid and disappointing, though not surprising. Yet, in late November, Cohen made a further confession to the court: he had lied to Congress about the president's business interests in Russia and contact with the Russian government. At his sentencing, Cohen gave no details on this but offered something of a plea and a warning.

"History will not remember me as the villain of his story," he said.

As much as Cohen played a part in a national drama, his case was a local affair. The prosecutors and defense attorneys watching this remarkable moment shared something beyond the experience litigating this case. Nearly every attorney in the courtroom worked as an Assistant U.S. Attorney in the Southern District of New York. Cohen's defense counsel, Guy Petrillo, had served as the chief of the Criminal Division, one of the office's ranking titles, reporting directly to the U.S. Attorney. Petrillo's associate, Amy Lester, prosecuted cases in the Southern District for nine years, including a tenure on the office's most prestigious criminal team, the Securities and Commodities Fraud unit. Prior to that, she clerked for a Southern District judge, Loretta Preska. The second seat for the Special Counsel's Office, Andrew Goldstein, ran the Southern District's Public Corruption unit in the months prior to joining the Mueller investigation. The judge, the lead special counsel prosecutor, and her junior associate were exceptional in that they were the only attorneys there who had not come through Manhattan's U.S. Attorney's Office. Cohen's case demonstrated that the Southern District is a place where tradition demands independence, whether that means pushing back against officials at the Department of Justice in Washington or—if the situation requires it—the president.

Several years earlier, I had my first direct experience with this power. It was on another grim December morning when I was summoned to the U.S. Attorney's Office for the Southern District of New York. The office sits at the edge of what was once the Five Points slum. Now it is known as Foley Square, the concourse of city, state, and federal buildings clustered north of city hall. The building doesn't look like much: a 1970s-era Brutalist block of sand-colored brick wedged between St. Andrew's church, a 172-year-old Catholic parish, and One Police Plaza, with a view cut off by the rear windows of the Manhattan borough president's office. If Manhattan could be said to have a utility closet, this was it.

The location's remove and its unremarkable facade suggest none of the history here. In 1789, George Washington nominated the first U.S. Attorney for New York, who, within a few short months, began prosecuting cases in what would become known as the Southern District. The first courthouse sat in the Royal Exchange at Broad and Water

Streets at Manhattan's southern tip, before migrating to Wall Street's Federal Hall and, later, the Old Post Office building, finally settling in Foley Square in 1936. Throughout this history, the Southern District has served as a bellwether for political and cultural shifts in the nation, a place where at times hysteria has fueled injustice and at others humility and vision have laid foundations for future generations. Southern District prosecutors sought and won the death penalty in the Rosenberg case. They sued to have copies of *Ulysses* destroyed before Random House could publish the book, an unsuccessful effort that yielded a historic First Amendment ruling. And one particularly ambitious U.S. Attorney, Rudy Giuliani, pursued criminals like the Gambino boss Paul Castellano and Wall Street's Ivan Boesky, before becoming New York's first Republican mayor in nearly three decades. More recently, the Southern District is where Bernie Madoff fought through crowds of paparazzi to receive a 150-year sentence and where, in the weeks after the release of Mueller's report, the public shifted some of its hopes and expectations that the office would deliver a version of justice the special counsel could not. Nicknames logically follow this historical record: there is "the Mother Court," a nod to the district's historical preeminence, and, more pejoratively, "the Sovereign District of New York." Within the nation's ninety-four federal districts—and their respective U.S. Attorney's Offices overseen by the Department of Justice—the Southern District has secured a unique autonomy.

When the Southern District's flack called me in for a chat with a senior prosecutor, a small measure of this history weighed on me. As I made my way across Foley Square, I fought a bracing December wind—as well as the feeling that generations of defendants, their counsel in tow, had made a similar pilgrimage. Dialogue between federal prosecutors and reporters typically occurs at well-scripted press conferences, a fake-oak lectern and Department of Justice placard establishing the appropriate distance from the scrum of reporters. Or in background conversations, where prosecutors seek to untether their names from the facts or slant they wish to push—an indiscretion most often reserved for *The New York Times* and *The Wall Street Journal*, outlets with the reach and pedigree to telegraph a message to the desired audiences. Truthfully, I had begged for a sit-down for months, assuming that I, like so many other journalists, would be ignored and avoided. For some reason, the U.S. Attorney's Office for the Southern District of New York relented. The ground rules, however, were clear: what we discussed would remain off the record. I passed through the layers of federal marshals, into the near-silent, unadorned office that houses some of the most powerful prosecutors in the world.

This was the era of Preet Bharara, the New Jersey–bred and Springsteen-loving Indian American U.S. Attorney. Bharara, then unknown to most Americans, reliably grabbed local headlines as a tough adversary: arresting Russian arms traffickers and spies, pursuing inside traders, targeting Albany's crony politics. He consistently downplayed his interest in elected office, but the public profile he maintained suggested that the Southern District was the beginning rather than the culmination of his political career. After his summary firing by President Trump in March 2017, he pivoted to a trade concomitant with politics: the media.

That day my appointment was with one of Bharara's underlings. The office spokesperson, a former network news producer, joylessly trailed me through a warren of cubicles leading to our interview. The job of federal prosecutor is powerful, though typically anonymous, and the route to the position is well worn. Most federal prosecutors in New York follow similar paths: a degree from an Ivy League law school, a top clerkship, two or three years in private practice under the wing of a former prosecutor, and finally the rigorous, multi-round interview process. To land the job is not a contest of intellect alone. It falls on judgment and temperament. A prosecutor needs to be comfortable with making decisions that carry the power to deprive people of their freedom. But a prosecutor should not relish this. It is a unique responsibility that follows from a unique type of power. The lowest-level federal prosecutor—the Assistant U.S. Attorney—enjoys some of the broadest authority in the government and is subject to the least amount of outside oversight. The power of an AUSA in the Southern District of New York, defined both by its jurisdiction and by its independence from Washington, belongs in a category unto itself.

The prosecutor I met with that day cut a dry, angular figure. He had a tidy, graying prep school haircut and a predictably firm handshake. His navy suit matched the pleather couch in his office. None of these, I should mention, are identifying characteristics. There is a deliberate uniformity among federal prosecutors. This serves a practical purpose: in court, federal prosecutors don't represent themselves—or even their offices—they represent the government. This uniformity can be seen in professional sports and, more subtly, the corporate world. But this particular transformation—the process of taking on the physical embodiment of the state—is essential to the federal prosecutor's identity. It allows prosecutors to project the appropriate formulation of fear and neutrality. Imagine a federal building human incarnate: commanding and impassive, any personality incidental and secondary, nonetheless holding unseen power. When I sat down, the prosecutor smiled. But it appeared to take some effort.

Every office makes use of status symbols. In Hollywood, there's the exaggeratedly large view of the hills and the condescendingly nice personal assistant. In the private equity world, you see the charity auction ephemera: the *Tyrannosaurus rex* skulls, autographed Les Pauls, framed Knicks jerseys—all dusted at night by nameless staff. In Liberia, where I traveled on and off for years completing my first book, bone-chilling air-conditioning signified status. Though this Southern District prosecutor had a window, he didn't have much of a view. The framed photographs on his wall were of the unmemorable federal variety: dark-suited officials clasping hands and grinning crazily toward the camera. The one thing I did notice was the baseball bat.

The prosecutor was eager to show it to me. The canned speech he gave me remains off the record; that bat he held while delivering it does not. It was a standard-issue wood Louisville Slugger. It showed no signs that it had ever been used to hit a baseball. Or a reporter, for that matter. The prosecutor stood up and palmed it mischievously. The image of a man in his late forties in a Brooks Brothers suit wielding a baseball bat in his office is open to interpretation. Perhaps the bat was some sort of tactile learning object. Or a concise physical metaphor for the power he wielded. I read the intent as a gesture to intimidate me. But the fact is that federal prosecutors inspire the most fear when they're pushing a wire cart stuffed with evidence into a courtroom.

Which is to say that a prosecutor's power lies in the precise, sustained, and overwhelming pressure the Department of Justice can bring to bear on a target. The brief, lurid history of the Trump administration is an object lesson in this. The nation's domestic politics have transpired against the backdrop of the special counsel's investigation. This is not a new story: national dramas have long turned on the work of federal prosecutors and the federal courts. In the Southern District, local stories have long seized onto the national consciousness—in large part, because prosecutors and judges here have the rare ability to turn Manhattan's dominant social, political, and economic hierarchies on their heads.

It was precisely that power that interested me and first drew me to report on the Southern District. But, as unique as this power was, the Southern District could not lay exclusive claim to it. Not even within New York City.

THE EASTERN DISTRICT of New York sits some three thousand steps over the Brooklyn Bridge. It is the scrappier younger sibling of Manhattan's venerable federal district. Its imprint on the American consciousness is without parallel. Much of our understanding of the American Mafia has been gleaned from testimony elicited by prosecutors and criminal defense attorneys examining witnesses on the stand in the Eastern District. It has been a center of gravity for national security cases from the Cold War through the post–September 11 era of counterterrorism.

The proximity of the two districts doesn't reflect their true distance. They exist worlds apart, each belonging to a particular social and political geography, each working within a distinct history. The Eastern District courthouse sits at the northern tip of Cadman Plaza, at the outer rung of downtown Brooklyn, Brooklyn Heights, and Dumbo, where the municipal grit of the Brooklyn borough president's office and state supreme court peters out into a leafy esplanade. The structure is handsome, but it could also be mistaken for a really nice post office. The humility extends into the U.S. Attorney's Office in the Eastern District, which—as it turns out—is housed in what once was a post office.

Several years after that sit-down in the Southern District, I walked up the worn marble steps of that old post office to sit down with a senior federal prosecutor from the Eastern District of New York. We met under similar ground rules: we would speak on background, which meant that I could quote him so long as I did not attribute the statement to him in an identifiable manner. I hadn't begged for the sit-down, just simply asked. As I walked through the drab, cluttered hallways to his office, the press officer was nowhere to be seen. When it came to reporters, Brooklyn prosecutors seemed to be wound less tight than their colleagues across the bridge. They didn't hesitate to say hello in the courthouse elevator, take a few minutes after a hearing to chip away at the arcana of a proceeding, even meet for a decaf coffee and a bagel at a diner for a background conversation. The Southern District, meanwhile, forbids its line assistants any interaction with the media—which sometimes led to absurd exchanges, as when a junior prosecutor turned on her heel at the sight of me in the elevator bank, rather than being forced to ride with me to the floor where we were both headed. The Eastern District prosecutor had cleared our meeting with his supervisors, explaining that he assessed me to be straight-forward. (A colleague of his put it differently: he told a group of law enforcement and intelligence officials not to worry about me because I write "nonfiction.") He decided to speak with me because he wanted to demystify his job, he said. To help Americans understand what the work of prosecuting crimes entails. To explain the need for secrecy and acknowledge the arguments that criticize law enforcement's broad-reaching powers. His window looked out on the bleating traffic piling up to cross the Brooklyn Bridge into Manhattan; his voice was steady, relaxed.

As he spoke, I noticed a wooden club sitting on his desk. It sat there unremarked upon, a memento of an investigation conducted overseas. It seemed an odd coincidence, but at no point in our conversation did this prosecutor reach for it.

AND THIS WAS the luxury of reporting on the federal courts in New York City: the luxury of comparison. The ability to stand up parallel institutions with aligned missions and similar enforcement environments side by side to see their fundamental differences and make the often-opaque process of seeking justice more transparent.

This book focuses on criminal practice—the area in which individuals most often find themselves in confrontation with the state. The text charts a distinct criminal landscape within the city. It structures itself much the same way the U.S. Attorneys' Offices organize themselves, through the major categories of crime, with sections devoted to organized crime, narcotics, white-collar crime, national security and terrorism, and public corruption.

This book is not about the law per se. It is about the impact of the law on the lives of people who make their work in it, and those who find themselves at odds with it. How we choose to define, prosecute, and punish crime offers a window into our politics and society. The stories in this book are told from the point of view of prosecutors, judges, jurors, defendants, and their counsel. This book does not provide definitive histories of each of New York's federal districts or U.S. Attorneys' Offices. Instead, it steps into a moment of time to report on the labor of the courts. The daily work of finding justice seen here is human, subject to all the intimacies that go with ambition, fear, sense of duty, and the need for retribution.

The Constitution did not establish an open judicial system. Instead, the founding fathers created a system where the public's right to access is balanced with the rights of the parties to a case, including the government, to maintain secrecy. The experiment of reporting this book—and at times stepping into the narrative—is an assertion of the public's right to participate in criminal justice. These stories attempt to push into the spaces hidden from public view—not just inside the U.S. Attorneys' Offices, but into closed courtrooms, judges' chambers, the lives and communities of the accused. And to map the personal and political terrain of major and minor criminal cases.

The ultimate subject of this book is power. It doesn't focus exclusively on the most powerful figures, but also looks at ordinary people and how they respond to the power of the law—whether that is the line prosecutor empowered to charge a crime or a criminal defense attorney charged with asserting a defendant's rights.

In *The House of the Dead,* Dostoevsky wrote, "The degree of civilization in a society can be judged by entering its prisons." If this book has a single premise, it is that the true measure of the justice within a society can be discovered by stepping into its courts.

Strange Spectacle

On February 3, 1865, Congress redefined the geography of federal law enforcement in New York City. After considering measures extending copyright to "photographs and negatives" and constructing a telegraph line "from Missouri to the Pacific Ocean," the Senate moved to House Bill 184, a piece of legislation that sought "to divide the southern District of New York." The Southern District had come into being nearly a century earlier with the passage of the Judiciary Act of 1789. Congress was then located at 26 Wall Street, and New York City was the center of federal power in the United States—all eleven of them. The act created thirteen federal districts (and thirteen judgeships), three circuits, and six Supreme Court justices overseeing federal law for a nation of 3.9 million people. The writers gave the district courts narrow power to address, among other things, "crimes and offences . . . committed within their respective districts, or upon the high seas; where no other punishment than whipping, not exceeding thirty stripes, a fine not exceeding one hundred dollars, or a term of imprisonment not exceeding six months, is to be inflicted."

By 1865, New York City's population had surged from 33,000 at the beginning of the century to 810,000. Perhaps more important, New York harbor had become the preeminent port on the East Coast, more than tripling the annual exports of Boston, the closest competitor, by

1860. The harbor wasn't only an engine of the city's economy; it supplied a steady stream of civil litigants into federal court. At that time, the Southern District accounted for one-third of the nation's caseload. More than anything else, the proposed creation of an Eastern District of New York was meant to cope with this overwhelming maritime litigation. The act called for Brooklyn, Queens, Staten Island, and Nassau and Suffolk Counties to be assigned to the Eastern District, while Manhattan, the Bronx, Westchester, and several upstate counties would remain in the Southern District, a geography that followed the contours of the East River and the Hudson.

The Senate debated the measure briefly. Much of the discussion centered on a question that would seem preposterous now: whether New York City had too few courts or too few lawyers. But one member of the New York bar worried about something else: that a city divided by two federal districts might harm the pursuit of justice itself by creating another court that would only encourage more litigants. A senator from Connecticut read a letter by an unidentified author. "I can imagine no public ground for such a measure, and mischiefs of the character in the administration of justice are sure to follow from this division of the port of New York into two judicial districts," he wrote. "We shall have the strange spectacle of two Federal judicial establishments holding courts within three miles of each other." It would be, in fact, just less than a mile and a half between the two courts, a distance more easily navigable with the opening of the Brooklyn Bridge five years later. The act cleared the Senate with a 26–7 vote, and that strange spectacle became a reality. What little controversy there was, was short-lived. There would be no shortage of lawyers or courts in New York or, for that matter, cases to appear before them.

The Southern District claimed its position as the preeminent federal district in the United States. It had a reputation for charting a path independent of Washington. For much of the next century, the Eastern District remained in its neighbor's shadow, a local counterpart to the New York court with national and eventually international recognition. The districts imprinted themselves upon our popular culture, even if only as the unnamed setting for the criminal cases in true-to-life dramas. The federal case (and Supreme Court affirmation) of the conviction of the Russian spy Rudolf Abel—who was exchanged with the U-2 pilot Gary Powers in a prisoner swap—was dramatized in *Bridge of Spies* (Eastern District). *The Godfather* trilogy was inspired by the rise of the Luchese and Gambino crime families in both districts. *Goodfellas* dramatized Henry Hill's account of the city's largest cash heist at the Lufthansa cargo terminal (Eastern District), while *Donnie Brasco* portrayed the FBI infiltration of the Colombo crime family (Southern District). *The Wolf of Wall Street* retold Jordan Belfort's rise and fall selling penny stocks, while *American Hustle* turned on the Abscam case (both Eastern District). Many of these stories planted the cornerstones of a twentieth-century American narrative tradition that would prove to be one of our most enduring cultural exports— the heroic journey of criminality and consequence under the American rule of law.

Prosecutors in the Eastern District rank in prestige among the nation's best, along with the Eastern District of Virginia and the District of Columbia. But everyone sits in the shadow of the Southern District of New York, which firmly remains the most competitive and coveted U.S. Attorney's Office in the nation. The reputation is deserved. Junior prosecutors in the Southern District are confident and meticulous and, typically, of distinction. Prosecutors in the Eastern District don't lack any of the academic or professional attainment of prosecutors in the Southern District. In general, the attorneys have gone to the same schools, clerked for the same judges, and practiced at the same firms before joining the government. What the Eastern District prosecutors do lack is the tradition of a cult of personality surrounding the head of their office. To be the U.S. Attorney in Brooklyn is to be a civil servant, albeit a high-ranking one; to be the U.S. Attorney in Manhattan is to be the most powerful law enforcement official in New York City—arguably the most powerful federal prosecutor in the country, undoubtedly the most autonomous.

The Eastern District includes a jurisdiction of eight million people. The Brooklyn U.S. Attorney's Office's criminal practice is divided into seven sections: Business and Securities Fraud, Public Integrity, Organized Crime and Gangs, International Narcotics and Money Laundering, National Security and Cybercrime, Civil Rights, and General

Crimes. (The office has an additional Long Island section devoted to criminal prosecutions.) The names of these sections reflect the office's enforcement priorities. U.S. Attorneys' Offices elsewhere in the country like Eastern Oklahoma and North Dakota may divide their practice simply between civil and criminal, with no particular specialization on enforcement areas. In larger and more diverse districts, like the Southern District of Florida centered on Miami, but also encompassing the Everglades, the U.S. Attorney dedicates sections of prosecutors to Environmental Crimes alongside National Security and Narcotics.

The Eastern District of New York sits on global boundaries—not only along the Atlantic coast and at airports like John F. Kennedy and LaGuardia, but in the immigrant communities that make their homes within the jurisdiction. Many immigrant communities throughout the district—concentrated in Queens, Brooklyn, and areas of Long Island—provide a nexus for international drug-trafficking organizations, ethnic gangs like the El Salvadoran MS-13 on Long Island, or organized crime groups like the remnants of La Cosa Nostra and the Vor, elements of the Russian mob. Terrorist groups like al-Qaeda and the Islamic State have found the district a potent recruiting ground among disaffected Americans and recent arrivals, while Eastern District jurisdiction over cyber criminals operating far from U.S. borders could easily be established once suspects stepped off a flight at JFK.

The office's proximity to Wall Street and Long Island's boiler rooms also drive the white-collar practice, while the naturally replenishing supply of state and city officials and police officers on the take keep the Public Integrity Section busy with cases.

How an office organizes itself can also signal the vision of the U.S. Attorney. In 2009, the Southern District's U.S. Attorney, Preet Bharara, announced the creation of the Terrorism and International Narcotics unit, which sought to address the "increasing nexus between narco-trafficking and terrorism." In 2012, the Eastern District underwent its own reorganization under then U.S. Attorney Loretta Lynch. She reordered the Violent Crime and Terrorism Sections with the new National Security and Cybercrime Section, a move she said borrowed from the office's approach on international organized crime groups to focus on state-sponsored and affiliated criminal groups.

With the 2014 nomination of Loretta Lynch to attorney general, the Eastern District surged to national prominence. Lynch was a widely respected candidate; she had developed a reputation as honest and hardworking. She attracted only a fraction of the attention that Bharara did while each served as U.S. Attorney, but her experience as a young federal prosecutor was defined by significantly higher-profile cases. Lynch distinguished herself with trials against the Green Dragons, a Queens-based Chinese gang, and Justin Volpe, an NYPD officer charged with sexually assaulting a man with a broom handle in a Brooklyn station house. As U.S. Attorney, she secured a $1.9 billion settlement from HSBC that drew criticism, both from the public and from Republicans in Congress, because executives at the bank escaped prosecution. Congress delayed Lynch's confirmation—putting her at the center of a showdown between the White House and the Senate on immigration—but, after waiting 165 days, held a vote with several Republicans crossing party lines to confirm her. As attorney general, Lynch remained connected to the Eastern District. Her debut occurred not at Justice Department headquarters but instead at the packed law library of the Eastern District U.S. Attorney's Office, where she and the FBI director, James Comey, announced the indictments of FIFA officials in a global corruption investigation. It was a celebratory scene that held little inkling of how the two officials' careers would collide in the coming year.

The geography had historically bred competition for cases ranging from organized crime to white-collar offenses to terrorism. When TWA Flight 800 crashed off Long Island in 1996—in international waters, but closest to the Eastern District—the Southern District under U.S. Attorney Mary Jo White pushed to lead the criminal investigation. "The joke at the time was that she claimed jurisdiction before the plane hit the water," said one former prosecutor, who no sooner than recounting that asked that his name be removed from the quotation. In early 2016, the arrest of the Sinaloa cartel leader Joaquín Guzmán Loera, a.k.a. El Chapo, thrust the jurisdictional competition into national headlines, before the case landed in then attorney general Loretta Lynch's former home, the Eastern District.

Jurisdictional rivalries come with the territory in New York City's law enforcement community and have become an essential feature of a senior federal prosecutor's job.

"If you were a section chief, you had to be good at fighting turf wars. There were a lot of them between the Southern and Eastern District," said Gordon Mehler, who served as the Eastern District's chief of special prosecutions in the 1990s. When it came to white-collar crime during that time, "the Southern District would have a bigger footprint and was stealing the Eastern District's lunch money with some degree of regularity." But by the time of the 2008 financial crisis, the Eastern District stepped forward to press the Department of Justice's first criminal prosecution of executives trading in mortgage-backed securities, while the Southern District demurred from pursuing cases tied to the economic collapse.

Competition among law enforcement agencies doesn't necessarily create market efficiencies. Stephen Fineman, a professor of organizational behavior, conducted fieldwork within several law enforcement agencies in New York in the early 1990s. He called jurisdictional disputes a "paradigmatic example" of "functional rationality and substantive irrationality." Fineman wrote:

> In New York City, such disputes often make justice a pawn in heated rivalries or more simply the function of geography or time of day. New York City has five different district-attorney jurisdictions and two federal-prosecutor jurisdictions . . . Every federal law enforcement agency, from the Federal Bureau of Investigation and the United States Marshals Service to the Immigration and Naturalization Services [*sic*], has major operations in the city, which has long been the national centre of organized crime, the principal east coast port-of-entry for narcotics, and a prototypical site for youth-gang violence . . . [O]ne of the paradoxes of law enforcement is that police of all sort need crime, the more vicious, the better, the more innocent the victim, the better, in order to demonstrate their prowess to their peers and make a plausible public claim of the necessities of their services. The rivalry between and within all law enforcement bureaucracies for "good" cases is fierce, often producing extremely frustrating outcomes.

Lynch came into national office at a moment when federal prosecutors have never been more powerful. While the U.S. Attorney puts a public face to the job of a federal prosecutor, the manual labor of bringing indictments and trying cases falls to Assistant U.S. Attorneys. These AUSAs, also called line assistants, can rise through the supervisory ranks to become section chiefs, overseeing teams of more junior prosecutors, but even the youngest assistant in a federal district wields significant power. With that title—and with approval of their supervisors—they are given the authority to charge and accept plea deals for federal crimes on behalf of the government. The crimes include those committed within the United States, as well as many where the defendants never set foot on U.S. soil.

This power is particularly prominent in our adversarial system of justice, tilting the process strongly in favor of the government—a statement that most prosecutors would reject, but judges, defendants, and their attorneys would accept. This wasn't always the case. Federal sentencing guidelines introduced in the mid-1980s significantly limited a federal judge's discretion in tailoring punishments to defendants. Even after a 2005 Supreme Court ruling made the guidelines no longer mandatory, the imbalance remained a feature of the system. In late 2018, Congress passed the First Step Act, a piece of broad criminal justice reform legislation, which further loosened some of the sentencing requirements placed on judges.

All incentives, within this guideline sentencing system, point toward cutting a deal on criminal charges—in all but the narrowest circumstances where the risk of a trial can be justified. Under this system, defendants who opt for a plea receive credit for "acceptance of responsibility," which triggers less severe sentences than those received by individuals convicted at trial. A defendant's primary leverage remains his willingness to take a case to trial, to publicly test the government's evidence and to force the U.S. Attorney's Office to direct resources to a case. But this is—in effect—a gamble. Defendants risk a greater sentence if they lose; this is the so-called trial tax. The prosecutor's power to charge and negotiate pleas, in particular, is the power to dictate the sentence. By selecting charges with specific guideline sentence ranges, the government sets the high and low end of the costs defendants face when they go before the judge to be sentenced. Defendants who take a plea receive credit for their cooperation and, in most cases, a significantly reduced sentence. The criminal indictment or charging information serves as an invitation to this negotiation, rather than to the beginning of a trial. Prosecutors argue that the plea negotiation system creates efficiency in a system overwhelmed by cases. Critics argue that this creates perverse incentives for defendants to plead guilty, even when innocent.

Both sides have a point, but the result is that federal courthouses are places not to see a trial but rather to watch a plea or sentencing. In 2017, 94 percent of federal criminal cases never went to trial. District judges around the country have voiced their frustration with the status quo. Judge William G. Young, a federal district court judge in Massachusetts, wrote, "Prosecutors run our federal criminal justice system today. Judges play a subordinate role—necessary yes, but subordinate nonetheless. Defense counsel take what they can get."

Among the most vocal critics of this is Judge Jed Rakoff, a Southern District federal judge (and former prosecutor in the office) who has argued for the abolishment of the sentencing guidelines, which would reduce the incentive to plea. In a 2014 *New York Review of Books* essay, "Why Innocent People Plead Guilty," he wrote, "Our criminal justice system is almost exclusively a system of plea bargaining, negotiated behind closed doors and with no judicial oversight. The outcome is very largely determined by the prosecutor alone."

That power extends to settlements with companies charged with criminal activities. Under Attorney General Eric Holder, companies negotiated significant fines instead of entering into protracted, public courtroom fights with the government. Critics pointed out that these agreements largely remove the judicial system from the process and that the individuals responsible for breaking the law escape consequences. In September 2015, Lynch's Department of Justice shifted tacks. In a memo, Deputy Attorney General Sally Yates announced, "One of the most effective ways to combat corporate misconduct is by seeking accountability from the individuals who perpetrated the wrongdoing." Yates was dismissed ten days into her tenure as acting attorney general by President Trump after she refused to allow the Justice Department to defend the administration's first executive order barring the entry of individuals from predominantly Muslim nations—the "travel ban"—on the grounds that it was not constitutional. But the policy of individual corporate accountability which bore her name remained active eighteen months into the new administration. In November 2018, Deputy Attorney General Rod Rosenstein softened the department's position. He announced that the requirement that companies pursuing settlements disclose every individual involved in wrongdoing was impractical and had stifled the resolution of cases. Going forward, the department would only require disclosure of those "substantially involved." Even in this slightly minimized form, this shift in policy forced companies to develop compliance systems to limit both their civil and their criminal exposure.

Another central element of the federal prosecutors' power is the sheer size of their statutory arsenal. The total number of federal criminal laws is unknown but has grown from fewer than two dozen at the nation's founding to more than 5,000 today, a number that—by a congressional estimate—still expands by nearly 500 statutes a decade. During the first five years of the Obama administration, Congress added 403 laws to the U.S. criminal code. The Trump administration passed more than 443 laws during the first two years in office, but the number of criminal provisions it added and eliminated has not been counted. The code covers crimes as varied as aiming laser pointers at aircraft and creating "animal crush" videos to disclosing personal information on public employees, witnesses, and informants. The overwhelming majority of these offenses are not charged in federal court with any frequency, but their existence serves to expand the power of federal prosecutors to investigate individuals. As John Baker, a Georgetown law professor, explained to the Senate Judiciary Committee in 2013,

> Very few prosecutors in major cities have time to go looking for things. They can't find what has already been done. That is not the case in Federal court. In Federal court, you convene the grand jury, and you go out looking. You got the defendant, potential target, and then you figure out, "Well, what has this person [done?]"

"What can we nail him on?" That is not the way local prosecutors work.

The grim absurdity of this power wasn't lost on prosecutors in the Southern District, according to the law professor Tim Wu, who cited a game played over "beer and pretzels" there:

> Junior and senior prosecutors would sit around, and someone would name a random celebrity—say, Mother Theresa or John Lennon. It would then be up to the junior prosecutors to figure out a plausible crime for which to indict him or her. The crimes were not usually rape, murder, or other crimes you'd see on Law & Order but rather the incredibly broad yet obscure crimes that populate the U.S. Code like a kind of jurisprudential minefield: Crimes like "false statements" (a felony, up to five years), "obstructing the mails" (five years), or "false pretenses on the high seas" (also five years). The trick and the skill lay in finding the more obscure offenses that fit the character of the celebrity and carried the toughest sentences. The result, however, was inevitable: "prison time."

Baker told the committee that this power impacts the ethos at work in U.S. Attorneys' Offices around the country: "There is a certain arrogance that pervades the prosecutors. And it goes with the territory, unfortunately. When you give anybody too much power, they are going to use it."

In this regard, Rudy Giuliani's story is both exceptional and instructive. Long before he became a national figure, he was a uniquely ambitious junior prosecutor in the Southern District. Line assistants typically focus on the rigors of bringing cases, but early on Giuliani veered to politics. He tied his career to the Republican Party, coming under the wing of the Ford administration Justice Department official Harold R. Tyler, a close friend of Judge Lloyd McMahon, for whom Giuliani clerked. At the outset of the Reagan administration, Giuliani served in Washington as an assistant attorney general under William Smith. His tenure there was brief—just three years—but he was an early architect of the War on Drugs, pushing Congress for greater military involvement in narcotics interdiction and, unsuccessfully, to merge the DEA and the FBI. He lobbied for the Southern and Eastern Districts of New York to create dedicated units to combat food stamp fraud. At one point, he drew criticism from his attorneys for meeting separately with executives from McDonnell Douglas while the Department of Justice was investigating the company.

The tough-on-crime policies Giuliani advocated while in Washington have not aged well. He pushed for more prison space for more convicts while rejecting the underlying factors of poverty and unemployment on crime rates. He proposed fighting violent crime associated with the heroin epidemic by attacking traffickers while calling the notion of decriminalizing heroin use "a vast social tragedy." These policies were ineffective and fraught with collateral consequences, but within a decade he would become the mayor of the nation's largest city—seeing the city through the immediate aftermath of the September 11 attacks. He left office a figure of profound influence, an apparent model for how the training and experience of being a federal prosecutor can lend itself to public service.

This type of influence can also have far-reaching effects on society. When Purdue Pharmaceuticals faced Justice Department scrutiny in the early years of the twenty-first century for the marketing of its opioid Oxycontin, the former mayor represented the company through his consulting group Giuliani Partners. A federal investigation determined that Purdue's founders and executives had not only been aware of the dangers of their drug but lied about its safety. Nonetheless, Giuliani prevailed upon the Justice Department to accept a plea deal that wouldn't require jail time or the admission of fault. Most important, the deal averted a public indictment, which would have revealed the findings of fact that linked Oxycontin to the root of the country's opioid crisis. This didn't just represent a personal reversal for Giuliani's get-tough approach on drug abuse; it presaged a vast social tragedy of the sort he had warned the public about. In the decade that followed, other manufacturers swelled both the legal and the black markets with opioids. In 2018, drug overdoses surpassed car accidents and heart attacks as the leading cause of death for Americans under the age of fifty. The following year, a Justice Department memorandum disclosed that three Purdue executives had been recommended for felony charges related to the marketing of Oxycontin; they pleaded guilty to misdemeanor charges. Yet, as Giuliani became President Trump's most vocal defender in the face of the special counsel investigation, these unseemly details were often drowned out.

The Southern District has provided a launching pad for scores of other national careers beyond Giuliani. The Supreme Court justices Felix Frankfurter and Sonia Sotomayor served there as district judges; Frankfurter also argued cases there as a prosecutor. The former attorney general Michael Mukasey started his career as a line assistant there, tried cases as a judge, and, eventually, assumed the top position at the Justice Department. Louis Freeh started his career as an FBI agent before joining the Southern District's U.S. Attorney's Office, then becoming a Southern District judge, before returning to the FBI as director. James Comey, who served as U.S. Attorney for nearly two years beginning in 2002, went on to become deputy attorney general and then the director of the FBI. Mary Jo White ran the office from 1993 to 2002, then the Securities and Exchange Commission. She also represented members of the Sackler family, who founded Purdue. Others have pursued politics, such as Charles Rangel, the twenty-three-term Democratic congressman from New York. Former prosecutors have also found themselves at the center of national political dramas acting as special counsels. These include Robert Fiske and Robert W. Ray, who each briefly led the Whitewater investigation, and Patrick Fitzgerald, a former senior prosecutor who went on to lead the Valerie Plame leak investigation that resulted in the conviction of the White House staffer Scooter Libby. And even those who remain in the districts, particularly those who rise to the federal bench, can have a systemic impact. Judge Shira Scheindlin—whom Mayor Michael Bloomberg excoriated as "that woman"—ruled the New York Police Department's "stop and frisk" policy unconstitutional in 2013. The decision fundamentally changed the nature of the relationship between the police and communities of color, who had been subjected to nearly 600,000 stops in 2011 and just 18,000 two years after. (Scheindlin started her career as a line prosecutor in the Eastern District.)

For each figure who went on to build a national profile from his or her time in the Southern District, a legion of colleagues carved out less conspicuous but no less powerful positions in the law. The former U.S. Attorney Robert Fiske left the prestigious firm Davis Polk to take on the less lucrative work of an Assistant U.S. Attorney, only to return to the firm when his public service career concluded. His career provided a template for a revolving door of prosecutors cycling between the U.S. Attorney's Office and Big Law. Top firms like Paul, Weiss, Davis Polk, and Skadden Arps feed into the U.S. Attorneys' Offices and also recruit experienced prosecutors.

The allure of the private sector is clear. The compensation for federal prosecutors tops out at approximately $164,200, in the range of what a junior associate makes in New York out of law school. Former Assistant U.S. Attorneys can command multiples of their parting government salaries the morning they enter into private practice. In particular, line assistants with experience prosecuting financial crimes like insider trading, Foreign Corrupt Practices Act claims, and money laundering leave government service with extensive litigation experience and other skills actively sought by Big Law.

A federal prosecutor can, in effect, switch sides. She can find a seat at the defense table representing companies against actions she spent much of her career prosecuting—benefiting not only from familiarity with the statutes and enforcement practices but also from her professional network in the Justice Department and working relationships with judges. Non-white-collar criminal defense—narcotics, racketeering, weapons violations—is often less lucrative but also a common career path. A significant majority of defense work conducted in each district is handled by either the Federal Defender's office or private court-appointed CJA (Criminal Justice Act) attorneys assigned to clients who are unable to pay for their counsel. Unlike in state and local courts, these attorneys are career defenders who tend to offer high-quality representation; in some instances, former federal prosecutors in private practice take on CJA cases.

Many former prosecutors view this commingling of public service and private practice as an asset, leading to efficiencies within the system rather than contributing to conflicts of interest. "I started my career in the private sector and then became U.S. attorney. I think I was a stronger U.S. attorney, and I frankly think I am a stronger Chair of the SEC, because of that experience," Mary Jo White, who served as acting U.S Attorney in the Eastern District and U.S. Attorney in the Southern District, told *Time* in 2014.

Federal prosecutors, in one sense, have a unique responsibility compared with other attorneys within the federal criminal justice system. Their obligation is not solely to their client, the U.S. government, but also to pursuing justice. This obligation to justice supersedes the need to secure a conviction, though the Department of Justice does not work from an explicit definition of "justice." Instead, it asks its prosecutors to conduct themselves in a manner that reflects fairness and effectiveness while promoting public confidence in their decision making.

"The qualities of a good prosecutor are as elusive and as impossible to define as those which mark a gentleman. And those who need to be told would not understand it anyway," the attorney general (and future Supreme Court justice) Robert H. Jackson said in an address in 1940. "A sensitiveness to fair play and sportsmanship is perhaps the best protection against the abuse of power, and the citizen's safety lies in the prosecutor who tempers zeal with human kindness, who seeks truth and not victims, who serves the law and not factional purposes, and who approaches his task with humility."

But if justice is an intangible value, success is not. In 2017, federal prosecutors secured more than 63,509 convictions against defendants in the 68,411 cases the Justice Department adjudicated—a 93 percent conviction rate that has remained largely static since 2010. The Southern and Eastern Districts routinely outperform this national average by one or two percentage points. The distinction may seem minimal, but the implication—both for defendants and prosecutors—is not. When a line prosecutor in New York City types a name on a charging document, there is only one expectation: victory.

Proving Grounds

A line of jurors, attorneys, and one defendant stood inside the entrance of the Thurgood Marshall U.S. Courthouse a few minutes before 9:00 a.m., waiting to pass through security. One man stood alone, holding a large black fedora, wearing a brilliant red tie and a look of cowed annoyance. He was Sheldon Silver, the former Speaker of the New York State Assembly, akin to the Speaker of the House in the state legislature in Albany. No one appeared to notice him. One by one, the crowd in front of him passed their briefcases and handbags through an X-ray machine and stepped through the lone metal detector, before surrendering their phones. The line was a small indignity compared with what he would face inside the courthouse.

Outside, the marble steps led toward Foley Square, the point in lower Manhattan where Lafayette and Centre Streets collide into Park Row. The square took its name from Thomas F. Foley, a saloon keeper who found success in politics, eventually becoming sheriff and one of the last Tammany Hall chieftains. The FBI, DEA, and Homeland Security all have offices within eyeshot of the gold leaf tower topping the U.S. courthouse. Behind it is the most recent addition: the Daniel Patrick Moynihan U.S. Courthouse, a twenty-seven-story tower where most matters before the Southern District of New York are heard. Moynihan once called architecture "inescapably a political art" because it "reports faithfully for ages to come what the political values of a particular age were." The courthouse cost $1 billion in 1994. An example of "uncontrolled and excessive spending" according to a General Services Administration audit. The higher floors reveal the gray, claustrophobic span of Manhattan and bridges connecting to Brooklyn. The entrance is largely hidden from view, accessible to those who have reason to be there.

This location has drawn Depression-era labor activists and Cold War anticommunists, civil rights marchers and the Ku Klux Klan, antiwar protesters and Occupy Wall Street.

H. Rap Brown, the Student Nonviolent Coordinating Committee leader, stepped out onto the square following his arrest on gun charges to declare, "Justice is a joke in America." In 1999, a decision by a two-judge panel paved the way for eighteen members of the Ku Klux Klan to stage a rally there, only to be surrounded by six thousand counterprotesters. Fifteen years later, in the summer of 2015, thousands gathered to protest the killing of Eric Garner by NYPD officers in Staten Island during his arrest, chanting, "I can't breathe."

This morning was calm and cool. A wall of TV reporters and video operators gathered to form an audience on the sidewalk, the sky overhead gray and still. The casual daily emergency of lower Manhattan—the relentless sirens, bleating horns, jackhammering construction sites—had yet to set in. In the corridors of the courthouse, the echoes of heels clicking across the marble floors broke the quiet.

Silver's trial was set to begin following a final selection of jurors. It was the signature event in the Southern District of New York for the year, one of two major public corruption prosecutions pursued by the office of Preet Bharara, the U.S. Attorney. He had targeted two of the three top power brokers in New York State government in Albany, the Democrat Sheldon Silver and the Republican Dean Skelos, leaving the third, Governor Andrew Cuomo, in the shadow of suspicion. Silver, who represented a historically poor Latino and Jewish section of Manhattan's Lower East Side that had long since been gentrified, rose to Albany's top legislative job employing a style that the broadsheets described as "laconic" (and the tabloids called "cagey"). He was not a politician to linger at the lectern, but little happened in New York State without his imprimatur. Months earlier, he had been charged with seven criminal counts related to bribes and kickbacks he'd received during his two decades as the Speaker. The charges came after the governor's office abruptly disbanded a commission tasked with rooting out corruption in the state capital—the timing suggesting that if Albany couldn't police itself, Manhattan's Southern District was more than willing to step in. Bharara's announcement of the indictment against Silver—and four months later Dean Skelos, the Republican majority leader of the state senate—represented a collision of powers in New York and pitted state government against federal law enforcement, elected officials against those under appointment.

. Bharara was the first first-generation immigrant to take the top law enforcement position in New York City, a remarkable feat that he achieved at forty. His family immigrated to a small town in New Jersey from India when Bharara was less than two years old. His family pursued the path to citizenship, striving to integrate into a largely white suburban community. It was there, at a public school, where he describes how his earliest lessons in patriotism came alongside his first experiences with racism. At age five, he had developed not only a strong identity as an American but also an innate sense of fairness. Like many schools in that generation, the day began with the Pledge of Allegiance. Each morning a student would lead the class. Though he was kindergarten age and spoke English as a second language, Preet waited and waited for his turn to lead the pledge. But the teacher never chose him. When he realized that the teacher didn't plan to call on him, he returned home and reported to his parents what had happened: his teacher had deliberately overlooked him. Bharara's father drove to the school and confronted the teacher, as he recalled, who denied ignoring Preet. The incident, which didn't tamp his sense of patriotism, became a binding memory of kindergarten.

Bharara excelled in academics, becoming valedictorian at his small private school before attending Harvard. He was also a fastidious student of pop culture, staying up late each school night to watch David Letterman, pursuing a master class in the talk show host's brand of self-deprecating yet cutting humor. The hours in front of the television in his childhood bedroom were not misspent: Preet's comfort in front of crowds—and before cameras—became his trademark.

When he joined the Southern District's U.S. Attorney's Office in 2000 under Mary Jo White, he had the requisite academic credentials for a young prosecutor—cum laude at Harvard, Columbia Law. He came to the office after serving in private practice at Gibson Dunn and started like all line assistants, handling piecemeal general crimes: drug and weapons charges, perjury, bank and postal fraud, escaping federal custody. One of Bharara's first trials wasn't in Manhattan but instead in White Plains, the Westchester County office. His supervisor, who watched as Bharara put on the case, noticed that unlike many junior line assistants Preet didn't betray his nervousness. It was a two-day trial involving a felon charged with possessing a firearm.

"He had a great sense of humor and kept his wits," said Mark Godsey, now a professor of law at the University of Cincinnati.

But, more important, Preet won the conviction.

Bharara would go on to try ten cases during his career as an Assistant U.S. Attorney. He gained experience investigating Colombian drug traffickers, as well as Italian and Chinese organized crime. In one case, his prosecution team secured eighty-two-year sentences for two defendants convicted of a string of violent robberies in Chinatown, the neighborhood abutting the Southern District courthouses. It was an example of what Bharara saw as the utility for prosecutions to target local violent crime and improve the lives of those in the community. But the convictions also came with a price. The prosecution relied on the testimony of a cooperator, Xiao Qin Zhou. Like most cooperators, Zhou had baggage. He acknowledged conspiring to commit more than forty robberies and shooting one victim, but Bharara's team was willing to work with Zhou in order to convict the two men. Six years later, Zhou returned to the Southern District. He had violated his plea agreement, robbing a man with a screwdriver just a few blocks from the courthouse where he had testified to secure his freedom. The outcome of the case reflected the Sisyphean challenge of law enforcement. But, in the end, this case—like most of Bharara's career as a line prosecutor— garnered little attention.

"It didn't seem apparent to me that he would become the prosecutorial colossus that he's become," said Gordon Mehler, a former prosecutor in the Eastern District who faced off against Bharara as defense counsel in an organized crime case.

In 2005, Bharara pivoted to politics—and Washington. He signed on as chief counsel to New York's senator Chuck Schumer. This wasn't Bharara's first exposure to Democratic politics. As a first-year associate out of law school, he volunteered for Mark Green during his successful campaign to become New York City's public advocate. A decade later, the position with Senator Schumer gave Bharara a more substantial role on a much larger stage. The senator served as a member on the Senate Judiciary Committee, chairing a powerful subcommittee with oversight on the courts and the Department of Justice. This also placed Schumer at the center of power within New York's legal community. Beyond his influence as a lawmaker, he was a kingmaker. He had the authority to recommend candidates for the most powerful jobs in New York City law enforcement: the U.S. Attorney positions in the Southern and Eastern Districts. A generation of public officials owed their positions, in one way or another, to Schumer. When Bharara arrived at Schumer's office in Washington, he took charge of a case far more significant than anything he had handled in the Southern District: the Senate Judiciary Committee's investigation into the politicized firings of U.S. Attorneys under the Bush administration. Bharara helped secure a victory far more significant than any he obtained in the Southern District: the resignation of Attorney General Alberto Gonzales.

As the U.S. Attorney, Bharara immediately attracted attention with high-profile prosecutions against a Democratic Party fund-raiser, the Lucchese crime family, and the accused U.S. embassy bomber Ahmed Ghailani. His style—quick-witted, confident, and strident—translated to many as brash, but he made a case that a U.S. Attorney should act as a deterrent voice of conscience for the public. He also targeted white-collar criminals including Galleon Group's Raj Rajaratnam. Nonetheless, critics argued that he was not moving quickly and forcefully against the banks responsible for the 2008 financial collapse. A series of insider-trading cases that followed rehabilitated the impression that Bharara was soft on Wall Street. He soon emerged as the most outspoken U.S. Attorney in New York City since Rudy Giuliani, which translated to a national profile; in 2012, *Time* featured him on the cover. When he appeared in public, Bharara used self-deprecation and humor to blunt the invariable conclusion that could be drawn from his presence: he was among the most powerful figures in New York and, in certain corners, the most feared.

Yet 2015 marked significant setbacks for Bharara. The president had overlooked him for the attorney general job in late 2014 (he publicly maintained he had no interest in the position). Instead, Bharara's counterpart in Brooklyn, Loretta Lynch, the comparably understated U.S. Attorney for the Eastern District of New York, was sworn in to the position in April. Lynch, who had also been recommended by Schumer, became the nation's first African American woman to rise to the Justice Department's top position—and also the first former Brooklyn U.S. Attorney to take the most powerful job in law enforcement—an occasion that momentarily pulled the national spotlight from the Southern District. Following Sheldon Silver's arrest, Bharara received a rare public reprimand. The judge in the case admonished him for statements he made to the press about the case. Then, days before the Silver trial was to open, the Supreme Court refused to hear an appeal on one of the office's signature insider-trading cases, forcing Bharara to drop seven cases pursued by his office. His once successful record on Wall Street apparently rewritten by higher courts, Bharara's legacy now focused on the upcoming public corruption cases targeting Albany. The tabloids speculated that Governor Andrew Cuomo would be next in the U.S. Attorney's sights without elaborating on what laws, if any, the governor had broken. As the Albany lawmakers' trial dates approached, Bharara's investigators had begun looking at targets nearly visible from his window at One St. Andrew's Plaza: city hall and the New York Police Department. The rumor mill spun that Bharara was laying the groundwork for an office even more powerful than the one he currently occupied.

That morning, jurors streamed into courtroom 110. It was a cavernous perfect rectangle with ceilings rising nearly thirty feet, walls of steel-black marble topped with polished wood colonnades and lined with corniced windows; large domed chandeliers hung from the ceiling, bathing the room in a soft yellow glow. The only glint of color in the room was the red, white, and blue of the American flag standing in the corner, embellished with gold tasseling. The prosecution and defense tables sat side by side and perpendicular to the jury box, as they would in a film, but unlike nearly every courtroom in New York City's two federal districts. The room fulfilled all cinematic expectations, but the crowd of jurors filled the gallery wearing street clothes and looking listless, clutching newspapers, novels, Sudoku books. Outside Silver paced the hallway awaiting the arrival of his legal team—all six of them. When he finally entered the room, his expression drifted from disinterest to helplessness, eyes darting under his rimless glass frames.

Silver was only the latest public figure to make the transformative journey through the gallery to the defense table in room 110. This was the same room where the Rosenbergs went to the trial that resulted in their death sentence and where Joseph McCarthy once conducted local hearings under klieg lights. But the history of the place seemed far from reach; it was just a Monday morning in November.

ACROSS THE RIVER in the Eastern District, a few hours later, courtroom 2AS of New York City's other federal courthouse hummed with activity. The setting was considerably less magisterial than the Southern District—a windowless room with scuffed flesh-toned walls; even the American flag seemed to be shrinking from recognition in the corner of the room. Defense counsel gathered around their table in the spare, harshly lit room, a casual clump of graying men in suits, waiting for their clients to be arraigned that morning. One defendant faced money-laundering charges, another armed robbery charges, and a third, a twenty-two-year-old man from Jamaica, Queens, named Ali Saleh, charges of material support for terrorism. Domestic-based terror plots tended to surface more often in the Eastern District, a function of the social geography of the jurisdiction but also an expression of the law enforcement priorities there. The Eastern District U.S. Attorney's Office had effectively cornered the market on domestic terrorism investigations through a close working relationship with the FBI and

New York's Joint Terrorism Task Force (JTTF). Saleh's case was only the most recent there involving individuals seeking to join the Islamic State; since September 11, no other district in the country had charged as many terrorist suspects as the Eastern.

Before the arraignment, the parties gathered quietly. The lead prosecutor, Saritha Komatireddy, an Assistant U.S. Attorney in her early thirties, conferred in the front row of the gallery with a colleague. Like Bharara's, her parents had immigrated to the United States, and she excelled academically, attending Harvard for both undergraduate and law school. Her parents were nonplussed with her decision to become an attorney, hoping that she would pursue medicine. But she saw the law as an intellectual feast, clerking for the now Supreme Court justice Brett Kavanaugh, when he was serving as judge on the U.S Court of Appeals for the D.C. Circuit, and joining the Deepwater Horizon commission as a member of the investigative team developing a report on the 2010 BP oil rig disaster and subsequent spill in the Gulf of Mexico. When she chose the path of becoming a federal prosecutor, it was not so much to play the role of enforcer as to grapple directly with the most challenging issues in the law.

Days earlier, she had argued a novel issue for the government. Her office had made a relatively routine request, through a search warrant, to obtain access to an iPhone confiscated in a methamphetamine investigation. Apple had cooperated with similar requests in the past; like many Silicon Valley companies, it maintained cordial relationships with investigative and intelligence agencies. This time the company refused. The Edward Snowden disclosures revealed that American technology companies that had worked with the government had also seen their technology infiltrated by the government. Tech giants suddenly faced public exposure on the issue of personal privacy. The government and Apple collided on this issue before a magistrate in the Eastern District, albeit in a low-stakes drug case.

Komatireddy dealt with a more routine matter in courtroom 2AS on this day, an arraignment. A few minutes before the judge arrived, a door opened along the wall. Susan Kellman, the court-appointed defense counsel, appeared and walked over to the Saleh family to confer. She was a fixture of both districts—a deft and at times passionate defender who had the warmth and toughness of a social worker. A moment later, marshals led in Saleh to his seat next to her. His slight frame draped in navy prison scrubs, beard overgrown and unkempt, lent him an almost elderly appearance, though he was college age. He turned to his family and smiled weakly before the marshals guided him to stand before the judge. Saleh's brother and a woman in a blue, gold, and silver abaya sat in the second aisle. The woman mouthed a prayer to herself, dabbing her nose with a tissue.

"Do you wish to enter a plea of guilty or not guilty?" the judge asked.

Silence.

Saleh averted his gaze.

The judge looked to Kellman, who conferred with her client. "He has no comment," she said.

"There's no response here?" the judge asked Kellman.

Kellman wasn't impressed. Saleh was not her first terrorism defendant, nor was he her first terrorism defendant who became shifty in the presence of the judge. Indeed, among the accused terrorists she represented, the facts in Saleh's case were unexceptional. Over the course of a year, he had taken to social media to declare his support for the Islamic State while making plans to join the group in Syria. He was just one of dozens of active threats the U.S. Attorney's Office was tracking with federal investigators. Like many other terror defendants before him, he made little effort to conceal his activities or intentions from federal authorities. In one Twitter posting, he declared, "I am ready to die for the Caliphate, prison is nothing." (FBI agents with New York City's JTTF relied heavily on Twitter and jihadist message boards as entry points into local terrorist threats.) Saleh eventually led federal investigators on a five-state trek as he repeatedly tried to board flights to Egypt and Qatar, before returning to New York, unsuccessful. The FBI finally arrested him at his home in Queens.

"He's not this shy outside of the courtroom," Kellman offered.

Komatireddy could do little to compel the defendant to speak. Saleh would eventually plead guilty. He would also be convicted of slashing a prison guard with a shiv. But his small act of defiance complete, he made a feeble gesture to his family as the hearing ended and the marshals gently turned him in the opposite direction, back to detention.

THIS WAS ONLY a slightly busier-than-usual day in the federal districts of New York. Upstairs, on the eighth floor of the Brooklyn federal courthouse, a retired FBI agent walked a weary jury through a set of thirty-year-old surveillance photographs of two Bonanno family associates standing outside a South Ozone Park social club. Across the hall, prosecutors and defense lawyers winnowed jurors in a tax evasion case against the owner of a construction company. On the fourth floor, a defendant in a sealed case who appeared on the court calendar as "John Doe" stood before the judge at a conference in a loan modification and flip scheme.

Back in the Southern District, a jury on the fourteenth floor of the Moynihan courthouse deliberated the case against two London-based bankers accused of manipulating a key bank exchange rate known as LIBOR—London Interbank Offered Rate. Ten banks had already paid $10 billion in settlements to U.S., U.K., and European authorities, but in pursuing the new Justice Department approach, the prosecutors pressed ahead against the individuals in a criminal trial. One floor above, a man named Allah Justice McQueen stood before Judge Shira Scheindlin to be sentenced for a much smaller fraud: scamming elderly people into paying what they believed to be bail money for a grandchild. He wore a suit, a handkerchief neatly folded in his breast pocket, as his attorney begged for a reduced sentence. The judge watched, her hand fixed to her forehead, the glint of her computer screen playing across her glasses, as his attorney tried to cast the situation in the best possible light.

"He did it. He admitted it," his lawyer offered sheepishly. "We're not saying he's an angel. He's not. But he's not the devil either."

SHELDON SILVER'S TRIAL resumed in room 443 of the Thurgood Marshall U.S. Courthouse, a compact but elegant courtroom with towering windows. *The New York Times* described Silver as a "genius for leveraging obscurity," as a figure who had transformed a tiny legislative district in lower Manhattan into a fulcrum of statewide power. As he sat hunched in the defendant's seat, he seemed to be longing for obscurity, any piece of action or dialogue that would draw attention from him. During his career, Silver had not cut this helpless figure; he was a political icon who inspired fear in his opponents and allies alike. He joined the state assembly in 1976, part of a post-Watergate rush of new blood into the state body, which included a young Brooklyn lawyer named Chuck Schumer. Silver was a young lawyer, the son of a hardware store owner, intent on putting his community of low-income Jewish and Latino families on the political map. By the time he rose to the Speaker's chair in 1994, he'd developed a reputation as pragmatic with outsize influence. His indictment had, for the first time, pulled back the curtain on the personal benefits his power had yielded.

That afternoon Judge Valerie Caproni interviewed prospective jurors in the Silver case. She chewed her words through a drawl, her head barely rising above her bench as she walked each person through a set of questions. The process elicited an intimate but decontextualized portrait of the group of New Yorkers: a fifty-year-old salesman from the Bronx volunteered that his vision had "green/red deficiency"; a twenty-seven-year-old Trinidadian American woman mentioned that she lost her father in the September 11 attacks and that her mother was the victim of a sexual assault but the family did not report the crime, because she was in the country illegally at that time; a sixty-three-year-old marketing executive from Westchester County acknowledged that after a car accident he'd been sued by a "woman from Queens" and "since I was a defendant I felt like I was being gouged."

When prospective juror #27 stepped into the jury box, she felt certain she had already been selected. Her name was Arleen Phillips; she was a fifty-three-year-old technician for Verizon from Mount Vernon, born in St. Thomas and raised in Brooklyn and the Bronx. She'd already been called to jury service twice that year; each time she avoided being selected. She figured her luck had to run out at some point, and, frankly, she looked forward to a break from work. The attorneys asked Phillips what she knew about the case and the defendant. She mentioned that she had heard about the trial on the radio during her drive in that morning but hadn't connected it to her jury duty. The names Sheldon Silver and Preet Bharara meant nothing to her, but she didn't see any reason to mention that. She stood to return to the jury room, where the showdown between two of New York's most powerful men would rest in her hands.

ORGANIZED CRIME

There are something like 5,000 men in this city today to whom this tremendous power is laid open, ex-convicts of the Mafia and the Camorra, fierce medieval criminals . . . [they] laugh at the feeble laws by which the Government of the United States seeks to prevent their entrance into the country and restrain their depredations afterward.

—"Italians Seek Protection Against Black Hand,"
The New York Times, September 4, 1910

1

Downthehole

June 17, 2013

Gaspare Valenti had just come from the doctor's office when he climbed into the passenger seat of his cousin Vinny Asaro's Mercedes. It was a few minutes after ten in the morning. Clouds began to bridge the sky as the cool of the morning burned off under the early summer sun. Later that afternoon, the heat would break with a thunderstorm, the clouds lashing the city with a warm rain, but for now the sky held the powder-blue promise of an early summer day.

He had been getting in and out of cars, driving around New York City, with Vinny for more than forty years. Valenti, sixty-six, was twelve years younger than Asaro and had spent his lifetime under his older cousin's wing—a relationship that could be seen when they stood side by side. "Gar," as Valenti was known, was wiry and balding, with rimless glasses and a side smile that scissored each word from his mouth. He was an also-ran to Asaro, a giant in size and reputation: broad shoulders, large hands, a face cut with hard angles, his hairline largely intact. Even now, as an elderly man, his presence towered over his younger cousin. For more than half a century, the men's fortunes rose and fell—sometimes together, other times apart—almost exclusively outside the law.

Their world was Ozone Park, Queens. A low-rise neighborhood eleven miles from midtown Manhattan that clung to the edge of the Belt Parkway, the artery that rounded Brooklyn into southern Queens then terminated along Jamaica Bay and John F. Kennedy International Airport. The tidy streets of spare detached homes showed little outward change in the men's lifetimes. The older homes were built from red brick in the 1920s; the more recent were wood frame and vinyl-sided. The main thoroughfare, Liberty Avenue, ran like a thread out of Brooklyn's Brownsville and East New York, splitting into 101st Avenue at the border of the boroughs, where overhead tracks of the A train rose aboveground in time for riders to catch a view of the gravestones of Bayside Cemetery. Below the elevated tracks ran a shaded stretch of auto body shops, saloons, and nail salons on the way to Cross Bay Boulevard. It was a neighborhood built for working people, some trying to get a foothold in New York City, others holding on to a place they once knew.

Subtle signs pointed to a fundamental shift here. Fading Hindu prayer flags hung out front of many homes where crucifixes once watched over dining room tables. The Catholic churches remained—Nativity, St. Mary's, and St. Elizabeth's—but newer houses of worship appeared: Redeeming Christ Baptist church, the Tulsi Mandir Hindu temple, and Masjid Al Aman. The backroom *ramino* games and numbers run by the local bookies now faced legitimate competition: tour buses full of gamblers plied the Resorts World Casino down the road at Aqueduct Racetrack. Few could have predicted a day when the Italians no longer ruled Ozone Park or when a cut of the card games went not to the boss but to Albany—legitimately.

The cousins came of age on the edge of all this in a postage-stamp-size Brooklyn neighborhood called the Hole. Or, *downthehole,* as the men pronounced it. It sat on the other side of the graveyard, across the four lanes of North Conduit Avenue. One wiseguy described it as looking like it "got hit with a meteor." That made great copy, but it wasn't quite accurate. *Downthehole* was a terminal point, a last shred of Brooklyn where the city, as if it were worn out from the sprawl of tenements and housing projects, seemed to fall to its knees, like a pack mule finding its end. As Blake Avenue dropped, the streets sank below sea level, the two- and three-family homes suddenly traded ground with vacant lots overgrown with swaying salt-marsh cordgrass. Silty pools of standing water overtook intersections at Ruby, Emerald, and Amber Streets, aspirational names for a stretch of urban wilderness unlike any other in New York City. Overturned dumpsters, abandoned mattresses, sun-faded boats resting in unhitched trailers, were the only signs of life other than chickens running through the flotsam and weeds not noticing that they're in the largest city in the United States. The Hole was probably the only place outside the Third World where you could hear a cock's crow one moment and the scream of a descending jetliner the next. A hell of a place to come from. For Valenti and Asaro, the whole point in life was to get out.

They didn't get too far. By the time the men hit retirement age, they had barely made it up the hill, into Queens. There they spent their days driving the streets together, checking in at one of the few remaining social clubs, stopping by the auto body shops, talking about the past only in the most oblique terms.

In the late 1960s, the cousins made their living in the Bonanno crime family—or, more accurately, the men made their livings through their association with the Bonanno clan. Gangsters didn't draw pay-checks or receive handouts from the family they belonged to. Their association only granted them the right to commit crimes provided they "kicked up" a portion of their earnings to the family. In exchange, men like Valenti and Asaro received protection from criminal rivals, the veneer of credibility that association with an established crime family offered, and the promise—though for many unattainable—of getting "straightened out." Which remained the only way to become a made member of organized crime.

The more sophisticated gangsters could see the top-down structure of the mob for what it was: a hustle. A means to distribute risk among the lowest-rung associates while concentrating the wealth within the few at the top of the hierarchy. Those out on the street got the worst deal; the ones committing the crimes, exposing themselves to retribu-tion and law enforcement, made the least money. The inequity encouraged a sort of criminal entrepreneurship: those cunning and violent enough rose above this crowd; those content to follow orders remained in the shadows and, often, ended up in jail or on the run. Asaro was the former; Valenti, the latter.

When the men came of age in the 1960s, the five families of the New York Mafia had little to fear from law enforcement. Those on the street ran the risk of arrest, but the leadership kept their distance and—in the eyes of the law—their hands clean. The FBI director, J. Edgar Hoover, refused to acknowledge the existence of the mob, even as Robert Kennedy, the young attorney general, dragged organized crime figures into the daylight of Senate hearings. This dissonance allowed the mob to thrive in New York and around the country.

The "life," as the wiseguys referred to it, was the only option Valenti saw. His mother made her living as a seamstress and his father as a home builder. Like most of their neighbors, they were content with the living they could make on the books. They followed a legitimate path that most Italian American immigrants did, turning a generation of manual labor into property, college education for their children, and the prospect of ascending to a profession. It wasn't glamorous, nor did it garner much respect. It was simply what was expected. When Valenti looked at the wiseguys in the neighborhood, his cousin Vinny, his uncle Mickey Zaffarano, he saw something different from the life of humble sacrifice. He understood them.

"Everybody has lust in their hearts," he said. "Some people have more lust."

Looking back, Valenti had some fond memories of the "life." At age nineteen, he pulled his first robbery out on Long Island. His cohorts told him to "come dressed"; he appeared in burgundy boots, corduroys, and a "see-sucker" jacket, as he described it. Taking a look at Valenti, his accomplice explained that "dressed" meant *armed*. (The take from the virginal score was $63.) As an intrepid gangster, Valenti didn't distinguish himself with his wits, and in the late 1960s his uncle Mickey caught wind of his nephew's activities and pulled the young man aside. Zaffarano, a Bonanno captain who owned the Pussycat Theater, a Times Square X-rated movie house, once served as the bodyguard to Joseph Bonanno, the godfather of the crime family.

"You want to continue in this life?" Zaffarano asked him.

"Yes," Valenti replied.

"Shave your mustache," Zaffarano said. "Act like a gentleman."

Valenti's first major test as a wiseguy came in 1968, he said. Asaro, then thirty-two, rang his cousin and asked for help. He needed access to one of the homes Valenti's father had built on 102nd Road. "We have to bury somebody," Valenti recalled Asaro saying. There wasn't much choice: Valenti let his cousin and another mobster, Jimmy Burke, into one of the nearly complete two-flats, then went upstairs and waited for several hours. Burke was the rare Irishman associated with the Italian Mafia, a feared associate of the Lucchese crime family, known as Jimmy the Gent.

At the house with Burke and Asaro, Valenti didn't see the body, but he knew whom it belonged to: Paul Katz, a warehouse owner who let the two mobsters store stolen goods at one of his locations—a spot where the NYPD later arrested both men in a raid.

After the men were released, Katz left his home one night, telling his children that he was going to meet some friends at "the candy store." He never returned. Federal investigators believe Asaro strangled Katz to death with a dog leash, then ordered his body thrown into the freshly dug hole in the basement and covered with lime. Valenti knew only what Vinny told him: "The guy was a rat." Asaro ordered his cousin to lay cement over the grave, according to Valenti.

The 1970s treated the cousins well. Valenti lived as a self-described "hustler" hijacking trucks, fencing stolen goods. He and Asaro ran with other wiseguys, including Jimmy Burke and Henry Hill, spending their nights at social clubs like Robert's Lounge and the Colonial House in Ozone Park.

The cousins had a complex relationship. Valenti took on small-time jobs for Asaro: selling pornography, hijacking trucks, delivering beatings. When Asaro finally got "straightened out," Valenti drove Vinny to the ceremony, he later recounted. Asaro took the oath of *omertà*—the mob's code of silence—in a mausoleum in a nearby graveyard, Valenti said. A code enforced with death. Asaro later had the pledge of "death before dishonor" tattooed on his arm, a branded reminder that he had risen from the field of associates to become a Bonanno soldier, a made man. Even though Valenti didn't get the call, his loyalty had paid off.

The decade would be marked by the Lufthansa heist, a $6.8 million robbery of cash and gold from the airline's warehouse at JFK airport, a crime immortalized in Martin Scorsese's *Goodfellas*. The score typified the audacity of the mob in New York and became a legend simply known as "Lufthansa." In the film, Robert De Niro portrayed Burke, crediting him with the 1978 robbery. Henry Hill, played by Ray Liotta in the film, eventually testified against Burke and Paul Vario, a Lucchese associate, and laid out the lasting narrative of the crime in Nicholas Pileggi's *Wiseguy*. When Hill died in 2012, he was the last of the known participants in the heist. Asaro had never been linked to the robbery, though he and Burke were close. Nobody had ever been convicted of involvement in it, though many alleged participants wound up dead. The story of the heist had never been told in a courtroom: this presented a tangible opportunity for the prosecutors to tackle an unsolved crime.

Looking at the map, you could see that the heist was a neighborhood job. Ozone Park was close enough to be strafed by jetliners throughout the day, barreling in toward JFK's runways. The targeted warehouse sat four miles down North Conduit Avenue from the Hole, where Asaro and Valenti had grown up. It represented the biggest score of their lifetimes. And it was right there in their backyard. Their lives together, and on the fringes of New York City, seemed to lead to that one moment. Eventually, Lufthansa would drive a stake between the men.

THE THIRTY YEARS AFTER the heist were less forgiving for the men, and for the mob in New York. The other pivotal moment in their lives came not in Ozone Park but in Washington, where Congress passed the Racketeer Influenced and Corrupt Organizations statute—or RICO—in 1970. RICO gave prosecutors a tool that they had lacked: a law that allowed the justice system to connect the crimes committed on the street by low-level gangsters to the bosses who organized and benefited from the activity. Prosecutors simply needed to show that crimes were committed within an "enterprise" to charge the individuals under RICO. The list of crimes, or "predicate acts," reads like a good week for many of the mob families: homicide, assault, robbery, kidnapping, forgery, counterfeiting, theft, embezzlement, illegal kickbacks, bribery, gambling, usury, loan-sharking, coercion, and extortion, among many other potential RICO violations.

Several forces converged to make this power shift possible. In 1968, Congress laid the legal foundation with legislation sponsored by Robert Kennedy, the Omnibus Crime Control and Safe Streets Act. Wiretaps and other electronic surveillance methods, which Title III of the act authorized, gave agents a tool to finally penetrate crime families and produce evidence. The witness protection program, created under the Organized Crime Control Act of 1970, enabled prosecutors to promise safety to witnesses who had reason to fear retaliation.

But the most potent innovation was RICO. The author of the act had never set foot in a courtroom as a prosecutor. G. Robert Blakey worked as a young staffer on hearings into organized crime and labor conducted by the Arkansas senator John L. McClellan in 1957, developing expertise in organized crime. Over the next decade, he helped engineer the definitive legislative breakthrough in battling rackets, the RICO statute. The act drew widespread support in Congress, but some representatives including New York's Mario Biaggi successfully petitioned for any reference to "organized crime" to be omitted from the statute. (Biaggi, a former NYPD officer who as a congressman campaigned against the use of the term "Mafia," would be convicted on corruption charges in the late 1980s.)

Before RICO, prosecutors had extremely limited powers to confront the mob. Mobsters facing prosecution could answer only to specific charges for individual crimes.

This approach limited the reach of law enforcement to the street-level toughs responsible for the manual labor of committing the crime on behalf of the mob family. Blakey crafted the statute to confront the structural strengths of the Mafia: the compartmentalized hierarchy that insulated the leadership from criminal charges. The law made four distinct acts illegal: using money made from crimes or using patterns of crimes ("rackets") to acquire an interest in a criminal enterprise, running an enterprise based on rackets, or conspiring to do any of these things. Previously, the courts treated each of these as a stand-alone crime linked directly to a perpetrator; by doing so, they viewed the offenses in near isolation from the organized crime group the crimes had been committed under. Under the new law, the government could charge a murder committed for a crime family as a stand-alone act and a RICO violation—exposing to harsh penalties not only the person pulling the trigger but the one giving the order. The law effectively built a bridge between low-level offenders and the leadership that organized the criminal activity. The other element of the statute was punishment: a RICO conviction meant not only harsh prison sentences but asset forfeiture that could bankrupt mob bosses.

Congress passed RICO on October 15, 1970. Yet prosecutors did not immediately put the law into use. Blakey found little enthusiasm among federal prosecutors in New York and Washington. He was a creature of Congress, rather than a prosecutor, someone who had honed his experience with organized crime in committee hearings, rather than in criminal trials. In the Southern District, after Blakey laid out his vision for how to use the new law, one of the prosecutors told him, "You don't know what you're talking about," then ended the meeting.

But the FBI had already started to shift its approach to organized crime. After Hoover's death in 1972, the bureau turned not only to technology like wiretaps but also to the greater use of undercover work. In 1976, the FBI authorized an undercover operation that would pierce the mob's sense of invulnerability. A young agent named Joseph Pistone assumed the identity "Donnie Brasco" to investigate the gem-fencing trade. Six years later, he reemerged as the first agent to penetrate organized crime. He had been embraced by the Bonanno crime family, which bore the disgrace of being the first family to be infiltrated by the feds. Once an esteemed part of the mob's ruling body, the Commission, the Bonannos and their underlings became the objects of suspicion. The evidence culled in Pistone's investigation led to the first major legal assaults on the mob in federal court, though Asaro and Valenti escaped implication. The law could now deliver decades-long sentences, and the Mafia began to face its most pernicious threat: betrayal.

It took nearly a decade before Blakey eventually found a receptive audience. Blakey, then a law professor, hosted a weeklong summer clinic at Cornell Law School in 1979 that drew a crowd of federal agents and prosecutors. He urged the men to abandon not only the way they had done their jobs but how they viewed the threat: the criminal wasn't the target; the enterprise was. Blakey also pressed another innovation: the aggressive use of wiretaps as a means not only to gather direct evidence for a prosecution but to develop evidence for more wiretaps. Through broad surveillance, investigators could develop a picture of how an organization operated. One of the Cornell attendees, an FBI agent named Jim Kossler, returned to the New York bureau and immediately implemented a new structure: there would be five teams dedicated to the mob—one for each of the crime families.

The rise of RICO set the stage for one of the great jurisdictional battles between the Southern and the Eastern Districts. Neither office had a clear claim on organized crime. The geography of the Mafia across New York City's five boroughs did not hew to any clear jurisdictional lines. While all five families were represented in each of the five boroughs, each maintained headquarters at locations in the city. In the early 1980s, the largest clan, the Genovese family, projected its strength from a modest East Harlem storefront—a location out of step with the departure of generations of Italian immigrants shuttled out as more recent arrivals from Puerto Rico and the Dominican Republic moved in. The Lucchese family had three distinct arms operating in Manhattan, the Bronx and Brooklyn, and New Jersey; while the Gambino family, which controlled the unions operating in supermarkets and butcher shops throughout the city, was run from the secluded mansion of Paul Castellano in Todt Hill, Staten Island. The Colombo family, once the public face of the Mafia under the leadership of Joe Colombo, had gone back to ground in south Brooklyn after the public assassination attempt on their leader; farther north, in Williamsburg, the smaller Bonanno family centered its activities.

The outer boroughs did favor many of the rackets organized crime relied on. A young prosecutor described to *New York* magazine the unique opportunity the Eastern District presented: "We're in mob heaven here . . . We've got two racetracks, the Brooklyn waterfront, two airports, and the home offices for five of the largest organized-crime families in the country."

The Southern District wasn't an organized crime backwater, though. In 1979, Robert Fiske, the U.S. Attorney from 1976 to 1980, tried Anthony Scotto, a local president of the International Longshoremen's Association and accused member of the Gambino crime family, in the second prosecution under RICO. (Prosecutors first used RICO in a California case against the Hells Angels, which had resulted in an acquittal months earlier.) Scotto stood accused of accepting kickbacks from companies seeking to do business on New York's waterfront. The case illustrated the reach of the mob into the highest levels of government; shortly before his indictment came down, President Carter invited Scotto to lunch. The trial also brought in a cast of witnesses testifying to Scotto's upstanding character, including two former New York City mayors, John Lindsay and Robert F. Wagner Jr., and the former governor of New York Hugh Carey. While Scotto and his co-defendant were convicted, each received a lenient sentence of five years. The political leaders who vouched for Scotto were never implicated in wrongdoing; U.S. Attorney Fiske made clear that the White House was not aware of the Southern District's investigation and that Scotto wielded no influence there.

Even as the FBI moved steadily against the mob, the U.S. Attorneys for the Southern and Eastern Districts found themselves in a familiar turf battle. Raymond Dearie, the top prosecutor in Brooklyn, had been skeptical of Blakey's vision of RICO and more rigorous in scrutinizing wiretap applications to go before the judges in the Eastern District. The Southern District became the favored option for FBI agents hoping to get a wire up against organized crime figures. The U.S. Attorney there, John S. Martin, did not actively seek out a rivalry with Dearie. Instead, the FBI found that it could lever the districts against each other to move a case forward. When Donnie Brasco emerged from his undercover operation in 1981, the case went to the office that had worked most closely with the bureau on the mob: the Southern District. Pistone first testified against the Bonanno family in 1982 in the trial led by the Southern District prosecutors Barbara Jones and Louis Freeh, who would later become the director of the FBI. The RICO conviction sidelined three Bonanno family leaders and forced the family from the Commission, the ruling body of New York's five families.

In 1983, a new U.S. Attorney for the Southern District arrived eager to prove his mettle against the mob: thirty-nine-year-old Rudolph Giuliani, who started his career as a line prosecutor in the Southern District during organized crime's ascendance. He had clerked in the district with Judge Lloyd F. MacMahon, the Southern District judge who gained notoriety for ordering Carmine Galante and other disruptive mob figures gagged and shackled during a 1961 narcotics trial. (MacMahon, one evening, found a severed dog's head outside his house. The horrifying discovery evoked a Sicilian adage: "To kill a dog, you don't cut off its tail; you cut off its head.")

Rudolph Giuliani became the U.S. Attorney in 1983, put up for the job by the Republican senator Alfonse D'Amato. He had returned from Main Justice in Washington, where he served as an associate attorney general in the Reagan administration. While in Washington, Giuliani made moves to prepare for his eventual return to New York. As a senior Justice official, he cut the prosecutorial staff in Martin's Southern District office, only to go on a hiring spree on his return. When a friendly colleague announced his retirement as the head of the Eastern District's Organized Crime Strike Force, Giuliani angled to install an ally as the replacement so that he would be in a better position to try the strike force's cases in the Southern District.

The strike force's new chief, a young Brooklyn-born prosecutor, Edward McDonald, had little interest in handing Eastern District cases to Giuliani's Southern District. "He called me up and asked me to have lunch. He expected me to be very appreciative—which I was," McDonald said. "He started talking about joint investigations, and the prosecutions would be in Manhattan, where there would be greater publicity, and I'm thinking, 'What kind of bullshit is this?'"

The truth: Giuliani had the power to boot step the Eastern District. He had forged alliances with the FBI and the New York State Organized Crime Task Force. When push came to shove, he simply went to the only source that could decide jurisdictional disputes: Main Justice. Giuliani had the contacts and influence to convince the attorney general that cases belonged in the Southern District. McDonald watched as Giuliani's office laid claim to some of the evidence and surveillance gathered for years by his task force. The biggest among these: the Commission trial.

Nineteen eighty-six was the year law enforcement shattered the status quo of mob influence in New York City. In the Eastern District, John Gotti and his brother faced trial on racketeering charges, while investigations into a JFK-based Lucchese trucking scheme had led to a series of extortion convictions, and a probe of the Bonanno-family moving industry racket resulted in the conviction of eight members under RICO. In the Southern District, a drug-trafficking trial targeting the Sicilian links to the New York mob—the so-called Pizza Connection case—had stretched over a year. Among these cases, the Commission trial was the most ambitious test of RICO to date.

"The [Commission] case should be seen as the apex of the family cases," Giuliani said before the trial. "It is an attempt, if we can prove our charges, to dismantle the structure that has been used since the beginning of organized crime in the United States."

The indictment targeted the leadership of the Mafia, naming bosses of four of New York's five families—Anthony Salerno (Genovese), Philip Rastelli (Bonanno), Carmine Persico (Colombo), and Anthony Corallo (Lucchese)—as well as underlings. A number of defendants died before trial: Paul Castellano had been murdered months before the trial began by John Gotti and his crew in a brazen afternoon hit in midtown Manhattan. Several other mob leaders passed away from natural causes. Those who remained faced charges. The indictment detailed a scheme that the Commission used to control significant players in the city's construction industry. The five families operated a syndicate under the District Council of the Cement and Concrete Workers union, a perch from which they fixed prices, extorted money, and solicited bribes. The mob's presence behind a union foundational to New York City's construction industry evoked its power and influence; in one estimate, construction firms paid an additional 10 percent to the mob to complete projects.

At the trial, the defense conceded a fact that had never been decisively acknowledged to a jury: the mob existed. The fact of La Cosa Nostra's existence, however, didn't prove the government's charges. Under RICO, the government had to prove that the enterprise was criminal in nature and those charged in the indictment participated in activities within the Commission. The prosecution team included Michael Chertoff, who would go on to run the Department of Homeland Security, and John Savarese, both young prosecutors in their early thirties who had attended Harvard Law and clerked for Justice William Brennan. Among the defense counsel, Carmine Persico, the Colombo boss, represented himself; he had already been convicted under separate extortion charges but faced even stiffer penalties under RICO. Aware that the government had dozens of hours of wiretapped recordings and a string of informants, the defense tried to minimize the impact of the evidence. Where the government saw racketeering, there was instead simple bid rigging. The question for the jury was whether to buy into the concept of RICO—to see the fact that crimes were committed within an enterprise as the separate crime of racketeering in itself.

The government couldn't rely on a case built on cooked concrete invoices and accounting books. The prosecutors needed to reveal the mob's dark side. The jury heard lurid testimony of the mob's secret initiation rite—a blood oath that involved slicing open an initiate's finger; he would then shake hands with the other members as the men passed around the burning image of a saint, swearing his loyalty under penalty of death. Later, the son of a Bushwick, Brooklyn, restaurant owner recalled how masked men pushed into the family's establishment and executed Carmine Galante, then head of the Bonanno crime family. Photographs of the murder scene showed the boss crumpled on his back, among broken glasses, in a pool of blood, his cigar still in his mouth.

After more than thirty trial days, the jury returned a guilty verdict for each of the eight defendants.

"It can no longer be passed off as a prosecutor's theory. It's been proven beyond a reasonable doubt there is a Mafia, La Cosa Nostra exists," Giuliani said after the verdict.

IN THE POST-RICO ERA, men like Gaspare Valenti and Vinny Asaro were left with little to chart a course. The men needed to navigate not only the wreckage RICO had left—the fractured allegiances of organized crime, the shattered air of invincibility surrounding the dons—but also more middle-class concerns: divorce, financial problems, and the churn of time that had altered their world. These lean years wore on the cousins. By Valenti's account, he got a raw deal from Asaro. For decades, he'd always kicked up his earnings, but he complained that he never got his "end" of the scores they shared. He was reduced to borrowing money to stay alive, gambling much of it away, and—after skipping out on his debts—fleeing to Las Vegas to make a new start, driving a limo, hustling, serving six months on a mail fraud conviction in the mid-1990s. He eventually burned through his luck out West. At a time in life when he should have been considering retirement, Valenti was expecting a child from a young girlfriend. He needed help. Valenti picked up the phone and called the only person he could rely on: Vinny Asaro. He asked his cousin whether he could safely return home.

Asaro had changed little when Valenti got back to New York. He rose to acting head of the Bonanno family, only to have his leadership revoked, federal investigators believed. Age and an inability to adapt had pushed Asaro to the margins of the neighborhood he once commanded. Time had not mellowed him in the least.

One day after Valenti's return, the two men drove through the neighborhood navigating the double-parked vehicles when Asaro came across a truck blocking a lane. Most New Yorkers dealt with traffic as a fact of life; it primed Asaro's rage. A year earlier, a car cut off Asaro at a stoplight in Howard Beach. Rather than hit his horn and roll down the window to let the driver have a piece of his mind, Asaro tracked down the driver and had local gangsters torch the car. Vinny Asaro might have been pushing eighty, but he was not to be messed with.

The FBI captured a recording of one such outburst, directed at a truck driver parked in traffic.

"These fucking motherfuckers!" Asaro screamed. "Whatta youse got a license? Youse gotta license to block everything? Youse gotta fuckin' license?"

"What are you reachin' for right there?" the driver asked calmly.

"What am I reachin' for? My COCK! My cock I'm reachin' for. Fuck you, you mothafucka. Come around the corner!"

"For what?" the driver responded.

"Cuz I'm gonna fuck you in the ass!" Asaro screamed. "Tell Charlie you fuckin' boss."

"Uh, that's okay. Thank you," the driver dismissed him.

Asaro threw the car into park and stormed toward the driver.

"Get out of the truck!" he screamed. "I'll shoot you in the fuckin' head."

"Go yell at someone else."

"Tell Charlie Vinny Asaro said it!" Asaro screamed. "I know where you sleep you cocksucka."

Asaro got back into the car and said nothing. Adele's sweeping voice poured from the radio, filling the car. Fifteen or twenty years earlier, Asaro's name might have meant something in South Ozone Park. But it had gotten to the point where he couldn't even persuade a driver to move his truck.

"At least you feel better," Valenti said, joking.

"Fuckin' cocksucka," Asaro muttered.

The two men had an easy rapport. But even in the best of times, Valenti could never escape Asaro's shadow. Now, in their twilight years, the men had little to look forward to from the front seat of a Mercedes on that June morning in 2013.

That very morning the FBI had descended on an address on 102nd Road where Valenti's father had built his modest two-story homes. The agents broke through the concrete floor of the basement, turning over the dirt, searching for the remains of Paul Katz. That was a name never to be spoken of between the men.

"What happened?" Asaro asked.

"The feds are all over—Liberty Avenue," Valenti responded.

"For what?"

"By, you know—" Valenti ventured.

"BAM?" Asaro responded, referring to the auto body shop the men hung out in.

"Yeah."

"For what?"

"I don't know."

"How do you know?" Asaro asked.

"I just came from—my doctor is there."

"Who they looking for? John there?" Asaro pushed.

"I'm talking about Liberty Avenue where . . ." Valenti let the sentence drop.

Asaro stopped the car and threw it into park. The cousins sat silently for a moment; then Vinny let out a long sigh.

"You know what I mean?" Valenti ventured.

Asaro cut him off. "No, I don't know what you mean."

He sat for a moment and then, as if he'd made a decision, said to Valenti, "All right, let me go, go ahead, go—"

"Where do you want me to go? What, what should I do?" Valenti asked, surprised.

"What should you do—what?" Asaro's voice rose.

"Nothin'."

"I'll see you later, Gar," Asaro said as his cousin opened the door and climbed out of the car. "Don't call me."

"All right, don't call you," Valenti repeated back.

Six months later, the feds would come back to Liberty Avenue. This time they were returning for Asaro. Their search on 102nd Road turned up bits of human bone and shreds of clothing. The FBI arrested Asaro and charged him with racketeering, extortion, and murder.

The government had more than physical evidence. It had a star witness: his cousin Gar.

2

Cooperation

Visitors stepping off the elevator on the twenty-third floor of the FBI's New York field office enter into a time capsule. An image of the late 1970s. Dun carpeting, tombstone-gray file cabinets, cubicles, and track lighting conjure an era of dot matrix printers and polyester ties. At the entrance, a sun-faded map of the five boroughs looks back from the bygone era, when Reggie Jackson and Tom Seaver built their legends across town and organized crime ranked among the Justice Department's top law enforcement priorities—when the New York bureau ran five independent mob squads: one for each of the families in La Cosa Nostra.

That was the past, though. After the September 11 attacks, the "LCN" squads, as the Mafia units are referred to, took a backseat to counterterrorism. By 2015, the bureau had collapsed the remaining teams into two squads: C-5 for the Genovese, Bonanno, and Colombo families and C-16 for the Gambino and Lucchese. The few squads from the organized crime unit that remained could look down on Foley Square from the symbolic perch of 26 Federal Plaza. It was the lone floor of the building that had yet to be remodeled—an almost symbolic overlook on a city continually changing.

The Sicilian mob had lost its preeminence in New York's under-world. Chinese, Russian, and Albanian enterprises spread across the five boroughs on more recent waves of immigration, taking root in Queens, Brooklyn, and the Bronx. The violence of these recent arrivals resembled that of their Italian predecessors: drug-turf kidnappings, leg-breaking beatings over gambling debts, double murders in crowded karaoke bars. Prosecutors in both the Southern and the Eastern Districts charged defendants linked to eastern European and Chinese groups with crimes as varied as murder, extortion, drug trafficking, and Medicare fraud. The Italian mob, for its part, had largely disavowed killings. "There was a time in the 1990s when the bosses came together and said, 'No murders,'" said Lou DiGregorio, the supervisory agent over the FBI's C-16 squad. Violence drew attention and hurt business.

The five families persisted in an altered, and much-diminished, form. At the end of the twentieth century, second- and third-generation Italian Americans had migrated to Westchester, Long Island, and New Jersey, breaking up the communities in New York City where the Mafia had thrived. The Genovese and Gambino families remained the largest, while the Lucchese, Colombo, and Bonanno families dwindled. The groups continued to be involved in the trade unions and the carting and waste industries; members were as likely to be charged with embezzlement and fraud as they were with loan-sharking and gambling.

To some extent, the mob professionalized—using unions to provide associates with no-show jobs complete with health care and benefits. The leadership adopted basic operational security measures, like leaving behind cellular phones and car key fobs for any sit-downs. They also relied on off-hours and weekend rendezvous when fewer agents would be available to surveil them. But these changes wouldn't forestall generational shifts that had made law enforcement's job significantly easier.

THERE WAS A TIME when it was nearly impossible to prosecute the Mafia. It wasn't just a matter of the impenetrable secrecy of the organization; there was a lack of political will and legal tools. Local police and politicians easily fell under the influence of the mob, while federal agents and prosecutors had neither the institutional support nor the laws necessary to be effective. In New York, the five families exploited this situation and rose to power, establishing a foothold in legitimate and illegitimate businesses, forging alliances with politicians and law enforcement, becoming part of the social fabric of immigrant communities. When Congress began investigating organized crime in the early 1950s, it was a clumsy, public-relations-driven effort with no real enforcement power behind it. The Senate hauled mob leaders like Frank Costello of the Luciano (later Genovese) crime family before camera-packed Senate hearings in 1951 and 1957. Hearings like this served little law enforcement purpose but functioned exceptionally well as political spectacle. The hearings drew shadowy figures out from the street and onto television screens around the country, delivering them into public consciousness. J. Edgar Hoover's position that the Mafia did not exist became impossible to maintain in the glare of the media age. But the vilification of the leadership helped create the illusion that federal officials were finally confronting the mob.

The RICO assault wouldn't begin for nearly two decades. The directive to take down the mob came from Main Justice, which created the Organized Crime Strike Force program in the late 1960s. The unit operated out of Brooklyn under Tom Puccio. While not part of the U.S. Attorney's Office, the strike force was associated with the Eastern District; any indictments generated by the group would be signed by the U.S. Attorney there. The force made its mark with the 1978 Abscam case—an FBI sting that netted six members of Congress and one senator in an elaborate bribery scheme. It then shifted its focus to the influence of the five families across New York's five boroughs. In the 1970s, the mob had expanded its grip beyond street crime and rackets into city industries from construction to waste handling and trucking.

While the Commission case represented a historic victory for Giuliani's office in the Southern District, prosecutors in Brooklyn suffered a humiliating defeat when they failed to secure a conviction against John Gotti.

Gotti was a defiant reminder of the mob's influence. He had already beaten three cases—two state, one federal. Unlike previous mob figures, Gotti relished the spotlight. He cultivated the image of the "Teflon Don" preening for tabloid photographers in designer suits, amplifying his myth to spite law enforcement. His outsize personality followed in his underworld dealings; he was a profligate gambler and unceasingly ambitious. The hit on the Gambino boss, Paul Castellano, not only secured Gotti's leadership over the family but also clearly signaled his ruthlessness. He was willing to break a cardinal code of La Cosa Nostra by targeting a mob boss, and he would do it in broad daylight. The killing took place a few minutes after five o'clock as the doomed Gambino boss was stepping out of his car to go into Sparks Steak House on Forty-Sixth Street in Manhattan's midtown. Gotti sent a message that he was a new type of mob boss.

He faced an unlikely nemesis: a bookish line prosecutor in the Eastern District, John Gleeson. Gleeson's tidy presence earned him the nickname the "Jesuit" among defenders he faced off against as a junior Assistant U.S. Attorney here. Born in the Bronx to an Irish immigrant family of seven children, Gleeson was raised north of the city in Westchester County and educated at Georgetown on an academic scholarship, a coming of age that reflected the promise of postwar white suburban America. But his career in the U.S. Attorney's Office became defined by some of the city's most notorious acts of murder and betrayal.

Gleeson ran roughshod over the New York mob during his nine years as an Eastern District prosecutor, but he pursued other criminals with equal vigor: one Jamaican drug lord he helped convict received a five-hundred-year sentence on a range of drug and murder charges. He fit into a distinct Department of Justice archetype: the understated academic prosecutor capable of destroying powerful underworld figures.

But Gleeson had unresolved business with Gotti. He had lost a case against the mob boss in 1987, the government's first significant RICO defeat at trial. Before bringing another case against Gotti in the Eastern District, U.S. Attorney Andrew Maloney and Gleeson had to fight off the Manhattan district attorney, Robert Morgenthau, and the Southern District U.S. Attorney, Otto Obermaier, who vied to indict Gotti in Paul Castellano's murder. The Gambino crew knew indictments were imminent; a wiretap picked up Gotti and Salvatore Gravano, a.k.a Sammy Gravano parrying where to expect the next case to come from, according to a recording shared with *The New Yorker*.

"If this is Gleeson again, this fucking rat motherfucker again," said Gotti.

"I don't think it's gonna be by Gleeson," Gravano said. "Somebody with more brains."

"Southern District," Gotti replied.

The tiebreaker for the case went to Washington. The head of the Department of Justice's Criminal Division would make the call; he was another understated federal prosecutor, Robert Mueller. Obermaier did not convince Mueller that the Southern District should leapfrog the Eastern District. Mueller notified U.S. Attorney Maloney that the case would go ahead with his team in Brooklyn. Early in the case, Gleeson took the reins in the government's case. He not only was a capable investigator behind the scenes but also proved to have a steady hand in the courtroom. One marshal recalled that when U.S. Attorney Maloney stumbled over his words to answer the judge in a pretrial hearing, Gleeson stepped up and spoke for the government. Leading the case, he achieved several victories before the trial—disqualifying Gotti's counsel, sequestering an anonymous jury.

But Gleeson made history when he brought in Sammy the Bull, as a cooperating witness. Gravano served as Gotti's deputy in the Gambino crime family, a position he ascended to after proving himself a skilled criminal and ruthless murderer. But his will to survive won out over his loyalty to the mob. Gravano famously told Gleeson at their first meeting, "I want to switch governments."

Gravano's move shattered one of the Mafia's last defenses: *omertà*, the code of silence. He became the highest-ranking made member of the Mafia to break with the vow that had protected the New York mob's five families. Other mobsters had flipped before the Gotti case, but none of Gravano's stature—or with the baggage that he carried. He had committed more murders than he could accurately pin down, a number around eighteen or nineteen. Gleeson turned that liability into an asset when Gravano took the stand. He linked Gotti to at least ten of the killings, including the Castellano hit that had placed Gotti at the top of the Gambino family.

This relationship between the government and a cooperator became archetypal, but it also came with a steep moral cost for the government; the prosecution had crossed a threshold, agreeing to work with a confessed killer. But when the jury convicted Gotti and the judge later imposed on him multiple life sentences, the partnership had paid off. Gleeson went before the judge and said of Gravano, "He has rendered extraordinary, unprecedented, historic assistance to the government."

Gravano, for all his crimes, received a five-year sentence.

Once Gravano broke the deadly taboo of cooperation, rats began to proliferate in the mob. By then, the ranks had been decimated by more than twenty years of successful RICO convictions, even as the FBI shifted its priorities elsewhere. The life held little appeal, even for the aging wiseguys who knew little else. Many of them pushed their sons toward legitimate professions, now that the barriers to mobility that once fueled the mob's growth had shifted toward other minority and immigrant groups. The FBI has found, however, the new generation of Italian mobsters to be a contradiction. They rely on the image of the mob, driven by the media and popular culture, to hold on to their few remaining rackets. Yet few live by the traditional code—and the violence it demands—that made the Mafia fearsome to begin with. These remaining Mafia figures typically face charges that reveal the lack of the sort of institutional influence that defined the power of prior generations: gambling, narcotics trafficking, and small-scale extortion. Despite this, the easy money and big lifestyle continue to draw some recruits. For some, the mob life is the only life they have known.

"We're not dealing with geniuses here," the supervisory agent Lou DiGregorio said.

IN THE FALL OF 2008, a man called FBI headquarters giving only the name Simon. A supervisor passed the tip on to Special Agent Adam Mininni, who worked with C-10, the LCN squad unit that covered the Bonanno family at that time. A month earlier, Mininni wasn't yet an agent. He had been working as an investigative analyst tasked with menial assignments like surveillance and listening in on prison phone calls. With his promotion came more responsibility and the opportunity to field tips like this. Mininni's supervisor, Nora Conley, asked him to drive out to a hotel near JFK to meet the walk-in. The trip from Foley

Square was just twenty miles to John F. Kennedy airport. In traffic, it could easily take more than an hour to make the looping arc through Brooklyn and Queens to arrive there.

This first meeting would be deliberately perfunctory. Mininni had explicit orders: check the guy out, get his name, Social Security number, date of birth—any identifying information that the agent could run through FBI databases to see who exactly Simon was, whether he had a record. That young agent's task required little else. He wasn't there to interrogate Simon, definitely not to cut any deals.

The man who arrived to meet Mininni bore a striking resemblance to Larry David. Reed thin, glimmering scalp. In place of the comedian's roguish charm was the unaffected swagger of the street. Simon was an artifact of an era when mobsters still ran the outer boroughs—an era when meeting with a federal agent was a violation punishable by death. Those days had passed, though the danger still existed. Simon handed his driver's license over to the agent. It read, "Gaspare Valenti." The name didn't mean anything to the agent yet, but it was a start.

SEVERAL WEEKS LATER on September 29, 2008, Valenti found himself in a roomful of feds. He was risking everything meeting with the government, but at Valenti's place in life everything wasn't all that much. A team filed into the room with Mininni, the FBI agent whom he had met out near JFK a week earlier, Nora Conley, his supervisor and longtime Bonanno squad agent, and two other agents with her, Jude Tarasca and John Robertson. The person who mattered was the guy wearing a suit: Greg Andres, the chief of the Criminal Division for the Eastern District's U.S. Attorney's Office.

Andres wasn't just any prosecutor. He might have been the picture of a clean-cut fed, forty-one with a slightly squeaky voice and neutral expression, but he had a reputation for putting mobsters in prison. Especially members of the Bonanno family. The jailed boss Joseph Massino testified that Andres "pretty much destroyed the Bonanno family" with indictments that targeted nearly one hundred associates, decimating their ranks. Andres would eventually rise to national prominence as the lead prosecutor in the trial of President Trump's campaign manager Paul Manafort, the first to stem from Special Counsel Robert Mueller's investigation into Russian interference with the 2016 presidential election.

His success didn't come without bruises. Andres rankled some as he built up his track record in the Eastern District. A Brooklyn district attorney once accused him of taking credit for work done by his office, calling Andres a "typically arrogant poker-up-his-ass, know-it-all fed." That year the attorney general would give the prosecutor and his team one of the department's top honors, the Distinguished Service Award.

Andres had also achieved an organized crime prosecutor's ultimate badge of honor: a plot on his life. In 2004, Vincent "Vinny Gorgeous" Basciano, the acting boss of the family, allegedly proposed killing Andres while in a holding cell with Massino while the younger boss was awaiting trial. The men had learned that Andres regularly ate at Campagnola, an Upper East Side Italian restaurant, and Basciano had planned to kill the prosecutor there. The plot was chilling for the federal law enforcement community in New York: Andres's wife, Ronnie Abrams, worked as a Southern District prosecutor who went on to lead the office's General Crimes unit and, in 2011, was appointed by President Obama as a judge in the Southern District. After that, Massino did the unthinkable for a boss in the New York Mafia: he offered to wear a wire to record jailhouse conversations with a soldier loyal to him. Massino wasn't able to get Basciano to repeat the threat on tape, but Basciano was convicted of a separate murder he acknowledged on the wire. The younger boss's attorneys rejected that their client had threatened the prosecutor, accusing the U.S. Attorney's Office of using the thinly sourced plot to bluster in the press. Basciano avoided the death penalty but received a life sentence at Florence, the super-max prison in Colorado.

To a man in Gaspare Valenti's position, Andres held godlike powers. He could offer salvation or guarantee damnation. Joseph Massino provided an object lesson in this. The mob boss had received two life sentences after his conviction for seven murders—before he began cooperating. Massino testified in two trials and provided Andres's team with a road map for several other prosecutions. While Valenti didn't yet know what Massino would get in return from the government, he knew that a man of Massino's position and power wouldn't do something for nothing. Massino, in the end, made the right call; the government released him in 2013.

Valenti was a nobody compared with Massino. But he had been turning his options over in his head for nearly two years before he picked up the phone to call the FBI. His life was unfulfilled and complicated. He was a senior citizen raising a school-age child yet estranged from his first wife and grown children; he had no money, no career prospects, and a shattered reputation. Valenti was never a made man; his lackluster career had been entirely defined by his association with his cousin Vinny Asaro. In the New York Mafia, this conferred on Valenti some status. It also put him in service to Asaro, doing his bidding, kicking up what little he made, while dealing with his cousin's blistering temper. As both men entered their retirement years, loyalty had few discernible dividends. Valenti wasn't worth anything on his own to the feds, but Asaro was.

The first thing Valenti said to Greg Andres was this: "I've been around Vinny Asaro for forty-two years."

Mininni watched the questioning play out between the prosecutor and the mobster. The agent had no idea who Asaro was, but the others seemed to. Valenti started discussing a lot of things: murders, beatings, shylocking, gambling, hijacking armored cars. Two things jumped out: he mentioned Asaro's involvement in the murder of someone named Paul Katz and the Lufthansa heist. This was compelling. But the FBI and the Eastern District had other interests.

"We were trying to see as a source that came in if he was someone that we could run proactively, like out on the street, and meet with other guys, members of organized crime and be able to get conversations and see what's going on on the street with illegal activity," Mininni later testified.

Andres had been through this again and again with the Bonannos. As distasteful as it might have been to outsiders, federal prosecutors needed men like Valenti. Convictions make careers, and cooperators make convictions—especially in mob cases. That has been the uneasy symbiosis between federal law enforcement and organized crime since Gravano. Cooperators—or "rats," as their peers called them—were the lifeblood of not only organized crime cases but any complex investigation. One of Andres's cooperators, "Good Lookin' " Sal Vitale, played a part in putting away more than fifty Bonanno family members, thirty-eight on murder charges. Even though he had taken part in eleven murders on his own, he received only a seven-year sentence.

Valenti came with much less baggage; he didn't have any murders directly tied to him. This fact would spare prosecutors the experience of reading letters from the family of murder victims at the same hearing where the government would ask a judge to show leniency to a cooperator who had done similar things. But Valenti had some problems. His ex-girlfriend had obtained an order of protection against him after she accused him of domestic violence. Valenti assured the prosecutors that the allegations were false, but he had violated the order, and the court charged him with contempt. Valenti wasn't alone among Eastern District cooperators accused of beating their wives and girlfriends. One cooperator admitted to getting physical with his pregnant girlfriend and mother-in-law. Prosecutors had a narrow interest in the moral character of cooperators. The question wasn't whether they had or had not beaten their wives and girlfriends but whether those allegations would undermine their credibility. Also, from a line-item standpoint, cooperators could be cost-effective. Once he signed up, Valenti would cost the FBI only $3,000 a month, a fraction of the cost of surveillance. The government decided to put Valenti back into circulation.

Within two weeks, Valenti returned to Ozone Park wearing a wire. He'd be on the street for another five years.

VINNY ASARO WAS NOT the priority for the FBI. He could still be seen in Ozone Park and Howard Beach but was not a focus for the bureau. Initially, Valenti went to work on younger investigative targets the bureau associated with the Bonanno family: Sandro Aiosa, Jack Bonventre, John Ragano, Danny Rizzo, and Vinny's son, Jerry Asaro. Special Agent Mininni juggled Valenti among his other cases, meeting him at secret locations, swapping out the recording device, and recording a preamble to time-stamp each set of recordings. The agents would also surveil Valenti. He was an aging wiseguy without even a no-show job who spent much of his time with Vinny Asaro sitting in front of a deli in a Howard Beach strip mall. Valenti kept the tape running.

Asaro, unaware that he was being recorded, confided in his cousin.

"Gar, I can't win," he said in 2010. He was broke, embittered by his loss of station in the Bonanno family, and losing the will to get out of the house each day.

Eventually, the focus of the FBI investigation shifted to Asaro. Mininni's weekly meetings with Valenti became daily debriefs. The investigators wanted more than the historical crimes Valenti had reported to them; they also wanted to be able to show that Asaro—even at his advanced age—was still active in the Bonanno family. The wires seemed to contradict that. Asaro openly complained about being shut out from Cafe Liberty, a mob-linked social club on Liberty Avenue.

"People hate me in there," he said. "I don't pay my dues."

Mininni's squad sought approvals for Valenti to participate in an "OIA," or "Otherwise Illegal Activity," that would connect Asaro to a racketeering conspiracy—a dispensation for an informant to break the law. This agreement required the signatures of both the top FBI official in New York and the lead federal prosecutor on the investigation. The proposed crime Valenti was to carry out was both pedestrian and reflective of the perverted notions of honor and loyalty within the Mafia. He was sent to shake down a relative of Asaro's for money from the sale of his godfather's home after his death. The property was nearly worthless, a $50,000 home that stood at Drew Street and Blake Avenue overlooking the Hole. Asaro thought he deserved a cut of the sale from the stepson who had inherited the property and sent Valenti to the man's office in Long Island City, Queens, to collect it. Valenti showed up unannounced and demanded $3,000. The line between extortion and family dispute was fuzzy, but the feds authorized Valenti to move ahead and threaten the man, Carmine Muscarella, an electrical contractor.

"Listen, you know Vinny. You know the situation," he told him.

"I know Vinny," Muscarella said.

"I don't want to have to bring up wiseguys and whatnot, but you already know that. I'm not here to be a wiseguy with you. I'm here as a gentleman with you. That's the way I hope it's going to end that way."

"You have nothing to do with the house," Muscarella said.

"I don't want to start getting upset over here, in your office," Valenti said, frustrated. As he began to get angry, he stood up and closed the office door.

Eventually, Valenti put Asaro on the phone with Muscarella.

"Vin, I'm gonna settle up with him, but I don't want to hear from him ever again," Muscarella said of Valenti.

"We're wiseguys. We don't take no bullshit," Valenti explained as if to apologize.

The two men met early the next morning at a Starbucks in Howard Beach, Queens, to finalize the shakedown. Muscarella handed over a check for $3,000, while the FBI looked on out of sight.

The FBI slowly began building a case against Asaro and his son, Jerry, along with three others; each believed to be members of a Bonanno family crew in Ozone Park. Valenti's recordings picked up the chaotic but also low-stakes grind of shakedowns and "beefs" the men were involved in. Despite being well into his seventies, Asaro boasted about getting into fights: poking a hood in the eye at Belmont race-track, tearing his shirt off to confront young men in front of a bodega, attacking a "muscle guy" after exchanging words in an office.

Lufthansa loomed large. Even though thirty-three years had passed since the heist, the crime's position in popular culture was unrivaled. But Valenti struggled to get any detailed discussion of the crime on tape. In February 2011, he and Asaro tooled around the neighborhood in the car when they came across Danny Rizzo, whom Valenti identi-fied as a Lufthansa co-conspirator.

The men made small talk. The changes to the neighborhood, the sputtering economy, the unfulfilled promise of life on the streets.

"It's life; we did it to ourselves, it's a curse with this fucking gam-bling. We never got our right money, what we were supposed to get, we got fucked all around, got fucked all around, that fucking Jimmy kept everything," Asaro said.

"They got money, but they're not spending it. From your lips to God's ears," Rizzo said. "That's my problem. I spent money."

"You got no problems, Dan, what'd you do, bet a number once in a fucking while? You should have all your fucking money," Asaro said.

"Yeah, once in a while I bet the number . . ." Rizzo trailed off.

The conversation offered several readings. On its face, a trio of washed-up mobsters bemoaned the lots they had drawn on a wire. But the mention of Jimmy Burke, Lufthansa's mastermind, offered a thin thread to the historic heist. As the prosecutors reviewed the hundreds of hours of recordings, the conversations were primarily evidence of the pathos of mob life, an insular world of little relevance.

Occasionally, glimmers of intimacy between the cousins came through on the tape.

"But how are you?" Valenti asked Asaro on one recording. "I mean when you wrote to me, remember that letter you wrote when you were away? I was in Vegas, that nobody talked to you, the girls, your son. Ever since then, what the fuck happened?"

"Not only me," Asaro said of his son. "He don't talk to his own kids. He don't call his own kids. He don't call nobody. He don't call his own wife, his mother. Very strange. I think that fuck—I think he had a nervous breakdown, that's what I think. That's what the fuck I think," Asaro said, going on to lament how he took care of people but got little in return.

"I mean you fucking run for everybody. You run for everybody." Valenti tried to assure him.

"I can't take this," Asaro said.

AS VALENTI CONTINUED to record his cousin for years, the most compelling evidence remained in the ground: the remains of Paul Katz. In the mid-1980s, he and Asaro's son, Jerry, had returned to 102nd Road to dig up what they could find of Katz. His body had disintegrated, leaving only bones and his corduroy clothing mixed with the dirt. The men packed the remains in cardboard boxes and planned to put them in paint cans to bury upstate. Valenti wasn't sure what the feds would find once they broke through the floor.

Katz left behind a wife and five children. Not only had the family lost their father, but they were forced to live in the dark as to what happened to him. On the night of his disappearance, Katz left his home to meet up with a man he had allegedly committed a robbery with, Joe Allegro. After nearly twenty-four hours, Katz's wife, Dolores, reported him missing to the police. The NYPD interviewed her three more times over the next month. Nothing she said linked her husband's disappearance to Asaro or Burke.

Forty-four years later, some five years into Valenti's cooperation, the FBI team broke through the floor of the home to exhume what remained of Katz. To passersby, it was an ominous scene that harked back to a lost era of New York, an FBI evidence team appearing on a quiet Queens backstreet. The search had a unique symbolic resonance in Valenti's story. The homes on 102nd Road were a testimony to his father's achievement as an immigrant arriving from Sicily—a tiny stretch of this vast metropolis built from his sweat and fortitude. The body entombed in the basement was not only a human being but also a grim memorial of the path that Valenti, the first-generation son, had chosen. Valenti didn't own the home, but he did possess the secret it held. When he ran out of options, he cashed in that secret to the FBI.

Sifting through the dirt, the agents found shards of bone and teeth—very little of the man Paul Katz once was. A few blocks away, Asaro sat with his cousin in his car as Valenti nudged him with incriminating questions. If he knew that Gar had been the one to betray him, he didn't let it on. There was little he could do.

Vincent Asaro drove off alone. In the months after his arrest and leading up to his trial, the only question was what Valenti would say to the jury. And would they believe him?

3

Lufthansa

October 19, 2015

The defense team was already waiting at 9:15 a.m. Elizabeth Macedonio sat at the head of the table applying lip gloss, while her colleagues, a paralegal, and the co-counsel, Diane Ferrone, watched for the judge—and their client, Vinny Asaro—to make an entrance. Assistant U.S. Attorney Alicyn Cooley walked into the courtroom carrying a *grande* Starbucks cup, stepping through the crowded gallery as if holding a chalice. She joined her colleagues Lindsay Gerdes and Nicole Argentieri, who sat at the head of the government's table. In the years that Valenti's investigation wound forward, Greg Andres had moved on: first to Washington to serve as a deputy attorney general, then to Davis Polk, where he joined as a partner. Cooley handed the coffee to Argentieri. This was her case.

Among the last people to enter were Kelly Currie, the acting U.S. Attorney for the Eastern District, and Robert Capers, who would be sworn in as Loretta Lynch's successor in the coming months. There were no available seats, so the two stepped past the bar to find a seat just behind the defense counsel. The appearance of the U.S. Attorney to hear the opening statements in a trial was almost customary. The relative rarity of the federal criminal trial made it a custom easy to keep.

Today's trial was its own milestone: it was the first organized crime case to go to trial since Loretta Lynch had left the office to become attorney general.

"Please be seated," Judge Allyne Ross said the moment she stepped into the courtroom.

SINCE THE FIRST JOHN GOTTI prosecution, mob trials have become a perennial event in the Eastern District. Over the last decade, more than a dozen trials have gone forward in Brooklyn, outpacing the Southern District as New York's de facto organized crime venue. But as the convictions depleted the mob's ranks—and the defendants went from notorious and feared to obscure and pathetic—the cachet that had come with prosecuting the mob also diminished.

What had remained more or less constant was media interest. Mob trials have consistently filled tabloid column inches with images of a hidden New York. Tales of murderous rogues like "Ronnie One Arm" and "Skinny Dom" and "Vinny Gorgeous," subterranean rackets, witness stand betrayals, reliably delivered drama and color in a courthouse where health-care fraud and drug mule cases tended to fill out the criminal docket. The Asaro case had drawn outsize coverage, though. The Lufthansa heist gave the trial a cinematic sweep. Reporters billed it as the penultimate trial for the dying New York mob, a strong peg but also wholly unverifiable. If anything, the trial had the sense of being the Eastern District's fall production.

Mob cases provide a proving ground for Eastern District line assistants eager to feather their résumés with vivid trial experience. Once a prosecutor makes the jump to the private sector, experience prosecuting the mob doesn't inherently lend itself to civil practice or even white-collar criminal defense; it virtually guarantees a lifetime of anecdotes that can be trotted out at client dinners.

The Asaro case was unique in that it was being tried exclusively by women: the defense, prosecution, and the judge. In many ways, this was not remarkable in the Eastern District. Women had defined both the U.S. Attorney's Office and the federal bench in Brooklyn for a generation—their careers often following the path from a federal prosecutor's office to a judgeship. Judge Reena Raggi, who was appointed to the bench by President Reagan at age thirty-five, had paved the way for a generation of women in the Eastern District. By the time the Asaro trial opened, women accounted for the majority of judges in the Eastern District. The district's chief judge, Carol Amon, and the judge presiding over the Asaro case, Allyne Ross, had come up as prosecutors in the U.S. Attorney's Office there—not to mention that Attorney General Loretta Lynch had followed a similar path. One of their colleagues, Patricia Pileggi, described the office as a strict meritocracy where gender played little role in determining an assistant's career path. "The government didn't have the luxury to discriminate against talented people," she said. "If you were good, you got good assignments." She recalled trying an Asian heroin-trafficking case while nine months pregnant. Her junior colleague was terrified that she would go into labor during the trial, leaving the prosecution in his hands. The defense counsel fashioned a legal argument from it, voicing concern that the jury would favor a visibly pregnant attorney. (They did not; one defendant was acquitted.)

Asaro's case pitted two deeply experienced organized crime trial attorneys against each other: Elizabeth Macedonio, a private defender, and Nicole Argentieri, an eight-year veteran of the U.S. Attorney's Office. Argentieri had joined the office from Skadden Arps in 2007, eventually climbing the ranks to become the acting chief of the Organized Crime and Gangs unit. She worked on a stream of Mafia cases and was part of a death-penalty case against Vincent Basciano, the Bonanno boss accused of plotting to kill Judge Nicholas Garaufis and the prosecutor Greg Andres. A juror told the New York *Daily News* that the push for the death penalty smacked of vengeance and "chest-thumping from the prosecutors." For the Asaro case, two junior prosecutors from her office joined her, Lindsay Gerdes and Alicyn Cooley, but Argentieri set the tone, in a dark suit with a Nehru collar and a bright, confident smile.

Elizabeth Macedonio had also come up trying Mafia cases—as a defender. At age forty-eight and nearly fifteen years out on her own as a criminal defense attorney, she'd only recently moved out of her Bayside, Queens, office to a high-rise office suite overlooking Wall

Street in lower Manhattan. Over her career, she had learned never to underestimate federal prosecutors. "When the federal government brings suit, it's custom fit," she said.

She had mentored under John Jacobs, an outsize personality who once represented Michael Franzese, a Colombo underboss known as the "Yuppie Don." (When Jacobs passed away, he asked that his cell phone number be etched into his tombstone.) He had introduced Macedonio to the organized crime fold. Over the course of her career, she had seen the Organized Crime Division of the U.S. Attorney's Office in the Eastern District lose its preeminence. Cases often relied less on concrete investigative discoveries and more on a revolving cast of serial cooperators.

"What happened with old-fashioned FBI work?" she wondered.

"Rats" were a constant in her career. She recalled doing trial prep with Jacobs at her home in the mid-1990s, while her five-year-old son played nearby with toy rubber snakes and mice. As the two attorneys discussed case strategy, they used the mob's favored term when mentioning cooperating witnesses: "rats." Weeks later, without a sitter, she rushed to Foley Square, her son in tow, for a pretrial hearing in the 1993 World Trade Center bombing case. Macedonio and Jacobs represented one of Sheikh Omar Abdel-Rahman's co-defendants. She huddled in the back of the courtroom with her son waiting for the hearing to begin. The table of defendants caught sight of the little boy—a rarity in federal court—then smiled and waved. Her son looked at the sheikh, who had a flowing silver beard, and asked, "Is that Santa Claus?"

"No," Macedonio told him.

He was quiet for a moment, then, remembering his mother speaking with Jacobs weeks earlier, asked, "Where are the rats?"

They'd show up in the Asaro case soon enough. At a glance, the scene in the courtroom was almost comical: a room full of stylish, attractive women arguing over the fate of a geriatric wiseguy—as if he'd been caught sneaking extra dessert at the rest home. The allegations were, instead, racketeering and murder. The attorneys maintained outward collegiality, but underneath lay a fierce sense of competition.

Macedonio didn't want to go to trial in this case. But Vinny Asaro was the last man standing in his indictment, after his son and the three other defendants had each taken a plea. Asaro had little interest in taking a plea, though. He didn't think he had five years left, so any sentence would amount to a death sentence. But Macedonio had to consider all of his options—even a guilty plea, though there was no such offer from the government for him.

"I tried very hard to resolve this," Macedonio said. "I think they were going for the headlines."

When Macedonio got her first look at the statements the government intended to introduce through its witnesses—referred to as the 3500 material—she felt for the first time that she could pull together a defense. The government had gone back to the well of serial cooperators to build its case against Asaro; she knew who these guys were and what they were about. Gaspare Valenti was a new name, and he appeared to be the star witness. It wouldn't be easy, but she had a plan.

MARSHALS LED ASARO IN. He wore an oxford, V-neck sweater, khaki trousers, and wire-rimmed glasses. The grandfatherly ensemble was not calculated to make him appear less imposing. He had almost cartoonishly villainous features that his clothing, not to mention his age, could only slightly diminish. He towered over his counsel, magnifying his imposing presence. Asaro simply told Macedonio, "I'm not wearing a suit."

Asaro projected none of the helpless air that seemed to hover over some criminal defendants in court. He sat and faced the jury box, flanked by security officers. For a moment, he seemed in awe of the scene. Everyone working on the case was aware of Asaro's voluble temper. The wired recordings showed that he made little effort to restrain himself, regardless of the audience or venue. For Macedonio, this was just another variable to handle in what she expected to be a challenging trial.

The truth was that old age had radically diminished Asaro. He'd already had a heart attack and triple bypass surgery. His condition worsened during incarceration. His legs and chest constantly ached and burned, eventually growing swollen. He was suffering from inadequate blood flow to his heart—angina—though he didn't know it at the time.

Judge Allyne Ross entered court, and the room rose to its feet. She smiled and took her seat on the bench.

Even within the history of Eastern District mob trials, the Asaro case stood out. The prosecution hung the trial narrative on Lufthansa, one of New York City's enduring mysteries. The robbery was significant not only as an unsolved crime that had bedeviled New York law enforcement. It also had been elevated into pop culture mythology. In the quarter century since *Goodfellas*, the public had been raised within the Scorsese mob vernacular. That film helped normalize organized crime's perverted pursuit of the American Dream, training audience sympathies to embrace underdog characters with unflinching capacity for evil: Henry Hill, Whitey Bulger, Tony Soprano. But a month before the trial began, Judge Ross ordered that a major climactic plot point of the film and the Lufthansa heist not be mentioned: the killings of four alleged accomplices. The prosecutors had no evidence of Asaro's connection to the murders, and their mention could prejudice the jury, the judge found. The government also questioned prospective jurors about their familiarity with the Scorsese film and other mob epics including *The Godfather* and *The Sopranos*.

These stories created a structural challenge for prosecutors. In a culture where audiences empathize with complex and conflicted mob bosses like Tony Soprano and Michael Corleone, how do you make a jury see the real-life organized crime members as they are within the eyes of the law: criminals? This task becomes only more difficult when the government's key witnesses are themselves crooks. Juries had not only to navigate the biases informed by pop culture but also to parse the thin distinction between those appearing on the witness stand and those led into the courtroom in handcuffs.

The government's first witness made this challenge clear: Sal "Good Lookin' " Vitale, once a trusted Bonanno family underboss exiled to the witness protection program for his second career as a government cooperator. He looked comfortable on the witness stand: dapper in a steel-blue suit with gleaming cuff links, projecting confidence border-.

ing on arrogance as he was sworn in. At the defense table, Asaro asked
to change seats. He wanted to get a better look at the witness.

Prosecutors and defense attorneys share one rule when it comes to
witnesses: never ask a question that you don't already know the answer
to. A trial is not a place to solicit surprises. Both the government and
the defense want to strictly control what information the jury sees, and,
to the extent possible, how the jury sees it. To achieve this, attorneys
rigorously prepare witnesses for testifying. They are forbidden to tell
witnesses what to say on the stand, but they have free rein to instruct
them what not to say. All of this preparation occurs outside the court—
whether in sessions at the U.S. Attorney's Office in the days before
trial or on the bench outside the courtroom moments before taking the
stand. The line between coaching testimony and rehearsing is decidedly
narrow and left largely to the attorneys to determine.

On direct examination, Vitale's first job was to break down the mob
lexicon. He did so with an economy of language that left all the hacks
in the gallery envious. A "walktalk" was a stroll down a side street to
avoid being wired up by the feds. "Hello/goodbye" described how well
one knows a passing acquaintance. "Argumentual" was a local form
of being argumentative. "Work" was murder. Even when Vitale listed
the crimes he had pleaded guilty to—"Murder, extortion, shylocking,
numbers, gambling, to name a few"—the list of sins had a sonorous
appeal. Even in explaining the difficulties finding work in witness
protection, he played up his part. "You're living in whatever . . . you
sound like a wiseguy from Brooklyn," he said. "Who's going to hire
a 65-year-old guy with a brand-new social security card." For sheer
entertainment value, he was a perfect witness. Cooperators, in many
senses, were the character actors of the Eastern District mob trial,
appearing in similar roles in multiple productions where the plotlines
were only faintly distinguishable. Vitale typified this. Macedonio
referred to the serialized relationship of cooperators with the government as "the FBI pension program."

That characterization had some accuracy. The next witness, the
admitted Bonanno and Gambino family associate Peter Zuccaro,
acknowledged testifying in five other cases. When he appeared at the
Asaro trial, he looked tan and relaxed, his gray hair swept high across

his forehead, wearing a charcoal-and-black tracksuit as if he were stopping by on the way to the gym. When Assistant U.S. Attorney Argentieri questioned Zuccaro, he calmly swiveled in his chair as he answered.

"To become an inducted member of organized crime, what are the requirements?" the prosecutor asked.

"Like I said before, loyalty, the whole family comes first. Gotta be a good earner. And a killer," Zuccaro responded.

The dialogue felt scripted, in part, because it was. Zuccaro had a near-identical exchange six years earlier with Assistant U.S. Attorney Evan Norris while testifying against the Gambino hit man Charles Carneglia.

"How does an associate become a made member of an organized crime family?" Norris asked.

"He's either a good earner or good killer," Zuccaro responded.

The repetition served a purpose. Federal prosecutors in the Eastern District had been remarkably effective against the Mafia because of cooperators. Yet in the decades between Sammy the Bull's betrayal of John Gotti and the testimony Joe Massino gave against Vincent Basciano, jurors' attitudes appeared to shift toward these types of witnesses. There were two distinct traps: the jury might not believe a witness, or the jury simply might not like a witness—and compensate the defendant with their sympathy. In the midst of the dozens of successful mob convictions in Brooklyn, there were also acquittals. In two separate cases involving murder charges—against Thomas "Tommy Shots" Gioeli and Francis Guerra—juries failed to return guilty verdicts. For the team prosecuting Asaro, a potential loss wasn't an abstract possibility. Argentieri had prosecuted Guerra's case.

But to Macedonio's mind, the government had stepped into a huge tactical error on the first day of trial by opening with Vitale. When Macedonio began to push him on the reality of his criminal past, the wiseguy caricature lost some of its luster. Vitale was damaged goods. When he sat down on the witness stand, his sins had become the government's. Vitale had pleaded guilty to eleven murders and received $250,000 in payments from the FBI while testifying in four trials. As defense counsel, Macedonio saw an opening.

She moved in to unearth the ugliness underlying Vitale's cooperation.

"Did you participate in a conspiracy to murder William Capparelli in the '90s? Do you remember that?" she asked.

"Who is William captain—who is—William who?" Vitale asked, incredulous.

"You tell me. You got coverage for it," Macedonio said, referring to Vitale's deal with the prosecution. "You had a pass on conspiracy to murder William Capparelli in the '90s."

"Does he have a nickname?" asked Vitale.

"I don't know," said Macedonio.

"Was that—what's his name again?"

"*William Capparelli,*" Macedonio repeated.

"I think—I don't think I participated in that murder." Vitale searched a bit. "I think I overheard the murder from Big Louie if I'm talking about the right individual. I don't know."

Macedonio waited for him to finish. "Too many murders to keep straight?" she asked.

Vitale recognized that he had walked right into that trap. "No, not really," he responded, dismissively.

Over the next few days, as witness after witness testified, Asaro fumed. He had remained faithful to his oath. His reward: a procession of witnesses who had violated the most fundamental tenet of La Cosa Nostra. He had, in effect, been isolated by the perverse conception of honor that he appeared to uphold. The witness accounts seemed to foreclose any possibility that Asaro could be innocent. Their testimony placed him in the Bonanno hierarchy, linked him to goods stolen from Lufthansa, portrayed him as a violent neighborhood tough running a protection racket, even showed him scamming a relative out of $250,000 at a family funeral. But while the testimony was dense with Mafia history—an encyclopedia of dead wiseguys, long-closed social clubs and hangouts, and legendary killings—the connections to Asaro often ran thin.

Macedonio leaned back in her seat throughout the trial, projecting a finely tuned annoyance. With each sidebar, she would rise out of her

seat like a teenager called to the front of the class, following her colleagues to the bench. Judge Ross had taken notice of Asaro's growing
exasperation. At one sidebar, she called Asaro to the bench to warn
that his behavior might hurt him in the eyes of the jury.

"I'm not questioning my lawyer's ability," he said.

"As a judge listening to the evidence, there is nothing she can do
with these witnesses, but she will argue for you at summation," Judge
Ross said.

"It might be too late, Your Honor," Asaro said.

Macedonio wasn't distracted by this. She tried to channel her client's frustration.

"Vin was fighting with everybody," she recalled. "I knew what I
had to do."

When Macedonio rose to cross-examine witnesses, her small-
ness cut a sharp contrast to her attitude. With each question, she
telegraphed that she understood cooperating witnesses' weaknesses.
These were not honorable men—not in the eyes of the law, or even in
the perverted lens of *omertà*. On cross-examination, she made each
man catalog his dishonor for the jury, the crimes he had committed
in the past, the trials he had testified at, the money he had made from
the government. She laid out the quid pro quo to the jury as a crime
in and of itself.

"The more you tell them, the more you lie, they give you more
money," she said.

WHEN GASPARE VALENTI APPEARED at the trial, he was no longer
in his cousin's shadow. Valenti wore a dark suit with a matching tie
and a folded pocket handkerchief. His glasses held a faint, seedy tint.
Asaro sat two dozen feet across the courtroom, his face fixed with
suppressed rage. Valenti's son, Anthony, sat on the left side of the gallery, where Asaro's wife and granddaughters held their vigil, sending
a silent condemnation. Gar's betrayal had blindsided Asaro; when his
indictment came down in 2014, his suspicions on the morning of the
Katz exhumation were realized. But in both men's lives—which had

been marked by disappointment and struggle—it was a predictable outcome.

Prosecutors do not announce that a single witness *is* their case, but the central pillars of the prosecution—the murder of Paul Katz and Lufthansa—rested on Valenti's shoulders. At first glance, Valenti appeared to be a lesser figure than Sal Vitale. Valenti hunched forward to the microphone to answer each question. He spoke in the same cartoonish Queens-ese that Vitale used, but with none of the swagger and indignation that punctuated each syllable of the wiseguy's testimony. Unlike that of the other cooperators, the ties between him and Asaro were not weak. The men had been bound together for half a century. Assistant U.S. Attorney Argentieri worked quickly to establish that connection with her questioning.

Valenti brought the jury back to the late 1960s where his story began with Asaro—*downthehole*—and into the provincial criminal world around South Ozone Park and Howard Beach. Robert's Lounge served as the crew's hangout during this era. It was where Valenti and Asaro ran with Jimmy Burke, Henry Hill, Tommy "Two-Guns" DeSimone (played by Joe Pesci), and others involved in the Lufthansa robbery. He testified that Asaro had shown up there after his arrest at Paul Katz's warehouse in 1968 saying, "We have to bury somebody."

"I was taken aback," he said.

He described how he brought Asaro and Burke to one of the homes that his father had built, off Liberty Avenue. Valenti testified that he sat upstairs for three hours, listening to the sound of a sledgehammer plinking against concrete. When the men were done, Valenti said, he went downstairs to spread lime over the body and pour concrete over the hole. Asaro listened to this testimony with his hands clasped together as if in prayer, watching from across the courtroom. The Katz family looked on a few yards away from the first row of the gallery.

Burke eventually bought the home where the men had entombed Katz, but the secret it held haunted him. A decade later while in prison, Burke ordered the body dug up. Valenti testified to returning to the home with Asaro's grown son, Jerry, and breaking through the floor again, to disinter Katz's remains, turning up fragments of corduroy, concrete, and bone amid the dirt.

"We put them in cardboard boxes," he said.

Macedonio asked for a break. As the prosecution team walked out toward the hallway, Assistant U.S. Attorney Argentieri leaned in toward the Katz family and asked, "Are you okay?"

On Valenti's second day of testimony, the questioning turned to Lufthansa. Argentieri set up a diagram with photographs of the men believed to be participants in the robbery, including Burke, Asaro, Tommy DeSimone, and Danny Rizzo. Valenti described how the group held a handful of planning sessions, but that the robbery was to be relatively straightforward: an armed holdup while the employees were on their lunch break. Asaro handed Valenti a hammerless .38, he testified, and said, "Don't dog it"—meaning, "don't run." Asaro and Jimmy Burke then drove off to watch the robbery from a distance. The crew drove up in a van, Valenti testified, rushed the security guard, and forced him to open the warehouse. The gang made their way to the break room and subdued the remaining staff. Within minutes, the robbers formed a chain to load box after box of cash, gold, and diamonds into the van. When the crew convened to count the take, it totaled more than $6 million. But the euphoria almost immediately gave way to fear. There was no honor among thieves. And the staggering amount of money at stake only made the threat more pressing. "We've got to be real careful now," Asaro warned Valenti, according to his testimony. "They'll look to kill us."

Valenti testified he never benefited from the job, but Asaro did. He had purchased a home and a Bill Blass Oldsmobile Mark V, Valenti said. Much of the money was kicked up to the mob leadership or stolen by other participants, but even as he was stiffed, Valenti fared better than others. "Some died, and some went missing," Valenti said, referencing the post-Lufthansa murders. Judge Ross instructed the jury to forget the comment.

Valenti testified for several days, providing a grim survey of life in organized crime following the heist. He recalled the killing of Richard Eaton, a drug dealer who had crossed Jimmy Burke. Hours before his death, Eaton dined on a meal of shrimp scampi at Afters, a mob nightclub that Valenti managed. Burke strangled Eaton and ordered Asaro to dispose of the body, Valenti testified. Asaro tasked his cousin with the job, according to his testimony, but Valenti was unable to break the frozen ground. Instead, he stashed the body in a trailer where Eaton was discovered by children several days later. As Valenti spoke, Asaro looked around the courtroom, perplexed.

"I could never eat shrimp scampi again," Valenti said. If it was meant to be a joke, it fell flat.

The most critical question a juror needs to understand about a witness is this: "Why is this person testifying?" Valenti turned to that on his second day of testimony, after recounting how he skipped New York for Las Vegas, leaving a trail of debts behind him. He remained in exile for nearly fifteen years, but in 2005, when he returned to New York, he had no money and an eighteen-month-old daughter. "I had a suit on, that's it," he said.

It took three years before Valenti approached the FBI. Asaro shut him out after his cousin's return, Valenti testified, because he had borrowed money from an associate but had not repaid it. Valenti just could not get ahead. "I was tired of that life," he said. "All I wanted to do was take care of my family."

The words appeared to sting Asaro. He grimaced and looked over, wide-eyed, to his counsel, his hands shaking in front of him. Diane Ferrone, co-counsel, tried to calm him. But Asaro's temper appeared to be boiling as if he were on the edge of the sort of outburst Judge Ross had advised him to avoid. Valenti's testimony wrapped for a break, and marshals calmly led Asaro back into the holding cell next to the courtroom.

THE TRIAL CONTINUED for another two weeks, but with each of the government's witnesses the evidence appeared to be further and further on the periphery of Asaro's life. Paul Katz's son Lawrence testified, recounting the phone call that prompted his father to leave the house. He was just five years old on the night of his father's disappearance, and there was little context he could offer connecting Asaro to the murder. More than thirty former FBI agents testified as well. They had conducted surveillance on Asaro and other Bonanno targets from the 1980s until weeks before his 2013 arrest. The photographs introduced provided period snapshots that could have been torn from a Scorsese film. Asaro, muscle-bound, outside a social club holding a pot of coffee or golf clubs, getting a kiss on the cheek from an associate, pulling up in a black Mercedes. One long-retired agent, James Parker, bore a remarkable resemblance to Günter Grass as he wearily explained photographs he had taken in May 1986; as he spoke, his eyeglasses drifted down the bridge of his nose. The evidence introduced was voluminous but archival.

TWENTY-ONE TRIAL DAYS after the jury had been sworn, the government's summation began on a Friday morning. Nicole Argentieri had let Assistant U.S. Attorney Lindsay Gerdes open the trial, and now Alicyn Cooley made the government's closing argument. She had considerable ground to cover—fourteen counts that stretched back to 1969, testimony from dozens of witnesses. Cooley was young and energetic, but nonetheless had an exhausting task. By the time she entered the fourth hour of her presentation, the jury had flagged, shifting in their seats, looking ahead blankly. Elizabeth Macedonio watched the clock. It was Friday afternoon, and there was no chance that Judge Ross would let the defense begin their summation this late in the day. By the time Cooley concluded her closing, she had been speaking for nearly seven hours. In that time, she had meticulously laid out the government's theory behind its evidence. But the government had also handed Macedonio a significant tactical victory. She would have the whole weekend to rework the defense team's closing argument.

The next Monday morning Elizabeth Macedonio stood in front of the jury. Diane Ferrone had set up a binder of materials on the lectern behind her co-counsel, but Macedonio held only a few sheets of notes in front of her as she began speaking.

"I remind you as he sits here now Mr. Asaro is still presumed to be innocent," she said to the jury. Her delivery lacked emotion, and she appeared, for a moment, nervous. It was a remarkable statement to make this late in the trial. The government had spent four weeks linking Asaro to one of New York's most historic crime families, connecting him to murders, beatings, and extortion, showing photographs of him with known organized crime figures, playing audio of him boasting of his position, decrying what he'd been owed. Yet Macedonio's statement was true: that presumption did not disappear until the jury had rendered the verdict. And, if only for a few minutes more, she set out to reinforce how Vincent Asaro remained to be seen in the eyes of the law: innocent until proven guilty.

This was the moment that Judge Ross had alluded to earlier in the trial—when Macedonio could confront the government's case head-on. Her strategy was simple: to turn the government's strengths into weaknesses. She called dozens of surveillance photographs of her client with mobsters "filler in order to bolster the testimony of cooperators." The photos didn't prove any crimes, she argued; in fact, they revealed that the government had *no proof* of any crimes. "What is the crime here?" she asked indignantly. "There is no such thing as guilt by association in this country."

The primary target of her anger was the cooperating witnesses. Not only were these men liars; they were paid liars, she said. She made their moral failings the government's. Macedonio wanted to stoke the outrage of the jury about what the "pension plan for organized crime" meant in practice: "government money going to career criminals responsible for dozens and dozens of deaths, assaults, drug sales, extortions and the list goes on and on. Every single one of these cooperators has been released from jail . . . The fact is they're despicable people, and they're all very accomplished liars." Not only was the government asking the jury to look the other way from the moral compromise in this relationship, but it was also asking the jurors to trust these men.

Macedonio reserved her harshest words for Gaspare Valenti. This was a man who had abandoned his wife and children *twice,* never repaid a debt, lied habitually—even in court—yet had never spent a single day in jail, she said. She pointed out that Vincent Asaro was not the first target that the FBI had sent Valenti after, but only after he couldn't build other cases in two years did he begin recording his cousin. "He baited Mr. Asaro with lines that the FBI gave him," she said.

"Can you imagine yourself spending years of your life sitting in a car with your cousin, just trying to set him up, just riding around trying to set him up with a crime so that you could collect money? That really takes a certain type of individual." It was a powerful summation. But after the government had put up seventy witnesses against Asaro, there was a futility to it.

In a criminal case, the government has the luxury of addressing the jury one last time before they begin deliberations. Nicole Argentieri rose to deliver the government's rebuttal. "Ask for the evidence," she said. "Look at it and test it yourself." She worked point by point to counter Macedonio's closing, aggressively moving through the evidence, translating the testimony with pantomime, at times wagging her finger at the jury, other times doling out figurative cash with her hands. As she closed, she stepped back and tried to frame the case for the jury.

"This is a story about fathers and sons. It's about tradition. It's about family. But for this defendant and his father and his son, family traditions go beyond how to string a fishing line and watching football on Sunday. The crime family is their family. And its traditions and even more strongly held. *Omertà*. Death before dishonor. The Mafia life," she said.

Argentieri was the portrait of a federal prosecutor in a conservative black suit and white blouse. The tinges of Staten Island in her voice made it clear that the world she spoke of wasn't alien to her. But her literary turn veered from the government's message. The jury needed to rely on the evidence and the evidence alone, she had told them. Yet her summation seemed to suggest that proving that Vinny Asaro was a criminal was enough to convict him of the crimes in the indictment. She closed with Asaro's voice—a final quotation from Valenti's wired recordings, of the defendant criticizing another gangster because he "never did a fucking piece of work in his life."

"Not like me," Asaro said on the recording.

Argentieri repeated it—*not like me*—pointing to her chest.

She let the phrase sit for a moment. "Thank you," she said before taking her seat.

WHEN THE ASARO TRIAL OPENED, the last of summer's heat had burned off into a few bright autumn days. By the time the jury came back in late October, autumn had dropped a cool gray blanket over the city. During the trial, Macedonio could do little as the government put up witness after witness. While the jury deliberated, she could only wait. Late in the second afternoon of deliberations, she received word that the jury had come back. It was not a good sign. The jury had not requested to see significant amounts of evidence. The quick decision suggested little, if any, deliberation on each of the counts. Macedonio had been doing this a long time and had seen many clients convicted of charges related to organized crime—including one client Argentieri had charged with ordering a killing. The Asaro case was different, though. She didn't understand why the FBI and the U.S. Attorney's Office were looking so deeply into the past when there appeared to be other active crimes to pursue. Unlike the verdicts of many of her other clients, a guilty verdict all but guaranteed that Asaro would die in prison.

THE ROOM FIXED its attention on the lone juror who stood to read aloud the verdict—Asaro, his attorneys, the government, the U.S. Attorney Robert Capers, the reporters gathered in the rows. For all the preparation, choreography, and performance of a trial, the moment the judge turned it over to the jury, she all but surrendered to unpredictability. And as the words cut through the quiet, the one outcome few, if anyone, predicted had come to pass. *Not guilty.*

Asaro looked at Macedonio, dumbfounded, searching for an explanation.

"Not guilty, you're free to go home," she said, equally stunned.

"I can't fucking believe it," he muttered.

The courtroom shared his disbelief. The jury had delivered a body blow to the prosecution team and the U.S. Attorney's Office, and rejected Gaspare Valenti's version of the truth.

The marshals quickly led Asaro back to the holding cell to begin the process of clearing him for release. Macedonio pulled herself back into the moment, instructing Asaro's family to head home, to avoid the growing crowd of press and onlookers outside the courthouse. A short time later, the defense team escorted Asaro through the lobby and into the waiting scrum of cameras.

"Free!" he shouted as he stepped out of the courthouse. He stopped to address the crowd, his arms around his two attorneys. "I'd like to thank the U.S. Marshals Service for treating me great," he said. "I can't say the same for the FBI."

Asaro followed Macedonio to her waiting Mercedes for the short drive home to Floral Park, Queens, the crowd trailing him, peppering him with questions. Before climbing into his attorney's car, he made one last joke. "Don't let them see the body in the trunk."

4

Retribution

March 22, 2017

A crowd gathered outside courtroom 2AS a few minutes before 2:00 p.m., in a hallway up the stairwell from the lobby of the federal courthouse for the Eastern District of New York. The wives and mothers seated on a bench outside the courtroom, holding their purses and eyeing the closed door, were sitting a specific form of vigil—waiting for the arraignment of a loved one to begin. Each had made a pilgrimage from the outer edges of Queens to Cadman Plaza to see their sons and husbands make their first post-arrest appearance before a magistrate. Defense attorneys leaned in quiet counsel with the women, offering glimmers of perspective, providing an ear to rehear the trauma of dawn arrests. A lone defense attorney sat with a dark-haired woman in her sixties and explained, "There's no better jail. There's only worse."

As an aside, it offered a reminder of an old defense attorney chestnut about clients facing federal prosecution: "They don't need an attorney; they need a priest."

A few minutes later Assistant U.S. Attorneys Lindsay Gerdes and Nicole Argentieri swept past clutching brown accordion folders; their determined expressions registered little acknowledgment of the audience. Elizabeth Macedonio followed several minutes afterward, a vividly printed scarf wrapped above the collar of a checkered wool jacket. Gerdes stood up from her seat at the government's table, took a few steps, then wordlessly dropped a piece of paper in front of Macedonio. Macedonio removed her jacket, pulled reading glasses from a case carried in her purse, and began examining the paper, her face a portrait of skepticism.

Early that morning, a team of FBI agents had rousted Vincent Asaro from his girlfriend's home in Richmond Hill, Queens, and placed him under arrest. The seven-page indictment was a stunning contrast to Asaro's prior charges. Rather than a sprawling RICO conspiracy capped off by a generation-defining heist like Lufthansa, Asaro was brought in on charges related to a five-year-old road rage incident in Howard Beach. Arson, specifically. The feds had located a man whose car had been torched on Asaro's orders. The victim described a surreal scene: After he had cut off Asaro in traffic in Howard Beach, the aging mobster chased him across the Belt Parkway and into South Ozone Park. Asaro continued to try to run the driver off the road, and at one point Asaro appeared to rope in another car to chase the driver, who frantically called the police. Asaro took off before the police arrived, but did not let it go. The next day, he called a Gambino soldier who he knew could run the plate on the driver who cut him off. Asaro then met the Gambino associate at a Howard Beach deli where the men got in a car together to go case the house of the driver. That night, in the dawn hours, a crew of three men, including John Gotti's grandson, doused the hood of the car with gasoline, tossing matches on the fuel to set it alight. The vehicle burned as the men made their escape into the night. It was an old-style Mafia tactic.

This wasn't the most compelling organized crime case; it wasn't even a glancing blow to the Italian mob in New York. But that didn't matter: the point was to bring in Asaro. The other defendants in the case, who were more than half a century younger than Asaro, were almost incidental to this purpose. They had been implicated in bank and jewelry store robberies. Around the same time, the Eastern District had been preparing a separate thirty-seven-count indictment against ten members of the Bonanno crime family, but none of the charges connected back to Asaro. Meanwhile, prosecutors in the Southern District announced a sprawling indictment against forty-six "leaders, members and associates" of the Genovese, Lucchese, Gambino, and Bonanno families, but many of those cases fizzled to time served or nominal sentences. Asaro's minor new charges only underscored how remote he was from what remained of the five families.

Around 2:20 p.m., six federal agents, including Adam Mininni, poured into a holding area along the courtroom wall. The men—they were all men—were unshaven and deliberately unkempt, dressed in post-arrest chic: hoodies, blue jeans, and Under Armour, badges hanging off their necks, over their hearts. Mininni looked as if he hadn't slept since the acquittal, his eyes darkened by rings, cheeks sunken, yet still boyish. The agents said nothing. Their attention fixed on Argentieri, who walked over and retrieved a gallon-size Ziploc bag filled with orange prescription bottles from one of the agents. As the clock ticked past 3:00 p.m., the gallery began to fill with reporters.

Asaro entered the courtroom wearing a North Face windbreaker and sweatpants, a wide-eyed look of bewilderment across his face. He had returned to a relatively anonymous life after the trial, living with his longtime girlfriend and her ninety-four-year-old mother in a modest two-story house in Richmond Hill, Queens, neighboring his old haunts of Ozone Park and Howard Beach. Asaro tended to his girlfriend's mother, who was deteriorating with dementia, cooking her meals and taking care of the household chores. His list of illnesses read like the warning on a pharmaceutical ad: heart disease, kidney disease, hepatitis C, liver disease, high blood pressure, high cholesterol, arthritis. When Asaro wasn't at doctors' appointments, he'd linger in the yard, watering the lawn, with his dog—until the dog died.

After the arraignment ended and Asaro was led back into custody, Macedonio could only think: "These charges are personal."

THE GOVERNMENT WANTED another bite at the apple—to get the justice that the jury would not deliver. Whatever the stated law enforcement purpose of Asaro's arrest was, it could be seen only through the lens of the defeat the prosecution suffered at trial. The accusations showed that five years earlier Asaro pulled enough weight in Howard Beach to effect an arson. But the pettiness of the offense also suggested that he was far from the height of his power in the Bonanno crime family. The Vincent Asaro whom Macedonio knew was a hot-tempered old man, adored by his granddaughters, and of no consequence to organized crime in New York. Argentieri saw him differently: Asaro strangled Paul Katz with a dog leash, he deprived the Katz children of their father in the earliest years of their lives, he left them with an unresolved absence that would haunt the family. The failure to deliver a guilty verdict only deprived the family again of any sense of justice.

There was very little Macedonio could use to fight. The likelihood that Asaro would prevail at trial again was remote. She sought to have him released on bond, putting together a $2 million bail package from assets belonging to Asaro's girlfriend and daughters. It had taken his last case nearly eighteen months to make it to trial. If Macedonio could secure her client's freedom while she litigated the pretrial issues, that might be as valuable as winning the case.

But the government did not want Asaro back on the street. The prosecutors surfaced allegations that made it all but impossible for Judge Ross to sign off on his release. Relying on a secondhand conversation from a jailhouse informant, the government accused Asaro of threatening to kill Assistant U.S. Attorney Argentieri.

"We need to do something about this bitch [referring to the prosecutor]," Asaro allegedly told another Bonanno soldier while incarcerated at the Metropolitan Detention Center.

According to the informant, Asaro also said to "not fuck it up like Vinny. We need to handle this"—a reference to Vincent Basciano, the former Bonanno boss who threatened to kill another Eastern District mob prosecutor, Greg Andres. The government used the grave threat to argue against his release pending trial, but the accusations also raised the stakes that Asaro might face additional charges in a superseding indictment.

Increasing the pressure even more, Argentieri almost immediately sought to have Macedonio removed from the case. The prosecution argued that Macedonio's representation of another accused Bonanno member, Ronnie Giallanzo, constituted a conflict of interest. (Argentieri was also prosecuting that case.) If Asaro wanted to cooperate with the government against Giallanzo to cut a deal on his case, his attorney would be caught between her duty to protect both clients. But the judge allowed Macedonio to remain on the case.

Unlike in his prior case, the government was interested in entering into plea negotiations with Asaro. Asaro wasn't going to be a rat, whether out of fealty to the Bonanno family or because whatever dirt he might have had wouldn't be sufficient to persuade the government to back down. That was enough. He took a deal where he could keep his mouth shut and avoid sitting through another trial. After nearly half a century on the streets, Vincent Asaro pleaded guilty to one federal charge: a single count of arson.

JUDGE ROSS HELD ASARO'S SENTENCING several days after Christmas in 2017. In the weeks before his sentencing, the prosecution was forced to withdraw their claims that Asaro had threatened Argentieri. In a filing, the prosecutors acknowledged that "the government discovered additional information regarding CS-1 that has cast doubt on his reliability."

As Judge Ross prepared to sentence Asaro, she decided to reveal her thinking on not just the immediate case but also his acquittal in the 2015 trial. The government had proved its case against Asaro, she said, and while she could only order punishment on the charges to which he had pleaded, she did have the discretion to depart upward. That is what she chose to do. Ross handed down a sentence nearly twice as long as the guidelines required of her: eight years in prison.

"I don't care what happens to me anyway," Asaro told the judge angrily. "What you sentenced me to is a death sentence."

ON MARCH 19, 2018, Gaspare Valenti stepped into Judge Ross's courtroom one minute before his sentencing was scheduled to begin. He entered from the chambers' doorway. That he wasn't led in from a holding cell, or walked freely through the courtroom's public doors, suggested a third option, a state of being somewhere between incarceration and freedom. This was the strange state of witness protection. Valenti's attorney, Scott Fenstermaker, walked one step behind him. Special Agent Adam Mininni followed, dressed for the occasion in a suit.

Valenti appeared tan and exhausted. He wore a lapis-blue suit jacket, a sweater underneath, and a white shirt with no tie. The swagger that he carried into Judge Ross's packed courtroom two years earlier had left him. The seats where family and friends scowled from the back rows of the gallery as he testified against his cousin now sat empty. Today as Valenti took his seat, he leaned forward over the table, as if waiting to hear a long-suspected diagnosis.

The sentencing of a criminal cooperator is not a moment that serves the government's narrative. It is when the government acknowledges the quid pro quo between prosecutors and men and women who commit the universal crime of betrayal. The Eastern District's U.S. Attorney's Office does its best to conceal these events, often docketing the defendant as "John Doe" and not including the hearings in press notifications. The new press officer for the office, John Marzulli, had covered the first Asaro trial in his last job as the Eastern District courthouse reporter for the New York *Daily News*. He knew the event would be of interest to a handful of reporters who covered organized crime and alerted us the morning of the sentencing. The prosecutors Nicole Argentieri and Lindsay Gerdes expressed surprise when a handful of reporters began to trickle in.

For Argentieri, the occasion had a salutary aspect. This was the final day of her career as a federal prosecutor. After nearly eleven years and after rising to become the chief of the Public Integrity Section, she was returning to Big Law, to the prestigious firm of O'Melveny & Myers. Lindsay Gerdes, her second seat throughout the Asaro trial, remained by her side. The Italian Mafia, or rather the remnants of the Italian Mafia, had defined Argentieri's career. In the tradition of Ed McDonald, John Gleeson, and Greg Andres, she'd left the five families much to fear. But, also in her predecessors' tradition, she was graduating to the more lucrative realm of corporate law.

If Argentieri reflected the office's tradition of strength against the mob, Valenti represented the diminished, defeated, yet still craven impulses of the Mafia. He had been moved to cooperate not so much by conscience as by desperation. That decision set him on the dangerous course of an active informant and, now, into witness protection. His sole connection to the world he had once known was his FBI handlers. Even Valenti's lawyer didn't know how to reach his client directly; everything needed to go through the bureau. His primary handler, Agent Mininni, became something like family to him, particularly because his son silently disavowed his father during the trial.

When Judge Ross entered, she smiled, an expression that looked both forced and sincere. Valenti pleaded guilty in secrecy in 2009, knowing that sentencing would someday come. He also knew that whatever assurances he'd received from the FBI or the government were just that.

When Judge Ross spoke, any fear about Valenti's fate left the room. She plainly remarked that "his lengthy testimony at the Asaro trial was wholly credible." That is to say, she did not doubt that Vincent Asaro not only was behind the Lufthansa heist but was a murderer.

"I view him as among the most valuable cooperators I have seen in twenty-five years on the bench," she said of Valenti. The sentence: probation.

It was an ignoble achievement. But in Gaspare Valenti's and Vincent Asaro's lifelong struggle to get out of *downthehole,* it was something.

DRUGS

The war has become institutionalized. It is no longer a special program or politicized project; it is simply the way things are done.

—MICHELLE ALEXANDER, *The New Jim Crow*

5

The Border

January 6, 2015

JetBlue Flight 780 touched down shortly before 10:00 p.m. It was the second of the airline's two daily flights between Montego Bay and New York's John F. Kennedy International Airport. The airport's holiday rush had begun to taper off. Sun-chasing tourists filled the evening's flight along with those, like Chevelle Nesbeth, for whom a trip to Jamaica marked a return to a home left behind years earlier. Nesbeth was a nineteen-year-old Southern Connecticut State University education major with straight shoulder-length brown hair highlighted with streaks, a trim dancer's build, and a wide telegenic smile. She stepped off the plane in a gray-and-maroon three-quarter-sleeve T-shirt, fitted acid-washed jeans, and red sneakers. The holiday break had given her a chance to see her father in Kingston and a boyfriend, who had paid her airfare, and, perhaps most comforting, the chance to break up the long East Coast winter with a Caribbean holiday. When she stood up from her seat in the sixth row, she hadn't even pulled a winter coat from her luggage to ready herself for the cold night.

Nesbeth waited more than thirty minutes for her luggage. Finally, a blue Michael Kors roll-along suitcase tumbled onto the baggage carousel. She had checked the larger of her two matching bags but had carried on the smaller roll-along. By the time the second bag appeared, the crowd from her flight had thinned to a handful of passengers. Next to her, a toddler in a navy stocking cap parka reached down to touch the carousel's silver slats as the last of the luggage cycled past. Nesbeth lugged her bag to the floor and pulled at the handle, which would only partially extend. She didn't fuss with it further, instead throwing her purse strap across her chest, pulling her hair back, and making her way toward the exit.

Nesbeth, like many immigrants in the New York area, had split her life between two worlds. She was born and raised in Jamaica, where she lived with her father. At age thirteen, she joined her mother in Connecticut. By the time she finished high school, she was a U.S. citizen and on her way to college. She lived at home with her mother in New Haven, where she worked a part-time job as a nail technician while attending school. After graduation, she hoped to teach and, someday, become a school principal. Jamaica remained a part of her identity. Many of her friends had roots on the island. She would shift into patois when speaking or texting with them, reverting to American English when she needed to.

The tiny, lush island nation, which boasts itself to be among the world's happiest places, has long struggled with poverty and violence. Much of this is fueled by the drug trade in locally grown marijuana and the transshipment of South American cocaine. In 2010, a request from the U.S. Attorney for the Southern District of New York to apprehend and extradite the gang lord Christopher "Dudus" Coke triggered a month of rioting in Tivoli Gardens, a Kingston neighborhood where the police held little authority. The unrest culminated in a massacre. Soldiers conducted a door-to-door assault on the neighborhood, killing more than seventy people. That violence contradicted the easygoing image of the island nation, but the duality of a wealth of natural beauty and a paucity of real opportunity is shared by other Caribbean countries such as Trinidad and Tobago, Guyana, and the Dominican Republic, which also wrestle with violence and crime. It fuels the migration toward the United States of those seeking stability and a more secure future. Nesbeth carried with her an American passport and all the possibilities that went with citizenship—a paying job, college, a career path. Jamaica was her home, but the United States was her future.

NESBETH CROSSED TWO BORDERS that night: the international border with the United States and the jurisdictional boundary of the Eastern District of New York. The Eastern District is an "airport district"—which is to say that a central feature of the jurisdiction's landscape is an international airport. On any given day, passengers originating from dozens of nations land there. In 2015, fifty-six million passengers transited through JFK, with more than two million passengers passing through that January alone. The flow of human traffic nearly matched the entire population of South Africa. The airport was also a locus for crimes native to a border crossing: immigration fraud; smuggling of money, counterfeit goods, and agricultural products; and, most frequent, narcotics trafficking.

Behind a doorway in Terminal 4, just past the arrivals hall and steps before the final point of entry into the United States, is the office of U.S. Customs and Border Protection. CBP, as the agency is known, serves as the beat cops that patrol the border between the United States and the rest of the world. That border takes many forms—the seventy-five hundred miles of land crossings along Canada and in the Southwest, the ports in Long Beach and Newark, and air transit hubs like Los Angeles, Miami, and JFK. Customs officers are not investigators trying to crack the inner workings of a criminal organization. Their jobs begin and end at the border, the sort of lunch pail enforcement of interdicting contraband and detaining those entering the country illegally. Once a CBP agent has made a stop, he hands off the investigation to Immigration and Customs Enforcement (ICE), a sister agency in the Department of Homeland Security.

Nonetheless, CBP's work at JFK offers a keen vantage point on the changing fortunes of the global drug trade. Before air travel, smugglers moved narcotics transited through Europe and Canada on steam liners docking on the Brooklyn waterfront. International air travel gave cocaine producers in Colombia and Bolivia and heroin sources in Afghanistan and Burma more immediate entry to the United States.

While overland and maritime routes allowed traffickers to move large quantities of drugs into the United States, commercial air travel provided cover for traffickers to enter the country. Each year Customs intercepted on average more than 61 tons of narcotics landing at the airport—nearly 340 pounds each day. The vast majority of shipments arrived as cargo through commercial shipping companies, akin to tossing a load over a fence and hoping the right person happened to pick it up on the other side. Nearly every drug turned up at JFK: small quantities of LSD, ecstasy, opium, and hashish and more significant amounts of crystal meth, ketamine, and steroids. Khat, the psychotropic leaf favored in the Horn of Africa, was the most commonly seized narcotic, followed by pharmaceuticals and chemicals used in the manufacture of methamphetamine. Cocaine, heroin, and marijuana, the troika of the international drug trade, ranked top among street narcotics.

Traffickers blended in smaller loads of these in the daily crowds of travelers. In the 1980s and 1990s, cocaine arrived this way exclusively from producing countries like Colombia and Bolivia: a Saturday evening flight from Bogotá could often yield half a dozen to a dozen seizures. With the rise of the Colombian cartels, trafficking organizations hired out the risky work to new players—with less capital and leverage. Distribution was first farmed out to Mexican couriers, but as local cartels gained power and developed their trafficking networks, the work fell to smaller players in nations across the southern reach of the United States: the Dominican Republic, Trinidad, Guyana, Jamaica.

AFTER RETRIEVING HER BAGS, Nesbeth approached the final point of entry into the United States. Waiting there was a Customs and Border Protection officer, Giuseppe D'Andrea. Officer D'Andrea was nearing the end of his shift. The officer had worked for CBP for six years, and even though he was on duty inside the terminal that evening, he wore his heavy navy Customs coat, his service weapon and handcuffs riding his hip, a trimmed five o'clock shadow across his face. A typical day involved processing hundreds of passengers and selecting fifteen to twenty bags for screening. During his entire career, after searching through thousands of bags, D'Andrea had discovered a load of narcotics only once. More often, people tried to smuggle in meats, cheeses, and vegetables from their native countries restricted under agricultural regulations. After Nesbeth presented her passport to him, he looked it over for a moment, then asked her to follow him to the secondary screening area.

Under the watch of several surveillance cameras, D'Andrea ran through several rote questions with her: *Were the bags hers? Had she packed them herself? Was everything in the bags hers? How much cash was she carrying? What was the purpose of her trip? How long had she been gone?*

Nesbeth answered calmly, in a friendly, matter-of-fact tone. She told Officer D'Andrea that she'd traveled from Montego Bay to Kingston to visit her father. That was true, but Nesbeth did not mention that she had also visited a boyfriend there—one who had paid for her trip and given her the new Michael Kors luggage to bring back to the United States.

As she spoke, Officer D'Andrea adjusted the bags on the examination table, a stainless steel horseshoe behind a desk with several monitors. Nesbeth unzipped the larger bag and briefly held on to the edge of it, as if she might be asked to zip it up again a moment later. Once D'Andrea began pulling her belongings out onto the table, her hands returned to her sides. He pulled a bottle from the bag, unscrewed the cap, and smelled the contents, before quickly closing it and setting it down. She wasn't the only traveler being examined late that evening. As D'Andrea moved through the contents of her larger suitcase, she could see another man hauling three large roll-alongs onto the table across from her.

D'Andrea peppered her with questions as he pulled clothing onto the table.

What do you do? he asked.

I work at a spa, Nesbeth responded.

He asked about her father, what he did for a living, occasionally glancing up as he emptied the last of her belongings onto the table. Nesbeth stood one step back from the table, following the items with her eyes, occasionally adjusting her purse on her shoulder. When she had rolled the suitcases toward the area, the officer noticed that the handle on the larger bag did not extend fully; this was not the reason he had stopped her, but it was a detail he registered, the sort of anomaly that warranted his attention. After unpacking her clothes and belongings from the larger of her two suitcases, D'Andrea unzipped the interior lining to examine the length of the roll-along handles. Nesbeth took a step back and rested her hands on her hips, peering into the suitcase. The officer produced a probe—a long metal shiv—and began hammering the handle. She grew alarmed.

Is something wrong? she asked.

Nope, he said, looking up and shaking his head.

Banging on the handle did not produce the hollow clanging sound that the officer expected. Instead, D'Andrea heard a muted thunking sound, which told him that there was something within the handle. He used the probe to penetrate the handle, and within moments a white powdery substance appeared. Officer D'Andrea immediately looked up, not at Nesbeth, then glanced over his shoulder before hastily tossing her clothes back into the bag. Moments later, he stepped from behind the desk and caught his supervisor's eye.

Bag, he said. *We need to do a passport check. There's something wrong with the passport.*

Something wrong with my passport? Nesbeth asked.

Chevelle, please follow me, D'Andrea said.

As she rolled her bags toward a locked door, two Customs officers fell in behind her.

CUSTOMS OFFICIALS GO to lengths to avoid the word "profile." Yet, from even before Nesbeth set foot on the JetBlue flight, she fit one of law enforcement's most enduring and legally substantiated profiles: the drug courier. The profile was created in 1974 by a Drug Enforcement Administration (DEA) agent, Paul Markonni, who developed seven characteristics common to couriers. The Markonni profile, which was never validated by quantitative data, has since been outdated by changes in the drug trade and post–September 11 security protocols. Yet several elements persist to this day in assessing potential targets to be stopped at the border including a passenger's point of origin, the presence of either too much or too little luggage for a trip, a passenger giving off the appearance of nervousness, unusually short itineraries or those booked recently, and the cash purchase of tickets. The Supreme Court heard a challenge on the use of profiling on suspected couriers in 1989. In *United States v. Sokolow,* an appeal brought by a convicted drug trafficker on the constitutionality of the search of his bags, the Supreme Court carved out an area under the Fourth Amendment specific to suspected drug couriers. The Court found that law enforcement needed only "reasonable suspicion" to stop and search individuals, rather than "probable cause" supported by specific facts. This decision gave considerable power to border agents, yet also magnified the hazard of targeting innocent travelers. This authority extended to physical searches. The most invasive of these, the use of X-rays, carried with it not only legal considerations but ethical concerns for the technicians and radiologists conducting the examinations—including the potential to make a "false positive" determination that results in someone's arrest and detention. Health professionals are aware that officers often rely on profiles rather than evidence to target the patients subjected to the test. (In a hospital setting, doctors who discover drugs inside individuals who are not under criminal investigation can choose to not disclose their discoveries to authorities but instead destroy the drugs.)

Through one lens, Nesbeth's journey looked innocuous—a Christmas visit to see her father. But mapped to the drug courier profile, several facts about Nesbeth jumped out. Hours before she boarded the flight for Jamaica, her $703.31 ticket was paid for in cash at JFK airport. While tourists favored Montego Bay as a destination to Kingston, both airports had a demonstrated record as transshipment points. The fact that she was departing Montego Bay alone also warranted scrutiny, because Customs officials viewed that as a resort destination more often frequented by couples and families, rather than single travelers.

Much of Nesbeth's travel information was contained in a passenger name record (PNR), a data file assigned to each air traveler that contains identity and booking information. A typical PNR is a cryptic all-caps output of itinerary and booking data. Occasionally a note about an interaction with the airline will appear. (For example, my PNR read, "WIFE CALLED TO SEE ABOUT CHG ONE DAY

EARLIER," at the end of an entry about a flight from Port of Spain to JFK that I asked my wife to change from the United States.) The PNR can go further to include "racial or ethnic origin, political opinions, religious or philosophical beliefs, trade union membership, health, or sex life," though the government only uses that information in "exceptional circumstances." PNRs had long been a key tool in interdicting drug couriers before the September 11 attacks, when U.S. authorities came to rely on the system to track and prevent suspected terrorists from entering the United States. This caused some controversy, and the U.S. government had to make a case for international cooperation. In Europe, for example, U.S. officials had to argue that authorities could implement the system without violating the European Union's stringent privacy regulations. Only after the successive terrorist attacks in Paris and Brussels did the European Union adopt the agreement to share PNRs among member states. Law enforcement agencies sought this to enhance their abilities to target suspect passengers electronically anywhere between forty-eight and twenty-four hours before they even arrive.

Once a passenger lands, the human surveillance begins. A dedicated unit—the Passenger Enforcement Rover Team—polices the arrival hall. These units look past the PNRs and passenger manifest information to pick out anomalies in the crowd, nervous or ill passengers, those walking with a stiff or stilted gait, or those wearing clothing, shoes, bags, and even hairstyles that offer a visual clue they may be used to smuggle drugs. For all the sophisticated technology brought to bear and the layers of human surveillance, the smallest detail could stand out and mean the difference between quickly clearing passport control and being questioned and searched—a detail like a roll-along handle that won't extend.

CHEVELLE NESBETH FOLLOWED the officers to a windowless room off the entry hall, pulling her luggage along with her. Inside sat a wooden desk, a single scuffed chair, and a wooden bench with a set of shackles; the walls were padded. Officer D'Andrea made no mention of his discovery. He wasn't certain whether the other passenger undergoing a search at the examination table knew her or had any connections to her. Once she and the bags were secured, he contacted Homeland Security Investigations (HSI), the squad of investigators who work along with Customs. HSI takes over once a discovery of contraband has been made to question a suspect further—in hopes of obtaining a confession or information on the trafficking organization.

Typically couriers have little connection to a drug organization beyond their immediate handlers. This compartmentalization serves the trafficker's interest; mules are seen as disposable and, given the likelihood of arrest, a potential liability. In some instances, couriers act as unwitting accomplices—either unaware that they are moving drugs or believing they are carrying something other than narcotics, like precious metals or stones. Lack of knowledge, however, doesn't provide a foolproof defense. If a prosecutor can show that a defendant did not know but was willfully ignorant of his or her crime—a legal doctrine known as "conscious avoidance"—then there is sufficient basis to convict that person.

Outside the interrogation room, an HSI investigator disassembled the extendable handles on each of Nesbeth's bags. He pulled wrapped packages of white powder from each handle. The packages together weighed in at twelve hundred grams, or about two and a half pounds. Officer D'Andrea took a small sample to conduct a field test. After a few moments, the results came back: the powder was positive for cocaine. When the investigator stepped into the room, he told Nesbeth about the discovery. The government was charging her with importing more than a kilogram of cocaine into the United States. She wasn't going home that night.

A few hours later, at the federal courthouse for the Eastern District of New York, the investigator swore the complaint before a magistrate judge on duty, charging that Nesbeth "knowingly" and "intentionally" brought the drugs into the country. This was the most average criminal charge in the Brooklyn federal prosecutor's office, a near boilerplate courier case that would be assigned to a junior Assistant U.S. Attorney and a federal public defender—the kind that generations of ambitious prosecutors working their way through the office's freshman year, known as General Crimes, had cut their teeth on. (Assistant U.S. Attorneys referred to the group of prosecutors who started in the office at the same time as their "General Crimes class.") There were few facts to dispute: the search and discovery of the cocaine had occurred under the constant gaze of surveillance cameras. D'Andrea had followed a nearly scripted dialogue with Nesbeth, leaving no novel legal terrain to explore: the legality of the search had been well established even up to the Supreme Court. Nesbeth's case was left to turn on a more fundamental question. Did Chevelle Nesbeth know she was carrying cocaine into the country? Did she, at least, have reason to know? More specifically, could the government prove either?

6

Trial Tax

June 16, 2015

Seated at the defense table, Chevelle Nesbeth looked minimized and harmless. She wore a dark cardigan and glasses, projecting a bewildered bookishness. Since her January arrest, Chevelle had returned to school, on bond, while the charges cast uncertainty over her future. School and work were two pillars of her life. Her mother immigrated to the United States to find a better life for her and her daughter, and the road to a better life was through education. Nesbeth upheld her part of that bargain: she showed herself to be a diligent student, navigating the fraught teen years as a recent arrival, studying, playing soccer, and, from the age of fifteen, working to buy herself the things she needed. By the time she entered college, Nesbeth had the ambition to match her work ethic: she wanted to be a teacher and principal. On the morning of her trial, her entire future seemed to hang in the balance.

Judge Frederic Block's courtroom was hardly a pressure cooker, either. The judge, a Clinton appointee who rose to the bench from a two-person law practice on Long Island, kept the formalities to a minimum. Block liked to interject—during opening statements, examinations, jury instructions—as if the jury were on a tour of the federal courthouse and happened to be asked to sit for a case. He adopted a friendly, educational tone, burying his *r*'s like a native New Yorker, softening any edge to the proceeding. When the jury sat that morning, he explained the mechanics of a criminal trial to them: who the parties were, how the evidence would be introduced, and, in the event someone needed to go to the bathroom, that they should raise their hand.

"Make believe we are in kindergarten class," he told them.

The prosecutor and the federal public defender, on the other hand, proceeded with dour seriousness. It was the second federal trial for Amanda David, the defense attorney, and the first federal trial for the prosecutor, Paul Scotti, though each had trial experience at the state level. Cases like this provided a sandbox for young prosecutors and defenders in the Eastern District to develop their trial skills. One day earlier, the entire General Crimes class of the U.S. Attorney's Office had sat in on jury selection to get a glimpse of how juries in the district looked. Eastern District panels differed from those in the Southern District, which drew from Westchester County and were peppered with recent arrivals who lived and worked in Manhattan. Here juries pulled in noticeable numbers from the people who made New York City run: sanitation and transit workers, corrections officers, cops, and their family members. There were also potential jurors from the communities most closely impacted by the drug trade and the police attention brought on by it. For all his preamble, Block did not let on that he was a critic of the drug war. Or that he thought the harm caused by mass incarceration outweighed the benefits of tough enforcement. Drug courier cases were the face of that war in the Eastern District and, as a tradition indigenous to the jurisdiction, a unique window into the war's folly. Block likened his role to a "traffic cop just waving the traffic on with no end in sight."

Perhaps the only thing remarkable about Chevelle Nesbeth's case was that she elected to go to trial. The act of asserting her innocence came with a political cost: a more severe sentence after a conviction. The government had charged her with two offenses: importing cocaine and the intent to distribute it, ratcheting up the pressure in a potential plea negotiation. That charging decision didn't necessarily follow from

Department of Justice guidance. In 2013, Attorney General Eric Holder distributed a directive to federal prosecutors to avoid overcharging certain "low-level" drug offenders. The Holder Memo, as it became known, directed a tempered use of charging power against nonviolent offenders with no criminal history or ties to drug organizations. Nesbeth appeared to be the exact type of defendant the attorney general had described.

But when the federal defender Amanda David rose to address the jury in her opening statements, she didn't want the jurors to weigh the policy at work. She tried to place the jurors in her client's shoes.

"It's early January, a few days after New Year's, a week or so after Christmas. Imagine that you are lucky enough to have escaped the frigid temperatures here in New York, the slush, the snow, and be able to enjoy all the trappings of the holiday season still. You are able to get out of New York, head to the sun, to the beach, to the Caribbean. It sounds fantastic, right?" she said. "For 19-year-old Chevelle Nesbeth, it seemed like a dream vacation."

But, David explained, it was the beginning of an "ongoing nightmare."

Like many teenagers, Nesbeth didn't fit tidily into adult perceptions. Her online persona presented a more complicated picture of her identity. Her postings were full of bluster, contradictions, and sexualized humor. She complained of boredom and philosophized about relationships. In the days after her arrest, her postings were circumspect. ("Start each day with a new hope, leave bad memories behind and have faith for a better tomorrow.") But in the months preceding her trial, she could be harsh and judgmental. ("Pregnant bitches that work fast food got the worst attitudes. Bitch you should've fucked a nigga with a job.") She occasionally drifted into patois ("Mi nuh like deal wid dat idiot ya enuh"). The photographs of herself she posted didn't reflect the sullen image in the courtroom: she appeared in sleek dresses, posing with friends at parties, her smile beaming, but never appearing in glasses.

But none of that information would enter in the trial. The objective of the defense was to limit the evidence that the government could put in front of the jury. In truth, the government knew Chevelle only in the narrowest sense. The prosecutors knew that when she had arrived at JFK that January night, Officer D'Andrea had made his discovery. The government didn't need to prove that she placed the cocaine there. It merely needed to prove that as she retrieved her luggage from the carousel and tried to extend her suitcases' handles, she knew—or should have known—that each carried a little less than three-quarters of a pound of cocaine.

METHODS OF CONCEALMENT for drug couriers have evolved with the drug trade. False-bottomed suitcases, modified shoe soles, molds sculpted to wrap around the limbs and torso of a courier. Objects like plates, jars—in some cases the hard exterior of suitcases—fabricated entirely from compressed cocaine. Liquid cocaine suffused into fabric to be extracted and reconstituted once safely inside the United States. Even dreadlocks spun around loads of narcotics. Traffickers have tried to innovate, finding means to transit drugs imperceptibly in with crowds of travelers clearing Customs.

The most relied-upon smuggling vessel is the human body. Those who swallow or insert drugs are referred to by CBP officials at JFK as "the Internals." The 1990 crash of Avianca Flight 52 from Bogotá in Cove Neck, Long Island, revealed the prevalence of this new class of smuggler. The crash left 65 of the 149 passengers aboard dead. As doctors examined two survivors with critical injuries, they made a startling discovery: some of the men were carrying dozens of sealed "pellets" of cocaine in their digestive tracts. Ten years later, on the same Avianca route from Bogotá, Customs officers discovered an emaciated sheepdog shipped as cargo. An X-ray revealed orange-size objects sewn into the animal's body—what turned out to be condoms filled with nearly $50,000 in cocaine. The officers removed the drugs, then adopted the dog and named him Cokie.

From the decades of interdiction efforts at JFK, Customs developed a "bag to body" approach with suspected traffickers. Officers begin their searches by looking at a passenger's belongings. They look out for anything misshapen, broken, or out of place—like a new screw on a worn suitcase. Sometimes the make of luggage signals a potential courier. Drug trafficking organizations function like any other business. When possible, these organizations buy in bulk, including the bags they intend to retrofit to carry concealed narcotics. Once a Customs official discovers a bag-borne load, the agency shares that data on seizures across points of entry in the event a trafficker is flooding crossings around the country with similarly modified bags. "Bag" couriers can carry larger loads of drugs but face greater risk of discovery. Loads of powdered cocaine and heroin tend to leave visible traces, even when they have been concealed. Scent is another giveaway; cocaine often gives off the unmistakable smell of nail polish remover, from the acetone used in its processing, while heroin gives off a telltale vinegar odor.

If an officer does not discover anything in a suspected courier's luggage, he will turn his attention to the traveler's body. Officers pat down passengers to determine whether they have strapped drugs to their person. Officers also scan the crowd in the immigration hall to see if there are any individuals with a stiff or awkward gait that may indicate that they are carrying drugs on their extremities. "Body" couriers bring smaller loads but require more intrusive efforts to determine if they are carrying—in particular, if the load is inside the courier. These "Internals" typically swallow pellets fashioned from condoms or the fingers of surgical gloves or insert objects in their rectums or vaginas. Investigators have two options to determine if a passenger has ingested drugs. If individuals consent, they can be brought to a JFK medical facility for an X-ray that will readily reveal the presence of pellets in their digestive tracts. Or the investigators can wait until suspects need to move their bowels. For these situations, Customs has a toilet—or "throne," as it is referred to by the officers—where couriers pass the contents of their bodies into a container. Whatever the suspect passes is pressure washed and handed over for testing. The greatest danger these couriers face is if part of their load ruptures. Sudden internal exposure to several grams of cocaine can trigger cardiac arrest within moments. Heroin, while also potentially fatal, moves more slowly through the system and, if Customs officers detect a rupture, can allow time for the courier to receive medical treatment.

"Drug couriers" is a politically correct term, one that has been adopted by the law enforcement community and criminal defense attorneys as an alternative to the more pejorative term: "drug mule." "Mule" is accurate in one respect: it captures the dehumanizing nature of the work. The men, women, and children who do this risk the gauntlet of international borders carrying a load of narcotics. Some couriers do not know or appreciate the risk they are undertaking, while others repeatedly play the odds. "There is an inexhaustible supply of under-educated, impoverished people in Latin America, Africa, and Asia who are ripe for recruiting to earn in a short time what is for them an enormous amount of money," wrote the former deputy chief probation officer for the Eastern District of New York. Mules earn a fraction of the profit but absorb the majority of the risk.

Not all couriers fit the description of the poor, disadvantaged surrogate. Many knowingly take the risk with the prospect for easy money. These include grandmothers, flight attendants, yeshiva students, and, in at least one case, a Customs and Border Protection officer who helped two couriers clear forty-five kilograms of cocaine through security in February 2017.

Each year the Eastern District U.S. Attorney's Office charges more than ninety couriers on a range of trafficking offenses; nearly all of these are individuals attempting to pass through JFK with a load of narcotics. In the month before Nesbeth's flight landed, the Eastern District had charged five traffickers: a Panamanian man with a false-bottom suitcase stuffed with nine pounds of cocaine, a man arriving from Guyana who had swallowed forty-five pellets of cocaine, a mother of four from Massachusetts returning from Jamaica with two pounds of cocaine hidden in her bag, a man who had been paid $6,000 to fly from Santo Domingo wearing a diaper packed with three and a half pounds of cocaine, and another man who had swallowed eighty pellets before boarding a flight from Kingston to JFK. Each of them was traveling alone from destinations in the Caribbean.

WHEN OFFICER GIUSEPPE D'ANDREA took the witness stand, he did not remove his coat. He wore the same uniform that he had worn the night of Chevelle Nesbeth's arrest six months earlier, down to the navy nylon patrol jacket. Over the course of his career as a Customs and Border Protection agent, he'd searched thousands of pieces of luggage, but he had never testified in federal court before. He looked as if he'd rather be anywhere else in the world. His posture, an uneasy hunch, gave the impression that the moment the judge dismissed him, he'd bolt for the door. He sat sullen and quiet.

The government would put up only three other witnesses: a DEA lab technician to confirm that the drugs seized were cocaine, a JetBlue employee to verify details of Nesbeth's itinerary, and an ICE agent to provide an estimated street value on the drug. D'Andrea was the only witness who had ever interacted with Chevelle. His role that day was not only to recount how he found the cocaine but to admit into the evidence the backbone of the government's case: surveillance footage of Chevelle as Officer D'Andrea searched her bags. But at the outset D'Andrea proved a difficult witness. The prosecutor struggled to get him through basic questions about his training and experience. He offered terse responses to each question; the judge continually asked that he speak more loudly. At one point—after the prosecutor asked how many bags D'Andrea inspected each day—Judge Block interjected.

"How does that work? You know, the jurors probably are curious. All of us travel . . . Is it a random selection process?" the judge asked as if to break the ice.

"Yeah, pretty much, depending on where you are coming from," D'Andrea responded. The officer was wrong, though he seemed to have misspoken rather than deliberately misled the judge. The process was not random but highly selective based on data in the passenger's PNR—as D'Andrea alluded to.

On cross-examination, the defender, Amanda David, tried to tease this out of D'Andrea. "As part of your job, you also look at— sometimes you look at flight patterns of the passengers?"

The officer acknowledged that he did. But neither the defense nor the prosecution pursued the issue; acknowledging that the profile of a courier existed ran the risk of alienating the jury, but confirming that Nesbeth's PNR fit the profile wouldn't help the defense case.

Surveillance video had captured D'Andrea's entire interaction with Nesbeth at JFK. The prosecutor played the video for the jury, stopping intermittently to ask D'Andrea to narrate what was occurring on-screen. It was a duplicative exercise, but when a portion of the tape played showing the officer hammering a hole into the handle, the prosecutor stopped the tape.

"After you punched a hole in the rail, what, if anything, did the defendant say to you?" Scotti asked.

"Nothing," D'Andrea responded.

"Prior to that, had you and the defendant been talking?"

"Yes," the officer said.

The implication was that Nesbeth fell silent because she knew that the drugs had been discovered. She began repacking her bag silently as if she expected to be sent on her way, while the officer moved to search the next piece of luggage. Both Chevelle and D'Andrea didn't register any reaction that she had just been caught smuggling cocaine into the United States.

The video left little for the defense to work with on cross-examination. David pursued her vacation-turned-nightmare trial theory, eliciting that Nesbeth's suitcases were packed with women's clothing and that when she arrived at JFK, she had no cash on her person. Both attorneys circled the central issue of the case, but only Chevelle could testify to what was in her mind.

THE GOVERNMENT DID HAVE evidence that could speak to her thoughts. Agents had confiscated Chevelle's phone at the time of her arrest and obtained a search warrant to go through its contents, including her text messages, which contained exchanges in Jamaican patois. At the outset of the trial, the government had not intended to introduce the messages into evidence but had provided them to the defense as part of trial discovery. Assistant U.S. Attorney Scotti knew the messages could cut both ways: some could help the defense, while others favored the government's case. The messages could fill one significant absence in the government's case: Chevelle's voice. While the defense had agreed that the messages were admissible, the parties had yet to resolve the process of interpreting them from patois into English. After the government's last witness stepped down, Assistant U.S. Attorney Scotti asked to address the issue with the judge. The trial had moved ahead efficiently so far but then ran into an unexpected hiccup on the question of whether the text messages would be admitted into evidence. As the parties approached the bench, Judge Block began to grow impatient.

"The best I can glean from your mumbling is that you have an incipient agreement on the admissibility of these," he told the attorneys. "I'm a little confused as to what went on."

Defense counsel Amanda David tried to explain that the issue wasn't the authenticity of the texts but their translation. "Now you don't want the jurors to hear them, even though you're agreeing that they are authentic. Is that what you're telling me?" Block demanded.

She again tried to narrow in on the issue of the translation. The judge cut her off: "You are not going to say anything more now. I gave you the opportunity. It sounds like gobbledygook to me."

David was pursuing an entirely legitimate objection: to bring in text messages in a language other than English would require two witnesses, a technical witness to testify to how the messages were extracted from the phone and a linguistic expert to verify their translation. Had the government's attorneys sought to do that, they were required to disclose that before the trial began. But Judge Block appeared unmoved. As he prepared to call the witness, Assistant U.S. Attorney Scotti spoke up.

"Your Honor, I do want to point out to the court one thing," he said. "The defendant herself, these are her own words. She could have interpreted it. But I do want to be clear that this was not part of the exhibit list."

The government was acknowledging fault. It took only a moment for the judge to consider the information. It was enough for him to reverse his decision.

"This is my ruling. I'm not going to let you do it. Your case is over," Judge Block said. "You have all your evidence in. You have your drugs.

You have everything else. And I don't know if you need any more. I was willing to try to accommodate you, but it's just too fuzzy for me to really get a handle on it. So we are not allowing it."

The case would go to a jury as is. Judge Block told the lawyers he would give the charges to the jury "as to whether she knowingly and intentionally imported cocaine, period. Is there any problem with that? That's what the case is all about," the judge said.

Knowledge was indeed the critical distinction that raised the standard of proof for the government. Assistant U.S. Attorney Scotti asked the judge for what seemed a slight modification to the charge, suggesting "that the defendant intentionally or consciously avoided knowing." The revision, however, raised a central concept in criminal law.

"Conscious avoidance?" the judge asked, referring to a legal doctrine that willful ignorance is not a defense.

"A conscious avoidance charge, I think, is appropriate here, Judge. The evidence here is that the defendant didn't know. So the lack of knowledge and all the surrounding circumstances here would argue that she did know. So if the defense itself is lack of knowledge, then the argument here that she made herself willfully blind so it would have been obvious."

It wasn't a straightforward decision for the judge. Block pointed out that while some pretrial motions alluded to the involvement of "a boyfriend," the government had not introduced any evidence at trial about how she came into possession of the suitcases with the cocaine. He wouldn't allow the prosecutors to put a conscious avoidance charge in front of the jury. In doing so, the judge effectively raised the bar for the government late in the trial. "It's a close call," he said.

The government was left with one option: to appeal to the jury's common sense. In the prosecution's summation, Assistant U.S. Attorney Scotti raised circumstances that could be inferred from the evidence: that someone had modified her suitcase, placed the cocaine inside its handles, and expected to retrieve it once the load arrived in the United States—and that the only way this could have been done was with Chevelle's knowledge.

"The drugs were inside; she was caught. She tried to get it through, and she was caught," the prosecutor said, asking the jury to convict her.

For her part, David attacked the circumstantial leap the government was asking the jury to make—to use what they saw in the surveillance video and what they heard from Officer D'Andrea to step inside her client's mind.

"There is no evidence of any bigger picture here because Chevelle is not linked to some bigger picture because she doesn't know. She absolutely doesn't know. This nineteen-year-old girl comes into the country with these bags after going to visit her family. Where is the bigger conspiracy?" she asked the jury. "Where is the evidence that she was part of some plan to bring drugs into the country? There isn't one."

The judge sent the jury to deliberate a few minutes before 4:00 p.m. Chevelle's case had been a very standard drug courier trial in Brooklyn's federal court. Trials like hers were often rote, exercising unglamorous and rarely novel dimensions of federal law. The U.S. Attorney and Homeland Security did not hold press conferences or even issue press releases to announce convictions of couriers. This reflected the primary function of the Justice Department as measured by case volume, which was to enforce the nation's drug laws and then to prosecute immigration offenses. The Eastern District's caseload roughly reflected that reality. Nearly a quarter of the U.S. Attorney's charges involved narcotics, and the most common lead charge in those cases, and in Brooklyn federal court, was what Chevelle had been charged with: 21 U.S. Code § 952, importation of controlled substances. In these cases, the courts performed as an efficient bureaucracy. Like most bureaucracies, it was, by design, impersonal. But for defendants awaiting a verdict, the moment was intensely personal; for many, it was the most consequential event in their lives.

AT 1:19 P.M. THE NEXT DAY, juror #1 sent a folded piece of paper notifying Judge Block that the jury had reached their verdict. Chevelle returned to the courtroom with her attorney; the prosecutor took his seat across from her. None of the jurors were interested in reading the verdict on each count aloud. Before the panel returned to the jury box, juror #1 finally agreed that she would do it. Nobody wanted to say the words.

Guilty on both counts.

Chevelle cried out.

She was still the college student who someday hoped to be an educator. But she was now something of greater and permanent consequence: a convicted felon.

The remaining question was for Judge Block. What sort of sentence would be just?

7

Collateral Consequences

May 26, 2016

When Chevelle Nesbeth returned to Judge Frederic Block's courtroom, her fate, like that of all federal defendants awaiting sentencing, lay in how the judge would interpret Congress's guidelines on punishment. She stepped quietly into the courtroom in a black blazer and a pink blouse; her hair pulled back with a headband. She glanced over at the few people sitting in the audience; a scowl flashed across her face; then she followed her attorney to the same table where she had heard the jury's guilty verdict nearly a year earlier. This day had been rescheduled for almost five months after the judge sought additional filings from the government and the defense on the appropriate sentence.

The language of federal sentencing is, in fact, arithmetic. It has been that way for nearly thirty years. Under federal sentencing guidelines, judges rely on an arcane scoring system to determine an appropriate sentence for a given crime. The calculation combines two sets of values: prior criminal conduct and what is called "the offense level," which runs from lesser offenses, like trespass (level 4), to the most serious offenses, first-degree murder (level 43). Determining the offense level is, within itself, a particularized task of assigning points to each element of a given crime—*was a weapon used (+2), was it an act of terrorism (+12)*. Points can also be taken away, for example, if an individual pleads guilty or, as in Chevelle's case, a person has limited involvement with the overall offense. The system attempts to quantify something inherently qualitative: the gravity of a crime.

Four voices weigh in on this process: the government and the defense outline a sentence that each believes is appropriate, the U.S. Probation Department creates a presentence report about the defendant, and the judge renders the sentence. The fifth—perhaps most influential—voice in this is Congress. The judge must operate within guidelines created by Congress in 1984. The legislation established the guidelines as part of a bipartisan push against crime championed by Senators Ted Kennedy and Strom Thurmond. Congress intended the new regulations as a check on sentencing disparities between judges and on criminals gaming the plea-bargain process. Instead, Congress created a rigid system that disempowered everyone in the judiciary, except for federal prosecutors. One of the system's earliest critics, the Eastern District judge Jack Weinstein, said that guidelines "require, in the main, cruel imposition of excessive sentences." Even a member of the commission that drafted the guidelines, Justice Stephen G. Breyer, eventually came to criticize their application. In 2007, a Supreme Court decision made those guidelines advisory, affording judges discretion to consider additional factors in determining the best sentence.

Those factors are called 3553(a) factors, a technical name that belies their purpose: to humanize the defendant. The judge can take into account the person before the court and what circumstances led the defendant to that moment. The judge can also consider the purpose of the sentence: *Will it speak to the seriousness of the crime? Will the sentence deter others? Will it protect the public? Will the sentence be a just punishment for the crime?* These questions open the door, if only slightly, for judges to exercise *judgment*.

Then there is the arithmetic portion. Once the judge takes all of this information in to calculate the criminal history and offense level, she turns to page 404 of the Federal Sentencing Guidelines to plot those values. There is a full-page chart that displays a cascading array of seemingly random number ranges. At a glance, the chart appears bland, as if it could be depicting crop yields. Those ranges are, in fact, the number of months a defendant is to be incarcerated. (Federal prison terms are counted in months, not years.) Down the page the number ranges climb, beginning at 0 in the upper left corner, continuing to 360 until the lower right corner, where the numbers finally terminate into a single word: "life."

Chevelle Nesbeth's sentencing calculation put her in the first third of that page, a very narrow range between thirty-three and forty-one months, which amounted to an approximately three-year prison term. But the truth was any federal conviction carried a life sentence.

JAIL TIME IS just one of the many penalties that come with a criminal conviction. There is a universe of separate—often open-ended—sanctions that felons face once their prison term ends. These collateral consequences, as they are referred to, extend far beyond the loss of the right to vote or sit on a jury. In the United States, state and federal laws outline more than forty-eight thousand sanctions that convicted criminals potentially face, some mandatory, others discretionary. These include well-known provisions requiring sex offenders to register and restricting felons from possessing firearms, but also lesser-known penalties as varied as forbidding felons to act as sports fishing guides (Alaska), work in public housing (Texas), or adopt a child (federal). Within the past fifteen years, legal scholars have renewed arguments that collateral consequences enacted by law effect something akin to a civil death—the systematic disenfranchisement of certain convicts practiced in sixteenth-century England and the colonial United States. Critics see these sanctions as an end run around sentencing laws, giving legislatures the ability to impose punishments far beyond what judges determine to be appropriate. These penalties disproportionately impact black Americans and, in some cases, were designed with the explicit purpose to disenfranchise these communities. Some of the most onerous collateral consequences are reserved for drug offenses—restrictions that target a felon's ability to obtain food and housing assistance, health care, and employment. The moment the jury returned a guilty verdict in Chevelle's case, her future was circumscribed not only by the social stigma associated with being a felon but also by an array of federal sanctions outlined for drug offenders.

The issue of profiling also impacted Nesbeth's sentencing. The fact that drug couriers at JFK tended to fit a specific profile led to an unprecedented agreement between the U.S. Probation Department and the U.S. Attorney's Office for the Eastern District, the two government parties within a jurisdiction that recommend sentences to the judge. After the U.S. Sentencing Commission rejected a 1993 proposal to view couriers less harshly under mandatory penalties, the two parties agreed to not throw the book at couriers arrested at JFK. Couriers tended to fit a specific profile: they are work for hire with only incidental connections to trafficking organizations; they have no personal stake in the load they carry; they are usually in the dark about the operations of the traffickers and have no power within the groups. This agreement—to view couriers as playing a minimal role in a drug conspiracy—in effect, reduced the potential sentence, which could be up to twenty years.

The government's original sentencing recommendations in Chevelle's case made no mention of collateral consequences. Assistant U.S. Attorney Paul Scotti treated the case like any other courier conviction, seeking a sentence within the guideline range. "The defendant's young age and lack of criminal history do not, on their own, remove this case from the heartland of drug importation cases," he wrote. (Scotti was not indulging a poetic turn. The federal sentencing commission describes guidelines "as carving out a 'heartland,' a set of typical cases embodying the conduct that each guideline describes.")

But Judge Block wasn't content with that heartland. He postponed the sentencing. He wanted the prosecution and the defense to consider whether the issue that would have the most lasting impact on Chevelle's life, the collateral consequences of her conviction, should be considered a 3553(a) factor. Was the harsh reality of being branded a convicted felon, in effect, punishment in and of itself?

THE BENCH IN THE EASTERN DISTRICT had been a center of discontent with federal sentencing guidelines since their inception. In 1993, Judge Jack Weinstein announced that he wouldn't hear any more drug cases, calling himself "just a tired old judge who has temporarily filled his quota of remorselessness."

"I simply cannot sentence another impoverished person whose destruction has no discernible effect on the drug trade," Weinstein said in a speech at the time. (A Southern District colleague, Judge Whitman Knapp, continued to hear drug cases but referred them to other judges for sentencing.)

Judge John Gleeson had taken on the issue of sentencing through another approach, the elimination of criminal records through expungement. Gleeson had been moved by the case of a woman he had sentenced for insurance fraud in 2002. Her crime was aberrational: she claimed injury in a staged car accident, and Gleeson sentenced her to fifteen months in prison. The woman, a nurse and mother of four, was a nonviolent offender who had remained out of trouble but couldn't find employment following her conviction. Gleeson pointed out that the continued punishment of this woman did not serve the public interest; if she wasn't working, she wasn't paying taxes, forcing her to turn to public assistance to provide for her family. In May 2015, he expunged her record. The government immediately appealed to the Second Circuit, the appeals court located on the seventeenth floor of the Thurgood Marshall Courthouse, which heard cases for the New York, Vermont, and Connecticut federal districts.

Judge Gleeson wasn't a patsy when it came to sentencing. Several months later, a defendant whom he had sentenced in 2001 sought expungement of his conviction for the embezzlement of Veterans Administration benefits. The man, George C. Cox, appeared in Gleeson's courtroom on a winter afternoon, dressed in red snow boots, khakis, and a knit sweater. He was in his late fifties and arrived in court without an attorney. He sought to explain the collateral consequences of his conviction: he wasn't able to get a job or secure a long-term place to live. When it came time for Cox to describe his offense, he fell apart. For more than a minute, he wept uncontrollably.

Gleeson didn't interrupt the defendant. The man's sobbing filled the courtroom as the judge, prosecutor, courtroom manager, and court reporter looked on. Cox eventually regained his composure, and Judge Gleeson asked him, plainly, "You wanna take a break?"

Gleeson had a reputation for fairness. He could also be described as streetwise. He knew when he was being hustled. Cox had stolen nearly $600,000 from the federal government over twelve years, devising an embezzlement scheme while working for the Veterans Administration. The scheme came apart after police arrested Cox following reports of a woman screaming for help in a Fort Lee, New Jersey, motel room; the cops discovered crack and marijuana on Cox, as well as documents pointing to the fraud. In his motion for expungement, Cox had glanced over the details of his offense. When the defendant finished his appeal, Gleeson spoke.

"Part of this is trust. Right out of the box you can't even level with me," Gleeson said. "The application is denied. This case doesn't even come close."

Cox, defeated, turned and walked out of the courtroom.

Every sentencing comes with risk for judges. Passing down an unduly harsh sentence can needlessly destroy a person's life; showing leniency stakes a judge's reputation on the future conduct of the defendant. In his decision to expunge the defendant's insurance fraud record, Gleeson asserted a power that few federal judges had dared exercise.

Chevelle Nesbeth's case remained within Judge Block's authority pending her sentencing. He sought input from both parties on whether he should consider the collateral consequences in determining her sentence. The government responded that it did not see the inevitable results of her conviction in her case as unwarranted. It attached a list of ninety-seven mandatory collateral consequences related to drug offenses. "The street drug trade is responsible for many of the tragic incidents and conditions plaguing too many communities in our region, including shootings, robberies, murders and the proliferation of gangs. Whether contemplated or not, the defendant and others who try to smuggle large quantities of illegal narcotics into the United States are acting in furtherance of that trade," the prosecutor wrote. He acknowledged that meant Chevelle would face challenges but asserted that "the defendant can achieve the same level of success in life regardless of her criminal conviction."

Chevelle's attorney was not as hopeful. Amanda David opened her memorandum with a quotation from Michelle Alexander's indictment of American criminal justice, *The New Jim Crow*: "Many of the forms of discrimination that relegated African Americans to an inferior caste during Jim Crow continue to apply to huge segments of the black population today—provided they are first labeled felons. If they are branded felons by the time they reach the age of twenty-one (as many of them are), they are subject to legalized discrimination for their entire adult lives." David outlined precisely how the conviction would radiate through Nesbeth's life after sentencing. She would be ineligible for specific forms of student financial aid and tax credits. She could lose her passport and ability to see her father in Jamaica. She could be denied work on the basis of her conviction alone. She could lose her driver's license and be denied food stamps. She would not be able to receive a certificate to become a teacher.

When Chevelle Nesbeth appeared before Judge Block for sentencing, he had to find a balance between consequence, mercy, and what the law itself would allow.

ON THAT MAY AFTERNOON, the parties stood before Judge Block, who appeared in his robe, a pair of reading glasses hanging around his neck. An air of nervous anticipation filled the courtroom. It was understood that the judge did not want to treat the sentencing as business as usual, but it wasn't clear how he would take any of the arguments into account.

The hearing kicked off with little fanfare as Block began tabulating Chevelle's offense level. "The base offense level is twenty-four, she gets four levels off because she is the classic courier. If she was involved as a minimum participant. That makes the adjusted offense level of twenty. And she doesn't get any credit for acceptance; she chose, as well is her right, to go to trial. So then we are dealing with a criminal history category of one, level twenty-six—thirty-three to forty-one months with the guidelines. Everyone I think is in agreement with that."

Chevelle stood by her attorney's side, listening and waiting. The attorneys had considerable ground to cover with the judge, but before Block went further, he stopped.

"Now, I will not put her in jail," he said. "I think it is unkind to string somebody along to the eleventh hour."

The relief was palpable, but the substance of the day's sentencing was intended to turn on the question not of Chevelle's freedom but of how the collateral consequences she stood to face would bear on her sentence, and those of similar defendants.

"I'm not exactly clear, Mr. Scotti, whether the Government believes or doesn't believe that you know collateral consequences under proper circumstances should be a 3553(a) factor?" he said.

Scotti was a relatively junior line assistant, but Block appeared to be asking for a statement that would speak to the government's position on a broad range of similar defendants.

"I don't want to commit the office in any way. Obviously, this is one particular case, one defendant. I'm one Assistant U.S. Attorney. The Court has chosen to take on a larger issue that is—" he said, trying to squirm out from under the question.

The judge let him off the hook. "I understand your position," he said. "If I had in front of me a Blood or Crip that was convicted of multiple murders, we would not be having this discussion. But this particular case, I think it is the ideal factual dynamic for the Court to address, you know, what I think had been neglected by the judiciary and lawyers for many years."

The judge meandered into a recent judicial history of the issue, pointing out that he wasn't alone in his view that collateral consequences should figure into some sentencing decisions; then, almost as an aside, he mentioned his sentence. "Separate and apart from all of that, I have considered collateral consequences in my sentence of one-year probation," he said, "which I will give her unless the defendant wants to talk me out of it."

The humor did little to soften the mood. Chevelle stood silently as the judge continued to speak.

"Candidly, I was looking for the right case to address this issue," he said, before addressing Chevelle directly. "Your crime was serious and inexcusable, and you don't get a gold star for doing that . . . I think that you can be a real good role model considering your past background and you can be an effective ambassador to help dissuade other young people, to even think about violating the code of law."

Judge Block gave her a chance to speak before pronouncing the sentence.

"I want to say, thank you," Chevelle said, in a near whisper.

"You have to try to speak louder," the judge said.

"I just want you to say thank you for your decision," she repeated, growing emotional.

Block had written a forty-two-page order on her sentencing, which concluded, "While consideration of the collateral consequences a convicted felon must face should be part of a sentencing judge's calculus in arriving at a just punishment, it does nothing, of course, to mitigate the fact that those consequences will still attach. It is for Congress and the states' legislatures to determine whether the plethora of post-sentence punishments imposed upon felons is truly warranted and to take a hard look at whether they do the country more harm than good."

"Try to calm yourself and compose yourself," he said to the defendant. "If the Circuit affirms Judge Gleeson then it will open the door for people like Ms. Nesbeth [to expunge their records]."

WITHIN A MONTH, the government filed notice that it would appeal Chevelle's sentence—ostensibly to seek a more severe punishment. The door that the judges in the Eastern District tried to open for low-level offenders like Nesbeth appeared to be closing again. The Second Circuit overturned Judge Gleeson's expungement order later that summer. Then, in early September, without any explanation, the government withdrew its appeal in her case. The prosecutor would let the judge's order stand. The government gave no reason for its reversal. The office's motives were a mystery even to Chevelle's attorney. The consequences she faced, collateral and otherwise, would stand as she returned to college to complete her degree. As would the court's acknowledgment that in cases like hers the actual sentence, in terms of opportunities lost and potential not realized, rarely fit the crime.

WHITE-COLLAR CRIME

Wall Street never changes, the pockets change, the suckers change, the stocks change, but Wall Street never changes, because human nature never changes.

—JESSE L. LIVERMORE

8

Override

By April 2013, Stefan Lumiere's brief, unsuccessful career at Visium Asset Management was coming to an intensely personal end. Visium was a $4 billion hedge fund with offices that looked out on the broad, wooded expanse of Central Park from twenty-two stories above midtown Manhattan. At any point in the day, one could step to the window to see the manicured wilderness of the park neatly hemmed in by avenues crowded with traffic. It was a vantage point on the city reserved for the wealthy and powerful—and a selling point for their office's address, 888 Seventh Avenue, which had become the preferred location for hedge funds and private equity in New York. Visium shared the building—and its breathtaking views—with Pershing Square Capital Management, the Soros Fund Management, Barrington Capital Management, and, five floors above, Level Global Investors, an upstart hedge fund charting a similar path of rapid success. For Lumiere, however, the location was a step down. When the fund moved in there he lost his office and was consigned to the trading floor with analysts ten years his junior. Like so many things at the fund, a professional slight carried a deeply personal resonance. Visium was a family business, but that family was coming apart.

Months earlier, Lumiere's sister's marriage disintegrated. Her husband of six years filed for divorce, setting in motion a bitter, public showdown over the couple's prenuptial agreement. This would have been of little matter for Stefan if his brother-in-law wasn't Jacob Gottlieb, the founder of Visium. Lumiere introduced Gottlieb to his sister and Gottlieb brought Lumiere into the fund; neither arrangement worked out. To make matters worse, one of the portfolios that Lumiere had responsibility for—the Credit Opportunities Fund—was losing money. Lumiere didn't want to resign, but he did want out of Visium.

On paper, Lumiere appeared to be a typical Wall Street analyst: born and raised in Manhattan, educated at private schools (Lycée Français de New York, Kent School in Connecticut), completing undergraduate at Tulane and an MBA at INCAE, a business school in Costa Rica, living in a co-op on Central Park South. He was stocky, well built, and handsome; at forty-three, he'd yet to go gray or lose his boyish expression. As a bachelor, he doted on his sister Alexandra and her two children. He was the type of brother who would settle into a Lifetime movie with his sister, rather than go off with his buddies to watch a football game. She would tell people, "Stefan works in finance, but he has a heart."

Lumiere had done well enough after two decades working on Wall Street. He took home $200,000 in salary each year, with a bonus subject to his performance—tied to how well the Credit Opportunities Fund did. Stefan didn't know how much his boss made, but he estimated that it was ten times his salary. His brother-in-law Jacob Gottlieb had a net worth of $103 million. This disparity offered a constant reminder that in the fiercely relative terms of his industry wealth equated with success. And when most compensation came through bonuses, it was distinctly possible to earn $200,000 a year and feel that you had neither.

Jacob Gottlieb had founded the fund eight years earlier, surrounding himself with those close to him including his brother, Mark, and his brother-in-law Lumiere. The child of Polish immigrants, Gottlieb grew up in Brooklyn, went to Brown, then studied medicine at NYU, before turning to finance. He was, by objective measures, a spectacular success. As a doctor, he arrived on Wall Street as an outsider; he worked his way up as an analyst, then a trader, before starting his fund with $300 million in assets, eventually growing Visium into a $8 billion hedge fund.

"He was a different person at that time," Lumiere recalled. "He seemed like a reasonable, kind person when I met him."

Visium's health-care-focused Visium Balanced Fund was the top performer, with its pharmaceutical strategy overseen by the firm's star portfolio manager, Sanjay Valvani. That fund, which consistently generated double-digit returns, had been nominated for an industry award weeks earlier. Gottlieb, meanwhile, planned to launch a new $500 million investment fund, part of a longtime strategy to expand Visium into a leader in a crowded field of hedge funds. The success did not carry over to Stefan's team.

It had been difficult for Lumiere to separate the rancor surrounding his sister's divorce from the deteriorating situation at Visium. Lumiere was responsible for the distressed assets portfolio of the Credit Opportunities Fund, which had raised $600 million from investors. His boss, Chris Plaford, was seven years younger but had a track record as a successful portfolio manager. He attended Indiana University's business school before working under Jacob Gottlieb at Balyasny Asset Management in Chicago, following his boss to Visium in 2005, where he made several million dollars as a portfolio manager. Plaford looked older than thirty-six, and in many respects his success had come early in his career. One day, Plaford was told that Stefan Lumiere would be joining his team. "He was Jake's brother-in-law, so I didn't interview him or anything like that," he later testified. Lumiere didn't like Plaford, and the other young analyst who joined the team, Jason Thorell, struck him as nervous and ambitious. It seemed clear to Lumiere that Thorell wanted his boss' job. On personalities alone, the team seemed hardly set up for success.

The fund touted its approach to investors as "capturing alpha through disciplined, fundamental research processes." What that meant, in practice, was picking securities that would generate a profit. There was no secret sauce to the Visium strategy—at least, within the Credit Opportunities Fund. Individual analysts, like Lumiere and Plaford, were responsible for finding value and making the right trades at the right moment. That task became increasingly difficult for the team.

Each month, the fund reported its performance to investors—a ritual that grew more distressing as the value of the securities in Lumiere's portfolio began to sink, pulling down the fund's overall performance. The fund had invested in a range of distressed assets—loans and bonds—held by a for-profit career-training school company, ATI Enterprises; a medical device company, China Medical Technologies; and Friend Finder Networks, an adult entertainment company. In late 2011, Lumiere, Plaford, and Thorell found another way to "capture alpha." Rather than report to investors the market value of the securities in their portfolio, the advisers would get an outside broker to quote a better price—a price that the Visium team provided. The men could then list that price as the "value" of the asset, a misrepresentation that overstated the Credit Opportunities Fund's performance and liquidity.

The trio didn't simply fabricate prices for the assets to execute the scheme. Lumiere turned to two friends who worked at smaller brokerages to quote price levels that his boss, Plaford, needed to show to Visium's valuation committee. This created the appearance for their internal compliance team that a third party had provided the valuation. It was a relatively crude scheme and, like most acts of corruption, rooted in a legitimate practice. Overrides—as they were called—allowed investors to value a security at a price other than what the markets report, essentially *overriding* the prevailing valuation. Rare circumstances warranted this. Over two years, the Visium team had done this more than 300 times; in 284 of those instances, their basis for doing so had been entirely fabricated.

"I was not part of the overrides," Lumiere said. "It was something that Chris and Thorell worked on."

Yet prosecutors would later show that Lumiere did his best to conceal his role in the overrides. He adopted low-fi operational security measures—speaking with brokers from his personal cell phone and, in two cases, hiring a messenger to carry a thumb drive with pricing data across Manhattan to a broker. Occasionally, the team went so far as to purchase securities at a higher price to lend credibility to their quotes—which traders called "painting the tape." The result: the value of the Credit Opportunities Fund would be inflated, and Visium would charge investors a management fee based on the fraudulent performance numbers. Under the impression that their investment was doing well, these investors would also be less inclined to pull their assets from the fund. Lumiere and his colleagues had broken the law, but the facts of their crime were buried deep within investors' statements.

By 2013, the efforts to prop up the Credit Opportunities Fund by replacing market prices with overrides had all but failed. The prospect of flaming out at his brother-in-law's hedge fund held the potential for both personal and professional humiliation. With the divorce and the fund's flagging performance, Lumiere's place at Visium had grown increasingly tenuous. That is when Stefan began recording his conversations.

STEFAN LUMIERE HAD BEEN at Visium for nearly two years when Preet Bharara was sworn in as the U.S. Attorney for the Southern District of New York. Bharara modeled the persona of his former boss Senator Chuck Schumer: folksy, quick-witted, and telegenic. Bharara commanded a room with seemingly little effort, moving confidently between the registers of humble public servant and intimidating enforcer. Like many prosecutors, he projected himself as approachable and eminently reasonable. Until someone disagreed with him.

As U.S. Attorney, Bharara set the tone for his tenure early. In a November 2009 address at New York University Law School, he made it clear that white-collar crime would be a priority for his office. "We work only blocks from Wall Street. Our subpoenas, I suppose, don't have to travel very far. Sitting in the financial capital of the world also provides something of a window into the workings of the financial markets and contemporary corporate culture," he said. Southern District prosecutors would pursue insider trading, Ponzi schemes, the legion opportunities for fraud—from accounting and bank fraud to health-care fraud—in the financial industry, Bharara promised.

Bharara's first significant white-collar prosecution targeted Raj Rajaratnam, the founder of the $8 billion hedge fund Galleon Group, and a jury convicted Rajaratnam for his role in a massive insider-trading ring uncovered by the SEC. (Rajaratnam received an eleven-year sentence.) The media interpreted the case as the opening salvo of a broader fight against Wall Street.

In 2012, Preet Bharara appeared on the cover of *Time* magazine under the headline "This Man Is Busting Wall St." The article featured a standing portrait of Bharara, arms crossed in a federal blue suit and red tie, framed perfectly by the arched entry of the Manhattan municipal building against a Gotham-esque overcast horizon. The piece credited Bharara as the prosecutor who "collars the masters of the meltdown"—in reference to the vilified caste of Wall Streeters believed responsible for the subprime mortgage crisis that spurred the 2008 financial collapse. It was grossly inaccurate.

Bharara's Securities and Commodities Fraud unit had largely looked past Wall Street institutions. It had secured only one conviction that touched on the crisis—a guilty plea by a Credit Suisse executive. The only federal prosecution that pursued Wall Street executives hocking mortgage-backed securities had, in fact, gone forward in the Eastern District. The real targets for prosecutors in the Southern District were not the Wall Street investment banks but the Connecticut and midtown hedge funds.

IN APRIL 2013, Stefan Lumiere dialed a former colleague with self-preservation on his mind. His sister's marriage had begun collapsing in 2010 and, stuck in the middle professionally and personally, he eventually met with his sister's divorce attorney. In that meeting, Lumiere said, he was warned that "Jake wants to destroy you." From that moment Lumiere began to document everything. On the call that day, he placed the man—a colleague named Philip—on speakerphone and pressed record. The conversation was awkward and stilted. Each party seemed to be circling the other warily. Visium had its secrets, and each man did not know the extent of the other's knowledge. Eventually, Stefan brought up the issue of pricing.

"Yeah. Hey, by the way, don't mention anything about what I told you about the, you know, the way that Visium portrays their P&L and shit like that," Lumiere said.

"Oh, well, which piece? But of course, I wouldn't. Whatever you and I talk about is between us," Phil responded.

"Yeah. No, yeah, the fucking bullshit marking of the book," Lumiere said.

"No, yeah, of course," Phil said.

"That will come out at some point," he told Phil. "If I decide if they're really trying to put the pressure—trying to throw me under the bus somehow."

"I would love to see you fuck them over," Phil responded.

"I can't do anything yet. I'll probably let things sit, but I mean, at some point, I think—I don't know, I think at some point the SEC will just hear about something. Guys are all, all fuckers, all of those—" Lumiere said.

"Nothing would make me happier than to see Jake get ass-fucked," Phil said.

"I would too, I would love it, love it. That narcissistic asshole," Lumiere said.

For all the bravado, Lumiere was devastated: his career had spun out. He'd gone from working twelve-hour days, to doing little work at all, all the while growing increasingly paranoid about his brother-in-law's intentions.

Within weeks of that call, Lumiere was out of a job, and the Credit Opportunities Fund was shut down. Investors had lost more than $9.5 million and paid more than $3 million in performance fees. But in the end, Lumiere hadn't been fired. That month he'd shown up at the office to negotiate his non-compete agreement as part of a departure settlement. Instead, Lumiere said, he was told to check his email. Visium's general counsel had notified him via email, "Given your expressed desire to depart the firm, we consider this a voluntary resignation and, accordingly, your employment has ended." Even with Lumiere's departure, the details of the mismarking scheme had yet to be discovered and might have remained a secret. But Lumiere's boss—Chris Plaford—had come under scrutiny for a crime synonymous with Wall Street's greed: insider trading.

———

IT WAS ONLY AFTER the Nixon presidency that American society finally began to confront the idea of white-collar crime. That term was first popularized by Edwin H. Sutherland, who published a 1940 essay, "White-Collar Criminality," that defined it as a crime from the "white-collar class, composed of respectable or at least respected business and professional men." Among the earliest advocates for a shift in enforcement was Robert Morgenthau, who as U.S. Attorney for the Southern District pushed to investigate the use of Swiss bank accounts by American companies. He did not view white-collar crime as it had historically been seen, as a moral offense with narrow impact. Morgenthau saw it as a threat to society as a whole.

"If the affluent flagrantly disregard the law, the poor and deprived will follow the leadership," he told a group of business leaders in 1968.

Before Morgenthau left office in the Southern District, he established the Business Frauds unit, among the first of its kind in the Justice Department. At the same time, the consumer advocate and frequent presidential candidate Ralph Nader drove the discussion of the "corporate crime wave," a shift in vernacular away from the class-laden language surrounding the issue of crime. He pressed the Department of Justice to create a division dedicated to white-collar crime, for Congress to pass laws barring the payment of bribes to foreign officials, and for federal judges to be educated on the impact of corporate crime.

New York, as the center of the financial markets, led the way. The post-Nixon U.S. Attorney for the Southern District, Robert Fiske, kept up the pressure not only to bring cases but to punish those who were convicted. He criticized the soft sentences given by judges who rationalized that "a businessman's fall from grace among his peers" was sufficient punishment because "people won't talk to him at a bar in his country club." (His Brooklyn counterpart, U.S. Attorney David Trager, directed his ire at the FBI, which he accused of "suffering from arteriosclerosis," and said that the bureau did not "have the ability or the people to do the job in the areas we consider priorities—official corruption and white-collar crime.")

The Business Frauds unit was the office's most senior team, drawing from the most talented assistants who had been prosecuting cases for at least four or five years. The junior prosecutors within the unit always started with lower-level white-collar cases; only after an assistant gained enough trial experience would he or she be assigned a case reaching into the executive suite. During U.S. Attorney Fiske's four-year tenure, the unit scored fifteen convictions of executives from major publicly held companies, as well as corporations themselves.

"It was the only district. It was the only district in the country that handled white-collar securities cases," said Ira Sorkin, the former director of New York's office of the Securities and Exchange Commission and defense counsel to Bernard Madoff.

At that time, Congress had not enacted many laws specific to corporate crime. The Securities and Exchange Commission dealt with many offenses through civil enforcement: pursuing fraud violations under Rule 10b-5 of the Securities Exchange Act of 1934. The Department of Justice prosecuted criminal cases through broad statutes like the mail fraud statute. Two elements defined this crime: the scheme to defraud and the use of the mail to execute the fraud. This loose definition captured a universe of potential criminal conduct. It also provided a looking glass for investigators to view previously undefined crimes. Congress passed the statute following the Civil War and, with it, vastly expanded the reach of federal prosecutors.

Similarly, there was (and continues to be) no law with explicit criminal penalties for insider trading. Prosecutors used the 1934 Securities Exchange Act to charge the first insider-trading defendant with securities fraud. Southern District prosecutors brought the case, and it involved an unlikely source: an employee at a printing company near Wall Street. The company printed tender offers that gave the employee, Vincent F. Chiarella, advance knowledge of corporate takeovers. A jury convicted him in 1978 of making $30,000 from trades related to takeover bids he'd learned about from his job.

The case also set in motion the developing body of law on insider trading. Two years later, the Supreme Court overturned Chiarella's conviction, finding that possession of inside information did not make someone an insider, that there needed to be a relationship between two parties. The Supreme Court further defined that relationship as the "tipper/tippee" relationship—that is, the provider and the recipient of inside information—and established that there must be a "personal benefit" to either party to constitute insider trading. The ruling, *Dirks v. SEC,* created a broad and loose standard but provided a lane for prosecutors to pursue cases against insiders who traded in information for material gain.

Around this time, insider trading entered the popular culture. Figures like Ivan Boesky and Michael Milken became cutouts for the mercenary greed of Wall Street in the 1980s. Both men pleaded guilty to charges following insider-trading investigations under U.S. Attorney Giuliani. During his term, Giuliani moved forcefully on white-collar crime, securing forty-one convictions from forty-six individuals charged in the Southern District between 1980 and 1985. The defendants weren't just those in the financial industries. Prosecutions targeted attorneys with knowledge of corporate transactions, a *Wall Street Journal* reporter privy to inside information, and, in one case, a psychiatrist who had traded on information shared by a patient. The insularity of the white-collar criminal practice community was also pronounced. Former Southern District section chiefs in private practice routinely faced off against assistants whom they used to supervise a few years earlier in the fraud unit.

AFTER VISIUM TERMINATED Stefan Lumiere, he met with his former colleague Jason Thorell at a crowded Manhattan restaurant looking out at Central Park. Thorell had the bearing of an Eagle Scout, sandy-haired with a strong jaw and clear smile. In Lumiere's absence, Plaford had turned to the younger trader to come back with the mismarked pricing—a role in which he'd grown increasingly uncomfortable. When Thorell took his seat, Lumiere noticed that he seemed jittery. Initially, Lumiere didn't trust him. He questioned whether Gottlieb had sent Thorell to gather information on Lumiere's plans. Over dinner, Thorell recounted how he had probed Visium's chief operating officer, Steven Ku, for details on the overrides—specifically about the source of the decision to mismark prices.

"He said the valuation committee determines the prices," Thorell said of their conversation. " 'We've never had any overrides'—he said this to my face."

It was preposterous to assert that. Thorell, Lumiere, and Plaford had made a practice of providing prices on their securities that overrode the prices set by the markets.

"What do you mean, no pricing overrides?" said Lumiere.

There was even a paper trail documenting the mismarked securities. Thorell had received a monthly "override" spreadsheet from his boss, Chris Plaford, detailing the prices to be mismarked.

"What do you think he's sending me that spreadsheet for?" Thorell said, pointing out the obvious.

"Even though Chris is manipulating the valuation," Lumiere replied.

"Yeah, definitely," Thorell said.

Days earlier, Thorell had reached out to Visium's owner, Jacob Gottlieb, in an email saying, "I would like to discuss a serious concern I have about the monthly pricing process." Gottlieb called Thorell to his office almost immediately and, according to Thorell, was visibly stressed as his trader explained his concerns. Thorell told Lumiere that he recorded the conversation with Gottlieb. New York State is a "one-party consent" state, meaning it is legal to record a person without his or her knowledge. The recordings would never go to a jury, but they provided a clear signal of Thorell's intentions. That evening, as he and Lumiere vented over plates of pasta, Thorell was also recording their conversation.

It was a uniquely Manhattan scene: amid the din of a midtown restaurant, two disgruntled hedge fund employees gathering evidence in search of an investigation that could someday use it. But beyond their clumsy machinations in trying to build evidence that both implicated others and exonerated themselves, each man faced the very real danger of prosecution. If and when federal officials caught wind of the scheme at Visium, only one thing would matter: who was the first man through the door.

Two years earlier, the passage of the Dodd-Frank Wall Street Reform and Consumer Protection Act had created the SEC's Office of the Whistleblower. The statute tied a financial award to those who voluntarily provided information, which went one step further than whistle-blower protections under previous laws. Whistle-blowers qualified for an award in the range of 10 to 30 percent of what the SEC collected from a successful enforcement. The information needed to be direct, or "original," and the award could be reduced if the whistle-blower was an active participant. At the time Thorell and Lumiere discussed their options with Visium, the program had received more than three thousand tips each year. The prior year the commission had awarded four whistle-blowers nearly $15 million in payouts for information.

When the two met again months later, in January 2014, the Credit Opportunities Fund had closed, and Chris Plaford, their boss, remained the last man standing from their team. Thorell no longer worked at Visium; he had left with the secrets of his former employers. Lumiere and Thorell discussed what that meant for their former employer.

"You got a lot of fucking shit to put him, put him out of business," Lumiere said.

Thorell replied, "I think."

"Well, first we can extort him," Lumiere began thinking aloud. "I'd love to be able to go to him and say listen, Jake, Chris, give us $100 million between the both of you."

(Later, Lumiere would contend that he said "can't" rather than "can" and that the statement was a "joke.")

"Personally I'm just interested in prison time," Thorell said.

At a meeting later that month, the men began discussing blowing the whistle together.

"I'm trying to educate myself right now because I didn't really understand anything that was going on," Thorell said.

"I mean that's how, that's how we operated," Lumiere said, as he began to explain how the mismarked asset price levels were determined. "Every month end, Chris would call me . . . and say these are the levels that you need to, that—that these are the levels that they are. Some of them I knew, some of them I didn't know and he always had an explanation for why."

"But that, the thing is that doesn't matter if he has an explanation because he's lying," Thorell replied. "You know that."

"Yes," Lumiere responded.

What Lumiere did not know, but what in hindsight appeared only too obvious, was that Thorell was wearing a wire. Not for his own edification this time, but for the FBI. He had turned himself in to the SEC months earlier. The SEC handed him over to the bureau's white-collar crime squad, who, in exchange for offering him immunity, then turned Thorell out to gather evidence on his former colleagues. He had been the first man through the door.

The real prize wasn't an SEC award; it was escaping criminal prosecution.

9

Market Justice

On the thirteenth floor of the 500 Pearl Street courthouse for the Southern District of New York, a gray Casio keyboard sits before a window in Judge Jed Rakoff's chambers. It seems an odd artifact for a federal judge. Rakoff is small and elegant; he has a trimmed silver beard and wears the type of stylish transparent-framed horn-rimmed glasses favored by architects and advertising executives. His voice has a low, cheerful rumble, bouncing with emphasis, as he makes his way—even in casual conversation—meticulously from one point to the next. Among the crowd of framed photographs behind his desk is one of him and the Supreme Court justice Sonia Sotomayor. The two are dressed comically as vaudeville-esque hobos for an appearance in the Courthouse Follies, an annual tradition in the Southern District, where the judge channels his remaining musical ambitions.

The keyboard sits across the room from his desk, which is piled neatly with motions, opinions, and articles, a physical and conceptual separation from his work as a federal judge. It serves as a reminder of the young attorney who arrived in New York in 1970 with split ambitions: to labor in law during the day and, at night, to summon his heroes Yip Harburg and Lorenz Hart while writing America's next great musical. Rakoff learned soon enough that in a young lawyer's life workdays bleed into nights and legal ambitions sometimes grow in spite of other dreams. That ambition led Rakoff to be among the nation's foremost experts on white-collar criminal law.

He has devoted his adult life to the justice system; as a district level judge he's worked exclusively in the Southern District of New York, but he has also sat on the Second, Ninth, and Third Circuits as an appellate judge. Over twenty years on the bench, Rakoff has earned a reputation as a fair but outspoken judge. From his perch in the Southern District, he not only took part in the genesis of modern white-collar criminal enforcement but also played a direct role in the development of the law.

Rakoff started his career as a prosecutor. He joined the U.S. Attorney's Office as an assistant in 1973, hired by the U.S. Attorney Whitney "Mike" Seymour. Rakoff came to the office with the usual credentials: Swarthmore, Oxford, Harvard Law, a clerkship on the Third Circuit. Seymour, a Republican appointee, offered him one comment in their interview—that Rakoff's beard might not play well with juries. Eager to dispel any counterculture associations, he shaved it before showing up for his first day as a government attorney—the very definition of an establishment job. Seymour greeted him, surprised after initially not recognizing him, then said, "What happened to that beautiful beard?"

Rakoff never saw himself becoming a prosecutor. Activist causes drew him in as a college student, and he imagined that, perhaps, one day he would work for the ACLU. But the culture of the Southern District almost immediately won him over. He saw in the office a robust tradition of independence and commitment to justice. His boss, Seymour, demonstrated this vividly. Seymour had been appointed by Nixon to succeed Robert Morgenthau. The national moment was tense. As U.S. Attorney, Morgenthau had several active public corruption investigations running when Nixon took office. Breaking with tradition, the Manhattan prosecutor refused to step down until a suitable replacement was put forward. Morgenthau found himself in a stalemate with Attorney General John Mitchell. It was only after the selection of Seymour, a Republican, that Morgenthau relinquished his position, allowing a new U.S. Attorney to take over the Southern District office in 1970. Three years later, when Rakoff joined as a line assistant, the office brought an indictment against Mitchell on obstruction of justice charges. Any U.S. Attorney who can prosecute his former boss, Rakoff thought, is the definition of independent.

"I very quickly came to learn that the tradition of the office was doing justice, which didn't always mean prosecution and didn't always mean taking the hardest [line] and did mean sometimes going after people at a very high level who might otherwise be ignored," he said.

Rakoff arrived at a moment of change in the U.S. Attorney's Office, and within the nation. It was the Watergate era. The American public had been forced to reconcile the idea that some criminals put a tie on each morning. Former U.S. Attorney Robert Morgenthau had recently created the Business Frauds unit, which soon became the Southern District's most selective unit of prosecutors. After paying his dues with all the other rookie assistants in what was known as the "Short Trials Unit" Rakoff, a preternatural high achiever, gravitated toward the most competitive job in the office. It was also among the most difficult. Prosecuting executives and business leaders required an entirely new set of skills other than what he'd learned trying street criminals.

"To go after people of that level requires a great deal of expertise," he said.

Rakoff went on to prosecute cases targeting a $34 million bank fraud and a $2.5 million foreign bribe scheme involving United Brands, eventually rising to become the chief of the unit in 1978.

Within two years, Rakoff jumped to the private sector. For him, the decision to leave the U.S. Attorney's Office was both timely and practical: he had kids he wanted to send to college someday, something he didn't envision doing on an Assistant U.S. Attorney's salary. Respected firms had only just begun to embrace white-collar criminal defense, which had traditionally been viewed as undignified work. He joined the nineteenth-century firm where Richard Nixon had started his legal career—Mudge Rose Guthrie Alexander & Ferdon—and was given a provocative mandate: take on as much white-collar criminal work as he could handle. There were two forces at play: On the one hand, stepped-up law enforcement efforts created a sudden supply of prospective clients, in effect creating a legal market that didn't exist on the same level a decade earlier. At the same time, the stigma attached to criminal defense work had begun to fade.

For Rakoff, the experience of sitting at both sides of the table prepared him for his next turn: a federal judgeship. Just as he never envisioned himself as a prosecutor, Rakoff did not see himself as a judge until he first began to argue before the judges in the Southern District. "There was no one who was a mediocrity—the range was from good judges to great judges. Edward Weinfeld, Inzer Wyatt, Harold Tyler Jr., Morris Lasker, I could go on. These were people, and you would be in their court, and you would say, 'Solomon lives again,'" he said.

Bill Clinton nominated Rakoff to the bench in the Southern District in 1995. Rakoff learned that the work of being a federal judge involved unpopular decisions, some of which he scarcely remembered, like the time he upheld a suspension against the Knicks players Larry Johnson and John Starks in the midst of the 1997 NBA play-offs, setting up the team's loss to the Miami Heat. In a district of influential judges, he showed an independent streak. In 1999, he rejected a set of plea deals involving illegal trading on the New York Stock Exchange. Three years later, he ruled that the federal death penalty was unconstitutional because of the risk that a "meaningful number" of innocent people faced execution. Rakoff's reasons were both legal and deeply personal: his brother had been murdered in the Philippines in 1985, which sent the judge on a journey of grief and reckoning with the justice of the death penalty. The Second Circuit reversed his decision; the defendants in the case in question, a drug murder conspiracy, received life sentences from Rakoff. That decision, attorneys who appeared before him said, all but ruled out Rakoff for consideration for the Supreme Court. Nonetheless, his independent streak persisted. In 2006, he ordered the Pentagon to release the names of detainees held at Guantánamo Bay. The financial collapse of 2008 filled his docket with the types of prosecutions that defined his career: white-collar cases.

WHEN THE VISIUM INVESTIGATION kicked off, the Southern District had been on a remarkable run of white-collar victories. In three years, the Securities and Commodities Fraud Task Force—as the Business Frauds unit had been renamed—had won seventy-three convictions. Hedge funds had flourished during the years Preet Bharara spent as a prosecutor and a congressional staffer—more than tripling from three thousand funds managing $200 billion to nearly ten thousand hedge funds managing $2.4 trillion in assets. Hedge funds were separate and distinct from traditional Wall Street investment banks and companies. Typically, these funds operated under an SEC guideline—Rule 506, regulation D—that allowed only sophisticated and accredited investors, including pension funds and high-net-worth individuals, to put cash into hedge funds. These funds were, as a result, less regulated than institutions that handled consumer investments. Hedge fund managers had greater liberty to use leverage and debt to trade, without having to meet the liquidity requirements established under the Securities Act.

While the hedge fund industry grew at a sprawling rate, with talented managers opting to start funds rather than remain at a firm, the world of high-performing funds was small and provincial. An early target of Bharara's office demonstrated this. Investigators focused on Primary Global Research, an information clearinghouse tracking various industries. Companies like Primary Global connected portfolio managers with subject area experts who worked closely with the companies the funds invested in. Prosecutors saw these "expert networks" as vehicles to traffic in insider information. Wiretaps put up by Bharara's prosecutors turned up inculpatory information on nearly fifty hedge funds. These relationships between expert networks and the hedge funds they served were self-governing and ripe for conflict. Antonia Apps, an Australian-born Southern District Assistant U.S. Attorney, who prosecuted several cases involving expert networks, saw that hedge funds lagged far behind the rest of the financial industry when it came to compliance with regulations and laws.

"I think they felt that they were outside of the purview of the watch of the regulators," she told a group of Harvard law students.

FOR ALL THE POWER in the federal justice system—and all the effort put into policing the hedge fund industry—the Department of Justice was nearly wholly ineffectual in its response to the 2008 financial crisis. Among the most vocal critics of this were members of the bench. Judge Rakoff saw the absence of significant prosecutions as a departure from historical practice. He would point to history that he knew well—both as an attorney and as a judge. The savings and loan crisis resulted in nearly eight hundred prosecutions of individuals, up to Charles Keating Jr., in the 1980s, followed a decade later by the accounting scandals at WorldCom, Enron, and Tyco, where the most senior executives and their corporations were held to account. Yet the collapse of 2008 did not yield similar criminal prosecutions. Senior executives, with few exceptions, appeared to elude law enforcement action.

A troubling early sign for the Justice Department's response to the financial crisis was the trial of two Bear Stearns executives in the Eastern District in 2009. The case served as a galvanizing event, though not in a manner the Department of Justice would have hoped. The two senior Bear Stearns executives, Ralph Cioffi and Matthew Tannin, were charged with lying to investors as their investments in the subprime mortgage market turned toxic. Prosecutors charged them with securities fraud related to $1.6 billion in losses from funds tied to mortgage-backed securities. The evidence investigators gathered created an image of two bank executives taking steps to minimize their losses while failing to warn investors of a collapse they came to see as imminent. "The subprime market is toast," Tannin wrote in an April 2007 email to his boss, Cioffi. (The boss transferred $2 million of his own money out of the fund but did not notify investors.)

The trial opened in October 2009, before the cause and effect of the housing market's role in the crisis was well understood and as "collateralized debt obligation" was becoming a media catchphrase. The prosecution entered the trial assuming that the jury's sympathy would be with the government, if only because the defendants had incurred losses upwards of $20 billion.

The case, which appeared before Judge Frederic Block, was marked by bitter pretrial litigation. The government accused the defense of destroying evidence, and the defense countered with charges of "extensive prosecutorial misconduct." Google had turned over an email recovered from Tannin's personal Gmail account—an account that his attorneys had advised him to close. The government said the email, which the defendant had sent to himself as a sort of journal entry, could be used as evidence that he was aware of the impending peril in the subprime mortgage market. Block showed little patience for issues that threatened to delay the trial and ruled that the defendant's Fourth Amendment rights had been violated when Google turned the email over to the government. The jury would never see it—or what the prosecution saw as evidence that the defense had attempted to keep the email out of the government's hands.

The trial didn't fare much better for the government. At one point, the judge interrupted testimony to probe a witness, an investor who lost money with the Bear Stearns fund, asking whether a $1 million loss would be "chump change" to an individual worth $100 million. The witness responded, "I probably would not use that term."

"Speaking elegantly as [you do] you would not use that term," Block replied. "Judges from Brooklyn might use it."

The prosecution knew their case lacked an essential element: a cooperating witness. The government, instead, needed to rely on emails to provide an insight into the intent of the defendants. One former Eastern District prosecutor familiar with the case said that the jury would not simply take the prosecution's interpretation of the evidence. "I don't think New Yorkers view the mob and Wall Street the way the rest of America does," he said. "New Yorkers have romanticized these people."

The jury acquitted the Bear Stearns executives of all charges.

"What Bear did was crystallize the problem. That you can't just take a bunch of emails and a shitty set of financial circumstances," the prosecutor said. "It is very, very difficult to establish criminal intent."

Rakoff saw in the loss a lack of experience. "The prosecutors weren't familiar with how to try those kinds of cases. It was kind of strange that it was brought in the Eastern District because that was not an office that had usually done these kinds of cases," he said. "The Eastern District had wanted to get in on the action. They thought there were going to be a lot of cases like this. Instead, they brought the only one. They lost it."

A former Eastern District prosecutor said that Washington was "eager to do these cases. They had chopped them up among different offices," but the department had set an extremely high bar for a case to be brought to a grand jury. Even in the Bear case, the prosecutor said, "I don't know how thrilled they were to charge."

Following the acquittals, the Department of Justice adopted a risk-averse approach to prosecuting large financial institutions. Prosecutors came to increasingly rely on "deferred prosecution agreements" to sanction corporate criminal conduct. These agreements, which first came into prominent use in the 1980s, sought to alter corporate culture without holding individual employees to account with jail sentences.

Both the government and corporations saw this scenario as a win-win. The Department of Justice avoided costly, time-consuming, and—perhaps most significant—potentially unsuccessful criminal trials in exchange for lump cash sums. This was the type of victory that could be trumpeted to the press, tied off with large round figures that sent the message of the federal government getting tough on corporate offenders. Corporations—like the repeat offender Pfizer—could avoid the embarrassment of seeing footage of their employees being frog-marched into federal custody on CNBC with their sinking stock price running on-screen in the chyron. As popular as the agreements have become—by one estimate the government puts forward on average thirty-five deferred prosecution agreements each year—they are seen as, ultimately, ineffective.

The public rarely learns about these settlements until the government and the company issue a press release. The facts would never be subjected to a jury or the general public. There would instead be an announcement of a fine and, in the occasional instance, a narrow acknowledgment of wrongdoing. Or none at all. The one signature the parties to these sorts of agreements needed—usually the SEC or a U.S. Attorney's Office and a corporate defendant—was that of a federal judge.

When Eastern District prosecutors brokered a deal with HSBC to avoid criminal prosecution, the matter fell to Judge John Gleeson to approve. The charges weren't a simple matter of some controversial bookkeeping or a nebulous transactional gray area involving complex securities. The bank had been accused of laundering money for violent

drug cartels in Mexico, among others. HSBC did not protest its innocence and take that matter to trial. The bank agreed to a $1.92 billion
fine and promised to implement reforms to stop the money laundering.
Gleeson was not willing to take either the government's or HSBC's
word that the parties would abide by the agreement. As if to remind
the parties gathered that a federal indictment isn't a transaction that
can be papered over by two consensual parties, he wrote in an opinion,
"A pending federal criminal case is not window dressing. Nor is the
Court, to borrow a famous phrase, a potted plant."

Gleeson pulled the reference from a heated exchange during the
Iran-contra hearings between Colonel Oliver North's attorney, Bren-
dan Sullivan, and Senator Daniel Inouye. Sullivan protested that he had
a right to object for his client—in particular, to hypothetical questions,
saying, "I'm not a potted plant. I'm here as a lawyer, that's my job."
Gleeson's use of the reference made clear that a federal judge had a job
to do as well, even when the parties cut a deal. He signed the order,
but with a caveat: he would oversee the agreement, requiring HSBC
and the government to update him quarterly on the bank's compliance.

Rakoff was similarly skeptical of the relationship between the
regulators and the regulated early on. In 2009, the SEC brought Bank
of America before Rakoff to seek approval for a $33 million settle-
ment involving bonuses the bank paid out following the acquisition of
Merrill Lynch—after the bank received nearly $40 billion in federal
bailout funds. Rakoff refused to sign off on it, calling the agreement a
"contrivance designed to provide the S.E.C. with the façade of enforcement and the management of the Bank with a quick resolution of an
embarrassing inquiry—all at the expense of the sole alleged victims,
the shareholders." (Rakoff later approved a revised settlement for $150
million.)

A watershed moment for Rakoff came when the SEC and Citigroup
sought his approval of a settlement in 2011. The parties had agreed to
a $285 million penalty for the bank's failure to disclose to investors
that it was selling mortgage-backed securities that it was also betting
against. Rakoff rejected the agreement, saying it was "neither fair,
nor reasonable, nor adequate, nor in the public interest." He used his

opinion to address the case, but more broadly the troubling status quo that had emerged:

> An application of judicial power that does not rest on facts is worse than mindless; it is inherently dangerous. The injunctive power of the judiciary is not a free roving remedy to be invoked at the whim of a regulatory agency, even with the consent of the regulated. If its deployment does not rest on facts—cold, hard, solid facts, established either by admissions or by trials—it serves no lawful or moral purpose and is simply an engine of oppression.
>
> Finally, in any case like this that touches on the transparency of financial markets whose gyrations have so depressed our economy and debilitated our lives, there is an overriding public interest in knowing the truth. In much of the world, propaganda reigns, and truth is confined to secretive, fearful whispers. Even in our nation, apologists for suppressing or obscuring the truth may always be found.

Again, the Second Circuit rebuked Rakoff, saying that he had "abused" his discretion in rejecting the settlement. But Rakoff's opinion had an impact. Other courts cited his decision in considering SEC settlements, putting pressure on the regulator to bring settlements that met the judge's higher standard of factual acknowledgment and accountability.

Rakoff's reversals on Bank of America and Citigroup carried meaning beyond the courts. He became a hero, a reflection of public anger that lingered following the financial crisis, but also a symbol that the justice system was not indifferent to popular sentiment—even if, at times, the law appeared to be.

10

No Victories

A year had passed since he left Visium. In that time, Stefan had tried to put the financial industry behind him, learning to work with his hands—carpentry, plumbing, and electrical work—as he gut renovated a Ninety-Sixth Street three-bedroom co-op that he had purchased before leaving the fund, putting in dark wood floors, a wall-to-wall white marble bathroom, and a kitchen with gleaming white cabinets and stainless steel appliances. It seemed the ideal location to settle down, perhaps get married and raise a family. Little good had come from meeting Jacob Gottlieb nearly a decade earlier: the years of Lumiere chasing success at Visium, his sister's failed marriage, and the nagging feeling that his former boss and brother-in-law sought revenge.

In late February 2014, a loud knock at the door woke Lumiere at his Central Park South apartment. He looked at the time—it was a few minutes after 6:00 a.m., as the sun was beginning to rise over Central Park. He opened the door to a man claiming to be an FBI agent. It was Special Agent Matthew Callahan, a member of C-1, the FBI's New York white-collar squad; he told Lumiere that he was there to execute a search warrant. A group of agents poured through the doorway, the beams of their flashlights illuminating a path in front of them. Lumiere stood there, shell-shocked, his girlfriend in bed in the next room. His mind searched to make sense of the scene, strangers rifling through his belongings looking for laptops and tablets. He wondered whether these men were agents at all, whether Jacob had sent a team to search his apartment and seize his files and recordings. Eventually, reality set in. Lumiere realized what was happening to him.

The agents had seized two computers, two tablets, an iPhone, and a series of USB sticks. Later, the agents would take a safe-deposit box that belonged to Lumiere. Stefan had locked items in there that required safekeeping: documents and copies of the recordings he had made. His options had suddenly narrowed: to cooperate with the government or fight.

THE EXECUTION OF a search warrant was an unwelcome rite for a select group in New York's financial industry. For several years, the hedge fund industry, specifically, had been under sustained pressure from both the SEC and the U.S. Attorney's Office for the Southern District of New York, with the collision of Preet Bharara and SAC Capital's Steve Cohen unfolding as a clash of centers of power in the city. On a November morning four years earlier, Lumiere—and everyone at Visium—had front-row seats for an FBI raid. A crowd of office workers filed out of 888 Seventh Avenue, nervously lighting up cigarettes. The men and women worked for Level Global, a hedge fund five floors above Visium's office. The investigation into Level would provide an object lesson in the power of federal prosecutors and the FBI.

Level's co-founder David Ganek was a profoundly wealthy man, a veteran of Cohen's SAC Capital, and an investor who at the peak of his career managed a $4 billion fund. Ganek knowingly filled out the caricature of a hedge funder. He owned a $19 million co-op where Jacqueline Onassis once lived at 740 Park Avenue—one of Manhattan's most exclusive addresses—and held a coveted seat on the board of the Guggenheim Museum. He and his wife, the novelist Danielle Ganek, ranked among the top art collectors in the country with a collection that included Richard Prince and Jeff Koons—facts conspicuously reported in *The New York Times, The New York Observer,* and *ARTnews.* David Ganek's wealth had always translated to a specific type of power in New York. The power to move freely in the upper reaches of the circles he cared about—finance, philanthropy, and the art world. That was taken away from him by the power of a federal prosecutor.

When Ganek arrived at the building, one of his employees told him, "The FBI is upstairs raiding our business."

On the twenty-seventh floor, special agents with the C-1 rummaged through Ganek's office, cataloging items as they seized them: a binder titled "Business Continuity Plan," a handful of notebooks, a spreadsheet detailing cash positions on June 9, 2009, a list of artwork owned by him and his wife, two envelopes containing instant message data, a copy of Level's Compliance and Procedure Manual. Simultaneous raids were also unfolding at funds in Connecticut and Boston. Within hours, the news of the daylight raids catapulted across the financial media; the next day *The Wall Street Journal* ran a front-page story, "Hedge Funds Raided in Probe." Within weeks, Ganek found himself standing before his employees doing the unthinkable, telling them that he was shutting down Level Global—that all of them would be losing their jobs. It would be fourteen months before Bharara's office announced indictments related to the raid. The Southern District charged Todd Newman of Diamondback Capital Management, a Connecticut hedge fund, and Anthony Chiasson, a founder of Level Global, in an insider-trading conspiracy. Ganek was not charged.

The lead prosecutor in the Level Global case—which went to trial as *United States v. Newman*—was a sober but genial Assistant U.S. Attorney, Antonia Apps. She had taken an atypical route to the Southern District; born in Australia, she studied at Oxford and Harvard Law before entering private practice. On the day she became a naturalized U.S. citizen in 2006, she applied to the U.S. Attorney's Office, joining the next year with more than a decade of private sector experience under her belt. She gravitated toward the Securities and Commodities Fraud unit, in part, because of an early mentor, Audrey Strauss, the first woman to ever lead the unit—at that time one of just three to ever head up the unit. The Level Global raids showed her just how vulnerable the hedge fund industry was to federal scrutiny—that, unlike large institutions, fund managers could not merely assure investors that they had systems in place to prevent illegal conduct; instead, they were forced to shutter their shops and return their assets to investors.

The Newman case was in many ways a typical "expert network" case. Anthony Chiasson, a Level Global founder, and Todd Newman, a portfolio manager at Diamondback Capital, were accused of making trades based on a tip on Dell relayed by a former Level Global employee. The employee, Sam Adondakis, had been granted immunity in exchange for providing critical testimony. The information behind the trade prosecutors had focused on originated several steps from Adondakis, passed by a former Dell employee to an intermediary working for the expert network. Level Global shorted Dell stock based on that tip, he would later testify. When the tech company reported poor performance, Level made $50 million.

Both Anthony Chiasson and Todd Newman were convicted. The trial seemed to exonerate Level Global's co-founder David Ganek. The government's primary witness, Sam Adondakis, testified that he had never provided inside information on Dell to Ganek, nor had he told the FBI that he had. An FBI agent testified to this fact days later. For those removed from the case, it seemed a minor footnote. But for Ganek, it was a stomach-churning revelation. The FBI had obtained a search warrant on his offices based, in part, on the representation that they had evidence of Ganek's involvement in the insider-trading scheme. The government's key witness and one of the lead FBI agents on the case now disavowed this. The search warrant was obtained based on a lie, or, in the more genteel phrasing favored by the courts, "deliberate misrepresentations." Ganek was left to consider the implications. Without that falsehood, the judge might have balked at granting a search warrant or signed off on a more narrow search that would not have touched his personal office, leaving him with room to assert his innocence to his most critical audience: his investors.

But the raid had not been narrow. The investment community was left to imagine what, if anything, the raid was evidence of. The publicity that followed proved fatal for the fund. For hedge fund executives like Lumiere, the Level Global raid demonstrated the raw, total destructive power of accusation. David Ganek had not been implicated in insider trading or indicted, but he lost his business.

"There's no victory here," he recalled thinking when he learned of the FBI agent's testimony. "There's only loss minimization."

C-1 took pride in its aggressive tactics. It pursued potential cooperators working in hedge funds as if they belonged to organized crime families. Special Agent David Chaves, a supervisor for the squad, described at a conference how his agents tracked a witness the investigators sought to flip, according to *The New York Times*.

"We would follow him every day for months," the agent said. "We would work out with him at lunchtime."

There was a more covert form of power, not discussed by Chaves, that the FBI brought to bear on investigations: leaks to the press. The agent, in fact, met regularly with reporters from *The New York Times* and *The Wall Street Journal*, disclosing nonpublic details about investigations over dinner, at coffee shops, often using his personal cell phone. The articles that followed broke details of investigations known only to the parties involved. The calculation was simple: coverage increased the public profile of investigations, ratcheting up the pressure on everyone—the defendants and the prosecution—to break any inertia surrounding a case, whether that meant motivating a defendant to plea or pushing the government to charge.

In February 2014, the month before Lumiere was served a warrant, a larger clash unfolded in the Southern District. A junior employee of SAC Capital, Mathew Martoma, went to trial, marking a climax in the ongoing contest between Steve Cohen and Preet Bharara. Martoma had helped the fund net a $275 million profit based on inside information on an Alzheimer's drug trial, according to prosecutors. Like Lumiere, Martoma had been approached by Special Agent Callahan. Martoma refused to cooperate, instead choosing to press his innocence at trial. Martoma wasn't alone: another SAC manager, Michael Steinberg, had just been convicted for trading on insider information on Dell in December 2013. (He received three and a half years.) The SAC Capital cases became defining prosecutions of Preet's tenure: the investigation resulted in a historic guilty plea by the fund and a $1.2 billion fine associated with criminal insider-trading charges. Cohen did not face charges, but six former SAC employees pleaded guilty to insider-trading charges. SAC Capital was effectively shut down by the investigation. After his four-week trial, the jury found Martoma guilty. He was convicted and sentenced to nine years in prison.

Three weeks later, Lumiere decided to cooperate. He traveled down to Foley Square to attend a proffer session at the U.S. Attorney's Office with Special Agent Callahan and the prosecutors. Stefan hoped that the government would see the situation as he did: that he'd done nothing wrong.

IN WHITE-COLLAR CASES, innocence is often a question resolved on appeal. Which is to say innocence is less a matter of facts determined by a jury than a question of how those facts are interpreted under the law by a panel of judges. The case that came from the Level Global raids—*United States v. Newman*—typified this. After Anthony Chiasson and Todd Newman were convicted at trial, the criminal definition of their conduct ended up turning not on the evidence but on the law. When the case went to the Second Circuit in 2014, something remarkable happened: the panel vacated the convictions and, in doing so, upended the status quo in insider-trading law. The appeals court hearing *Newman* found that there needed to be a more clear quid pro quo for an inside tip to be criminal, finding that the government "must prove beyond a reasonable doubt that the tippee knew that an insider disclosed confidential information *and* that he did so in exchange for a personal benefit." This decision tightened the standard established in 1983, under the Supreme Court case *Dirks v. SEC*. For many on Wall Street, the decision stepped in to clarify a hazy area of securities law; for many regulators, it legalized a universe of conduct that prosecutors had successfully pursued for decades.

It was an outcome that the prosecutor in *Newman* did not anticipate. Apps went on to argue the appeal. She sensed the government would face a tough fight when she saw the three-judge panel selected to hear the case. When she appeared before the court in April 2014, the hostility to the government's argument was immediately apparent. She relished forceful questioning, yet that day she felt as if she were arguing for her life. Not only was *Newman* significant to her office, but it was the capstone of her career in the U.S. Attorney's Office. By the time the panel had finished their questions, Apps knew that she had lost. She did not think that the judges would reverse the decision on the issue of personal benefit, which had been settled for more than thirty years under *Dirks;* instead, the government presumed the case would be sent back to the lower court. To its surprise, the decision erased the criminal convictions of the two men charged.

The *Newman* decision was only the latest setback in Preet Bharara's campaign against white-collar crime. Several months earlier, a jury handed the Southern District U.S. Attorney's Office its first insider-trading acquittal, breaking Bharara's run of victories. The case, against Rengan Rajaratnam, the brother of the Galleon Group's founder, had been marked by clashes between the government and the judge, Naomi Reice Buchwald, whom the prosecution accused of "effectively direct-ing a verdict for the defense." After questioning the strength of the case, the judge dismissed several charges, an unusual move; then the prosecution withdrew several other charges. For the remaining charges, the judge limited the evidence the government could use, disallowing facts that had been introduced to support the dismissed counts. It was logical, but also fatal to the government's case. At a going-away party for one of his prosecutors following the verdict, Bharara called Buch-wald the "worst federal judge," according to *The New York Times.* The U.S. Attorney qualified the statement as a bad attempt at humor in a private setting. The comment broke from the decorum and mutual respect that defined the working relationship between his office and the bench, and several judges in attendance heard it firsthand. Bharara wrote an apology letter to the judge after the comment became public.

Nonetheless, the *Newman* decision's position at the vanguard of insider-trading law was short-lived. Across the country, in the Ninth Circuit—which covers much of the western United States—another case moved ahead. Bassam Yacoub Salman, a defendant who had pro-vided information to his brother-in-law, appealed his insider-trading conviction under the new standard, which required a more stark quid pro quo. He argued that because the information had been given to a family member, there was not sufficient evidence to show any personal benefit that would rise to the criminal threshold. It was an opportu-nity for another appeals court to sign on to the Second Circuit's more restrictive view of insider trading, but the Ninth Circuit declined to do so. The opinion offered little comment on the *Newman* ruling other than to say that "doing so would require us to depart from the clear holding of *Dirks*," referring to the long-established standard. The prose of the Ninth Circuit's opinion was polite and spare. The single adjective "clear" offered the only suggestion of a deficiency with the other circuit's finding. The member of the panel who authored the opinion was visiting from New York's Southern District, Judge Jed Rakoff.

The decision created a circuit split, and both decisions—*Newman* and *Salman*—moved to the final arbiter, the Supreme Court. In October 2015, just as Sheldon Silver was going to trial, the Court declined to hear *Newman,* effectively leaving in place the restrictive definition that prosecutors would need to charge insider-trading cases. The decision forced Bharara's office to drop a case against Michael Steinberg, the highest-level executive from SAC Capital to face charges, and six cooperating witnesses, including Level Global's Sam Adondakis, who had pleaded guilty to insider-trading crimes, vacating his conviction. The courts had erased any legal consequence that followed from the Level Global raid, leaving only the extralegal impact that forced Ganek to shutter his business. It was an odd coda to Bharara's reputation as Wall Street's enforcer. The hedge fund industry might have been vulnerable to the public mechanics of federal investigations, but the cases Bharara's prosecutors had won were equally vulnerable to appeals courts.

BY THE TIME STEFAN LUMIERE sat down with prosecutors in March 2014, the government didn't need another cooperator. Visium's Jason Thorell had been working for the FBI for a year. He initially walked into the SEC as a whistle-blower, but the regulators saw that the conduct he disclosed went beyond civil enforcement and could bring criminal charges. Not only had Thorell's historical information implicated his two colleagues in the mismarking scheme, but he had also agreed to wear a wire as part of an active investigation. Thorell ended up recording hours of conversations with former Visium colleagues. Among these was an inadvertent confession from Lumiere.

The investigation went further than the price manipulation: Lumiere's boss, Chris Plaford, had also traded on insider information in

2010—a fact that implicated Visium's star portfolio manager, Sanjay Valvani. At forty-four, Valvani was a dashing and respected investor with a Brooklyn Heights brownstone and a palatial home in the Hamptons. News of the investigation broke in April with a six-hundred-word *Wall Street Journal* article that reported, "The U.S. attorney's office has targeted Sanjay Valvani, a current partner and portfolio manager who focuses on pharmaceutical shares, the people familiar with the matter said."

Valvani's attorney fired off an angry letter to the prosecutors, accusing the government of "leaks to the press concerning highly significant details of the above-referenced investigation" and saying "the article discloses what . . . is almost certainly career-ending information." The letter highlighted the leak that "Mr. Valvani is the target of a federal criminal insider trading investigation . . . [and] that charging decisions would be expected in the short-term." It noted that Valvani had been placed on leave by Visium, "because the article identifying him as the target of the criminal investigation made it too difficult for him to do his job—instantly decimating his reputation and likely ending forever his heretofore unblemished and highly successful 15+ year career in the securities industry." The letter identified two articles from separate investigations where information had been "leaked to the Wall Street Journal in prior insider trading investigations involving your office and the same group of FBI agents involved in our matter."

The article didn't mention the mismarking scheme or Lumiere. A week before he turned himself in, his boss, Chris Plaford, had pleaded guilty to a seven-count sealed information of wire and securities fraud charges. On June 16, when Lumiere arrived to surrender to authorities, he looked around and didn't see any of his colleagues from Visium.

"Where's Jake? Where's Ku? Where's the rest of the Credit team?" he remembered thinking. "Why am I the only one here?"

Lumiere wasn't alone, though. Agents had also taken Valvani into custody—the two men didn't work together and Lumiere didn't know him very well. When Lumiere passed him in the hallway after each had been taken into custody, Valvani didn't appear concerned. Lumiere recalled him as coming off as "cocky" given the circumstance.

The two men were arraigned that day. The case would be assigned to Judge Rakoff, joining an already crowded docket of financial crime cases. But Lumiere would be the only one to return to the Southern District. Five days later, Valvani took his own life.

When Lumiere heard of Valvani's death, Stefan's first thought was that he had been murdered. But, the death had been ruled a suicide by the medical examiner. In a suicide note, he proclaimed his innocence. He left behind a wife and two school-age daughters. Within days, Visium ceased to operate as a hedge fund.

The destruction for Lumiere had nearly been complete. His sister's divorce from Jacob Gottlieb came to a public conclusion: a New York appeals court ruled in the husband's favor that the couple's prenuptial agreement would remain in place, leaving her with $1.6 million from the nearly $200 million fortune Gottlieb had amassed. Lumiere had his own battle in front of him to convince a jury that between Jason Thorell, Chris Plaford, and himself he was the innocent man.

11

Questions of Innocence

T he month before the Visium trial was set to begin before Judge
Rakoff, two events took much of Wall Street by surprise. The
first seemed to vindicate Preet Bharara and the Securities and
Commodities Fraud unit, while the second raised new questions about
the Southern District's aggressive campaign on financial crime.

In early December 2016, a decision came down that appeared to
settle the lingering ambiguity surrounding the law on insider trading.
The Supreme Court issued an opinion on the *Salman* case unanimously rejecting the narrow definition of the crime under *Newman*—
specifically the terms of how each party needed to benefit from the
exchange of information. Justice Samuel Alito, who wrote the decision, found that Salman's "giving a gift of trading information to a
trading relative is the same thing as trading by the tipper followed
by a gift of the proceeds." Bharara issued a self-congratulatory statement: "The court stood up for common sense and affirmed what we
have been arguing from the outset—that the law absolutely prohibits
insiders from advantaging their friends and relatives at the expense of
the trading public." Rakoff's decision before the Ninth Circuit had set
up the issue perfectly for the higher court to consider by splitting with
New York's Second Circuit. This left a tension in securities law that
the high court needed to resolve. While traders and their attorneys

hoped that some of *Newman*'s ambiguity would survive the Supreme Court's ruling, the decision was viewed universally as a victory for federal prosecutors.

The second event revealed the extralegal yet devastating tactics by law enforcement in targeting white-collar defendants: media leaks. For two years, *The Wall Street Journal* and *The New York Times* had been reporting on a case implicating William "Billy" Walters, a professional gambler, in an insider-trading scheme involving Dean Foods, the national food and dairy company. The investigation—which touched on the pro golfer Phil Mickelson and the investor Carl Icahn—did not become public until an indictment was unsealed in May 2016. But several months later on December 16, the prosecutors in the case wrote a striking letter to the judge. It acknowledged that "during an interview conducted by the U.S. Attorney's Office in preparation for the hearing the Court ordered in this case, a Special Agent with the Federal Bureau of Investigation admitted that he was a significant source of confidential information leaked to reporters at both the *Wall Street Journal* and the *New York Times* about the underlying investigation."

The admission was not unprompted; the court had ordered an evidentiary hearing on potential misconduct by the government. The revelation also tied directly back to Visium. Walters's attorney in the case, Barry Berke, had represented Sanjay Valvani, the portfolio manager for Visium's health-care fund. Examining the *Journal* and *New York Times* coverage of each case, Berke had deduced a pattern of leaks, which prompted him to file a motion accusing the government of having knowledge of the disclosures and allowing them to continue. The allegations that appeared in the press shared an attribution that they were sourced anonymously to "people familiar with the matter." The pattern appeared to go back even further. In the weeks after the Level Global raid in 2010, the *Journal* ran a series of articles suggesting that arrests were imminent. Some of the same reporters who authored the Walters pieces had also written the Level Global stories, which precipitated the collapse of the fund.

After reading the filing, the judge in Walters's case called the parties into court for a hearing. "I will say that I've learned a lesson here. I reviewed the defendant's motion. I was somewhat skeptical that the

allegations could possibly be true," said Judge Kevin Castel of the claim
that the FBI had leaked to the *Times* and the *Journal*. "I wasn't cynical
enough to think that I was going to learn of deliberate disclosures by a
special agent of the FBI and deliberate disclosures after the fact of leaks
became known within the bureau and the U.S. Attorney's Office."

In fact, the government disclosed that it had referred the matter to
both the FBI's Office of Professional Responsibility and the Department of Justice's Office of the Inspector General for potential criminal
investigation. "Those referrals are now pending," the government
wrote in its filing, and the agent "declined to meet with us further
without counsel."

Berke made clear that the leaks were not isolated. "The leaking
agent, as well as many others involved in the story, were involved in
some of the most high-profile insider trading investigations that pre-
dated the time period we are talking about," he said.

"I just want to take one lawyer: me," he responded, describing how
he had represented another hedge fund analyst years earlier who had
been suspended from his job after a *Wall Street Journal* article.

The analyst was never charged, Berke said, but the article connected
to his current client, Valvani, because it involved the "same leaking
agent, same squad of the FBI . . . same reporters."

He also made it clear that the leaks had an impact beyond the legal
process. "Mr. Valvani was put on leave from his position, and it started
a stream of very lengthy articles about his culpability based on what
we believe to be the same group involving the same leaking agent about
Mr. Valvani, your Honor." Berke did not need to say what everyone
in the courtroom knew. Unlike the other clients that he referenced,
Valvani had committed suicide.

(There were other unintended consequences of leaks from the unit.
The *Journal* published a similar article by one of the reporters, Michael
Rothfeld, detailing pre-indictment allegations surrounding several
financial institutions, including Goldman Sachs, Blackstone, and Och-
Ziff, being scrutinized for Foreign Corrupt Practices Act violations
related to investments courted with the Qaddafi family. That article
threatened to expose a confidential informant providing information

to a separate unit of the FBI and investigators in the Eastern District of New York, according to the informant.)

Initially, the government took steps to conceal the leaking agent's name, redacting it from court documents in the Walters case and simply referring to him as "the Special Agent." But eventually the source accused of the leaks came to light. It was not a low-level special agent but instead one of the senior members of the FBI's white-collar squad, Supervisory Special Agent David Chaves. The agent's seniority compounded the ugliness of the revelation. The U.S. Attorney's Office for the Southern District and the FBI's elite white-collar squad suddenly appeared out of lockstep, the investigative agency pushing for an aggressive approach on suspects, while the prosecutors moved cautiously ahead. This wasn't only a breach of the clear hierarchy that governed the prosecutor-investigator relationship. It undermined a critical principle that prosecutors swore to uphold: to not simply win cases but to act in the interest of justice.

The accusations that the FBI had both lied and unlawfully leaked material to the press reverberated through the financial community. In particular, Chaves's proximity to the Level Global raids, which had received damaging coverage in the press, did not sit well with David Ganek. Since then, he had been consigned to a similar fate as his former boss, Steve Cohen, working on the margins of the financial industry, investing his own money. Ganek met with the attorney Barry Scheck, the founder of the Innocence Project and part of the team who obtained an acquittal for O. J. Simpson, to discuss what, if any, options he had. Ganek had never been charged, yet he had lost his business and reputation—what was the remedy to that? When Scheck and his colleagues reviewed the facts in the Level Global case, they were stunned by what they saw as a lie by the FBI agent in the affidavit seeking a search warrant for Ganek's office. The claim that Ganek had direct knowledge of Adondakis's tip helped establish probable cause to approve the warrant but would be refuted on the witness stand by both the analyst and the agent. That—and the apparent leaks to *The Wall Street Journal*—suggested deliberate misconduct that opened the door, ever so slightly, to liability on the part of the government. With

Scheck, Ganek filed a lawsuit against Bharara and twelve of his deputies and line prosecutors, as well as FBI agents and their supervisors,
accusing them individually of violating his rights under the Fourth and
Fifth Amendments.

The case hinged on the allegations of misconduct. Prosecutors and
federal agents are typically protected from civil suits under a doctrine
of qualified immunity, which shields them from litigation in cases
where there is not a clear violation of constitutional rights. Ganek
would need to show that the defendants knowingly broke the law in the
course of the investigation—an extraordinarily high threshold needed
to overcome any claims to immunity. The district judge in the lawsuit
cleared one hurdle for Ganek, allowing the case to proceed to discovery, a decision the government quickly appealed to the Second Circuit.

The lawsuit immediately raised questions about the ethics underpinning Bharara's office's investigations into Wall Street. *The Wall
Street Journal* published an editorial titled "Preet Bharara's Methods"
that concluded, "Mr. Bharara isn't the first ambitious prosecutor to
abuse his discretion, but perhaps there will be fewer in the future if
Mr. Ganek succeeds." The case remained in the background at the end
of 2016 as Stefan Lumiere's prosecution approached its trial date, an
unseemly sideshow that would only be resolved by the Second Circuit
in the coming months.

IN EARLY JANUARY 2017, Jason Thorell arrived at 500 Pearl Street
to testify against his former colleague. Three years had passed since he
first wore a wire and recorded Lumiere. In that time, he had made the
most significant trade of his career: exchanging the secrets of Visium's
Credit Opportunities Fund team for immunity from prosecution. That
day he walked through the gallery, where Lumiere's mother and sister
sat, before taking the stand, cowed but attentive. The puerile decep-
tions, the clumsy machinations, the rivalries, and the bitterness terminated that winter afternoon in the quiet of Judge Rakoff's courtroom.

Lumiere had chosen to go to trial. His proffer session, by his own
account, had been a disaster. His attorneys escorted him into a conference room at the U.S. Attorney's office where a crowd of more than

fifteen prosecutors lined the walls. The room was a pressure cooker. From the outset, the questioning was aggressive. Lumiere said that he "just went in there and told them what I knew." But, the line assistants questioning him weren't satisfied. Lumiere felt like the prosecutors wanted to yell a confession out of him.

"Things got heated. And they pulled me from the room," he recalled, of his legal counsel. "My attorney said this was over."

The morning Lumiere's trial opened, he felt confident. The decision to not plead guilty had been simple for him. "How can they possibly win when I didn't do anything?"

White-collar cases live and die on witness testimony that shows not only wrongful conduct but that the participants knew their actions were illegal. Intent is the ultimate quarry of a white-collar prosecutor at trial. The government must demonstrate to the jury that the defendants' actions were not simply unethical or dishonest but criminal. This is largely a nonissue in the drug and immigration cases that tend to dominate federal dockets. But the criminal statutes white-collar prosecutors utilized were ambiguous, a fact that criminal defense attorneys relied on to carve out reasonable doubt.

But before the government could introduce Thorell's testimony with any impact, the prosecutors needed to offer a clear definition of the crime. The prosecution led the jury through a stultifying catalog of evidence: compliance manuals, pricing spreadsheets, emails, pitch books, and Bloomberg terminal messages. The jury had to acquire the lexicon that the Visium team worked within: terms like "net asset value" (NAV), "level 3" assets, "generally accepted accounting practices" (GAAP). The stream of financial minutiae seemed endless. At one point, Judge Rakoff dozed off for a moment, before his clerk roused him—and the judge sent the clerk to fetch a cup of coffee.

Thorell faced questioning from Assistant U.S. Attorney Joshua Naftalis. His line of inquiry tried to situate Lumiere at the center of the criminal activity, acting as the middleman between Thorell and Plaford. On the stand, Thorell came across, much like Lumiere, as a pathetic figure of privilege—endowed with good looks, education, social status, but lacking the moral strength to refuse to go along with a conspiracy. Thorell described the paralysis he experienced when his boss, Chris Plaford, in a closed-door meeting instructed him on how to provide the cooked pricing to Visium's valuation committee.

"I was at a loss. I was overwhelmed," he testified. "I had never been in a situation like that before."

Thorell, however, wasn't a passive participant. He had moved the fraud forward through his efforts. At one point, he reached out to a broker he worked with in the past to provide fabricated prices for the team to submit to the valuation committee. Once Plaford approved the cooked numbers, Thorell handed them off to Visium's operations team. But, as he testified, Thorell positioned himself at the bottom of the totem pole, following orders from both Plaford and Lumiere while going through a slow moral reckoning of his crime.

His most damning testimony came when the government played the recordings Thorell had made of Lumiere. Stefan had sat silently through the trial, a flat presence, indistinguishable from the attorneys he sat with at the defendant's table. But as the recordings played for the jury, his voice came through: confident and vindictive. The tone damaged Lumiere almost as much as the content. His defense counsel had asserted during the opening that Stefan didn't fully grasp Plaford's mismarking scheme, but the recordings directly contradicted this.

In one recorded conversation, Lumiere explained to Thorell that he and Plaford worked together to falsify the valuations and how Plaford always provided a justification for the new price.

"The thing is that doesn't matter if he has an explanation because he's lying. You know that," Thorell pressed.

"Yes," Stefan responded.

Christopher Plaford eventually took the stand on January 17, 2017. The former hedge fund portfolio manager's journey to Judge Rakoff's courtroom began with an unannounced visit by the FBI two and a half years earlier, in the fall of 2014. Two agents arrived at his eight-thousand-square-foot home tucked away on the five-acre estate where he lived with his wife and daughter in Bedford, New York, a wooded and wealthy suburb in northern Westchester County. Plaford first reacted to the agents with fear. When they began asking him questions about mismarking assets and insider trading, he did the only thing that he felt he could do: lied. When he accompanied his lawyer to the

U.S. Attorney's Office for the Southern District in 2015, he had time to think about it. But he lied again.

"It took me a while to come to terms with what I had done," he testified.

The government, which is often quick to charge potential witnesses with lying to a federal agent, looked past Plaford's lies. He had more value to them as a cooperating witness. Assistant U.S. Attorney Patrick McGinley asked, "While you worked at Visium did you commit crimes?"

"Yes," Plaford said.

Plaford's cooperation was atypical. He was senior to Stefan and, by his admission, had committed more crimes—not only the mismarking fraud and insider trading, but also lying to federal agents. He led the jury through Lumiere's role directing and executing the scheme. The testimony foreclosed the possibility that Stefan was unaware that his conduct was illegal—but Lumiere hoped that the jury would see Plaford's account the same way he did: as lies. The guilty pleas from Lumiere's two colleagues only solidified the idea that the Credit Opportunities Fund team knew full well what they were engaged in, though. "You could convict on the words of one of them alone," Assistant U.S. Attorney Naftalis told the jury during his closing.

Lumiere's counsel, Eric Creizman, used his summation to try to divert the jury's attention from his client—pointing to the lax policies at Visium, the government's failure to prove that he intended to mislead investors, the fundamental inequity that Lumiere's colleagues, who stood to gain more from the alleged crimes, faced less consequence. He had a point. The most substantive difference between Lumiere and the two men who testified against him was that he'd asserted his innocence at trial. Watching this, Lumiere quietly seethed. He felt that his counsel had failed him—that Creizman hadn't called exculpatory witnesses, properly cross-examined the government's witnesses, or sufficiently objected to speculative testimony. After deliberating less than two hours, the jury showed that Stefan had miscalculated. The men and women convicted Lumiere on all counts.

———

AFTER LUMIERE'S CONVICTION, David Ganek also finally got his day in court, though as a plaintiff, rather than as a defendant. On a gray March morning, a three-judge panel at the Second Circuit heard arguments as to whether his lawsuit against Bharara and others could proceed. Ganek sheepishly took a seat in the third row of the appellate courtroom, his teenage son by his side. Even though the Second Circuit and the Southern District sit in the same building, the appeals court makes the district look like the underdressed younger sibling. Outside each courtroom is a waiting room with a coatroom, leather couches, and wood furnishings—resembling a university club or upscale funeral home. The courtrooms are smaller but more regal. Instead of wooden benches in the gallery, the audience looks on from armchairs. There is no jury box, witness stand, or entrance for defendants in custody. This isn't a place for facts to be weighed. It is where the law is argued.

Yet, once Ganek's hearing began, the government almost immediately asserted a fact that had not been alleged in an indictment or proven at trial.

"It is not contested that investigators had reason to believe that four individuals at the fund including Mr. Ganek and his co-founder received and traded on inside information," Sarah Normand, from the Southern District's Civil Division, told the judges. "Given his undisputed trading activity and his central role at the fund he was at the heart of the criminal activity"—she stopped to correct herself—"the *suspected* criminal activity that was under investigation."

The government argued that even without the false information used to authorize the search, a judge would have granted a warrant to search Ganek's office. Though, Normand added, "we do not concede that there was any false statement in this warrant affidavit."

In other words, Bharara's attorneys would not cede ground that there had been wrongdoing that led to the Level Global raid—or any conduct that entitled Ganek's lawsuit to proceed to discovery.

His attorneys did not see how the government could make the argument. "There's nothing about this search warrant, and the scope of the search, and the *Wall Street Journal* leak that is fair or reasonable under qualified immunity." The panel of judges looked on skeptically.

They could not find any precedent that showed how an FBI agent's lie violated an individual's constitutional rights.

"The notion that there is no remedy for officers of the United States to lie in an affidavit is extraordinary," Ganek's attorney, Nancy Gertner, argued, pressing the appeals court to allow Ganek's lawsuit to move forward. "This [lawsuit] is the only remedy. This is about accountability."

A small crowd of reporters followed Ganek out of the courtroom after the hearing ended. He conferred for a moment with his public relations representative, then walked over to the gaggle, smiling. It would be months before the appeals court issued its decision. That the court had heard the appeal in the first place was a small but significant victory for Ganek.

"One of my main reasons for bringing this case was to air these issues," he said. "It's out of my hands."

The appeal remained in the panel's hands for the next six months. The panel dismissed Ganek's lawsuit, finding that even without the FBI agent's misrepresentation, there was enough probable cause to authorize the raid on Level Global. Bharara, who had seen so many of his cases thrown out on appeal, could only thank the Second Circuit. He would be spared the public spectacle of being a U.S. Attorney dragged through the courts by someone targeted in an investigation out of his office.

ON A JUNE MORNING in 2017, Stefan Lumiere hobbled into Judge Rakoff's courtroom, leaning on a brass-handled cane, his right foot in a gray plastic orthotic boot. Otherwise, he blended into the crowd of clean-cut white men in dark navy suits and black leather dress shoes. A crowd had assembled in the courtroom; the women in Lumiere's life lined the front row: his mother, sister, girlfriend. Friends, colleagues, and four reporters filled in the remaining seats.

The room was claustrophobic with anticipation that day, but much of the tension had dissipated by the time the parties convened. Two weeks earlier, many of the same people had gathered in Judge Rakoff's courtroom expecting Lumiere to be sentenced. Rakoff had adjourned the original hearing after he was not satisfied with the government's calculation of the loss Visium investors suffered as a result of Lumiere's role in the mismarking scheme. When it came to sentencing, the investors' losses had a direct impact on how the defendant's sentence would be calculated, adding points to the guideline range based on the size of the victims' losses and the defendant's gain. The parties agreed that the scheme resulted in a gain of between $1.5 and $3.1 million, even though Lumiere walked away from Visium with nothing more than a paycheck.

Rakoff had a visceral distaste for the sentencing guidelines, and his essays in *The New York Review of Books* advocated for eliminating them. He didn't shy away from the opportunity to take a shot at Congress for boxing him in with mandatory minimum sentences or the U.S. Attorney's Office for charging cases that invoked those consequences— most often seen with drug offenses. He blanched at the quantitative focus of the sentencing guidelines, saying the point-based system "give[s] the mirage of something that can be obtained with arithmetic certainty." In white-collar convictions, where the size of the loss has a multiplying effect on the sentencing math, Rakoff pointed to "the utter travesty of justice that sometimes results from the [g]uidelines' fetish with abstract arithmetic, as well as the harm that guideline calculations can visit on human beings if not cabined by common sense."

The purpose of the hearing for defense counsel was to stress his client's humanity. In the months since his conviction, Lumiere's relationship with Eric Creizman imploded—Stefan speculated that his attorney had thrown the case, an accusation that he'd make in court filings, alleging that his attorney was secretely colluding with Gottlieb and Visium's counsel. (Creizman would not comment on the specific allegations, citing the potential for future litigation.) As Lumiere looked on at his sentencing, his reading glasses sliding down his nose, the new attorney, Jonathan Halpern, stood, reed thin and projecting a folksy honesty. "He's a good soul and honorable soul," he said of his client, though he went on to qualify that, describing Lumiere as also "a hapless soul, someone who was a working stiff." The circumstance bore that out: of those involved, Lumiere had benefited the least from the scheme but stood to lose the most.

Halpern referred to the eighty letters of support that Lumiere had marshaled for his sentencing, from friends, family, even his nine-year-old niece and ten-year-old nephew. Unlike many defendants who face sentencing on organized crime, narcotics, or terrorism offenses, Lumiere had not been isolated by his criminality. The letters painted a portrait of a supportive community, a community willing to look past this crime, to welcome Lumiere and help him return to a modest position of standing. Rakoff interrupted Halpern. "There's no question that he has wonderful friends," the judge said. "Certainly I'm going to factor that in."

But, he continued, that factor cut both ways. The presence of a strong community "also does pinpoint the willfulness and intentionality of the conduct."

Halpern tried to distance Lumiere from the "caricature and stereotype of some folks who work in hedge funds."

"I don't share that stereotype," Rakoff said, interrupting again. Calling the evidence in the case "overwhelming," he said, "The court totally agrees with the jury's verdict."

Then for the benefit of the attorneys and the record, he laid out his thinking. In white-collar cases, he said, the research shows that stiff sentences don't necessarily add up to more deterrence but that some incarceration did accomplish that goal. The audience waited for the punch line, which Rakoff offered almost as an aside: Lumiere would face prison. It was important, he said, to send the message that "you can't buy your way out of this."

The government's response was brief. Assistant U.S. Attorney Patrick McGinley returned to the two damning recordings of Lumiere, where he laid out his vitriol for his brother-in-law and hope to extort him.

"This crime was the defendant's brainchild," McGinley said. "This is not a hapless soul. This is not a working stiff."

Before pronouncing the sentence, Rakoff gave Lumiere the opportunity to speak. He rose from his seat, but Rakoff instructed him to sit.

"I understand I have been convicted," he began, his voice plain with a slight upward intonation. Lumiere was not in a position to apologize for his crime, because he had yet to appeal. Instead, he described the embarrassment that his family had suffered and the uncertain future he now faced. "My accomplishments are for nothing," he said.

"Mr. Lumiere is lucky in some respects as a white-collar defendant," Rakoff began. He pointed out that, unlike many drug charges, securities fraud did not carry a mandatory minimum sentence, which, he said, was more "typical of a brutal regime than a proud American system." After pointing out that Lumiere's guideline calculations suggested a seven- to nine-year sentence, he signaled that he'd depart significantly downward, criticizing the "number-crunching gibberish that constitutes the sentencing guidelines." In fact, in the Southern District, judges had increasingly moved away from sentencing guidelines in white-collar cases: in 2003, more than 70 percent of these sentences adhered to guidelines; but by 2012 just 30 percent did.

"I came into the court this morning with a sentence of two years," Rakoff said. Then he asked Lumiere to stand: "The sentence of this court is eighteen months in prison."

Lumiere's expression changed little, but his family members looked visibly relieved. After the hearing, he stepped out into the bright, sunlit hallway outside Judge Rakoff's courtroom. Friends and family members surrounded him with quiet consolations. He would be required to report to prison in early September. It wasn't a moment without hope. Other hedge fund analysts pursued by Preet Bharara before him—from SAC Capital, Level Global, Diamondback—had seen their convictions overturned on appeal.

Lumiere's attorneys filed their notice of appeal a month later. Yet, shortly after he reported to prison, Stefan's counsel withdrew his appeal, allowing his conviction to stand.

TERRORISM

Terror is only justice: prompt, severe and inflexible.

——MAXIMILIEN ROBESPIERRE,
Report upon the Principles of Political Morality

12

Hijra

Imran Rabbani was not far from the mosque when he realized that he was still being followed.

The intersection of Twentieth Avenue and the Whitestone Expressway was empty. The seventeen-year-old sat in a Jeep Cherokee with two friends, waiting for a red light to turn in a vaguely suburban stretch of College Point, Queens, on an overpass along a wide boulevard lined by square office buildings and empty parking lots.

It was just past 4:00 a.m. In little more than an hour, sunrise prayers would begin; the men were en route to the mosque to open it in time. At the wheel was a young imam who went by the name Faisal Shah; across from him sat Imran's friend Munther.

Behind their truck, an unmarked sedan idled. The car was indistinguishable from the others that Rabbani had seen: late model, American made, windows tinted. The headlights burned clearly in the rearview mirror.

A week earlier in Brooklyn, the young men had seen the same thing. As Imran and several others pulled away from a mosque in Cypress Hills, another car followed them. These mysterious cars seemed to be a near-constant presence in recent months. Imran did the only thing he could think to do: he called 911.

The NYPD could do little with his complaint: *a teenager calling in to report that a car was following him.* Imran was persistent, though. He had even snapped a picture of the license plate of one of the vehicles and brought it to the police. The cop told the teenager that it came back last registered to a business that had closed more than a decade earlier.

This didn't help quell the young men's paranoia. Imran and his friend Munther started carrying knives when they went out. Months earlier, Imran had purchased three military-style folding knives from Amazon, including a Smith & Wesson serrated knife. Imran had troubles with the law in the past, but none of his run-ins involved violence. If anything, he was the type of teenager burdened by his conscience. To the point where he felt that he had done wrong. But the more persistent whoever was following him became, the more frustrated he grew.

The light had yet to turn green when Rabbani and Munther made their decision. The time had come to do something about this. Imran reached for the door and stepped out into the street. As he made his way toward the car, he kept his knife in his pocket. His friend did not. For a second, the handle of the knife flickered in Munther's palm. The driver threw the vehicle into reverse as Imran and his friend closed in.

THE FIRST SIX MONTHS of 2015 marked a disturbing trend for prosecutors in the Eastern District of New York's national security unit. The team, known as the National Security and Cybercrime Section, had broken up two domestic cells of Islamic State supporters in Queens and Brooklyn with New York's Joint Terrorism Task Force—a consortium of law enforcement and intelligence agencies. Those cases sat within a broader national trend of ISIS-related cases that peaked in April 2015 with sixteen new federal prosecutions. New York had been the epicenter of these cases, and the Eastern District handled the vast majority of ISIS investigations and prosecutions. The tempo of prosecutions reflected the intense pressure on law enforcement to prevent an attack in New York.

The attack on the offices of *Charlie Hebdo* in Paris had raised the specter of another potential mass-casualty incident in a Western city, perhaps even on U.S. soil. But the most significant threat the Islamic State posed domestically was not an external operation executed by a fighter with experience waging jihad in Iraq or Syria. Instead, U.S. law enforcement officials feared an attack carried out by an adherent recruited, radicalized, and mobilized entirely online. It would be six months before ISIS supporters staged an attack in San Bernardino and a year later at the Pulse nightclub in Orlando. While ISIS was relatively new, the threat the group posed was not.

One prosecutor particularly attuned to this threat—and to the pressure of disrupting potential attacks—was Assistant U.S. Attorney Seth DuCharme. He was the rare prosecutor to emerge from the rank and file of law enforcement: DuCharme started his career as a deputy U.S. marshal at the courthouse, before heading to Fordham Law, doing a stint in private practice, then returning to the Eastern District when he joined the U.S. Attorney's Office. His path there set him apart from many of his colleagues, and—in an office of studious and canny litigators—it was the culture of investigators he most readily identified with. DuCharme didn't present himself as a streetwise federal agent. He had a soft demeanor and small frame, coming across as affable and approachable, with a disarming half smile that curled across the right side of his mouth. After he joined the U.S. Attorney's Office, he rose through the ranks as a line assistant to become the chief of the Eastern District's National Security and Cybercrime Section.

The pace of national security investigations in the Eastern District rarely let up. One prosecutor took a poetic turn to describe the thrill and purpose of hunting spies and terrorists as an antidote for the "glassy-eyed meaninglessness" of corporate law, where the best you could hope for was a life of "suburban ennui . . . a boat. A mistress. Alimony." It was an opportunity to work within an area of law that those in the private sector rarely, if ever, touched on. Many prosecutors spoke of "the mission" in near-religious terms—to explain the devotion to service where fulfillment could only truly be found through complete dedication. In the next breath, they would often acknowledge the sacrifice that came with it: being a counterterrorism prosecutor didn't pay well—in relative terms. Senior district attorneys, mid-level NYPD officials, and even Department of Sanitation managers took home more than many prosecutors responsible for preventing terrorism and espionage. After one put in a decade or so rising into the managerial ranks, the Assistant U.S. Attorney salary hit its ceiling at $164,003, a little less than a first-year associate made at the firms many prosecutors leave to take the job. One wistfully expressed how he wanted to spend his life in law enforcement but knew that it wouldn't be fair to his wife and children. With law school loans, mortgages, the impending prospect of college tuition, the groaning cost of living in New York City and the surrounding suburbs, the functional choice that most prosecutors eventually faced was between affording college or continuing to serve the country.

Until that time came, national security prosecutors enjoyed the job's unique perk: when it came time to confront a national security threat, they had a uniquely powerful place at the table with other decision makers. In New York, that actual table was in a conference room at the headquarters of the Joint Terrorism Task Force in Manhattan's Chelsea neighborhood, where the FBI, NYPD, CIA, Homeland Security, Immigration and Customs Enforcement, and representatives of the military, alongside prosecutors from both districts, convened to assess the current threats facing the jurisdictions. The fallout from the September 11 attacks had conditioned the national security establishment toward actions rarely used in the past—whether that meant extraordinary rendition to a third-party country, a "kinetic" strike on a target overseas (or, in other words, a targeted killing), or an arrest. No national security officials, including prosecutors, wanted to be connected to a judgment call to leave a suspected terrorist alone if doing so would then pave the way for an attack. Or that would lead to the reemergence of a terrorist figure who had been in their sights. It was left to the government lawyers to assess these risks and weigh them against those associated with a public prosecution.

In terrorism cases, losing was not the risk; an indictment all but guaranteed a conviction. The risk was disclosure of secrets. Prosecutors had the dual responsibility for protecting intelligence sources and capabilities while marshaling the most compelling evidence to make their cases. Often investigations touched on the intelligence world and involved unseemly alliances with people who had done despicable things; these truths presented a threat not necessarily to a jury's verdict but instead to the United States' moral standing. The ideal counterterrorism case involved the least exposure to the public: a plea hashed out behind closed doors and allocuted to a judge, the narrative controlled by the government from beginning to end. An even more ideal case would play out in a trial with little or no exposure of intelligence information, while the government maintained control over the story line. In our adversarial justice system, where trials were contests of narratives, this did not happen often.

The first terrorism case DuCharme worked involved two friends, not unlike Munther and Imran. Two men from the working-class outer-borough neighborhood of Bensonhurst, Brooklyn, Betim Kaziu and Sulejmah Hadzovic, had traveled to Egypt in 2009 in hopes of linking up with al-Shabaab in Somalia or al-Qaeda in Pakistan.

DuCharme went into the case having lost his first two trials. He'd spent a year and a day in General Crimes, doing the bread-and-butter work of a line prosecutor, negotiating pleas and securing convictions with minimal complications—"clean hits," as some in the office referred to them. In the two cases DuCharme took to trial—a drug courier case and a postal fraud case—the defendants were acquitted. The results didn't deter him. Nor did they disqualify him from a promotion. Soon after, he joined what was then called the Violent Crimes and Terrorism unit or, as one former member described it, "where the cool kids went." The section had, in fact, become the desired destination not only for ambitious prosecutors but for agents in the FBI's New York office seeking to prosecute terrorism cases. DuCharme's section chief, Jeffrey Knox, was credited with cementing the close relationship between the bureau and his team, raising the stature of the office as a leader in national security prosecutions.

The Kaziu investigation came to him not as a historical case where he would need to unearth the evidence of a crime committed. It was a live-threat investigation of an inchoate terrorism offense that had potential to develop into a domestic attack or an attack on U.S. interests abroad. Both of the suspects were American citizens. The notion that the men could obtain training abroad and return to New York to wage an attack wasn't an abstract hypothetical. Months earlier, local officials had arrested a Patchogue, Long Island, man named Bryant Neal Viñas in Peshawar, Pakistan. He had spent more than a year training with al-Qaeda in the mountains along the border with Afghanistan. Viñas plotted with al-Qaeda leadership to bomb the Long Island Rail Road but was intercepted overseas before he could return to the United States. The two suspects in DuCharme's case ventured to Cairo, not the typical jihadi way station, then split up: Kaziu dropped off the map, while Hadzovic returned to the States.

DuCharme partnered with Shreve Ariail, then a young prosecutor who had joined the office from Skadden Arps, the white-shoe law firm. He had followed his father's path to the law, through Davidson and the University of Virginia Law School. Shreve then clerked for a federal judge in the Eastern District of Virginia before moving to New York to join Skadden Arps. Like his father, who briefly served as a Cold War–era CIA officer, Ariail was drawn to the national security mission. The Eastern District would not have seemed the place to pursue that work just a few years earlier, but by the time he joined the U.S. Attorney's Office in 2007, the national security practice was ascendant. After doing his requisite time in General Crimes prosecuting gang and drug cases, he joined the team.

The two cut a strong contrast: Ariail carried himself like laid-back southern gentry, without the drawl but with the genteel bearing and pedigree; DuCharme wore a suit like an obligation. Whatever aggressiveness DuCharme brought as a former federal marshal with street experience chasing down fugitives, Ariail matched with that of a corporate litigator; he was charming but strident, willing to cede cordiality but never a point of contention. The men split responsibility for the suspects in the investigation: Ariail would cover Kaziu, and DuCharme would take Hadzovic. The government had limited visibility on Kaziu's movements—he returned to Kosovo, the country of his family's origin—but Hadzovic quietly resumed his life in Brooklyn.

Even though he was a junior counterterrorism prosecutor, DuCharme made a gut decision. He got into a car with two investigators, John Ross and Hugo Smith, and knocked on Hadzovic's door in Brooklyn. It was unorthodox. DuCharme had little leverage going into the conversation but also felt a 24—ticking bomb—scenario unfolding with the other defendant, Kaziu, off the map. DuCharme had experience arresting suspects as a marshal, but an arrest wasn't the objective: he needed to determine whether Hadzovic was a threat and, if not, whether he would come in to help the government. When the young man opened the door, DuCharme told him, "We know you were involved in something very serious and you have a choice to make. You can do the right thing, and you can help us, or you can await the consequences, but this isn't going away."

Hadzovic—or "Sulee," as DuCharme came to call him—invited the men in. Within days, the young man was actively cooperating with the JTTF and DuCharme's Eastern District team, helping facilitate the arrest of his close friend in Kosovo. DuCharme and Ariail took the case to trial against Joshua Dratel, who one prosecutor described as "the dean of the terrorism bar," and David Stern, another career criminal defense attorney, before Judge John Gleeson. They put Sulee on the stand to testify on the conspiracy to join a terror group. A jury convicted Kaziu, and Judge Gleeson sentenced him to twenty-seven years.

The Kaziu case was the prototypical Eastern District domestic terror prosecution. But it would be overshadowed by another, more dramatic investigation known in the office as "High Rise"—a case prompted by intelligence on an imminent plot to stage an attack in New York. The intelligence implicated a former Queens resident, Najibullah Zazi, who at one point worked a coffee cart in lower Manhattan not far from ground zero. The JTTF disrupted an active plot to launch a suicide attack on the New York subway system, tracking three suspects—Zazi and his friends Zarein Ahmedzay and Adis Medunjanin—to an apartment two blocks from Rabbani's house as they made final preparations to build and deploy bombs in backpacks. The men grew up in Pakistani, Afghan, and Bosnian immigrant families and had attended Flushing High School together before venturing to Pakistan to receive training from al-Qaeda. The plot unraveled over the course of a dizzying weekend in September 2009 as FBI and NYPD counterterrorism investigators zeroed in on Zazi and his co-conspirators. Even as Kaziu went to trial and DuCharme scored his first trial victory, the case remained in the shadow of High Rise.

If High Rise involved the dramatic disruption of a plot in its final hours, Kaziu represented something less glamorous: a case where the government dictated the tempo and preempted any escalation. It also showed DuCharme something an aggressive prosecutor could easily overlook. Not every suspect taking steps toward jihad ultimately chooses to follow that path.

IMRAN WAS THE THIRD of five children in the Rabbani family. They lived together in a one-bedroom apartment on the fourth floor of a featureless brick building in Flushing, Queens. The family did not stand out there. Flushing was an immigrant community several miles directly east from the heart of Manhattan. Most New Yorkers ventured to the neighborhood for two landmarks on its industrial periphery: Shea Stadium (now Citi Field), to see the New York Mets play, and Arthur Ashe Stadium, to watch the U.S. Open tennis tournament. Despite growing up down the street from both, Imran hadn't had the chance to experience either.

Flushing centered on the crowded, kinetic Chinatown on Main Street, the terminus of the 7 train line, just a few blocks from the front door of the Rabbani family's brick-faced apartment block on a side street that pulsed with traffic. The Chinese community made up the majority in Flushing, but residents from more than seventy countries made the neighborhood their home including dozens of families from Pakistan, where the Rabbani parents had emigrated from. The Rabbani children, like many of the children from immigrant families in the neighborhood, were born American citizens.

Imran attended John Bowne High School, an inner-city public high school filled with first-generation children. Nearly one in three students dropped out of John Bowne, and a little more than 50 percent went on to college. But the Rabbani sons had bucked these trends. Inam, the eldest son, went on to St. John's University, where he graduated magna cum laude before attending law school there. The second son, Ikram, was John Bowne's 2013 valedictorian. He went on to Dickinson College on a full scholarship. Unlike his older brothers, Imran didn't distinguish himself academically. Instead, when people discussed him, they often mentioned his character. He was handsome and well built and had grown a neatly trimmed beard while still in high school. A teacher remembered him as "extremely intelligent and sophisticated" but also a "loving, supporting, and caring person," one who would linger after class to wait for a girl he had befriended. When a close friend's mother desperately needed an organ transplant, Imran helped the friend lose weight so that he could qualify as a donor. The cliques at John Bowne separated along racial and religious lines, but Imran easily traversed these social boundaries. Many of the students at John Bowne were from struggling families and lacked direction, often growing up in strict and insular households with immigrant parents. Many students ditched classes and blew off academics, but Imran pushed his friends to take their educations seriously, to recognize the limited opportunity they had and to make good on it. Some friends saw Imran's concern for others as a weakness, a dangerous naïveté: "He could not see the worst in others. He always saw the best in everyone."

Imran wasn't without his difficulties. Unlike his focused and accomplished older brothers, he rebelled. At fourteen, he snuck out of the house and stole his neighbor's car, taking it for a joyride in a nearby Home Depot parking lot to spin doughnuts. The police pulled Imran into the 109th Precinct, but after a few tense hours they released him into his parents' custody. It wasn't Imran's parents who were most upset with him but his eldest brother, Inam.

Inam was serious and career-minded. He hoped one day to serve as a military lawyer and had little patience for indiscipline. He interrogated his younger brother, demanding to know why he would do something so reckless. But as Imran tried to explain himself, his older brother only heard lies. Enraged, Inam told his brother that he would never speak to him again. For two years, the brothers lived together in the Rabbanis' small apartment without exchanging a word.

The Rabbani children didn't have the luxury of an adolescence without direction. They faced a complex set of pressures unique to the children of immigrant parents. To come of age in New York City was to grow up in between worlds. Their parents and the elders in their community belonged to a different past, with different customs and histories. In the younger generation, they saw the unfamiliar influences of not only American culture but also secular life. To those closest to them, these children were too American to be seen as Pakistani. To outsiders, they were too Pakistani and Muslim to be seen as American.

Yet the Rabbanis made some effort to bridge this gap for their children. When the boys were in grade school, their father brought them into Manhattan to Dylan's Candy Bar, a sugary version of heaven for children with rows of jelly beans, jawbreakers, licorice, and even a bubbling fountain of chocolate. It was a rare splurge for the Rabbani family, for whom money was always tight. Their father, Ghulam, drove a limousine for a living, while their mother remained at home raising the children. When the boys became old enough to work, they would eventually contribute to the household expenses. The trip to the Manhattan candy store was a small but significant journey, yet not for the reasons their parents intended. A man confronted the Rabbani family and, in front of his young children, told Ghulam, "Go home, sand nigger."

New York was their home—the only home that the family had ever known. Their parents were naturalized American citizens, and the children's ties to Pakistan were, if anything, cultural. Imran's older brother described their predicament: "If I don't belong here. And I don't belong there. And no one wants me anywhere. Then where do I go?"

One place of belonging was the local mosque, the Muslim Center of New York, a marble edifice on a residential street off Kissena Park. The mosque had been founded forty years earlier by a small group of Pakistani immigrants, joining Flushing's mosaic of faiths. On the short walk from the Rabbanis' apartment, one could pass the Free Synagogue of Flushing, the Hindu Center Temple, and the Boon Church, a Christian congregation from the Oversea Chinese Mission. On Fridays, Imran would attend prayer at the mosque. The mosque's director noticed that when Imran arrived there, he smiled and greeted everyone he passed, offering his respects. The Rabbani family were known and well regarded in the community. In early 2015, seventeen-year-old Imran became increasingly pious, devoting his time to volunteer work, raising money for the mosque's charitable efforts, and bringing meals to those in need. He also became close to a neighbor who had graduated from John Bowne with his older brother, a lanky, talkative college student named Munther Saleh.

The young men knew what it was to grow up as first-generation Americans. Saleh's father, who was from Jordan, worked at the local grocery, and the family lived in an apartment across the street from the store, just several doors down from the Rabbani family apartment. Saleh attended Vaughn College, an aeronautics school overlooking LaGuardia Airport. He had branched out from the community in Flushing, befriending young Muslim men throughout New York and New Jersey. And that year, Munther had looked even further afield for companionship: he made contact with the Islamic State.

BY EARLY 2015, ISIS had achieved a key strategic innovation: the ability to use social media to project its message globally and target recruits. A little more than a year earlier, the group was just one faction among many in the Syrian civil war, an al-Qaeda affiliate of murky beginnings. Then it began waging a series of devastatingly indiscriminate attacks across Syria and Iraq before emerging under a new name: Islamic State. Al-Qaeda broke with this upstart, in part in a dispute over this new breed of violence. The elder terrorist organization disavowed the newly minted group's brutal tactics and rigid extremism. The group's leader, Abu Bakr al-Baghdadi, an Iraqi who had spent time in U.S. custody during the occupation, had little need for the al-Qaeda brand; in fact, the group set itself apart from al-Qaeda's atomized and stateless presence by doing something unconventional: occupying territory and establishing a geographic footprint. He called for Muslims to make *hijra*—religious migration—to Iraq and Syria, where ISIS claimed to have established a caliphate. This initially served the purpose of drawing fighters to the battlefield in Syria and Iraq, a journey that was more tenable for fighters in Europe and the Middle East but attracted Americans—in particular, young men.

Imran's friend Munther Saleh didn't struggle to find the path toward radicalization. While studying in college, he gravitated to other Muslims online. Saleh discussed politics and eventually became more vocal in his personal beliefs—beliefs that grew increasingly radical. In September 2014, he posted a message online saying, "I fear that AQ could be getting more moderate." Saleh had struck up a friendship online with Junaid Hussain, a young hacker from Birmingham, England, who had operated under the name "TriCk." Hussain had also adopted a nom de guerre, Abu Hussain al-Britani, and lived no longer in the United Kingdom but in Raqqa, Syria, where he led digital operations for the Islamic State.

Hussain, for his part, had been in touch with ISIS aspirants in California, Massachusetts, Minnesota, North Carolina, Ohio, and Rhode Island, men and women who did not hew to a clear profile other than growing radicalized online. ISIS fighters who made it to the battlefield tended to be reasonably well educated, though only about 10 percent had any experience waging jihad. That summer, nearly eight hundred foreign fighters a month flocked to the caliphate after Baghdadi's call for *hijra*.

Around this time, in early 2015, Imran also began researching the Islamic State. The group projected a simple idea: a separate society of Muslims living under Islamic law. In many respects, this represented the antithesis to Flushing, a polyglot community where each individual was entitled to abide by his or her own set of cultural and religious beliefs. Even more so, the Islamic State represented an alternate reality to the secular United States, where economic and racial barriers often blocked the paths toward societal acceptance for the children of immigrants. The Islamic State message offered things that young men coming out of adolescence into adulthood craved: belonging, honor, and, above all, absolute moral certainty. After watching a documentary on ISIS, Imran shot Munther a message.

"I've been looking more into it," Rabbani wrote to his friend. "You can tell me more about it . . . it just makes sense."

"U mean establishing Islam the same way the Prophet did? We can meet up whenever ur free," Saleh responded.

"Yeah and dude it's like their doing it step by step and perfectly," Imran wrote. "The exact ways and rules of the prophet."

―――――

ON THE NIGHT of July 12, 2015, Imran invited Saleh to a Queens mosque with other friends. The young men had been invited to pray, then to take part in a religious discussion late into the night. The conversation turned to the Islamic State. Saleh was outspoken about his support for the group, but Imran didn't share his friend's outward enthusiasm—or interest in undertaking *hijra*. But Imran did believe that Muslims in the United States were being unfairly targeted. He could point to his own experience. The mysterious vehicles trailing his movements. He could only speculate that it was the FBI. And that the agents were monitoring not only his movements but also his communications. But to his mind, he'd done nothing wrong.

But he had researched and discussed the ideas of the Islamic State, some of which appealed to him. Imran was still a high school student, but he knew that in the United States he had the right to his thoughts and his own words.

The group left the mosque after midnight. A crowd piled into a Jeep Cherokee, some for a ride home, the others to go to a mosque in College Point to catch a few hours of sleep before the call to prayer. As dawn approached, only Munther, Faisal, and Imran remained. The men noticed that they had again picked up a surveillance vehicle. The Jeep pulled into a car wash. Then, to evade their tail, the driver flipped the headlights off before flooring it through a parking lot. The car gave chase, following the Jeep as it blew through several stop signs. Each maneuver the Jeep pulled, the surveillance mirrored, falling in behind the men as they continued toward the mosque.

By the time the men had pulled up to the stoplight on the overpass at Twentieth Avenue and the Whitestone Expressway, they decided they'd had enough. Why were they being followed? they wondered. Even if the driver behind them was FBI, what were Imran and his friends doing wrong?

When Imran and Munther stepped out of the Jeep, the driver behind them immediately threw the car into reverse. Seeing the car begin to retreat, Imran and his friend returned to the Jeep. But the car didn't flee the scene. Almost immediately, the vehicle pulled back in behind them, closer. The two friends again jumped out of the Jeep. For an instant, Munther had pulled his knife out, but he did not open it to reveal the blade. As they moved toward the car to demand the driver explain himself, another car appeared.

A federal agent bounded out with a gun, ordering the men to stop.

The agents rifled through the men's pockets, where they discovered a knife on Munther; Imran's was tucked in his waistband.

Before the sun rose that morning, federal agents had taken him and Munther into custody. Unlike Imran, Munther had taken clear direct actions to support ISIS. Weeks earlier, he'd helped send off a friend from JFK on his way to join the Islamic State. With another friend he had conspired to stage a Boston Marathon–style attack with a pipe bomb.

The young men faced "2339B" charges, conspiracy to provide material support to a terrorist organization. Imran Rabbani became the first minor charged with attempting to support the Islamic State in New York City.

13

702

August 13, 2015

Judge John Gleeson was running late. The courtroom deputy stood up to make an announcement, breaking the quiet murmur of the courtroom: the judge would arrive at three o'clock; thirty minutes after the hearing's scheduled start. No explanation, but none was needed for one of the most respected judges in the Eastern District of New York.

Outside a clear blue summer afternoon unfolded across Cadman Plaza, the open tree-lined esplanade in front of the courthouse. Lawyers and paralegals took in the moment in rolled shirtsleeves, jackets flung over the shaded park benches. Children in matching summer camp T-shirts fanned out across the artificial turf soccer pitch in front of the war memorial; their voices carried into the sound of the invisible traffic passing over the Brooklyn Bridge.

Upstairs, in courtroom 6CS, the shirtsleeves, ties, and jackets of the men and women waiting to appear before the judge remained intact. The parties filtered in subdued but smiling: two criminal defense attorneys, three Assistant U.S. Attorneys, interns, and a probation officer in tow, and in the back row of the courtroom two federal agents. The room felt light, only a tinge of nervous energy. The lawyers settled, pulling filings from their briefcases and handbags, bantering like old acquaintances as they waited for the judge.

The occasion was simultaneously serious and routine in the Eastern District of New York: the sentencing of a terrorism defendant.

JIHADIST TERRORISM DOMINATED our politics for more than a decade after September 11. But before the World Trade Center attacks, terrorism lacked a fixed definition in the United States. The historian J. Bowyer Bell described the prismatic nature of the term saying, "Tell me what you think about terrorism, and I will tell you who you are." The term began appearing frequently in American newspapers directly before and after the Civil War, describing vigilante violence carried out by anti-abolitionists and, eventually, the Ku Klux Klan. It was also invoked to frame the actions of John Brown and John Wilkes Booth. By the turn of the twentieth century, editors and reporters applied the term more liberally, describing conduct as varied as violence between political parties in Louisiana or interfamily warfare in Kentucky.

In New York, terrorism was a criminal concept—often aligned with an immigrant underworld. In 1903, the *New-York Tribune* wrote, "Terrorism and blackmail are the favorite methods by means of which the Mafia, the anarchists, the Camorra, the Nihilists and most of those other kindred secret societies of the old world organized under the mantle of politics for crime." The line between organized crime and organized labor had also blurred in the early twentieth century, in part because of the shared reliance on racketeering, extortion, and the attendant violence of each. When a bombing on Wall Street in 1920 left thirty-eight people dead and hundreds injured, the daily papers characterized it as an act of terrorism. Reports blamed "unionists" for the bombing, but the perpetrators of the attack—and their objective— remain a mystery to this day. In 1935, a window-smashing ring organized by the American Federation of Master Barbers prompted "an investigation of a campaign of terrorism" aimed at forcing price increases among nonaffiliated barbers. Describing a racket targeting Brooklyn bakeries in 1937 by a figure named Lupo the Wolf, the *Times* wrote that the "conviction marked the end of a system of terrorism that plagued hundreds of bakeries for several years." Both cases resulted in conspiracy charges.

When violent political groups like the Weathermen and the Symbionese Liberation Army emerged in the early 1970s with kidnappings, robberies, and bombings, they were not branded as terrorists. The press favored terms like "radicals," "leftists," and "militants" even as academics began to develop conceptual frameworks to discuss "urban terrorism."

It wasn't until the 1980s that the term again entered general use; even then, it referred to violent nationalist groups. In response to a series of bombings across the city by Puerto Rican, Cuban, and Croatian groups, the FBI and the NYPD stood up the first Joint Terrorism Task Force in 1980. It assumed an idea that would later be heavily debated: that terrorism was a law enforcement issue. After the first World Trade Center bombing and the September 11 attacks, the JTTF expanded and focused on the threat posed by jihadist groups. The unit eventually pulled personnel from nearly every local and national law enforcement and intelligence agency, most notably the NYPD, FBI, CIA, and NSA. These last two agencies only substantively came into the picture after September 11, when investigators tracking terror suspects finally gained access to information developed by the intelligence community. The force of some five hundred investigators evolved into three distinct branches: Branches B and C comprise the group's respective extraterritorial, WMD, and "special tactics" units, while Branch A became responsible for operations in New York City. From their Chelsea command center, members of the task force tracked real-time threat information, while investigators from the NYPD's counterterrorism units and the FBI navigated the delicate jurisdictional terrain across the city's five boroughs.

The federal courts also got into the terrorism business after Congress passed the Foreign Intelligence Surveillance Act in 1978. Counterterrorism investigators relied on FISA to conduct surveillance; it was as integral as the passage of Title III provisions on wiretaps in dismantling the Mafia. The case that broke ground in the early 1980s did not involve Islamic extremists. Instead, it was the prosecution of four Provisional Irish Republican Army members in the Eastern District on charges of transporting explosives. The case, *United States v. Duggan,* led to an appeal that would shape national security law for three decades when the Second Circuit first ruled FISA constitutional in 1984. That decision laid the groundwork for the use of classified evidence in criminal trials. In 1986, U.S. Attorney Rudolph Giuliani made a foray into national security, pursuing a sprawling fifty-five-count indictment against seventeen individuals linked to $2 billion in arms sales to Iran—which allowed him to tie the transactions to international terrorism. But after news emerged that the United States had also sold arms to Iran, Giuliani's prosecutors dropped a majority of the charges out of fear that they could not show that the sale did not have the tacit approval of the Reagan administration. In 1987, the Eastern District U.S. Attorney, Andrew Maloney, pressed terrorism charges on a separate front, winning bombing conspiracy convictions against several members of the Jewish Defense League, a militant group founded by Rabbi Meir Kahane. The first significant trial involving Islamic terrorism came after the 1993 World Trade Center bombing, when the U.S. Attorney for the Southern District of New York, Mary Jo White, won convictions against nine defendants charged with the attack. In the eight-month trial, she turned to a Civil War–era statute, the Seditious Conspiracy Act of 1861—a law enacted to counter the threat posed by Southerners rejecting the authority of the Union—to charge the men, adherents of the Egyptian cleric Sheikh Omar Abdel-Rahman.

In the years leading up to the September 11 attacks, White prosecuted several other terrorism cases, from the conspiracy to bomb the U.S. embassies in Tanzania and Kenya to the Manhattan assassination of Meir Kahane. In hindsight, the contours of the emerging al-Qaeda threat could be seen. One inmate charged with the embassy bombings attacked a guard at Manhattan's Metropolitan Correctional Center (MCC), stabbing him in the eye with a sharpened comb and causing a severe brain injury. The attacker, Mamdouh Mahmud Salim, served bin Laden directly and had helped found al-Qaeda.

As perceptions of terrorism evolved, federal prosecutors' statutory tool kit also changed. In 1994, Congress passed a law targeting support for terrorism conspiracies and crimes—whether the violence went realized or unrealized. The next year the most significant act of domestic terrorism in U.S. history, the Oklahoma City bombing, prompted Congress to expand terror prohibitions with the Antiterrorism and Effective Death Penalty Act of 1996. The act contained two key sections, 2339A, which barred "providing material support to terrorists" preparing or carrying out an act of violence, and 2339B, outlawing material support for "designated terrorist organizations." The latter criminalized a much broader array of activities not necessarily tied to a specific plot or attack. Yet prosecutors didn't gravitate toward either statute: 2339A had a narrow focus, while the expansive provisions of 2339B had yet to be tested before September 11, 2001.

In the months following the September 11 attacks, federal prosecutors and the FBI responded both to the immediate al-Qaeda conspiracy, in a prosecution against the "20th hijacker," Zacarias Moussaoui, and to the perceived threat of Islamic terrorism, in a case against John Walker Lindh, an American who fought with the Taliban. The Justice Department brought both cases in the Eastern District of Virginia, a jurisdiction home to prosecutors with existing expertise on al-Qaeda, as well as a background in handling classified evidence. But Attorney General John Ashcroft and the FBI director, Robert Mueller, had explicit marching orders from the White House: law enforcement's priority was not to investigate terrorist attacks after the fact but to prevent them from happening.

Within months of the attacks, the federal courts in New York became a battleground over what role the judicial system should play, if any, in combating terrorism. In May 2002, federal agents arrested Jose Padilla, a Brooklyn-born al-Qaeda member, in Chicago. He was brought in secret to the Southern District as a material witness in the attacks, where he remained in federal custody long enough to be assigned a defense attorney. But—without any notice—then the Southern District U.S. Attorney, James Comey, turned Padilla over to be housed at a military prison in South Carolina. It was an extraordinary moment. Prosecutors, by nature, fight to preserve their jurisdiction; in New York City, those instincts are honed by the fierce competition among the two federal districts and the neighboring New Jersey district. After the White House designated Padilla an "enemy combatant," Comey not only surrendered Padilla to Washington's fiat; he handed him over to the Department of Defense. The Office of Legal Counsel had created the term to remove constitutional protections and obligations under the Geneva Convention for al-Qaeda fighters. Padilla, an American citizen, had been removed from the federal judicial system without due process. (Comey left the Southern District to become the deputy attorney general the next year.)

In the Southern District, Padilla provided a potent test to the administration's underlying legal theory: he was an American citizen who had been arrested on U.S. soil but denied the most basic due process rights. Did the president have the authority to take those away from a citizen by merely invoking the term "enemy combatant"? That question, and the habeas petition filed by Padilla's attorneys, first appeared before the Southern District judge Michael Mukasey. The judge backed the defense's right to sue for access to their client, but supported the president's authority to remove "enemy combatants" from the criminal justice system, provided the government had evidence to support that designation. Mukasey appeared to defer to the broad executive powers the Bush administration sought after the September 11 attacks. (Bush would later nominate Mukasey to head the Justice Department.) Even with that important concession, the ruling left the White House dissatisfied and defiant. On appeal, the Second Circuit rejected the notion that the executive branch had the power to sidestep due process by classifying defendants with what amounted to a rhetorical flourish. Padilla's fight shifted to South Carolina, where the Defense Department held the accused terrorist. The Supreme Court was poised to take up the question. Instead, federal prosecutors indicted the accused terrorist—making the questions of his status as an "enemy combatant" moot. The Bush administration averted a Supreme Court ruling that would have clearly articulated the scope of executive powers. In 2006, the Supreme Court issued a decision in *Hamdan v. Rumsfeld* that found the military commissions set up to try accused al-Qaeda members violated the Geneva Conventions, whether or not the detained was an American citizen.

The Southern District seemed an obvious venue for criminal cases related to the September 11 attacks. The World Trade Center towers fell blocks from Foley Square, and after the 1993 bombing at the towers a Manhattan judge and jury heard the case against the plotters in that attack. Yet, when the Obama administration sought to shift the cases from the Bush administration's military tribunal system at Guantánamo to the Southern District, another branch of government stepped in: Congress. In 2011, buried deep in the National Defense Authorization Act, Republicans opposed to the Obama administration's intent to criminally charge those involved in the September 11 attacks inserted a provision that made the transfer of military detainees onto U.S. soil illegal. The Obama administration viewed the maneuver as a power grab, depriving the president of the ability to pursue a key policy objective—and campaign promise—of closing Guantánamo. A decade after the attacks, the question of venue in terrorism cases—which was legal in nature—became a political one.

Yet the Guantánamo cases represented jihadist terrorism's past. The Obama administration confronted a new brand of terror, which had yet to reveal its face. When that time came, New York's federal districts became the nation's leading legal battleground for terrorism cases. The prosecutors and investigators working in Brooklyn and Manhattan had powers unimaginable a decade earlier: to conduct broad surveillance, to marshal evidence shrouded in classification, to reach not only across the globe but back in time to pursue targets of their choosing. After the attacks, the Patriot Act also made 2339B into a more potent tool for prosecutors, defining support as "expert advice or assistance," which exposed those in contact with designated terrorist organizations, including charitable groups and NGOs, to criminal liability. Two years later, following the Supreme Court case *Humanitarian Law Project v. Ashcroft*, Congress refined that language to mean "specialized knowledge."

The decades-long process of redefining terrorism gave law enforcement the power to look both inside the United States and far beyond our borders for threats. The mandate to prevent future attacks included destroying terrorist networks by any means necessary—including through use of the courts. Most of the accused in the New York courts are Muslim men, though the defendants include several women. Often, they have connections to immigrant communities in the outer boroughs. In some cases, prosecutors and federal agents have plucked suspects from abroad who had never set foot inside the United States before their arrest.

In the Eastern District, the National Security and Cybercrime Section soon replaced Organized Crime as the coveted assignment among ambitious prosecutors. Since the September 11 attacks, the U.S. Attorneys in Brooklyn and Manhattan have charged ninety-three and one hundred defendants with terrorism offenses, respectively, leading the third-busiest district, the Eastern District of Virginia, by thirty defendants. Over a decade of trying cases following the September 11 attacks, an uncharitable yet accurate distinction came to set the New York districts apart: the Eastern District typically charged terrorism cases before an attack; the Southern District often did so afterward.

THAT AUGUST AFTERNOON, the lead prosecutor, Assistant U.S. Attorney Seth DuCharme, stepped from the government's table to greet one of the investigators. DuCharme always made a point to check in with the agents and marshals working the courthouse. One of his longest-standing defendants, Agron Hasbajrami, a twenty-nine-year-old architect from Peshkopi, Albania, convicted on two counts of material support for terrorism, was to be sentenced that day. Hasbajrami fit the profile of a typical material support defendant in the Eastern District: a young, disaffected Muslim man living in Brooklyn. He arrived in the United States on a green card in 2008. His isolation and disillusionment grew as he struggled to gain a foothold in New York from his apartment in Bensonhurst. Hasbajrami also began to feel that he was being targeted, he said. He was approached by at least one Albanian-speaking stranger he believed was an FBI informant. Hasbajrami felt that he picked him out because "he was a young man with a beard attending mosque." Hasbajrami eventually did make online contact with someone presenting himself as a jihadist recruiter. Their relationship progressed from words to action over time—from ruminations on joining jihad to concrete steps. Eventually, he wired the recruiter funds, then purchased a one-way ticket to Turkey, intent on joining the fight against Americans in Pakistan. In the end, he didn't get any farther than a departures terminal at JFK.

Hasbajrami had been communicating online with the FBI all along. Investigators skillfully led him across the border between fantasy and reality, building the evidence that would support a criminal charge and giving sufficient basis to arrest him before he boarded his flight. Hasbajrami pleaded guilty and received a fifteen-year sentence in 2013. Soon after, his criminal case had jumped off the rails and directly into the national debate raging around warrantless surveillance and the unresolved constitutional questions involving criminal cases using evidence obtained through these means.

THE DAY'S SENTENCING also provided a window into the tight-knit terrorism bar in New York City. DuCharme sat with two junior assistants, Saritha Komatireddy and Peter Baldwin, while others from the U.S. Attorney's Office found seats in the gallery. Zainab Ahmad, a striking prosecutor with a reputation for flipping terrorism suspects, looked up from a stack of filings to see her colleague Shreve Ariail as he stepped into the courtroom to find a seat among the onlookers. After the courtroom deputy announced the delay, the two prosecutors stepped outside quickly. Minutes later they snuck back into the courtroom with iced coffees, concealing the contraband drinks. Just a day earlier, Ahmad had appeared before Gleeson for another terrorism sentencing: Lawal Babafemi, an al-Qaeda propagandist, rendered from Nigeria after he had trained and fought with the terrorist group in Yemen. The judge sentenced him to twenty-two years. It was another in a string of terrorism convictions Ahmad had helped secure; she would leave the office, to go to Main Justice, before joining Special Counsel Robert Mueller's team, after the 2016 election.

Summer had already been busy for the Eastern District national security team. For the first time in DuCharme's career as a national security prosecutor, there were so many cases that he needed more than just a defendant's last name to recall the details of each. DuCharme and Ariail were prosecuting three al-Shabaab fighters rendered from Djibouti to Brooklyn; the case was referred to as DJ3 by the investigative team. Separately, Ariail was leading a prosecution against a wily Nigerien al-Qaeda operative who was flushed out of Libya during the

2011 intervention. Ahmad was working a murder case: French special forces had captured a Malian smuggler believed to be responsible for the murder of an American diplomat in 2000. But the Djibouti, Libya, and Mali arrests were historical cases, investigations that the Eastern District had opted into years earlier before the rise of the Islamic State.

The Boston Marathon bombings ushered in a grim new threat for law enforcement: jihadist terror plots originated and carried out domestically. It fell to the JTTF to ensure that no similar plots came to fruition. DuCharme and his colleagues had to act at the precise moment when the defendants broke terrorism laws without committing an act of terrorism. This required discerning whether a person was truly on a path toward violence or harboring a daydream—a daydream protected under the Constitution. Even then, investigators took into account whether there were off-ramps that a would-be jihadist could take, whether there was a supportive family or community that could act as a deterrent. If the government did decide to do something, the task fell to either the intelligence community, the military, or federal prosecutors. The objective was the same for each: to eliminate a threat. Once a suspect left the United States, the options expanded: the government could tip off friendly intelligence services to hold a suspect, sometimes indefinitely, or conduct a military strike.

The legal option was powerful but also demanding: each count under the material support statute carried a potential fifteen-year sentence, not to mention the years of litigation involved in resolving a terrorism case. And even with conviction rates for ISIS-related offenses nationwide at 100 percent, there was no guarantee of success. Even as terrorism cases became routine in the Eastern District, there was no such thing as a routine terrorism case. Intelligence and law enforcement agencies conducting counterterrorism investigations often wanted to avoid the mess of a trial, the discovery obligations the process entailed, and the potential exposure of sources and methods. Once prosecutors charged a defendant, they needed to pursue convictions with equal effort, whether the accused was a seasoned al-Qaeda fighter or a high school student from Queens. But in the zero-sum game of preventing terrorism, parsing distinctions between those two things was dangerous, both to the public and to a prosecutor's career.

"It's a major burn on resources," said Don Borelli, former assistant special agent in charge of the New York Joint Terrorism Task Force. "The reason they're getting arrested is because we don't have anything between the school counselor and the FBI."

The other resource demand created by the rise in terrorism cases in New York was for experienced defense counsel. At the table opposite the government sat one of Hasbajrami's three attorneys, Joshua Dratel. He leaned back in his chair, looking down across his nose at a filing, cradling the back of his head with one hand—as if to hold in the information he was absorbing. He looked up, occasionally, to greet someone with his big, toothy smile. Brooklyn bred, a Yankees fan who mingled yellowing paperbacks on baseball statistics with the dusty law guides on the bookshelf of his Manhattan office, Dratel has defended some of the most significant terrorism clients both in federal court—at that point almost exclusively the Southern District—and at Guantánamo Bay, where he appeared as the first civilian attorney. He graduated from Harvard Law School in 1981 and, unlike many criminal defense attorneys, never did a stint as a prosecutor. Even as his law school groomed graduates along three paths into corporate practice, academics, or government service, Dratel took the less traveled route directly into criminal defense. In more than thirty years practicing law in New York City, he said the trajectory of his career had largely been dictated by the crusades taken on by the government, whether it was against corrupt public officials, mob bosses, drug traffickers, or terrorists. Dratel had no affinity with Islamic extremism, but he was a fundamentalist on one point: if the government was going to bring charges, it had an obligation to prove them. At that point in his career, he had represented more than forty defendants accused of terrorism offenses, dating back to several Provisional IRA defendants in *United States v. Duggan* in the early 1980s. He appeared as counsel at Guantánamo during the first military commission trial for the Australian al-Qaeda fighter David Hicks.

When it came to national security, Dratel saw his job as much the same as Seth DuCharme's: to prevent attacks against the United States. But the attacks Dratel focused on were on the Constitution, the Bill of Rights, due process, and the proper function of the criminal justice system. National security, in his view, meant much more than the physical security of our people and country. It involved protecting our institutions. These are as worthy of providing security to as our people and landmarks are. Prosecutors and those in law enforcement often question the credibility of critics of aggressive approaches to counterterrorism investigations—from running informants to warrantless electronic surveillance to the reliance on classified evidence. These are arguments that can be made only by those free from the responsibility of protecting the public, they say. Yet Dratel had staked his career and reputation on making these arguments on behalf of defendants accused of crimes of terrorism. In New York, where the reminders that three thousand people lost their lives in such an attack can turn up in voir dire or in dinner party conversation, this wasn't an academic position. A needlepoint of the pre–September 11 skyline that hung in Dratel's conference room seemed to acknowledge this. It was stitched with the phrase "Old lawyers never die . . . they just lose their appeal." The otherwise hammy joke set against that image of the silhouette of the Twin Towers took on the unexpected weight of Dratel's experience.

Seated next to him was his co-counsel, Michael Bachrach, a baby-faced defense attorney two decades younger who was known as a gifted appellate attorney. Like Dratel, he was a native New Yorker, raised in Greenwich Village, where he went to school at Friends Seminary; later he attended Sarah Lawrence College, where he studied poetry. Bachrach had represented other accused terrorists in the past including Ahmed Ghailani, a Tanzanian convicted on one conspiracy count in the Southern District for the 1998 U.S. embassy bombings. The Ghailani case was in some regards typical of the Southern District—a high-profile prosecution that followed an act of terror. Bachrach recalled trying to establish a rapport with Ghailani. He explained to his new client that he was Jewish but had attended a Quaker school. It wasn't clear whether an East African would even know what a Quaker was—no less the distinctly New York confluence of social influences in Bachrach's upbringing—but to his surprise Ghailani said, "Like *Witness?*" a reference to the Harrison Ford film set in Pennsylvania's Amish country.

"I loved that movie," he recalled the al-Qaeda associate saying.

The threat of terrorism had changed significantly since the Ghailani case—as had law enforcement's capabilities. But Bachrach's job had remained much the same: to ensure that his client's rights had not been violated.

The courtroom doors opened, and an attorney, beaming, briefcase in hand, breezed in alone with a rush of air.

"ZEE-SUE," said one of the feds to his colleague in the gallery.

It was an onomatopoeia indigenous to the federal courts in New York City. Steve Zissou, defender of local drug kingpins and international drug lords, global terrorists and their homegrown counterparts. His client, Bryant Neal Viñas, had become the Eastern District's most prized cooperator on al-Qaeda, a relationship that was entering its seventh year. Zissou greeted his colleagues, clasping hands and leaning in to kiss women on the cheek. His broad shoulders cut a sweeping, dapper figure that—even at sixty—projected brash confidence, reminiscent of the Wes Anderson character that shares his name, without the cluelessness. (Zissou had, in fact, settled with Anderson on the use of his name in the film.) Though Zissou had been absent from the last plea hearing, he had been instrumental in securing Hasbajrami's assent.

He nodded to Bachrach, his junior partner on the Ghailani case. ("Generally I let him carry the file and get me coffee," he joked of their working relationship at the time.) He slowed his step as he approached Dratel, extending his hand: "Do you mind if I say hello to *your* client?"

It was a friendly joke. Two weeks earlier, the defendant had tried to fire Zissou.

A DOORWAY IN THE CORNER of the courtroom opened. Without a knock to announce his entrance, Judge John Gleeson stepped into the room. He wasn't wearing a robe. Instead, he stepped up to the bench in a dusk-blue suit and lavender tie. Everyone abruptly stood. Even after Gleeson took his seat, he waited for several moments before directing the small audience to sit.

Gleeson projected an imposing presence from the bench. He also gave the sense that he was a reasonable man. His career ran as a vivid thread through the story of the modern Eastern District. Even at sixty-two, with wavy dark hair and prominent ears, he retained a youthful, wholesome bookishness. His career as a prosecutor was remembered through a single case: Gotti. And with that success was the unsavory alliance made with a man like Sammy "the Bull" Gravano. Yet, as a judge, Gleeson resisted easy description.

His brand of judgment came across in the frank, humorless prose of his decisions. That voice mirrored how he spoke in court, where he often relied on the inertial impact of simple sentences. When attorneys argued that he, as a judge, didn't have the authority to rule on a matter, he wrote simply, "They are wrong." When acknowledging the stark circumstances of an armed robber who came before his court seeking a sentence reduction, Gleeson was similarly blunt. "Holloway has eight grandchildren he's never seen." On the bench, he was compassionate and skeptical, not easily tied to the underdog, nor prejudiced toward the office he once served.

Gleeson had a track record on national security. In one case, he largely dismissed the claims of Muslim men challenging their detention as illegal aliens following the September 11 attacks. The suit named Attorney General John Ashcroft, Director of the FBI Robert Mueller, and Immigration and Naturalization Service commissioner James Ziglar, as well as more than two dozen employees of the Metropolitan Detention Center accused of mistreatment. The Department of Justice was a small community, and Gleeson had a history with some of these men. When Gleeson was still a prosecutor, Mueller, then an official at Main Justice, had played the tiebreaker in the Southern District's fierce battle to take the John Gotti prosecution. Mueller surprised everyone when he let the case move ahead in Brooklyn under Gleeson and his Eastern District boss, Andrew Maloney. A decade later, organized crime was a distant threat, and the men had changed seats.

"National emergencies are not cause to relax the rights guaranteed in our Constitution," he wrote in his ninety-nine-page decision, but he also acknowledged the limited power of the courts to drive the response to national security interests. "Regarding immigration matters such as this, the Constitution assigns to the political branches all but the most minimal authority in making the delicate balancing judgments." The decision outraged civil rights advocates who saw it as laying the legal foundation for an internment program akin to the World War II–era detention of Japanese Americans. The case, nonetheless, moved forward—in amended form—to the Supreme Court, in part because of the due process and equal protection claims that Gleeson left open.

The Hasbajrami case presented a novel constitutional question. More than a year after the defendant's sentencing, Seth DuCharme sent a letter to Hasbajrami at the medium-security prison where he was being held. It notified him "that certain evidence and information, obtained or derived from Title I or III FISA collection, that the government intended to offer into evidence or otherwise use or disclose in proceedings, in this case, was derived from acquisition of foreign intelligence information conducted pursuant to the FISA Amendments Act." This was a standard notification, but Hasbajrami should have received it long before he pleaded guilty.

The anodyne language undersold the revelation. The government had planned to use evidence gathered through the warrantless wiretap program—specifically, through PRISM, the NSA surveillance capability revealed by Edward Snowden. Previously, such a search required a court order. But two pieces of legislation, the Protect America Act of 2007 and the FISA Amendments Act of 2008 (FAA), removed that hurdle for agents and prosecutors. Specifically, a provision of the FAA—section 702—permitted the NSA to target non-U.S. individuals outside the country with bulk data collection for the purpose of gathering "foreign intelligence." U.S. law enforcement could then search this repository of "702 material"—without a warrant—for evidence of criminal activity of people living inside the United States. Technically, it was a very novel approach that allowed federal investigators access to reams of historical data. Most significantly, Justice Department officials believed that "702" collapsed the wall between law enforcement and the intelligence community, a contributor to the September 11 attacks. But the constitutional question remained. Was this an "unreasonable" search under the Fourth Amendment? The simple fact was that intelligence agencies had broadly expanded their powers to collect communications without a warrant, including those belonging to American citizens. From a civil libertarian's point of view, a federal agent could search and read through an American's messages without seeking a judge's approval to do so. Hasbajrami's fairly run-of-the-mill Brooklyn terror case suddenly found itself at the center of a national debate.

The revelation opened the door, if only a crack, for Hasbajrami. The path toward freedom for Hasbajrami, as narrow as it was, was through an appeal to the Second Circuit and—perhaps—the Supreme Court. If a court found that the evidence, which initially led investigators to him, was obtained through unconstitutional means, then his conviction would be vacated. Hasbajrami's case no longer represented an imminent threat—if it ever really did—but it remained unfinished business in the Eastern District.

PLAINCLOTHES COURT OFFICERS LED Agron Hasbajrami in from a paneled doorway along the wall. He looked bedraggled and slouching, like many would-be jihadis who appear in federal court; his untended beard made him appear much older than his thirty-one years. A good defendant is a quiet defendant, defense attorneys often say. Hasbajrami was not a quiet defendant. He had made a practice of writing letters to Gleeson, enclosing articles on everything from the IRA to the Norwegian mass murderer Anders Breivik. "A word is itself a shell, a holder of meaning," he wrote in one. "But the meaning is liable to change regard [sic] our perception our understanding. This is both the problem and the solutions."

In federal terror investigations, words aren't complex. They lack the elliptical paradox Hasbajrami described to the judge. This was keenly true in the era of electronic surveillance. Words are easily converted into data that can be stored, analyzed, mapped, and searched—where terms like "jihad," "virgins," and "wedding" project a distinct signal from the noise. In law enforcement terms, these words represent danger. Strung together in the wrong way, with the wrong context, the wrong intent, they become evidence.

While Hasbajrami might have been impetuous, he wasn't dim. The specter of a potential thirty-year-to-life sentence loomed over him in the months following his arrest. A plea would halve that. This was the so-called trial tax—the uniquely powerful system of incentives that prosecutors wield. Despite his misgivings, Hasbajrami pleaded guilty in 2012. Thirteen months after he had first been sentenced to fifteen years in prison, he'd received the letter from DuCharme acknowledging the government's error—seemingly too late to make any difference. The government called this "untimely," "far from ideal," and eventually "an unfortunate mistake"; Hasbajrami's lawyers weren't inclined to believe that. He had the choice to start over again, to risk trial. His counsel had decided that the best shot at freeing their client wasn't by putting him—an accused terrorist—in front of a jury. It was by pleading out once more, then appealing the basis of his conviction.

As Hasbajrami's—now second—sentencing approached, the Eastern District courthouse wound down into an August lull. From prison, Hasbajrami resumed his letter-writing campaign to Judge Gleeson. Hasbajrami wrote that his plea was "unvoluntary" and singled out Zissou, telling the judge that the attorney had ordered him to plea. "You will plea [sic] guilty. If you don't plea [sic], I am not coming to trial with you. You will go pro-se. Even if I come I will say you are guilty," Hasbajrami wrote that Zissou said. "Do you have a mental problem that you don't want to plea?"

Gleeson denied Hasbajrami's request to fire Zissou but made clear that Dratel would be lead counsel for the sentencing. The constitutional appeal—which Dratel had yet to file—loomed large. But the more immediate question remained whether Hasbajrami would receive the same fifteen-year sentence. Or whether Gleeson would use his discretion to impose more time.

Gleeson had seen men in Hasbajrami's position before. He'd sat as the judge in five post–September 11 terror cases and had other defendants awaiting trial before him. At the guilty plea weeks earlier, Gleeson's tone with Hasbajrami was patient yet vaguely exasperated. He explained that under the deal Hasbajrami faced twenty years and a lifetime of supervised release.

There was an element of theater in the moment. Hasbajrami's case was one of three in the country where disclosures on the use of FISA evidence raised constitutional issues. A Somali-born man named Mohamed Osman Mohamud, who also had not been notified of the

702 evidence, tried to attack his conviction at trial. He attempted to set off what he believed to be a car bomb in 2010 in Portland (FBI investigators had provided the decoy van). In a Colorado case, an Uzbek man, Jamshid Muhtorov, who had resettled in the United States as a refugee, was the first defendant to be notified that Section 702 NSA surveillance would be used against him. He sought to have the surveillance-born evidence suppressed at his upcoming trial for providing support to the Islamic Jihad Union. These men had parallel stories. Not just of government targeting, surveillance, and apprehension, but of exile from their homelands and disillusionment with the United States. And each had taken clear steps in supporting terrorism. Now their stories were linked by this constitutional issue.

When it came to the constitutional claims in Hasbajrami's case, Gleeson hadn't shown his hand on whether he thought the defendant had a viable argument. Several months earlier, Hasbajrami's attorney had appeared before the court with two attorneys from the ACLU, Patrick Toomey and Jameel Jaffer. Both prosecution and defense had argued the constitutional issues in filings with Gleeson, but the hearing provided an opportunity for them to make the case in person. The ACLU argued that the FISA Amendments Act violated the Fourth Amendment: that the Constitution protected privacy interests for those in the United States communicating abroad, that a warrant would need to be sought to obtain this type of information, that the sweeping and broad targeting methods constituted an unreasonable search.

DuCharme welcomed the litigation as an opportunity—post-Snowden—for the government to demystify state surveillance powers. While DuCharme felt an obligation to protect the methods he and his colleagues used to hunt suspected terrorists, he recognized the collateral damage of the secrecy surrounding them. The failure to communicate with the public engendered distrust in the government that frankly, he felt, was unwarranted. Other national security prosecutors expressed frustration at the pushback from the civil rights community on 702 collection, because the other warrantless alternatives—conducting physical surveillance and bumping up on a target with an informant—were arguably more invasive.

"We want people to have confidence in the integrity of our programs, the reasonableness of our programs and the constitutionality of our programs," he said to Gleeson, arguing against Hasbajrami's motion to suppress statements obtained through warrantless surveillance.

Hasbajrami's other defender, Michael Bachrach, stood to counter the constitutional point. When it came time to explain section 702 surveillance to Gleeson, Bachrach also turned to a film:

> There is a movie and a book right now that is very popular. It's called *American Sniper*. And I think a sniper is a good analogy to the FAA program. A sniper targets a very specific target who is supposed to be a foreigner or an enemy of the state. The FAA ostensibly targets, if it's working properly, a noncitizen abroad. But the way the FAA does it is, instead of using a sniper's rifle, it uses a machine gun. Instead of using a scope, it puts on a blindfold. And instead of targeting foreign persons abroad, it turns around with the machine gun and just sprays across at anything it can hit on U.S. soil. That is not constitutional, Your Honor. That is not consistent with the Fourth Amendment. And it's certainly not consistent with when the defendant individually specifically, in this case, is a U.S. person who at all times relevant to this case is on U.S. soil.

Gleeson denied Hasbajrami's motion. He didn't issue a ruling immediately, so his rationale remained unclear. Once Hasbajrami pleaded out, Gleeson wouldn't need to rule. The case would then belong to the Second Circuit. And the judge's views on the government's surveillance powers would remain his own—which left the remaining task of Hasbajrami's now second sentencing.

At a sentencing, a defense attorney's job is to surface every conceivable piece of positive information about a client. Even before a defendant comes to court, the judge is papered over with letters from friends, family, and colleagues. In some cases, the family will make a showing, prostrating themselves in the front row of the courtroom, dressed as if attending a funeral, a focused desperate anticipation written into their expressions. At sentencings where defenders have little material to work with, the counsel can only repeat slight variations on the same facts and themes, running the clock as if the longer they speak about their client, the more likely the judge will see the humanity of the captive.

At this point, having taken his guilty plea twice and sentenced him once before, Gleeson was more than familiar with Hasbajrami's humanity. Dratel could only ask him to impose the same sentence he had once before. "It was reasonable then. And the same sentence is reasonable now," Dratel said.

DuCharme wouldn't cede that ground to the defense counsel. Hasbajrami's reversals had dragged out the case three years longer than anyone had anticipated. The impending appeal only promised further delay of a final resolution. In a moment of candor, DuCharme alluded to the fact that his office had more immediate national security issues to deal with than Hasbajrami.

"When this defendant came to our attention, we were in a brisk counterterrorism landscape and, frankly, that landscape has only become more challenging," he said. The office cut a plea with Hasbajrami, DuCharme said, to "allow us to redirect our attention to other terrorist threats . . . we struck a bargain that we thought was a fair one.

"Now we've got a chance to do this again," he said. "We ought to give the judge discretion to impose a sentence."

Hasbajrami looked on silently. There was little he could do or say in that moment. Gleeson looked down and said, "I'm going to impose a sentence of sixteen years, just so you know the punch line."

His original sentence of fifteen years would stand. But Hasbajrami's claim against Zissou required the judge to act.

Gleeson called Hasbajrami's allegation "false . . . preposterous . . . a lie."

"The last year of your sentence you can chalk up to that statement, Mr. Hasbajrami," Gleeson said.

With that, Agron Hasbajrami's four years appearing before Judge Gleeson came to an end. The parties filed out into the hallway. Dratel fielded questions from reporters, like a college professor chatting with eager students after class. The other 702 cases had split results: the Supreme Court declined to hear the case involving Mohamud in Portland, while the Uzbek refugee Muhtorov was convicted after six years of pretrial litigation, which he appealed to the Tenth Circuit. Has-bajrami's ultimate fate, in fact, wouldn't be decided by Gleeson—or any Eastern District judge for that matter. The Second Circuit would hear his case in the coming months. DuCharme and his colleagues, meanwhile, stepped into the elevator together to walk across the street and get back to work.

14

Shkin

The defendant's shouts bled through the door and into the
courtroom. Clapping, banging, screaming, guttural utterings,
affronts to the quiet decorum of a federal court. Assistant U.S.
Attorney Shreve Ariail paced along the government's table at the center
of the room. The commotion continued. A few moments earlier, the
defense attorney David Stern had disappeared behind the door in an
attempt to speak with his client. He returned, a look of exasperation
painted across his face as he reentered the courtroom, taking his seat
next to his co-counsel Joshua Dratel, who was quietly studying a set
of papers. Ariail didn't know what was going on behind the door. He
did know that on the way across the bridge from the MCC in Manhattan, the defendant had tried to kick out the marshal's van window.
And then he tore his pants off, which would make it difficult for the
defendant to appear. The defense attorneys were worried about their
client's sanity, but Ariail was worried that the defendant was trying to
sabotage any chance for a trial.

This case had been dragging on for nearly five years. But it was
important for the government to prove that it could succeed in federal
court.

In the summer of 2011, Ariail set off on this journey, boarding a van in Palermo, Italy, and settling in for the three-and-a-half-hour journey to a prison complex in Agrigento, a small Sicilian city on a rocky plateau overlooking the Mediterranean. A group had traveled with him: the FBI special agents Burt LaCroix and Greg Paciorek with New York's Joint Terrorism Task Force, the Justice Department's Rome attaché William Nardini, a government Hausa translator, and Ariail's supervisor from the Eastern District of New York, David Bitkower. If all went as planned, in a few hours this group of agents and prosecutors would be interrogating a senior al-Qaeda suspect. Ariail, then thirty-five, was witty and intense, with a self-deprecating charisma. This softened an otherwise unapologetic competitive drive that often exasperated defense counsel. He had played linebacker during college—a conference all-star for two years—and, even in routine hearings, tended to scan the courtroom as if he were looking for a clean tackle.

The day after taking office in January 2009, President Obama signed an executive order ordering the closure of the detention facility at Guantánamo Bay. The action, which was the president's fourth executive order, placed the attorney general in charge of the complex process of reviewing each detainee and coordinating with the other branches of government on how best to remove them from Defense Department custody. This represented a clear departure from the Bush administration's failed experiment with the military tribunal system, but also a step into the politically uncertain prospect of bringing accused al-Qaeda members out of a secret system and into the public arena.

Shortly after that, the office assigned Ariail to the Guantanamo Review Task Force, to assess the legal options for detainees. He was one of fewer than a dozen federal prosecutors from around the country assigned to work on this controversial objective, pairing up with the intelligence community and other law enforcement agencies to parse through the detainees' cases, selecting among them those viable for prosecutions in federal court. Among the most damning issues surrounding the detainees was torture: the presence of physical violence during detention and interrogation threatened the viability of any prosecution. The task force eventually pitched Attorney General Eric

Holder on military commission cases the office felt it could win in federal court. The group's report ultimately presaged Holder's showdown with Congress, which stepped in to effectively outlaw civilian trials for Guantánamo detainees.

The counterterrorism landscape looked very different in 2011. Even after the death of bin Laden, the future of al-Qaeda and its franchises remained an active question for law enforcement. Meanwhile, the Arab Spring had drastically altered the political balance throughout the Middle East. At first, there appeared to be a positive shift toward democracy. But as regimes began to crumble, Islamist groups seized on the emerging power vacuums to draw in recruits from throughout the region and North Africa. In West Africa, Boko Haram and al-Qaeda in the Islamic Maghreb similarly exploited weakly governed spaces to wage terror attacks and seize territory. Libya appeared to be next to crumble. The Qaddafi regime struggled to hold on to power, yet few people asked what, if anything, would follow his eccentric if stable brand of autocracy and what that could mean for the security of Europe and the United States.

The task force wasn't Ariail's only exposure to accused terrorists. Weeks before arriving in Italy, Ariail had just won his first conviction in a material support case against Betim Kaziu, the Brooklyn man who had traveled to Cairo intent to link up with a terror group, and had seen how conventional law enforcement could work as a counterterrorism strategy. Arriving at Agrigento, Ariail and his team had a nearly unheard-of opportunity: to question a first-generation al-Qaeda operative who hadn't been tainted by detention at Guantánamo.

EARLIER THAT SUMMER, the *Excelsior,* a cruise liner, docked in Lampedusa, Italy. The ship's passengers weren't tourists on holiday but hundreds of migrants arriving from Libya. As civil war unfolded in Libya, the regime opened the door for migrants to make the short but dangerous journey across the Mediterranean to Europe. Displaced Africans had flooded the closest destination, the arid island of Lampedusa, the southernmost in the Sicilian chain, for several months: the first wave fleeing the Tunisian uprising less than one hundred miles from the island's cliff-bound shoreline, the second wave pouring in from Tripoli. The journey was nearly twice that distance, but close enough to lure thousands of Africans targeted with reprisals in the waning hours of Qaddafi's regime.

Aboard the *Excelsior,* a man paced an upper deck alone. A dark-skinned African with a round face, broad nose, and recently trimmed beard, wearing a dark blue track jacket and royal blue pants. He carried with him a Koran. An antiterrorism officer posted to the ship noticed there was something different about this figure. He was alone and didn't appear to be connected to any particular group of passengers. The officer's primary concern that evening was the potential for ethnic violence. The fractious mix of twelve hundred passengers from North and sub-Saharan Africa was watched over by only fourteen security officers. His team had also separated the single women from the single men to prevent sexual assault. It was outside that holding area where the officer first took notice of the man. He approached the officer and, in English, said, "Water?"

The officer noticed a scar on both sides of the man's arm—what appeared to be exit and entry wounds from a bullet.

The officer gestured to the passenger's arm and asked in English, "What happened?"

The passenger lifted his shirt to reveal more scars. He had not been arrested or even detained, but he explained to the officer that he had received the scars "fighting American soldiers." He was an al-Qaeda fighter, he boasted. *Ibrahim Suleiman Adnan Adam Harun Hausa.* He even had a nom de guerre: Spin Ghul, which translated to "white rose" in Pashto.

Several weeks later, Ariail and the team of Americans arrived in Agrigento. The prison was a football-stadium-size complex on a hillside above a city dotted with palm trees and fifth-century ruins. Inside the courtroom, the American team stepped into a distinctly Sicilian scene: the chamber sat beneath the prison complex. This was a precaution against the type of bombing that had killed Italy's top Mafia prosecutor in the 1980s. The room was nonetheless relaxed. Other than the Americans, only a handful of people were seated in the vast space built to conduct mass trials of mafiosi. Ariail noticed that the judge overseeing the proceedings wasn't wearing a robe. He wasn't even wearing a tie. He presided with an open shirt collar as if he were having coffee at a sidewalk café. When the proceedings did pause for a coffee break, the team didn't move to a windowless kitchen with a paper cup coffee machine. Instead, the prison housed a fully appointed bar where a barista served espresso and cappuccino in immaculate porcelain dishware. If the attorneys weren't on duty, they could order a glass of wine or Campari.

The name "Spin Ghul" meant something to the team. When the FBI first received the call from the Italians earlier that summer about a mysterious African who had turned up in custody, the Americans had intelligence on a fighter of that name and knew that at a minimum what he had to say was important. Hausa had been cooperative with the Italians, but there were no guarantees that he'd feel the same about speaking to Americans, particularly after a long summer in an Italian prison. Washington fast-tracked a mutual legal assistance request for approval by the Italians, and, surprisingly, the approvals came within a few weeks. But as Ariail and his colleagues prepared for the inter-rogation, they knew that they'd likely get only one bite at the apple. Each question would count.

When Hausa, who shared a surname with his language group, was led in, he sat on a large stool and began listening. He wore the same track pants and looked tousled, less like a prisoner than an indigent traveler waylaid on his journey. As Ariail explained Hausa's *Miranda* rights, the words were sent through a translation daisy chain: into Ital-ian for the judge and the African language for the suspect, then going back through the process before being finally translated into English.

"Are you FBI, CIA, or police?" Hausa asked Ariail.

"No," he said. "I'm a lawyer with the Department of Justice in the United States."

Then Ariail clarified: "The attorneys who represent you in Italy are both Italian. And I want to just make it clear that you can consult with your Italian attorneys if you have questions."

"I'm not concerned with, uh, the Italian lawyers or the Italian judge," Hausa responded. "I want to be handed over to the Americans."

It was a bold statement. Hausa had never intended to travel to Italy nor the United States for that matter.

"I'd first like to ask you," Ariail began. "When did you first go to Afghanistan?"

"Two weeks before September 11," Hausa responded.

He spoke with the Americans for several hours. His journey to jihad had begun in Saudi Arabia a decade earlier, Hausa explained. As a Nigerien, he had been raised as a foreigner in the kingdom. He first heard the call to jihad at age twelve. His boyhood imagination built up the mujahideen fighting the Soviets in Afghanistan into heroes. When he was old enough, he longed to join them. Eventually, that desire carried him to Pakistan and the mountains of Afghanistan. His timing to join the next phase of jihad could not have been better. As the September 11 attacks unfolded in New York and Washington, he found himself in an al-Qaeda guesthouse in Afghanistan, a recruit for the next phase in the war.

As the Nigerien responded to Ariail's questions, an even more remarkable story line emerged. Hausa recounted how he had trained and fought for al-Qaeda as a frontline soldier until being wounded. He convalesced for several months in Pakistan, during a critical period in the development of al-Qaeda's strategy. His journey put him into direct contact with some of bin Laden's most trusted deputies including Abu Zubaydah, Abdul Hadi al-Iraqi, and Abu Faraj al-Libi. The group directed its operatives to expand globally in order to strike Western targets with acts of terror. Hausa then returned to Africa for two years—surveilling American diplomatic targets in Nigeria. His objective was twofold: to launch an attack modeled after the 1998 embassy bombings and to meet with local al-Qaeda affiliates to strike alliances. By 2005, to be an al-Qaeda member meant to live as a global fugitive. After Nigerian officials arrested a cohort returning from a trip to Pakistan following a meeting with the terrorist group's leadership, Hausa fled to Niger and then crossed into Libya en route to Europe. Qaddafi's security forces arrested him almost immediately. He spent the next six years imprisoned.

The confession he had made aboard the *Excelsior* about fighting

Americans wasn't a hollow boast. Hausa described in detail cross-ing the Pakistani border to stage rocket attacks at an American base situated in an Afghan valley. He recounted how an American unit stumbled onto their encampment, setting off a close-quarters firefight with Hausa and his two comrades. The battle quickly escalated into an artillery bombardment that left him wounded and one of his fel-low fighters dead. Hausa's memory hadn't faded in the intervening years: he described an Apache helicopter circling before the fighting began and, later, an F-16 overflying his position but not dropping any munitions. It was just one of the thousands of firefights in the decade-long war. But Hausa could not remember the date. As Ariail tried to narrow in on this vital piece of information, the translator said that it was at a time when "Ramses the Fifth" visited American forces in Afghanistan.

The American team could make little sense of the reference. Was it a nickname? An alias? The name of an operation? As they pulled apart the translation, it became clear that Hausa had tried to say "Rums-feld," not "Ramses." The then secretary of defense had visited Kabul in August 2003, a fact that provided the team with a critical window to narrow their search.

During breaks in the proceeding, the team of Americans searched for information to corroborate Hausa's claims. Ariail and Bitkower came across a two-part interview published by the Combat Studies Institute at Fort Leavenworth with an Eighty-Second Airborne officer, Major Gregory Trahan. The details in the transcript roughly lined up with elements of Hausa's story. In it, the major described a mission to locate the source of rocket fire that had been targeting Trahan's forward operating base near Shkin, a hamlet along the border with Pakistan, on August 25, 2003. His platoon eventually located the posi-tion on a hillside outside the village.

"When we got there, we found a camp that had been set up. There were canteens all over the place. There were burlap sacks that these guys were using for either camouflage or sleeping bags . . . Right then, that's when we started taking machine gun fire," the interview read. Another element in his platoon spotted three fighters near Trahan's position, he recounted.

When the prosecutors returned to the courtroom, they pressed Hausa for details of the ambush. He didn't hesitate.

"We were face to face when I started shooting at the American, uh . . . I took that grenade and threw it at them," he said.

The transcript from Trahan's interview offered a parallel version, albeit from a different perspective: "Some guys popped up from behind a hillside about 50 meters away from me, and they threw hand grenades and fired AK-47s at me. I was hit twice in the right leg and once in the left leg. One bullet also went into my helmet, grazed my head and then lodged on the outside."

Hausa described how he had "heard one of the American soldiers talking possibly on a radio. I think, uh, he was, uh, talking to some of the individuals at the base that's close to us."

Trahan's testimony continued: "I crawled back to where my FSO [fire support officer] was . . . told him to call for fire for effect on the location I pointed to."

The three al-Qaeda fighters were quickly overwhelmed by the American counterattack. One blast killed a fighter nearly instantly. Both Hausa and the remaining fighter sustained blast injuries when they decided to evacuate, to escape the artillery barrage. "We could hear, uh, Apaches, and we could hear rounds, other rounds also coming to our direction."

When the fighting stopped, two Americans were dead, Airman Ray Losano and Private Jerod Dennis. Trahan's platoon suffered several other casualties; medics evacuated the major, who had been shot several times. His deployment came to an end on that hillside, but he would return to Afghanistan. Hausa, for his part, barely escaped the battlefield with his life.

Typically, war stories end like this. Survivors walk away. The life-altering experience of combat leaves them with little more than their memories. But Ariail and his team at Agrigento wanted to write a new chapter. The memories of that ambush on a hillside outside the village of Shkin, Afghanistan, would become evidence to charge Hausa with murder.

The following March, the Italian government authorized the extradition of Adnan Harun Hausa to the United States. That, in and of itself, reflected a new chapter in counterterrorism cooperation between the two countries. Their relationship had deteriorated after the CIA botched a rendition operation in Milan in 2004. The agency kidnapped Abu Omar, an Egyptian cleric, off a city street near his home and rendered him into Egyptian custody, where he claimed to have been tortured. An Italian court convicted the operatives involved in absentia, and in September 2012 the nation's highest court upheld the guilty verdict, leaving open the question of whether Italy would seek the extradition of American citizens involved in the operation.

Yet the Italians went ahead with Hausa's extradition. When he landed in New York, he knew nothing of the country's legal system. Or about the rights that the Constitution guaranteed criminal defendants. His knowledge of American justice had been defined by the extrajudicial system created by the CIA and the Department of Defense with black sites and detention facilities at Bagram Air Base and Guantánamo. He could reasonably expect his career as an al-Qaeda operative to end in one of two ways: he'd be assassinated in a drone strike or a covert raid, or he'd be detained, indefinitely, deprived of due process. That had been the fate of the original members of al-Qaeda whom he knew from his pre–September 11 days in Afghanistan. The Obama administration Justice Department had no intention of transferring Hausa to Saudi or Nigerien custody. Nor did it seek to imprison him at a black site or Guantánamo Bay. It had an entirely different idea: an open trial in the Eastern District of New York.

UPON HIS ARRIVAL in Brooklyn, Hausa continued talking. He had been arraigned in secret on a six-count indictment including the conspiracy to murder U.S. nationals and providing material support to al-Qaeda. He then sat down with Ariail and an FBI agent, accompanied by Joshua Dratel and David Stern, more than twenty times to negotiate a plea. (Ariail had gone to trial against Stern in the Kaziu case.) The meetings provided a window into al-Qaeda's external operations while detailing Hausa's efforts to coordinate with West African terrorist groups and case potential American targets in Nigeria. But after nearly two years, Hausa suddenly stopped cooperating.

In May 2013, he finally appeared before Judge Edward Korman in an open courtroom. Korman, a seventy-year-old former U.S. Attorney in the Eastern District, had some experience with terrorism defendants. More than twenty years earlier, FBI agents found the judge's name alongside the name of his Eastern District colleague Judge Jack Weinstein on a list of Jewish public officials maintained by El Sayyid Nosair, the man convicted in the assassination of Meir Kahane. Hausa had no interest in appearing before him. He looked dejected and defiant as it dawned on him that he was not going to Guantánamo to, in effect, join al-Qaeda's Martyrs' Row. He immediately made a demand of the judge.

"Hand me over to a military court, so I would know what is going to happen to me. Even if I die like Osama Bin Laden," he said.

Korman had no authority to do so. While Congress had forbidden the transfer of al-Qaeda suspects held at Guantánamo to the United States to face trial, there was little it could do to stop someone like Hausa from appearing in a civilian court. Hausa's appearance in Korman's courtroom was a quiet repudiation of the American military tribunal concept but also a propaganda defeat for al-Qaeda, who relied on Guantánamo as an enduring symbol of injustice.

The al-Qaeda manual gave operatives clear instructions on how to confront the legal process: counter the prosecution's efforts with misinformation and deception by filing false complaints of mistreatment and torture. An article in al-Qaeda in Yemen's magazine published following Hausa's capture in Libya further instructed detainees that "brothers should also try to appeal to the prison administration with every issue or demand—for if you do not preoccupy them, then they will preoccupy you . . . you will find that they will try to avoid you and will not try to confront you in order not to have to solve your problem. They will feel that they are winning, while actually, you are the ones who benefit." Prison, in al-Qaeda doctrine, was an extension of the war, and Guantánamo Bay was the final battlefield for the group's luminaries like Khalid Sheikh Mohammed, Ramzi bin al-Shibh, and Abu Zubaydah. Hausa wanted to be among these men.

"I have something to say," Hausa cut in. "It is possible that you're forgetting something. I am a warrior, and the war is not over." The defendant meandered, asking for the return of his Koran and stating that "the CIA came and worked on me in Libya."

During captivity, by Hausa's account, the CIA sought to recruit him as "a secret agent." He also claimed to have met with French and Italian intelligence officials. Hausa's recollection of this time—which includes allegations that he was injected with psychoactive drugs and subjected to a machine that could read his mind—remains unverified. (The Department of Defense investigated similar allegations made by terrorism suspects in its custody and found that some had been administered drugs as treatment for mental health conditions, then interrogated, but did not conclude the purpose of the drugs was to aid interrogation.) U.S. officials also acknowledged that the CIA did provide Hausa with a copy of the Koran while he was in custody.

(Hausa, in fact, had lost a Koran on the battlefield at Shkin. It was among the detritus picked up by Trahan's men after the firefight. When the unit prepared to leave Afghanistan, nobody had claimed the items. A private packed the Koran, as well as prayer beads, a knife, and an ammunition rack, as a memento of his deployment to bring home. In 2012, the FBI tracked down the soldier. He showed them the footlocker of his keepsakes from Afghanistan; the agents bagged each as evidence. After each had been turned over, a forensic technician with the FBI examined the Koran. On the first pass, the analyst found one fingerprint. On the second pass, she found five readable prints. Each matched Adnan Harun Hausa.)

Hausa's attorney, Susan Kellman, could do little to stop her client. He hovered closely to implicating himself before the court but remained hung up on the issue of the Koran.

"The Koran I had was a special Koran," he said.

Kellman clarified: "It has like commentary or something, Your Honor . . . like the Talmud."

It was a moment far outside the al-Qaeda martyrdom narrative. An operative standing in an American courtroom, represented by a Jewish woman who likened his holy book to the commentary provided to the Torah. But it was lost on Hausa.

"Yeah," he agreed.

The judge did not have the authority to hand Hausa over to the military unilaterally. Nor was that the government's interest. Hausa had been brought to the United States to face the criminal justice system. He found a new battlefield.

FOR FOUR YEARS, Adnan Harun Hausa continued to wage his jihad from solitary confinement on 10 South in Manhattan's Metropolitan Correctional Center—focusing his anger on the federal court system. He did everything in his limited power to derail the proceedings. He stopped bathing to make handling him more unpleasant for prison officers, an IRA tactic. Eventually, Hausa refused to cooperate with his lawyers, shouting them down and, at the sight of his lone female attorney, Susan Kellman, becoming enraged.

At the May 2016 status conference several months before the trial, Hausa fought with guards and marshals as they forced him into a vehicle to be transferred to the courthouse. The new judge overseeing the case, Brian Cogan, attempted to move ahead with the conference with Hausa's shouts audible through the door. When Cogan relented to have the defendant appear via video feed at a subsequent appearance, Hausa sat quietly in his cell, then, after learning that he was being broadcast to the courtroom, resumed shouting until the judge had to silence his microphone. Judge Cogan ordered the trial to proceed in the defendant's absence, which he would have access to via a live video feed, a team of two translators softly repeating the proceedings back to him in his native language, Hausa.

Hausa's obstructionism sabotaged his defense as well. His refusal to cooperate with his attorneys made it impossible even to begin the process of investigating the government's allegations. Had he been forthcoming, the defense would have faced the daunting prospect of conducting an extraterritorial investigation in some of the most dangerous places on the planet for Westerners to venture: the border regions of Afghanistan and Pakistan, post-revolution Libya. But the team did see Hausa's defiance as a potential defense—that years of torture, brutal detention, and isolation had left his sanity shattered.

The question of Hausa's competence had been litigated in the weeks before his trial. The government presented three experts to affirm that he was sufficiently sane to face a trial, while the defense countered with a lone psychologist offering a dissenting view. That psychologist, Dr. Jess Ghannam, shared a language with the defendant: Arabic. Ghannam opined that the court should view Hausa's behavior in a cultural context that the other psychologists lacked the ability to perceive. Ghannam, a Palestinian American, concluded that some of Hausa's conduct—public defecation and masturbation—was such an affront to Islam that each indicated he had paranoid schizophrenia. During cross-examination Ghannam faced withering questioning from the government about the psychologist's political activism on U.S. policy in the Middle East. Eventually, the judge ruled that because of these opinions he was "not credible." The judge, instead, found Hausa competent. He relied in part on his observations of the defendant, who had shown the ability to modulate between cooperation and tantrums.

"It is the game he plays," Judge Cogan wrote in his decision.

HAUSA WASN'T ALONE in his preference for Guantánamo Bay. By the time his case went to trial, the new American president, Donald Trump, championed the prison as an emblem of a get-tough approach to terrorism. His administration had rejected the Obama administration's view that the prison should be shut down, the remaining prisoners released or tried. After winning the Nevada primary, Trump promised to keep Guantánamo Bay open, saying, "We're gonna load it up with some bad dudes, believe me, we're gonna load it up."

Trump's vision stopped at that. There was no discussion of legal process, no recognition of the complex diplomatic negotiations required to release suspects, no acknowledgment of the most damning fact: military commissions did not function as effective courts of justice. Attorney General Jeff Sessions had a longer history with the issue. As a member of the Senate Judiciary Committee, he consistently endorsed Guantánamo and the military tribunal system—visiting Camp X-Ray in 2002, rejecting claims of systematic abuse in 2005, and at the outset of the Obama administration warning of the dangers of returning to a "pre-9/11" approach to prosecuting terrorists. His views on the subject were out of step with the law. The Supreme Court rejected one argument that Sessions relied on—that the pre–Geneva Convention tribunal prosecution of eight German saboteurs in 1942 provided a legal template for military commissions. The attorney general harbored a troubling and simplistic view on detainee abuse, arguing that guards do occasionally "overstep their bounds . . . [i]t happens in American prisons every day" but that conduct should be dealt with at the individual level and was not a policy concern. Sessions's belief that Guantánamo kept Americans safe had also been rejected. The prison had created a symbolic language of injustice for an entire generation of jihadists. The orange jumpsuit pictured on bound, blindfolded, and kneeling detainees at Guantánamo first appeared in al-Qaeda's videotaped execution of the American contractor Nicholas Berg in 2004. From there it became a staple of ISIS execution videos, worn by Western hostages like James Foley and Steven Sotloff and Syrian and Jordanian captives. A Pentagon official told Congress in 2015 that the orange jumpsuits were "believed by many to be the symbol of the Guantanamo detention facility." Federal trials of terrorism suspects had yet to produce such resonant imagery.

Few attorneys in the United States understood the importance of this as viscerally as Joshua Dratel. Five years before Hausa's case went to trial, he wrote a forceful rejection of the use of these tribunals in an essay for *The University of Toledo Law Review*, arguing, "The military commissions constitute a shipwreck forever grounded on unfriendly and unforgiving shoals—not only legally, but also logistically and in the court of international opinion. There they should remain, a curious archaeological artifact standing as an object lesson to insufficient and myopic planning and equally inept implementation." He identified several "myths" associated with tribunals: that the courts were better suited to handling classified material, better vehicles for delivering justice, that convictions would come easy, and sentences would be harsh, that the tribunals better served long-term national security interests and would show the world that terrorists were in a separate, distinct criminal category. The commission's record spoke for itself: in the fifteen years after September 11, more than 550 defendants accused of terrorism-related crimes had been tried before federal courts with little incident. In that same time, tribunals had completed three prosecutions; two were reversed on appeal, with one having a single charge—for conspiracy—reaffirmed.

Perhaps the most binding criticism, that al-Qaeda would manipulate our democracy's trial system to provide terrorists a soapbox for propaganda, had yet to materialize. Hausa, for his part, refused even to attend his trial as it opened in March 2017, nearly six years after his arrest. The judge declined to compel the defendant's presence. Hausa's absence seemed to show what little opportunity for propaganda he saw in a federal trial.

ON THE FIRST DAY of the trial, Assistant U.S. Attorney Matthew Jacobs, the most junior member of Ariail's prosecution team, took on the responsibility of delivering the opening statement. The government had won a small victory in securing an anonymous jury pool. The panel of jurors, casually dressed and, for the moment, paying close attention, watched the young prosecutor approach the jury box.

"The defendant is an Al Qaeda terrorist whose mission is to kill Americans," he said.

In any other trial, the prosecutor would then turn and point to the defendant seated at the table with his counsel. Instead, that seat sat empty.

Before the trial began, the judge had given a brief explanation of the defendant's absence and instructed the jury to infer nothing from it. Instead, Jacobs pointed the jury to a photograph. The image, a mug shot, left little to the imagination: in it Hausa stared blankly at the camera, eyes half shut, a faint beard and his dark-coffee complexion reflecting the camera's flash. Appearances matter in criminal trials. In fact, defendants had the right to appear in civilian clothes at trial— a right secured with a 1976 Supreme Court ruling—and to connect with a jury on the most basic level, as a human being sitting within the same room. The photograph heightened the aura of danger around Hausa.

Susan Kellman tried to defuse some of the tension in the courtroom as she rose to deliver her opening. She approached the jurors with a smile. In her mid-sixties, Kellman channeled the image of a funky aunt, wearing a multicolored jacket and her hair in a blond bob. Her voice was friendly but carried an edge, familiar but firm. She opened with a story: she spent the day before, a Sunday, at the gym with a friend walking the treadmill. Her friend suggested they go to a movie, but Kellman explained that she had a trial—her client was an accused terrorist, in fact.

"How do you sleep with yourself?" her friend asked in New Yorkese.

"Here in America every defendant is presumed innocent," Kellman explained to the jury. Her job was to act like a lifeguard, protecting clients from drowning in a "sea of prejudice."

Turning to Hausa, she said, "Our client pledged his allegiance to Al Qaeda," offering a shrug. "If you convict him of material support, so be it."

She ceded significant ground on the terrorism charge but did not yield the other, arguably more serious offenses. Those the government would need to prove.

But she warned that did not change the obligation of the jury. "You will not allow prejudice to be a substitute for truth."

DURING A LUNCH BREAK, Jerry Dennis sat alone on a wooden bench across the street from the Eastern District courthouse, drawing on a cigarette and taking long sips from a cup of cola. He wore his light bomber jacket open, a gingham button-down underneath, a baseball cap that read "OU Law" covering his scalp from the sun. His son, J. Renley Dennis, attended Oklahoma University's law school. Underneath his shirt, dog tags bearing the name of his other son Jerod Dennis hung from his neck along with a bronze arrowhead. It was on a bright clear spring day like this thirteen years earlier that his son was killed on a hillside along the Afghanistan and Pakistan border.

Dennis had been sitting through testimony in the case against Adnan Harun Hausa for a day and a half. But this morning had been particularly difficult. One after another, members of his son's unit took the witness stand to recount the events of April 25, 2003. Several strode into court in their dress blues, rows of medals lined up across their chests, Airborne pins affixed below their pockets; others appeared in

off-the-rack suits; a medic wore blue jeans and a pressed shirt. None of
them had difficulty recalling the furious minutes of that day.

The testimony was building toward Jerod's last moments. His father
had heard the story in pieces from different members of the unit since
losing his son. But he'd never heard the day stitched together, detail
by detail, from multiple perspectives. Jerry likened it to listening to
people recount a car accident, minor variations of facts that ultimately
align into a tragic result. As he sat on the bench, waiting to return for
the final testimony of the day, he recounted the impact of losing a son.

"I wasn't right for a while there," he said, his voice a gentle, husky
drawl. He marveled at the ability of the human mind to persevere—his
eyes lifting a little. His face was rugged and sun worn, a tightly cropped
gray mustache barely visible as he spoke. The army was Jerod's idea,
his father recalled. At seventeen, Jerod took a military aptitude test
at high school, and soon after a recruiter turned up at the house. The
soldier asked Jerry's permission to take his son to the recruiting center
in Oklahoma City. The recruiter needed Jerry's signature to take Jerod
on the trip. Dennis had done his service, a combat tour in Vietnam in
1968. He knew what that signature meant: Jerod could not only go
to Oklahoma City but enlist. Sure enough, when Jerod arrived at the
recruiting center, he called his parents. He wanted to become a soldier.
Jerry tried to put the decision off until his son came home so that they
could talk it over with his mother. Jerod couldn't wait.

"You know how kids are," he said, smiling faintly. He stubbed
out his cigarette, stood up, and returned to the courthouse to take the
elevator to Judge Cogan's courtroom.

Gregory Trahan took the stand in his army service uniform, pressed
blue slacks and a dark navy jacket with gold detailing and an array of
medals across his chest. In a typical criminal case, the only article
of clothing in a courtroom that carries deference is the judge's robe—
a symbolic separation from the rest of the participants that also serves
as a reminder of the judge's loyalty to the law and the Constitution.
The military uniform introduced a new element to the jury, a separate
moral order from the criminal justice system.

The uniform also symbolized the challenge the defense faced at
trial. The witnesses called that day were combat veterans who were,

by their status in society, unimpeachable. The defense attorney's role is to do just that: to impeach witnesses, to establish reasonable doubt around any evidence the witnesses brought into a case. It is one thing to hold a convicted mobster over the barrel for testimony he provides against a former boss; it is another to press a decorated combat veteran on testimony against a client perceived to be an enemy of the state. The issue also heightened the fundamental weakness of the defense case: the absence of the defendant. Without hearing a word of testimony, one could reasonably infer from Colonel Trahan's presence that he was a hero and from Adnan Harun Hausa's absence that he was a coward.

The judge, Brian Cogan, recognized the issue. But he also recognized that the uniform left him few good choices. "I've had police captains come in here in uniforms and lots of chest candy on it," he told the attorneys at sidebar before the testimony began. "I think to single out the U.S. military to tell them how to dress would not be appropriate."

Over the next six hours, the jury heard detailed testimony of the combat on April 25, 2003. Trahan was now a colonel. But he recalled the last moments of his command at Firebase Shkin, when he stepped to the edge of a slope and into gunfire.

"If you could visualize walking in a, you know, rain shower then looking down at the pavement and seeing the water kind of jump up," he said, stoically. "That's what I saw all around me."

As Assistant U.S. Attorney Melody Wells questioned him, he recounted seeing the enemy within "ten to fifteen meters" of his position. "I remember, ma'am, was that they had a bushy beard that's—and were kind of dark-skinned, like they had been in the sun for a long time," he said.

Trahan described being quickly cut down by the fire. "I was shot twice in my right leg, once in my left leg, and then a bullet entered inside my helmet and then grazed around and behind and then ended up lodging it in the left side of my helmet, ma'am," he said.

In his testimony Conrad Reed, a sergeant, recounted the moment Trahan fell. "All I saw was from the back of [Trahan's] body from the legs was generally a, like, a red mist like kind of spray out from behind him as we heard gunfire kind of pick up again," he said.

"I saw his legs come out from underneath him, he hit the ground and rolled back behind the rocks that he was behind," David Cyr, a sergeant, testified. He remembered seeing his commander on the ground grimacing in pain and ran to his aid. Trahan was still conscious, absorbing the fact that he had led his element directly into the enemy's line of fire. The image rattled the young soldier assessing his injuries.

"Sergeant Cyr, calm the fuck down," the commander said.

By the time Trahan was evacuated down the hill, he was drifting in and out of consciousness as the firefight raged on the hillside above them.

Lee Blackwell, a twenty-one-year air force veteran, testified in civilian clothes. But he sat straight up, his posture fixed as if he were appearing before his commanding officers. He and Ray Losano were the only two airmen on the scene that day. Their role was to guide any aircraft brought in for air strikes. But, he recounted, within moments of leaving their vehicles, the men found themselves under fire "from all different directions, hand grenades, AK-47s, RPGs."

Blackwell appeared nervous, speaking quickly, as he described for the court calling in air support, instinctively falling back on military jargon.

"I told Ray, I said, 'Call Tombstone, tell them troops in contact, and we'll 1972 enable,' " he said.

The prosecutor questioning him, Matthew Jacobs, steered to the events unfolding on the ground. Blackwell paged through his memories, describing how he and Losano sprinted for cover at a nearby Humvee, where the two lay down next to the front tire, watching insurgents approaching, firing on their position. When Blackwell opened the Humvee door to speak to the driver, bullets slammed into the vehicle's armor, he recalled, while he stood on the opposite side. He heard Losano call out that two F-16s were five minutes away. As he was telling Losano to use his backpack as cover, a bullet struck the Humvee's .50-caliber machine gunner in the helmet, knocking him unconscious. Blackwell had climbed into the vehicle to help the gunner when he felt the Humvee door slam on him.

"I'm looking through the window, really thick glass, and I can see Ray sitting back. He is kicking at the door," he recalled. "He is holding his face, a lot of blood. He has been shot in the face."

The courtroom was quiet.

"Ray is pulling at me, clawing at me," Blackwell continued, describing how he held his friend while calling for a medic. "And told him, Ray, [I] love him, I was proud of him. I told him his family loves him. I told him to hang in there, told him to calm down. He was losing a lot of blood."

Ray Losano's death could be felt in the courtroom. It was the weight of raw emotion pressing down on Blackwell's voice—the pride of doing his job in combat mixed with the loss that thirteen years had yet to heal.

Even before the jury heard this testimony, the parties had litigated the details of his recollection. Facts, not emotion, were to be presented to the jury—to the extent the two could be separated.

"There are certain parts of the testimony, in particular, Blackwell's testimony with respect to very graphic testimony about the injuries suffered by Mr. Losano, and we don't think that's necessary to prove anything in the case," Dratel argued.

Shreve Ariail explained that "it is likely that the bullet that entered Raymond Losano's jaw either was shot from the defendant's gun or another al-Qaeda fighter within proximate range to the defendant very close to him."

Judge Cogan had to decide as to what facts the jury would hear. Airman Blackwell had held his partner's face together as he bled to death; the bullet destroyed Losano's jaw and passed through his neck. He was quick and precise in his ruling: "Shot in the face definitely. Shot in the jaw, that's okay. I even think it's okay, profusely bleeding. That's okay. But pieces of the jaw, where they are, I don't think we need that." The jury did not need to hear further details to establish enemy fire had killed Losano.

As the firefight raged, Private Jerod Dennis arrived on the scene in the cab of a Toyota Hilux. He watched his fellow soldier struggling to save Losano's life.

The medic, David Simmons, spoke softly. "Private Dennis was pulling security on the vehicle. He was up in the standing-up area, just watching out, point of security for us," he said.

"I attempted to treat Losano—" his voiced seized slightly.

"Just tell us what you did," Judge Cogan cut in, gentle but firm, trying to stanch the emotion in the memory.

Simmons described trying to breathe for Losano, but the extent of his injuries made it impossible. "I didn't see any life in him," he recalled.

Conrad Read recalled how Dennis's Hilux passed his vehicle moving toward the fire. Trahan, lapsing in and out of consciousness, had ordered the men, including Private Dennis, Specialist Eddie Comacho, and Sergeant John Setzer, to head toward the firefight to evacuate the wounded. Thirty seconds later, Read heard "an explosion of gunfire and different weapon systems . . . what sounded like RPGs as well as machine gun fire."

Trahan's deputy, First Sergeant Brian Severino, testified that he had arrived at the bottom of the hill with a second quick reaction force to collect casualties when he heard the same burst of gunfire. It seemed to go uninterrupted for nearly twenty seconds. Soon after, a new round of casualties arrived.

"They had told me that one of our soldiers was not accounted for at this point in time," he said, his voice breaking.

"Put another question, please," the judge told the government.

"Do you remember the name of the soldier?" Assistant U.S. Attorney Wells asked.

"PFC Jerod Dennis," Severino said.

Jerod's father and brother sat listening to the testimony in the second row of the gallery, eyes fixed on the witness.

Another soldier with the quick reaction force, Victor Graf, came across Setzer and Comacho; the sergeant had a wound to his jaw that made it impossible for him to speak. Comacho told them, "Dennis was out there."

Graf came upon an eerie scene. The Hilux sat empty at the top of the hill. A lone M4 rifle lay on top of the truck; hundreds of shell casings littered the ground surrounding the vehicle. The spent rounds appeared to be from enemy weapons. He looked over the lip of the hill and began making his way down in search of the missing private, whispering Dennis's name as he moved through the terrain. He spotted in the distance what he thought was a pair of red sweatpants. As he approached, he noticed American combat boots and realized that blood had soaked through the pants. He had found PFC Dennis.

"He was—he was real lethargic, he was moving slowly on his own. He wasn't saying anything to me. I just looked at him, and I said, 'Buddy, we found you. We're going to get you out of here,'" Graf recalled.

The soldiers carried Dennis up the hill to be evacuated by helicopter with Setzer, Reed, and an Afghan soldier. "His skin was, like, a whitish gray color. He was receiving rescue breathing from the medics that were on the helicopter," said Reed, who had suffered shrapnel injuries. "The medics were not going to be able to treat anybody else because of them being busy trying to keep Private Dennis alive."

The men were taken to FOB Salerno, then to Bagram. The moment their helicopter landed, medics rushed Dennis into surgery.

"Did you ever see Private First Class Dennis alive again?" Assistant U.S. Attorney Matthew Jacobs asked.

Reed responded, "I did not."

HAUSA'S THREE ATTORNEYS SAT listening throughout the day, only offering occasional objections. They chose not to cross-examine any of the soldiers who had survived the ambush. The government did not introduce testimony from the two men who had witnessed the moment Dennis was mortally wounded, Setzer and Comacho. The three Americans in the Hilux that rushed into the firefight received the Silver Star for gallantry. Judge Cogan pressed the government on the need to put up multiple witnesses recounting the battle.

"I think I really understand this battle at this point, not that it isn't riveting: it is, but do the other witnesses really have more to add?" he asked.

Only Trahan and Blackwell had testified to seeing any of the enemy, but their remembrances fell well short of an identification that would be admissible.

But after the gunfire subsided that day, the uninjured soldiers from the quick reaction force fanned out to secure the hillside. One enemy fighter lay dead; his leg nearly severed from a blast injury. The soldiers stripped his pockets of anything that could offer intelligence. They discovered other belongings strewn about the hill: a compass, a nine-volt battery used as a detonation switch, waterproof matches, needle-nose pliers, prayer beads, and a leather-bound Koran—a bloodstained copy that years later would reveal Hausa's fingerprints.

When the jury began deliberations seven days later, they had heard testimony from a stream of witnesses: FBI agents, an al-Qaeda expert, a military investigator, an Italian police officer. Beyond his exhaustive confession, Hausa had left bread crumbs of evidence linking him to al-Qaeda, in email accounts, in notebooks discovered in raids on al-Qaeda, on hard drives. The government's closing dutifully cataloged the evidence; it required little translation or interpretation. When it came time for the defense to address the jury, David Stern rose to speak to Judge Cogan.

"We are not going to make a closing statement. We want to go directly to charge," he said.

The government attorneys looked stunned and angered, but they could do little. The absence of the defendant had already disrupted the balance of the trial. Unlike the pretrial litigation, the trial had been more performative than adversarial. The defense's refusal to make a summation left the jury with little choice but to fill in their silence with speculation. Had they given up in the face of overwhelming evidence? Or were they protesting the legitimacy of the trial? The jury returned to their room to deliberate. They remained there for a little more than two hours before returning a guilty verdict on each of the five charges.

The defense had not capitulated so much as narrowed their efforts. It was not clear whether their client had even consented to their representation. If they could not defend their client explicitly, they could defend him by confronting the process by which the government sought to bring him to justice—a task the team carried out even following Hausa's conviction when Stern filed notice of an appeal with the Second Circuit. Cogan made clear that the case against Hausa hadn't been lost by his attorneys. But Stern and the others, recognizing that perhaps Hausa's only chance at freedom would be through arguing that his attorneys had provided inadequate representation, withdrew as appellate counsel.

"The weight of the evidence was so substantial that defendant's appointed counsel—three of the most respected criminal defense attorneys in this district—made the unusual (but understandable and strategic) decision to waive closing argument," Cogan wrote in an opinion after the trial. "Any factual defense they articulated in closing could have only sounded incredible."

NEARLY A YEAR LATER, Adnan Harun Hausa remained committed to his jihad. He refused to appear before Judge Cogan to hear his sentence. A few minutes before the judge took the stand on a February morning, two monitors positioned on either side of the courtroom flashed to life to reveal a heavy slate-gray cell door with the number 4 stenciled next to a small rectangular glass window. Hidden behind that door was Hausa, invisible to those gathered in the courtroom, invisible to the outside world. His struggle remained with him there.

Jerry Dennis did not return to hear the sentence read. But his son spoke for the family.

"Your anger, your rage," said Jordan Dennis, "all of that is just background noise to the true tragedy here: Jerod's absence. Our loss."

The men who had survived the battle at Shkin rose one by one to speak. After that day, each man went on to fight his private war. Their voices briefly held the courtroom, the quiet murmur of the interpreter translating into a microphone offering accompaniment. When the statements concluded, Judge Cogan pronounced that Hausa would spend his life in prison.

The sentence, like those who had suffered losses on the hillside at Shkin, ensured that his war would also never end.

15

Hijra II

September 22, 2015

Without a word, Ghulam and Kehkashan Rabbani took their seats in the second row of the gallery in Judge Margo Brodie's courtroom. Their son Imran waited behind a wood-paneled doorway, seated alone in a holding cell. On that early summer morning two months earlier, his entire life had changed in an instant. Moments after he opened the Jeep's door and took a few steps toward the vehicle that had been tailing them, another unmarked sedan sped up to the scene. Men in plain clothes jumped out, pointing weapons at Imran and Munther. The two teenagers immediately lay down on the pavement. After a few shouted words, Imran was able to confirm who had been following the teens for weeks: it was the FBI. Imran was ten days away from graduating from high school when he found himself in handcuffs and, as the sun began to rise, on his way to FBI headquarters in Manhattan to be interrogated. His parents arrived hours later, in hopes that the government would let their son go, just as he had been when he took his neighbor's car for a joyride as a fourteen-year-old. They told him to tell the investigators everything. Instead, the government held Imran in solitary confinement for nearly six months, based on the nature of his charges.

That September morning, his mother covered her head with a dark shawl while his father wore a knit skullcap. They seemed to shrink within the emptiness of the courtroom. There were no other reporters or spectators. Seth DuCharme stepped inside the courtroom and took a seat. He wasn't prosecuting this case, but because he was the deputy chief of the National Security and Cybercrime Section, Imran's case fit within the growing catalog of active investigations DuCharme's team had been pursuing.

But the office hoped to keep the proceedings secret. That morning, Imran appeared under a pseudonym—John Doe—and the details of his arrest remained under seal. The public information on his case was limited to the public calendar, which noted the time of his appearance before the judge, and the docket, which indicated that a defendant had been charged under the material support for terrorism statute. A terrorism arrest often triggered a press release and a statement from the U.S. Attorney and the FBI special agent in charge. With Imran, there was silence. Officially, this was because he had been a minor at the time of his arrest. But to the government, he represented a potential cooperating witness for its cases against Munther Saleh who had ties to other aspiring jihadists.

Judge Brodie entered and took the bench. She was a regal African American woman in her late forties, and she spoke with a dull, slightly pissed-off effect. She made little effort to conceal her impatience when attorneys, whether for the government or defense, spoke. But when she took the opportunity to address the room, her disposition opened ever so slightly. She had followed the well-worn route to become a judge in the Eastern District, working her way up the ranks of the U.S. Attorney's Office, eventually becoming the deputy chief of the Criminal Division there, before being put forward under the Obama administration for a judgeship. As Brodie stacked papers in front of her, the courtroom manager asked, "Is everyone here part of the case?"

I stood up and recited a script, citing the presumption of access to criminal proceedings, and asked that the judge not close the courtroom. In a few short months, I'd attended eleven similar "John Doe" hearings in the Eastern District and had been kicked out of nine of them. I expected the judge to offer no basis for sealing the courtroom, other than to say the "reasons cited in the government's filings." Those reasons—whether they were to protect classified information or avoid a disclosure that could undermine an investigation—remained between the judge and the government. Instead, Judge Brodie said that she was granting the government's request to seal the courtroom because the matter concerned a juvenile.

"You have to leave. This is a closed proceeding," Judge Brodie said.

As an FBI agent followed me out of the courtroom, Mr. and Mrs. Rabbani kept their gaze fixed toward the door, waiting for their son to appear.

THE FBI HAD NO INTENTION of arresting Imran and Munther on the morning of June 13. The young men's decision to confront their surveillance set the case in motion, forcing the hand of the U.S. Attorney's Office to bring them in to be arraigned on a Saturday.

Imran had put himself on a collision course with the government once he came under Munther Saleh's wing. Saleh had opened the door of radicalization for him, but more important he made the idea of *hijra* real for Imran. Earlier that spring, Saleh had accompanied a friend to John F. Kennedy International Airport to board a flight to Amman, Jordan, en route to join the caliphate. The man, Nader Saadeh, was a twenty-year-old dual citizen of Jordan and the United States who had been living in Rutherford, New Jersey. The departure was meant to be the first leg of Saadeh's journey to join the Islamic State. Several years earlier, Saleh had befriended Nader and his brother, Alaa, who shared an apartment in New Jersey. The men bonded over jihad, ruminating on traveling abroad to join the "Mahdi's army." The younger brother, Nader, had begun the transformation into fledgling jihadist, growing out his beard and darkening his eyes with eyeliner, while plotting to return to Jordan as an entry point to join the caliphate. One of his high school friends, a gifted musician named Sam Topaz, converted from Judaism to Islam while growing increasingly infatuated with the idea of jihad. In this group, a small but determined cell of ISIS sympathizers began to approach the dangerous divide that separated jihadist fantasy from reality.

The reality was that making *hijra* was an exorbitant expense. Munther speculated that it would take several months for him to pull together the funds to travel to the Middle East. Topaz, a community college dropout who lived with his mother, worked at a restaurant to try to secrete away funds for a trip. Only Nader had any success in his preparations. His brother purchased a ticket to Jordan on his credit card, and his father wired him cash from Oman. But it wasn't clear whether Saadeh's parents wanted him closer to be in a better position to prevent their younger son from joining the Islamic State. In the days before his departure, Nader had been flooded by messages from his mother and relatives begging him not to join the group. "Stay home and let go. Fear God in your mother and seek her approval," one wrote. "Believe me, my dear, the time of jihad is not with those people."

By early 2015, more than thirty Americans in thirteen states had been intercepted by law enforcement for attempting to join ISIS abroad. Similarly, European and Turkish officials had also moved against the pipeline of even larger numbers of fighters streaming to the battlefield. The Jordanians were among the United States' closest allies in the war on terror. After the terror group immolated a Jordanian pilot alive who had been shot down while conducting air strikes over Raqqa, Syria, public opinion in that country only further coalesced around the cause of defeating the Islamic State. As routes into the caliphate from Jordan and Turkey became more dangerous for fighters, the Islamic State shifted its message.

"There is no excuse for any Muslim not to migrate to the Islamic State," Baghdadi said. But he offered an outlet for those unable to make the journey. "Joining is a duty on every Muslim. We are calling on you either join or carry weapons [to fight] wherever you are."

Almost immediately after dropping Nader Saadeh off at JFK, Munther Saleh told a contact he met online that he was in New York City and was "trying to do an Op." He had emailed himself instructions on how to build a pressure cooker bomb, the same type of device used in the Boston Marathon bombings, and he also purchased a digital watch. Munther then set a meeting with a friend on Staten Island, Fareed Mumuni, whom he had begun to meet with to plan an attack. Saleh grew paranoid that he was being followed. As he rode the subway to South Ferry in lower Manhattan to board the Staten Island Ferry, for the short journey across New York harbor, he took steps to evade anyone who might have been surveilling him on foot. And Saleh was right. The FBI had been tracking him since early spring.

Their plan had moved to the stage where Saleh sought religious counsel. He again reached out to his contact in the Islamic State, Junaid Hussain, and asked about a friend "who is planning on hitting a black cop car with a pressure cooker, the black car keeps following him." Saleh was referring not to Imran but to Mumuni, who apparently also believed that law enforcement was tracking him. The attack would serve to avenge those who had been captured and prevented from joining the Islamic State, Saleh explained.

"Is it permissible for him to do the attack and die purposely in the process?" Saleh asked.

"If he has no other way to fight them, he can," Hussain wrote back.

Saleh replied, "I told him the same thing."

Imran remained on the periphery of these conversations.

"How was the meeting with your guys?" Rabbani asked in a phone call.

Saleh initially didn't know what he was referring to.

"You got tea with them . . . Tea, wink, wink, tea," Imran said. "Your buddies, man, Staten Island."

"Oh yeah, it was awesome," Saleh said.

Saleh didn't mention his plans to Imran during the call. Instead, the two went on to lament the limits of peaceful protest. "It's so sad to see people think posting on Facebook or protests actually do something for Palestine," Rabbani wrote, saying that he'd gone to three protests against the occupation and "screamed my voice out."

"Not a single thing changed," he added. "I did nothing."

"Look at the examples of prophets, not many prophets achieved greater expansion and success except that they broke the rules," Saleh responded.

The two men sensed that they were being surveilled, not only physically, but electronically. They switched over to an encrypted messaging application to communicate.

Munther's friends in New Jersey, meanwhile, had begun to grow concerned—and paranoid. Nader Saadeh had not been heard from since departing JFK. In fact, on his arrival in Jordan officials detained him as part of a "national security" investigation.

"One of his friends snitched on him," Alaa, his brother, told Sam Topaz, speculating that Munther might have tipped off authorities. "I'm hoping it's not because if it is . . . I think I'm going to kill someone."

He warned his friend, "Lay low. And don't talk to nobody."

But somebody had already talked. Nearly two months earlier, the Saadeh brothers' roommate approached the FBI to report concerns about the young men's growing interest in the Islamic State. In late April 2015, agents with the Joint Terrorism Task Force began running the roommate as an informant on Alaa and Nader at their Rutherford, New Jersey, building. The informant attended a "going away dinner" for Nader at a restaurant in late April, taking pictures of the event and handing them over to the FBI. Nader had shaved his beard in preparation for his journey, to appear less readily identifiable as an observant Muslim and potential ISIS sympathizer.

This was not the first tip the FBI had received connected to the men. Sam Topaz's mother had come forward months earlier, concerned that the Saadeh brothers were influencing her son toward following the Islamic State. In April, the FBI returned to Topaz's mother. She then identified another person who had been in contact with her son: Munther Saleh.

By late April, the JTTF had begun working the case as a developing domestic ISIS plot. Prosecutors obtained court authorization to conduct electronic surveillance of the men, accessing their email and social media accounts and their text messages, as well as tapping their phones. The conversations included not only the Saadeh brothers in New Jersey but Saleh and his contacts with Fareed Mumuni and Imran Rabbani. When Nader traveled to JFK in early May to depart on his evening flight to Jordan, the informant went with him and the others. This gave the FBI direct access to, as amateurish as it might have been, an ISIS cell that had just taken an affirmative step to join the caliphate overseas.

Electronic surveillance revealed information the FBI would later present as the contours of a domestic attack plan. The intercepted online activity indicated that Saleh and Imran had "searched online for a pressure cooker, a crock pot, a sewing machine, a chemistry model, a drill, a lava lamp, an LED light, a garden hose, a pipe or pump, a pipe or exhaust, a saw, propane, and a watch" and "notable New York City landmarks and tourist attractions," an agent wrote in a court submission. Saleh and Mumuni appeared in recorded calls discussing "money" and arranging their meeting in Staten Island, for what agents feared was a planning session on an upcoming attack. Around this time, Imran Rabbani had zeroed out a bank account that he shared with his father, withdrawing $1,000 from an ATM. The FBI had no visibility on what, if anything, Rabbani intended to do with the cash.

The surveillance seemed to suggest the men had the motivation and intent to commit an act of terrorism. But before their arrest, prosecutors had not determined that the government had enough evidence to charge the men. Beyond Munther escorting Nader Saadeh to JFK for his journey to Jordan, the steps each had taken had remained within the realm of the hypothetical. The government could not take further risks. The morning after the arrests on the overpass, FBI agents, M4 rifles strapped to their chests, descended on the Staten Island home of Fareed Mumuni. A melee broke out. As the agents moved in to cuff him, Mumuni reached for an agent's weapon, grabbing the trigger grip. As one agent fought him off, Mumuni pulled a kitchen knife that he'd wrapped in a T-shirt and thrust it into the torso of one of the agents several times. The tip of the knife snapped off from the force, but the agent, who was wearing body armor, escaped serious injury.

The attack, however, dispelled any illusion that this cell consisted solely of wannabe jihadists. Prosecutors in New Jersey, meanwhile, moved on the remaining members of the group. The officials detained and charged Samuel Topaz and the Saadeh brothers, including Nader, who was brought from Jordan to face charges in the United States. Imran, though on the periphery of all of this, faced similar consequences to the other defendants. Each would be charged under the material support for terrorism statute.

IMRAN RABBANI'S ATTORNEY immediately realized how serious the situation was when Judge Brodie assigned the case to him. Richard Willstatter had been practicing criminal defense for thirty years, his earliest years in practice spent in the Bronx as a Legal Aid attorney. He now served on the Criminal Justice Act Panel—a reserve of private defenders who took on indigent clients who could not be represented by federal defenders in the Eastern and Southern Districts. The work wasn't nearly as lucrative as pulling in clients to his private practice, but the prosecutors in both offices kept the panel busy with a steady stream of defendants.

Willstatter discussed his work with carefully presented portions of contempt and caution. Like many criminal defenders, he channeled a near-constant exasperation with the posture of the government. When it came to directly criticizing its conduct, he became lawyerly. Yet when he learned that Imran's parents had consented to their son's questioning at FBI headquarters in the dawn hours after the arrest, he grew livid. Not at the parents, but at the FBI.

"They brought the parents in. They told the kid, 'This is really going to help you to talk to us,'" he said. "It didn't."

Imran gave up Munther soon after the interrogation began. He told the agents that his friend wanted to join ISIS and that somebody needed to stop him. When Imran tried to distance his actions from Munther's, the agents didn't believe him. He tried to explain to the agents that he wasn't aware that law enforcement was trailing him. The government had intercepted conversations to disprove that. When the agents finally pressed him on whether he sympathized with ISIS, he denied that he did. But at that point in the conversation, Imran had given the agents little reason to believe him.

The interview was a disaster. Imran should have said nothing, but his parents pressed him to cooperate. Willstatter felt that the agents took advantage of the Rabbani family's anxiety and insecurities as recent émigrés.

"If it were my kid, I would've said, 'Don't say a goddamn thing to these people,'" said Willstatter, who like many New Yorkers used profanity as punctuation. "'And you: Mr. Agent. Fuck you. My kid isn't talking to you. We love America, and we're not saying anything

to you. You know what we love? We love the Fifth Amendment of the
United States Constitution. Have a nice day.' "

The news of Imran and Munther's arrest immediately circulated the
mosques in Flushing. This was not the first time a terrorism case had
rocked the community. The Najibullah Zazi case loomed large in the
neighborhood as an example of how members of the community could
find themselves implicated in the conduct of others. That investigation
had pulled in not only the three men charged with terrorism but an
imam who worked at a nearby funeral parlor and had spent time with
the suspects. That man, Ahmad Wais Afzali, was eventually convicted
and deported for tipping off Zazi that the police had been looking for
him. During the Friday prayer following Imran and Munther's arrest,
the imam at the Rabbani family's mosque, Abdelghani Benyahya,
stepped to the lectern to deliver a sermon. His message: the dangers
of hatred.

"Brothers and sisters, we are losing our children every day in different ways. Some are misguided, some dig a trap, some got into something, and that's because of us. We as individuals, as a community,
as a society, as scholars, as anyone," said Benyahya. "The hatred is
spreading everywhere, and we cannot stop it. We are putting out the
fire with our own hands, and there's no way to stop it unless we start
learning how to love each other. We have to. This is the only solution
that we have."

But, appearing before Judge Brodie that morning, Willstatter faced
the immediate task of convincing her that the government should be
required to charge his client as a juvenile. The government seemed to
want it both ways in the case. For the purposes of sealing the courtroom, Imran was a juvenile, but when it came to the charges, it asked
the court to try him as an adult, though he had been arrested a month
before his eighteenth birthday. Imran's arrest meant a personal tragedy:
he spent his graduation day from John Bowne incarcerated at a juvenile
facility outside Newark, New Jersey, held in solitary confinement. The
goal was to keep him in custody pending trial. When the government
argued for Imran's detention, it marshaled a disturbing allegation:
Imran's computer had evidence that he had researched online for components to build a bomb.

In a sealed affidavit by an FBI agent, the government laid out this claim. The government had already detailed its accusations against Munther. He had sought instructions on how to build a pressure-cooker-style device like those used at the Boston Marathon bombings, according to intercepted emails. At first glance, this squared Imran with the broader conspiracy of Saleh and Mumuni, and it held the potential to destroy Willstatter's defense theory that Imran was a child, guilty of falling in with the wrong friend, but little else.

After the detention hearing, Willstatter pressed the prosecution to see the evidence. The government pushed back, insisting that the information on Imran's attempt to obtain bomb-making supplies remained classified. National security cases had this unique tension: security classification forced the defense to fight for evidence that would otherwise be available to them under disclosure requirements. Frequently, the judge had to rely on good faith representations from the government about why the evidence should be withheld from the defense, even defenders who had been cleared to see classified material. A judge had to balance the rights of the defendant against the govern-ment's need for secrecy. In the blunt arithmetic of national security, this meant choosing between protecting one individual or exposing many more to hypothetical danger. Judges often chose the lesser risk. But defense attorneys who worked national security cases saw the aggregate impact of this. It tilted the balance built into the adversarial system of justice toward the government; it alone, after all, held power to classify and declassify information. This impacted not only the pros-ecution's approach to a case but also that of the investigators. Agents could aggressively pursue suspects knowing that the defense counsel's ability to confront their evidence faced significant—and in some cases insurmountable—challenges.

But five months into Imran's detention, the judge compelled the government to turn over its evidence of his online search for bomb materials. Willstatter received raw data, he said. The FBI had imaged Imran's hard drive—made an exact copy of his computer's contents—and pulled out the information it viewed as inculpatory. The materials turned over to Willstatter included images of a lava lamp and a digital pressure cooker called an Instant Pot, which the government relied on to support its claim that Imran was seeking out materials to build a bomb. The government provided no context for the image files. They weren't matched to search queries or to specific instructions to construct an explosive. The lava lamp, in particular, seemed ridiculous to Willstatter. (In fact, when heated to high temperatures the lamps explode and send lethal glass shrapnel.) To test the government's allegations, he hired a forensic expert to map the images the prosecution provided him to their location on Imran's hard drive.

The expert did not locate the images in Imran's search history. Instead, Imran had received the images in emails sent by Amazon. Spam. It was unclear whether Imran had even opened them. The government did not volunteer this fact to the judge.

The prosecution was on the verge of winning their motion to try Imran as an adult, a victory that would carry an array of even more severe consequences and ratchet up the pressure on him to take a plea. But Richard Willstatter had a different idea: he wanted the government to drop the charges.

16

DJ3

August 2012

There's an epistemological problem at the center of counterterrorism. Do efforts to stop terrorism instead create more terrorists? The stock criticism of military action—in particular of drone assassinations, a sometimes effective tactic for eliminating a discrete threat—holds that these strikes only engender greater anger and hatred on the ground. But as law enforcement's counterterrorism strategies began to overlap with intelligence operations and direct military action, this criticism carried over to criminal justice. Surveillance, informant recruitment, sting operations—each created collateral damage among the innocent people and entire communities who found themselves targeted by investigators. The moment when a would-be jihadi collides with the state's counterterrorism apparatus becomes an almost universal milestone in the radicalization process—whether that collision comes with an overture by an intelligence officer or in an interrogation by a criminal investigator. But when it comes to the law, this problem isn't just one of action; it is one of perception. When does the state's power to define terrorism under the law become the power to, in effect, create terrorists?

THREE YEARS BEFORE Imran Rabbani appeared before Judge Brodie, two Americans arrived at a sweltering detention center at a classified location in Djibouti. They traveled to this tiny nation on the Horn of Africa to conduct a series of interviews. Weeks earlier, local officials had raided a guesthouse in Djibouti City, rousting a group of young Somali men from their sleep. Somali migrants were common in the capital, a way station for the dangerous journey across the Gulf of Aden into Yemen. With a civil war in Somalia raging, it was difficult to distinguish between refugees and combatants fleeing the fighting. Security officials ordered the men from their beds, then loaded each into a truck before rolling out onto the roadway to the secret facility.

The Americans were interested in three men from this group. For several years, the CIA and Joint Special Operations Command (JSOC) had been conducting a quiet war in the Horn of Africa and Yemen, relying on drones and small teams of special operations forces to assassinate the leadership of al-Qaeda in the Arabian Peninsula and al-Shabaab, the terror group fighting the fragmented national government in Somalia. It was a tertiary war to those in Iraq and Afghanistan, but a war that flushed the Somali men into custody in Djibouti. These three Somalis differed from the others: each held a European passport, one from the United Kingdom, two from Sweden. The danger, from the perspective of Western security services, was that battle-hardened fighters with European passports could return home, their commitment to violent jihad intact.

Among those detained was Mahdi Hashi, a handsome twenty-two-year-old Londoner with bright teeth and searching eyes. In 2009, Madhi had left London for Somalia, a country that he had fled as a child but understood little about. Like many young Somali men in the diaspora, he had written off his homeland as an international embarrassment, the rightful object of scorn. By 2006, that perception had shifted slightly. A new faction had emerged, the Islamic Courts Union (ICU), a rival Islamist government that offered a different vision for Somalia: a post-clan theocracy that promised to unite all Somalis under sharia law. Somalia had been lawless for Hashi's lifetime, so even the harsh brand of religious law the ICU propounded had some allure. News filtered back that their territory in Somalia was stable, safe, and thriving—in part due to the ICU's armed wing al-Shabaab, which translated in Arabic to "the youth." Hashi felt only anger toward his father's generation, but in the emergence of the ICU he saw something different for Somalia: hope.

The country also presented an alternative to the United Kingdom, particularly the streets of Camden Town, his north London neighborhood. The British security services actively surveilled young Muslim men in immigrant communities whom the state believed to be moving down the path of radicalization. On occasion, the security services tried to recruit informants. In 2009, while working as a volunteer in London, Hashi told *The Independent* of an unsettling encounter he had had with an MI5 agent named Richard as he tried to board a flight at Gatwick Airport en route to Djibouti.

"He warned me not to get on the flight. He said, 'Whatever happens to you outside the UK is not our responsibility,'" Hashi said. It was hard to discern whether that was a warning or a threat.

The Djiboutians deported Hashi shortly after his arrival. When he landed back in London, Richard met him again.

The whole thing had been stage-managed by British officials. "He said it was [the U.K. authorities] who sent me back because I was a terror suspect," Hashi told *The Independent*. Hashi accused the intelligence officials of blackmail, he said. They responded that they were giving him an opportunity to clear his name.

"'By cooperating with us, we know you're not guilty,'" he said, recounting the offer.

The British authorities had reason to be concerned. They had surveilled Hashi with Bilal al-Berjawi and Mohamed Sakr, two Britons who had received combat training in Somalia in 2006 and whom the government was tracking as recruiters for al-Shabaab. In many respects, Hashi fit the profile of an aspiring jihadi: he was a teenager from a first-generation immigrant family. He used drugs regularly but also gravitated toward the features of his identity that separated him from British society: his Somali roots and Islam. His language skills and travels—Egypt, Syria, Djibouti—put him within reach of international terrorist groups, who prized Western recruits.

In December 2009, Hashi returned to Somalia for the first time since his exodus from the civil war as a child. Even though he had been born in Mareerey, a river town midway between Mogadishu and the Ethiopian border, he was considered a foreigner in Somalia. Like many of those who had flocked to Somalia from the West, he joined the group that saw his foreignness as an asset, rather than a liability: al-Shabaab.

Unlike other foreigners who had joined, Hashi had made little name for himself in al-Shabaab. He did not appear in propaganda videos, nor did he recruit fighters from his London neighborhood. He left no record of participating in military operations with the group. The only thing that distinguished him was the company he kept. He was seen with Omar Hammami, a popular American al-Shabaab leader. Hammami cut an outsize presence among the *muhajireen*—the foreign fighters— jousting with journalists and sympathizers on social media, drawing attention from the U.S. national security establishment.

Al-Shabaab's embrace of foreigners had a brief honeymoon. Hashi's links to the West became a cause for suspicion within the al-Shabaab leadership. The group would later turn on Hammami and kill him. Drone strikes had also killed the two men whom Hashi knew from London, al-Berjawi and Sakr, in January and February. After those strikes, al-Shabaab placed Hashi in custody, locking him in a window-less cell, under a cloud of suspicion that he and others had tipped off the Americans.

Hashi's al-Shabaab captors cut him loose in June. But he wasn't relieved. He believed that his former comrades simply wanted to surveil him, to track whether he was, in fact, spying for the foreign powers who had been conducting drone strikes on the group's leadership, then—if need be—assassinate him. Hashi simply wanted to go home. He called his mother to help arrange his return to London. That would be impossible, his mother told him. The family had received a letter saying that the government had revoked Hashi's British citizenship. Soon after, al-Shabaab executed three men in town. Each had con-fessed to spying for American and British intelligence.

Crossing into Djibouti was a calculated risk. Hashi potentially faced a fate similar to the accused spies' if he remained in Somalia. Yet he had no country to return to. He decided to make the journey with two other men, Ali Yasin Ahmed and Mohamed Yusuf, Somali-born al-Shabaab fighters who held Swedish passports. The Swedes once figured more prominently in al-Shabaab but in the climate of paranoia now feared reprisals for American strikes. After smugglers carried them across the border, Djiboutian officials arrested the men a few days after they slipped into the capital. Soon after, the U.S. government was alerted to their presence.

The Americans returned to the facility to question the three men nearly a dozen times. One of the interrogators was Arab; the other was white. Each time the men questioned the detainees a single Djiboutian officer accompanied them. Hashi had seen this man torturing one of the Swedes, but he did nothing in the presence of the Americans. The two Americans asked the same questions his Djiboutian interrogators had, but Hashi came to feel that these men were different. He felt that they would protect him from the officers at the prison and the sort of treatment he'd seen meted out to other prisoners. Eventually, he talked. Soon after, the two Americans disappeared, never to return.

In early September 2012, a new American team arrived. The two men identified themselves as FBI agents. They explained that they wished to speak with Hashi. Before the interview began, they did something that none of Hashi's prior captors had: the agents advised him of his right to counsel.

THE MOST PIVOTAL MOMENT in Mahdi Hashi's life—and in the lives of the two Swedes—had occurred in Washington four years earlier. In 2008, Secretary of State Condoleezza Rice had designated al-Shabaab a foreign terrorist organization, adding the Somali group to a list that included al-Qaeda, Hezbollah, and groups like ETA (the Basque separatist faction) and the Real IRA, an offshoot of the inactive Irish Republican Army. That designation was more than a diplomatic flourish. It made the men's association with al-Shabaab prosecutable under the material support for terrorism statute. That statute had been revised under the Patriot Act so that its jurisdiction was no longer limited to the United States but applicable to activity anywhere in the world.

While al-Shabaab had never staged an attack on U.S. soil, it had demonstrated intent to kill Americans. Al-Shabaab fighters fired mortars at a visiting congressional delegation in Mogadishu that included Representative Donald Payne. Since appearing in 2006, the group had morphed from a local Islamist insurgent force staging attacks on the transitional government and Ethiopian forces deployed in Somalia to a regional al-Qaeda affiliate striking Uganda and Kenya with terrorist attacks.

Two years after the U.S. government designated the group a foreign terrorist organization, al-Shabaab staged its most serious external attack to date: simultaneous suicide bombings in Kampala, Uganda, at two separate locations showing the World Cup final. The attacks, which killed dozens of people including an American citizen, were seen as reprisals for the presence of Ugandan troops in Somalia. The bombings, as well as a rash of kidnappings of Westerners, also demonstrated a willingness to adopt al-Qaeda tactics previously seen in Europe, Iraq, Yemen, and Pakistan in the Horn of Africa.

Most troubling to U.S. officials was the appearance of American Somalis on the battlefield—disaffected young men like Hashi—a trend that the FBI had been tracking for several years. In May 2011, African forces shot two suicide bombers at the gates of their base in Mogadishu: they discovered one of the bombers was a twenty-seven-year-old former gang member from Minneapolis, Farah Mohamed Beledi. In 2012, the group made their alliance with al-Qaeda official, exchanging public pronouncements with Ayman al-Zawahiri, the Egyptian who had taken control of the group following bin Laden's assassination.

Hashi and the two Swedes fit within a broader effort targeting al-Shabaab as a terror group with ambitions outside Somalia. On one front, there was military force. Shortly before the men's arrest, the Obama administration acknowledged in a letter to Congress that "in a limited number of cases, the U.S. military has taken direct action in Somalia against members of al-Qa'ida, including those who are also members of al Shabaab, who are engaged in efforts to carry out terrorist attacks against the United States and our interests." The details were more striking. Since 2007, U.S. forces had fought a low-level war in Somalia, waging more than a dozen attacks using AC-130 gunships, attack helicopters, covert ground forces, naval firepower, and, for the first time in 2011, drone strikes. The Obama administration inherited this war but rather than disengage from the prior administration's policy soon escalated the conflict.

On the other front, was the legal approach. As al-Shabaab's message drew sympathizers from both outside and within the Somali community in the United States, particularly in Minneapolis, the FBI moved to disrupt the flow of recruits. Of the more than ninety-five terrorism plots disrupted by American authorities between 2009 and the time of these arrests in 2012, ten had connections to al-Shabaab. The United States also relied on third countries to chip away at al-Shabaab's growing influence. The Somali men were not the first al-Shabaab fighters to be turned over to the Americans by the authorities in Djibouti. In 2007, a Somali jihadist, Abdullahi Sudi Arale, believed to be a courier between al-Qaeda in Pakistan and Islamists in East Africa, was transferred to Camp Lemonnier in Djibouti before being brought to Guantánamo Bay. (Human Rights Watch and Amnesty International confronted the government in Djibouti on its cooperation with the United States, according to a diplomatic cable published by WikiLeaks.) Two years later, a legal attaché from the Department of Justice sat down with Djiboutian officials to discuss a new way forward. The United States proposed that the Djiboutians work with American law enforcement on an "informal" case-by-case basis, without necessarily going through diplomatic channels.

By the end of the summer of 2012, the two countries found such a case: it involved Mahdi Hashi and the Swedish men Ali Yasin Ahmed and Mohamed Yusuf.

WHEN SETH DUCHARME and Shreve Ariail took on the prosecutions against the Somali men, it represented a calculated risk. The defendants had popped up on the grid with troublesome threat profiles. The question was this: What was the best way to manage that threat?

Direct action was one option: the Somalis, had they indeed made their way to al-Qaeda in the Arabian Peninsula in Yemen, could have been eliminated in a single drone strike. They could have also been left to languish in Djiboutian custody, though that ran the inherent risk of the men finding their way to freedom—whether through diplomatic entreaties by the Swedish government or by the porous nature of incarceration in that part of the world.

DuCharme and Ariail saw in the fact pattern the elements of a criminal prosecution. The FBI agents returned from Djibouti with what amounted to confessions, though it was not clear that the men were aware that they had committed a crime prosecutable in the United States. Even before the FBI interviewed the men, they were known quantities to the intelligence services in their home countries. The Swedes, in particular, had been subjected to electronic surveillance before they left their adopted nation to return to Somalia to fight. The prosecutors had witnesses who could place those men in combat and on the battlefield, opening them up to not only material support charges but weapons charges that carried severe penalties. Hashi was less visible, but the prosecutors had a witness to testify to his association with Omar Hammami, the outspoken American al-Shabaab fighter who remained at large. If anything, Hashi's relationship with Hammami made him a compelling target as a potential cooperator if the government was ever in a position to charge the American. But when it came time to draw up the indictment on the men, DuCharme was brief. In a terse three-page indictment, the three men were charged with two crimes: conspiracy to provide material support to a terrorist group and the use of firearms. For all those working the case, it came to be called DJ3.

Mahdi Hashi landed in New York several weeks after the grand jury handed down the indictment. He did not fully understand why he was in the United States or the process that brought him there. Neither did the two Swedes, who also had been rendered to New York. Even before the FBI interviewed the men in Djibouti, one of them, Yusuf, had been told by his captors that they were being held "because of the U.S."

The Justice Department's official counterterrorism strategy aimed to "prevent, disrupt, and defeat terrorist operations." Yet these men represented unlikely candidates for an external operation: only two of them had a valid passport, and, more important, they were deserters. The men posed no immediate threat that the United States needed to "prevent."

But the men did have value to the Americans. Their disaffection with al-Shabaab made Hashi and the Swedes appealing targets for investigators to "disrupt and defeat" the group. If the prosecutors could flip any of them, the government could open a window into al-Shabaab and, potentially, provide evidence at trial. In the prior three years, al-Shabaab prosecutions had flooded the federal system with eighteen cases in Minneapolis alone—the city with the nation's largest concentration of Somali expats. Any cooperators who could place American citizens or residents in the ranks of al-Shabaab with their testimony would be a prize for prosecutors. But without an attorney, the men had little means to understand their value as cooperating witnesses.

Their experience in Djibouti had tainted Hashi and the Swedes. Their jailers made little effort to follow international law during their detention. Yusuf had been stripped to his underwear and held in a ten-by-twelve-foot cell with five others, according to a sworn statement he provided. The men in the cell warned him that they had been tortured, shocked with electrical current, and sexually assaulted with bottles in their rectums. When he was pulled from the cell for questioning, he first refused to speak, but the interrogators threatened him with the types of torture that he had heard about. Ahmed, the other Swede, also recounted his ordeal in a sworn statement. He said his jailers told him that they would "take away my manhood" and that "human rights don't exist here."

Hashi had already spoken with the FBI at length before he arrived in New York. These interrogations provided some reprieve from the suffering of his captivity in Djibouti. Otherwise, he remained in the cramped, fetid cell he shared with two others, sleeping on the hot marble floor, eating meager portions of beans, bread, rice, and pasta. His experience with the Djiboutian interrogators was only marginally better than the Swedes'. His captors blindfolded Hashi and stripped him to his underwear, threatening to rape him or beat him. They never did, though. The threats weren't idle: he watched nine prison guards subdue a prisoner, force him to the ground, and punch and kick him repeatedly in his testicles. He'd seen Ahmed, one of the Swedes with whom he'd been arrested, gagged and blindfolded, hung upside down by his ankles, and beaten with computer cables by guards. The first Americans Hashi sat with—whom he believed to be either CIA or JSOC—didn't threaten him, but the Djiboutians warned Hashi that the Americans tortured those who didn't cooperate. Hashi felt there was little left for him to do but talk.

He told the men about al-Shabaab, about the role he played in the group, about other members. When the FBI appeared again in September, he told them much the same. He'd waived his rights under *Miranda*—such as they were in a classified prison thousands of miles from the United States. Whether he understood the significance of that action isn't clear, but everything he said to the agents carried a different weight from his prior statements to the men he believed to be intelligence agents: what he told the FBI could be used in a court of law.

Hashi didn't know it, but the Swedes had made a similar calculation. Fearing torture at the hands of the Djiboutians, the men cooperated with the Americans. In New York, their situation immediately improved. Their cells were, by comparison, clean. They had traded cramped shared quarters for complete isolation and the constant glare of overhead lights. Each man had a toilet and a sink. And they were fed on a regular basis, though in some cases days would go by without a meal from their American jailers. The most material change to the men's situation occurred several miles from the jails when they were brought before a federal judge to be arraigned on terrorism charges. This carried a universe of potential consequences, but in the immediate moment it guaranteed each man something that he had previously been denied: a lawyer.

MAHDI HASHI SAW his predicament in binary terms. As a young man, he'd been given a "red pill/blue pill" choice between two worlds, either to live as a collaborator in the United Kingdom or to return to Somalia—a journey that would require he choose a side in the nation's civil war. He chose the latter, not just to return to the land of his birth,

but also to become a husband and father and to join the youth—
al-Shabaab—who had received the call to jihad to restore Somalia to
Islamic rule.

The material support statute doesn't parse motives. Nor does it
distinguish between the die-hard extremist and the accidental terrorist. In the complex and, at times, hazy world of violent extremist
groups, it is a blunt instrument. When Hashi met with his attorney,
Mark DeMarco, for the first time, the young Briton insisted on his
innocence of any crimes against the United States. That was a reasonable conclusion for someone who was unfamiliar with the extraterritorial reach of the law. DeMarco understood that reach, and he knew
how unforgiving an indictment on terrorism charges was. He'd lived
through the experience of thinking he had won a material support
case at trial, only to have a jury return a guilty verdict in a few short
hours. In that case, which was also an extraterritorial prosecution,
his client received a life sentence. Terrorism charges carried an inherent prejudice so strong that many defense attorneys saw a trial as an
unacceptable risk. Hashi had his challenges as a client: How do you
ask a man to plead guilty to breaking the laws of a country he'd never
set foot in? Especially when none of the evidence showed any intent to
harm Americans? He also faced a separate and equally perilous legal
fight: to preserve his U.K. citizenship. He had received a form letter
from the U.K. government confirming what his mother had told him,
that he had been determined to be "involved in Islamic extremism and
[to] present a risk to the national security of the United Kingdom." The
basis for that determination, the letter said, was secret.

DeMarco first sought to suppress his client's statements from evidence. But Hashi wasn't completely clear on whom he had given statements to. He had first spoken without receiving a *Miranda* warning,
yet he was mistaken about the identity of his American interrogators.
They were not CIA but FBI. That questioning lasted nearly two weeks,
but those statements were inadmissible. It wasn't until a "clean team"
of FBI agents arrived in late September that he received his *Miranda*
rights. Everything Hashi had told them this time could be used against
him, but DeMarco hoped to have as much of that testimony thrown
out as possible—on the basis that his client could not truly consent to

speak without an attorney while being held by the Djiboutians. The government pushed back, arguing that the statements were voluntary and that Hashi and the Swedes had waived their rights. In the government's submissions, Shreve Ariail argued that officials could corroborate this on the ground in Djibouti. But any extensive litigation around conditions of the men's custody threatened to create a sideshow for the government, shifting the focus from the threat the defendants posed as accused terrorists to their allegations of torture at the hands of U.S. allies. The government eventually gave in, agreeing that it would not use the statements taken in custody. This nullified the issue, if only for a moment.

David Stern was appointed to represent Mohamed Yusuf, the oldest of the men, who was twenty-nine when he was arrested. Stern was disturbed by the government's posturing in the case. The U.S. Attorney at the time, Loretta Lynch, had said, "The defendants were committed supporters of al Shabaab, a violent terrorist organization, who used high-powered firearms and participated in combat operations and al Shabaab's suicide bombing program," while the FBI New York official George Venizelos said, "These defendants are not aspiring terrorists, they are terrorists. They did more than receive terrorist training: they put that training to practice in terrorist operations with al Shabaab." Those statements went a good deal further than the allegations in the indictment. Soon after, the government filed a superseding indictment enumerating those charges in five counts.

The government had, in fact, developed evidence that the Swedes were active combat fighters in al-Shabaab, having trained under the wing of a regional al-Qaeda commander. In the summer of 2009, the men had fought against Somali transitional government forces and African peacekeepers to seize control of Mogadishu. At one point, a mortar blast injured Yusuf. Although neither of the men had participated in al-Shabaab operations outside Somalia, Yusuf later appeared in an al-Shabaab propaganda video, his face wrapped in a checkered balaclava, exhorting recruits to join jihad. At one point, he draws his finger across his neck as he swears to carry out revenge against the Swedish cartoonist Lars Vilks: "And to my brothers and sisters, I call you to make Hijra, and if you can kill this dog Lars Vilks, then you will receive a great award from Allah."

And even though the case involved alleged conduct committed a continent away, the government had also been building a case based, in part, on witnesses. In one court submission, Ariail revealed that they hoped to use testimony from "at least one foreign civilian witness who is located abroad and may also be unavailable as a witness in the United States." The judge authorized that these witnesses be deposed overseas, an extreme, taxpayer-funded measure that required both the prosecution and the defense teams to travel to Kampala, Uganda, for the deposition because the witness was not permitted to travel to the United States.

As the deposition approached, Hashi had misgivings about his attorney. He wanted to fire DeMarco and, at one point, sat down to write Judge Sandra Townes a letter. But in a status conference before the deposition, he instead tried to address the issue with her directly.

"I've had a few issues with my lawyers for the past—" he interjected.

"I'm not discussing that now. I said I will have a hearing and, hopefully, I'll have your letter," the judge said, cutting him off.

"So I come once to the court appearance, and you don't talk to me? I don't get to talk?" he said, growing frustrated.

"I anticipated you will be sending me the letter," she responded.

"I've been sitting here two years and a half. I've never spoke. I've never, ever spoke. Let me speak," he implored.

"You may send the letter, Mr. Hashi," she replied.

"The first time I speak and you do this, right? It's an embarrassment," he said, dejected.

Hashi's isolation was growing more acute. Guards at the MCC discovered a "drop note" in the recreational area that contained the phone number of Hashi's wife in Somalia and his mother in the U.K.; it also contained what they believed to be a coded message. Phone calls were rare, but when Hashi did speak to his mother, he did his best to remain positive, never complaining.

Hashi's co-defendants were also buckling under the pressure of incarceration. The conditions of the Bureau of Prison's detention program often applied to terrorism suspects, Special Administrative Measures—known as SAMs, were onerous; one called it "a different form of torture." Each man spent twenty-three hours a day in his cell. Their lone hour of recreation was spent in a separate cage down the hallway from their cells. One regulation forbade the men to read anything other than new copies of books; once the men were finished reading a book, the prison officials destroyed it. When Ali Ahmed tried to take his own life with a disposable razor, the jail responded by taking away his phone privileges for three months. He was being punished for "possessing an unauthorized item."

IN FEBRUARY 2015, nearly two and a half years after the men had been brought to the United States, their case returned to Africa. In Kampala, at a Ministry of Justice building, Susan Kellman, David Stern, and Mark DeMarco sat down with Shreve Ariail and Richard Tucker from the government, as well as two FBI agents, an NYPD detective, and a Ugandan prosecutor, Joan Kagezi. When the witness, a Rwandan named Mugisha Mohamoud, entered, it became clear why he had not been permitted to travel to the United States: he was an al-Shabaab member convicted for helping plan and execute the 2010 World Cup suicide bombings. He'd played a small but important role in the attacks that left more than seventy people dead and seventy more injured. Mohamoud helped smuggle explosives across the Kenyan border into Uganda before his arrest. Though the Ugandans had captured him, the bombings went forward. The attacks killed one American, Nate Henn, a twenty-five-year-old NGO worker from North Carolina, while six other Americans with a Pennsylvania church group were injured. Soon after the bombings, Mohamoud flipped.

For the defense attorneys, Mohamoud's presence was breathtaking. He had pleaded guilty to his role in the attacks and provided testimony against his former compatriots before Ugandan courts. He had also met repeatedly with the prosecution team for questioning while in prison. But the objective was not to bring Mohamoud to face trial for Henn's death or the attempted murder of the other Americans; he was to be a witness against Hashi and the Swedes.

Mohamoud offered the government an inside view of al-Shabaab. He described how the group functioned, who the key players were, and what sorts of tactics—including suicide bombings—the force relied on. He painted a picture of a sophisticated organization with concrete ties to al-Qaeda. Critical to the government's case, Mohamoud spent time at an al-Shabaab training camp at the same time as the Swedes, at a moment when the leadership preached a shift toward external terrorist operations. He, however, offered no direct testimony about Hashi.

The deposition ground forward for two days. A video feed broadcast the proceedings live to FBI headquarters in New York, where the defendants sat with co-counsel. In Kampala, the room teemed with tension. The jet-lagged attorneys didn't have a federal judge present to act as a buffer for their frustrations; they found themselves talking over each other's objections, nerves boiling to the surface. The decorum of a federal court enforced a functional respect for the opposing party, but each side found that difficult to muster in Kampala, where a local magistrate looked on powerless to intercede with the bickering Americans. When Kellman cross-examined Mohamoud, she zeroed in on the moral concession that had brought the case to Uganda in the first place.

"Would it be fair to say that for participating in planning the murder of seventy people, you got off pretty easy? Am I right?" Kellman asked. "Do you know that if you were prosecuted for those murders in the United States you could get the rest of your life in prison or the death penalty?"

"Objection," Ariail said.

But Mohamoud had already responded to both questions with a simple "no."

The team returned to New York bruised from the experience but without a clear victor. The government would not be walking into a trial empty-handed, but its key witness, Mohamoud, carried with him considerable baggage. A trial date loomed just a few short months in the distance, but before then the judge would decide whether to suppress the confessions the defendants had made in Djibouti. If the government continued to press to bring those statements in, the defense could call witnesses for a pretrial hearing to answer to the allegations of torture the men put forward. Eventually, DuCharme and Ariail made the call to move ahead without the statements. The government wasn't required to explain its rationale, but prosecutors needed to weigh the risks that a public suppression hearing would carry, by exposing their witnesses to cross-examination and, most significantly, exposing themselves to a loss even before the case went to trial. The defense faced stronger headwinds: their clients were not only accused of terrorism; the evidence told a story of radicalization and violence that few juries would parse for nuance. Going to trial meant a conviction; a conviction meant a sentence far beyond anything that the men would receive by pleading guilty. Despite their belief in their innocence, despite their professed lack of intentions to harm the United States, despite the certainty of more prison time, the men decided to do that. On a sunny May afternoon, more than nine hundred days since a grand jury had indicted the men, they appeared before a new judge assigned to the case, John Gleeson. Each man entered a plea of guilty for conspiracy to provide material support to a terrorist organization.

IN EARLY JANUARY 2016, Mahdi Hashi's two co-defendants returned to Judge Gleeson's courtroom for sentencing. The gallery filled in a little before 2:00 p.m. with FBI agents, other assistants from the Eastern District's national security team, and a handful of spectators. Mark DeMarco, Hashi's counsel, took a seat behind the federal agents and waited for the judge to enter. As was his custom, Gleeson appeared without a robe, in a pale blue suit and silver tie.

The defendants had submitted letters in anticipation of their sentencing. "My decision to join al Shabaab had nothing to do with America or what was happening in Iraq or Afghanistan. I never had any intention in the past, nor do I possess now any present intention to cause any harm to the United States now or in the future," wrote Ali Yasin Ahmed.

Assistant U.S. Attorney Shreve Ariail described the case as "a negotiated resolution." The path to a guilty plea had been hard fought by both sides. At one point, plea negotiations broke down, and the defense pressed for the U.S. Attorney's Office to return to the table. The government, for its part, acknowledged the limits of its evidence: it did not indicate that any of the men had made any clear, specific threat to any American citizens. It had evidence of unseemly associations—with leaders and low-level fighters who had participated in al-Shabaab's play for power, a terror campaign marked by assassinations, suicide attacks against civilians, and the steady strategic shift toward international attacks. Each side had risk to manage: the government faced the risk that just one juror could be convinced that the men were engaged not in terrorism but in a cause to liberate their homeland. The defense faced the risk that the jury would convict less on the strength of the evidence and more on the power of a single word.

Eventually, the two sides returned to the table. The men faced thirty years to life under the indictment, but the government agreed to a maximum sentence of fifteen years in exchange for a guilty plea. The government and the defense can negotiate a specific sentence that the judge, if the judge accepts the agreement, must impose—a so-called 11(c)(1)(C) plea agreement. But this wasn't one; the parties had simply negotiated a standard plea. Yet when Assistant U.S. Attorney Shreve Ariail spoke to the court at the sentencing of the two Swedes, he argued that there had been a consensus on a fifteen-year sentence.

"I think every single one of us who agreed to the resolution, in this case, did agree with the full expectation that the defendants would be sentenced to fifteen years and after that be deported without litigation, and that's the bargain we struck," he said.

"No, it's not," Judge John Gleeson said, cutting him off.

Ariail seemed to realize his mistake instantly. "That we struck, Your Honor, I apologize, *ourselves.*"

"It's important to understand that in a circumstance like this, the judging is not over," Gleeson reminded the prosecutor. "There's no binary dimension to this at all. By that, I don't mean to buy into any notion that these men were either freedom fighters or terrorists, they are a little bit of both."

The defense had raised the conditions of the men's detention. Susan Kellman recalled Djibouti. "I want to speak to the government's—I'll call it back-handed representation of the rough, rough treatment that our clients experienced," she said. "To use the word 'rough' is unfair and dismissive. The government was there. They can't refute that. They can't refute that there were five other near naked men in our client's, in Mr. Ahmed's cell, no mattress, no change of underwear, no change of clothing, over the course of three months. The government calls this rough but nothing more. I think it's more properly characterized, Your Honor, respectfully, as inhumane."

Kellman had tuned her outrage to navigate the narrow space decorum would allow; she did not raise her voice, but nor did she lower it. It held a firm, controlled anger. She described the impact SAMs had on her client, which kept Ahmed in total isolation and required him to be in a cage when they met. She recounted an incident when she struggled to get a point through to her client and, because of the caging, couldn't see whether her words registered.

" 'Would you do me a favor and just give him a crack in the head, like just make sure that he's there, make sure he's heard what I've said?' " she recalled asking the guard. "As I was leaving the area, the cage was, in fact, opened and I saw the guard put his arm around my client's throat and in a very caring way, give him what I call a noogie, just let him have a moment of human contact, and I saw my client's eyes glaze over and I thought to myself what are we doing to human beings here in Brooklyn?"

The hearing had gone sideways, both on the issue of the men's treatment and on the inadvertently indelicate suggestion that the government had settled the sentence. Several federal agents in the gallery shifted in their seats as several years of their work investigating the Swedes hung in the balance.

"It is my job to do the judging," Gleeson reminded the government. "The sentence is eleven years in the custody of the Attorney General."

WHEN IT CAME TIME for Hashi's moment to address the court two weeks later, he asked Judge Gleeson whether he could stand. Unlike the Swedes, he had yet to be sentenced. The fact that Gleeson had not given the men fifteen years, as had been inferred from the plea agreement, offered some hope. Hashi was a wiry twenty-six-year-old, a wispy beard growing from his chin, the navy prison scrubs swallowing his frame. His accent betrayed his upbringing in London, in the immigrant hub of Camden Town, but also carried the rolling intonation of Somalia, which at times muddled his English.

Hashi spoke for several minutes. He recounted how he grew up in exile and returned to Somalia at a moment when he perceived the Islamic Courts Union would restore order to the nation. How he stayed with his grandmother outside Mogadishu, in al-Shabaab-controlled territory, and felt compelled to join the group after seeing the order and safety they brought, compared with the chaos and absence of the rule of law in government-held Mogadishu. Al-Shabaab was the future, he felt. And, for these reasons, Hashi signed on.

As he recounted this, the courtroom fell quiet. It seemed as if the audience were privy to a conversation going on between just two men, John Gleeson and Mahdi Hashi.

"I've asked this question a lot of times," Hashi continued. "Do I regret joining al Shabaab? Do I regret leaving the UK? And the truth is: absolutely. With every fiber in my body, with every suffering I go through every day—me and my family go through." He spoke about how he, too, had underestimated the impact of solitary confinement: the migraines, the loss of appetite, the tunnel vision. "Your Honor, I don't have no animosity towards the United States. I never have, none whatsoever. I don't bear any ill feelings towards the prosecution here—I view the attorneys, Mr. DuCharme, Arial and—," he stopped.

"Tucker," the judge cut in.

"Forgive me, Tucker," Hashi completed.

"That's all right. A lot of people forget his name," Gleeson said, making a rare joke.

"I just see them as people who are trying to do their job the best way they can in times of trials and tribulations, in times of chaos and confusion. And I respect that," Hashi said.

Gleeson and Hashi appeared to have some rapport. Weeks earlier, when Hashi pleaded guilty, he asked whether he could inquire of the judge what would happen to him on his release. Hashi would be deported following his prison term, but could not return to the U.K. Gleeson could only tell him what the legal process was, not where he would end up. "I told you I could answer your questions. The first one you ask, I can't even answer. Sorry about that."

"Another scenario," Hashi asked. "If Somalia as we know, if it spirals down deep into a civil war and I don't have the citizenship of Britain, then am I sent to Somalia?"

Gleeson could not be certain. "I'm 0 for two in these questions," he said.

"I think the answer is yes, Your Honor," Ariail said.

Unlike the Swedes, who would be able to carry into prison an image of the place they would be at the end of their terms, Hashi found a new type of isolation: uncertainty.

"It's kind of hard to make plans when you don't know exactly where you are going," Hashi said as he closed his statement. "I stand before you today and ask you for leniency in judgment."

He was a young man and an admitted terrorist, but the brutality he had suffered, and the uncertainty of his future, made this plea for mercy before the court tangible. Gleeson registered little with his expression, asking for the government's response.

DuCharme was not going to make the same misstep that his colleague had weeks earlier. Instead, he seemed to read the room and understand the profound effect of Hashi's words. DuCharme started softly.

"We asked ourselves what more could we have said that would be helpful to the court? And I think the answer to that question is not much, but a little," he said.

DuCharme pointed to the last hearing: "something that really struck me, Judge, that you said," DuCharme said, referencing the Swedes' sentencing. "I thought to myself if Judge Gleeson views some of this conduct as part freedom fighter, I failed. I'm not doing my job. I'm not communicating effectively what the ideology is and what al Shabaab is really trying to do."

DuCharme then laid out a passionate and forceful repudiation of al-Shabaab. And, in doing so, he offered an implicit defense of the expansive legal powers underpinning the Justice Department's counterterrorism strategies. He rejected that Hashi was ignorant of the group's barbaric tactics when he joined; he raised the specter that Hashi had been stopped before he could link up with another terrorist group in Yemen, where al-Qaeda in the Arabian Peninsula operated and had demonstrated the capability to strike American targets. But in the end, DuCharme acknowledged the evidence, or lack thereof, that made Hashi distinct from his co-defendants.

"I can't put a gun in his hand," he said. "I have got no evidence that he personally engaged in acts of violence."

DuCharme explained the government's position. "I think I have not conveyed adequately what I think is a critical consideration. And that is the difference between someone with no anti-American animus going to al Shabaab to participate in an internecine civil war as opposed to someone who joins al Shabaab to participate in and been demonstrated to participate in the kind of atrocious conduct you have described with that anti-American animus."

DuCharme concluded that if he didn't succeed, "then shame on me."

Gleeson watched impassively as the prosecutor finished.

"You empowered me to do a little judging myself," Gleeson said, after noting the quality of the work by both sides.

"This is not a black-and-white situation. I see your side of it," he said, speaking to Hashi. "I do think you are slightly less culpable than your two co-defendants."

The legal approach to uncomfortable facts was to confront them as problems of language. The words "freedom fighter" and "terrorist," as Judge Gleeson rightly pointed out, are not binary propositions. Yet to engage the nuance of these ideas was to willingly enter into moral terrain neither the government nor the defense could navigate without endangering its position. The government's formulation that Hashi, Yusuf, and Ahmed had been subjected to "rough" or even "inhumane" treatment only called attention to the absence of the word that the men and their attorneys used to describe their experience: "torture." It was a word with clear statutory meaning, one that implicated U.S. treaty obligations, if not our basic sense of decency. The law seemed weakest in these moments, something approaching superstition or belief in magic when language was thrown back at difficult facts in an attempt to change their essence.

My mind drifted to a moment a decade earlier, when I stood in the ER of a combat hospital in central Iraq on a November evening. Some forty miles away, a battle for the control of Fallujah raged, providing a steady stream of casualties throughout the night and day. That day the doctors had treated tattooed and doped-up marines with gunshot and blast injuries, as well as filthy, bearded jihadis with festering wounds. At some point, two helicopters descended to the concrete landing pad next to the hospital, and nurses wheeled in the newest patient: a little girl, wrapped in a foil blanket, twisting with agitation. The flight crew relayed that she had been discovered alone in a field, apparently laid out there for a passing American patrol to pick up. My son was one and a half at that time; I estimated her to be at least twice his age.

But it was difficult to guess. Her face had been blasted open and blackened by a fragment from an explosive. I'd seen dozens of injured men over the course of the prior days, some with imperceptible injuries, others with horrific wounds. I had watched in awe and admiration as the nurses and doctors, a confident group of Americans and Australians, confronted each case dispassionately, often under the harassment of intermittent rocket and mortar fire. But the sight of this nameless girl left each of us shaken. There was the horror of her injury. But the real horror each of us confronted was the fact that she had been left alone. The head and neck surgeon, a circumspect Irish-Catholic air force lieutenant colonel from Newark, New Jersey, tried to make sense of this. He pieced together the events that might have brought her to the ER. The fragment that struck her face was traveling at a low enough velocity that it did not kill her but retained enough energy to destroy her face. He could infer that she was some distance from where the munition exploded, but close enough to be within the blast radius. Each of us knew that the marines and the army had been bombarding Fallujah for days. The insurgents, as the residents and jihadis drawn to the fight came to be called, fought back with small arms, RPGs, mortars, and IEDs. Who was responsible for this little girl's condition? Was it an errant fragment from a U.S. artillery strike? Or had the shrapnel been thrown off by an IED? The truth was that each side treated Fallujah as an open battlefield. Any military-age male was seen as a combatant. Any civilian, even a little girl of indeterminate age, should have long evacuated. This girl's crime was circumstance, but the punishment didn't acknowledge this. The lieutenant colonel, a man who owed much of his gifts and talents to the U.S. military, confronted the bitter irony that he'd now use them to repair what military planners would describe as collateral damage.

A decade later, the task before Judge Gleeson didn't seem all that different, the frustrating work of upholding American values in the midst of a war. The sentencing—and Hashi's experience—sat on the continuum with other extralegal tactics of the war on terror. Human and electronic surveillance, the coercive pressure of intelligence services, the drone assassinations, the torture by client states, the unseemly alliances with former enemies—all of which had been memorialized in the court record. These facts lent an ugliness to the outcome. None of these things belonged anywhere near an American courtroom. One could imagine that under a different political order many of these acts could be charged as crimes in their own right. These ugly measures taken in this war were unworthy of the men prosecuting the case and of the judge considering punishment. The only point left to argue was whether these steps were necessary.

As Judge Gleeson imposed his sentence, no one celebrated. Hashi would spend the next nine years in prison before confronting his uncertain fate. The moment was sad and imperfect. It left the unsettling sense that this may, in fact, be what justice looks like.

17

Hijra III

August 8, 2016

Imran Rabbani looked anxious but relieved. His oversize navy prison sweatshirt hung off his lean, broad-shouldered frame; his face unshaven and scruffy, but smiling. He appeared strong. But with a glance over to the gallery, his face betrayed some boyishness. Family, friends, members of his mosque, and a teacher from John Bowne High School looked back at him, without a word. The women and girls wore hijabs and flowing ankle-length dresses, their legs crossed at their ankles; the young boys sat with them. The men found a separate row, some in suits, the elders with graying beards wore *shalwar kameez,* the traditional trouser and shirt worn in Afghanistan and Pakistan. He could see his older brother Ikram sitting stock straight among this crowd, in a black suit and black shirt, scanning the courtroom, his long hair pulled back into a ponytail. Just eleven people had shown to see Imran sentenced, but their presence filled the first four rows of the gallery, and it had the psychological effect of balancing the moment toward him. As the marshals led him to his seat, Imran placed his hand to his heart to acknowledge those who had come for him.

The journey to this moment was hard fought. Richard Willstatter had determined that the FBI's allegations that Imran had been searching for bomb-making materials had no substance, but almost immediately after that the case suffered a setback: Judge Brodie ruled that the prosecution could proceed as an adult criminal case. Willstatter had been trying to avoid this. He weighed his options. He could appeal the judge's ruling, drawing out Imran's pretrial detention months, or perhaps, as much as a year longer. Or he could pitch a deal to the government. With his client's nod, he chose the latter.

"I think this case is not really a terrorism case," he recounted telling the prosecutors. Remarkably, the government attorneys agreed, or at least agreed that they did not want to go to trial to prove that it was. The prosecutors were willing to drop the most serious terrorism charges, but Imran would need to plead to the lesser offense, conspiracy to impede a federal officer. That charge carried a potential sentence of just more than three years, far less than the fifteen-year guidelines of the material support charge.

The Eastern District did not drop terrorism charges, as a practice. If prosecutors brought an indictment on terrorism-related offenses, they intended to prove it. But Imran's case stood out. The confrontation on the overpass rewrote the timeline of the investigation. The government had little choice but to charge him based on the evidence it had obtained at that moment—even if it was too weak to sustain the terrorism charge. A few weeks could have made a world of difference in his case. Not only would he have turned eighteen, but potentially he could have followed Munther further down the path of radicalization. Or he could have disengaged from his friend, returning to the last days of his high school career, his dalliance with radicalism a regrettable phase. Nobody would ever know which direction he would have chosen. Imran was left to consider these hypotheticals in solitary confinement. The government was left with a body of evidence that was damning, both in its implication and in its ambiguity.

The evidence against Munther Saleh and Fareed Mumuni was, by comparison, unassailable. Saleh had been apprehended as a fully radicalized supporter of the Islamic State preparing to conduct an attack. Surveillance intercepts and the testimony of cooperators had established these facts. Mumuni didn't even attempt to shield his allegiance. Instead, he tried to kill a federal agent—an act that the government viewed as a terrorist attack. There was no ambiguity surrounding these men; there would be no plea deal for them. To avoid trial, they pleaded guilty to all charges before Judge Brodie. Mumuni received twelve years, Saleh thirteen.

The government asked Judge Brodie to use her discretion to sentence Imran at the higher end of the guideline range, around three years in prison. The prosecutors argued that during the few months Imran fell under Munther's wing, he demonstrated "conduct indicating an increased interest in physical violence coupled with jihadist ideology" and "frequent association with an individual planning a domestic terror attack in support of ISIL." But Imran's attorney stressed that the government had relied on "false allegations" from the FBI to argue for his pretrial detention. The government did not respond directly to this allegation in its filings, but in arguing that Imran should receive a stiff sentence, the prosecutors didn't again try to prove that Imran had anything to do with a bomb plot. The FBI allegation hung out there, unresolved. There was no acknowledgment of error or wrongdoing. The government leaned out too far in front of the facts, and as a result Imran had been held for months in solitary confinement under the unsubstantiated belief that he was a dangerous terrorist. There was no recognition of fault, no sanction from the court, no acknowledgment that anything untoward had occurred.

Before Judge Brodie sentenced Imran, she allowed him to make a brief statement. He rose tentatively to speak.

"Your Honor, it's been a long haul, and it's been quite a journey. I spent about fourteen months in jail and five or six of those months in solitary," he said. Imran had turned to books and philosophy during his incarceration. He had even won a moot court competition among the juvenile inmates held at his facility; the law professor who ran the program considered Imran among the most gifted students she had ever taught. He haltingly quoted Socrates from the *Apology* to the judge, saying, "The unexamined life is not worth living." Before Judge Brodie, he made his argument for leniency thoughtfully, not falling into a trap many defendants do of blaming others, but opening with a strong acknowledgment of his fault.

"I made a mistake of getting out of that car and running at the law enforcement officer. I made a mistake, and I want to sincerely apologize if he's in this room. I don't know him, but if he's in this room, I'm sorry . . . I'm ready to leave. Your Honor, I'm ready to make something of myself. I'm ready to stand up on my own feet. Sorry," he said as his voice tensed up with emotion.

"Take your time," Judge Brodie said firmly.

Imran continued, "I have disappointed many people in my life, including my family and, most importantly, myself . . . I want to do something. Something good. Something good that affects the entire community and my own family as well as myself."

Imran's words hung in the air. His parents kept a stoic vigil, while his brother's face projected hope and concern. There was nothing further to say. The judge would have the final word.

Brodie took a moment before she began. Her approach to the case had been evenhanded and, at times, inscrutable, modulating between the grave recognition that the charges involved terrorism and a recognition that Imran was, in many senses, still a boy.

"The government argues that I should consider the fact that it exercised its discretion and allowed Mr. Rabbani to plead to a lesser charge of conspiracy to impede a federal officer, rather than the more serious charge of conspiracy to provide material support to a foreign terrorist organization," she began. "The problem I have with this argument is the fact that it's not clear to me that the government could have proven the more serious charge here against Mr. Rabbani, at least not based on the evidence I have seen, either at the hearing or in the submissions to me . . . [W]hile Mr. Rabbani's conduct demonstrates that he was, in fact, being led down the wrong path by Saleh, nothing in his conduct demonstrates that he conspired to provide material support to ISIL."

It was not an outright repudiation of the government's case but the closest the court would get to suggesting that Imran had been wrongly charged. She also acknowledged the uncertainty around what could have happened.

"I don't know what would have happened if you weren't stopped that night. It's possible that you would have gone down that path and you would be in a very different situation before the Court. It's also possible that you could have recognized that was not the path for you," said Judge Brodie.

As she sentenced Imran to twenty months, fourteen of which he had already served, it became clear that she did not see him as a threat, nor did she feel his conduct warranted the harsher sentence the government sought. Brodie hadn't let Imran leave that day with his parents, but the day he would be home was months, not years, in the future.

SETH DUCHARME HAD WATCHED Rabbani's case as a supervisor. Imran's story had become all too familiar for him as his office picked up on the thread of young men throughout Brooklyn, Queens, and Long Island moving down the path toward radicalization. Some of these men would be charged with crimes, while others would hang indefinitely at the precipice of crossing over into terrorist conduct. He knew the capabilities of his office. The agents he worked with built strong cases; the prosecutors he supervised won convictions. That was the Eastern District's well-earned reputation.

But his experience with his earliest case, Kaziu, made clear that bringing the full weight of the Justice Department's prosecutorial power didn't match every threat. Some defendants needed to be incarcerated, needed to be removed from society to ensure that they didn't harm the public, while others required merely counseling or mental health care, a job, an opportunity to step back into the fold of American society. He and his colleague Melody Wells, who had tried the Adnan Harun Hausa case, proposed something that Saudi Arabia and Jordan had pursued: building an off-ramp for would-be jihadists. The idea involved using the infrastructure of the national security establishment to identify potential threats but working with the private sector to intervene and give these young men an alternative. It was an innovative but risky idea. Not only for public safety, but for DuCharme's career. One attack would disprove the thesis with catastrophic effect. The safest route was to eliminate the threat, to prosecute every case, to win the conviction, and to move on. But DuCharme knew that was neither smart nor, necessarily, just. He also knew that other, more systemic threats endangered U.S. national security, that as potentially lethal as the Islamic State threatened to be, every minute spent tracking that threat was a moment not spent anticipating new attacks from new adversaries. The program he helped found, the Disruption and Early Engagement Program, launched shortly after Imran was sentenced and began the quiet work of confronting terrorism through other means than the federal justice system.

The Trump administration marked a natural break point for the Eastern District national security team. It wasn't a matter of being fired or forced to resign with the new president. For many it was time to move forward with their careers, whether that meant Washington, another U.S. Attorney's Office, or the private sector. The mission had also shifted away from the threat of a local ISIS-inspired attack toward the types of transnational cyber operations that had become increasingly commonplace and effective, including within the presidential campaign. Ariail returned to the South, as a visiting scholar at the University of Virginia, where he taught a law course on the role of the federal prosecutor and a course on prosecuting terrorism. The change of pace was welcome. He traded his tailored suits for blue jeans, blazers, and Red Wing boots. But he blanched at the public nature of academia; when a student asked to tape a lecture, his prosecutorial reflexes kicked in, emphatically denying the request. Or, when he assembled a panel of military, intelligence, and national security law leaders to speak at the university, he was stunned to see top national security reporters from *The Washington Post* and *The New York Times* crash the event. (He politely ushered them from a post-panel discussion working lunch.) After a year, he took a position more attuned to a low-key public profile but in proximity to the action: he joined the CIA as the Deputy General Counsel for Litigation and Investigations.

DuCharme, for his part, remained in the Eastern District. For a moment, rumors circulated that he would be tapped for the U.S. Attorney job. After the Trump administration dramatically dismissed the forty-six appointed U.S. Attorneys around the country in March 2017, the political nature of the role became a source of concern. Some line prosecutors wondered whether the job would now require a loyalty test from the president, particularly in jurisdictions with a clear nexus with the Trump organization, which the Southern and Eastern Districts had. The position went, instead, to an Eastern District veteran who had been working as in-house counsel for a technology company, Richard Donoghue, who was widely respected both by prosecutors and by defense counsel. Soon after returning to the office, he appointed DuCharme chief of the Criminal Division, the top criminal position in the office. But he held on to that job for only a year. In March 2019, he moved to Washington to serve as counselor to the attorney general, William Barr.

THE FOLLOWING SUMMER, Richard Willstatter stepped out into the stands at Citi Field on a gray rainy afternoon. He had no idea whom the Mets were playing, and he didn't really care. He was a Yankees fan, and the weather seemed to be acknowledging that fact. With him was Imran, who had moved home just a mile away from the stadium after his release from prison. Willstatter remarked that the scene was kind of "fucked-up," but the two would make it through the American ritual, eating hot dogs and zoning out to the rhythms of the game. Imran didn't seem to mind the drizzle. He was as he had always been with his lawyer: polite and grateful.

Willstatter wasn't given to emotional ruminations about his clients. The work of a criminal defense attorney in New York's federal courts could be grinding and at times appear futile. But each case carried the opportunity to right a wrong, whether it was to protect a teenager from being branded a terrorist for the rest of his life or take a kid who grew up in the shadow of one of baseball's monuments to his first major-league game. The details of the game were forgettable for Willstatter, but what it represented to him was not.

"You know how many clients I've taken to a Mets game at Citi Field?" he said. "One: Imran Rabbani."

PUBLIC CORRUPTION

We have the best government money can buy.

—MARK TWAIN

18

Juror #27

November 3, 2015

P ower."
   "Greed."
   "Corruption."
The trial of New York State assemblyman Sheldon Silver opened with three words.

From Arleen Phillips's seat in the front row of the jury box, the prosecutor's words hammered into the rhetorical ground like foundation pilings, breaking the quiet of the room with her forceful voice.

Phillips never expected to be sitting there. When she learned she had been called as a juror, one thought went through her mind: "Oh, crap."

Shortly after 7:30 that morning, she left the Mount Vernon two-story building where she lived with her mother and sixteen-year-old daughter, and drove in along the FDR, passing under the three bridges connecting to the Queens and Brooklyn waterfronts. Phillips always drove: the subway made her claustrophobic, and she knew this route well. For years, until 2002, she had commuted to an office in lower Manhattan on Pearl Street next to the Southern District courthouse. Phillips recalled one morning when she stood up from her desk to look across the hallway. From the window, she saw smoke pouring from a hole in one of the World Trade Center towers. By the time she went back to her desk to get her pocketbook, a second plane had struck the south tower. There was no hesitation. Arleen immediately got in her car to drive home. At some point near the Bronx, she finally looked in her rearview mirror. A smoldering cloud loomed over lower Manhattan. She asked for a transfer out of the office soon after. Fourteen years later, on her first morning of jury duty, Phillips was happily surprised when the parking lot attendant recognized her and offered her a discount.

That morning the gallery had quickly filled with press, spectators, and members of the Southern District's U.S. Attorney's Office, implicitly segregating themselves from one another, speaking in low tones. Stragglers walked across the hall to watch the proceedings in an empty courtroom with a single television monitor. The trial of Sheldon Silver marked a climax in the careers of both the assemblyman and his foil, U.S. Attorney Preet Bharara. But for Phillips, the return to lower Manhattan had thrust her, yet again, into the center of a political clash far outside her control.

As the trial opened, a bit of relief set in. The prospect of being out of work for a few weeks didn't bother Phillips. She felt the other jurors shared that sentiment, though she scarcely knew the seven women and four men impaneled with her. She looked forward to using the time to strike up friendships. Her nerves eased when the trial shifted from the imposing courtroom 110 to a smaller courtroom on the fourth floor. It was more brightly lit, intimate, with carpeted floors and mahogany finishes.

Public corruption cases, like insider trading and other financial crimes, pose a distinct narrative challenge for prosecutors. Unlike in cases against drug traffickers or organized crime figures, the government needed first to wipe away the veneer of legitimacy, as thin as it may be, that the defendant enjoyed as a member of the political or business community. As with white-collar crimes, the critical component for a prosecutor to prove was intent—a challenge that often involved creative methods of establishing circumstantial evidence, said Arlo Devlin-Brown, who supervised the case against Silver prosecuted by Carrie Cohen, Howard Master, and Andrew Goldstein. (Devlin-Brown served as chief of the Public Corruption unit for the Southern District, a rank he had obtained after trying the case against SAC Capital's Mathew Martoma.)

"When I was in the Securities Fraud unit, people definitely read *The Wall Street Journal* and the [*New York*] *Times* Business section. Then as Public Corruption's chief, I got delivered to me the *Daily News* and the *New York Post*," he said. "The tabloid writers would have stories all the time. They'd dig in some public record or city councilman's NGO. Politics makes it easier for investigative journalism; part of the system is that there's lots of enemies. In Wall Street, people cling together in large part of shared desire not to feed into investigative reporting on the industry." Public corruption crimes were typically complex, folded into transactions that would appear innocuous, even typical, in isolation. But once threaded through other interactions and conversations, a criminal pattern could be revealed. For the next thirty minutes, the government sought to do just that.

The courtroom sat silent. "This case is about a powerful politician who betrayed those that he was supposed to serve in order to line his pockets. Year, after year, after year Sheldon Silver was on the take," Cohen said.

SPEAKING TO THE JURY that morning was Cohen, the voice of the government in the Silver case. But the presence more keenly felt in the room belonged to Preet Bharara, the U.S. Attorney for the Southern District, sharply dressed in a trim suit and with bright, clear eyes rung with dark circles. The Silver case represented more than an isolated prosecution of a political figure. It was a repudiation of the culture of corruption in New York State politics and the ineffectiveness of the governor, Andrew Cuomo, in confronting it. In 2013, following a failed effort to push an ethics reform bill through the state legislature, the governor launched an anticorruption investigation—the Moreland Commission—focused on the New York State Senate and Assembly. He chose a veteran Southern District prosecutor, Danya Perry, to lead an investigation into the myriad conflicts of interest and improprieties that plagued the body. At the core of the investigation was a fact of how state government operated: being a lawmaker was a part-time job—which meant legislators could find sidelines elsewhere. One-third of these elected officials generated more than $20,000 in income from outside sources, yet there was an absence of oversight to determine how and when those positions crossed the line into pay-to-play political influence. Even before the commission kicked off, Bharara's prosecutors had charged a dozen legislators in other investigations. But with a powerful Southern District alum at the commission's helm, more charges—against more senior figures, including those close to New York's governor, Andrew Cuomo—seemed likely.

Then, in March 2014, Cuomo disbanded the commission, as part of an agreement to secure the passage of the ethics bill through the state legislature. An interim report issued by the group fell short of naming names but left little doubt of the potential for criminal charges. The governor was able to claim that he had achieved his original purpose of confronting Albany's culture of corruption by pushing an ethics bill. But in doing so, Cuomo had also placed unwanted scrutiny on some of the state's most powerful figures including the Republican Dean Skelos, the state senate majority leader, and Sheldon Silver, the Democratic Speaker of the assembly. Bharara responded to Cuomo's actions almost immediately: he ordered the commission to preserve its documents and sent members of his office in a van to take the materials compiled during the investigation. Eleven months later, a grand jury indicted Silver.

The Silver trial presented an opportunity for Bharara to play the role of political reformer. The case and the parallel trial of the Republican majority leader, Dean Skelos, promised a succession of headlines to divert from Bharara's reversals on Wall Street. He lauded the charges at a press conference. After providing a rote acknowledgment that the charges were allegations, Bharara added some color: "For many years New Yorkers have asked the question 'How could Speaker Silver, one of the most powerful men in all of New York, earn millions of dollars in outside income without deeply compromising his ability to honestly serve his constituents?' Today we provide the answer. He didn't."

The judge in the case, Valerie Caproni, drew the obvious parallel. She criticized Bharara in an opinion: "The U.S. Attorney, while castigating politicians in Albany for playing fast and loose with the ethical rules that govern their conduct, strayed so close to the edge of the rules governing his own conduct that Defendant Sheldon Silver has a non-frivolous argument that he fell over the edge to the Defendant's prejudice."

THE PUBLIC CLASH OF TWO of New York's most powerful figures before the trial had little impact on Arleen Phillips until she was called as a juror. She listened intently as the prosecutor Carrie Cohen forcefully laid out the government's case. The charges rested on two distinct corruption schemes. The first involved a seemingly positive cause: mesothelioma research. Silver had directed state funds into research of the rare cancer, which stems from asbestos exposure. But in an ethical pirouette, he had done so after a researcher referred patients suffering from the disease to the law firm where Silver worked, resulting in bonuses paid to Silver. The second scheme involved a straightforward kickback. Silver directed two of the state's largest real estate developers to hire an attorney whom he recommended, and that attorney then paid Silver a kickback for the referral. When legislation on high-stakes real estate issues like rent regulation and tax-exempt financing packages came before the state assembly, Silver pushed the developers' positions. Teasing out the quid pro quo was critical for the government's case. Cohen and her colleagues had to prove that the parties understood the transactional nature of their relationship. That the exchange of money, as veiled as it was through patient referrals and third-party payments, guaranteed political favors.

Trial days began with rituals for Cohen. The night before she read her opening aloud to herself in her Manhattan kitchen, working through the text several times to get the tone and delivery right. The next morning there was coffee—skim milk and one raw sugar—and a stop at Drybar, a Tribeca hair salon, for a blowout and one final read-through of her opening. This had nothing to do with vanity for her: it cut through the stress that crescendoed in the days leading up to trial. She read through her closing as a stylist brushed out her golden hair that fell below her shoulders. Cohen had developed this ritual over more than a decade as a prosecutor, first in the state Attorney General's Office under Eliot Spitzer, when he was New York State attorney general, then in the U.S. Attorney's Office for the Southern District. She always returned to a spare aesthetic at trial. Dark, conservative skirt suits—she never wore pants to trial—unassuming shoes. Cohen learned this not as a prosecutor but as a junior associate working for Judith Vladeck, an employment and labor law attorney who won groundbreaking civil cases that pushed for equal rights for women under the law. Cohen wanted jurors to focus on her words, not her appearance. She was not Carrie Cohen in that moment: she was the government.

The allure of the courtroom struck Cohen long before she entered law school. At high school in Great Neck, Long Island, an elective class on the Fourth Amendment set her on a path to the Silver trial. The teacher conducted the class like a law school course—addressing students by their last names, conducting the class through the Socratic method. Cohen had never encountered anything like it before. Her father was a psychologist, her mother a photographer. When she was growing up, the family didn't debate the events of the day over the dinner table. She did well in school and played lacrosse, but until that moment she'd never felt truly engaged in learning.

That curiosity carried her through undergraduate and law school, but also into motherhood. Like Phillips, Cohen was a working mother. She had juggled the demands of her legal career starting a family with her husband, a writer. At one point, she spent six months in Bhutan with her husband and their newborn daughter. He worked on a book, but Cohen did not stay at home. Instead, as the country prepared to transition from a monarchy to a democratic system, she helped the nation's chief justice work on a penal code and rules of evidence. When the family returned, she gave birth to three sons while working her way to become the lead public integrity prosecutor at the Attorney General's Office and, later, rising through the ranks in the Southern District to become a senior prosecutor.

That first day of trial her husband, mother, and children, ages five, six, twelve, and fourteen, sat in the audience of Judge Caproni's courtroom listening to Cohen deliver the opening in the most significant trial of her career. It wasn't a one-off, though. The kids had grown up in the

Southern District, visiting their mother at the U.S. Attorney's Office or stopping in at hearings and status conferences, meeting judges and FBI agents. At a moment when the cultural conversation turned on how working mothers could find the elusive "work-life balance" and "lean in" to achieve success, Cohen's children came to see their mother's role as a prosecutor as an essential feature of her identity—and her colleagues as a part of the extended family.

Cohen threaded a needle in her opening. Not only did she need to persuade the jury to believe her narrative, but the narrative had to align with a distinct theory of the prosecution: that Sheldon Silver's conduct constituted extortion and fraud. The government needed to show that his dealings deprived his constituents of the "honest" services he owed them as an elected official. Prosecutors relied on fraud as a catchall charge in the white-collar criminal world. In political corruption trials, it was often easier to prove than bribery, which required a jury to find a more explicit quid pro quo between parties. Cohen's narrative needed to convince the jury, but it also needed to survive an appeal.

When Arleen sat down with the jury that morning, she resolved to keep her mind open about this man and the charges he faced. As she listened, she objected to the word "scheme." It suggested that two people were involved. Silver was the only defendant in the courtroom, sitting there not entirely expressionless. His face fell slack with the gravity of age, his large pouty lips shut, with angular cheeks that gave his face a strangely geometric aspect. She, instead, began organizing the government's accusations in her mind as "scenario one" and "scenario two." The prosecutor's opening also left her intimidated. It wasn't the weight of the evidence that she'd hear at trial but the prosecutor's demeanor. Cohen wasn't just strident; she looked mean to Phillips. That morning, Cohen's tone was grave and strong, the strict economy of her language leaving little doubt as to the seriousness of the charges. Phillips's negative impression, nonetheless, began to color each word from the prosecutor's mouth.

Opening statements serve a different purpose for the defense. They remind the men and women of the jury of the most basic fact of the U.S. criminal system: that defendants are presumed innocent. The power of accusation is strong, and the run-up to even the most pedestrian trial

can overwhelm the presumption of innocence. The plain aesthetics of
the justice system seemed oriented toward the opposite conclusion—the
grim-faced and bored marshals and court officers, the hushed utter-
ances of the attorneys, the lengthy jury questionnaire and pregnant
questions at voir dire, the unexplained dismissals by the judge, and
the defendant, in the midst of this, helplessly shackled by accusation.
In a widely publicized trial, particularly of a powerful individual, that
presumption must fight even harder to find footing with the jury.

As Cohen spoke, that presumption took root with Phillips. She
listened to the opening, the state's troubled history of corruption, the
clashes among the ambitious and powerful, the silencing of the self-
described voices of conscience. Phillips could only think, "Just because
someone's accused of a crime doesn't mean they committed the crime."

19

Post-Tammany

New York City has contended with perfidy and graft since its founding. But corruption has also provided consistent fuel for the ambitions of politicians and the reformers confronting them. The career of William "Boss" Tweed, the chief of the city's Tammany Hall political machine, typified this. Manhattan's Lower East Side bookended Tweed's life, as it did for Sheldon Silver. He climbed the ranks of city government to eventually become the commissioner of public works, a role that overshadowed the mayor. Tweed used his office not only to enrich himself but also to champion the poor in an era of debtor prisons. He treated corruption as an essential function of government. Bribery, bid rigging, kickbacks—each had an uncanny ability to adhere to projects directly involved in the construction of the five boroughs, from the introduction of electricity to Brooklyn to the proposals for the first mass transit projects. Tweed's undoing came in 1873 with revelations that he had embezzled $10 million from the construction budget of a new county courthouse. (The building was to cost $250,000 but ran to $15 million.) He was convicted on more than one hundred counts of fraud—in the unfinished courthouse, no less.

Just one year later, Tweed walked free. To confront this apparent impunity, the governor, Samuel Tilden, launched the Tilden Commission to pursue the money stolen from the city's coffers and jailed

Tweed once again. It marked an ignominious end for one of the city's most notorious political leaders. Soon after, the Tammany chief died in the Ludlow Street Jail. Tilden used this experience to look beyond New York politics. In 1876, he ran for the U.S. presidency, winning the popular vote but losing the electoral college by a single vote to Rutherford B. Hayes.

Outside New York, the city's culture of corruption raised concerns about the viability of the American political system. "If they are content to be ruled and looted by whiskey-shop politicians, outsiders are not called upon to waste any sympathy on them. Unfortunately, however, they are not the only sufferers," *The Hartford Courant* wrote in 1885. "The enemies of the democratic idea point to New York as proof that popular institutions, even if practicable in thinly settled agricultural states, will not work in the case of great cities."

The Tweed conviction was not an isolated event. Instead, it provided a template for the ambitious in New York City: a visible campaign against public corruption provided a strong platform to pursue higher office. Less than a decade later, a twenty-five-year-old New York State assemblyman representing Manhattan followed Tilden's example to launch a career based on political reform.

The young assemblyman turned again to Tweed's old fiefdom, New York City's Department of Public Works, eventually uncovering widespread corruption in the Ludlow Street Jail, including a mysteriously generous contract by the city's sheriff to two men who cut the rope for hangings. The assemblyman used the public outrage to push a bill that wrested appointment power from Tammany aldermen and delivered it to city hall, allowing the mayor to staff his administration. The assemblyman followed this powerful blow to the political machine with a failed mayoral bid, though he was more successful in the other offices he sought: as governor of New York and, in 1901, as president of the United States. His name was Theodore Roosevelt, and while his record as corruption fighter was less known than his heroics during the Spanish-American War, his political street fighting in New York was more instrumental in laying the groundwork for future office.

Forty years later, two truths remained about corruption in New York. It was a persistent fact of political life in the city, and fighting

corruption—or more accurately promising to fight corruption—
continued to provide a viable path to power. Thomas Dewey, who
made his name convicting the mobster Lucky Luciano, held several jobs
as a prosecutor—as the senior Assistant U.S. Attorney in the Southern
District and as a special prosecutor in Manhattan's New York County.
When he turned to politics, he campaigned as a political reformer. In
1937, he ran for Manhattan district attorney by singling out one of
the last Tammany figures as a political enemy—Albert Marinelli, the
county clerk with ties to the underworld. Dewey described his campaign in moralistic terms that seemed to presage Bharara's rhetoric:
"This is not a political issue. There can be no difference of opinion on
the questions involved. Gorillas, thieves, pickpockets, and dope ped-
dlers in the political structure are not the subject of argument. There is
nothing political about human decency." (Marinelli would be indicted
in the Eastern District the next year for harboring a fugitive.) Dewey
won that election, then followed the path to New York's governorship
and two unsuccessful bids for the White House.

Corruption scandals touched the most obscure organs of city
and state government, often perennially. The NYPD (in 1894, 1960,
1970, 1981, 1998, and 2016), the Department of Buildings (in 1871,
1957, 1975, and 2008), the Taxi and Limousine Commission (1981
and 1992), the Sanitation Department (1967), the Parking Violations
Bureau (1986)—each endured graft inquiries and convictions. Federal
prosecutors were not immune to probes: in 1961, Elliott Kahaner, the
acting U.S. Attorney for the Eastern District, was prosecuted in the
Southern District for unlawfully seeking to influence a federal judge to
dismiss an indictment against a mobster. Investigations also penetrated
executive offices. During the 1970s, the Eastern District pursued
prosecutions against a Nassau County district attorney, a Queens city
councilman, and, most notably, the six congressmen and one senator
convicted in the Abscam investigation.

During Robert Morgenthau's two tenures as U.S. Attorney for
the Southern District of New York during the Kennedy, Johnson,
and Nixon administrations, he received credit for focusing the office
on white-collar crime—including public integrity prosecutions—
for the first time. Morgenthau found himself a decade in front of

a national trend. The emerging practice targeting wrongdoing in the establishment—from Watergate to the Church Commission— prompted the legal scholar Jack Katz to describe prosecutors as "executive moral entrepreneurs." He wrote,

> While legislators were essentially inactive in their legislative capacity, prosecutors have developed the legislative capacities of their offices, expanding public attention toward white-collar crime by "making law" and bringing "unprecedented" cases.

The shift in focus toward public corruption cases was epochal. In 1974, federal prosecutors achieved indictments on 291 federal and 36 state officials. A decade later those figures jumped to 563 federal and 79 state officials charged. In 2015, those figures were at 458 and 123 officials, respectively.

Rudy Giuliani rose in the ranks as this shift unfolded. During the early 1970s, he worked up from a line assistant in the U.S. Attorney's Office to become chief of the office's narcotics and special prosecutions unit and, eventually, to become the number three in the office: the Executive Assistant U.S. Attorney. He served alongside others who would also ascend the ranks of the New York legal community, including Jed Rakoff and Naomi Buchwald, judges in the Southern District, and Ira Sorkin, former director of the New York SEC office who later defended both Jordan Belfort and Bernard Madoff. In this group, Giuliani was singularly ambitious. As a young prosecutor, he gained notoriety with a blistering cross-examination of a Brooklyn congressman accused of taking a kickback to help an airline secure a route improperly. After a lunch recess, the representative, Bertram L. Podell, pleaded guilty. By all appearances, it looked as if Giuliani broke the congressman on the stand. The truth was more mundane: the plea had been in the works for some time but had only been approved by the Department of Justice after his testimony began. Giuliani's theatrics were immaterial to the case but useful in crafting his persona.

Before running for mayor, Giuliani targeted some of the city's most powerful Democrats in a public corruption case. He took the extraordinary step to personally prosecute a case against two Democratic Party leaders, Donald Manes, the Queens borough president, and Stanley Friedman, the Bronx party chief, charging the men with a bribery and extortion racket connected to the city's Parking Violations Bureau. Before he could pursue the case, Giuliani fought off a competing probe launched by District Attorney Robert Morgenthau, a Democrat who once served as the U.S. Attorney for the Southern District. The decision to push the federal case first came in a meeting with the rival prosecutors and Judge Whitman Knapp, who had served in the District Attorney's Office under Thomas Dewey. Morgenthau grew outraged, according to a defense attorney at the meeting, telling Knapp, "You forgot where you came from."

Once Giuliani won the jurisdictional battle, he turned to the press. Media coverage and Justice Department leaks plagued the case to such an extent that the judge made another extraordinary decision: he allowed the trial to move to New Haven, Connecticut, to secure an impartial jury. (Manes never went to trial; he plunged a kitchen knife into his chest as investigators closed in on him.) Giuliani won the case and within two years used the example in his own campaign for mayor—as a Republican—declaring on the steps of Tweed Courthouse, "If the Mayor [Ed Koch] had not turned over the Parking Violations Bureau to two of the biggest crooks in the city's history, there would have been $200 million to $250 million more in revenues." He would lose his first bid to become mayor, but Giuliani returned to win the office twice, before establishing himself as a national Republican Party figure and an early champion of Donald Trump's presidential campaign.

When Preet Bharara launched his office's campaign against public corruption late in his tenure as U.S. Attorney, it carried echoes of Giuliani's pivot to political crime toward the end of his tenure, but also the earlier drives by Roosevelt and Dewey. Bharara spoke to a group of Kentucky legislators at an ethics panel, describing his efforts against Albany as targeting a "caldron of corruption." He saw the role of the prosecutor to break the status quo where even those who didn't take part in graft kept silent. The financial crime that Bharara's office made a name prosecuting had a conceptual and personnel link to the high-profile public corruption cases it eventually pursued.

As Skelos and Silver went to trial, Bharara's investigators turned closer to home, probing centers of power in New York City, the NYPD and the Office of the Mayor. The office closely scrutinized Mayor Bill de Blasio's fund-raising practices but did not bring charges. Instead, it would issue a statement that acknowledged "allegations of misconduct" against the mayor for soliciting "donations from individuals who sought official favors" and that fell short of exonerating him. Prosecutors did find evidence sufficient to charge—and convict— one of the mayor's donors, Jona Rechnitz, and another man, Jeremy Reichberg, who had plied the NYPD with bribes. But the Silver trial remained the primary test of Bharara's ambitions to confront the political establishment.

Sheldon Silver was only the latest political leader in Albany to face federal charges. Joe Bruno, the former state senate majority leader, had endured a five-year odyssey in the Northern District of New York and the Second Circuit. His case offered some hope for Silver and caution for the prosecution team. Bruno was convicted in 2009 under the same "honest services fraud" statute Silver faced charges under, only to have his verdict overturned, his two-year sentence vacated, and the case sent back for a retrial. The higher court ruled that though Bruno had received consulting fees in conflict with his role as a legislator, his actions did not meet the standard of criminal conduct. Bruno fought to avoid going back to trial but returned to court in 2014. Prosecutors tried him for a second time and lost. Bruno, if anything, served as an object lesson for reform-minded prosecutors. Corruption cases needed to be fought on two fronts, first the evidence, then the law. Unlike drug and violent crime, what appeared to be corruption to many was often not seen that way in the eyes of the law. The law required that the defendant cross a profoundly blurry line between unethical and illegal conduct. A trial prosecutor would first need to prove his or her case to the jury. That case would then need to withstand the scrutiny of an appeals court, to determine whether the jury had convicted the defendant of criminal acts, rather than ethical breaches.

EVEN BEFORE SHE TOOK on the Silver case, controversial clashes had defined Judge Valerie Caproni's career. At just under five feet tall, she was often heard more clearly than seen in courtroom 443. From her perch on the bench, she looked down on the attorneys, jurors, and accused. When they looked back at her, often the reflection on her glasses and short brown hair and the soft contours of her face seemed to float in place Oz-like as she leaned back in her chair, her robes bunching over her shoulders.

Caproni's legal roots were in Brooklyn. After a brief stint at Cravath, Swaine & Moore, she joined the Eastern District's U.S. Attorney's Office as a junior prosecutor, where she eventually led the Criminal Division. She worked the federal investigation into one of the city's most divisive episodes: the murder of Yankel Rosenbaum, a Jewish scholar who was killed during the Crown Heights riots. After state prosecutors failed to convict the suspect, Lemrick Nelson, Caproni won a federal civil rights conviction against him. (An appeals court threw out the conviction, citing the judge's jury selection process; Nelson was later convicted on separate charges.)

She earned a reputation as a relentless prosecutor: when a young Chinese gang member charged with murder in a botched ransom plot claimed he was a juvenile, Caproni pursued capital charges and won a court order to use X-rays to determine whether he was, in fact, an adult (and eligible for the death penalty) through a process called forensic age estimation. (He was; he pleaded guilty to receive a life sentence.) During the investigation into the crash of TWA Flight 800, she subpoenaed a freelance journalist's phone records without receiving approval of the attorney general, forcing the Justice Department to acknowledge one of its prosecutors had broken its regulations. In 1999, while at the Securities and Exchange Commission, she and the then Eastern District chief Assistant U.S. Attorney, Loretta Lynch, found themselves in competition for the U.S. Attorney's job. Senator Schumer nominated Lynch.

Caproni didn't avoid clashes in her private sector work. Early in her career, she served as the general counsel for the New York State Urban Development Corporation. During her time there, the group fought to take control of and condemn parts of a thirteen-acre swath of Times Square. Under Caproni, the corporation won a six-year legal battle that gave the state the power to move ahead, paving the way for the redevelopment that converted the carnivalesque red-light district into a family-safe tourist center. Later, she jumped from the Securities and Exchange Commission to representing JPMorgan Chase for its involvement in the Enron scandal.

Her final stint in federal law enforcement, as general counsel for the FBI, also met with controversy. She was among several top Justice Department officials who had received early warnings on detainee abuse at Guantánamo Bay and in Iraq and were criticized for not acting more forcefully. She faced more criticism for obtaining phone records of journalists without authorization (again) and for the bureau's misuse of nearly three thousand "national security letters" to authorize surveillance. When Barack Obama nominated her to a federal judgeship in the Southern District in 2013, the Republican senator Chuck Grassley, ranking member of the Senate Judiciary Committee, probed this last issue extensively, before voting unsuccessfully against her confirmation. By the time Sheldon Silver appeared before her, she had lived through dozens of high-stakes showdowns in federal courtrooms and congressional hearings. As a judge, though, this was her first significant trial.

ON THE FIRST DAY of the trial, Sheldon Silver's attorneys introduced a distinctly New York City defense theory—one that combined both legal acumen and raw chutzpah. The lead defense counsel, Steven Molo, laid the accusations not on his client but on a fundamental flaw with New York State's legislative system.

"New York legislators, the Senate, and the assembly are part-time. So we have people right now serving in the New York legislature—one is a farmer. We have a veterinarian. We have an auctioneer. We have a pharmacist," he explained to the jury. "It's impossible, absolutely impossible, for a member of the assembly to do his or her job and to go out, make laws, deal with people, do the job that a person in the assembly does, and not have some form of conflict of interest."

He walked through the government's accusations line by line, not rejecting the facts, but attacking the premise. This was not corruption, he argued, this is what politics looks like.

"That may make you uncomfortable," he continued. "But that is the system that New York has chosen, and it is not a crime. The prosecutors here are trying to make that a crime. It is not."

Molo seemed to be ceding the ground vigorously fought in most trials, the evidence. Instead, he was asking the jury to take an interpretive leap with the evidence.

Yet when the witnesses began appearing, the perception of unequivocal wrongdoing became difficult to fight. Dr. Robert Taub, the Columbia University mesothelioma research director, described his relationship with the assemblyman as mutually beneficial if not reliant on a clear quid pro quo.

"I gave referrals to Mr. Silver in order to develop a relationship whereby he would help fund mesothelioma research and help those patients," he said. Taub received his first grant of $250,000 after Silver became the Speaker. Silver, for his part, received a check for $175,000 for the referrals he provided to Weitz & Luxenberg, the law firm. In total, Taub's research would receive $500,000 from New York State under Silver's direction.

Taub had requested a third grant of $250,000 from New York State to fund his research. He described how the assemblyman appeared at his office unannounced soon after. Silver arrived to tell him that he would not be giving the grant.

"I can't do this anymore," Silver said, according to Taub's testimony. Instead, Silver found alternate ways to help Taub, providing his children with references for jobs and internships, diverting money to Taub's wife's charity. The patient referrals continued, resulting in $3 million in payments to Silver.

In some ways, New York City corruption had achieved an enlightened state. The crimes didn't involve hangmen rigging the bids on a rope for the Ludlow Street Jail. This was cancer research and legal advocacy. To get to the victims of this scheme, jurors needed to look past the patients who stood to benefit from it.

Arleen Phillips wasn't convinced that Silver had done anything wrong. She could see that the doctor was uncomfortable testifying, as if he felt conflicted about betraying a man he considered a friend. It seemed plausible to her that this was not a "scheme," as the government described it, but instead a function of the men's relationship.

The real estate allegation was more difficult for Phillips to reconcile. On its face, the conduct looked like a friend doing a favor for another friend: Silver referred business from two of New York State's larger real estate development companies, Glenwood Management and the Witkoff Group, to a law firm founded by his childhood friend Jay Goldberg, a real estate tax specialist. But the companies did not know that Goldberg kicked back a portion of their legal fees—approximately $835,000—to Silver.

The prosecution, defense, and judge all agreed on one thing when the jury returned to deliberate: each juror should rely on common sense.

"There is no magic formula that you should use to evaluate the evidence," Caproni said. "You should not leave your common sense at home. The same types of judgments that you use every day in order to make important decisions in your own life are the judgments that you should bring to bear on your consideration of the evidence in this case."

Cohen reiterated that point in her opening, "First, listen carefully to the evidence as it comes in during the trial. Second, listen and follow Judge Caproni's instructions about the law. Third, use your common sense, the same common sense you use in your everyday lives."

Her colleague Andrew Goldstein echoed it in his summation. "You know the *quid* and the *quo* are connected. It is obvious; it is common sense. Why did Sheldon Silver do it? He did it for the money. He did it for the money."

Even Steven Molo made the same, somewhat meandering, appeal in his closing. "Use your common sense. What kind of bribe scheme is it where the person taking the bribes thinks it is a bribe, [yet] where the person giving doesn't, or the person giving the bribe thinks it is a bribe but the person taking it doesn't. What kind of extortion is it when the person allegedly being extorted doesn't think they're being extorted. It is ridiculous."

The jury returned to the deliberation room on a Tuesday before Thanksgiving. Over the course of the two-week trial, Arleen Phillips began thinking of jurors by nicknames: a woman who always discussed her evening plans became the Socialite; another woman who read throughout the trial, the Quiet Mouse; an outspoken woman, the Loudmouth Bandit; and a juror who seemed to follow the woman's lead, Mini-me.

The group immediately went around the table to poll a verdict on the mesothelioma scheme. Each juror came back "guilty." Except for Phillips.

She could only say, "I'm not sure."

"It's common sense!" one of the jurors told her.

The judge gave the jury thirty-five pages of jury instructions, which she read to them for nearly two hours before deliberations began. The instructions laid out that the government needed to prove "a bribe or kickback was sought or received by Mr. Silver, directly or indirectly, in exchange for the promise or performance of official action." Substantively, Arleen wasn't sure whether Dr. Taub and Sheldon Silver had engaged in a quid pro quo. She felt that her other jurors saw the two men's relationship in the worst possible light. But beyond the evidence, Phillips felt her fellow jurors showed little patience for her position. Many seemed eager to resolve the case before Thanksgiving. At one point, "two jurors seemed to be ganging up on her. One of the jurors kept raising her voice," an anonymous juror told a political website, *City & State New York*.

"I'm like, wait a minute, am I not allowed to have an opinion here?" she recalled. "What is this? They're all on this 'common sense.' Other people are chiming in around them. One person says to me, 'Didn't you hear the trial?' I was like, 'Excuse me, so you're saying I don't have common sense?'"

She later tried to put her experience into words in her journal. "Everyone did not look at the evidence. Some people entered the deliberation room already convinced that he was guilty," Phillips wrote. "I felt it was an attack! One person's voice is always loud. Instead of asking me in a respectful quiet manner; I was asked why with attitude, and an irritated, annoyed and disapproving tone."

Phillips went into what she called "shut-down mode" and decided to participate no longer. While her fellow jurors were discussing, she sent the judge a note that said, "I am wondering if there is any way I can be excused from this case, because I have a different opinion," she wrote. "I'm feeling very pressured, stressed out . . . told that I'm not using common sense, my heart is pounding and my head feels weird."

Arleen hoped to hear from the judge quickly, but instead the note threw the courtroom on its heels. The government wanted Arleen replaced with an alternate juror, while Silver's counsel—confronted with the possibility of a hung jury—sought to keep her.

Arleen did not know that a jury could deadlock. The jury instructions were clear that a verdict required unanimity but made no mention of what happened if a jury could not arrive at a verdict. She hoped that she could talk with Judge Caproni. "I just wanted someone to tell me that it was okay for me to say, 'I don't agree with the prosecutors when it comes to scenario one.' That's all I wanted. I wanted someone to tell me that it was okay for me to have the opinion I had and that I could stay with that opinion through the whole case," she said.

Arleen never had that meeting. In fact, she wasn't the only juror to write to the judge. One juror sought clarification whether the New York State Assembly had a code of conduct, while another raised a potential conflict of interest. The judge didn't speak directly to Arleen but did address the potential conflict of interest.

The jurors left for the holiday without arriving at a verdict. For Arleen, the experience had become intensely personal. At times during deliberations, she felt as if she were on trial, as if she needed a lawyer to represent her. She drove home from court seething, scrapping any plans to make pies for Thanksgiving, breaking from her tradition. She struggled to sleep over the weekend and prayed for clarity. Arleen recalled hearing a voice inside her saying, "Regardless of whether he's guilty or innocent, when you return on Monday, you have to look through the evidence, you have to go through as much evidence as you need to look at to make your decision. That's what I did."

On Monday, November 30, 2015, she returned to the jury room. Two other jurors approached Arleen and offered to review the evidence with her. Phillips pored over Sheldon Silver's disclosure forms with them. She did not find a clear reference to the money he had received related to Dr. Taub's referral or through Jay Goldberg. Earlier in the trial, she had felt that if there was truly a scheme, those men should also have been indicted. But the apparent efforts of Sheldon Silver to conceal the nature of the relationship offered the closest thing she could find to evidence of a quid pro quo. Shortly before 3:00 p.m., she notified her fellow jurors that she would vote "guilty" on both schemes.

As the foreperson read the verdict, Phillips didn't look at Sheldon Silver. She heard murmurs and applause from the gallery and felt disappointment wash over her.

"In a perfect world, I would've gone not guilty for the first part, guilty for the second part," she said, but felt grateful to be leaving her fellow jurors. "It's difficult to monitor people's emotions, past experiences, current experiences. You don't know what you're getting into [in] a jury pool."

20

Reversals

May 3, 2016

U.S. Attorney Preet Bharara took a seat on the aisle of the last row of courtroom 318. The sentencing of Sheldon Silver was scheduled to start in two minutes in the cavernous courtroom at 40 Foley Square. With the entrance of the Southern District's top prosecutor, the gravity of the room shifted, heads craning to make out his presence among the slate of gray and blue suits. Bharara didn't acknowledge this. Instead, he quietly thumbed through his phone as he sat alongside three colleagues, doing the same.

At the front of the room sat Sheldon Silver, the convicted former New York State assemblyman. He occupied the third chair at the defense table with an elderly slump, having hobbled through the gallery minutes earlier, dramatically letting out a breath before pausing to acknowledge a single supporter in the crowd. The resigned expression he wore seemed to be made smaller by the tension holding the room. The thirteen rows in the audience were filled; federal agents stood along the rear wall, choosing not to take a seat. The court security officers led the in-house press corps into the jury box, then filling in the public and other media behind them in the gallery, setting an unspoken hierarchy among the observers for the day's sentencing.

Carrie Cohen took her seat at the prosecution table. Few knew it beyond her colleagues, but her career as an Assistant U.S. Attorney would end within the week. She planned to return to private practice at the firm she had spent a year at early in her career, Morrison Foerster. The decision had been heartbreaking for her children. The day after the Silver trial opened, her seven-year-old son had proudly presented the cover of the *New York Post* to his class; the headline echoed a spin on the words she delivered to the jury ("Power. Greed. And Loads of Corruption"). Her children struggled to reconcile how she could go from prosecuting those accused of crimes to representing the same people. For Cohen, it was the right time.

Silver had been the capstone of her career in public service. It embodied what she saw as the Southern District ethos: the relentless pursuit of the truth and the justice that it demanded. With public corruption cases, the stakes were particularly high. The decision to charge an elected official imputed the will of the people who placed that person in a position of power. Silver was not the only official she had won a conviction against. She had also been part of the team that prosecuted Alan Hevesi, the New York State comptroller who served twenty months in prison on corruption charges. Cohen didn't measure her achievement by convictions alone: some of her proudest decisions were those cases where she declined to pursue charges. She wasn't alone in her departure to the private sector; her supervisor Arlo Devlin-Brown would move to Covington & Burling in August 2016. The migration for a senior Assistant U.S. Attorney to a lucrative partnership at a private firm is so fundamental that it goes unremarked upon. But as the epilogue to a conviction where a jury found that a public servant had used his office for pecuniary gain, it struck an ironic coda.

The guideline range that Judge Caproni calculated called for a sentence between twenty-one and twenty-seven years.

"I am not going to impose a guideline sentence in this case," said Judge Caproni, noting that it would be "draconian" to do so and "unjust" given Silver's age. Bharara did not look up from his phone as the judge spoke.

"The government is asking that the Court impose a sentence on this defendant that is higher than any sentence imposed on other New York convicted state officials," said Cohen, her voice booming. As she spoke, Bharara looked up and directed his attention, for the first time, to the sentencing. Cohen sought more than fourteen years, the harshest punishment a New York political figure had received—William Boyland, a Brooklyn assemblyman sentenced in the Eastern District in 2015.

"If we could address one other point the defense raised in its submission, that there is a lack of discernible harm—and that's a quote . . . Your Honor, nothing could be farther from the truth," said Cohen, the anger in her voice palpable. "The defendant here caused specific and massive harm; harm to the people's faith in their government, harm to our rule of law, and harm to our democracy."

When Steven Molo began speaking, he countered the government's strident tone with a plainspoken, slightly plaintive approach.

"The Court must consider every convicted person as an individual, and it must consider every case as a unique study in human failings," he offered up. "Those aren't my words. Those are the words of the Supreme Court of the United States."

Molo portrayed his client as a lifelong, beloved public servant in declining health. He reiterated the effect of the corruption that Silver had been convicted of: a cohort referred mesothelioma patients to a top law firm, medical research received funding, the legislature passed tenant-friendly legislation. In relative terms, had Silver committed such severe crimes? Bharara watched closely as Molo spoke.

"I want to highlight three cases," Molo began. "The first is the McDonnell case, which was just argued before the Supreme Court of the United States . . ."

"Very different facts," Judge Caproni cut him off.

Molo, gingerly, made his point that Bob McDonnell, who had received "lavish gifts" and "shopping sprees" for his wife, was sentenced to only two years. He mentioned the thirty-month term Bob Ney, the Ohio representative implicated in the Jack Abramoff scandal, received. Finally, he mentioned Joe Bruno, the former New York State Senate leader, sentenced to two years. Silver's attorneys offered up these as examples of leniency, though the catalog of perfidy in our politics left the room dispirited.

Sheldon Silver rose to speak. His attorney had recognized that

Silver's personality came across as "droll" and "Sphinx-like." Arleen Phillips had waited for a moment like this throughout the trial, an opportunity to hear the Speaker's voice as a measure of his character. He pulled the microphone close, standing, defeated, in a gray suit with an American flag fixed feebly to his lapel.

"Without question, I let down my family, I let down my colleagues, I let down my constituents, and I am truly, truly sorry for that," he said.

It was a deflating recitation. And the judge took a little pause before moving into her sentence.

"Here's the thing about corruption: It makes the public very cynical," she said.

Judge Caproni highlighted the question she faced: "Is Sheldon Silver a basically good and honest person who just went astray, which is what the defense argues, or is he fundamentally corrupt, as the government argues?"

She went through the letters and the evidence in the case and pointed out a recurring theme: Silver had gone to great lengths to conceal the schemes that the government charged him with.

"Mr. Silver, those are not the actions of a basically honest person. Those are the actions of a scheming, corrupt politician," she concluded.

Caproni announced the sentence: twelve years and a $1.75 million fine. Sheldon Silver stared straight down. Preet Bharara did not look up from his phone. The Speaker would not need to report to prison until his appeal had been addressed.

The crowd scrambled from the courtroom, reporters making their way to the elevators and stairwells.

Outside the Thurgood Marshall Courthouse, the cold spring afternoon had a sky the gray of the courthouse steps. A dense scrum of cameramen and photographers had set up a watch on the sidewalk, handicapping which exit the convicted Speaker would emerge from. *Would he walk out the front door of the courthouse and descend the steps in an almost metaphorical fall from grace? Or would he chance the side exit, thrusting himself immediately into the crowd on the sidewalk?*

A lone photographer stood on a ledge overlooking the scene, a keen but dangerous vantage point, before a court security officer shouted him down. As the press corps rushed out of the building, the photographers snapped into a frenzy. The word that Silver would depart the side door shot through the crowd like a bolt. In an instant, dozens of bodies pressed forward around the doorway, holding DSLRs and video cameras above the crowd, blindly hoping to capture an image.

Whatever decorum had held together the sentencing in courtroom 318 vanished on the sidewalk. Silver appeared in the doorway on the side of the courthouse, immediately confronted by the wall of people, the flash and blink of cameras reflecting in his glasses. His face appeared unchanged, expressionless; only his body language suggested fear and panic. Reporters shouted questions across the sound of shutters snapping. The crowd made no path for him, forcing Silver to push into and then through the photographers. The swarm followed him as he made his way toward Centre Street. Passersby stopped to take in the carnivalesque scene, pulling their phones from their pockets to document the chaos. The one attorney accompanying Silver waved down a passing yellow cab. In a moment, the Speaker climbed in, fixing his gaze forward, as the crowd stopped in its tracks. The cab pulled away, taking the former Speaker back toward the district he once represented.

IT WOULD BE another ten months before the Second Circuit heard Silver's appeal and another four months, in July 2017, before the panel issued its decision. In that time, the Supreme Court had reinterpreted the law on honest services fraud in the McDonnell case. The Court unanimously took a charitable view of corruption. The use of influence, like making introductions and setting up meetings, no longer qualified as "official acts" of government, which could expose a political leader to criminal liability. The Court required that the defendant take overt steps to exercise that influence, to violate the statute, whether that meant taking an official action or pressing another official to do so. This narrower view of the law gave prosecutors a way forward. But it highlighted the divide between how the law functions and how the public expects it to function. The Supreme Court ruled on the language of the existing statute, but in doing so endorsed an extremely reductive view of how political influence operates. In Sheldon Silver's case, the mesothelioma grants and the real estate legislative input had acts of government attached to both. The appeals court, nonetheless, ruled that Judge Caproni had instructed the jury on an overly broad and incorrect definition of the law, and it vacated the conviction and remanded the case back to the district court.

The circuit's decision that morning surprised Arleen Phillips when she first heard about it. "I felt all along that he shouldn't have been convicted," she said. "At least for part one."

The circuit court vacated Bharara's signature public corruption conviction. For all the crimes that the government had gone to such pains to show that Sheldon Silver had committed, none of them broke the law. It seemed that all the appeals to common sense that the government had made of the jury were misplaced. Common sense would offer little guide in defining corruption under the law.

Yet a year later, the office tried Sheldon Silver again. Both Arleen Phillips and Preet Bharara watched the case as private citizens, no longer attached to the trial as a juror or a prosecutor. President Trump had removed Bharara with the dismissal of other U.S. Attorneys around the country, a traditional succession that was confused by the president's private assurances that Bharara would remain in the job. For twenty hours, Bharara held on to his position—uncertain of whether he had, in fact, been fired. The confirmation came with a request for his resignation.

Sheldon Silver's second trial offered Phillips proof that the charges of corruption were not true. The new trial was an opportunity for the government to pull another jury, one more willing to convict Silver. When Phillips learned that the jury had convicted Silver yet again in May 2018, she reflected on the blunt politics at play.

"He lost his job," she said. "So I think he's received his punishment."

It was a statement that unintentionally aligned the fates of the two men, the former New York State Assembly leader and the former U.S. Attorney for the Southern District of New York.

Epilogue

January 28, 2017

On a Saturday night eight days after the inauguration, I sprinted across Cadman Plaza Park toward the doors of the Eastern District courthouse with only a notebook in hand. The Trump administration's executive order barring entry of citizens from several Muslim-majority nations—the travel ban—had set in motion chaos at ports of entry around the country, including John F. Kennedy International Airport, where an unknown number of travelers had been detained. While the president's supporters greeted the order as an election promise kept, the ban sparked protests at airports around the country. An emergency hearing had been called less than an hour earlier. A palpable shock hung in the air outside the federal courthouse, where a small crowd began forming, looking in the doorway, unsure whether they were allowed in.

I knew that the hearing concerned the executive order but understood very little beyond that. By the time I made it to Judge Ann Donnelly's fourth-floor courtroom, a crowd had collected at the door. The reporters and a single courtroom artist filed into the jury box, while immigration attorneys in slapped-together suits and New Balance sneakers began to fill out the gallery, joined by a dozen or so protesters, a few holding signs. The parties to the case were already seated at the attorneys' tables, though it wasn't yet apparent who the lawyers were. The courtroom manager entered from behind the bench, and at the sight of the crowd taking their seats, she stepped forward to issue a warning. "There will be no talking. No signs. No rustling," she said. "You will be kicked out."

Judge Donnelly entered carrying papers under her arm, and after the counsel took their seats, the manager called the case: *Hameed Khalid Darweesh v. President Donald Trump.*

The parties addressing the judge were Lee Gelernt and two colleagues from the ACLU; three Assistant U.S. Attorneys, led by the chief of the Eastern District's Civil Division, Susan Riley; and an attorney from Main Justice, Gisela Westwater, who joined by phone.

An attorney's race, ethnicity, or apparent faith didn't seem particularly relevant when reporting in the Eastern District. The courthouse, the U.S. Attorney's Office, and, to some extent, the defense bar reflected the diversity of the district. Some generalizations could be made: federal agents skewed heavily white, and if you were a defendant arraigned on terrorism charges for seeking to join ISIS, there was a strong likelihood you'd be assigned a nonreligious Jew as a lawyer. Race, gender, creed, sexual orientation, and physical abilities rarely surfaced in discussion. One of the most impressive prosecutors in the Eastern District was deaf, but that fact, like any of these other aspects of identity, seemed incidental, rather than a basis to define or assess him. The discriminatory tenor of the executive order made identity suddenly relevant. The government counsel on this evening consisted of an African American woman and two white men, one of whom wore a yarmulke, as observant Jews often do. They had arrived in court to defend an executive order that singled out a religious group, Muslims. The diversity so fundamental to the Eastern District's jurisdiction and the identity of those who worked the courts here seemed to have taken a turn down a darkened corridor as a value embraced under the new administration.

"All right. We're here considering an emergency stay application in a removal case. I just have a couple of questions about status," said Judge Donnelly, who had been nominated to the bench one year earlier.

Riley, the chief of the Eastern District's Civil Division, responded tentatively: "This has unfolded with such speed, both the executive order and the actions taken pursuant to the executive order, that we haven't had an opportunity to address any of the issues."

The government attorneys projected none of the confidence or preparedness typical of federal prosecutors. Riley responded haltingly, glancing at her colleagues and pausing to allow the attorney on the phone from Main Justice an opportunity to respond.

"I do recognize that you haven't really had a chance to review all of this but that's, I think, why they're asking for the stay," Donnelly responded impatiently.

The two plaintiffs named in the ACLU complaint had been freed. The government hoped that this would make further argument moot.

"What exactly are plaintiffs arguing are the various statuses of these individuals?" Westwater asked over speakerphone.

Donnelly cut her off. Hundreds of others had already been impacted by the order. "Well, let me just put it this way. I mean, if they had come in two days ago, we wouldn't be here, am I right?"

The ACLU attorneys conferred quietly at their table before Gelernt rose to speak. "I was just passed a note that the government is literally, as we speak, putting someone back on a plane back to Syria."

Donnelly frowned. Federal judges typically controlled the clock in a case, and few relished making important decisions under the gun. She gave the government a chance to make its case as to why she should allow this to happen.

"The government does not have sufficient information about this person or the circumstances, Your Honor, to be able to have a position," Westwater said, her disembodied voice nearly inaudible.

The government had shown up to court without an argument. The Trump administration had exercised its presidential power for the first time, yet the government's lawyers could not defend the legality of the action the White House chose to take. There seemed to be an incongruity in the courtroom. On the one hand, there was the law, governed by customs and traditions taken as fundamental to the parties gathered there. On the other, there was government by fiat, the willing of policy into existence, irrespective of the law and of those who make it their life's work. Riley and her colleagues sat there, stunned that they found themselves in the position to defend an impulse that held their very existence in contempt.

Judge Donnelly struggled to conceal her irritation.

"Well, that's exactly why I am going to grant the stay," she said, exasperated.

The clock read a few minutes before 9:00 on a Saturday night in Brooklyn. A first-year federal judge had just defied the president. The audience murmured ecstatically and began to celebrate, and the judge shouted, "No, no, no, no. Not a word. Not a word!"

The executive order had created its own circus; she would not let it turn her courtroom into one. The gallery fell into giddy silence, smiles and a few tears appearing on faces in the crowd.

Lee Gelernt bounded out of the courtroom, met by his sister, Michelle, a federal public defender who had represented El Chapo in a courtroom down the hallway a few days earlier. It was a reminder that as large and imposing as the idea of the justice system seemed, in New York it remained a small, familial society. She beamed with pride at the sight of her brother. The two piled into an elevator with a handful of reporters, who pressed the ACLU lawyer for clarification on the scope of Judge Donnelly's order. Gelernt poised his glasses on top of his head and, in a dispassionate, lawyerly response, began to explain the mechanics of how the order impacted the country. When the group stepped off the elevator and into the lobby on the first floor, the roar of a crowd emanating from outside the building suddenly broke the quiet.

Gelernt looked at his sister sheepishly, then stepped outside. The dozen or so protesters had grown to several hundred, pressing toward the entrance of the building, cheering and shouting. The crowd hushed itself as the ACLU attorney appeared, leaning in to hear what he had to say.

"The judge, in a nutshell, saw what the government was doing and gave us what we wanted, which was to block the Trump order," Gelernt shouted. "The key tonight was to make sure that nobody was put back on a plane."

The crowd broke out into a cheer. Someone had the presence of mind to assemble an ad hoc marching band, the clatter of a snare drum, trumpet, and tuba punched the air of a hazy January night. Gelernt and his colleagues pushed through the scrum. He knew that when the government returned to court, the Assistant U.S. Attorneys would be better prepared. But he had yet to fully appreciate the impulses of the Trump administration. In the next year, Gelernt's attention would turn far beyond the Eastern District's border at JFK to the southern border and to sanctuary cities, where the administration pursued an unprecedented policy of removal and family separation and where the ACLU would stage its most persistent challenges to executive power. That night he could enjoy the celebration only for a moment before returning to work. He and his colleagues walked off through the mist.

But the crowd remained, dancing and shouting, euphoric, the impassive face of the Eastern District federal courthouse watching over them.

A WEEK LATER, a parallel scene would play out in Manhattan on a chilly and clear Sunday afternoon. Thousands of New Yorkers gathered at the Battery in sight of the Statue of Liberty to protest the new administration's travel ban. Near sunset, the crowd marched through the shaded streets of the financial district shouting, "This is what democracy looks like!" their voices echoing between the empty office buildings. The route terminated at the steps of the Southern District's Thurgood Marshall Courthouse.

There the crowd of families, young people, and the elderly gathered in the day's fading light, a sense of calm quieting the scene. The lurid drama of the Trump presidency would continue in a courtroom overhead in the coming year: the president's personal attorney, Michael Cohen, would be sentenced in a criminal conviction that reached directly back to the president. But the crowd wasn't prescient. Their journey was instinctual. It acknowledged an unspoken American truth felt by the crowds at Cadman Plaza a week earlier. The courts are where we still turn to address the most fundamental human longing: justice.

Acknowledgments

Sitting down and writing a book can be solitary and, at times, a bit isolating. But the process of completing a book is a communal effort and, at least in this case, the chance to share in the insight, talent, and generosity of others.

I'd like to express gratitude and acknowledge the contributions so many others made to this book. Some people can't be named. They nonetheless took the initiative and time to speak with me. Often these people did so with no discernible benefit and, in some cases, a measure of professional or personal risk. Many others fielded my queries and acted as sounding boards on a range of issues including Adam Perlmutter, Joshua Dratel, Steve Zissou, Susan Kellman, and Elizabeth Macedonio. Several attorneys represented me or lent advice on access issues including David Schulz, Thomas Sullivan, Katie Townsend, and Zachary Margulis-Ohnuma. The public affairs professionals at the Departments of Justice and Homeland Security also deserve recognition for the day-to-day work of ensuring some measure of transparency to the activities of the government: John Marzulli, Dawn Dearden, James Margolin, Stephanie Shark, Kelly Langmesser, Wyn Hornbuckle, and Anthony Bucci. I am also grateful to staff at the courthouses, the security officers and the clerks, who are often the first point of contact for people stepping into the justice system—their professionalism and courtesy did not go unnoticed each morning I showed up to attend court.

I owe this opportunity to my editor Andrew Miller and the wonderful team at Knopf, including Sonny Mehta, Zakiya Harris, Dan Novack, Katie Schoder, Josie Kals, Danielle Plasky, Rose Cronin-Jackman, and Maris Dyer. Andrew and I have been working on books for a decade and his skill and composure as an editor have shaped me as a writer and reporter.

I'm also grateful to my agent, Eric Lupfer, for his keen perspective and pragmatism. He molded this idea from a conversation in his office one afternoon, through the proposal process and into the early drafts until the book took shape as a completed manuscript. Also, the team at WME, Anna DeRoy, Erin Conroy, and Alicia Gordon, have represented this book enthusiastically throughout this process.

I'm also indebted to my colleagues and friends—the folks who have been generous in large and small ways, whether picking up an assignment, speaking to my class, fielding my calls, or giving me the space to work. This list is, by definition, incomplete: Ben Nicholl and Nellie LeCren, Vanessa Gezari, Mark Schone, Katie Roiphe, Reyhan Harmanci, Matthew Cole, Maureen Callahan, Evan Ratliff, Patrick Keefe, Maryam Saleh, Seamus Hughes, Megan Twohey, Dan Bennett, Paul Janzen, Mike Moore, Peter Kline, Douglas McGowan, Daniel Ahearn, the O'Connell brothers, Presston Brown, Benjamin Provo, Jens Fleming, and Gabriel Cole. In all this I remember my dear buddy Travis J. Peterson.

This may seem silly, but it is sincere: I could not have completed this book without Upright Coffee and the friends I've made there including Haly Bei and Sean Doyle.

My family have made the greatest contribution to this book. My mother, Maureen Dwyer, sisters Jeanne Pyrz and Maria Nasharr, and brothers Joe and Pat Dwyer have happily tolerated a writer in the family since I can remember. Harriet Dominique, Lizzy and Terrel Ross, and David Magid have continued this support. My kids, Ruby and Clyde, have put up with their fair share of inconvenience because of my job—but the pride I feel for them drives me each day. Sarah, my wife, is my partner in all things—our twenty-three years in love and friendship are written into each word in this book.

Notes

A Note on Sources

Directly across from the courthouse for the Eastern District of New York, at the entrance to Cadman Plaza Park underneath a towering stand of London plane trees, you'll find a set of park benches. They aren't much to see—weathered wood planks bolted to matte iron legs that loop into near perfectly circular armrests. Robert Moses created this design for the World's Fair in 1939. Since then they've become ubiquitous in New York City's parks, suitable monuments to his legacy: not particularly comfortable, but, given no other options, fine.

These benches became something of an office for me while reporting this book. A good spot to gather notes, drink a coffee, and strike up conversations with people headed into the courthouse in between hearings. The benches also provided an ideal vantage point to watch the traffic between the U.S. Attorney's Office and courthouse doors. A steady parade of line assistants, and, on occasion, the section chiefs or even the U.S. Attorney made the two-hundred-yard journey between the offices where they investigated their cases and the courtrooms where they brought their evidence and argued the law. After a year or so, I could begin to read the day's docket by watching who was moving in and out of the courthouse. And I got the greatest kick on the rare afternoons when I saw a judge passing through the park, breathing the same air that you and I do. I was never trying to break news, to divine grand jury proceedings, or pull a scoop out of my conversations with people. But I was trying to get past these titles like "federal prosecutor" and "defense counsel" or "judge," which effectively carry meaning about the institutions each serve, but tell you very little about the people who actually do the job. My hope was to understand the human experience of the courts and this unique human process of seeking justice. The only way to do that was to show up every day, to familiarize myself with the rhythms and rituals of the courthouse, and make my face familiar to the people who work there.

The primary source material for this book is the reporting I did in court. I began writing about the federal courts in New York in 2009 but started dedicated reporting for this book in May of 2015. Since then, I've spent thousands of hours attending hundreds of conferences, hearings, and trials in both the Southern and Eastern Districts, making daily visits to the courthouses during the first two years reporting this book. The vast majority of cases I followed did not make it into this text. These did, however, introduce me to many of the characters and the histories of each district. The cases I covered opened doors to different worlds that were often a subway ride or short drive away: JFK and the surrounding neighborhoods of Ozone Park and Howard Beach, the gleaming midtown offices of white-shoe firms and hedge funds, the less appointed shared work spaces of defense attorneys in lower Manhattan and Bayside, Queens, public housing communities in the northern Bronx, immigrant neighborhoods in Bensonhurst, Brooklyn, and Flushing, Queens, academic panels at the law schools of Fordham University and New York University, George Washington University's Program on Extremism, and the University of Virginia's Batten School of Public Policy. These hours are memorialized in eight black notebooks and in daily files I would write to myself to capture the moments, big and small, that I'd just experienced in the courthouses. My reporting is not cited explicitly in the "Notes" that follow, but it forms the foundation of this book. The notes, however, seek to detail the interviews, documents, and published source material I relied on to write this narrative.

This book benefited greatly from the work of daily reporters who covered the courthouses including John Marzulli, Nate Raymond, Benjamin Weiser, Stephanie Clifford, and others. I learned not only from the stories each published prior to the inception of this book, but also from working the same hearings, trials, and press conferences, and studying how each distilled these sometimes stultifying and obtuse events into readable, relevant work. I've also included a bibliography listing some of the books that informed my reporting, but I owe a distinct debt to Selwyn Raab for his comprehensive chronicle of La Cosa Nostra, *The Five Families*.

There are always missed opportunities when reporting a project this length. I've indicated throughout the notes the instances where sources either declined to speak to me or did not respond to requests for interviews. Nothing should be inferred from any party's decision not to engage with the reporting process of this book. In some cases, individuals had a professional obligation not to speak with a journalist. In other cases, the decision is personal and has nothing to do with the factual issues at stake. And in others, subjects made a judgment that speaking to me would not serve their interests.

One absence from the reporting in this book should be noted: the federal defenders offices in Manhattan and Brooklyn. The work of New York City's federal public defenders deserves a dedicated book. The nature of the offices' caseload and the caliber of their attorneys are without parallel. I was grateful to the federal defenders who would speak to me briefly to clarify relevant facts and issues raised in a case, before begging off on a request for an interview. The Brooklyn defenders office did initially respond to a request to speak with a senior attorney, going as far as to schedule that meeting. The attorney, however, canceled and never responded to further requests. The offices have far more urgent matters to attend to than questions from an author. But, unfortunately, without the engagement of the office I was not able to tell the important story of their work.

Another missed opportunity in this reporting process came with the Freedom of Information requests I made of the Department of Justice and its components, including the Bureau of Prisons. The department does not fulfill its obligations under the statute willingly. As a result, none of the multiple requests that I made, which were completed by the department, yielded anything of substance. This was not because the documents I sought were not relevant to my research, but because they were often redacted to the point of abstract minimalism. One example: I sought memoranda from the Department of Justice's Office of Professional Responsibility on employees of both the Southern and Eastern Districts. I received five reports on allegations of misconduct totaling more than 65 pages—every name, identifying feature and detail of the report had been blacked out. The same was true of a request on courtroom closures—I received hundreds of pages detailng requests to close courtrooms in the districts. Yet, again, they were redacted into nothingness. The frustration of seeing the department flout their obligations under the FOIA was only outdone in the instances when the department altogether ignored these obligations—which it continues to do in requests that remain pending to this day, several years after their first submission.

Finally, a number of people spoke to me without attribution. In the cases where I went off the record or on background with sources I did so by balancing their need for anonymity with the public interest in reporting the information or perspective they could provide. Parties to criminal cases often have professional obligations that restrict their interactions with the press. In other cases, office policies forbid, or circumscribe, contact with reporters. My guiding principle in making the decision to rely on a background or anonymous source was fairness. If, for example, a prosecutor not permitted to speak publicly about a case needed to go on background to explain the decision-making process behind an action, in that case I felt justified in agreeing to those terms. Alternatively, if a source chose to speak on background to trash their opponents (or, in some cases their own colleagues) I made a point to not rely on those statements.

Also, it should be noted: none of the text or quotes within this book has been approved by the subjects prior to publication. Often attorneys seek quote approval as a ground rule for conversations. I do not read back quotes to interview subjects, so in those cases I opted to not directly quote those sources, but instead paraphrase or seek out similar statements in the public record.

There are also dozens of interviews that are not directly cited in the "Notes" with current and former federal agents, prosecutors, criminal defense attorneys, defendants, informants, and subjects of investigations who were never charged. These interviews were essential in not only forming a base of knowledge for me to report more deeply in the Southern and Eastern Districts, but also in understanding the culture of ethos of this part of the legal community.

In these citations, I've strived to be transparent, accurate, and complete without unnecessarily exposing sources; any errors are mine alone.

Prologue

4 **This day's sentencing covered two sets of criminal charges:** *United States v. Michael Cohen,* U.S. District Court, Southern District of New York, Manhattan Division, "Government's Sentencing Memorandum," Dec. 7, 2018.

6 **When the Southern District's flack:** Senior federal prosecutor, interview by author, Dec. 22, 2010.

7 **This was the era of Preet:** Preet Bharara did not respond to requests for an interview.

10 **Several years after that sit-down:** Senior federal prosecutor, interview by author, Sept. 19, 2016.

Strange Spectacle

13 **The act created thirteen federal districts:** Russell R. Wheeler and Cynthia Ellen Harrison, *Creating the Federal Judicial System* (Washington, D.C.: Federal Judicial Center, 1989), 4.

13 **By 1865, New York City's population:** "Total and Foreign-Born Population New York City, 1790–2000," NYC.gov, accessed Jan. 5, 2018, www1.nyc.gov.

13 **Perhaps more important, New York harbor had:** Edward Glaeser, "Urban Colossus: Why Is New York America's Largest City?," *Federal Reserve Bank of New York Economic Policy Review* 11 (Dec. 2005): 7–24, accessed Jan. 5, 2019, doi:10.3386/w11398.

14 **More than anything else, the proposed:** Cong. Globe, vol. 56, pt. 2, ed. John Cook Rives and George A. Bailey, 983.

16 **In 2009, the Southern District's U.S. Attorney:** U.S. Department of Justice, May 3, 2018, accessed Jan. 5, 2019, www.justice.gov.

16 **She reordered the Violent Crime:** U.S. Attorney Loretta Lynch to Entire Staff, July 30, 2012, "Criminal Division Reorganization, Appointments and Transfers," nylawyer.nylj.com.

17 **When TWA Flight 800 crashed:** Robert E. Kessler, "The Blast on Flight 800: Prosecutors Rushed to Stake Claims," *Newsday*, July 25, 1996.

18 **"If you were a section chief":** Gordon Mehler interview by author, Sept. 24, 2015.

18 **"In New York City, such disputes":** Stephen Fineman, *Emotion in Organizations*, 2nd ed. (London: Sage, 2000), 235.

19 **Congress passed the First Step Act:** German Lopez, "The First Step Act, Congress's Criminal Justice Reform Bill, Explained," *Vox*, Dec. 11, 2018, accessed Jan. 7, 2019, www.vox.com.

20 **Both sides have a point:** Executive Office for U.S. Attorneys, *United States Attorneys Annual Statistical Report* (Washington, D.C.: U.S. Department of Justice, Executive Office for U.S. Attorneys, 1996), www.justice.gov. (The 2018 statistics have not been released by the Trump administration.)

20 **"Prosecutors run our federal criminal justice":** *United States v. Gurley,* Criminal Action no. 10-10310-WGY, U.S. District Court, D. Massachusetts, "Sentencing Memorandum," May 17, 2012.

20 **"Our criminal justice system is almost":** Jed S. Rakoff, "Why Innocent People Plead Guilty," *New York Review of Books*, Nov. 20, 2014, accessed Jan. 7, 2019, www.nybooks.com.

21 **But the policy of individual corporate accountability:** Chris Bennington, "Personal Liability Trend Continues: Health Care CEO Gets Jail Time for Fraud Scheme," Bricker Eckler LLP, July 10, 2018.

21   **In November 2018, Deputy Attorney General Rod Rosenstein:** "Deputy Attorney General Rod J. Rosenstein Delivers Remarks at the American Conference Institute's 35th International Conference on the Foreign Corrupt Practices Act," U.S. Department of Justice, Nov. 29, 2018, accessed Jan. 7, 2019, www.justice.gov.

21   **The total number of federal criminal laws:** U.S. Congress, House of Representatives, Committee on the Judiciary, *The Crimes on the Books and Committee Jurisdiction: The Over-criminalization Task Force of 2014,* 113th Cong., 2nd Sess., 2014, 2–3.

21   **The Trump administration passed:** "Library of Congress," Congress.gov, accessed Mar. 19, 2019, www.congress.gov. (Query: Refined by Legislation 115 (2017–2018) Became Law).

22   **His tenure there was brief:** Edward T. Pound, "U.S. Fraud Unit to Start Inquiry in New York City," *New York Times,* Sept. 5, 1981, accessed Jan. 8, 2019, www.nytimes.com.

23   **When Purdue Pharmaceuticals faced Justice Department:** Barry Meier and Eric Lipton, "Under Attack, Drug Maker Turned to Giuliani for Help," *New York Times,* Dec. 28, 2237, accessed Jan. 8, 2019, www.nytimes.com.

23   **In 2018, drug overdoses surpassed:** Lee Zeldin, "The Leading Cause of Death: The Heroin & Opioid Abuse Epidemic," March 5, 2018, accessed Jan. 8, 2019, zeldin.house.gov.

23   **The following year:** Barry Meier, "Sackler Testimony Appears to Conflict With Federal Investigation," *New York Times,* Feb. 22, 2019, accessed March 19, 2019.

24   **The decision fundamentally changed:** Brentin Mock, "How Police Are Using Stop-and-Frisk Four Years After a Seminal Court Ruling," *CityLab,* Aug. 31, 2017, accessed Jan. 8, 2019, www.citylab.com.

25   **The former U.S. Attorney Robert Fiske:** Robert B. Fiske, *Prosecutor Defender Counselor: The Memoirs of Robert B. Fiske Jr.* (Kittery, Maine: Smith/Kerr Associates, 2014).

25   **The compensation for federal prosecutors:** "Office of Diversity and Inclusion: A Diverse Workforce," U.S. Office of Personnel Management, Jan. 2018, accessed Jan. 8, 2019, www.opm.gov.

26   **"I started my career":** Massimo Calabresi, "SEC Chair Mary Jo White Talks to TIME in Exclusive Interview," *Time,* April 3, 2014, accessed Jan. 8, 2019, time.com.

26   **Instead, it asks its prosecutors:** "9-27.000—Principles of Federal Prosecution," U.S. Department of Justice, Dec. 7, 2018, accessed Jan. 8, 2019, www.justice.gov.

26   **"The qualities of a good prosecutor":** Robert H. Jackson, "The Federal Prosecutor: An Address," Second Annual Conference of United States Attorneys, Great Hall Department of Justice Building, Washington, D.C., April 1, 1940, accessed Jan. 8, 2019, www.justice.gov.

26   **But if justice is an intangible value:** U.S. Attorneys' Office, "Annual Statistical Report 2017," www.justice.gov.

Proving Grounds

27   **He was Sheldon Silver, the former:** Sheldon Silver did not respond to requests to interview him.

29   **Bharara was the first first-generation immigrant:** Bharara did not respond to requests to interview him both during and following his tenure at the Southern District of New York.

29   **The incident, which didn't tamp:** Preet Bharara, "Con Jobs: From Inmate to Entrepreneur (with Catherine Hoke)," *Stay Tuned with Preet,* Oct. 12, 2017, accessed Jan. 8, 2019, www.cafe.com.

29   **Bharara excelled in academics:** Jeffrey Toobin, "The Showman," *New Yorker,* May 9, 2016.

29   **He was also a fastidious student:** Preet Bharara, "The Problem of Power in Hollywood (with Judd Apatow)," *Stay Tuned with Preet,* Nov. 16, 2017, www.wnycstudios.org.

30   **When he joined the Southern:** U.S. Congress, House of Representatives, Committee on the Judiciary, Preetinder "Preet" Bharara, Questionnaire for Non-judicial Nominees, May 13, 2009.

30   **"He had a great sense of humor":** Godsey interview by author, July 6, 2017.

30   **In one case, his prosecution team:** *United States of America, Appellee, v. Xiao Qin Zhou aka Viet Guy aka Viet Boy aka Vietnamese Boy, Lin Li aka Yi Jun aka Crazy Chung, Chun Rong Chen aka Yi Non, Li Wei aka Yi Guan, Li Xin Ye aka Pai Fot, and Hing Wah Gau aka Yi Hei, Defendants, Chen Zi Xiang aka Yi Soon aka Yi Soon Gang and Lin Xian Wu aka Ah Oo, Defendants-Appellants,* 428 F.3d 361, 2005 U.S. App. LEXIS 23599 (U.S. Court of Appeals for the Second Circuit, Nov. 1, 2005, decided), advance.lexis.com.

31   **Bharara helped secure:** Neil M. Barofsky, *Bailout: An Inside Account of How Washington Abandoned Main Street While Rescuing Wall Street* (New York: Free Press, 2013), 41–42.

32   **Then, days before the Silver:** Michael Bobelian, "As Preet Bharara Drops Seven Insider Trading Charges, Some Enforcement Might Move Out of New York," *Forbes,* Oct. 23, 2015, accessed Jan. 10, 2019, www.forbes.com.

34   **since September 11, no other district:** Trevor Aaronson and Margot Williams, "Trial and Terror," *Intercept,* April 17, 2017, accessed Jan. 9, 2019, trial-and-terror.theintercept.com/.

35   **In one Twitter posting:** *United States v. Ali Saleh,* U.S. District Court, Eastern District of New York, Case no. 15-MJ-886, "Criminal Complaint," Sept. 16, 2015.

37   *The New York Times* **described:** Jim Dwyer, "For Sheldon Silver, It's Another in a String of Small-Number Victories," *New York Times,* July 14, 2017, A18.

37   **He joined the state assembly:** Linda Greenhouse, "Unorthodox Newcomers Reshaping the Assembly," *New York Times,* April 18, 1977, accessed Jan. 9, 2019, www.nytimes.com.

37   **By the time he rose:** Ian Fisher, "With Cuomo's Loss, Speaker Is Top Democrat in Albany," *New York Times,* Nov. 22, 1994, accessed Jan. 9, 2019, www.nytimes.com.

37   **When prospective juror #27:** Phillips, interview by author, Feb. 15, 2016.

1. *Downthehole*

41　**Gaspare Valenti had just come:** *United States v. Vincent Asaro,* U.S. District Court, Eastern District of New York, Case no. 14-CR-26, "Memorandum in Law in Support of the Government's Motion In Limine to Admit Certain Evidence Against the Defendant at Trial," May 27, 2015.

44　**Zaffarano, a Bonanno captain:** Joseph D. Pistone, *Donnie Brasco: My Undercover Life in the Mafia,* with Richard Woodley (New York: New American Library, 1988).

47　**The list of crimes, or "predicate acts":** Jason D. Reichelt, "Stalking the Enterprise Criminal: State RICO and the Liberal Interpretation of the Enterprise Element," *Cornell Law Review* 81, no. 1 (1995), scholarship.law.cornell .edu. Also *Criminal RICO: 18 U.S.C. §§ 1961–1968 (A Manual for Federal Prosecutors)* (Washington, D.C.: U.S. Department of Justice, 2016), prepared by the Staff of the Organized Crime and Gang Section, U.S. Department of Justice, Washington, D.C., 2015.

47　**Wiretaps and other electronic surveillance:** Selwyn Raab, *Five Families: The Rise, Decline, and Resurgence of America's Most Powerful Mafia Empires* (New York: Thomas Dunne Books, 2016), 175.

47　**Over the next decade:** Gregory J. Wallance, "Outgunning the Mob," *ABA Journal,* March 1, 1994.

47　**The act drew widespread support:** Frank Northen Magill, *Chronology of Twentieth-Century History: Business and Commerce* (London: Fitzroy Dearborn, 1996), 2:1012.

47　**Biaggi, a former NYPD officer:** Robert D. McFadden, "Mario Biaggi, 97, Popular Bronx Congressman Who Went to Prison, Dies," *New York Times,* Dec. 21, 2017, accessed Jan. 9, 2019, www.nytimes.com; Richard Reeves, "Ex-cop Makes His Move to Take Over the City," *New York,* Dec. 11, 1972, 42–50.

47　**The law made four distinct:** G. R. Blakey and Brian Gettings, "Racketeer Influenced and Corrupt Organizations (RICO): Basic Concepts—Criminal and Civil Remedies," *Temple Law Quarterly* 53 (1980), scholarship.law .nd.edu.

48　**Under the new law:** Raab, *Five Families,* 693.

48　**"You don't know what you're talking about":** Wallance, "Outgunning the Mob."

49　**He urged the men:** Ibid.

49　**In the early 1980s:** James B. Jacobs, *Busting the Mob: United States v. Cosa Nostra,* with Christopher Panarella and Jay Worthington (New York: New York University Press, 1994), 70.

49　**The Colombo family, once the public face:** Michael Franzese, *I'll Make You an Offer You Can't Refuse: Insider Business Tips from a Former Mob Boss* (Nashville: Thomas Nelson, 2009), 75.

50　**"We're in mob heaven here":** Nicholas Pileggi, "Gangbusters," *New York,* July 25, 1983.

50　**Prosecutors first used RICO:** Nathan Koppel, "They Call It RICO, and It Is Sweeping," *Wall Street Journal,* Jan. 20, 2011, accessed Jan. 9, 2019, www .wsj.com.

50 **While Scotto and his co-defendant:** Robert B. Fiske, *Prosecutor Defender Counselor: The Memoirs of Robert B. Fiske Jr.* (Kittery, Maine: Smith/Kerr Associates, 2014), 102–6.

50 **When Donnie Brasco emerged:** Ralph Blumenthal, *Last Days of the Sicilians: At War with the Mafia* (New York: Times Books, 1988).

51 **MacMahon, one evening, found:** Raab, *Five Families*, 204.

51 **When a friendly colleague:** Edward McDonald, interview by author, Dec. 10, 2015.

52 **Nineteen eighty-six was the year:** "The Mob on Trial: A Union Dissident Is Beaten as Ordered," *Newsday*, Sept. 10, 1986, New York ed., 26–27.

52 **"The [Commission] case should be seen":** Jacobs, *Busting the Mob*.

52 **The indictment targeted the leadership:** Arnold H. Lubasch, "Mob's Ruling 'Commission' to Go on Trial in New York," *New York Times,* Sept. 7, 1986, accessed Jan. 10, 2019, www.nytimes.com.

52 **The mob's presence behind:** Sam Roberts, "Mafia Infiltration of Business Costing Consumers Millions," *New York Times,* Dec. 19, 1985, accessed Jan. 10, 2019, www.nytimes.com.

53 **At the trial, the defense:** Michael Oreskes, "Commission Trial Illustrates Changes in Attitude on Mafia," *New York Times,* Sept. 20, 1986, accessed Jan. 10, 2019, www.nytimes.com.

53 **The prosecution team included:** "The Mob on Trial," *Newsday,* Sept. 12, 1986.

53 **Where the government saw racketeering:** Margot Hornblower, "Secret Tapes Cited as Crucial Evidence in U.S. Mafia Trial," *Toronto Star,* Sept. 21, 1986.

53 **The jury heard lurid testimony:** Arnold H. Lubasch, "Ex-Mob Leader Tells of Slaying Father's Killer," *New York Times,* Sept. 24, 1986, accessed Jan. 10, 2019, www.nytimes.com.

54 **"It can no longer be":** "3 Mafia Chieftains Are Convicted," *Sun Sentinel,* Nov. 20, 1986, 3A.

2. Cooperation

58 **The violence of these recent arrivals:** Author data set of organized crime cases in the Southern and Eastern Districts of New York.

58 **"There was a time in the 1990s":** Belle Chen, Bill Vredenbergh, and Lou DiGregorio (FBI New York), interviews by author, Jan. 2016.

58 **The groups remained involved:** Author data set of organized crime cases in the Southern and Eastern Districts of New York.

60 **Gleeson ran roughshod over:** Confirmation Hearings on Federal Appointments: Hearings Before the Committee on the Judiciary, U.S. Senate, 103rd Cong., 1st Sess., Confirmations of Appointees to the Federal Judiciary, Aug. 24, 1994.

60 **He had lost a case:** Selwyn Raab, *Five Families: The Rise, Decline, and Resurgence of America's Most Powerful Mafia Empires* (New York: Thomas Dunne Books, 2016), 395.

60 **Before bringing another case:** Ibid., 428.

60 **The Gambino crew knew indictments:** Jeffrey Toobin, "More Brains," *New Yorker,* Nov. 24, 2014, accessed Jan. 10, 2019, www.newyorker.com.

61 **One marshal recalled that when:** Craig Donlon interview by author, Jan. 6, 2016.

61 **"I want to switch governments":** Peter Maas, *Underboss: Sammy the Bull Gravano's Story of Life in the Mafia* (New York: HarperCollins, 1997).

61 **Gravano's move shattered one:** John Gotti and Salvatore Gravano, *The Gotti Tapes: Including the Testimony of Salvatore "Sammy the Bull" Gravano* (New York: Times Books, 1992).

63 **The jailed boss Joseph Massino:** Colin Moynihan, "Death Penalty Sought in Basciano Trial," *New York Times*, May 24, 2011, accessed Jan. 10, 2019, www.nytimes.com.

64 **"typically arrogant poker-up-his-ass":** Tommy Dades and Mike Vecchione, *Friends of the Family: The Inside Story of the Mafia Cops Case*, with David Fisher (New York: Harper, 2010).

64 **Andres had also achieved:** Andres, interview by author, Jan. 19, 2015.

64 **The younger boss's attorneys rejected:** *United States v. Vincent Basciano*, U.S. District Court, Eastern District of New York, Case no. 05-CR-060, "Defendants Memorandum in Support of Motion to Suppress the 'Massino' Tapes and to Dismiss the Indictment."

66 **One of Andres's cooperators:** "Betrayed by a Mafia Underboss," *New York Times*, Oct. 28, 2010, accessed Jan. 10, 2019, archive.nytimes.com.

66 **This fact would spare prosecutors:** John Marzulli, "Bonanno Rat Dominick Cicale Gets Break of a Lifetime for Helping Nail Vinny Gorgeous Basciano," *New York Daily News*, April 9, 2018, accessed Jan. 10, 2019, www.nydaily news.com.

66 **Valenti wasn't alone among:** *United States v. Vincent Asaro*, U.S. District Court, Eastern District of New York, Case no. 14-CR-26 (SR) (ARR), "Memorandum of Law in Support of the Government's Motion In Limine to Preclude Certain Evidence at Trial," Sept. 15, 2015.

68 **In February 2011, he and Asaro:** Ibid., "Memorandum of Law in Support of the Government's Motion of Limine to Admit Certain Evidence Against the Defendant at Trial," May 27, 2015.

69 **Occasionally, glimmers of intimacy:** Ibid., "Exhibit: Recording 22— 7/14/2011," Oct. 9, 2015.

70 **After nearly twenty-four hours:** Ibid., "Defendant Vincent Asaro's Memorandum of Law in Support of His Motion In Limine," Sept. 16, 2015.

70 **The NYPD interviewed her:** Ibid., "Opinion & Order," Oct. 7, 2015.

3. Lufthansa

73 **Judge Reena Raggi, who was appointed:** "Reagan Picks Lawyer for Office in Brooklyn," *New York Times*, May 15, 1986, accessed Jan. 10, 2019, www .nytimes.com.

73 **By the time the Asaro trial opened:** "The United States District Court for the Eastern District of New York (1990–2014)," U.S. District Court, Eastern District of New York, May 2015.

73 **"The government didn't have the luxury":** Pileggi, interview by author, April 7, 2017.

73   **She worked on a stream:** John Marzulli, "Jury Kills Case, Acquits Alleged
      Colombo Guy in Two Gangland Murders," *New York Daily News,* July 12,
      2012; Tom Hays, "Ex-Mob Boss Takes Stand Against One of His Own," *New
      York Law Journal* (Online), April 13, 2011.

73   **"chest-thumping from the prosecutors":** John Marzulli, "'Schoolboy' Feds'
      Death Wish: Basciano Juror Says Push to Execute Thug 'Waste of Time'
      Authorities 'Wanted Him Dead Because He Threatened Their Guy,'" *New
      York Daily News,* July 4, 2011.

73   **Elizabeth Macedonio had also come up:** Macedonio, interview by author,
      March 8, 2015.

74   **When Jacobs passed away:** Susannah Cahalan, "The Dead Ringer," *New York
      Post,* Dec. 21, 2008, accessed Jan. 10, 2019, nypost.com.

75   **"I tried very hard to resolve this":** Macedonio, interview by author, March 8,
      2015.

76   **He was suffering from inadequate:** *United States v. Vincent Asaro,* U.S.
      District Court, Eastern District of New York, Case no. 17-CR-27 (ARR),
      "Defendant's Sentencing Memorandum," Dec. 11, 2017.

76   **But a month before the trial began:** John Marzulli, "Judge Throws Out Any
      Reference to Gruesome 'Goodfellas' Murders in Upcoming Trial for Gangster,
      Vincent Asaro," *New York Daily News,* Oct. 7, 2015, accessed Jan. 10, 2019,
      www.nydailynews.com.

78   **When Macedonio began to push him:** Macedonio, interview by author,
      March 8, 2015.

83   **Paul Katz's son Lawrence:** John Marzulli, "Son of Man Allegedly Strangled
      to Death with Dog Chain by Mob Boss Vincent Asaro Testifies at Lufthansa
      Trial," *New York Daily News,* Nov. 3, 2015.

88   **"I'd like to thank":** Tom Hays and Michael Balsamo, "Aging Mobster Vincent
      Asaro Acquitted in 1978 'Goodfellas' Heist," AP, ABC7 New York, Jan. 12,
      2018, accessed Jan. 10, 2019, abc7ny.com.

4. Retribution

90   **the Eastern District had been preparing:** "Ten Members and Associates of the
      Bonanno Crime Family Indicted for Racketeering and Related Charges," U.S.
      Department of Justice, Aug. 18, 2017, accessed Jan. 10, 2019, www.justice
      .gov.

91   **Meanwhile, prosecutors in the Southern District:** *United States v. Pasquale
      Parrello,* U.S. District Court, Southern District of New York, Case no.
      16-CR-522-RJS, "Criminal Docket," Aug. 1, 2016.

92   **"We need to do something":** *United States v. Vincent Asaro,* U.S. District
      Court, Eastern District of New York, Case no. 17-CR-27 (ARR), "Letter in
      Opposition to the Defendant Vincent Asaro's Bail Application as to Vincent
      Asaro," May 16, 2017.

93   **"I don't care what happens":** Larry Neumeister, "Mobster Sent to Prison in
      Road Rage Arson Case; Judge Cites Evidence of Role in Legendary Airport
      Robbery," Associated Press, Dec. 28, 2017.

5. The Border

99   **She stepped off the plane in:** *United States v. Chevelle Nesbeth,* U.S. District Court, Eastern District of New York, Case no. 15-CR-18 (FB), "Exhibits 17 A-C," May 24, 2016.

100 **After graduation, she hoped to teach:** *United States v. Chevelle Nesbeth,* U.S. District Court, Eastern District of New York, Case no. 15-CR-18 (FB), "Opinion," May 24, 2016.

100 **The tiny, lush island nation:** "Jamaica Is Third Happiest Nation on Earth," Jamaica Information Service, Aug. 26, 2013, accessed Jan. 10, 2019, jis .gov.jm.

100 **The unrest culminated in a massacre:** Mattathias Schwartz, "A Massacre in Jamaica," *New Yorker,* July 10, 2017, accessed Jan. 10, 2019, www.new -yorker.com.

101 **In 2015, fifty-six million passengers:** "January 2015 Traffic Report," Port Authority of New York & New Jersey, accessed Jan. 10, 2019, www .panynj.gov.

102 **Each year Customs intercepted:** "Drug Seizures—New York Field Office— 2010–2015," U.S. Customs and Border Protection Freedom of Information Act Request 2016-052676, author's collection, Sept. 1, 2015.

102 **The officer had worked:** *Nesbeth,* Case no. 15-CR-18 (FB), "Transcript of Criminal Cause for Trial," June 16, 2015.

104 *Is something wrong?:* Ibid.

104 **Banging on the handle did not:** Ibid.

105 **The Court found that law enforcement:** Steven K. Bernstein, "Fourth Amendment: Using the Drug Courier Profile to Fight the War on Drugs," *Journal of Criminal Law and Criminology* 80, no. 4 (Winter 1990): 996–1017, accessed Jan. 10, 2019, doi:10.2307/1143688.

105 **The most invasive of these:** A. Pinto et al., "Radiological and Practical Aspects of Body Packing," *British Journal of Radiology* 87, no. 1036 (April 2014), doi:10.1259/bjr.20130500.

105 **Health professionals are aware:** Ramdas Prabhu et al., "Radiology of Body Packers: The Detection of Internally Concealed Illegal Materials," *Applied Radiology: The Journal of Practical Medical Imaging and Management,* accessed Jan. 10, 2019, appliedradiology.com.

105 **In a hospital setting:** Ibid.

105 **The fact that she was departing:** Craig Sanko (chief of Customs and Border Protection), interview by author, Aug. 12, 2015.

105 **For example, my PNR read:** "Passenger Name Record, John David Dwyer," Department of Homeland Security Freedom of Information Act Request, author's collection.

106 **The PNR can go further:** "Passenger Name Record (PNR) Privacy Policy," U.S. Customs and Border Protection, June 21, 2013, accessed Jan. 10, 2019, www.cbp.gov.

106 **PNRs had long been a key tool:** *United States of America, Appellant, v. Tunya Reginera Poitier, Appellee,* 818 F.2d 679 No. 86-1616, U.S. Court of Appeals, Eighth Circuit, July 30, 1987; "DHS U/S Beardsworth Meets with Spanish

Officials About Passenger Name Records," WikiLeaks, July 29, 2005, accessed Jan. 10, 2019, wikileaks.org.

106 **Only after the successive terrorist attacks:** "EU Ministers Approve PNR Legislation," Euronews, April 21, 2016, accessed Jan. 10, 2019, www.euro news.com.

6. Trial Tax

110 **Block likened his role:** Frederic Block. "R/IAmA—I Am Frederic Block, a Federal Trial Court Judge in the U.S. District Court for the Eastern District of New York, Author of the Tell-All Book 'Disrobed: An Inside Look at the Life and Work of a Federal Trial Judge.' AMA," Reddit, Sept. 27, 2012, accessed Jan. 10, 2019, www.reddit.com.

111 **"Start each day with a:** @Potential_Gal, Twitter January 17, 2015.

111 **"Pregnant bitches that work:** @Potential_Gal, Twitter February 2, 2015.

111 **"Mi nuh like deal wid:** @Potential_Gal, Twitter February 22, 2015.

112 **The officers removed the drugs:** Craig Sanko (chief of Customs and Border Protection), interview by author, Aug. 12, 2015.

114 **"There is an inexhaustible supply":** Tony Garoppolo, "Treatment of Narcotics Couriers in the Eastern District of New York," *Federal Sentencing Reporter* 5, no. 6 (May/June 1993): 317–18, doi:10.2307/20639604.

114 **officer who allegedly helped two couriers:** *United States v. Fernando Marte,* U.S. District Court, Eastern District of New York, Case no. 17-MJ-123 (RML), "Transcript of Criminal Cause for Trial," Feb. 8, 2017.

114 **Each year the Eastern District:** U.S. District Court, Eastern District of New York, Cases Charged Under 21 USC 952, author's analysis, Aug. 4, 2016.

119 **the primary function of the Justice Department:** "U.S. Attorneys Annual Statistical Report 2016," U.S. Department of Justice, 2017, accessed Jan. 10, 2019, www.justice.gov.

119 **Nearly a quarter of the U.S. Attorney's charges:** "Eastern District of New York Prosecutions: January–August 2017," TRACFED, accessed Jan. 10, 2019, tracfed.syr.edu/.

7. Collateral Consequences

121 **The language of federal sentencing:** Frank O. Bowman III, "The Failure of the Federal Sentencing System: A Structural Analysis," *Columbia Law Review* 105, no. 4 (May 2005): 1315–50, accessed Jan. 10, 2019, www.jstor.org.

122 **Congress intended the new regulations:** "How to Lock Them Away," *Wall Street Journal,* Jan. 5, 1987, 16.

122 **One of the system's earliest critics:** Nat Hentoff, "Judge Breyer: Lots of Room for Dissent," *Washington Post,* June 4, 1994, A19.

122 **Even a member of the commission:** Linda Greenhouse, "Guidelines on Sentencing Are Flawed, Justice Says," *New York Times,* Nov. 21, 1998, accessed Jan. 10, 2019, www.nytimes.com.

122 **There is a full-page chart:** "2015 U.S. Sentencing Guidelines Manual," U.S. Sentencing Commission, Nov. 1, 2015, accessed Jan. 10, 2019, www.ussc.gov/.

123 **In the United States, state and federal laws:** "National Inventory of Collateral Consequences of Conviction," Justice Center: The Council of State Governments, accessed Jan. 10, 2019, niccc.csgjusticecenter.org/.

123 **Within the past fifteen years:** Michael Pinard, "Reflections and Perspectives on Reentry and Collateral Consequences," *Journal of Criminal Law and Criminology* 100, no. 3 (Summer 2010): 1213–24, accessed Jan. 10, 2019, scholarlycommons.law.northwestern.edu.

123 **Critics see these sanctions:** Gabriel Jackson Chin, "Race, the War on Drugs, and the Collateral Consequences of Criminal Conviction," *Journal of Gender, Race, and Justice* 6 (2002): 253, ssrn.com.

123 **These penalties disproportionately impact:** Michelle Alexander, *The New Jim Crow: Mass Incarceration in the Age of Colorblindness* (New York: New Press, 2016), 144.

124 **drug couriers at JFK tended:** Tony Garoppolo, "Treatment of Narcotics Couriers in the Eastern District of New York," *Federal Sentencing Reporter* 5, no. 6 (May/June 1993): 317–18, doi:10.2307/20639604.

124 **"The defendant's young age and lack":** *United States v. Chevelle Nesbeth,* U.S. District Court, Eastern District of New York, Case no. 15-CR-18 (FB), "Sentencing Memorandum," Sept. 10, 2015.

124 **The federal sentencing commission describes:** "U.S. Sentencing Commission Guidelines Manual," U.S. Sentencing Commission, Nov. 1, 2018, accessed Jan. 10, 2019, www.ussc.gov.

124 **In 1993, Judge Jack Weinstein:** "Making Sense of Sentences," *Washington Post,* May 1, 1993, accessed Jan. 10, 2019, www.washingtonpost.com.

125 **"I simply cannot sentence":** "Senior Judge Declines Drug Cases," *American Bar Association Journal* (July 1993).

125 **Her crime was aberrational:** Jesse Wegman, "A Federal Judge's New Model for Forgiveness," *New York Times,* March 16, 2016, accessed Jan. 10, 2019, www.nytimes.com.

126 **"The street drug trade is responsible":** *Nesbeth,* Case no. 15-CR-18 (FB), "Sentencing Memorandum," Jan. 26, 2016.

129 **Block had written a forty-two-page order:** Ibid., "Opinion," May 24, 2016.

8. Override

133 **By April 2013, Stefan Lumiere's brief:** *United States v. Stefan Lumiere,* U.S. District Court, Southern District of New York, Case no. 16-CR-483-JSR, "Government's Sentencing Memorandum," May 16, 2017.

133 **Visium was a $4 billion hedge fund:** "Visium Asset Management," Wayback Machine, accessed Jan. 10, 2019, web.archive.org.

133 **At any point in the day:** "Visium Asset Management," Spin Design, accessed Jan. 10, 2019, www.spindesignny.com.

133 **For Lumiere, however, the location:** Stefan Lumiere, interview by author, February 6, 2018.

134 **This would have been of:** Jacob Gottlieb did not respond to requests for an interview.

134 **Gottlieb brought Lumiere into the fund:** Lumiere interview; also *Lumiere,* Case no. 16-CR-483-JSR, "Letter from Richard M. Lumiere, MD," May 8, 2017.

134 **Lumiere didn't want to resign:** Ibid., "Exhibit: Email from David Keily to Stefan Lumiere, FYI: Stefan Lumiere: Your Resignation from Employment with Visium Asset Management, LP."

134 **He was the type of brother:** Ibid., "Letter from Erica Lumiere," May 7, 2017.

134 **She would tell people:** Ibid., "Letter from Alexandra Lumiere Gottlieb," May 11, 2017.

134 **His brother-in-law Jacob:** *Jacob Gottlieb, Appellant-Respondent, v. Alexandra Lumiere Gottlieb, Respondent-Appellant,* 2016 NY Slip Op 00613 (138 AD3d 30), Jan. 28, 2016.

134 **This disparity offered a constant:** Lumiere interview.

134 **The child of Polish immigrants:** Imogen Rose-Smith, "The Quiet Ambition of Jacob Gottlieb," *Institutional Investor,* Aug. 2012.

135 **Visium's health-care-focused Visium Balanced Fund:** Simone Foxman and Katia Porzecanski, "Visium to Shut Four Remaining Hedge Funds as Manager Charged," *Bloomberg,* June 17, 2016, accessed Jan. 10, 2019, www.bloom berg.com.

135 **His boss, Chris Plaford, was seven:** Through his counsel, David Smith, Chris Plaford declined to be interviewed.

135 **"He was Jake's brother-in-law":** *Lumiere,* Case no. 16-CR-483-JSR, "Trial Transcript," Jan. 17, 2017.

135 **Lumiere didn't like Plaford:** Lumiere interview.

135 **It seemed clear to Lumiere that:** Ibid. Also, Jason Thorell did not respond to requests for an interview.

135 **The fund touted its approach:** "Visium Asset Management—Investment Process," Wayback Machine, accessed Jan. 10, 2019, web.archive.org.

136 **The fund had invested:** *Securities and Exchange Commission v. Stefan Lumiere,* U.S. District Court, Southern District of New York, Case no. 16-CV-4513, "Complaint," June 15, 2016.

136 **The men could then list:** *Lumiere,* Case no. 16-CR-483-JSR, "Government's Sentencing Memorandum," May 16, 2017.

136 **Over two years, the Visium team:** Ibid.

136 **"I was not part of the":** Lumiere interview.

137 **"We work only blocks from Wall Street":** Preet Bharara, U.S. Attorney, "Address on White Collar Crime," New York University Law School, Nov. 19, 2009.

138 **In 2012, Preet Bharara appeared:** *Time,* Feb. 1, 2012.

138 **It had secured only one conviction:** Jesse Eisinger, "Why Only One Top Banker Went to Jail for the Financial Crisis," *New York Times,* April 30, 2014, accessed Jan. 10, 2019, www.nytimes.com.

138 **In April 2013, Stefan Lumiere dialed:** *Lumiere,* Case no. 16-CR-483-JSR, "Transcript," Jan. 17, 2017.

138 **From that moment Lumiere began:** Lumiere interview.

138 **"Yeah. Hey, by the way":** Ibid., "Exhibit 1231-A.wav/1231-T.pdf," Jan. 9, 2017.

139 **For all the bravado, Lumiere was:** Lumiere interview.

139 **Within weeks, Lumiere was out of a job:** Ibid., "Government's Sentencing Memorandum," May 16, 2017.

139 **Instead, Lumiere said, he was told to:** Lumiere interview.

140 **That term was first popularized:** Edwin H. Sutherland, "White-Collar Criminality," *American Sociological Review* 5, no. 1 (Feb. 1940).

140 **"If the affluent flagrantly disregard":** John J. Goldman, "Law and Order: Nixon Faces N.Y. Dilemma," *Los Angeles Times,* Dec. 19, 1968.

140 **He pressed the Department of Justice:** "Nader Asks Creation of Justice Division on Corporate Crime," *Wall Street Journal,* Aug. 25, 1975.

140 **He criticized the soft sentences:** Arnold H. Lubasch, "Leniency Decried in Business Crime," *New York Times,* Aug. 1, 1976, accessed Jan. 11, 2019, www.nytimes.com.

140 **His Brooklyn counterpart, U.S. Attorney David Trager:** Selwyn Raab, "U.S. Attorney Calls F.B.I. 'Out of Step,'" *New York Times,* July 4, 1976, accessed Jan. 11, 2019, www.nytimes.com.

140 **The Business Frauds unit was the office's:** Jed Rakoff, interview by author, March 17, 2016. Also, Ira Sorkin, interview by author, Aug. 12, 2015.

141 **During U.S. Attorney Fiske's:** Robert B. Fiske, *Prosecutor Defender Counselor: The Memoirs of Robert B. Fiske Jr.* (Kittery, Maine: Smith/Kerr Associates, 2014).

141 **"It was the only district":** Ira Sorkin, interview by author, Aug. 12, 2015.

141 **The Securities and Exchange Commission:** Patrick Radden Keefe, "The Empire of Edge," *New Yorker,* Oct. 13, 2014, accessed Jan. 11, 2019, www.newyorker.com.

141 **The Department of Justice prosecuted:** Stuart Taylor Jr., "Law's 'Stradivarius'; Inside Trader Ruling Saves Mail Law as Key Tool for Federal Prosecutors," *New York Times,* Nov. 19, 1987, accessed Jan. 11, 2019, www.nytimes.com.

141 **Prosecutors used the 1934 Securities:** Taylor Essner, "Insider Trading in Flux: Explaining the Second Circuit's Error in *United States v. Newman* and the Supreme Court's Correction of That Error in *United States v. Salman,*" *Saint Louis University Law Journal* 61, no. 1 (2016): 117–42, www.slu.edu.

141 **A jury convicted him in 1978:** Edwin McDowell, "Printer's Conviction as Insider Is Upheld," *New York Times,* Nov. 30, 1978.

141 **The Supreme Court further defined:** Adam C. Pritchard, "*Dirks* and the Genesis of Personal Benefit," *Southern Methodist University Law Review* 68, no. 3 (2015), ssrn.com.

142 **During his term, Giuliani moved forcefully:** James Sterngold, "Wall Street Crime and Its Dividends," *New York Times,* April 27, 1986.

142 **Former Southern District section chiefs:** Barbara Bradley and David Clark Scott, "The Inside World of Insider-Trading Counsel," *Christian Science Monitor,* Feb. 27, 1987, accessed Jan. 11, 2019, www.csmonitor.com.

142 **Lumiere noticed that he seemed jittery:** Lumiere interview.

143 **"I would like to discuss":** *United States v. Stefan Lumiere,* U.S. District Court, Southern District of New York, Case no. 16-CR-483-JSR, "Email 'Meeting' from Jason Thorell to Jacob Gottlieb," June 24, 2014.

143 **Gottlieb called Thorell to his office:** Ibid., "Transcript," Jan. 13, 2017.

143 **That evening, as he and Lumiere:** Ibid.

143 **The statute tied a financial award:** Michael H. Hurwitz and Jonathan Kovacs, "An Overview of the SEC's Whistleblower Award Program," *Fordham Journal of Corporate and Financial Law* 21, no. 3 (2016).

144 **The prior year the commission:** U.S. Securities and Exchange Commission, *2013 Annual Report on the Dodd-Frank Whistleblower Program,* www .sec.gov.

144 **Later, Lumiere would contend:** *Lumiere,* Case no. 16-CR-483-JSR, "Motion Under 28 USC 2255 to Vacate, Set Aside, or Correct Sentence by a Person in Federal Custody," Oct. 5, 2018.

9. Market Justice

146 **On the thirteenth floor:** Jed Rakoff, interview by author, March 17, 2016.

148 **"To go after people of that level":** Ibid.

148 **Rakoff went on to prosecute cases:** "New Chief of Fraud Unit Named by U.S. Attorney in Manhattan," *New York Times,* Jan. 27, 1978.

148 **He joined the nineteenth-century firm:** Peter H. Stone, "Law Firms No Longer Scorn White-Collar Criminal Cases: White-Collar Legal Work Rosy in Defense Area," *Washington Post,* Nov. 3, 1985, F7.

149 **he upheld a suspension against:** Richard Sandomir, "Effort to Delay Four Bans Is Rejected," *New York Times,* May 17, 1997.

149 **Three years later, he ruled:** Robert F. Worth, "Prosecutors Oppose Judge in Ruling on Death Penalty," *New York Times,* May 17, 2002, B3.

149 **Rakoff's reasons were both legal:** Jed S. Rakoff, "Will the Death Penalty Ever Die?," *New York Review of Books,* June 8, 2017, accessed Jan. 10, 2019, www .nybooks.com.

149 **The Second Circuit reversed his decision:** Julia Preston, "Killers Get Life Sentences, in Setback to Justice Dept.," *New York Times,* Aug. 6, 2004, accessed Jan. 11, 2019, www.nytimes.com.

149 **In 2006, he ordered the Pentagon:** Julia Preston, "Judge Orders U.S. to Supply Prisoner Names," *New York Times,* Jan. 24, 2006, A15.

149 **In three years, the Securities:** James B. Stewart, "SAC Case Is Testing a Classic Dilemma," *New York Times,* June 1, 2013.

150 **Hedge funds had flourished:** Lloyd Dixon, Noreen Clancy, and Krishna Kumar, *Hedge Funds and Systemic Risk* (Santa Monica, Calif.: Rand, 2012).

150 **Hedge fund managers had:** Christopher Geczy, "The Future of the Hedge Fund Industry," in *After the Crash: The Future of Finance,* ed. Yasuyuki Fuchita, Richard J. Herring, and Robert E. Litan (Washington, D.C.: Brookings Institution Press; Tokyo: Nomura Institute of Capital Markets Research, 2010).

150 **Wiretaps put up by Bharara's prosecutors:** Michael Rothfeld, Jenny Strasburg, and Susan Pulliam, "New Arrests Expected in Insider Probe," *Wall Street Journal,* Dec. 1, 2011.

150 **These relationships between expert networks:** Antonia Apps, interview by author, May 31, 2017.

151 **Judge Rakoff saw the absence:** Rakoff, interview by author, March 17, 2016.

151 **Prosecutors charged them with securities fraud:** Zachery Kouwe and Dan Slater, "2 Bear Stearns Fund Leaders Are Acquitted," *New York Times,* Nov. 11, 2009.

151 **The boss transferred $2 million:** Grant McCool, "Ex–Bear Stearns Manager Did Not Lie—Trial Lawyer," Reuters, Oct. 15, 2009.

151 **The prosecution entered the trial:** Former Eastern District prosecutor, interview by author, May 30, 2017.

151 **The government accused the defense:** *United States v. Cioffi,* U.S. District Court, Eastern District of New York, Case no. 08-CR-451, "Transcript of Proceedings Before the Honorable Frederic Block," Oct. 8, 2009.

152 **The trial didn't fare much better:** *United States v. Cioffi,* Nov. 2, 2009, 2353.

152 **The prosecution knew their case lacked:** Former Eastern District prosecutor, interview by author, May 30, 2017.

152 **One former Eastern District prosecutor familiar:** Former Eastern District prosecutor interview by author, May 30, 2017

153 **As popular as the agreements:** Jed Rakoff, "Justice Deferred Is Justice Denied," *New York Review of Books,* Feb. 19, 2015.

154 **HSBC did not protest its innocence:** Carrick Mollenkamp, "HSBC Became Bank to Drug Cartels, Pays Big for Lapses," Reuters, Dec. 11, 2012, www .reuters.com.

154 **As if to remind the parties:** *United States v. HSBC USA, N.A. and HSBC Holdings PLC,* U.S. District Court, Eastern District of New York, Case no. 12-CR-763, "Memorandum and Order," April 6, 2015.

154 **In 2009, the SEC brought Bank of America:** U.S. Securities and Exchange Commission, Office of the Inspector General, *Investigation of the Circumstances Surrounding the SEC's Proposed Settlements with Bank of America, Including a Review of the Court's Rejection of the SEC's First Proposed Settlement and an Analysis of the Impact of Bank of America's Status as a TARP Recipient,* Case no. OIG-522.

154 **Rakoff refused to sign off:** Ibid.

154 **He used his opinion to address the case:** *Securities and Exchange Commission v. Citigroup Global Markets,* U.S. District Court, Southern District of New York, Case no. 11-CV-7387, "Opinion and Order," Nov. 28, 2011, www.nysd .uscourts.gov.

155 **Again, the Second Circuit rebuked:** *Securities and Exchange Commission v. Citigroup Global Markets,* U.S. Court of Appeals for the Second Circuit, Docket nos. 11-5227-cv(L), 11-5375-cv(con), 11-5242-cv(xap), "Opinion," June 4, 2014, www.gpo.gov.

155 **But Rakoff's opinion had an impact:** Amanda S. Naoufal, "Is Judge Rakoff Asking for Too Much? The New Standard for Consent Judgment Settlements with the SEC," *American University Business Law Review* 2, no. 1 (2012): 183–207.

10. No Victories

156 **In that time, Stefan had tried:** *United States v. Stefan Lumiere,* U.S. District Court, Southern District of New York, Case no. 16-CR-483-JSR, "Letter from Richard Lumiere, MD," May 8, 2017.

156 **Little good had come from meeting:** Lumiere interview.

157 **Stefan had locked items in there:** *United States v. Stefan Lumiere,* U.S. District Court, Southern District of New York, Case no. 16-MJ-3812, "Criminal Complaint," June 14, 2016.

157 **Ganek knowingly filled out the caricature:** Ganek, interview by author, March 6, 2017.

157 **He and his wife, the novelist:** Katya Wachtel, "Meet David Ganek, the Second Highest Profile Hedge Fund Manager Involved in the New Scandal," *Business Insider,* Nov. 23, 2010, accessed Jan. 11, 2019, www.businessinsider .com; Landon Thomas Jr., "Most Wanted on Museum Boards: Hedge Fund Managers," *New York Times,* Dec. 13, 2006, accessed Jan. 11, 2019, www.ny times.com.

158 **When Ganek arrived at the building:** "David Ganek: Delivering Alpha Unfiltered," CNBC, Sept. 16, 2016, accessed Jan. 11, 2019, video.cnbc.com.

158 **She had taken an atypical route:** Harvard Law School, "A Talk by Antonia Apps," Oct. 23, 2015, accessed Jan. 11, 2019, www.youtube.com.

159 **The search warrant was obtained:** *David Ganek v. David Leibowitz et al.,* U.S. District Court, Southern District of New York, Case no. 15-CV-1446, "Memorandum and Order," March 10, 2016.

160 **Special Agent David Chaves, a supervisor:** David Chaves did not respond to a request for an interview.

160 **"We would follow him every day":** Alexandra Stevenson, "After SAC Plea, Fellow Funds May Pay," *New York Times,* Nov. 6, 2013, B1.

160 **The agent, in fact, met regularly:** Case 1:16-cr-160338-PKC, Document 59, filed Dec. 20, 2016.

160 **He was convicted and sentenced:** Susan Beck, "The Year's Most Interesting Cases: Changing Technology Sparked a Range of Memorable Lawsuits—but So Did Some Timeless (and Thorny) Legal Issues," *American Lawyer,* Jan. 1, 2015.

161 **He traveled down to Foley Square:** *United States v. Stefan Lumiere,* U.S. District Court, Southern District of New York, Case no. 16-CR-483-JSR, "Letter to Assistant Attorney General Leslie R. Caldwell," Dec. 26, 2017.

161 **The appeals court hearing** *Newman:* *United States v. Todd Newman, Anthony Chiasson,* U.S. Court of Appeals for the Second Circuit, Docket no. 13-1837-cr (L), "Opinion," Dec. 10, 2014.

161 **This decision tightened the standard:** Jon Eisenberg, "How *United States v. Newman* Changes the Law," *Harvard Law School Forum on Corporate Governance and Financial Regulation,* May 3, 2015, accessed Jan. 11, 2019, corpgov.law.harvard.edu.

162 **The case, against Rengan Rajaratnam:** Charles Levinson, "Tensions Between Prosecutors, Judge Flared in Insider-Trading Trial; Angry Letters in Rengan Rajaratnam Case Show a U.S. Attorney's Office on the Defensive," *Wall Street Journal,* July 14, 2014.

162 **The U.S. Attorney qualified the statement:** James B. Stewart, "Some Fear Fallout from Preet Bharara's Tension with Judges," *New York Times,* April 16, 2015.

163 **Lumiere's boss, Chris Plaford, had also traded:** *Securities and Exchange Commission v. Christopher Plaford,* U.S. District Court, Southern District of New York, Case no. 16-CV-4511, "Complaint," June 15, 2016.

164 **News of the investigation broke:** Christopher M. Matthews and Gregory Zuckerman, "Insider Trading Is Focus of Probe into Visium," *Wall Street Journal,* April 8, 2016.

164 **Valvani's attorney fired off an angry letter:** *United States v. William T. Walters,* U.S. District Court, Southern District of New York, Case no. 16-CR-383-JSR, "Letter from Barry H. Berke to Assistant United States Attorney Ian McGinley 'Re: Grand Jury Investigation of Visium Asset Management LP,'" April 25, 2016.

164 **On June 16, when Lumiere arrived:** Lumiere interview.

165 **the death had been ruled:** Levy, Rachael. "Behind the Life and Death of a Star Money Manager Accused of Insider Trading," *Business Insider,* September 29, 2016, acessed March 14, 2019, www.businessinsider.com /behind-the-life-and-death-of-visiums-sanjay-valvani-2016-9.

165 **His sister's divorce from Jacob Gottlieb:** Julia Marsh, "Wife Stuck with Prenup and 'Only' $1.6M of Hubby's $54M Salary," *New York Post,* Jan. 29, 2016, accessed Jan. 11, 2019, nypost.com.

11. Questions of Innocence

166 **Justice Samuel Alito, who wrote:** *Salman v. United States,* Supreme Court of the United States, Case no. 15–628, argued Oct. 5, 2016, decided Dec. 6, 2016.

166 **Bharara issued a self-congratulatory statement:** "Statement of U.S. Attorney Preet Bharara on the Supreme Court's Decision in Salman v. U.S.," U.S. Department of Justice, Dec. 6, 2016, accessed Jan. 11, 2019, www.justice.gov.

167 **"during an interview conducted":** *United States v. William T. Walters,* U.S. District Court, Southern District of New York, Case no. 16-CR-383-JSR, "Government Letter to Judge Castel," Dec. 16, 2016.

168 **"Those referrals are now pending":** Ibid.

168 **The *Journal* published a similar article:** Michael Rothfeld and Jean Eaglesham, "U.S. Probes Och-Ziff Fee Paid in Libyan Dealings," *Wall Street Journal,* Dec. 5, 2014, accessed Jan. 11, 2019, www.wsj.com.

168 **That article threatened to expose:** Confidential informant, interview by author, Nov. 24, 2015.

170 **"Mr. Bharara isn't the first":** "Preet Bharara's Methods," *Wall Street Journal,* March 29, 2015, accessed Jan. 11, 2019, www.wsj.com.

172 **He had moved the fraud forward:** *United States v. Stefan Lumiere,* U.S. District Court, Southern District of New York, Case no. 16-CR-483-JSR, "Opinion and Order," April 19, 2017.

172 **The former hedge fund portfolio manager's:** Ibid., "Transcript," Jan. 17, 2017.

173 **He felt that his counsel:** Ibid., "Motion Under 28 USC 2255 to Vacate, Set Aside, or Correct Sentence by a Person in Federal Custody," Oct. 5, 2018.

176 **He blanched at the quantitative focus:** Jed S. Rakoff, "Why the Federal Sentencing Guidelines Should Be Scrapped," *Federal Sentencing Reporter* 26, no. 1 (Oct. 2013): 6–9, doi:10.1525/fsr.2013.26.1.6.

176 **In white-collar convictions, where the size:** *United States v. Adelson,* U.S. District Court, Southern District of New York, 441 F. Supp. 2d 506, 507 (2006).

176 **Creizman would not comment:** Email to author, March 14, 2019.

178 **In fact, in the Southern District:** Jillian Hewitt, "Fifty Shades of Gray: Sentencing Trends in Major White-Collar Cases," *Yale Law Journal* 125, no. 4 (2016), accessed Jan. 11, 2019, www.yalelawjournal.org.

12. *Hijra*

181 **In little more than an hour:** Richard Willstatter, interview by author, Jan. 9, 2018.

181 **At the wheel was a young imam:** *United States v. Imran Rabbani,* U.S. District Court, Eastern District of New York, Case no. 15-CR-302-MKB, "Sentencing Memorandum by John Doe," July 7, 2016.

181 **These mysterious cars seemed:** Ibid.

182 **The cop told the teenager:** *United States v. Munther Saleh,* U.S. District Court, Eastern District of New York, Case no. 15-CR-393-MKB, "Letter from Munther Omar Saleh to Judge Brodie," Oct. 13, 2017.

182 **He kept a list of the things:** *Rabbani,* Case no. 15-CR-302-MKB, "Sentencing Memorandum by John Doe," July 7, 2016.

182 **The light had yet to turn green:** Imran Rabbani did not respond to requests for comment; Munter Saleh declined to comment on the details of his case.

182 **The first six months of 2015:** The following chapters are based, in part, on interviews with current and former prosecutors and FBI agents conducted on background by author, various dates.

182 **Those cases sat within a broader:** Karen J. Greenberg and Seth Weiner, "The American Exception—Terrorism Prosecutions in the United States: The ISIS Cases, March 2014–August 2017," Center on National Security at Fordham Law, Sept. 2017, accessed Jan. 11, 2019, news.law.fordham.edu.

183 **One prosecutor particularly attuned:** Seth D. DuCharme, "The Search for Reasonableness in Use-of-Force Cases: Understanding the Effects of Stress on Perception and Performance," *Fordham Law Review* 70, no. 6 (2002), ir.lawnet.fordham.edu.

183 **One prosecutor took:** Current national security prosecutor, interview by author, Sept. 9, 2015.

184 **After one put in a decade:** "Administratively Determined Pay Plan Charts," U.S. Department of Justice, Jan. 8, 2018, accessed Jan. 11, 2019, www.justice.gov.

184 **With law school loans, mortgages:** Based on author interviews with current national security prosecutors, Sept. 9, 2015, June 10, 2016, and Oct. 15, 2017.

184 **Until that time came, national:** Senior national security prosecutor, interview by author, Aug. 25, 2017.

185 **"where the cool kids went":** Ibid.

186 **Like his father, who briefly served:** "John H. Ariail Jr., Co-founder of Sport and Health Clubs, Dies at 68," *Washington Post,* Feb. 11, 2011, accessed Jan. 11, 2019, www.washingtonpost.com.

187 **DuCharme had experience arresting:** *United States v. Sulejmah Hadzovic,* U.S. District Court, Eastern District of New York, Case no. 9-CR-648-MKB, "Transcript," April 15, 2015.

188 **Nearly one in three students dropped out:** "John Bowne High School (25Q425)," School Quality Guide—Online Edition, New York City Department of Education, Jan. 2016, accessed Jan. 11, 2019, tools.nycenet.edu.

188 **The second son, Ikram:** *United States v. Imran Rabbani,* U.S. District Court, Eastern District of New York, Case no. 15-CR-302-MKB, "Sentencing Memorandum by John Doe," July 7, 2016.

189 **Many students ditched classes:** Ibid., "Letters of Support," July 7, 2016.

189 **For two years, the brothers:** Ibid.

189 **They faced a complex set:** "Community Responses to Anti-Muslim Hatred," Clarke Forum, Feb. 13, 2017, accessed Jan. 11, 2019, clarke .dickinson.edu.

190 **Their father, Ghulam, drove a limousine:** Ibid., "Sentencing Memorandum by John Doe," July 7, 2016.

190 **Their parents were naturalized:** "Community Responses to Anti-Muslim Hatred," Clarke Forum, Feb. 13, 2017, accessed Jan. 11, 2019, clarke .dickinson.edu.

190 **The mosque had been founded:** R. Scott Hanson, *City of Gods: Religious Freedom, Immigration, and Pluralism in Flushing, Queens* (New York: Empire States Editions, an imprint of Fordham University Press, 2016).

190 **He also became close to a neighbor:** Richard Willstatter, interview by author, Jan. 9, 2018.

191 **Then it began waging a series:** Michael Pizzi, "In Declaring a Caliphate, Islamic State Draws a Line in the Sand," *Al Jazeera,* June 30, 2014.

191 **The elder terrorist organization:** Tricia Bacon and Elizabeth Grimm Arsenault, "Al Qaeda and the Islamic State's Break: Strategic Strife or Lackluster Leadership?," *Studies in Conflict and Terrorism,* Oct. 6, 2017, 1–35.

191 **This initially served the purpose:** J. M. Berger, "Social Media: An Evolving Front in Radicalization," Brookings Institution.

192 **Hussain, for his part, had been in touch:** According to Seamus Hughes, deputy director, Program on Extremism, George Washington University.

192 **ISIS fighters who made it:** Brian Dodwell, Daniel Milton, and Don Rassler, "The Caliphate's Global Workforce: An Inside Look at the Islamic State's Foreign Fighter Paper Trail," Combating Terrorism Center at West Point, Jan. 18, 2018, accessed Jan. 11, 2019, ctc.usma.edu.

192 **"I've been looking more into it":** *United States v. Imran Rabbani,* U.S. District Court, Eastern District of New York, Case no. 15-CR-302-MKB, "Sentencing Memorandum by USA as to John Doe," Aug. 3, 2016.

193 **Why were they being followed:** Ibid., "Letters of Support," July 7, 2016.

194 **The agents rifled through the men's pockets:** Ibid., "Sentencing Memorandum by USA as to John Doe," Aug. 3, 2016.

13. 702

196 **The historian J. Bowyer Bell described:** Alex Schmid, "Terrorism—the Definitional Problem," *Case Western Reserve Journal of International Law* 36, no. 2 (2004), scholarlycommons.law.case.edu.

196 **It was also invoked to frame:** Randall D. Law, *The Routledge History of Terrorism* (Abingdon, Oxon: Routledge, 2015).

196 **"Terrorism and blackmail are the favorite methods":** "How Mafia and Other Like Societies Get Funds: Terrorism, Blackmail," *New-York Tribune,* April 26, 1903, A16.

196 **Reports blamed "unionists" for the bombing:** "Inquiry Ordered into Explosion," *Christian Science Monitor,* Sept. 18, 1920, 2; "Unionists Blamed for Wall Street Explosion: New York Newspaper," *Los Angeles Times,* Nov. 12, 1920.

196 **In 1935, a window-smashing ring:** "Six Labor Leaders Guilty of Sabotage: Officers of Master Barbers Group Convicted of Terrorism to Force Price Rises," *New York Times,* Feb. 29, 1936.

196 **Describing a racket targeting Brooklyn:** "Lupo Aide Guilty in Bakery Racket: Geoghan Says the Conviction of Alagna Ends Long Terrorism Against Tradesmen," *New York Times,* Jan. 22, 1937.

197 **The press favored terms like:** Phillip A. Karber, "Urban Terrorism: Baseline Data and a Conceptual Framework," *Social Science Quarterly* 52, no. 3 (1971): 5.

197 **In response to a series of bombings:** Mary Jo White, "Prosecuting Terrorism in New York," *Middle East Quarterly* (Spring 2001): 11–18.

197 **These last two agencies only:** "The Department of Justice's Terrorism Task Forces: Report Number I-2005-007," U.S. Department of Justice Office of the Inspector General Evaluation and Inspections Division, June 2005, 46, accessed Jan. 11, 2019, oig.justice.gov.

197 **The force of some five hundred investigators:** "Terrorism Prosecutions: Lessons Learned and Future Challenges," Center for National Security, Fordham University, YouTube, Oct. 6, 2014, accessed Jan. 11, 2019, www.youtube.com

198 **That decision laid the groundwork:** Stefan Sottiaux, *Terrorism and the Limitation of Rights: The ECHR and the US Constitution* (Oxford: Hart, 2008).

198 **But after news emerged:** Stuart Diamond, "Big Arms Smuggling Case Stalls, Tangled in Legal and Political Troubles," *New York Times,* July 17, 1988.

198 **In the eight-month trial:** Richard Perez, "A Gamble Pays Off as the Prosecution Uses an Obscure 19th-Century Law," *New York Times,* Oct. 2, 1995.

198 **In 1994, Congress passed a law:** Charles Doyle, "Terrorist Material Support: A Sketch of 18 U.S.C. 2339A and 2339B," *Congressional Research Service,* www.fas.org.

199 **The latter criminalized a much broader:** Emma Sutherland, "The Material Support Statute: Strangling Free Speech Domestically?," *Civil Rights Law Journal* 23, no. 2 (2013), accessed Jan. 11, 2019, sls.gmu.edu.

199 **Yet prosecutors didn't gravitate:** Bradley A. Parker, "Material Support and the First Amendment: Eliminating Terrorist Support by Punishing Those with No Intention to Support Terror?," *City University of New York Law Review* 13, no. 2 (2010), 10.31641/clr130203.

199 **The Justice Department brought both cases:** Jeffrey K. Tulis and Stephen Macedo, eds., *The Limits of Constitutional Democracy* (Princeton, N.J.: Princeton University Press, 2010).

200 **The Office of Legal Counsel:** Karen J. Greenberg, *Rogue Justice: The Making of the Security State* (New York: Crown, 2016), 71–75.

200 **Comey left the Southern District:** Chris Smith, "Mr. Comey Goes to Washington," *New York,* Oct. 20, 2003, accessed Jan. 11, 2019, nymag.com.

202 **Since the September 11 attacks:** Trevor Aaronson and Margot Williams, "Trial and Terror," *Intercept,* April 17, 2017, accessed Mar. 15, 2019, trial-and-terror.theintercept.com/.

202 **One of his longest-standing defendants:** *U.S. v. Hasbajrami,* U.S. District Court, Eastern District of New York, Case no. 11-CR-63, "Letter from Ahmet Hasbajrami and Meriban Hasbajrami to Judge John Gleeson," July 6, 2012.

202 **He was approached by at least one Albanian-speaking:** *United States v. Agron Hasbajrami,* U.S. Court of Appeals for the Second Circuit, Case no. 17-2669, Jan. 30, 2018.

204 **If the government did decide:** "Terrorism Prosecutions: Lessons Learned and Future Challenges."

204 **And even with conviction rates:** Newsroom, "Trump Calls Terrorism Trial Process 'a Joke,' Despite Hundreds of Convictions," *Fordham Law News,* Nov. 3, 2017, accessed Jan. 10, 2019, news.law.fordham.edu.

204 **Intelligence and law enforcement agencies conducting:** "Terrorism Prosecutions: Lessons Learned and Future Challenges."

205 **"It's a major burn on resources":** Borelli, interview by author, Oct. 16, 2015.

205 **He looked up, occasionally, to greet:** Dratel, interviews by author, June 8 and Nov. 13, 2015.

206 **These are as worthy of providing:** Joshua L. Dratel and Karen Greenberg, *The Enemy Combatant Papers: American Justice, the Courts, and the War on Terror* (New York: Cambridge University Press, 2008).

206 **Like Dratel, he was a native:** Michael Bachrach, interview by author, May 20, 2015.

208 **Mueller surprised everyone when he let:** Howard Blum, "How the Feds Got Gotti," *New York,* Nov. 1, 1993, 50–59.

208 **"National emergencies are not cause":** *Turkmen v. Ashcroft,* U.S. District Court, Eastern District of New York, Case no. 02-CV-2307, "Memorandum and Order," June 14, 2006.

209 **The government had planned to use:** *U.S. v. Hasbajrami,* U.S. District Court, Eastern District of New York, Case no. 11-CR-63, "Opinion," March 8, 2016.

209 **Previously, such a search required:** Elizabeth Goitein (co-director, Liberty and National Security Program, Brennan Center for Justice at New York University School of Law), *The FISA Amendments Act: Reauthorizing America's Vital National Security Authority and Protecting Privacy and Civil Liberties,* U.S. Senate, Committee on the Judiciary, June 27, 2017, accessed Jan. 11, 2019, www.judiciary.senate.gov/.

209 **Most significantly, Justice Department officials:** Shreve Ariail, "The High Stakes of Misunderstanding Section 702 Reforms," *Lawfare,* Dec. 8, 2017, accessed Jan. 11, 2019, www.lawfareblog.com.

209 **The simple fact was that intelligence agencies:** Goitein, *FISA Amendments Act.*

211 **The government called this "untimely":** *Agron Hasbajrami v. United States,* U.S. District Court, Eastern District of New York, Case no. 13-CV-6852, "Memorandum in Opposition to Motion to Compel Discovery," Aug. 8, 2014.

211 **A Somali-born man named Mohamed:** "SCOTUS Declines Hearing for Oregon Christmas Bombing Case Marred by Entrapment, Warrantless Surveillance Claims," *District Sentinel News Co-Op,* Jan. 9, 2018, accessed Jan. 10, 2019, www.districtsentinel.com.

212 **In a Colorado case, an Uzbek man:** Evan Perez and Michael Martinez, "In a First, U.S. to Use NSA Surveillance Against Terror Suspect," CNN, Oct. 26, 2013, accessed Jan. 10, 2019, www.cnn.com.

212 **He sought to have:** Keith Coffman, "U.S. Prosecutors Seek to Halt Pretrial Release of Uzbek Terror Suspect," Reuters, June 28, 2017, accessed Jan. 10, 2019, www.reuters.com.

212 **Other national security prosecutors expressed frustration:** Background conversation with current and former national security prosecutors, May 9, 2017.

14. Shkin

217 **A group had traveled with him:** Transcript of the Statements of the Defendant, United States v. Ibrahim Suleiman Adnan Adam Harun Hausa, Sept. 14, 2011.

217 **The day after taking office:** Executive Order 13492, 3 C.F.R. 1 (2009).

218 **The group's report ultimately presaged:** "Final Report: Guantanamo Review Task Force," U.S. Department of Justice, Jan. 22, 2010, accessed Jan. 11, 2019, www.justice.gov.

221 **As the Nigerien responded to:** *United States v. Ibrahim Suleiman Adnan Adam Harun,* U.S. District Court, Eastern District of New York, Case no. 12-CR-134, "Government's Memorandum of Law in Support of Motion for an Anonymous and Partially Sequestered Jury," April 8, 2016.

222 **As Ariail tried to narrow:** Ibid., "Transcript of Statements of the Defendant," Sept. 14, 2011.

224 **The agency kidnapped Abu Omar:** Peter Bergen, "Exclusive: I Was Kidnapped by the CIA," *Mother Jones,* March/April 2008, accessed Jan. 10, 2019, www .motherjones.com.

224 **Upon his arrival in Brooklyn:** *Harun,* Case no. 12-CR-134, "Government's Memorandum of Law in Support of Motions In Limine to Admit Evidence and to Preclude an Improper Defense," Nov. 14, 2016.

225 **More than twenty years earlier, FBI agents:** James C. McKinley Jr., "Suspect in Kahane Slaying Kept List of Prominent Jews," *New York Times,* Dec. 1, 1990.

225 **The al-Qaeda manual gave operatives:** *United States v. Usama Bin Laden,* U.S. District Court, Southern District of New York, 126 F. Supp. 2d 290, "Declaration of Jihad Against the Country's Tyrants—Military Series Al Qaeda Training Manual, Exhibit GX-1677."

225 **An article in al-Qaeda in Yemen's magazine:** "The School of Yusuf," *Sada al-Malahim* (Echo of the slaughter), Jan. 2008–April 2009.

226 **The Department of Defense investigated:** Robert Beckhusen, "U.S. Injected Gitmo Detainees with 'Mind Altering' Drugs," *Wired,* June 3, 2017, accessed Jan. 11, 2019, www.wired.com.

228 **Ghannam faced withering questioning:** *Harun,* Case no. 12-CR-134, "Order," Feb. 24, 2017.

228 **"We're gonna load it up":** Network, Right Side Broadcasting, "Full Event: Donald Trump Nevada Watch Party & Victory Speech," YouTube, Feb. 23, 2016, accessed Jan. 11, 2019, www.youtube.com.

229 **The attorney general harbored a troubling:** Cong. Record, 109th Proceedings and Debates of the Congress, 1st Sess., vol. 151, June 16, 2005, no. 80.

229 **A Pentagon official told Congress:** Patricia Zengerle, "U.S. Official: 'No Coincidence' Islamic State Victims in Guantanamo-Like Jumpsuits," Reuters, Feb. 5, 2015, accessed Jan. 11, 2019, www.reuters.com.

229 **"The military commissions constitute a shipwreck":** "Symposium Article: The Military Commissions Act of 2009: Military Commission Mythology," *University of Toledo Law Review* 41 (Summer 2010).

230 **In fact, defendants had the right:** *Estelle v. Williams,* Supreme Court of the United States, 425 U.S. 501 (1976).

15. *Hijra* II

240 **Instead, the government held Imran:** *United States v. Imran Rabbani,* U.S. District Court, Eastern District of New York, Case no. 15-CR-302-MKB, "Letters of Support," July 7, 2016.

243 **After the terror group immolated:** Alice Su, "It Wasn't Their War: How Jordanians Came to Oppose ISIS," *Atlantic,* Feb. 5, 2015, accessed Jan. 12, 2019, www.theatlantic.com.

243 **Almost immediately after dropping:** *United States v. Fareed Mumuni,* U.S. District Court, Eastern District of New York, Case no. 15-MJ-00554-VMS, "Affidavit: FBI Special Agent Christopher J. Buscaglia," Sept. 17, 2015.

243 **Munther then set a meeting with a friend:** *United States v. Munther Saleh,* U.S. District Court, Eastern District of New York, Case no. 15-CR-393-MKB, "Objection to Presentence Investigation Report by USA as to Munther Omar Saleh Containing Response to Defendant Saleh's Objections," Jan. 5, 2018.

244 **The two men sensed that they:** *Rabbani,* Case no. 15-CR-302-MKB, "Sentencing Memorandum by USA as to John Doe," Aug. 3, 2016.

244 **Munther's friends in New Jersey:** *United States v. Alaa Saadeh,* U.S. District Court, District of New Jersey, Case no. 15-MJ-7200-CLW, "Criminal Complaint," June 26, 2015.

245 **But somebody had already talked:** Ibid.

246 **The intercepted online activity:** *Mumuni,* Case no. 15-MJ-00554-VMS, "Affidavit: FBI Special Agent Christopher J. Buscaglia," Sept. 17, 2015.

246 **Around this time, Imran Rabbani:** *Rabbani,* Case no. 15-CR-302-MKB, "Letters of Support," July 7, 2016.

246 **As one agent fought him off:** *United States v. Munther Saleh,* U.S. District Court, Eastern District of New York, Case no. 15-CR-393-MKB, "Sentencing Memorandum by USA as to Fareed Mumuni," April 19, 2018.

247 **He told the agents that his friend:** *Rabbani,* Case no. 15-CR-302-MKB, "Sentencing Memorandum by USA as to John Doe," Aug. 3, 2016.

248 **"Brothers and sisters, we are losing":** Jum'ah, June 16, 2015, www.youtube.com.

248 **When the government argued for Imran's detention:** *Rabbani,* Case no. 15-CR-302-MKB, "Sentencing Memorandum by John Doe," July 7, 2016.

249 **He had sought instructions:** *Saleh,* Case no. 15-CR-393-MKB, "Sentencing Memorandum by USA as to Fareed Mumuni," April 19, 2018.

250 **In fact, when heated to high:** "Can Lava Lamps Explode with Lethal Force," *MythBusters,* Sept. 18, 2014, accessed Jan. 11, 2019, www.discovery.com.

16. DJ3

253 **The whole thing had been stage-managed:** Robert Verkaik, "Exclusive: How MI5 Blackmails British Muslims," *Independent,* May 21, 2009, accessed Jan. 11, 2019, www.independent.co.uk.

255 **That statute had been revised:** John De Pue, "Fundamental Principles Governing Extraterritorial Prosecutions—Jurisdiction and Venue," *Extraterritorial Issues* 55, no. 2 (March 2007): 5–6.

256 **Al-Shabaab fighters fired mortars:** "Somalia: Somali Islamist Group al Shabaab Claims Responsibility for a Mortar Attack on U.S. Congressman," *Asia News Monitor,* April 14, 2009.

256 **Most troubling to U.S. officials:** *United States v. Mahdi Hashi,* U.S. District Court, Eastern District of New York, Case no. 12-CR-661, "Government's Memorandum of Law in Support of Motion for an Anonymous, Partially Sequestered Jury," Nov. 11, 2014.

257 **The details were more striking:** "Somalia: Reported US Covert Actions, 2001–2016," Bureau of Investigative Journalism, accessed Jan. 11, 2019, www.thebureauinvestigates.com.

257 **Of the more than ninety-five terrorism plots:** "Terrorist Arrests and Plots Stopped in the United States, 2009–2012," Immigration—United States Senator for California, accessed Jan. 11, 2019, www.feinstein.senate.gov/.

257 **In 2007, a Somali jihadist:** "Abdullahi Sudi Arale—the Guantánamo Docket," *New York Times,* accessed Jan. 11, 2019, www.nytimes.com.

257 **Human Rights Watch and Amnesty International confronted:** "Godj Welcomes Engagement with Department of Justice," WikiLeaks, Oct. 8, 2009, accessed Jan. 11, 2019, wikileaks.org.

258 **Even before the FBI interviewed:** *United States v. Ali Yasin Ahmed,* U.S. District Court, Eastern District of New York, Case no. 12-CR-661-JG-LB, "Motion for a Taint Hearing," March 31, 2015.

259 **In the prior three years:** Trevor Aaronson and Margot Williams, "Trial and Terror," *Intercept,* April 17, 2017, accessed Jan. 9, 2019, trial-and-terror .theintercept.com/.

259 **The men in the cell warned him:** *United States v. Mohamed Yusuf,* U.S. District Court, Eastern District of New York, Case no. 12-CR-661, "Affidavit," Sept. 16, 2014.

259 **He said his jailers told him:** *United States v. Ali Yasin Ahmed,* U.S. District Court, Eastern District of New York, Case no. 12-CR-661, "Affidavit," Sept. 19, 2014.

260 **Hashi felt there was little:** *United States v. Mahdi Hashi,* U.S. District Court, Eastern District of New York, Case no. 12-CR-661, "Affidavit," Sept. 16, 2014.

260 **Hashi didn't know it:** *Ahmed,* Case no. 12-CR-661-JG-LB, "Transcript," Jan. 15, 2016.

261 **DeMarco understood that reach:** Mark Demarco, interview by author, July 18, 2017.

261 **He had received a form letter:** *Ahmed,* Case no. 12-CR-661-JG-LB, "Letter in Response to Defendants Request for Status Conference Regarding SAMs as to Ali Yasin Ahmed, Mahdi Hashi, Mohamed Yusuf—Exhibit 5," Sept. 22, 2015.

261 **They were not CIA but FBI:** Ibid., "Memorandum and Order," March 24, 2015.

262 **The government eventually gave in:** Ibid., "Second Motion for Hearing on Tainted Evidence Derived from Illegal Interrogations or Arrests, First Motion to Suppress Photographs Taken While in Foreign Custody by Ali Yasin Ahmed as to Ali Yasin Ahmed, Mahdi Hashi, Mohamed Yusuf," March 31, 2015.

262 **The U.S. Attorney at the time, Loretta Lynch:** Ibid., "Memorandum in Opposition re First Motion In Limine for an Anonymous and Semi-sequestered Jury," Nov. 18, 2014.

262 **Yusuf later appeared in an al-Shabaab propaganda video:** www.youtube.com.

262 **At one point, he draws his finger:** *Ahmed,* Case no. 12-CR-661-JG-LB, "Letter Responding to Factual Objections as to Ali Yasin Ahmed, Mahdi Hashi, Mohamed Yusuf," Jan. 8, 2016.

263 **In one court submission, Ariail:** Ibid., "First Motion to Take Deposition of Foreign Government Representatives by USA as to Ali Yasin Ahmed, Mahdi Hashi, Mohamed Yusuf," Oct. 15, 2014.

263 **Guards at the MCC discovered:** Ibid., "Letter in Response to Defendants Request for Status Conference Regarding SAMs as to Ali Yasin Ahmed, Mahdi Hashi, Mohamed Yusuf," Sept. 22, 2015.

263 **Phone calls were rare:** Ibid., "Letter Supplement Prior Sentencing Memoranda as to Ali Yasin Ahmed, Mahdi Hashi, Mohamed Yusuf," Dec. 2, 2015.

263 **Hashi's co-defendants were also buckling:** Ibid., "Sentencing Memorandum by Ali Yasin Ahmed as to Ali Yasin Ahmed, Mahdi Hashi, Mohamed Yusuf," Dec. 3, 2015.

264 **One regulation forbade the men:** Ibid.

264 **When the witness, a Rwandan named:** Ibid., "Videotaped Deposition of Mugisha Mohamoud, Volume I & II," Feb. 24–25, 2015.

264 **The attacks killed one American:** Chris Reinolds Kozelle, "American Killed in Uganda Was Dedicated to Service," CNN, July 14, 2010, accessed Jan. 10, 2019, www.cnn.com.

266 **"My decision to join al Shabaab":** *Ahmed,* Case no. 12-CR-661-JG-LB, "Sentencing Memorandum by Ali Yasin Ahmed as to Ali Yasin Ahmed, Mahdi Hashi, Mohamed Yusuf," Dec. 3, 2015.

266 **The government, for its part, acknowledged:** Ibid., "Letter Responding to Factual Objections as to Ali Yasin Ahmed, Mahdi Hashi, Mohamed Yusuf," Jan. 8, 2016.

17. *Hijra* III

279 **After a year, he took a position:** Confirmed by Department of Justice spokesperson Mar. 12, 2019.

18. Juror #27

283 **When she learned she had been called:** Phillips, interview by author, Feb. 15, 2016.

284 **As with white-collar crimes:** Devlin-Brown, interview by author, Nov. 21, 2017.

285 **"When I was in the Securities Fraud unit":** Ibid.

286 **One-third of these elected officials:** "Serving Two Masters: Outside Income and Conflict of Interest in Albany," New York Public Interest Research Group, Reinvent Albany, and Common Cause New York, Feb. 2015, accessed Jan. 12, 2019, www.nypirg.org.

287 **Trial days began with rituals:** Cohen, interview by author, Oct. 18, 2016.

19. Post-Tammany

291 **The building was to cost:** Sara Hodon, "Tammany Hall: A Legacy of Corruption," *History Magazine,* Aug. 2010, 25–27.

291 **He was convicted on more than:** "A Brief History of the Tweed Courthouse," NYC.gov, accessed Jan. 10, 2019, www.nyc.gov.

292 **"If they are content to be ruled":** "The Looting of New York," *Hartford Daily Courant,* Dec. 3, 1885, 2.

292 **His name was Theodore Roosevelt:** Edward P. Kohn, " 'A Most Revolting State of Affairs': Theodore Roosevelt's Aldermanic Bill and the New York Assembly City Investigating Committee of 1884," *American Nineteenth Century History* 10, no. 1 (2009): 71–92, doi:10.1080/14664650802299909.

293 **In 1937, he ran for Manhattan district attorney:** "Marinelli Indicted by Federal Jury in Hiding of Falci," *New York Times,* Jan. 26, 1938; Thomas Dewey, "A Politician & Political Ally," Speech Vault, Oct. 24, 1937, accessed Jan. 12, 2019, www.speeches-usa.com.

293 **Dewey won that election:** Selwyn Raab, "Why Federal Attorneys Are the Gang-Busters Nowadays," *New York Times,* March 8, 1987.

293 **Federal prosecutors were not immune:** Jack Katz, "The Social Movement Against White-Collar Crime," *Criminology Review Yearbook* 2 (1980): 161–85, www.sscnet.ucla.edu.

293 **Investigations also penetrated executive offices:** Ibid.

294 **"While legislators were essentially inactive":** Ibid.

294 **In 1974, federal prosecutors:** U.S. Census Bureau, "Statistical Abstract of the United States of America," Census Bureau QuickFacts, July 23, 2015, accessed Jan. 12, 2019, www.census.gov.

294 **A decade later those figures:** U.S. Department of Justice, Federal Prosecutions of Corrupt Public Officials, 1970–1980; Report to Congress on the Activities and Operations of the Public Integrity Section, annual, www2.census.gov.

294 **In 2015, those figures were at 458:** "Report to Congress on the Activities and Operations of the Public Integrity Section for 2015," U.S. Department of Justice, accessed Jan. 12, 2019, www.justice.gov.

294 **He took the extraordinary step:** Richard J. Meislin, "Friedman Is Sentenced to 12 Years in Corruption Case," *New York Times,* March 12, 1987, accessed Jan. 12, 2019, www.nytimes.com.

295 **The decision to push the federal case:** Gerald Lefcourt, interview by author, Aug. 5, 2015.

295 **Media coverage and Justice Department leaks:** Alan Dershowitz, "When Prosecutors Violate Confidentiality," *New York Times,* Oct. 12, 1987; Richard J. Meislin, "The City Will Wash Its Dirty Linen in Hartford," *New York Times,* June 15, 1986.

295 **Manes never went to trial:** Richard J. Meislin, "Manes's Death: A Frantic Call, a Fatal Thrust," *New York Times,* March 15, 1986.

295 **"If the Mayor [Ed Koch] had not turned over":** Frank Lynn, "Giuliani Pledges to Appoint a Panel to Fight Corruption," *New York Times,* Aug. 9, 1989.

295 **Bharara spoke to a group:** Rebecca Davis O'Brien, "Preet Bharara, in Kentucky, Rails Against Corruption," *Wall Street Journal,* Jan. 6, 2016.

296 **Instead, it would issue a statement:** "Acting U.S. Attorney's Statement on de Blasio," *New York Times,* March 16, 2017, accessed Jan. 10, 2019, www.nytimes.com.

297 **She worked the federal investigation:** Joseph P. Fried, "Crown Heights Case 'Very Difficult,'" *New York Times,* Jan. 30, 1994.

297 **An appeals court threw out:** Patricia Hurtado, "Retrial in a Fatal Riot; U.S. Court Faults Jury Selection in Crown Heights Case," *Newsday,* Jan. 8, 2002.

297 **She earned a reputation as a relentless prosecutor:** Andreas Schmeling et al., "Forensic Age Estimation: Methods, Certainty, and the Law," *Deutsches Ärzteblatt,* Jan. 29, 2016, doi:10.3238/arztebl.2016.0044.

297 **He was; he pleaded guilty:** Associated Press, "X-Ray Proves Murder Defendant Is at Least 20, Doctor Says," *Orange County Register,* Dec. 8, 1995.

297 **During the investigation into the crash:** Allan Wolper, "Justice Dept. Admits Violation," *Editor & Publisher,* Sept. 27, 1997, 10–11.

297 **In 1999, while at the Securities and Exchange Commission:** Joseph P. Fried, "As Federal Prosecutor Quits, Aspiring Successors Rush In," *New York Times,* June 12, 1999.

298 **Under Caproni, the corporation won:** Richard Levine, "State Acquires Most of Times Square Project Site," *New York Times,* April 19, 1990.

298 **Later, she jumped from the Securities and Exchange Commission:** Edmund Sanders, "Lawmakers Turn Heat on Bankers," *Milwaukee Journal Sentinel,* July 24, 2002.

298 **She faced more criticism for obtaining:** "F.B.I. Obtained Reporters' Phone Records," *New York Times,* Aug. 9, 2008.

298 **"New York legislators, the Senate":** *United States v. Sheldon Silver,* U.S. District Court, Southern District of New York, Case no. 15-CR-93 (VEC), "Transcript," Nov. 3, 2015.

300 **Silver referred business from two:** Ibid.

301 **"It's common sense!" one of the jurors:** "Journal Entry by Arleen Phillips," author's collection, Dec. 2, 2015.

301 **"two jurors seemed to be ganging up":** Zack Fink, "Inside the Jury Room: How 12 Jurors Found Sheldon Silver Guilty—After Deliberations That Nearly Fell Apart," *City & State New York,* Jan. 14, 2016.

301 **"I'm like, wait a minute":** Phillips, interview by author, Feb. 15, 2016.

301 **While her fellow jurors were discussing:** *Silver,* Case no. 15-CR-93 (VEC), "Exhibit 8."

20. Reversals

305 **She wasn't alone in her departure:** "Chief of the Public Corruption Unit for the SDNY Joins Covington," Covington & Burling LLP, Aug. 8, 2016, accessed Jan. 10, 2019, www.cov.com.

306 **William Boyland, a Brooklyn assemblyman:** Nicholas Casey, "William Boyland Jr., Ex–New York Assemblyman, Gets 14-Year Sentence for Corruption," *New York Times*, Sept. 18, 2015, accessed Jan. 10, 2019, www.nytimes.com.

308 **The Court required that the defendant:** "*McDonnell v. United States:* Statutory Interpretation," *Harvard Law Review,* Nov. 2016, accessed Jan. 10, 2019, harvardlawreview.org.

Selected Bibliography

Alexander, Michelle. *The New Jim Crow: Mass Incarceration in the Age of Color-blindness*. New York: New Press, 2016.

Arrigo, Bruce A., ed. *Encyclopedia of Criminal Justice Ethics*. Los Angeles: Sage Publications, 2014.

Barofsky, Neil M. *Bailout: An Inside Account of How Washington Abandoned Main Street While Rescuing Wall Street*. New York: Free Press, 2013.

Brandt, Charles. *"I Heard You Paint Houses": Frank "the Irishman" Sheeran and the Inside Story of the Mafia, the Teamsters, and the Last Ride of Jimmy Hoffa*. Hanover, NH: Steerforth Press, 2016.

Eisinger, Jesse. *The Chickenshit Club: Why the Justice Department Fails to Prosecute Executives*. New York: Simon & Schuster, 2018.

Godsey, Mark. *Blind Injustice: A Former Prosecutor Exposes the Psychology and Politics of Wrongful Convictions*. Oakland, CA: University of California Press, 2018.

Fiske, Robert B. *Prosecutor Defender Counselor: The Memoirs of Robert B. Fiske Jr.* Kittery, ME: Smith/Kerr Associates, 2014.

Kolhatkar, Sheelah. *Black Edge: Inside Information, Dirty Money, and the Quest to Bring Down the Most Wanted Man on Wall Street*. New York: Random House, 2018.

Kroger, John. *Convictions: A Prosecutor's Battles Against Mafia Killers, Drug Kingpins, and Enron Thieves*. New York: Farrar, Straus and Giroux, 2008.

Lawless, Joseph F. *Prosecutorial Misconduct: Law, Procedure, Forms*. Newark, NJ: LexisNexis, 2018.

Natapoff, Alexandra. *Snitching: Criminal Informants and the Erosion of American Justice*. New York: New York University Press, 2011.

Pistone, Joseph, with Richard Woodley. *Donnie Brasco: My Undercover Life in the Mafia*. New York: New American Library, 1988.

Raab, Selwyn. *Five Families: The Rise, Decline, and Resurgence of America's Most Powerful Mafia Empires*. New York: Thomas Dunne Books, 2006.

Ripelli, Donato, and David S. Barry. *The Scorpion and the Frog: High Times and High Crimes*. Beverly Hills, CA: New Millennium Press, 2003.

Saviano, Roberto. *Gomorrah: A Personal Journey into the Violent International Empire of Naples' Organized Crime System*. New York: Picador, 2008.

Stuntz, William J. *The Collapse of American Criminal Justice*. Cambridge, MA: Belknap Press, 2013.

Turow, Scott. *One L*. New York: Penguin, 2010.

United States Sentencing Commission Guidelines Manual. Washington, D.C.: United States Sentencing Commission, 2016.

Zirin, James D. *The Mother Court: Tales of Cases That Mattered in America's Greatest Trial Court*. New York: American Bar Association, 2016.

A NOTE ABOUT THE AUTHOR

Johnny Dwyer is a reporter living in New York City and the author of *American Warlord*. He teaches at New York University's Arthur L. Carter Journalism Institute. He has written for *Esquire*, *The New York Times*, *Rolling Stone*, *The Intercept*, and other publications.

A NOTE ON THE TYPE

The text of this book was set in Sabon, a typeface designed by Jan Tschichold (1902–1974), the well-known German typographer. Based loosely on the original designs by Claude Garamond (ca. 1480–1561), Sabon is unique in that it was explicitly designed for hot-metal composition on both the Monotype and Linotype machines as well as for filmsetting. Designed in 1966 in Frankfurt, Sabon was named for the famous Lyons punch cutter Jacques Sabon, who is thought to have brought some of Garamond's matrices to Frankfurt.

Composed by North Market Street Graphics,
Lancaster, Pennsylvania

Printed and bound by Berryville Graphics,
Berryville, Virginia

Designed by Cassandra J. Pappas